THE SHAPE OF DEATH

A rippling series of pops shook the creature. Its muzzle shortened as the face flattened into something vaguely human. The creature shook one last time, violently, then promptly scrabbled up into a squat. A purple light blazed in its eyes. Black lips peeled back from teeth that had taken on the jagged serration of a carnivore's bite.

The goat-thing looked left and right, then bowed its horned head toward Will. "Pray thee, tell me, who would you be?"

Will pulled himself into a crouch. "I'm Will."

"Will, Will, one more to kill." The beast cocked its head and looked at him sidelong. "He comes not without anticipation, this bastard who will save a nation."

The youth shifted his shoulders as a shiver ran up his spine. "What are you?"

"Nefrai-laysh, at your beck and call." The goat-man sketched a little bow. "I serve she who commands them all."

"You're a Dark Lancer!"

"That much is clear, but not why I'm he.." The *sullanciri* pointed at Crow, Resolute, and Oracl.... "Beware these three, my little Will. They ...... , they mean you ill. A key to a lock is .... they stop and look at thee."

"He's lying to you, ..., his bow at the ready.

Three creatures ....nole. The two larger ones, with m..... .....humanoid bodies, emerged with longkn..... ..hey dove straight at Crow and Resolute. The ...... a bit smaller and covered with brown fur, leaped at Will. . . .

BOOKS BY MICHAEL A. STACKPOLE

*published by Bantam Books

FORTRESS DRACONIS

Book One of the DragonCrown War Cycle

Michael A. Stackpole

BANTAM BOOKS

This edition contains the complete text
of the original trade paperback edition.
NOT ONE WORD HAS BEEN OMITTED.

**FORTRESS DRACONIS:
BOOK ONE OF THE DRAGONCROWN WAR CYCLE**

A Bantam Spectra Book

PUBLISHING HISTORY
Bantam Spectra trade paperback published December 2001
Bantam Spectra mass market edition / November 2002

SPECTRA and the portrayal of a boxed "s" are trademarks of
Bantam Books, a division of Random House, Inc.

Library of Congress Catalog Card Number: 2001037969.

ISBN 0-553-57849-9

Published simultaneously in the United States and Canada

PRINTED IN THE UNITED STATES OF AMERICA

OPM   10 9 8 7 6 5 4 3 2 1

This book is dedicated to all those who patiently waited for it.

ACKNOWLEDGMENTS

Without the patience and forbearance of Anne Lesley Groell and Liz Danforth neither this book nor my sanity would exist. I can never fully repay the debt I owe them for this work.

THE NORRINGTON PROPHECY

A Norrington to lead them,
Immortal, washed in fire
Victorious, from sea to ice.

Power of the north he will shatter,
A scourge he will kill,
Then Vorquellyn will redeem.

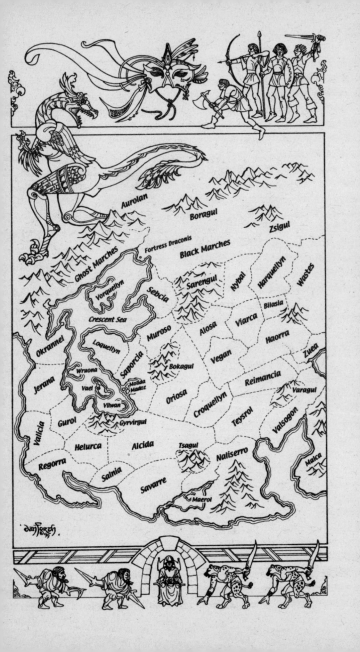

CHAPTER 1

Will shivered in the wet and rain, but clenched his jaw so his teeth would not chatter. The drops came down big and fat; colder, too, than he expected even so late in summer. They splashed against the tiled roof, spattering him and pockmarking the shifting surface of the puddles down on the street. The threadbare scrap of a blanket beneath which he huddled shielded him from their buffets, but let their cold soak straight into him.

The youth had no question that being elsewhere would be preferable—certainly warmer, if nothing else—but he refused to move on. Though he risked catching his death of cold by remaining, running away would kill him as well. *I do this, and everything will be okay again.*

He raised the blanket a mite and shook his head, letting water spray off his long brown hair. Leaning his head to the right, he let some water drip out of his ear and listened. The drumming of the raindrops hid most all sounds, but little bits of laughter drifted up from the public house's common room down on the ground level. He shifted slightly to his right, making no more noise than a squab might scrabbling for dry amid the roof's red tiles. Peering down from the roof's ridge, he could no longer see yellow light peeking out from behind the attic room's shuttered window.

Will couldn't help but let a smile blossom on his face. *'Bout damned time.* Throwing off the blanket, he began to unwind the knotted rope from around his waist. As he coiled it on the roof, he nodded slowly and whispered to himself.

> *Damn the Vorks,*
> *Damn their eyes.*
> *Let them drink,*
> *I'll have their prize.*

As poetry went, he knew it wasn't much, but felt the little verse was the seed of something larger. It would be a piece of the great saga minstrels would sing about his life. *And sing they will, of Will the Nimble, King of the Dimandowns. I'll make them forget Marcus, Scabby Jack, and Garrow; I'll even make them forget the Azure Spider.*

He crawled out along the roof's beam to where a piece overhung the alley. He looped the rope over the end of it, then snugged it tight. Tugging on it twice to assure himself it would hold, he started down it, letting the rope slide between his toes until he could rest his weight on a knot. Little by slowly he descended, reaching out to touch the building and kill any swing on the rope. Finally he hung there, right in front of the attic window.

The dagger he drew from the sheath at the small of his back slid neatly into the gap between shutters. Will worked it up, and between two rusty nail heads, his blade met the latch. Lifting easily, he slipped it and the shutters sagged outward, opening with a lazy sigh.

The thief shook his head as he resheathed his dagger. *Stupid Vorks deserve to lose their prize.* As anxious as he was to get his hands on it, he didn't reach for the shutters immediately, but waited a bit more, listening. *No time for mistakes now.*

He'd been pleased with how well the plan had come together, and he was fair certain Marcus and Fabia would be, too. He'd woven it together from things he knew they'd forgotten, like Fabia talking glowingly about the Vorquelf Predator, leader of the Grey Mist, as if he were King Augustus warring against the north. Predator would tell all that he hated men, and he'd only ever showed Will the cold side of a sneer and the fast-hard of a fist; but to hear Fabia tell it, he loved the warmth of a woman. He'd favored her with his attentions forever ago, when she wasn't so fat that only Marcus would have her.

She told tales of his having a treasure that she'd never seen, but she knew it was there. Once she'd awakened deep in the night, still drunk, and had seen his face backlit in the glow of something he cupped in his hands. Fabia said he smiled wider than he ever had in her arms. When she asked him what it was, he said she was dreaming, and in telling the tale to the younglings she'd allowed as how she likely was dreaming, since Predator would have long ago drunk up anything so precious.

Will always had believed her telling of the story as a dream until there came a time he thought on it for a while. Then he sought out the woman Predator was currently using. Lumina laughed when Will clowned for her, and cooed over the little things he'd steal and give her, be they bits of pastries or a bright button. She'd reward him with a kiss, clearly assuming that he had a crush on her. The fact that he did didn't keep him from his mission, and eventually she was coaxed into revealing a tale close enough to Fabia's that Will knew the Vorquelf *was* hiding something valuable.

It hadn't been hard for Will to convince himself that whatever the treasure was, it was meant to be his. For as long as he could remember—which went a bit further back before Marcus and Fabia had taken him in, but not much—he'd hated the Vorquelves. The exiled elves had long ago claimed the Downs as their own domain in Yslin. As hard times hit, the area around the Downs began to decay. Beggars and thieves, whores and the halt—most all men—came to live in the shadows of the city heart. Their neighborhoods became called the Dim, and Hightown folks dismissed the whole area as the Dimandowns. The Vorquelves constantly fought against the growing human population, and the only time human officials came into the area was to press-gang the unwary into crewing on galleys sailing the Crescent Sea.

Will's hatred for the Vorquelves found an ally in Marcus. Will could remember how the man had brought him into their home, a big building in the Dim, and had housed him with other children. Marcus taught them about thieving and worse, then sent them out into the city. In return for bringing back spoils, the children were fed and clothed and not beaten too often. Those who were especially good were taken to the Harvest Festival in the autumn, though the recent affairs in no way matched what Fabia talked about in her stories of festivals past.

Marcus and Fabia had always done for Will, but he did remember that they'd not always done so for everyone. The girls, when they reached a certain age, were trained for other things. Lumina hadn't been one of them, but plenty of Will's sisters plied the liftskirt trade. The boys, when they reached what Marcus called "willfulness," went away, never to be seen again.

Over the years, the age when willfulness manifested seemed to get younger. Beatings and kids getting vanished seemed to come more frequently with every new cycle of songs devoted to the master thief, the Azure Spider. Will could remember the days when Marcus used to claim with pride having been the Spider's mentor, but of late he'd been bitter and resentful. He took those feelings out on his male charges—many of whom, Will suspected, Marcus believed would betray him and leave for glory as the Spider had done.

Will had no intention of doing that, and hoped pulling off a job like this, which would have been worthy of the Azure Spider, would impress Marcus. He knew that planning and executing this theft would likely brand him as willful, but he hoped that by bringing the treasure to Marcus, he'd show how loyal he intended to be.

He'll have no excuse to send me away, none at all.

Confident that nothing lived or breathed in the darkened room, Will opened a shutter, grabbed the inside of the casement, and pulled himself in. He kept hold of the rope with his toes, so it slithered in after him. Crouching by the window, water dripping into a puddle beneath him, Will studied the room carefully. He dearly wished his heart would stop pounding so loudly in his ears, but the tumult of drunken conversation from below would have hidden the approach of a dragon.

Staying low, and spreading his weight out on his hands and feet, Will scuttled across the floor. Lamplight from below bled up through cracks between planks, striping chairs, bed, and wardrobe with a soft yellow glow. Small and light though he was, he knew the uneven boards would be creaking with his passage, but he felt certain those sounds went unheard.

He made his way to the wardrobe and carefully felt around the base molding. Lumina said she'd seen Predator kneeling there, his body washed in silver, but had thought nothing of it. Tracing his fingers along the baseboard, Will sought a catch or lever to reveal a hidden compartment. He found nothing so sophisticated.

His fingers caught against a piece of the base that jutted out just a hair. Hooking his fingernails into the gap, he teased it free without so much as a squeak. A little block of wood as long as his hand came free. In the cavity behind it he found a leather pouch heavy enough for a silver or two, and a lighter velvet pouch. The latter had something in it, but he couldn't tell what.

He slipped the leather pouch beneath his belt and knew

he should head out before examining his other find, but he needed to make certain he really *had* gotten his hands on Predator's treasure. Slender fingers unmade the knot holding the bag shut, then peeled the velvet away, letting a blinding argent light shine forth.

Will squinted against the brilliance, at once entranced and puzzled. The treasure looked like a leaf—he knew it was from a tree, but what kind he had no idea since trees were few in the Dimandowns. The leaf blazed with a silver light and appeared to be metal, but had none of the heft it would have had if cast in silver. More impressively, it had the supple texture and flexibility of a living leaf.

Don't know what it is, but it is a treasure! For the barest of moments Will considered tucking it back in its hidey-hole. Just having disturbed it felt somehow wrong—and the idea that taking something that didn't belong to him was *wrong* had seldom occurred to him before. At the same time, it also felt wrong for this leaf to remain shut up in a little hole. He sensed another purpose to it, as if there was something he was supposed to do with it.

Suddenly shouting arose from below and something shattered against the floorboards. Ale sprayed up through a crack. Wet as he was, he couldn't really feel it hit him, but he could smell it. In an instant he knew the silver light had been seen by someone below, and that the thundering came from feet on the stairs leading to the upper floor.

Without a second thought, and with skill born of more than a decade's thievery, Will stuffed the leaf into the bag and tucked it in his belt. He darted toward the window, tumbling a chair in his wake, and dove for the rope as the room's door burst inward. The rope bumped and slithered, knot by knot, out behind him, chased by the curses of a Vork, who hit the chair and fell. Out into the night Will sailed, snapping his legs up, hoping he could loop his way back onto the roof.

Though his feet came up above the level of the roof, he couldn't get far enough over to land there, so he twisted around as he descended again on a short, tight arc. A waiting Vork smiled, reaching out for him as he returned. Will kicked one of the shutters around, slamming it flat against the Vork's face, spilling him back into the room.

As quickly as he could, controlling his fall more than actually climbing, he let himself down, and reached the alley seconds before a sword sliced the rope free from above. Will crouched, found a rock with his right hand, and sent it flying up at the window. The pale face that had been leering at him snapped back into the darkness.

Will darted off along the alley, hitting the street and cutting right. That route would actually take him deeper into the Downs, which he figured would confuse the Vorks. He ran as fast as he could, splashing through puddles, leaping over the dead bodies of animals, hoping the battering rain would aid him by erasing all traces of his passage.

Aid him it did in some ways, for nothing could have tracked him by sight or scent as the rain washed away his spoor almost instantly. Even so, the rain betrayed him in more important ways, which he slowly came to understand as he raced past cloaked figures skulking through the streets, and close by soaked curs that barked and howled at him. *This is not the way to go.*

The Downs had been called the Downs because the city of Yslin sunk to its lowest level there. At high tide some of the streets would flood, and although high tide lay hours yet away, the day's downpour had flooded streets into brown rapids thick with debris. The street along which he ran dipped into a raging torrent.

His course blocked, Will turned north, dashing toward an alley mouth. He could hear his pursuers after him and knew he should toss away his loot. The leather bag with coins he tugged free of his belt and dropped behind him without a second thought. When his fingers touched the velvet bag, however, it felt warm and dry and he knew he wouldn't let anyone take it from him. *Not them, not Marcus. Not anyone.*

Will put his head down and started running in earnest when the rain's second betrayal occurred. He sprinted through a puddle that hid in its murky depths a missing cobblestone. The youth caught his right foot in the hole and stumbled, smashing his right knee into the roadway. The cobblestones, while soaked by the rain, had not been softened, so the blow drove a jolt of pain up and down his leg. His ankle twisted before his foot came free. He rolled over onto his back, clutching his knee in both hands.

Cold rain splashed his face, and colder laughter rang in his ears. A knot of Vorquelves towered over him. The silver moonlight made them into ghosts, and what he could see of their faces indicated they were most malevolent. One bled from a cut on his forehead—Will took some joy in knowing his rock had flown true—and another's nose looked to be swelling.

Predator leaned down and grabbed Will by the front of his tunic. "Should have known it was you. No one else would have been so stupid."

"Stupid was making it so easy."

The Vorquelf, his sapphire eyes glowing in the moonlight, raised a fist. "I won't be easy on you, little Will. Give it back."

It struck Will as peculiar that Predator didn't just pull the bag off his belt. It was there in plain sight; Will could feel its warmth against his right hip. He wanted to tell Predator to take it, but that idea died quicker than a lightning flash.

"You'll never find it now. It's halfway to the sea."

Predator screamed and his fist fell heavily. Will caught it on the right side of his face and saw stars. He didn't think he'd been hit that hard, but he found himself on the ground again, his face throbbing.

A rasped, edged voice cut through the ringing in Will's

ears. "I told you, years ago, if you ever touched one of them, you'd regret it."

Predator whirled to face a hulking human silhouette limned in silver, but before he could square around, a fist flew and caught the Vork straight in the face. Predator's nose cracked sharply. The Vorquelf stumbled back and splashed down in the puddle. From the way his body bounced and his arms and legs flopped, Will knew Predator had been senseless before he hit the ground.

The other Grey Misters pulled back away from the figure, hands falling to the hilts of daggers and swords. *Poor fool should have stayed out of what wasn't his business.* Will gathered his legs beneath him as best he could and began to inch away, then his head and shoulders butted up against something solid. He looked up, saw a massive Vork looming above him, and yelped.

The other Vorquelves looked down at him, then their heads rose as they studied the elf standing over him. One of the Grey Misters raised his hands, open and easily. "We don't want any trouble, Resolute, but he stole something from Predator and we can't have that."

"This stripling stole from you?" Resolute laughed, and the mere sound of it seemed to stagger some of the Misters. "What was it he stole?"

The Mister shrugged. "Don't know. Predator said it was important."

Resolute dropped to one knee and plucked the velvet pouch from Will's belt. Will grabbed for his forearm, but his cold, wet fingers found no purchase on the Vorquelf's thickly tattooed flesh. "That's mine."

"Is it, now?" Resolute stood and opened the bag. Silver light poured out over his face, illuminating argent eyes and a snarl. The Vorquelf's hands closed the bag quickly, then he took a step into the middle of the Misters and kicked Predator hard in the ribs.

"Get him out of here, the lot of you. He's jeopardized everything with his greed. Get him gone before I kick his belly through his spine." The Vorquelf spun and pointed a finger at Will. "And you, you're going nowhere."

The anger in his voice froze Will where he was. The Misters each grabbed an ankle or wrist and dragged Predator away. As they hauled him off, Resolute kicked water at them, hissing curses in Elvish. The other figure, which Will discovered to be a white-haired man with a thick white beard, crouched down beside him.

"How's that knee?"

Will shrugged.

The man looked up at Resolute. "Think he's the one? Hardly washed in fire, here."

The Vorquelf nodded, the thick stripe of white hair on his head glistening with rain. "Yes, but a piece of Vorquellyn he did redeem."

Will shook his head. "What are you talking about?"

Resolute tied the velvet bag to his belt. "You'll learn, eventually."

"Maybe I won't."

The Vorquelf and the man both hauled him to his feet. "You will learn, if all things turn out the way they are meant to."

"And if they don't?"

"You aspire to what, boy? Growing up to be the Azure Spider, the Prince of Shadows? You want to be a master thief?" Resolute slowly shook his head. "Your life is wasted. Having it shortened will just save you pain."

CHAPTER 2

Will didn't like the sound of what Resolute had said and wanted to snap a remark that would hurt him, but he was mindful of two things that stopped him. The first was the way Resolute had kicked Predator. The Vorquelf was clearly not in a good mood, and Will did not want to become the focus of his ire.

The second was that Resolute obviously would hit harder than Predator.

Will had wanted to protest that what Resolute said wasn't true, but the word "wasted" kept bouncing around inside his head. *Will the Nimble, King of the Dimandowns.* That concept mocked him as he stood there, wet and aching, with his right eye swelling shut. But he'd been hurt before, laughed at before, told he was nothing before, so there was something else eating at him.

The man threw a corner of his cloak over the youth's shoulders. "He's shivering and probably hungry."

Resolute nodded. "C'mon, boy, let's go."

Will limped along a few steps, letting the cloak slip off him, then stopped.

The Vorquelf paused and looked back at him. "You can walk along with us, or I will *march* you along, boy. Your choice."

Will's nostrils flared. "My name is Will."

"I'm Resolute, this is Crow. Now move."

The youth frowned. "One thing."

"And that is?"

Will reached out a trembling hand. "Let me carry the leaf."

The Vorquelf's head came up. "You think I'm going to trust it to a thief?"

Crow laid a hand on Resolute's shoulder. "He did get it. He can't run off."

Resolute's eyes became crescent slivers of silver. "You lose this, boy, and you'll wish Predator hadn't been stopped."

The youth raised his chin and snorted. "Predator could have never made me give it up. I won't lose it."

Resolute knotted the bag securely, then handed it to Will. "Come on, then."

Grinning like a fool, Will held on with both hands.

> *The leaf is shining,*
> *Glowing bright,*
> *In my caring,*
> *Clung-to tight.*

The man's head came up, the hint of a smile gracing his lips. "Let's go, Will."

The man let Will get in front of him, but the youth really didn't feel Crow was there to stop him from running. He chuckled to himself, knowing he'd bolt at the first opportunity, but the throbbing in his knee told him that opportunity would be a little while in coming. Besides, the man had mentioned food, and going back to Marcus all wet and hurt and without anything to show for it would just get his other eye blacked. *Might's well have a full belly.*

The warmth from the bag spread into his hands and Will started thinking on what Resolute had said. It seemed to him that the desire to be the King of the Dimandowns *had* been a worthy goal, but that had been before he saw the leaf and touched it. And then, when Resolute had taken the leaf from him, he was left all hollow inside. He knew then that he'd been meant to steal the leaf. For what purpose he had no idea, but he sensed there was one. *And that purpose is mine to fulfill.*

These thoughts occupied him as Resolute led the way through the Downs to an inn that didn't look nearly as decrepit as the other Vork haunts. Will seemed to remember having been in that place once before and having been chased away with a brown bucket of floor sloppings dumped over him. As they entered the common room Will saw the emerald-eyed bartender scowl at him, but the Vorquelf's expression eased into something shy of a smile as Crow closed the door behind them.

Crow pulled his cloak off and hung it on a peg. His white hair had been gathered back into a thick braid that was knotted with a leather cord from which dangled a rainbow of feathers. His beard ran along his jaw and flushed full at his chin and moustaches, but left visible an old scar down his right cheek. Above it another scar ran up into his hair. The brown of his buckskin clothes ran lighter than the color of his eyes, save where the rain had soaked his shoulders and wrists. The sword he wore had a brass hilt with leather bindings and a big angular pommel. Daggers rode on his right hip, in his left boot-top, and, if Will wasn't missing anything, in a sheath on his right forearm, up his sleeve.

Will couldn't begin to guess at his age. The man looked ancient—*must be at least forty*—but a fair bit of life still burned in his eyes. Crow's-feet crinkled the corners of those eyes, nicks and cuts had scarred his cheek, nose, brow, and ears, but he didn't seem the sort of man to be wasting away, drinking off scartales in some Dim squalor-squat.

The way he'd moved through the streets, and the power with which he hit Predator suggested to Will that the man wasn't as old as he first appeared. There was no doubting at all that he'd seen a lot of life, and Will figured the man was more than content to let his coloration disguise him. Plenty of folks would look at him and dismiss him for being old, but Will determined that wasn't a mistake he'd make.

A shiver shook Will then, and it wasn't from the cold. Conversation, which had been in Elvish and unintelligible to him save for the odd curse or two, had died. He turned away from Crow and saw two dozen Vorquelves staring at the man with expressions that ranged from friendly to respectful. Not a few were tinged with fear. Whispers started, but Will caught little of them, save for a name.

Kedyn's Crow.

The youth turned back and looked at Crow again. "You're Kedyn's Crow?"

"Crow fits better, Will."

Resolute laughed. "He's more afraid of you than he was of Predator, Crow."

Will shook his head, lashing his face with wet strands of hair. "Not afraid." He shivered again. "Really."

Crow smiled and guided Will toward a table, which Vorquelves quickly vacated. "Sit down. I'll get you something warm to eat."

"Yes." Will sat, still clutching the bag to his chest. "And, sir, thank you, sir."

His hasty comment sparked laughter from the Vorks, who went back to their drinking and eating. Will ignored them and stared after the broad-shouldered man speaking Elvish with the bartender. *Kedyn's Crow!* If there were a more famous man, aside from King Augustus of course, Will didn't know of him. Minstrels in the Dim sung of his exploits, of his traveling north to the frozen plains of

Aurolan, killing hoargoun and temeryces. *Those feathers, they have to be from some of the frostclaws!*

Kedyn's Crow didn't seek fame for himself, but was known from when he and his companions—*I know who the Vork he runs with is now*—saved a Jeranese caravan from marauders, or showed up in a snowbound Murosan village and fought off Aurolani raiders or . . . The one Will liked best talked about Kedyn's Crow hunting through the Ghost March, killing off a vylaen general that Chytrine was using to lead an army down into Okrannel. Will wasn't certain where any of those places were, save for being far away, but he'd reveled in hearing those adventures.

Crow returned to the table and set a wooden bowl full of steaming stew in front of Will. Beside it he placed an earthenware mug from which steam likewise rose. "Eat slowly,"

Will nodded and tucked the bag inside his tunic, then grabbed the wooden spoon, stuck it into the stew, and shoveled up a mouthful. The stew tasted okay, though the cook clearly didn't know what he was doing because it was way too thick to be proper stew. The food's warmth started to seep out of his belly into the rest of him. He grabbed the mug in both hands and gulped down a big swallow of the mulled wine, then sat back and burped.

Crow raised an eyebrow. "Slowly, Will. No one is going to take it away from you."

Will nodded, not sure if Crow was talking about the food or the leaf. About the time Will realized he'd sooner give up the food than the leaf, Resolute came to the table. He brought with him two mugs of ale, one of which he handed to Crow. In his wake trailed another Vorquelf.

This Vorquelf brought a smile to Will's face. Even though his eyes were a solid light blue, he dressed as if he were a real elf. Red hair hung in two braids at his temples and was long elsewhere in the current elven fashion; his clothes had been cut along the lines of those worn by dandies in Hightown. Will couldn't see a scar or tattoo on him, and his straight nose had clearly never collided with a fist or shutter. The Vorquelf remained slender and didn't have a speck of dirt on his clothes or under his fingernails.

And the rings on his slender fingers . . . Will knew he could have them off in the blink of an eye, and could even nick the gold coins in the pouch at his belt—for gold weighed much more than silver and made itself apparent to the trained eye.

"Is this the boy?"

Resolute grunted. "No getting anything past you, is there, Amends? And he's not a boy, he's almost a man."

"Small for a man yet."

Crow laid a hand on Will's arm. "Do you know how old you are?"

Will shook his head. "Fire took my mother, they tell me. Aunts kept me until I ran away. Been in the Dim since then. Around."

Resolute rapped a fist sharply on the table. "Your *age,* boy, not your life story."

Will jumped, then frowned. "Fifteen years, maybe more, but not much. I'm just small."

The clean, red-haired Vorquelf narrowed his eyes. "Are you sure this is the one? He doesn't look it."

"Of course he doesn't, with his face swelling like that. Predator hit him."

Amends snarled. "He'll pay for that."

"He already did."

Amends nodded, then pointed deeper into the common room. "Charity, fix the boy's face."

Will turned around as a chair scraped against the wooden floor. A slender elf, not much taller than himself— a mere slip of a girl with golden hair and full sea-green eyes—got out of her chair and approached him timidly. She met his glance for a second, then seemed to look away. *No black dot to their eyes, not easy to tell where she's looking.* Still, she came to him and stroked the right side of his face with her left hand.

He couldn't see what she was doing, given as how that eye had almost swelled shut, but he could feel it. His flesh tingled in the wake of her caress. Heat leaped from her hand into his face and he began to smile. He noticed it didn't hurt his cheek to do so, and then his right eye opened.

He looked up and saw a trace of pain pass over her features. "What? I didn't do it. What's wrong?"

She shook her head. "Nothing."

Crow squeezed his right forearm. "She used magick to heal you, and it's not without a cost. She took the pain of your healing on herself."

Will blinked. "But why?"

Charity smiled at him. "For what you will do, in thanks."

"What I will do?" He frowned and looked at Crow. "What does she mean?"

The man shook his head. "It's too soon to worry about that, Will. Just get yourself outside of that stew, then we'll see if you can have the lend of a bed. Thank you, Charity."

Will stared after her as she walked away. "Not going to have her do my leg?"

"And have you able to run?" Resolute laughed mirthlessly. "You'll be fine to sit a saddle tomorrow."

Amends' head came up. "You're not leaving tonight?"

Resolute studied his mug of ale. "Done enough for one evening."

"But this is important. If you don't get him there . . ."

Crow raised a hand to stop the discussion. "Good Amends, forgive us. Resolute would prefer not to insult me, but these old bones need sleep before I can head out."

The red-haired Vorquelf blushed from his throat to the tips of his pointed ears. "Forgive me, Kedyn's Crow. I meant no offense, it is just . . ."

"Don't worry yourself, Amends." Crow chuckled lightly. "I vowed to see to the liberation of Vorquellyn in my lifetime. You should rejoice that my age means that event is going to be sooner rather than later."

"If people will let us be about our duty." Resolute shook his head quickly, spraying a little water from the strip of white hair running from his forehead to the nape of his neck. "Now leave us alone or make yourself useful ordering up roadbread and drymeat for us."

Amends nodded solemnly. "Of course, of course. You'll be leaving when? Dawn? Noon?"

Crow shrugged. "Dawn if the rain breaks, noon if it doesn't. No one wants to ride in the cold wet too long."

"Of course not, no." Amends tapped a finger against his lips. "Reason, Sagacity, round up some supplies for them, see if you can find clothes for the . . . manling."

Two other Vorquelves left their tables, pulled on oilskin cloaks, and vanished into the night. It surprised Will that they moved so quickly to Amends' orders, since he didn't look nearly strong enough to be their leader. As much as Will didn't like Predator, he figured Predator would have been able to whip Amends easily.

That was the way of things in the Dim, after all. The strong ruled. Predator would have been on top until someone like Resolute decided to topple him. Marcus had been supreme until the Azure Spider went on to greater glory. *After that, even Scabby Jack and Garrow challenged him. He's got nothing—'cept for me, that is.*

Amends stared down at Will again, his face closing up. "I pray he is the one. Gods speed you on your journey. And good luck to you, William."

Will looked up from his bowl, the dripping spoon halfway to his mouth. "I'm not William." He glanced from side to side, reading shock on all three faces. "I'm just Will."

Resolute set his mug down and cocked an eyebrow at the boy. "Will? Nothing more? Why are you blushing, boy?"

"No reason." Will frowned and looked back into his nearly empty bowl. "I'm Will."

"You're certainly stubborn, *Will.*" Crow's voice came easily, lightly, with a touch of friendliness to it. "You've forgotten, I think, what Resolute and I saved you from. You've forgotten what Resolute has trusted you with. You'll trust us with your name, won't you?"

Will lowered his spoon to the bowl again. "You'll laugh."

The man shook his head. "No, not at all."

Will snarled and pointed his spoon at Resolute. "He will."

"Better me laughing, boy, than having to get it out of you *my* way."

That sent a shiver down Will's spine. "Just this once." His eyes narrowed and he waved the spoon back and forth like a dagger. "My name is Wilburforce."

Resolute and Crow gave no sign of their reaction to his name, but Amends exhaled loudly. "Oh, yes, yes; perfect. Thus ends one debate."

Will frowned at Crow. "There's a lot here you're not telling me."

"There will be time, on the road, to answer your questions."

Will licked the spoon off and brandished it again. "On the road to where?"

Resolute snorted. "Does it matter to you? It's away from here."

"Maybe I don't want to go."

"It's not like you have a choice." The large Vorquelf smiled carefully, wrapping one massive hand over a scarred fist. "You're going, Wilburforce."

Crow waved away Resolute's comment. "Think of it as an adventure, Will. Who among your friends has been to the mountains? We'll go there, see a friend, then you can come back here if you wish."

"I don't know." Will tried to keep his face impassive, but his voice rose a bit at the end, and a nervous smile tugged at the corner of his mouth. He swiped a sleeve over it to hide it. No one he'd known had been out of the environs of Yslin, save maybe Marcus, and Marcus had never been to the mountains.

A fitting first adventure for Will the Nimble?

"I'll get to ride a horse?"

"Several."

Will nodded and scraped at the bowl with his spoon. He recalled well the tales of children snatched from the streets never to be heard from again, but the wariness engendered by those tales faded. The kindness in Crow's voice, the insistence in Resolute's, and the warmth of the bag pressed against his ribs, those three things in no way suggested he'd be safe on the trip, but they did tell him he had nothing to fear from his traveling companions.

Besides, the little hint that there might be danger—and he'd picked that up from dozens of things, not the least of which was Resolute's not telling Amends about the leaf—sent a thrill through him. He'd grown up in the roughest part of Yslin. There was nothing in the wilderness he was going to fear.

"Okay," Will said. "To the mountains we'll go."

CHAPTER 3

Resolute and Crow led the way up the stairs and along a corridor to a room at the back corner of the inn. The rain beat a steady tattoo on the tile roof, which Will didn't find unusual. The fact that the roof didn't leak did surprise him, however, as did the size of the room. It fit a big bed *and* a chest of drawers, with a little side table and spindly chairs in the corner. A candle burned on the table, and one of the chairs creaked mightily as Resolute sat in it.

Crow hung the wet cloaks up on the pegs behind the door, then nodded toward the bed. "Go ahead, Will. Strip those wet clothes and wrap yourself up in a sheet. Can't have you catching a cough."

Will, having been raised in a pack of urchins, didn't suffer from modesty. Wet clothes flew in all directions leaving him naked, when a gentle knocking came on the door. Crow answered it, and Will smiled at Charity through the opening. The Vorquelf blushed and turned her head, handing Crow a neatly folded parcel of clothes. Crow thanked her and closed the door behind her.

He tossed the clothes onto the bed. "There you go. You'll want to get dressed."

Will, holding the leaf-bag in his hands, blinked and looked up. "But it's time for sleeping, right?"

Resolute snorted. "Not going to be getting much sleep tonight, boy. Get dressed."

Crow had crossed to the window at the rear of the inn. "Looks clear."

Sitting on the bed, Will pulled some oversized trousers on. "I don't understand. You told Amends . . ."

The man stretched. "Amends does not understand much about our kind, Will, and accepts that the white of my hair and beard means I might as well reside in a grave. It's useful to let him and others assume I'm capable of a bit less than I am."

"We told Amends what we wanted him to hear, boy." The Vorquelf tossed Crow his cloak. "By now the story is circulating that we found you and that we'll be leaving tomorrow. In the morning this place will be filthy with people. They'll be here to see you. Most of them will want you to succeed. A few won't. And a couple will want you dead."

Crow shrugged his cloak on. "I'm not sure about the last, Resolute."

The Vorquelf scratched at the back of his neck with a big, scarred hand. "You know there are those who think we're fools, the two of us. They think we might anger the enemy, and that appeasing her by informing on us might be the quick way to get Vorquellyn back."

Will pulled a dry woolen tunic on. "What are you talking about?"

The Vorquelf's lip curled up into a snarl. "What do you know of the world, boy?"

"I know a lot."

"Tell me."

Will hesitated for a second, then looked over at Crow, who gave him a reassuring nod. "Well, I know that Augustus is king because he beat Chytrine's army a long time ago.

That's where he found Queen Yelena. And I know the Vorks don't have a home because Chytrine kicked them off it. I know all about the Azure Spider and how he stole the heart of the Wruonan pirate queen, Vionna. I mean, I know more about him, but that's one of the best stories I know. And, and . . . I know that the smith down on South Street is carrying on with the wife of the baker on Sparrow Road."

Resolute's head came up and his expression softened. "That's it, that's all you know?" He swung his left fist around and slammed it into the wall, cracking the plaster. "It's impossible, Crow. If he's the one . . ."

"Calm yourself, my friend. You know as well as I do that neither of us knew the Azure Spider was on Wruona." The man laid a hand on Resolute's shoulder and smiled. "If Will's the one, it's our job to educate him."

"Crow, in another lifetime I couldn't teach him enough."

"It's not that dire, Resolute." Crow looked over at Will. "What do you know of the *sullanciri*?"

The youth shivered. "Everybody knows about them. Everybody thought they were heroes but that's not true. They wanted to have King Augustus use his army to take over the world, but he chased them off, all ten of them, the treacherous dogs. They ran away and went to Chytrine and fed her their souls. She gave them magickal powers and everything. They're led by the Norringtons, father and son, just as they were led back in the time of the war. All of them are there except the one who betrayed them."

The Vorquelf nodded slowly. "Do you know their names?"

"Heard a couple, maybe. Ganagrei, Nefrai-kesh—he leads them. Not good to mention them because you might bring them."

Crow nodded. "It's wise to be cautious."

"Well, I'm wiser than they were, that's for sure." Will snorted. "The traitor, Hawkins was his name, he was the one who talked them into leaving Augustus. He fooled them all, you know. He lured them north, sabotaged their mission, then lost his nerve when he met Chytrine and she wanted to reward him for his work. He ran away, then tried to cover up for his evil. King Augustus had once called him a friend, but he banished him. I heard a story that he threw himself into the Crescent Sea, killing himself before others could hunt him down. He serves Tagothcha, shooting harpoons into ships with a magick bow, dragging them down."

The youth smiled. "I bet he killed himself because you two were hunting him. He knew he couldn't escape justice, right?"

Crow's face closed and Resolute's fist hit the wall again, but not as hard. Still, little bits of plaster rattled to the floor. Both of them seemed numbed by what he had told them. The ferocity they'd showed in combat, the confidence they'd displayed talking to Amends, had drained away. Crow suddenly looked old, the fire in his eyes dulled.

"Was I wrong?"

Resolute's eyes had widened in the sort of dismay a child experiences when a cherished myth is exploded.

Will shivered. "Um, you asked. I told you, but you *asked*."

Crow recovered himself first, and nodded slowly. He kept his voice even and warm, despite the little bit of a quiver that echoed through his words. "You should understand, Will, that Resolute and I lived during the time of the last war with Chytrine. What you have told us does not match our memories. For the past quarter century, we've been looking for a way to fulfill a prophecy and defeat Chytrine. We've been so focused on what we were doing, we've missed how the history has changed."

"What do you mean it's changed? Chytrine is this evil woman who wants to take over everything." The youth frowned. "She has all these monsters fighting for her, and the *sullanciri*, of course, and weapons like dragonels. The other armies didn't kill her because she ran from King Augustus, and she's been waiting to avenge herself. But you know that because you're heroes. You two stop her. I have heard your stories sung by lots of minstrels."

Resolute growled as his eyes narrowed. "A song is entertainment, boy, not a recitation of facts. It might make us heroes here in the Dim, but that means nothing in Hightown or the rest of the world."

"What I told you isn't right?"

"History's a mosaic, boy, bits of the truth mixed with lies. Lies people had to tell, so they wouldn't be afraid." Resolute rubbed at his fist, brushing plaster dust from it. "Augustus did defeat an army and win a queen. That's true. The rest of it, though . . . wishful thinking."

Will picked up the leaf-bag and rubbed it. "What does that history have to do with me? Why would someone want to kill me?"

Crow held up a hand to forestall Resolute's comment. "There are some things we cannot tell you, Will—until we know you need to hear them. It could be you're just a thief who stole a leaf. . . ."

The youth smiled. " 'Just a thief who stole a leaf,' I like that rhyme."

The man chuckled just a bit. "No surprise there, I think. If you are the person we hope you are, then we will eventually be able to explain everything to you. If you are not, a chance comment could doom the person who *is* the one we want. Do you understand?"

"I think so." Will nodded and shoved his feet back into wet boots. "It's like the story of the twin princes. They couldn't let the one who had been raised away from the castle know who he was because folks wanted to kill him." His head came up. "You're not saying I'm a prince or anything, are you?"

Resolute laughed aloud, with just a hint of cruelty. "You're no prince, boy, not in the least."

"Oh." Will suspected they might be lying to him, but he also decided not to let them know he knew. He shrugged his shoulders and stood, wincing at the squishiness of his boots. "Just as well, since a prince will get as soaked in the rain as a thief, but a thief can tolerate it."

Through the window and out across rooftops they went in the rain and dead of night. For an old man and a big Vork, the two of them moved pretty well. Will followed the paths they picked out, primarily because his knee was still tender enough to make the more demanding route he would have chosen a bit dangerous. He wasn't so much worried about hurting himself as he was about damaging the leaf, which surprised him.

They descended to the streets and reached a stable where three horses were quickly saddled. Grain and other supplies were loaded on six more horses, then all of them were led out in a string behind Resolute's horse. Will ended up riding a brown gelding, which seemed to be a docile creature. Will had no complaints about that because the last time he'd tried to ride a horse, the owner had arrived before he'd gotten away and the beast had reared, tossing Will off. Limping back to Marcus had not been any fun.

Crow took the reins of Will's horse and led it along through the city. The rain slackened to a drizzle, and mist began crawling through the streets. They skirted the southern edge of the Dimandowns, then left the city through the western gate. The guards there barely roused themselves to watch them pass. Resolute flipped them gold-coin lullabies to encourage their return to sleep and forgetting about the trio's passage.

They rode west for a while, but with the clouds so thick and black, Will could not mark time by the moon's passage. He only knew they'd gone a long way when they headed off toward the northwest, along a track through hills of tree stumps. In a little valley they stopped at an abandoned woodsman's hovel and stabled the horses in a cave dug into the hillside.

His two companions saw to the horses, so Will entered

the cabin and found a dry patch of floor to curl up on. A little flutter of fear ran through him, but the warmth pulsing out from the leaf-bag kept his worries at bay. Quickly enough he surrendered to a full belly and exhaustion, dreaming of great adventures that evaporated by the time he wakened.

Morning came bright and Will rose with the speed of the sun. Lazily wiping sleepsand from his eyes, he stepped over Crow's sleeping form and wandered out into the daylight. He found Resolute snarling whispered curses in Elvish, crouched near the cabin. In the field before it, rabbits gamboled amid stumps. They twitched their ears and wrinkled their noses, grazing ten yards away from the cabin, and a yard away from some contraption set in the field.

Will frowned. "What's that thing?"

Resolute frowned. "It's a deadfall trap that should catch us breakfast."

"A rabbit? You can eat them?"

The Vorquelf arched an eyebrow. "You've never . . . ?"

Will shook his head. "S'posed to taste like cat." He squatted down and fingered some rocks in the dry soil at the cabin's entrance. "Why don't you just kill one?"

"That's what the snare is for, boy. Now keep your voice down. You don't want to scare them off."

The youth snorted, then whispered, "Ain't my voice keeping them away, it's that thing you made." He hefted a dark stone. "Me, I'd just throw a rock at it."

"Would you? Well, then, how about an easy target?" Resolute pointed off at a plump rabbit. "That one, with the white blaze . . ."

Before the Vorquelf finished his sentence, Will shifted his stance, dropping to his right knee a lot faster than he should have. He whipped his right hand forward, side-arming the stone. It whizzed through the air, clipping the rabbit in the side of the head. The creature flopped over on its flank and twitched, but before it stopped, Resolute had darted forward, snatched it up, and wrung its neck.

Will clenched his teeth against the pain in his knee, determined not to show Resolute any weakness. He was paying the price for showing off, and was damned glad the rock had actually hit its target. *If I'd missed . . .*

The Vorquelf glanced at him, then nodded. "Nice throw."

Will shrugged and rose slowly. "Bigger than most rats, anyway. Hope it's better eating."

"It will be." Resolute jerked a thumb at the field. "Once you collect up some firewood, we can cook it."

"But I got the rabbit."

"True, but getting breakfast wasn't your job. Gathering firewood is."

"But you never told me."

"You never asked." Resolute stooped and drew a knife from his boot-top. "Won't take me long to skin and prepare it. Once you get firewood and some water, we'll be ready for breakfast."

Will frowned. "Why is that my . . . ?"

"Out here, boy, there are things I can do that you cannot. If I'm doing your chores, I can't do mine." Resolute tossed him a flaccid waterskin. "You want me doing my chores around here. Now get the firewood and mind the frostclaws."

"Frostclaws?" Will's eyes narrowed. "There aren't any frostclaws around here. They're all up north. And I'm not a child that you can scare with such stories."

"No? Come here, little boy." Resolute led him around the side of the cabin, toward the cave where their horses had been kept, then squatted down and stabbed the point of his knife into the ground. "See this track here?"

The youth came over and lowered himself onto his left knee. The Vorquelf pointed to a trio of parallel lines, with the centermost a bit longer and thicker than the other two.

The lines weren't terribly distinct, just shallow marks in the dirt.

"That's a frostclaw track? It's not much."

"You've lived your life on cobblestones, so now you learn something." The Vorquelf pointed back along the path Will had taken to reach his side. "See your boot print? See how crisp the heel mark is? The ground is still moist from the rain. As that print dries out, the edges will crumble, and the wind will erode it. If the rain comes again, it'll melt the edges, leaving your heel print just a shallow oval in the dirt. The rain melted the edges of these marks. They're likely less than a week old."

"But . . . frostclaws, they can't be here. King Augustus, he made sure that wouldn't happen." Will shivered, and suddenly realized he was well away from the city where he'd grown up. He was out and exposed and there were horrible things in the wild that he wanted nothing to do with.

"Boy, the world you know is a mosaic, remember? Some pieces are true. Augustus did make the world safe for a while. He kept Chytrine back, *for a while*. Over the years, she's gotten stronger, bolder. She sends frostclaws, vylaens and gibberers this far south, testing, probing, searching and scouting. She'll be coming, and soon."

Resolute stood and, with one swift knife stroke, gutted the rabbit. "Augustus bought the world a generation in which to prepare for her to come back. If you're any example of what's waiting for her, that time has been utterly squandered."

CHAPTER 4

Will heard the sharp crack of Resolute's openhanded slap against his thigh before the pain registered. His eyes snapped open. He grabbed for the saddle with one hand, the other tightening down on the rope lead. He steadied himself and raised his head, little pops crawling up his spine bone by bone.

"I've got the horses." He raised his hand to show the rope looped around it several times. "I've got them."

Resolute remained stone-faced in profile, silhouetted against the dimming western sky. "Not the horses I'm worried about, boy. Night's coming on. Frostclaws will be about."

Will shook his head to clear it from the logginess his brief saddle-nap had caused. The way Resolute left off speaking told Will that the Vorquelf expected something of him, and expected him to figure it out. He'd been left to do a lot of that over the past three days, amid fetching and carrying, caring for the horses, cleaning up, and learning to memorize every birdsong, animal call, beast track, and plant.

Plants! He'd had to learn them by leaf, flower, fruit, root, scent, taste, and medicinal powers. Will had gotten to hate flowers and trees, and was longing to be back in some civilized place where plants were restricted to parks and gardens. Many times, Resolute had even awakened him by thrusting some plant under his nose and demanding that he identify it instantly.

It hadn't been all bad. Resolute would let him chew *metholanth* leaves to ease some aches and pains—though the supply of *metholanth* was never sufficient, or his pains were overabundant. Every night Will had collapsed exhausted and aching. In the mornings he woke stiff and sore, moving even more slowly than Crow did.

So, what is it the Vork wants now? Will blinked his eyes and looked around. With night coming on they should be seeking shelter. Usually, by this time of the day, they'd have already ridden off the main road to some hovel or cave his two guides already knew about. Those tracks, though, had headed off through forest for the most part, and now grassy fields lay on both sides of the road.

The road itself had widened, and the plants weren't meadow grasses. They were something else, something Will didn't recognize, but he could see that they were arranged in rough rows. He wasn't sure what that meant, but he knew it wasn't natural. *And if it ain't natural, that means . . .*

The young man smiled, discovering that even those muscles ached. "Someone planted these plants. There are people about. Maybe even a village or something."

Resolute's chin came up. "And?"

"And?" Will shrugged, his shoulders sagging forward. "And, and . . ."

"Think, boy, *think*."

"We can take shelter with them?"

"No, no, no!"

"We can't?"

Resolute turned in his saddle and waved away Will's question with the flick of a hand. "This is hopeless, Crow. I accepted that we might have to train him, but he's incapable of learning."

Crow chuckled as his horse trotted forward and drew abreast of the two of them, trapping Will between them. "You learned these lessons, my friend, of necessity, at a younger age. You'd not been raised in the Dimandowns. He's not a stupid lad, just a tired one."

"I'm too tired to be tired."

Crow patted him on the left shoulder. "The fields have you thinking ahead, Will. That's good, but you also need to think back. What do the fields tell you?"

"I'm going to have a harder time finding firewood?" Will shook his head. Something else niggled at the back of his mind.

"You see, Crow. He focuses on himself."

"Easy, Resolute. Why is that, Will? Why will finding firewood be harder?"

"No trees." He sighed heavily, then it hit him. His head came up. "No trees because someone cut them down for firewood. No trees means no forest. No forest means no frostclaws because they like the forest." Will glanced over at Resolute. "You tried to trick me by telling me frostclaws would be about."

"How do you know they won't?"

The youth frowned, started to point at the fields, then snarled. "I don't *know*, but it makes sense. Is that wrong? Are they going to be around?"

Resolute shrugged. "Some, yes. There will be sheep about, some goats, cows, chickens, and horses. That's what they will be going for."

"So I wasn't wrong?"

"Not completely, but it took you far too long to figure it out." The Vorquelf tapped his own skull with a finger. "You have to always be thinking, always be aware. The world would just as soon see you dead as not, and legions would like to be doing the killing."

The Vorquelf touched his heels to his horse's flanks and trotted ahead along the road. Before them, it curved between two low hills, then started a descent into the valley. A little breeze came up from that direction, bringing with it the hint of woodsmoke, confirming the presence of a village nearby.

The youth looked over at Crow. "Why is he so hard on me? I didn't do anything to him. I got him the leaf, remember? He should be thanking me."

The man's eyes glittered with the last of the day's dying light. "Remember how he said life was a mosaic?"

"Hard to forget when he says it all the time. 'Here's another piece to your mosaic, *boy*.'"

"You almost sound like him." Crow scratched at his bearded chin. "For Resolute, you're a piece in his mosaic, but his mosaic is a map, a map to a goal. He wants to make sure you fit. He hopes you do—because *if* you do, he's that much closer."

"Okay, I understand that, but shouldn't he be careful with me, not being all . . ." Will wanted to say "cruel," but he flashed back on thrashings Marcus had given him for little harmless things. "I mean, he's being hard, you know?"

Crow nodded slowly. "Always has been. When I first met him he wasn't any easier on me. For Resolute, that piece of the mosaic has taken on a shape in his mind. He wants you to fit that shape. You weren't quite what he expected, so he's doing what needs to be done."

"But what about what I want?"

The man laughed aloud. "Have you ever gotten what you want, Will? Do you even know what you want, beyond a bed and a full belly, maybe some *metholanth* or a cup of watered wine?"

"Yes, well, no, but . . ." Crow's question shot through him and echoed around inside, emphasizing how hollow he felt. Then the warmth of the leaf slowly trickled in to fill him. "I want the leaf."

Crow leaned to the right and dropped his voice to a whisper. "The care you take with that leaf, and the fact that Predator couldn't see it there on your belt, is probably what has kept Resolute from using you as frostclaw bait. You want that leaf because the leaf wants you."

Then the white-haired man straightened up and asked a series of quick questions, forestalling any questions Will might have asked in return. "Now, the things that you've learned here, have they hurt you or helped you? Has the labor been that hard, or just different from what you're used to? Is Resolute any harder on you than your former master?"

Will answered each question in his mind the second it was asked, and he didn't like the answers. The stuff he'd learned . . . Well, just knowing about *metholanth* was a help; and the other stuff would make it easy to figure out what to steal from a herbalist. Getting water and wood, cleaning up; those chores weren't as hard as ones he'd outgrown in Marcus' family. And Marcus as a taskmaster, well . . .

He snorted and decided to say nothing instead of letting Crow know he was right. That really annoyed Will about the two of them. When Resolute was right, he would hammer Will with that fact, over and over. But Crow, he'd just kind of slip it in like a stiletto. You wouldn't feel it going in, he wouldn't even twist it, but you'd know it was there when you moved against it.

They rode on, the only sounds coming from the creak of leather, the clop of hooves, the jingling of tack, or the crunch of a horse chewing a bit. Around the curve and on down they went, riding in Resolute's wake. Ahead of them, the Vorquelf had stopped his horse in the middle of the road. Beyond him, by a hundred yards or so, a bonfire burned on the road. The fire silhouetted three men facing the Vorquelf, and Will counted five others standing on the village side of the fire.

The village itself sat astride the road. At the far end, another fire burned, cutting off the western route. Fences of stone or split rails guarded the village perimeter, but none of them came even close to being as strong as the walls of Yslin. Most of the buildings were low affairs made of sod, with thatched roofing—though the tallest, a two-story house, had a tile roof and light blazing out through sloppily hung shutters.

Resolute let the other two pull parallel with him before they continued in toward the fire. Will quickly recalled one of Resolute's road lessons and glanced down and away from the flames. The men behind it would have no night vision, so if the trio chose to ride around it, their pursuers would be blind. Only the three men facing them would be able to see what they were doing. One wore a sword, the other two carried pitchforks.

The man with the sword raised a hand. "Hold there, strangers."

Crow rode up toward him slowly, stopping five yards back. "Strangers? I thought the men of Alcida greeted travelers as friends."

"Might in some other times. Who be ye, and what be you wanting in Stellin?"

"We're just travelers, my friend, my nephew, and I. We're heading into the mountains." Crow kept his voice even and light. "We were hoping to find lodging and fodder here."

The villager nodded toward Resolute. "He's a Vorquelf?"

Resolute threw back his cloak, exposing well-muscled arms covered in dark tattoos. "That should be obvious."

"Well, we'll not be wanting your kind hereabouts." The villager dropped a hand to the hilt of his sword. "You can push on and tell your mistress we're not gonna be taken like Ingens was. We may not be big, but . . ."

One of the other men stepped forward, squinting, then rested a hand on the speaker's shoulder. "I remember this one. Come through about twenty year ago. Had a woman of his kind with him, and a young fella with them. That would be you?"

Crow nodded. "We were bound into the mountains, as we are now. Has it really been twenty years?"

"Close enough, right afore Augustus' face started showing up on coin." The older man half smiled. "Quintus, they'll be no trouble."

Quintus frowned. "How can you say that?"

The old man tapped his nose. "They don't have the stink of the pack on 'em, and there ain't but one Vorquelf working for Chytrine and this one ain't her."

"There's trouble, it's on your head."

The man rubbed a rough hand back over his bald pate. "Least then there'd be something on it."

Quintus snorted a laugh, then jerked a thumb toward the heart of town. "Hare and Hutch is our inn; they have a stable. Other travelers in, so might be the stable is full. Tell the boy to take the other horses to my barn. Be gone in the morning, will you?"

Crow nodded. "With the sunrise."

"Then I'll see you going out as I go in." He gave them a nod. "The peace of Stellin be on ya, and a plague on your souls if you break it."

CHAPTER 5

Will wasn't quite certain why Resolute didn't demand he accompany the stableboy to take care of their horses, but he welcomed the relief from his chores. He grabbed his rolled blanket and the flaccid saddlebags that carried his threadbare change of clothes, then followed the other two into the Hare and Hutch. *After so long on the road, back to normal will be good.*

But the village tavern, he discovered upon entry, escaped normal by leagues. It certainly had the look of a normal tavern, with entry through a sheltered door, then steps down into the common room. One short wall of the rectangular building stood close by on the right, with a set of stairs marking the far right corner and leading up to the next floor. Huddled beneath the stairs lay the bar, and a doorway through the long wall led out to the kitchen at the back. It had a roof and a hearth, half walls and a dirt floor.

The common room opened to the left, with a big hearth and roaring fire on the left wall. Benches took up those corners, with some long tables and other round ones filling the main space. Will could feel the fire's heat from the doorway and welcomed it, though the fire did seem a bit big for a summer's evening.

Resolute hung his cloak on the pegs by the door, dropped his bag beneath it, then relieved Crow of his burdens and likewise disposed of them. The low hum of conversation dipped for a moment, then picked up with some intensity. Will felt himself tensing, for in the Dim, the Vorquelf's showing himself in a human haunt would have caused an immediate fight.

The added energy drained quickly from the conversation, but Will didn't get a sense of fear holding the people at bay. As he tried to figure out what was at work, he began to notice other things, such as the floor being clean and well kept, with new boards laid down to replace old and rotted ones. As for the barkeeper, his clothes had clearly been laundered—and recently. The clientele didn't seem drunk, and he heard no catcalls as a young woman wove her way between tables to deliver wooden tankards of frothy ale.

He finally hit upon it. The people were smiling, none of them hooding their eyes or watching their fellows for weakness. The taverns he'd known were wolves'-dens. *Here they're sheep. Farmers, herders, working for a living, taking time here to share stories.* It sent a shiver down his spine.

Crow, leaning his right flank against the bar, waved his left hand toward Resolute and Will. "We were told, my companion, nephew, and I, that you might have room available here for a night's lodging."

The tavernkeeper, a burly man with a ring of black hair running round his head, ran a hand over unshaved jowls. "Well, the last room, it was taken by that gentleman and his niece, but they've not paid as yet. . . . Oy, you." He flicked a stained dishrag toward two people seated at a round table.

An older man turned toward the bar, raising an eyebrow, but Crow reached out and took hold of the barman's wrist. "That's all right. You'd be having space on the floor here, near the fire?"

The barman nodded. "Plenty of room there, yes; silver a head, and that gets you an ale tonight and porridge in the morning."

"Done, then." Crow went to open his pouch, but the barman shook his head. "We'll settle up before you bed down. You'll be wanting some stew, won't you? And bread, some cheese?"

Crow nodded. "Please."

"Have it ready in a bit."

Crow smiled at his companions. "There we are, set for the night."

Will nodded, barely hearing Crow. He looked around the room, eyeing each person in there. He quickly sorted prosperous from poor, which he found easy given that most of the farmers wore not so much as a ring. The prosperous had coin pouches, but most were as empty as his saddlebags. Having seen how trusting the barman was in dealing with Crow, Will assumed most of the people were drinking on credit, and that a fair amount of debt was paid off in stew-makings, cheese, and flour.

Being bumped in the back by Resolute jolted Will from his thoughts and propelled him in Crow's wake. They threaded their way over to a circular table near the fireplace. The old man, who wore a blue cloak that had seen better days, nodded a welcome to them and waved them to the open chairs.

Crow thanked him. "I'm Crow, this is my nephew, Will, and my friend, Resolute."

The man half rose from his chair and shook Crow's hand, then nodded to Will and Resolute. "I am Distalus and this is my niece, Sephi. We're on our way to Yslin, where she'll be apprenticing to a weaver."

Will nipped around past Crow and took the seat next to Sephi. "I'm Will."

The girl blushed. "Sephi." Had she been standing, she would have towered over him, and seated she still appeared taller, but Will didn't mind. Her raven hair fell to mid-back.

Hazel eyes sparkled with reflected firelight, set in a pretty face marred only by a small scar above her right eye.

Distalus raised his mug in Crow's direction. "That was good of you, sir, not to evict us."

Crow shrugged easily. "We've been on the road, so warm will do for us. You've a long journey ahead, and few places will be this nice."

Will let his saddlebags slip to the floor and dumped his cloak on top of them. "Have you been to the city before, Sephi?"

She shook her head and gave him a little smile. "My uncle says it is a wonderful place, and that I will love it." She wrapped her small hands around the barrel of her mug. "I can hardly wait."

The young thief smiled and was about to launch into a story of the city, when Crow elbowed him. He turned to look at his older companion. "What?"

"You've better things to be doing, like helping the barkeep bring us our stew." Crow glanced at Distalus. "More ale for you, as long as Will is going to be fetching it?"

"Well, now, very kind, sir, very kind. Traveling is a dry business and Master Julian's ale is good."

Crow flicked two fingers toward the barman. "Two more ales, please, for our friends. Will, go."

Will nodded, then flashed Sephi a quick smile. He got up and moved around her chair, daring to let the fingers of his left hand brush her shoulder. In paying more attention to her than where he'd tossed his cloak, he tripped and fell heavily against Distalus, catching himself before smashing his slowly healing knee into the floor.

"Beg pardon, sir." Will pulled himself up and straightened his shirt, then made his way to the bar. He twisted his hips left and right, nipping through the narrows of chairs pushed back from tables. He made his journey a display of agility, hoping to dispel the image his fall had left in Sephi's mind.

Julian looked at him with a critical eye. "You be spilling

any of this, and you might's well eat it off the floor, for you're paying for it."

"I will be careful."

"Be double that, lad." Julian hefted a tray of ale mugs, leaving another with stew bowls and bread for Will. The youth trailed after the barman, occasionally peeking out from behind his girth to see if Sephi was watching him. She was and giggled. Will cut around Julian and served Resolute first, then Crow and himself last. He put his bowl down where he'd have to scoot his chair closer to her to eat it, and put the bread in the middle of the table.

Julian accepted the tray from him, then trapped both of them beneath his right arm. He counted on his fingers. "Well, now, I'm making that six silvers you're owing, sir. And you, sir, for the girl and you, lodging and ale, that's three silvers."

Distalus' hand went to his belt, then he blinked and looked up. "My purse seems to be gone."

Resolute's silver eyes narrowed. "Boy, give it back."

Will, who had a spoonful of stew halfway between bowl and eaten, froze. "I didn't take it."

"Don't lie, boy." The Vorquelf's voice took on a chill. "I won't have it."

The spoon returned to the bowl and Will slowly stood. He deliberately opened his hands and held them out away from his sides. "Search me. I didn't take anything."

Distalus shook his head. "I'm sure the boy didn't . . . as my niece will agree, I get forgetful. Probably just in my bag in the room."

Crow laid a hand on Resolute's forearm, then fished a gold coin from the pouch on his belt. The coin rang solid as he flicked it with his thumb into the air. Julian caught it easily, then held it at arm's length to study it on both sides.

"New-minted Oriosa." The man snapped the coin down on the table, leaving the masked profile of King Scrainwood easily visible. From a pocket on his apron he pulled a short metal rod with a knob at one end and a point at the other. He pressed the small part on Scrainwood's eye and leaned hard on the knob. The rod gouged the eye, disfiguring the face.

Julian smiled, then slipped coin and punch back into his apron pocket. "There, that will fix him. Enjoy your food. You've more coming if you want, or a silver yet."

"Thank you." Crow nodded to him. "You're stabling our horses as well, so we will owe you more."

With a nod the barman retreated, then Distalus raised his new mug of ale. "I'll pay you back. I have the silver in my bags."

"I'm not worried."

Will frowned. In his life he'd not seen that many gold coins, and had held fewer, and not for very long. A few he'd seen had the eyes gouged or crossed on a face, but he never knew why. "What he did to that coin, why?"

Distalus' eyes brightened. "I would have thought everyone knew the tale of how Scrainwood became a king, and where his allegiances lie." The man raised his voice a bit, drawing attention from the tables around him, suddenly sounding much more like a storyteller than a . . .

I don't know what *he is.*

The man quaffed a bit of ale, then wiped his mouth with the back of his hand. "Maybe you know, lad, maybe you don't, but Scrainwood of Oriosa joined good King Augustus in war against Chytrine a quarter century ago. Some say Scrainwood fought, others that he never fought. Some say not too many died to protect him and others that he cowered; but none deny he was there at Fortress Draconis. And there it was he stayed, while King Augustus routed an Aurolani army in Okrannel. And he was there when the coward brought news of the heroes sent to destroy Chytrine."

A quiet had fallen over the common room, with only the hiss and snap of the fire, or an occasional soft belch heard around Distalus' words. The man's eyes glowed and he smiled, looking at his listeners, nodding and smiling.

Whatever he was, it included being a storyteller, and Will didn't mind that his question started the story. He figured he'd not been alone in not knowing, but even if he was, the story was a good one to hear and others were enjoying it.

"Well now, then, it was fifteen years ago, a decade past the loss of our heroes and Augustus winning a bride, that the first of the new *sullanciri* came south. Word had come, filtered down through the Ghost March, in the mouths of renegades who pledged themselves to Chytrine, that her nine new Dark Lancers could not be stopped. They gave a date and a place and a target: Queen Lanivette of Oriosa would die in her castle in Meredo. Came that day, all dark and cold, cold as winter, wet as fall, the clouds weeping, wind keening; mourning her while she still breathed.

"Troops guarded the castle, ringed it with steel. Heroes and those who wished to be heroes came to keep her safe. Come the appointed hour, they saw naught but lightning. They thought themselves safe then. Yet as they hooted and hollered, cheered and rejoiced, guess what they saw, lad, guess!"

Will, caught up in the story, shook his head. "I don't know."

"They saw a terrible thing, lad, the most horrible thing they'd ever seen." Distalus raised his hand, shaping a tall tower in the air. "Lightning, it struck the tallest tower, scattering men, spilling them from battlements to be dashed to red pieces on the courtyards below. In its wake stood a fiery horse, with long dragon's wings, and on it a specter, with a long flowing cape. It appeared to be feathered, but each feather was a tongue of flame. He hoisted above him a shrouded body and cast it down. It bounced from crenels and catwalks, unwrapping as it went. Queen Lanivette's body, broken and rent, headless, lay before her keep."

Distalus' voice lowered, his telling paused for a moment as he drank, then he peered into the depths of his ale and continued. "The guards and the heroes, they rushed into the castle, opening the Grand Hall. They found but one man there, Scrainwood, her son. He stood dripping in a puddle of his own piss. In his hands he held his mother's severed head, staring at it as she stared at him. He didn't speak, but just trembled. Then someone closed her eyes and that broke the spell. He collapsed and when he regained his senses, a week later, his hair had gone white.

"Since that day, two things are true of Oriosa. The first is that their last hero, Leigh Norrington, went north to kill his own father, the *sullanciri* who had slain the queen. That hero, though, chose blood over nation. His father had become Nefrai-kesh and he was turned to be Nefrai-laysh, the tenth of the new *sullanciri*. As they once led an army against Chytrine, now, father and son, they prepare to lead an army against us."

A bit of a hubbub began, but Distalus merely lifted a hand and it quieted. "The other thing, lad, is that Scrainwood fears the *sullanciri* who put him on the throne so much that he dare not oppose them. His mother had steeled her nation for another war, but he has let it rust. Everyone knows Oriosa is a safe haven for Aurolani scouts, and that foul magicks can let Scrainwood see through the coins bearing his face. So we blind them to rob him of this sight, and deprive Chytrine of her spy."

Distalus punctuated his story with a gulp of ale. Others did the same, then calls came for refills, which kept Julian very busy. The old man glanced over at Crow. "You knew the tale, yes?"

Crow nodded slowly. "But the telling, that was good. The part about the urine—your embellishment or . . ."

The storyteller licked his lips. "Had the story from a soldier who was there."

Resolute tore a hunk off a small loaf of bread. "This is how you make your living, then? Telling stories?"

"I do a little of everything, but now I'm taking my niece to the city. Might stay here for a bit, though. It depends, I guess." Distalus jerked his head toward Julian. "If he makes me an offer, we might stay. I have a number of thirsty tales. Tonight was just a taste."

The Vorquelf nodded. "And people pay to listen to tales of Chytrine?"

Distalus shrugged. "She's very popular. She's the villain of a thousand stories, each worse than the last. Everyone fears her, of course, fears her coming to a place like Stellin to destroy it. Some folks assume it's plain greed, others thinks she has a more sinister motivation. To me it doesn't matter—all answers are right. I have no doubt she wants to lay waste to the southlands. *Why* she wants to do it is not my concern."

Will frowned. "But if you knew why, couldn't you stop her?"

The man canted his head for a moment, then nodded. "An interesting observation, young man. I suspect we shall never know her motivation, but perhaps a tale hinting at it might be very popular indeed. I shall think on it. Thank you."

With that, Distalus stood and held his hand out for Sephi. "Come, child, we shall retire early so the crowd will thin and our friends can sleep. Good evening to you. Sleep well."

Will frowned as the girl left, but then she turned back toward him and gave him a little finger-wave that Distalus could not see. This brightened his heart and put a smile on his face.

A smile so broad even the landing of Resolute's hands on his shoulders couldn't kill it. The Vorquelf had used the distraction Sephi supplied to slip from his chair and come up behind Will. The youth started to rise and Resolute spun him around. Will's chair clattered to the ground and he fell forward against the Vorquelf for a second, then Resolute hoisted him from the floor by his upper arms.

"Where did you put his money?"

Will shook his head. "I didn't steal it."

Resolute shook him once, hard. "You did. You took it when you tripped."

"No, I didn't." The youth's nostrils flared. "I tripped, truly tripped, and caught myself on him. I didn't take his money."

"It was a clumsy attempt at a theft that anyone could have seen through, boy."

Will kept his voice low, but an edge slid into it. "I'm much better than that, Resolute."

"A regular Azure Spider are you, boy?"

"Not yet, but I am good!" Will flipped his right wrist and a pouch heavy with coins clunked down in the middle of the table. "I'm that good."

The Vorquelf dropped him, then felt his own belt. "Just now? You took that from me, just now?"

Will nodded as he appropriated Sephi's chair. "Yes. And I didn't take Distalus' coin because he didn't have any."

Resolute snatched his purse from the table and retied it to his belt. "The fact that you know that, though, means you would have taken it."

Will blinked. "If a hart crossed your trail, you'd shoot it."

Resolute's hands curled down into fists. "If you cannot understand the difference, boy . . ."

Crow turned in his chair and leaned forward, resting his elbows on his knees. "The difference is this, Will. Resolute would shoot the hart, but only if he needed the food. You didn't need the money. You don't need to steal."

"But that's what I do." Will shrugged. "I'm a thief."

"Not anymore, Will." Crow poked a finger against his breastbone, spearing the pouch in which lay the leaf. "The theft of that ended your old life. You're meant for better now."

CHAPTER 6

Will spent a restless night there on the floor of the Hare and Hutch. Early on he was too warm, then too cold, with parts of his body going numb from sleeping on this knotted piece of wood or that. He tossed and turned and, half asleep as he was, would have welcomed a kick from Crow or Resolute that would have wakened him fully.

Worse than the physical conditions were his dreams. In little bits and pieces he could see things he knew were not meant for him. He felt himself springing from the saddle of a flaming horse that furled its wings. Tongues of flame formed his cloak, leaving scorched patches on the red carpet. He marched along toward the throne, seeing a defiant woman there—one who looked like Sephi. They spoke, cordially at first, but always strained, then harsher. The woman waved him away and he reached out, grabbing her throat. With the ease of thumbing a head off a flower, he decapitated her, then placed her head in her son's hands.

When he caught sight of himself in a mirror, he wore Crow's face, but much younger.

That dream nearly woke him all the way, but then simple idylls seduced him back. He and Sephi, or sometimes the Vorquelf, Charity, would walk hand in hand through spring fields, with grasses and flowers dancing in a warm breeze. He could feel his ardor rising, and he could see it burning in the eyes of his companion, then an icy blizzard would break over the meadow, washing his sight away in an ocean of white. When he could see again, the object of his desire had been transformed into a woman of ice who radiated cold, both attractive and repellent for in her embrace he would find cold comfort and agonizing death.

Finally, after hours of such horrid visions, morning came. Julian's daughter—Malva, she whispered, was her name—wakened him when she stirred the coals in the hearth and added wood to it to build the fire up again. Will somehow propelled himself to his feet, made use of the outhouse, then volunteered to split wood. *As long as I am going to be tired, I should have a reason for it.*

Julian's wife—though not Malva's mother, who had died of summer's-fever two years back—prepared breakfast for the family, Crow's party, Distalus and Sephi. Distalus entertained them all with some information about the Gold Wolf, a female bandit given to raiding down out of the mountains. Will would have preferred tales of the Azure Spider, but the stories Distalus told were harrowing enough to bring Will fully awake, and he wondered if they'd encounter her on their way into the mountains.

Crow settled up their account, paying for the keeping of the horses, then they quit the inn. Julian and Distalus sat closely, speaking quietly as they left. Sephi did wave to Will and watched him go, but when he looked back one last time, she had turned to listen to Julian.

Saddled up, they headed out of Stellin and along the road west for a bit, then cut to the northwest on their journey's fourth day. They skirted a salt marsh, then started working their way up into the mountains. The trail they used seemed to be seldom traveled and mostly overgrown.

"Been a while since anyone came this way."

Resolute shrugged. "A year."

"Two, I think, my friend."

The Vorquelf turned in his saddle. "Are you sure?"

"We left here end of summer, having helped harvest, then wintered in Jerana, spring in the Ghost March. Summer again south, but not back in the mountains, then Muroso this last winter."

"The years, they blur together."

"You have more to remember than I do, Resolute."

"It's no excuse." The Vorquelf gave Crow a grin. "And you are right about when we were here last."

Will cleared his voice. "Where exactly is here?"

Resolute's smile died. "What difference does it make to you, boy? You know nothing of the world so you can't figure out where to put this place in your vision of it."

"Maybe I want to learn." Will pointed to the trail in front of them. "Want to know how I know no one has come this way in a while? There, those blue-cups, they're already flowered for the year and will be making those seed pods that will let them spread seeds out further. Plants would have been trampled if riders had come this way."

The Vorquelf snorted. "A child could have figured that out."

"Sure, but not me, not without what I've learned so far."

Resolute remained silent for a moment, then nodded. "You're in the Gyrvirgul, near the Crescent Sea. Does that mean anything to you?"

Will almost said that it did, but hesitated. *If I do, he will ask what and I will be stuck for an answer.* "Means I'm a long way from home. Means we might see Gyrkyme."

"I doubt that. The Winged Ones keep to the highest mountains more inland." Resolute pointed toward the southwest where, in the distance, clouds shrouded tall peaks. "I doubt we will see this Gold Wolf either."

"Why not? You've got gold."

The Vorquelf glanced quickly at the pouch tied to his belt. "We'd be slim pickings for a bandit such as that."

The youth started to ask Resolute to explain his comment, but stopped and thought about it. Distalus' tales had been sketchy at best, mostly describing her as a beautiful and powerful warrior woman who led a host of horsemen. They raided throughout the Alcidese border with Helurca, according to Distalus, with Stellin being at the extreme edge of their range.

Will frowned mightily. "Something isn't right with the Gold Wolf."

Crow turned from watching the packhorses strung out behind them and smiled. "What makes you say that?"

"Okay, look, we have three people, nine horses. We can find a hovel or pitch a tent and let our horses crop grass and give them grain when they need it. We kill a rabbit and roast it, we find roots and other edible plants. That's fine for us, but as big a group as she has—even if you figure Distalus was lying—would need more food, more fodder."

The older man nodded. "And this leads you to conclude?"

"I'm not sure, but the people of Stellin seemed to thrill to stories of her, not cringe from them like they did the stories of Chytrine." He shrugged. "They're not afraid of this Gold Wolf."

"Not in the least, so we won't be either."

"But how can she be a bandit raider, with the folks she should be raiding not being afraid of her?"

Resolute snarled. "It's an impossible question to answer, boy. Next time we see Distalus, perhaps he can make up an answer for you."

Crow laughed. "Next time we see Distalus he'll be in a tavern in the Dim, drinking what little profits he has from selling Sephi."

Resolute nodded. "She was a pretty one."

That simple comment recast the whole evening for Will. "She's going to Yslin to be a liftskirt?"

"Likely, though she probably does not know it." Crow shook his head. "Her parents might not even know it. Distalus gave them some money, told them there would be more, and they suddenly have one less mouth to feed."

"I wish I *had* stolen his money."

The Vorquelf laughed. "So the thief looks down on a procurer?"

"There is honor among . . ." Will's protest died beneath the hellish glare of Resolute's argent stare. "She should have a choice."

"She'll get one. It just may not be easy." Crow nodded further up the trail, where it climbed up a hill and around to the left. "Almost there."

Will looked back toward the east, thinking he could actually see Stellin, but knowing he could not. "We should have done something."

Resolute ducked beneath a low maple branch. "There was nothing to do, boy. If we fail in our mission, her fate won't matter."

"And that mission is?"

The Vorquelf smiled cruelly. "Seeing if you're steel or bronze, boy. If you're the one, you'll save the world. If you're the other, you'll be lucky to save yourself."

The trail took them up and around through a narrow pass where stones scraped both of Will's shins as he rode. After a short while it opened into a small copse of birch, then down into a vale that made Will's breath catch in his chest. He let his horse wander off the trail and start cropping grasses while he just sat in the saddle and stared.

Until this journey and his education by Resolute, Will had not known one plant from another. While his trip had not been long, he had absorbed a great deal. He'd even been able to identify his leaf as looking like something from an oak, though the silver metal matched nothing he saw growing in field and forest.

At least until now . . .

Rows of silverwood trees lined the trail into the vale. Other plants clung to these trees, bursting with gorgeous flowers, lush and plump and colorful. Bushes were ripe with berries that looked like raspberries, but were pumpkin orange. Other flowers and undergrowth seemed familiar, but somehow more vibrant, more green, more alive than plants not a league back down the road.

Crow rode over and took the reins from Will's hands. "Come on, this is nothing."

That comment surprised Will. "What is this place?"

"The shadow of another place."

Crow nudged his horse's ribs with his heels and the two animals trotted forward through the silverwood arbor. At the bottom of a slight hill, the trail curved around to the left, through plots of cultivated soil. Will recognized none of the vegetables hanging from those plants, but the chickens that scattered as they rode up seemed quite common. He saw a pen with goats and sheep in it further along, but no farmhouse to go along with the fields and livestock.

Crow reined up behind Resolute and the packhorses, near the mouth of a cave. A female elf emerged from it. Will supposed she was a Vorquelf, since her eyes were almost entirely copper, but they had a white dot at the center of each. Those dots flicked back and forth, as if she were watching them dismount, but Will saw that her gaze followed sounds, not people.

He wondered for a moment if she were Resolute's wife. He doubted any female would be stupid enough to want Resolute for a husband, but having him for one would explain why she lived in a place that was hard for him to visit.

Resolute crossed to her and dropped to a knee. He took

her right hand in his and kissed it. "Our absence has been unforgivable."

She patted his head gently, as if he were a dog. "Forgiven because it was unavoidable. I have seen where you have been, Resolute. And Kedyn's Crow, he still travels with you."

Crow swung from the saddle and hugged the elf. "It has been too long."

She freed herself from his embrace. "And this one you've brought. Who is he?"

Her voice caressed his ears and his heart began to pound faster. Will didn't know who she was, but for Resolute to kneel before her meant she was important. Still, Will didn't need that evidence to know how special she was. Something inside of him realized they shared a kinship, a bond.

Will slid from the saddle and fished the leaf-bag from within his tunic. He held it out. "I'm Will, a courier. This is for you." As much as he didn't want to surrender it, he also knew, deep down, that it was never meant to be possessed. It was meant to be put to a use, and she was the one to use it.

"I am Oracle, and I thank you, Will." Her slender fingers stroked his hands as she accepted the pouch from him. She smiled, and Will felt certain it was because of the leaf. "Wilburforce, yes, a wonderful name. I intended no disrespect."

"I, um, th-thank you." Will found his mouth suddenly dry. "No problem."

"Good." The word came softly from her mouth, then she closed her eyes and opened the bag. The silver leaf seemed to shine more brightly than ever before as she brought it into her hands and the full light of day. She clasped it flat between her hands, the silver so brilliant that light fled through her flesh, outlining her bones in black. "Yes, oh, yes, this is an important piece. Come, now, come with me."

She turned on her heel and all but ran into the cave. Will started after her, but Crow grabbed his shoulder. "Slowly, Will. She knows the cave well and the darkness does not bother her."

The youth nodded. "Her eyes. She's blind, isn't she?"

Resolute growled. "Some sight is gone, but she sees what she must see."

Will frowned. "Can't you ever just say yes?"

"Some questions just don't have simple answers, boy."

Crow gave Will's shoulder a squeeze. "Yes, she is blind. She has been for a number of years now."

Will's eyes widened. "How did it happen?"

Resolute, half hidden in the shadow of the cave, scowled. "She did it to herself."

"What? Why?"

"Here's an answer that's simple for you, boy. . . ." Resolute's voice echoed from inside the cave as he disappeared. "She didn't want someone else using her eyes."

CHAPTER 7

Will followed Resolute into the cave and passed through a narrowing before the path cut to the left. There it widened somewhat into a flat ovoid space several yards across at the widest point. A small fire guttered in a makeshift fireplace fashioned of stones. It generated more heat than light, with the smoke rising to fill the chamber's low roof. A bit farther along the path, the smoke, like water pouring gently over a dam, streamed out and rose through a crack in the cave's roof.

The Vorquelf's bulk blocked Will from seeing into the next chamber, but he knew it was going to be something spectacular. Light, a greenish silver, glowed around Resolute's outline. Resolute ducked his head to make it through a small opening and Will followed, his head unbowed.

Then he stopped, his breath frozen in his lungs.

For the whole of the journey to the mountains, Resolute had ground on about how little Will knew about the world. Will had learned from him, at times grudgingly, other times gratefully; but never had Will let go of his conviction that he knew far more than Resolute suspected or would ever know himself. The cavern into which he walked stripped that smugness away from him.

He felt as lost as a wandering toddler in the streets of Yslin.

The soft brilliance of glowing minerals and lichens illuminated the cavern, which Will guessed was big enough to house four of the Hare and Hutch inns. Pillars of flowstone upheld a dark roof within which sparkled lights like stars. He even thought he recognized some of the constellations, but so many seemed alien to him.

More remarkable than a night sky set in stone was the cavern itself. As Will took a step forward he felt as if he were moving through something fluid—not as dense as water, but certainly not air. He really could feel it pressing against him, softly and gently, like the weight of a light blanket. It didn't hurt or make him uncomfortable, yet it dragged on him the way the air did on a humid day.

All around him, throughout the cavern, things hung in the air. Leaves and branches, here and there, as if they were the only visible part of trees hidden by an invisible fog. By his feet he saw the skeleton of what he took to be a rabbit, painstakingly reconstructed, with a moth-eaten cape of fur draped over it. Beyond it, springing from atop a rock, another skeleton hovered in mid-leap, clawed paws ready to rend the rabbit. Looking at it Will could almost see the muscles layered on its bare bones, the rippling of them and how that would shift the color of the hunting predator's coat.

Yet more impressive than the bones and branches were the murals. At first Will could not tell what they were because when he looked at them from the entryway, all he saw was a slender stripe of color. As he moved further into the room, however, the colors spread out into long rectangular landscapes and vistas. Through them—some were painted, others the product of chalk or of bits and pieces of stone and leaf mosaics that just hung there in the air—he could see how a boulder had been transformed into an ocean headland, or a stone spire became the edge of a valley. And as he stared longer at any one picture, the reality that defined it seemed to fade. The colors mixed and fused, then bled into depth. He wanted to reach a hand out and through them to touch the place they represented.

Resolute caught his left wrist before he could touch a painting. "Don't."

"No? It seems so real."

"It is, or *was*." Resolute's voice broke ever so slightly, surprising Will. "How much do you know of magick, boy?"

Will felt his rebellion returning, but he only shrugged.

Oracle turned from where she had been brushing a light blue circle of paint onto what was, for all Will could see, air. "Resolute, you make it sound like an accusation. Wilburforce would know nothing of magick, for he has not had the opportunity to be trained."

Part of Will wanted to frown with her use of his full name, but from her mouth it sounded right. It wasn't used the way Marcus and some of the others had, to scold or ridicule him. *The way she says it makes it fit me.*

Oracle smiled at Will and opened her hands, leaving the brush and small bowl of pigment she'd been using hanging in the air. She stepped around them, opening her arms to encompass the whole room. "This is a place of magick, a very special place, and you are now one of two men who knows of its existence."

"Thank you?" Will's confusion knitted his brows together. "Why would you trust me?"

"We have to, Wilburforce." She turned and nodded toward Resolute. "The acorn, please."

The Vorquelf dug into a small pouch on his belt and produced an acorn. It looked like many others Will had learned to identify on his trip, save that it had a red-gold sheen to it instead of brown or green. Resolute flipped it toward Oracle. The acorn traveled quickly through the first half of its arc, then slowed and started floating, as if it were a feather caught on a whisper.

Oracle opened her right hand, splaying long pale fingers, and the acorn came to rest in the center of her palm. "This acorn came from the very tree that produced the leaf you found, Wilburforce. In magick, many things are linked. Some links are natural, such as the link between a leaf and a tree. Do you understand?"

Will nodded.

"Some links are forged. By way of example, this acorn is something Resolute has carried for two years. It contains traces of him, much as a stone you'd held in your hands for hours would have some of your warmth."

Will nodded, then realized that because she was blind, she could not see him. "I understand."

Resolute snorted. "She knew. Heard your brain rattling in your skull."

Oracle closed her eyes and sighed. "Your impatience, Resolute, must it color everything?"

Resolute started to answer in Elvish, but Oracle frowned. "In the common tongue. He should hear this."

"If we must." Resolute's nostrils flared. "Perhaps my impatience need not spill over, but we do not know if he is the one we need or not."

"The acorn led you to him, did it not?"

"The acorn led me to the leaf, and you said the leaf would lead to him. This boy could just be a link in a chain."

She smiled and opened her eyes slowly. "It was not easy for me to blind myself, yet you refuse to even see."

Will fidgeted. "You may be speaking words I understand, but, um, I don't understand."

"Understanding will come, Wilburforce." She turned a circle, almost gaily, with the hem of her white robe flaring out, her long white braid arcing behind her. "This place we created from bits and pieces of our homeland, Vorquellyn. You know the story: a century and a quarter ago the Aurolani host overran the island and we were driven out.

When elves are about your age, they are bound to the land of their birth through a ritual. It makes us responsible for our homeland, ties to it so we feel its pain. Those elves who were bound to Vorquellyn were in such agony because of the island's rape that they abandoned the world.

"This left the unbound—Resolute, Amends, me, others—to wander the world and fight for our homeland. We hoped, a human generation ago, that the war against Chytrine would free Vorquellyn, but it did not. So we began to act covertly. Here we bring together artifacts of our old home, for those things link us to it. As we get more, the link grows stronger."

Will glanced back toward the outside. "The trees, they were grown from seeds from Vorquellyn?"

"No, Wilburforce, things from Vorquellyn we bring in here. Those plants came from other elven homelands, though originally were grown from Vorquellyn stock." She shrugged. "We had hoped that growing them here might allow us to establish a homeland. While they do provide a link, it is a weak one, since conditions here are not the same as they were on our island. In this cave, however, the power grows. I can sometimes hear the breakers, feel the sea breeze, smell flowers and fruits."

Resolute scratched along his unshaven jaw. "To create this place—the idea for it came from a series of prophecies Oracle uttered at the time of the war—we demanded keepsakes from the Vorquelves. Some, like Predator, held out. As we get more, the power grows."

"Why not just go to Vorquellyn and get what you need?"

Resolute began with one of his low and sinister laughs, but a frown from Oracle cut him off. "Wilburforce, these things came from Vorquellyn *before* the taint settled over it. Anything from there now would serve to warn our enemies of our presence, and we cannot have that."

The youth nodded slowly. "How am I part of this?"

The blind Vorquelf sighed and turned away from him.

"Follow me." As she walked deeper into the cavern, she swept past the edge of one mural and descended from view.

Will trailed after her quickly and hurried down a narrow stairway that had been crudely hacked from the stone. Glowing lichen marked the top of the passage, though he was in no risk of hitting his head. It twisted right and then left again, descending sharply during the last twenty yards, and opened into another smaller chamber that he figured was roughly below the heart of the room above. Lichen and minerals also provided illumination here, and for the barest of moments, Will envied Oracle her blindness.

Big, bloody murals covered the walls and ceiling of the chamber. They coiled like rainbow vipers around stalactites and stalagmites. Nothing hung in the air, but the hideous and apocalyptic nature of the images would have clawed themselves free from the paintings were they not anchored to the walls. Men and elves, urZrethi, Gyrkyme, and other races, bestial and otherwise, fought in pitched battles against each other. Bodies and pieces thereof filled holes in the riot of combatants, with some later images being painted over earlier ones.

In the midst of all this violent chaos, one small section of wall had nothing on it but a human silhouette outlined in gold. Oracle drifted through the room toward it, then tucked her hands in the opposite sleeves of her robe and bowed her head. "This, I believe, is your part in it. Yours is the face meant to be painted here. We do not know for certain if you are the one we seek or, as Resolute allowed, only a link to that person. Determining if you are or not could be dangerous, very dangerous."

Will glanced back at where Resolute filled the only exit to the chamber. "I have no choice in the matter?"

Oracle's head came up, her face expressionless. "You have choices, always. If this is your destiny, then the next step is crucial."

"And if not?"

"Then your destiny is unknown to me, but I wish you

well with it." She closed her eyes. "It would be best if you were not compelled."

Resolute cracked his knuckles.

Will sighed, mostly because that was the easiest defense against the shiver running up his spine. The magick in the place intrigued and scared him, but wonder washed over the top of his fear. The fact that Oracle, blind as she was, had been capable of doing all she had impressed him, because the only blind he knew were beggars. Beggars were as rats to wolves when measured against thieves, but Oracle would have astounded even the greatest thief Will knew.

Still, the fear lurked there. "I will ask you my question, Oracle. I know what Resolute will answer, since, for him, my death is never far away. What you will do is learn if I am the one you want, right? And this is going to be deadly dangerous?"

She smiled slowly. "Only if you are the one we seek. But if you are, we will do all we can to save you."

No sigh came to quell the shiver this time. Will turned to look at Resolute. "If I am not, I'm not leaving this place, am I? You didn't trust Amends. You can't trust me."

The large Vorquelf folded his arms over his chest and shrugged. "Spending the rest of your life here would be better than in the slums of Yslin."

However long you'd let me live. Will wanted to feel angry or scared at the prospect of being trapped here or slain, but he could not. Just as he knew the leaf had wanted him to carry it away, somehow he knew his place was here. That almost made him laugh. Every orphan Marcus had taken in harbored the same fantasy. Someday someone would come and reveal to them who they really were, would show them to their rightful place in the world. For him it had been his mother who would have escaped the fire, survived and become Vionna, the pirate queen, with the Azure Spider as her consort.

Now I have what we all wished for, but it doesn't come free. The way Resolute watched him told Will that the

Vorquelf expected him to try to run. Will put his chances at being able to escape the Vork as small, but part of him wanted to try anyway.

Another part of him, a larger part, balked. There was something in the way Oracle had said they would do all they could to save him that told him how important he was to them. *If I am not the one they want, I would be a link in the chain.* Suddenly he found for himself the theme of the saga of Will the Nimble. His story would be one of exploits strung like pearls, and now he had a string. He would help restore Vorquellyn—wherever that was—and he knew he would do it because everyone else had failed for a very long time.

He nodded and exhaled slowly. "What do we have to do?"

Relief painted a smile on Oracle's face. "Come over here and stand in this basin, Wilburforce."

Will complied as Resolute exited the chamber. The youth found an iron ring had been half-sunk into the center of a shallow depression in the rock, which was ten feet in diameter. Around the rim had been painted an uneven red line. He toed the rusty ring and found it both heavy and solidly affixed to the ground.

An angry bleat and the clicking of goat's-hooves on the stone brought him around. Resolute reentered the room and stepped aside as Crow led a goat at the end of a stout length of chain into the chamber. The two warriors exchanged silent glances, then Crow smiled.

"I had no doubt Will would agree. I thought I would save time." Crow led the goat over to the depression, then fastened its chain to the ring, leaving it six feet of play. The creature seemed docile enough, coming over to sniff at Will, then gently butting him.

Oracle entered the depression and the goat came to her. She stroked its neck, then brushed a thumb over its forehead. The Vorquelf drew a slender poniard and slashed a little cut above and between the goat's eyes. The creature bleated and jumped back to the length of its chain, with blood welling in the wound. Its hooves scrabbled against the smooth stone, but gained little purchase, and the goat went down.

"Give me your left hand, your heart hand, Wilburforce."

He complied and felt the sting of the blade being dragged over his palm.

Oracle pointed to the goat as it rose unsteadily to its feet. "We need to forge a link between you and it. Place your wound against its, let the blood comingle. Go, do it, there is little time to lose."

Will trailed his right hand over the chain and closed with the goat. By the time he got to it and laid his hand on its forehead, Crow and Oracle had cleared the depression. Oracle and Resolute, standing together at circle's edge, held hands and Resolute's tattoos began to glow with a vibrant purple hue. A quarter circle away, Crow had strung a small horse-bow made of a silver-blond wood, and had nocked an arrow with a wide razored broadhead that had been washed in silver.

Will swallowed hard. "I'm ready."

Crow winked. "You'll do fine."

Resolute's argent eyes narrowed. "I think he will. I think we will succeed. The question is, how much will they make us pay for that success?"

Then Oracle began to speak.

CHAPTER 8

The words trickled sibilant and lyrical from Oracle's mouth. Some would ring high and clear, like the peal of a crystal bell, while others would rumble cart-heavy through a cobblestone street. Each word spilled into the air and seemed to hang there. Will thought he caught glimpses of them, illuminated in the glow of Resolute's tattoos.

As the sounds floated in the air, they linked themselves into chains. Echoes reinforced them and drew them in, further, surrounding Will and the goat. The youth kept his hand pressed against the creature's forehead, ignoring the warm wetness that connected them. His hand tingled, as if the echoes of words had funneled down into the wound and through it into the goat.

Oracle's words began to speed up, building in intensity, too. The rhythm solidified, making sounds pulse with power. Will could feel the air tighten, grow into the hard-edged sensation of crisp winter nights. Something in it cut at him, drawing no blood but taking something of him with it anyway.

The goat suddenly twisted away from Will, severing their contact. Will spilled onto his buttocks and started scuttling away from the creature as it reared up on its hind hooves, feet scrambling for purchase. The chain pulled taut and the goat slipped, crashing down hard onto its side. It writhed there, its bleating becoming more urgent and shrill, then tightening down into a hideous croaking.

A rippling series of pops shook the creature. Its spine straightened, amplifying the twitching of the legs. Its muzzle shortened as the face flattened into something vaguely human. The hooves lengthened on the forelegs, becoming two fingers that grasped the chain tightly. The pelvis shifted and the legs became more human in construction.

Worse than the physical changes was the creature's scent. The goat had not smelled particularly sweet, but the wretched miasma drifting out from it now choked Will. In it he caught hints of meat many days green and his flesh began to crawl as if maggots were burrowing beneath it.

The creature shook one last time, violently, then promptly scrabbled up into a squat with the chain tugged into a straight line. A purple light blazed in its eyes, and those eyes twitched, slowly focusing. Black lips peeled back from teeth that had taken on the jagged serrations of a carnivore's bite.

The goat-thing looked left and right, then bowed its horned head toward Will. "Old friends I see, but I know not thee. Pray thee, tell me, who would you be?" The voice came softly, but full of ridicule and with an annoying hiss.

Will pulled himself into a crouch and jammed his cut palm against his thigh. "I'm Will."

"Will, Will, one more to kill." The beast cocked its head and looked at him sidelong. "He comes not without anticipation, this bastard who will save a nation."

The youth shifted his shoulders as a shiver ran up his spine. "What are you?"

"Nefrai-laysh, at your beck and call." The goat-man sketched a little bow. "I serve she who commands them all."

"You're a Dark Lancer!"

"That much is clear, but not why I'm here." The *sullan-ciri* pointed at Crow, Resolute, and Oracle in turn. "Beware these three, my little Will. They mean you harm, they mean you ill. A key to a lock is what they see, when they stop and look at thee."

"He's lying to you, Will. It's his way now." Crow took a step to the edge of the depression, his bow still at the ready. "He can't be trusted."

"Is this the pot calling the kettle black, you who stuck the knife in my back?" The beast's eyes narrowed as it reached out and pinched a link of the chain, severing it. "I've never forgotten, never will. When the time comes, you're mine to kill. I won't forget, though the time's not yet. Still, for you, something fun to do!"

Nefrai-laysh reached back with its right hand and inscribed an oval in the air, as high as the crouching beast could reach and as wide as a man's shoulders. A thin purple line glowed in the air in his talon's wake, then the beast jammed an elbow sharply back into the heart of the oval. The reality within it shattered as might have a looking glass, leaving a black hole hovering in the air.

Before the beast had a chance to leap into that hole, Crow's arrow split its breastbone and pinned its heart to its spine. At the same time three creatures came boiling out of the hole. The two larger ones—their humanoid bodies covered with mottled fur—emerged with longknives drawn. They dove straight at Crow and Resolute. The third, a bit smaller and covered with brown fur, emerged from the hole and leaped at Will.

The nasty little poniard in its right hand had been raised for a killing thrust.

Without thinking, Will rolled onto his back, then kicked out with both feet, catching the creature full in the chest. Ribs cracked and the creature flew backward. It crashed down hard, but bounced up quickly. It flexed its hand, unsheathing claws even before it had regained its balance. It snarled and stumbled back a step, trying to get its feet beneath it.

Then it slipped on the chain.

Links rattled as they shot out from beneath its feet. The creature started to fall and reached out to steady itself, but missed the grab at the edge of the hole. At least, that was what Will thought had happened—but this was before he could see that the creature's thumb had started to fall on the cave side of the hole.

The hole's edge caught the creature midway between shoulder and hip, slicing up into its chest with the ease of a willow-whip slashing through air. The upper half of its torso, severed cleanly, disappeared into the hole while the lower half thrashed its legs, spraying blood and a twisted cord of guts into the depression.

To his right, Crow sidestepped a longknife thrust, then grabbed his attacker's wrist and twisted, locking the arm. Crow's left arm came down, cracking the silverwood bow on the joint. The elbow snapped wetly under the assault. Crow flung the howling creature aside and, in one fluid motion, bent and scooped up the longknife. He gutted his foe as it straightened up.

Oracle had reeled away from the creature rushing at Resolute. The tall Vorquelf drew a longknife with his right hand and parried the lunge coming at his belly. Then he struck lightning-fast with his left hand, slamming a fist into the creature's throat. It gurgled and stumbled back, raising a hand to its crushed windpipe. Batting aside a weak slash, Resolute stabbed down with his longknife, sinking the blade deep between shoulder and throat. Blood spurted when he wrenched it free, and the creature collapsed.

Will had just started to turn and look at the portal when a heavy weight landed on him. The goat-thing straddled him, grabbing handfuls of his tunic, pulling his chest upright while its body trapped his thighs against the ground. It shoved its muzzle forward until they were nose to nose, and blood dripped from its mouth onto his face.

"Will, my Will, remember if you can, come after me, you'll die not yet a man." Blood sprayed with each word, flecking Will's face. "Pain is all you'll know, all you deserve, unless from this path you swerve. Come with me now, come and serve. . . ."

"Not for all the sorrow in the Dimandowns!" Will snapped off the arrow in the creature's chest and stabbed the broken end through its neck. The beast reared back, one hand raised to its throat, mouth working, but words just bubbling red. It raised a forelimb to strike him, but before the blow could fall, Resolute kicked the creature in the face, spilling it back off Will.

The youth crawled back behind Resolute's legs and peered out at the goat-thing. It lay there, at the feet half of the other creature, its coat turning black and melting away. The overwhelming stench of rotten meat accompanied the effervescent decay of its flesh, leaving white bones rising from a black puddle like the skeleton of a ship beached on black sand.

A flicker of purple light leaped from the empty eye sockets and shot through the portal. The opening closed down tight, into a tiny dot, which then fell with a splash into the fetid puddle. The fluid boiled furiously for a second, then drained away through sharp cracks in what had previously been the depression's smooth bowl.

Will shivered.

Resolute looked down at him and nodded grimly. "You did better than I expected."

The youth's stomach heaved, spewing out what little remained of their last road meal.

The Vorquelf grabbed the back of Will's tunic and hauled him up by one hand. "Wipe your face, take a deep breath."

Crow held up a hand. "Take it easy with him. That wasn't what any of us expected."

Will wiped his mouth off on his sleeve. "Was that really a Dark Lancer? Is he dead?"

The older man dropped into a crouch at the edge of the

bowl, resting his bow across his knees. "It was part of him, a part he was able to project here."

"A part of him we summoned here." Oracle came over and stared blindly down at Will. "Forgive me for putting you in such danger, Wilburforce. In using the goat as part of the link, we thought we would be able to sever the link by killing the goat. It is not a common magick, but one that has worked for ages; though it did not work here."

Resolute set Will down at the edge of the pit. Will forced himself to look at Oracle and away from the remains of the goat. "Why didn't it work?"

The Vorquelf mage shook her head. "Chytrine is an able sorceress herself, so she may have unraveled the spell and found a way to change it. Clearly she has made Nefrai-laysh very strong. We will be more careful in the future."

"More careful? More careful?" Will blinked with disbelief. "If Chytrine can create *sullanciri* like that, with powers like that . . . I mean, some of them are supposed to already be dead, right? And they can do magick."

The man held his hands up. "Easy, Will. The *sullanciri* are indeed powerful. They were once our champions, yes, but they are not invincible."

Resolute nodded solemnly. "They're not impossibly powerful, either. They can be killed, and killing them hurts Chytrine. You hurt Nefrai-laysh here, sticking him the way you did. Chytrine knows she has to be careful, too."

The youth nodded slowly. It seemed the appropriate response, though he really understood very little. "What did it mean, his coming here? Was that good or bad? I mean, obviously bad, but if he's dead . . ."

Crow sighed. "He's not dead, though this might have hurt him a bit. He will be tired. And this ability to change himself into other things, it's fitting, since he could be whomever he needed to be when he needed it. He'll be very dangerous."

Resolute snorted. "Save that he can't change who he is at the core, and that is where we will kill him."

The Vorquelf sorceress stroked Will's hair softly. "As for his coming here, this is good. It means you are the one we're looking for, or are linked very strongly to him."

"Quick lesson for you, boy." Resolute hauled the creature he'd killed into the depression and tossed it at Will's feet. "This is a gibberer or gibberkin. Chytrine uses them for soldiers. Somewhat strong, not terribly smart, but mind those jaws. That muzzle can bite clean through an arm. They die, but they die hard."

Will blinked. "But you and Crow handled them so easily."

Resolute lowered his face to Will's. "We lost Vorquellyn a long time ago. I have been killing gibberers ever since. I am well schooled in killing them, and ply that trade at every opportunity."

"I think they were a bit disoriented as they came through." Crow shrugged easily. "The thing you killed was a vylaen. Smaller, smarter, almost like a child in a bear costume at festival, but capable of using magicks. Chytrine uses them to lead forces around. This wasn't a planned attack, clearly, or more would have come through; many more."

"I don't like the idea of that." Will shook his head. "I want to go home and forget all of this. Let me go, please."

Oracle knelt and wiped his face with the sleeve of her robe, leaving it stained with blood. "There is no forgetting, Wilburforce, no running, no hiding. This is a time of destiny, and your part in it has just begun to unfold. And while this may seem to be a disaster to warn of more disasters, there is good here, too."

The youth shivered again, and choked down more vomit.

CHAPTER 9

When he slept that evening, Will slept shallowly and woke easily. Bad dreams did not haunt him, but the worry that he might succumb to them did slow his returning to sleep. He knew he had nothing to fear immediately, for Crow stood watch at the mouth of the cave and Resolute slept within the Vorquellyn chamber. He'd been allowed to unroll his blanket in the alcove Oracle called home, but after supper and a short nap, she was nowhere to be seen.

Will sat in the darkness and thought about what had happened in the lower chamber. The images of war and death and dying sent a chill down his spine, though not because of their gruesome nature. Blood and gore were nothing new to Will. The Dimandowns saw violence every day, whether in a street brawl, or a cart smashing some child, or to the entertainments offered in dingy playhouses. Murder, assault, rape, cannibalism; these were all things he knew of—and most of them from dark faery tales whispered in the night.

But something about the murals in the lower chamber had more substance than night-whispers, an actor convulsing on a stage, or even blood trickling through the gutter. The painting oozed hatred. Each stab stung him, each thrust opened a hollow in him. He didn't so much feel the pain of the wounds as much as he felt the loss of the lives.

Every one of those people will die because someone else hates.

He threw back his blankets and stalked quietly through the Vorquellyn chamber. He expected an immediate and hostile challenge from Resolute, but silence marked his passage. Deep in the chamber, in the shadow of a picture that turned a stone into a forested hill, the Vorquelf slept soundly, with a blanket of gibberer pelts covering him.

On down to the lower chamber Will went and found Oracle there, painting away. He paused in the entrance, not willing to disturb her, but from the way she moved, he knew that was unlikely. She worked quickly, dabbing paint here and there, spreading individual dashes of color all over a wall, then she would shift to another paint-pot and splash another hue in places. She let the color define what she wanted to display, with the images slowly coming into focus as more and more of the stone disappeared.

One part of her mural had been completely finished and it shocked Will. Where there had only been a silhouette before he now looked at himself. He wore a stony expression and subtle shading worked details of the rock below into him. It almost seemed as if he were walking out from the rock or, worse, that he'd been trapped in it. As horrible as that might seem, however, it did not make him shiver.

The mural she still worked on, though, did tighten his flesh. As yet unpainted towers stood limned with red and gold fire. A dragon, in silhouette only, hovered in the sky above the tallest tower, breathing a stream of fire at it. On the ground and battlements of the walls surrounding the towers, armies clashed. Wizards cast spells and gibberers stood in ranks shouldering odd weapons that spit fire. Men opposing those gibberers fell back, as if struck with invisible arrows.

Swords and pikes, bows and arrows, armored warriors with lances charging atop massive horses, these things still played a part in battle. Creatures with split skulls littered the ground. Oracle returned to them, anointing them with scarlet paint. More than once a curl of red erased a previously painted head, or opened a rent in pristine armor. It almost seemed as if Oracle were somehow watching the battle's progression and changing details as people lived or died.

As that thought occurred to Will, Oracle stooped to get more paint and revealed images of himself and Crow and Resolute. Resolute was magnificent and defiant, with gibberer bodies piled high around him. Even so, a pike had been thrust into his back, and a gibberer was raising him from the ground. And Crow, he bled from the poxy sort of wounds the gibberkin weapon created. His arrows had wrought havoc with their line, but Will could see Crow would die before the last of the Aurolani troops.

Of himself he saw little, for the space surrounding him remained bare stone. He didn't understand why that was, or what it might mean. He took a step into the chamber to get a better angle on a flurry of work Oracle had begun near his image.

She whirled, the pot of yellow paint flying from her left hand. The pigment streaked out, like the tail on a shooting star. Will started forward, reaching a hand out to catch it, but the pot slowed in its trajectory and hung there, mocking his effort to save it.

Oracle stared at him, her brows furrowed, but a smile beginning to grow on her face. "You see it, you see it, so everything changes." She stepped forward, plucked the pot out of the air, then scooped the spilled paint back into it. The few drops she missed fell to stain the stone floor.

A heavy hand landed on Will's shoulder. The youth spun and found Resolute standing there, wearing an expression he'd not seen on the Vorquelf's face before. "Come with me, Will. You've seen enough for tonight."

Will blinked, wondering if the *sullanciri* Nefrai-laysh had somehow been able to take over the Vorquelf's body. "But, what she's painting . . ."

The Vorquelf turned Will around and gave him a gentle shove back into the passage to the upper chamber. "Ever since her eyes . . . Oracle always was a seer. Now what she sees are snips and tittles of the future."

The youth tried to twist back to point at the mural, but Resolute blocked his line of sight and kept him moving. "So you'll be speared on a pike, and Crow will be killed?"

"The future is not easy to unravel. Think of your life as a single thread. Mine, too, and Crow's. Stretch that thread out from here to the horizon. How far along it can you see?"

Will shrugged. "A bit, I guess."

"Well, that siege she's painting, that's a point where many threads will come together. Think of it as a knot of threads. Some will end there, some will continue on. Seeing a knot of lives tangled in the future is easy for Oracle. Seeing where each thread will enter and leave, that is more difficult."

"So you're saying that from that mural I should assume there will be a siege of towers? That much we know, but what happens we don't know?"

"That is my read of things, yes." They emerged into the Vorquellyn chamber. "I will not worry too much, but I will sharpen my blades. You, I think, should go and get some sleep."

The youth frowned and turned to look at Resolute as the Vorquelf settled himself down on a blanket. "You have always yelled at me, called me boy. What's going on? Is it because I am the person you were looking for you're being nice to me?"

Resolute's silver eyes half shut. "No, not that; nor will you find me nice to you in the future. My job is to keep you alive, and to help you become the person we need to save the world from Chytrine. I guess, from the perspective of the steel, the blacksmith is very cruel; but there is only one way to forge a sword.

"As for my being nice to you, well . . ." The Vorquelf opened his arms. "For the first time in over a century I sleep in a place where I can look out at a vista I knew from my youth. Just for a bit, a tiny bit, I know the peace I knew then. It won't last long."

Will nodded. "I'm sorry."

Resolute's head came up and he regarded Will openly. "So am I, but I won't let myself be seduced by this peace. My life is dedicated to restoring Vorquellyn, so others can know this, too."

The edged growl returned to his voice. "And you, boy, are the sword that will win me what I want. So until you are perfect, you will be worked."

"And if I don't want to be worked?"

Resolute's silver eyes tightened. "Understand one thing, boy, I need your bloodline more than I need you. If I have to get you on a dozen women so I have your children to train, I will do it. That future Oracle is painting down there is one I would like to change. That goal is more important than you. You will help, or like every other obstacle in my path for the last century, you will be swept aside."

Will found the return of the nasty Resolute something of a comfort, but hardly something that induced easy sleep. He tossed and turned for a long time, his thoughts racing. Part of him thought that being asked to get children on a dozen women would be fun—and certainly in keeping with aspects of the Will the Nimble saga he had envisioned. Still, he realized that Resolute would choose the women and was pretty certain the Vorquelf's process would drain all the fun from the enterprise.

Supervision wasn't something Will figured he wanted in the midst of such intimacies.

Eventually he did fall asleep, and all too soon found Crow shaking him awake. Their horses had been saddled and prepared for a ride while Will had been allowed to sleep. He came to awareness slowly and gathered his stuff together. The rumbling of his stomach reminded him of the fact that his last meal had not made it all the way through his system. When he recalled why, however, his appetite died.

Will tossed his bedroll behind his saddle and looked up at Crow. "I guess all that's left is for me to say good-bye to Oracle."

"Resolute will do that for you."

The young thief frowned. "Why can't I? I mean, she isn't angry that I saw her working last night, is she?"

Crow shook his head. "No, not angry, just exhausted. There are prophecies that involve you or someone of your blood, which makes you very important to the future. Right here, right now, you're akin to a pebble dropped into the pond of the future. This close to Oracle, all she sees are the initial splashings. The further you ride away, the more perspective she will get. She'll need that, and we'll need that perspective."

Will nodded for a half second, then his eyes narrowed. "That's not the only reason, is it?"

"What do you mean?"

He pointed back toward the cavern. "If I go down there and look at what she has painted, I might see things I don't like. I might do things to make sure those futures do not come about, right? That would ruin everything."

"That's an interesting insight. I don't let what I see in there concern me, though. Oracle sees events, but not outcomes. Resolute and I talked about the tower under siege. We're fairly certain that is Fortress Draconis, so we're going to head there. How things turn out, well, that will depend upon what we do when we get there."

Resolute strode strongly from the cavern. "Mount up, boy, we have to ride."

Will hauled himself into the saddle. "Did Oracle say good-bye?"

"Something like that." Resolute swung up into his saddle. "She said to ride east to the Rivenrock, then south. If we hurry . . . Well, we best hurry."

CHAPTER 10

Riding quickly through mountain forests was not an easy task. The route they chose consisted of narrow trails that meandered across hillsides, followed bare-rock streambeds, and otherwise flowed with the landscape. Based on what Will had learned heading into the mountains, he assumed their current path had started as a game trail, and the minimal amount of blazing suggested very few people used it at all.

They rode as hard as they could, pausing only to water their horses and switch mounts. During one of the switches, Resolute tossed a heavy, quilted leather surcoat to Will, nearly knocking him down. Iron studs dotted the buckskin garment. Will held it up to his shoulders, with the hem falling to his knees, and knew he could have pitched it as a tent for himself and still had room to stable his horse.

"Yes, it's big, but it's the best we've got." Resolute slipped a rustling coat of ringmail over a padded leather surcoat. "Put it on, boy, belt it tight at the middle, and use some leather straps to tie it off at your wrists."

The black tone of Resolute's words made Will comply without complaint. The surcoat hung on him very loosely but still managed to trap much of the midday heat. He tied it off at wrists and waist as instructed, which left the sleeves billowing over his forearms and a flaccid flap of leather hanging down to his groin over the belt.

Resolute secured bracers on his own forearms, then tossed Will a gibberer longknife in a scabbard. "Slide it in your belt, across the back. Now try drawing it."

The weapon's hilt projected just past his right side at waist level. Will grabbed the hilt and slid his hand wide. The blade came out cleanly and easily. The thief whipped the blade's point up and found the longknife's weight was perfect for a quick slash.

"He draws it well, Resolute, but chances are that's the biggest knife he's ever brought to hand." Crow strung his silverwood bow. "He's better at throwing. Give him some of your bladestars."

Resolute opened a saddlebag and tossed Will a leather pouch that landed heavily and clanked when he caught it. The elf pulled out another and tied it to his belt, at his right hip. From it he drew a four-pointed metal star that had been forged from broken tips of gibberer longknives. He held it between fingers and thumb, pulled his hand back, then whipped it forward.

The spinning silver weapon thunked into the bole of a sapling thirty feet away.

Will blinked. "That throw. You could have killed a rabbit without your snare."

"I'm not of a mind to be eating what I kill with these." The Vorquelf snorted. "Mind, boy, they're sharp, and the red stain in the blood-groove, that's a nasty poison. Cut yourself and start tingling, well, sing out *fast*."

All three remounted horses and headed out. Crow, at the back, kept his bow in hand, but his arrows remained in the saddle quiver in front of his right leg. The packhorses trailed him. Resolute, riding point, opened a twenty-yard lead on the other two, but held up so they constantly remained in sight of each other. Despite the caution he was taking, they did set something of a quick pace, with the sun only just beginning its descent toward night when Rivenrock came into view on a distant hill.

The morning's ride had been quiet and easy, but since arming themselves, tension had risen. Every birdsong Will heard got matched up against what he could remember from the trip into the mountains. *Was that really a berrysparrow, or a signal?* Worse were the times when all they could hear was the sound of their own progress. He didn't know what had scared the local creatures away, but he was finding it easy to imagine some huge Aurolani army slinking its way through the next valley over, led by a twisted goat-thing.

At Rivenrock Resolute dismounted. In the shadow of a huge dolmen, he studied tracks on the ground, then pointed south, along the line of the slab that had been sliced off the standing stone. "Gibberers, close. We have to move fast, but be careful."

The southern trail took them down a mountain meadow and toward a dark wood. Will strained his ears, listening for anything like the sound of battle. He watched their destination, looking for any sign that they were riding into an ambush. The jingle of tack and the pounding thunder of horses' hooves made listening difficult, and the woods' darkness remained impenetrable to his sight. His heart began to race and he wiped his hand off on the thigh of his armor.

The woods blotted out the sun, and Will's eyes took a couple of seconds to adjust to the gloom. By then his horse, swiftly following Resolute's mount, had crested a little hillock and started a quick descent into a wooded bowl with a stream crossing the path.

In an instant Will knew this place would be perfect for an ambush. The stream's running red with blood confirmed this conclusion, as did the growls of the gibberers who tore at the bodies and scattered baggage on either side of the stream. Snarls and snaps, quick yips and pitiless, guttural laughter filled the bowl.

As one of them turned, bloodied muzzle baring gore-stained teeth, an arrow flew past and took the creature in the shoulder, spinning it around. Somehow the gibberer remained upright, then Resolute's horse hit it with a shoulder. The gibberer careened all loose-jointed into a knot of its fellows, dumping them into the swollen vein at the bowl's heart.

Will fumbled with the flap of the bladestar pouch, then looked over to see a gibberer on a hillside aiming a crossbow at him. Will pulled back, tugging the reins. The bolt hit hard, yanking him from the saddle. He crashed down on the far side of the path, crushing a bush beneath him. Dust rose to choke him and he wanted to vomit.

He was fairly certain that if he did, the bolt would be the first thing he expelled.

Will lay there for a second, waiting for the agony sure to come from a quarrel coring him like an apple. His short life passed before his eyes, and he found pitifully little that was memorable. Only the recent events seemed worth clinging to, but they mocked him. *Perhaps this is what Oracle didn't want me to see.*

He waited for the pain, but it didn't come. All he felt were the stings and scratches of the bush. It didn't make any sense to him, but if he wasn't dead yet, he was determined that Will the Nimble would do more than die.

He rolled off the bush, letting it spring up behind him, giving him some cover, and came up into a crouch. The bolt hung leechlike from his leather surcoat. It had missed his flesh, but tangled in the excess material, pulling him off his horse's back. Will tugged it free with his left hand and cast it aside. Then he shifted his feet, bringing his right flank back, and fingered open the bladestar pouch. One of the cool metal weapons came easily to hand.

Will rose, and saw the gibberer who had shot at him still

bent over reloading its crossbow. The thief whipped his hand forward. The poisoned metal star whirred through the air and stuck the gibberer full in the thigh.

It looked up at him for a heartbeat, then its body convulsed and it flopped to the ground.

Another arrow from Crow's bow split the spine of a gibberer rushing at Resolute. The Vorquelf had dismounted and fought with a longknife in each hand. He parried one stab low with his left, then thrust through the gibberer's throat with his right. Ripping the blade free, he spattered blood across another gibberer's face. A lunge made the most of the temporary blindness that resulted, then a rush by three gibberers drove Resolute back.

Will boiled into this fray. None of his training, either with Resolute or before, had formally addressed fighting. But Will's very existence in the Dimandowns had demanded fighting—perhaps not on a daily basis, but commonly enough that he'd learned what he could and could not do. Throwing rocks, keeping the enemy at a distance, this he did best, but when forced in close, he knew there were no rules, no honor.

The first gibberer noticed him when Will splashed into the stream, his longknife raised for a slash. The gibberer started to turn, bringing its own blade around for a cut, but Will got there first. His blade hacked open the back of the creature's right thigh. Blood coated his knife—the stark contrast of the blade's cold silver edged by a red ribbon exploded in his mind.

Then something hit him hard across the shoulder blades. It pitched him forward, launching him into the air. Will's blade went flying. The thief tucked his shoulder as he started to come down, thinking to roll to his feet, but he bumped up hard against something that stopped him. His head and shoulders on the ground, and his feet in the air, Will saw a limping gibberer start toward him.

Worse yet, an arrow flew past the gibberer, barely nipping the tuft of hair from one of its ears.

Will twisted around and came down on his knees. He grabbed a stone with his right hand and threw it at the gibberer. The beast cackled as it batted the rock aside with an open paw. Will shuffled back, in the shadow of the corpse that had stopped his roll and pitched another stone at the gibberer.

The Aurolani creature slapped that missile out of the air, giggling hideously as Will retreated again. It waved its longknife at him, then jabbed the air twice, punctuating each motion with a ringing laugh.

A third time Will threw. The gibberer flicked its paw at the missile, then shrieked. The bladestar had stuck it all the way through, with the sharp silver point spiking out the back. The gibberer dropped its longknife to pluck the star out, but before it could, the poison took hold. The creature dropped to the ground and thrashed its life out in the bloody stream.

Will started forward, intending to scoop up the gibberer's knife and help Resolute, but saw almost immediately that wasn't necessary. One gibberer spun away, hands futilely attempting to stop blood spurting from a slashed neck. The other staggered as Resolute stabbed his left longknife deep into its thigh. His other blade came up, over, and down in a crushing blow that pulped the gibberer's skull. The creature melted into a boneless pile of mottled fur.

The fact that he wasn't needed was not what stopped Will from moving forward. Something tugging at his left ankle accomplished that. He turned and tried to jump back, but caught his heels on a rock and went down hard. A bloodied hand kept grasping at his boot as the body attached to it slowly emerged from a pile of animal skins, like a caterpillar undulating from a cocoon.

Wide white eyes stared at him from a face that was a mask of blood. The jaw worked, but no sound came out of the mouth. Then Will realized he could see the person's teeth, all of them, and that what he had taken as a blood-clotted beard ... *By the gods, they peeled his face off, left it hanging ...*

The youth reeled away and vomited. On his hands and knees he tried to crawl away, but shudders shook him violently. He could hear the faceless man inching toward him, through the sand. He could feel fingers scrabbling against his boot, clutching him by the heel. He moved away a foot or two, shying from a dead gibberer in the stream.

Suddenly death lay everywhere around him, choking him. He heaved again, his vomit annihilating the dark bloodstain in the sand. He shoveled a handful of sand over it, then let another handful drift down from his hand, breathing deeply of the dust. It made him sneeze, clearing his nose of the scent of blood and sickness.

But I can still smell death.

Someone crouched in front of him. "It's over, Will, all over."

Will slumped onto his right hip, but refused to look back toward his feet. "The man back there."

Crow shook his head. "He's gone now. He might have been in a lot of pain, but at least he lived long enough to see his torturers die."

"But, what they did to him." Will shivered. "They peeled his face off."

"Crow, get over here!" Resolute, on one knee beside a different bundle of skins, pointed his left hand at the hillside. "Will, *metholanth*, now!"

The order pumped steel into his limbs and coursed fire into his muscles. Will scrambled to his feet and ascended the hillside quickly, on hands and feet. Grabbing tree roots and bushes he pulled himself up, anxious to be away from the carnage. He found the *metholanth* bush and stripped off several branches, then laid hold of the main stem. Letting his anger and fury course through him, he tugged and twisted, yanked and pulled. He ripped the bush from the ground in a shower of earth, unbalancing himself. He crashed onto his back and rolled down the hill, bouncing off trees, bumping over logs.

Reaching the floor of the bowl, Will leaped the corpse that had grabbed at him and skidded to a stop beside the body Resolute and Crow worked on. They'd stripped away the young woman's furs. She had several cuts that he could see on her legs and arms, one across her belly, and another on her forehead, but none seemed deep. Crow used a damp piece of cloth to wash away the blood.

Resolute stripped leaves off the bush and started to chew them. He glanced at the uprooted bush, then at Will, and shook his head. "You have a mouth, boy. Chew."

Will nodded and started chewing leaves into a green pulp. The *metholanth*'s aroma managed to clear his head a bit, then he spat the pulp into Resolute's left hand. The Vorquelf smeared the paste across the girl's belly.

As Crow turned her head and started cleaning up her face, Will recognized her. "That's Sephi."

Crow nodded. "It is. The faceless one over there is probably Distalus. The other two are probably local trappers hired on as guides."

Will blinked. "But they were going to Yslin. What are they doing here?"

"Good question, boy. If we save her, we might get an answer." Resolute snorted and jerked his head back toward the stream. "A better question is, 'What are gibberers doing here?' If you have an answer for that, I'm more than glad to listen."

CHAPTER 11

They sent Will to collect their horses, which he was able to do in short order. He did find tracks that indicated Sephi and the others had ridden into the area, and found one dead horse that had been shot with a crossbow. Of the others—and he assumed there were at least four more—he saw little sign. When he returned with the horses, he reported what he'd seen.

Crow, who was just finishing up bandaging Sephi's forehead, took the news with a nod. "If we are lucky, the horses ran off and will find their way to the meadow below Rivenrock."

"And if we aren't?"

"They won't fill the temeryces' bellies completely, so the frostclaws will be back looking for another meal."

Resolute looked up from the dead huntsman he was searching. "These bodies should suit them just fine. Can she sit a horse?"

The older man nodded as he pulled a blanket over her.

"If she wakes up. Otherwise we'll have to tie her into the saddle."

"She doesn't have much time, so you'd best get her dressed and ready to go." Resolute untied the belt on the corpse and slid buckskin trousers off him. Despite some blood, they seemed to be in good shape. "Put these on her. They'll be big, but warm. Boy, look through their baggage, see what you can find."

Will bent to the task he had been given immediately, for two very good reasons. First, it appeared Resolute was content to deal with bodies and Will really didn't want to do that himself. Second, he was hoping that in the baggage he would find reasons why Distalus and Sephi hadn't made it to Yslin.

He started by gathering up and going through Sephi's things. The clothes that remained in her baggage had all been folded neatly, and having been dumped from the back of a bucking packhorse had done little to disturb that arrangement. He found a small wooden box that contained pens and ink and some paper, but none of it had any writing on it. That wouldn't have mattered since Will couldn't read more than a word or two, anyway. A small, flat piece of cedarwood with a groove at one narrow end had been tucked inside the bag and smelled pretty good—and Will had seen similar things in chests in the city, so he knew it was there to keep bugs out.

Deciding he'd seen all there was to see in her stuff, he started through Distalus' bags. He wasn't sure what to make of the fact that the old man's things had been untouched by the gibberers. The fact that his clothes had been similarly folded suggested that Sephi had packed for both of them. He found another box of writing tools and a leather-bound journal. He opened it and found faded brown ink on the tan pages. Some drawings decorated the pages, including birds and plants, but a lot were of cities and towns. The words eluded Will, but at the point where a slender wooden slat had been used as a bookmark, he thought he recognized a sketch of Stellin. He also found another of the cedar pieces, again with a groove in the narrow end.

Of considerable interest to him, though, was a pouch heavy with coins—some gold, most silver. He opened it and spilled a number out. Several were from Alcida, a few more from Savarre, and even one from Helurca. Another random lot selected from the purse yielded coins from Naliserro and Salnia, Jerana and Saporicia.

Will frowned. It struck him as very odd that he didn't have any coins from Oriosa. While it was true that relations between Oriosa and Alcida were coldly cordial, Oriosan silver could still be easily found in the purses he pinched in Yslin. Oriosan coinage was common enough that the barman in Stellin hadn't blinked when Crow produced a gold crown and Distalus had seemed quite familiar with it.

He bounced the octagonal Jeranese silver piece in the palm of his hand. It had striations along the edges, and the image of the sailing ship seemed correct, but something was just not right about the coin. Will thought for a second, then pressed the coin up against his right eye. By squinting, he caught it between cheek and eyebrow, holding it easily in place.

Will widened his eyes and let the coin drop with a clink into the pouch of coins. He fixed it to his belt, then tossed most of Distalus' clothes out. In that half of the saddlebag pair he stuffed the book and piece of cedar, as well as some bags of meal and jerky that had fallen from a rent sack. He added more food to the other side, supplementing what Distalus had already carried, then knotted the saddlebags securely.

He restocked the provisions in Sephi's bags, then brought her bags over to where Crow was slipping her into a dark brown leather tunic. He set them down next to her. "I'm going to take the rest of their provisions and restock our bags. Should be ready to go pretty soon."

Crow nodded. "Good idea. Move things around so she can have the black mare. Saddle over there should fit."

Will laid Distalus' bags on the back of his own horse, then moved things around. Resolute came over, and gave him a hand. While they worked, Will reported what he'd found, though he did underestimate the coin count and didn't tell Resolute he thought the Jeranese coin was a counterfeit based on its size. The Vorquelf, for his part, did not make any pretense at concealing the things he'd taken from the bodies: some coins and nine of the gibberer longknives.

The youth smiled. "If you want, I can wash up the bladestars and resharpen them for you."

Resolute shook his head. "No, leave them there, Crow's arrows as well. We do that. It lets Chytrine know who it is who has killed her motley bands. Crow has picked the habit up from me. You killed two, did you, boy?"

Will nodded. "Bladestars, both."

"Yes, I saw the one who greeted death with an open hand. You were very lucky."

The young thief blushed. "I know."

The Vorquelf glanced back at the bodies in the bowl. "I killed four—five if you count the one Crow shoulder-shot. He feathered another one, which leaves us one unaccounted for. The hunters died in the initial shot from the ambush. Distalus had a quarrel in him and Sephi looks as if she was just dragged from the saddle."

Will shrugged. "Distalus managed to get one before he died."

"No doubt, but *how* he did it is interesting. Come with me."

He followed in Resolute's wake even though the Vorquelf's course took them straight over Distalus' corpse. Past him, lying on the side of the bowl, a gibberer remained where it had fallen, its arms and legs bent in odd directions. Will had no doubt it was dead, and the hole in its chest, right over where its heart should have been, clearly was the cause of death.

The hole had been burned there. Crispy, charred flesh crumbled as Resolute tapped the body with his toe. "Burning there and up here, at the muzzle. The thing snorted fire before it died. Whatever hit it burned its heart and lungs out."

"In Oracle's mural I saw these weapons that spat fire."

Resolute nodded. "I know about those. This is not the sort of wound they cause. Distalus, it seems, was a sorcerer, but we knew that already from the look of him."

Before the Vorquelf could expand on that remark, Crow gave out with a shout. "She's awake."

The two of them trotted over to where Sephi was sitting up, with Crow assisting her. He supported her shoulder and elbow on the left side while she held her head in her hands and drew her knees up. She moaned a little, then began to cry.

Crow stroked her black hair. "The threat is over now, child, at least for a little while. We have to ride, though. We have to get away from here. Can you ride?"

She sniffed, wiped her nose on the sleeve of her tunic, then nodded. She started to get up and Will took her right hand to help her. He ducked beneath her arm and wrapped his left arm around her slender waist.

She smiled down at him and mouthed, "Thank you."

Will beamed. "Over here, Sephi, the black mare—as black as your hair."

Sephi half giggled at the rhyme, then clamped her mouth shut for a second, pressing her lips into a thin line. "What about Distalus?"

Resolute cut off Will's nascent reply. "He died in your defense."

Will led her on a course to the horses that spared her the worst of the carnage, then Resolute took her by the waist and lifted her onto the mare's saddle. He tossed the reins to Will. "You'll be leading her horse. Girl, you have to hold on to the saddle to stay in it. We'll be going quickly because we want a good distance between here and where we will camp tonight."

She glanced at the bodies. "You're not going to bury them?"

"No time."

"Our things?"

Resolute shook his head. "Will gathered up what he could tell was yours, but the gibberers destroyed anything they couldn't understand."

The girl seemed to take that comment at face value. Will wondered why Resolute was lying to her, but knew challenging him in front of her was a bad idea. *If Distalus was a sorcerer . . . but, wait, couldn't she be a sorceress? What if she killed the gibberer?* A little thrill ran through Will at the thought, though she did look rather young to have mastered what he assumed to be a powerful spell.

Resolute again took the point and Crow brought up the rear, with the packhorses trailing out behind him. This left Will riding ahead of Sephi, with a bit of a buffer between them and their elders. Will kept turning back in the saddle to make sure she was awake and upright. Weary though she appeared to be, she managed to stay in the saddle pretty well, and Will did appreciate the shy smiles he got when he checked or offered a "mind this branch, Sephi."

They rode all afternoon and into early evening, stopping only to water the horses. As dusk came on, Resolute led them into a rock-strewn canyon. They made a cold camp there, shutting the horses up in what had long ago been a mine of some sort, using piles of tailings as breastworks.

Will broke out roadbread and dried meat from their supplies, figuring to save the things he'd taken from the dead men so as not to remind Sephi of what had happened to her. Everyone ate quickly and quietly. Resolute assigned the first watch to Will and told the thief to wake him when the crescent moon touched a distant rock spire.

The youth sat on a pile of rocks. He wore his armor, and as the day cooled into night, he was glad it retained heat. A scabbarded longknife lay across his thigh. From the tailings he drew sharp-edged, flat rocks. He ground them against other, harder rocks to edge them, or size them better to his hand, then slipped them into the bladestar pouch on his belt.

"I couldn't sleep."

He turned and looked at a blanket-shrouded Sephi. Shadows masked her face, reinforcing the illusion of distance he'd gotten from the smallness of her voice.

"Not a surprise, after what happened."

She shook her head once, listlessly. "I don't really know what happened. Cletus, he was in the lead, he just flew from his saddle. Numitor cried out from behind and then they pulled me from the saddle. I don't remember anything more until you found me. I was lucky you came along."

"It wasn't luck, really."

"No? Tell me." She came forward, then seated herself at his feet. Her right hand came from inside the blanket and snaked itself around his left ankle. She leaned against him, with her cheek on his knee. "How did you know where to find us?"

Will started to tell her about Oracle and what Resolute had seen that made them ride east and south at Rivenrock, then hesitated. He'd not seen what Resolute saw, nor had the Vorquelf told Will about it. That moment's hesitation gave him a chance to think, which was good. The overwhelming weight of questions about what she and her uncle were doing in the mountains, with him being a sorcerer and all, stoked the fire of Will's curiosity to the point where it became suspicion.

So Will resorted to doing what he did well: he lied, effortlessly and completely. "My uncle and his friend, they are hunters, very good hunters, better than those trappers guiding you. Well, my father, he's a famous noble, very famous, you would know him if I told you his name but I can't because of an oath, you understand. My father wanted me to learn the ways of hunting gibberers and their kith. So we were in the mountains, hunting, and cut across the track of the ones hunting you, but we caught up too late."

Her right hand rose to hook fingers over the top of his knee, her palm resting flat against the inside of it. "Oh, that you could have been there sooner. Did you have success in the mountains?"

"Oh, yes, I learned a great deal. Did you know that *metholanth* grows wild? I picked that which they smeared on your cuts."

"Thank you." Sephi turned her head and gently kissed his knee. "I feel much better."

"I wish I could have done more." Her kiss and her hand were combining to make Will a bit uncomfortable, and he was very glad his armor slopped well over his belt and down into his lap. *Either that knock on her head addled her more than any one of us has imagined, or she wants me thinking about things other than thinking.*

Will wanted to succumb to her charms. Rescuing beautiful damsels and having them reward him with their favors had always been a key ingredient in the saga of Will the Nimble. And the tailings, spread with enough blankets, wouldn't be that uncomfortable. Sephi was even acting interested, and Resolute *was* threatening him with the needs of getting children on someone.

The problem for Will was simple, however: Sephi wasn't acting right. He could understand her being grateful, but of the three she could show her gratitude to, he was putting himself at the bottom of the list. *Except in the category of being young and gullible.* He had no doubt that if he were the person she likely saw him as being, she'd have him distracted with a lick and a kiss, and have him telling her everything for more of the same.

Because Will himself knew how useful distraction could be when cutting a purse, or in a quick snatch-theft, he had no trouble identifying diversionary tactics. Her questions, while seeming to be harmless, would have had him reveal Oracle's presence and the Vorquellyn cave. Given what he'd been told about it by Resolute, Oracle, and Crow, it was a secret he wasn't going to surrender no matter how pretty the questioner or dire the torture.

"Sephi, how is it that you and your uncle were in the mountains?"

"The hunters heard my uncle tell a tale or two in Stellin the day after you left. They told him of a minor noble in the mountains who paid well for taletellers. They were leading us there but I think . . . I mean, I suspect they intended to kill Distalus and have me for themselves."

Her voice became a harsh, choked whisper. She accompanied her admission by hugging his legs with both arms, letting the blanket slip from her shoulders. "Praise be to Erlinsax you got there to save me."

Will reached down and lifted the blanket over her shoulders again. "Yes, Sephi, thank Erlinsax we were wise enough to be hunting, and Arel that we were lucky enough to find you."

He patted her shoulders and smiled in the darkness as she stroked her cheek against his knee. *I don't know what your game is, but I'm very glad I know how to play.*

CHAPTER 12

Resolute had them up and moving by the earliest light, when pink and gold stole into the sky's dark blue vault. Crow had relieved Will some time after Sephi had left him. Her departure came after he asked more questions than he answered. Will then stretched out on his bedroll and woke only when Sephi moved her bedding beside his. They ended up sharing a blanket and he was glad for her warmth.

Resolute led the way out of the rock field and southeast. He explained that he wanted to make Stellin by nightfall or, failing that, find a croft where they could defend themselves. He said it all very matter-of-factly, but something in his voice made Will shiver.

By mid-morning they found the burned-out remains of a farm. Charred timbers lay in a jumble at the base of a stone chimney. The windows were empty kohl-rimmed eyes into the soul of the fire-blackened home. A fresh row of five graves in front of the house let them know the family's passing had not gone unnoticed.

More important than the house and graves, however, was the sign that had been left on the big oak tree out back of the house. A gibberer had been tied to the tree, hand and foot—and again around the waist. They could tell from the bloating that the creature had been dead for days, but there was more than enough left to identify what it was.

And to see the mark branded into its hide. Covering his nose with the sleeve of his armor, Will rode close enough to see the maggots writhing in some of the rents in the gibberer's flesh. The mark looked to him like the paw print of a wolf, with glyphs above and below it.

He reined his horse away. "What is it?"

Resolute shrugged and Crow shook his head.

Sephi's voice came dully. "I've seen it before. It's the mark of the Gold Wolf. Either she killed this gibberer because of the deaths here, or she killed the family and is trying to make people think the gibberers did it."

Crow pointed back at the farmhouse. "The graves. Why bury your victims?"

She lifted her shoulders and let them drop. "I only know what my uncle heard and told me."

"Doesn't matter." Resolute shaded his eyes with a hand. "We still need to make Stellin. We've wasted more than enough time here as it is."

On their ride in toward the town they found two more abandoned farms, but no more graves. The buildings had been looted but not burned, and showed ample signs of habitation by gibberers. Will learned to study their tracks and, amid them, found signs of frostclaws and vylaens as well. While he did not doubt they were actually present, he found it disturbing that so many seemed to be roaming about.

Commenting on that fact only brought a scowl from Resolute and an admonition to ride faster. Even though they traveled swiftly, and largely in silence, the sun's fading light stretched their shadows toward Stellin. Will took it as a bad sign that the fires on the road had been replaced with ranks of sharpened stakes long enough to impale a horse. Further back, behind breastworks of wicker and dirt, three men in ragged armor brandished pitchforks and scythes.

One of them moved from behind his shelter and dropped a hand to the hilt of a sword. "Begone!"

Resolute reined his horse up short and vaulted from the saddle. His ringmail hissed as he crossed to the man in two quick strides. The farmer tried to draw his sword, but Resolute caught his wrist before the weapon cleared the scabbard. With a savage twist, Resolute wrenched the arm around and drove the man to his knees.

"Stupid pup. You won't stop anything here." The Vorquelf waved a hand contemptuously at the stakes. "This might stop cavalry, but gibberers won't be riding. They'll slip through. And frostclaws, they'll vault them in a leap and open you from throat to loins before they touch ground again."

One of the other two men moved to help his comrade, but Crow spurred his horse forward. He had his bow out and an arrow nocked. "I don't want to make your next step your last."

The second farmer stopped and anguish washed over his face. "We're just trying to save our families."

Resolute's voice slashed at the man on his knees. "How? By driving people away? You figure that if the gibberers get us out here, somehow they won't get into the town? They won't want to?" He twisted the farmer's wrist. "Was that it?"

"Resolute, this isn't helping."

The Vorquelf nodded in response to Crow's remark and released the man's wrist with a shove that dumped him face first onto the roadway. "Where are the people gathered?"

"Hare and Hutch."

"That's where we'll be, then. How many more outposts like this?"

The downed man struggled to his knees and rubbed his wrist. "Three more, one in each direction."

Resolute walked over and pulled up enough of the stakes to let their horses pass through. "Two of you go to the nearest ones, send a runner to the furthest. Have them make fires of their stakes, then pull back to the center of town. Get lookouts high to watch for things moving against the fire. Go, now. Do it."

The Vorquelf walked his horse through the gap, then swung into the saddle again. In front of the tavern he dismounted again and pounded his fist against the door. From the shouts and shrieks inside it seemed some of the townfolk took his pounding for that of an Aurolani battering ram, but someone did draw the bar back and open the door.

Resolute marched straight in, with Sephi, Will, and Crow in his wake. "Who is in charge here?"

A man near the fireplace stepped forward and Will recognized him as Quintus, the man who had challenged them on their way into town before. The people crowded into the inn's common room looked from the man to the Vorquelf and back. "I am. I remember you. No room here for you. You should have stayed in the mountains."

A child started crying and hugged himself to his mother's skirts. Will could feel the fear in the room shift into hatred. Resolute drew himself up to his full height, his stripe of white hair brushing the ceiling. This elicited a couple more frightened cries from children, and more than one adult refused to look at him.

Crow stepped forward. "Listen to me. We're not in the mountains, we're here. In the mountains we killed gibberers who ambushed this girl and those traveling with her. Resolute and I have spent a great deal of time killing gibberers. We can help you, but we need to know how many there are and where they're coming from."

A dozen voices started at once, then Quintus slammed a pewter mug against the fireplace mantel. "You see, they are everywhere. These are the lucky ones, the ones who made it into town when they heard of farms being raided. The unlucky ones, the ones the gibberers attacked, they're upstairs—the survivors anyway. The things have run off our livestock. They come in packs of a dozen or more. Tightening a noose around us, they are."

Crow nodded. "You'll want to get most of these people upstairs, along with a few men. If the gibberers make it to the roof and start to burrow through the thatching, you'll want to kill them. Your best men should be down in here, though, since most of the fighting will be here. We have horses. We'll need to stable them."

Quintus' eyes half shut. "The stable's all yours."

Will felt a shiver run down his spine. The tone he heard in the man's voice was the same he'd heard countless times from the mouths of the homeless. They knew they were dying and the only thing they had left was some illusion of dignity. Quintus was clearly clinging to that, which made sense since Stellin was a town of farmers, suddenly faced with a problem that needed warriors.

Crow slowly nodded. "I understand. We'll be leaving the girl here."

"Let me come with you."

Crow shook his head. "Here you might survive."

Resolute snorted. "Just so you'll know, your stakes are now burning so your lookouts can see where they are coming from. If you're lucky, the fires will keep them out of your town." He turned and roughly spun Will around to face the door, then gave him a shove. "Move, boy; to the stable."

Will half turned to bid Sephi a farewell, but Resolute eclipsed his view of her. The youth made his way out of the tavern and gathered the reins to his horse. He tugged gently, bringing the horse around, then took up the lead for the pack animals as well.

He glanced at Crow, who led his own horse and the one they'd given to Sephi. "They're all going to die in there, aren't they?"

"I hope not."

"Why leave Sephi with them, then?"

"Because, boy, her chances of survival in there are far better than ours in the stable."

Will looked up at Resolute. "If the stable is a death trap, why are we going to be there?"

"If we stay in the tavern, our horses die and we will never get to Fortress Draconis. If there are enough gibberers to be raiding farms, we'd never make it out of here on foot." The Vorquelf led the way around the tavern to the stable behind it. "In there it will be panic and chaos, which will be a problem. Killing isn't a business where panic is useful."

Will got the stable door open. The building was solidly constructed, though a few of the siding boards did not fully fit, or were missing. Deeper than it was wide, it rose two stories, with the upper one consisting largely of a hayloft. A loading door was built into the front wall, but was closed. That door, along with the wide door at ground level, were the only ingresses. Two of the dozen stalls were in use—one for storage of tools and old tack, the other with a broken-down farm horse.

Resolute surveyed the stable and shook his head. "Boy, get the horses put away, but don't unpack them."

"But it won't be good for them to stand here loaded up all night. I mean, that is what you've taught me, right?"

The Vorquelf's silver eyes became slits. "Boy, if by some miracle we are here in the morning, we will rest them then. Chances are they'll be a gibberer feast. If we get the chance to run, we don't want to be saddling and loading horses."

"We'd run?" Will led his horse to a stall and guided it in. "But we would leave Sephi behind."

Crow, having ascended a ladder to the hayloft, crouched at the upper floor's edge. "The only way we run is if the raiders torch the town or find themselves occupied and give us that chance." He moved forward, opening the upper door a crack. "They have the fires burning, but looks like they're not abandoning their posts."

The Vorquelf snarled as he closed a horse in a stall. "Fools. They should have listened to me. I've killed more gibberers in one day than they'll see in a lifetime."

The older man laughed. "Would you have taken their advice, were you in their position?"

"If they knew better than I did about something, yes."

Will smiled over at him. "You mean there might be something you don't know everything about?"

"Don't be smart, boy. I know much more than you do about anything."

"Then you can tell me why Chytrine is attacking Stellin."

Resolute's expression hardened. "I don't know her mind, boy. It could be she is just being capricious. Attacking Stellin will do little for her, save creating fear. Some people may decide that King Augustus can't defend them, and that will create unrest for him. It could be that she wants him sending troops here, to the west, while she does something else in another spot. None of that matters, though, as her troops are here, now, and we have to deal with them."

The inhuman cry of agony that split the early evening stopped Will's retort. He'd never heard anything like it. It sent a shiver down his spine that grew into the heart of his bones like black ice. "Is that a frostclaw? A vylaen?"

Resolute shook his head. "Just a farmer dying. Came from the south, so they'll be coming past the stable before they reach the inn."

Will ran to the stable door and began to pull it shut.

"Leave it open a crack."

"Why?"

Resolute led another horse into a stall. "If you're a military leader and you find a building shut, what do you do?"

The youth shrugged as he guided a horse to a stall. "Open it. Send a group in."

"And if it's open?"

"A scout."

Resolute nodded. "Good, boy, and when that scout doesn't return?"

Will slowly smiled. "Another couple, who we kill, then he sends a bunch."

"More to kill." Resolute dragged along the string of packhorses and started slotting them into stalls. "Crow, do you see them?"

"Don't have your eyesight, my friend, but in the distance, yes." Crow stood and stretched. "Coming before full night; they're being very bold. I guess they don't fear anything here."

Resolute's grin became purely predatory. "Their mistake." He pulled a coil of rope from a wall peg and tossed it to Will.

"Tie this to the base of that post there, then stretch it across to that other post. Leave it slack for now, but when the time comes, you'll pull it taut and tie it off here."

Will caught the rope and nodded. "When they rush in, they'll trip. I can hold it, you know."

"No you couldn't, boy, but it doesn't matter if you could. You'll have your hands full killing those who fall." The Vorquelf opened the pack on one of the horses and pulled out the longknives he'd taken from the gibberers in the mountains. He left two near the post where Will was to be standing, then hung others from posts or rested them on shelves where they could come easily to hand.

"Mind a question, Resolute?"

"What, Will?"

"Crow has a sword. Why don't you have one?"

Resolute snorted. "Do I tell him the truth, Crow?"

"Some of it, perhaps, but quietly."

In the brief bit of silence that followed Crow's comment, Will could hear the sound of someone beating his fists on the tavern door. Demands to be let in rose in tone, with curses punctuating them as the voice became more shrill. Then a sizzling sound began to rise. Something brilliant and green flared outside, outlining Crow in emerald light, then subsided.

As did the yelling.

Resolute came over to Will. "Crow will signal you when to tighten the rope. When they fall, just slash and stab. Be quick, very quick."

"I will be. Quick and nimble."

The Vorquelf nodded thoughtfully. "The reason I use longknives is because that's what I used to kill my first gibberkin. On Vorquellyn, when I was not yet even your age. A longknife worked then, and so far, nothing better has come along. If you find something that would be better, let me know."

Crow's whisper carried down through the darkness. "Get ready, my friends. This will either be the longest night of our lives, or the last one. Either way, as long as we're killing Aurolani forces, it will be time well spent."

CHAPTER 13

Despite the nightmarish cacophony of howls and snarls from the gibberers filling the air, Will actually heard the first gibberer before he saw it. Before hiding behind the barn door, Resolute had gone to the stalls with a shovel and mucked out a sour, dripping mass of straw and manure. He spread this near the doorway and let the odor fill the stable.

The gibberer sniffed at the cracked-open door and paused. Some of the horses shifted in their stalls and one neighed. The sniffing intensified, then the Aurolani creature poked his head into the stable. It looked about, its tufted ears up and alert, but the stamping of hooves clearly caught all of its attention. It pushed the door open just a little and slipped inside, its paws pressed back against the door so it could ease the door shut and survey the bounty it had found.

It never heard Resolute move. Its ears didn't so much as flick back as the Vorquelf struck, dropping a canvas feedbag over its muzzled head and roughly jerking it backward. The gibberer's paws came up to claw at the bag blinding it.

Resolute drove the dagger he'd chosen for close work into the creature's back with serpentine speed. The gibberer at first stiffened, then uttered a muffled sigh and slackened.

Leaving the blade in his victim because it would be useless in the coming melee, the Vorquelf dragged the corpse into the corner and unhooded it. He picked up one of the longknives and returned to his place by the door to wait.

Will dried his hands yet again on his thighs. Outside the stable a snarl-storm raged. He could hear yips and snaps from the gibberers. Crashes came from other buildings as homes were looted. In some places green light flashed again and again. Human voices—a mix of panic and command—played in counterpoint to the gibberer noise, but command slowly gave way to panic.

Part of him hated waiting. It seemed so unheroic, even cowardly. It didn't matter that to charge out into the village would be suicidal. Somehow it seemed wrong that they weren't killing gibberers as fast as they could.

Another part of him knew that holding the stable would allow them to tie up and destroy more of the Aurolani raiders than they could in the tavern. Still, the fact that vylaens out there had magick meant that their fight would be shortened unless Crow could shoot the sorcerous creatures.

His pulse pounded in his head in rough syncopation with the undulating din outside, for the gibberers had clearly determined the whole of the village's population had gathered in one spot for protection. Will flexed his hands, then wrapped them tightly around the rope. *Pull hard, tie it off, and then cut and cut and cut...* Soon, he knew, his time would come.

Two more gibberers came, perhaps a bit bolder because the rest of the village lay abandoned, or a bit more wary because of the tang of blood in the air. They came through the doorway faster than the first—ears up, longknives drawn, and eyes bright.

Resolute hooded one and whirled it off into the stable

wall. The creature hit hard and rebounded, but managed to stay on its feet. The second cleared the door and slashed at Resolute, catching the Vorquelf in the flank. Resolute hissed, then slashed back. His longknife bobbed an ear, clipped the skull, and staggered the gibberer.

The one-eared beast stumbled back through the door and raised an alarm. Resolute spun and batted aside a weak slash by the hooded gibberer. Abandoning his longknife, the Vorquelf pulled the creature close to him, got a good grip on skull and muzzle. He wrenched the gibberer's head around with a crackling pop, touching chin to spine, and let it drop.

From above, Crow called down to Will. "The rope, now, Will!"

Will hauled back, tightening the rope six inches above the floor. He quickly looped it around the post and knotted it. Resolute took that time to kick the stable door shut, then crossed the center area and filled his empty hands with two longknives.

"Crow, how many?"

"A good little knot of them. Eight, ten, maybe. And, yes, there, a vylaen, but no frostclaws." Boards creaked above as Crow stood and drew back on his bow. "Get down. The vylaen's going to blast the door."

A sizzling hiss built, and green light shot in at the doorway. The spell slammed into the stable door, flinging it open. A black scorch mark wreathed in green flames marked the door's center. The ball of verdant fire skipped off the burning door and flew deeper into the stable. It slammed into a wall, exploding it outward, scattering fiery splinters into the street beyond.

Gibberers, howling and hooting, barking and yowling, boiled through the doorway. The tripline jerked the initial three down into a heap. Two more following collapsed onto that mass of mottled fur and steel. Another gibberer vaulted its fallen comrades, but a quick slash from Resolute sent both halves of it spinning off into a dark corner.

With a longknife in each hand, Will darted forward. He stabbed indiscriminately, making up for in quantity what Resolute might have managed with a single precise thrust. He chopped at necks when they were exposed, and stomped on paws grasping for longknives. He lost himself in the need to do damage, punctuating his actions with the crack of bones, the whistle of a blade, or the silence of a growl muted with steel.

He moved as quickly as he could, but the new gibberers coming to the stable approached with more caution and did not trip. Some never made it into the stable as Crow's arrows took them in the street. The others oriented almost immediately on Resolute, as his twin blades were clearly wreaking havoc. One, however, bared its fangs and came at Will.

The thief ducked its initial slash and spun away, putting his back against a post. The gibberer slashed again, this time missing Will but sinking its blade into the post, trapping the weapon. Will laughed and stabbed it deep in the thigh with one blade, and knew he could easily carve its heart out before it ever got its longknife out of the post.

The gibberer didn't even try to free the longknife. Its open-pawed slap snapped Will's head around and spun him toward the door. The thief caught his ankles on the rope and went down. Despite the ringing in his ears, and the taste of blood in his mouth, he did have the presence of mind to roll. He used the momentum to come up on his feet, but as he completed the maneuver a wave of dizziness washed over him and he careened drunkenly into the street.

Spinning around, he dropped to one knee and looked back at the tavern. An arrow-stuck vylaen was struggling to its feet. Other gibberers dashed toward the stable, but the one he'd stabbed came limping back out. It had its left paw jammed against the spurting hole in its thigh, and a gore-streaked longknife in its right paw.

Shaking his head in a futile effort to clear it, Will looked down at his empty hands and felt betrayed. When he looked up again, the gibberer had gotten closer to him than he would have thought possible. The creature backhanded him with its bloody paw, sprawling him on his back, then raised the longknife for a thrust to the heart.

Suddenly the gibberer bounced back, the longknife spinning in air. A spear had lanced down into its chest at an impossibly sharp angle. For the barest of moments, when the spear burst from its back and stabbed into the ground, it held the gibberer upright. The beast gurgled a bloody scream, then wrenched the spear free of the earth with its spasmodic jerking. The gibberer collapsed to the ground at Will's feet.

The longknife thumped down beside it.

An earsplitting screech split the night. Will caught sight of a winged creature arcing back up into the darkness. She seemed to him part ghost, so quickly did she fade, and part fantasy—for she had been long, lithe, and beautiful. Despite the evidence of the twitching gibberer at his feet, Will wondered if he'd seen her at all, or if she were wholly an illusion.

Coming up on one knee, he got his confirmation of her reality. The vylaen between stable and inn spun to track her flight, green fire kindling in its palms. The Aurolani magicker croaked and hissed in some arcane tongue and started to point skyward.

Will fingered open the bladestar pouch and immediately whipped one of the missiles at the vylaen. It caught the beast in the shoulder, wringing a yelp of pain from it. The yelp seemed to spoil the spell, for the green fire died, and the poison ensured that a second later the vylaen did as well.

His yelp, however, had summoned help. Four gibberers with longknives drawn ran into the street behind the tavern. They surveyed the damage with a sniff and never paused as they came at Will. A bladestar in the stomach slowed one, then dropped him. An arrow from the stable's loft whirled another around into a slack-limbed heap of flesh. Resolute's emergence from the stable with his twin blades dripping blood stopped the other two in their tracks. Their ears flicked back and forth, then they turned and ran back toward the front of the inn.

Gibberers started yelping, panic filling their voices. In the background came a deep bass rumble. It came from outside the village, but Will hadn't been able to place it by the time Resolute reached him and hauled him to his feet. "What is that?"

"Horses, a lot of horses." The Vorquelf jerked him back toward the stable. "I don't know what's happening, but it has the gibberers scared, and that's something I like."

They retreated to the stable and shut the door. The rumbling rose to crest over the sounds of gibberers. Will watched through the hole blasted in the stable's side and caught brief glimpses of horsemen racing into the village. He couldn't see if they were killing the gibberers, but he suspected so from the shouts and snarls he was hearing.

He scrambled up the ladder to the loft to get a better look and slid over beside Crow, who had opened the door wider. From that vantage point they could see the roadway in front of the tavern. Horsemen gathered there, reining back anxious chargers, reporting and waiting on orders. They all gave their attention to their leader, and Will found his gaze drawn to her as well.

He wasn't sure why, but he told himself that it wasn't because she was beautiful—though there was no denying she was easy on the eyes. She sat astride a majestic black horse with gold-washed ringmail over it. Her long, white-blonde hair had been pulled back into a thick braid that snaked out from beneath her gold helm. The snarling-wolf visor had been raised, revealing a face with noble features, from the high cheekbones and strong chin to the long, straight nose and full lips.

The way she sat the horse, too, demanded attention, for even her long surcoat of gold ringmail did not stoop her shoulders or bow her back. She sat straight and tall, listening intently, nodding curtly, then pointing and barking orders that riders immediately carried out.

Her voice, when it reached him, had a richness that belied its higher pitch. The sentences came short and must have been clear, since no one questioned the orders. The swiftness with which her orders were obeyed suggested a confidence in her that would have seemed improbable, given how young she appeared.

Will started to comment about that when Crow shoved him roughly aside. In an instant the older man drew an arrow back to his cheek and let fly. A second too late, Will recovered himself and grabbed Crow's leg, hoping to upset his aim. It struck him as inconceivable that Crow could have gone insane and shot her, but there seemed no other explanation for his action.

Then, looking to see if she was unharmed, Will saw a dying vylaen spill out of the alley across the square. Green fire poured from its hands like oil, lighting the way for a small group of gibberers. Howling furiously, the Aurolani troops threw themselves at the horsemen, and the last glimpse Will caught of the golden woman was to see her drawing a heavy saber and spurring her horse into the midst of the enemy.

Crow grabbed Will by the collar and spun him around. "Get down to the horses now. Resolute, we'd better move fast. These riders are chasing the gibberers out of town."

The Vorquelf nodded and started leading horses from the stalls. "We'll head south."

Will climbed down the ladder, then jumped the last two yards. "Why not wait and talk to her?"

"We don't know her or why she's here; and we don't need to be delayed by some bandit queen." Crow, with his bow and quiver slung over his left shoulder, swung from the ladder into the saddle of his horse. "Worse case, they demand ransom from us and we're stuck."

"Agreed." Resolute boosted Will into the saddle, then

handed him the lead for the packhorses. "Follow Crow south; I'll catch up with you."

"What are you going to do?"

"They're chasing gibberers. I'll give them something unusual to chase." The Vorquelf knelt beside a gibberer body and tugged down its lower lip. He smiled, then stuck thumbs into its nostrils and pressed his fingers against its eyes. He started chanting in a low voice and one of the tattoos on his left forearm started to glow. The gibberer shook like a flag in a stiff breeze, then rolled to its feet and ran off through the hole in the stable wall. The fact that it lacked most of its right arm and had a gaping wound on that side of its chest didn't seem to bother it at all.

Resolute pointed at the door. "Go, go quickly. Couple more of these decoys and we'll be clear. We ride south for near a day, then it's east, northeast, Fortress Draconis bound."

CHAPTER 14

The arrow flew close enough to Alyx's face that she could feel the wind of its passing. She instantly sighted back along the flightline and picked the stable hayloft as the source of the shot. The guttural gasp coming from her left, however, served to distract her from seeking out the assassin.

A vylaen, its heart pinned to its spine by a black-fletched arrow, staggered from an alley and toppled in the dust. The green fire of aborted Aurolani magick trickled from its paws. In the fire's light she saw the gleam of feral eyes hidden deeper in the alley. Yanking Valor's reins to the left, she spurred him forward into the gibberers rushing to attack. She drew her saber with the ring of steel on scabbard, then slashed down.

A cloven-skulled gibberer dropped to the dirt. Valor's charge battered another back, then Alyx shattered the arm a third gibberer had raised to ward off a blow. It howled, and the return cut that stroked its throat ended that protest in a froth of red bubbles.

Alyx looked up as a gibberer's silhouette rose on a rooftop. The moon's light glinted coldly from a longknife's edge. The creature gathered itself to leap down on her. She brought her sword up and stabbed toward the creature, knowing she'd impale the gibberer even as it knocked her from the saddle. *At least, if he is dead when we land, it's one problem solved.*

Before the gibberer could leap, however, a screech sounded and a winged figure swept through the air. The braided rope loop she carried settled around the gibberer's throat and jerked him backward off the roof edge. With a powerful beat of wings, the Gyrkyme struck for the sky, letting the noose tighten, then dragged the strangling gibberer from Alyx's sight.

Other riders plunged forward, driving the gibberers back into the alley or along the road. Some of the Aurolani beasts managed to cut and dodge, prolonging their lives, while others who relied on speed to escape quickly writhed at the end of sharp lances. Alyx's troops offered the gibberers no more mercy or quarter than the Aurolani had offered the elves of Vorquellyn or the people of Okrannel. They hunted them down and slew them ruthlessly, not out of any sense of vengeance, but with the righteous fury of a people defending their kind against predation.

Alyx reined Valor around and trotted him back toward the city square. The Gyrkyme landed in the center of the grassy patch, furling brown wings. Her folded wings towered above her head. Brown spots dappled the ivory down that covered her body from toes to crown. Darker down did surround her large amber eyes, trailing down into her cheeks as might tears. Save for a brown loincloth and a brown leather halter, the winged woman remained naked.

Alyx smiled at her. "How many left in the town, Peri?"

The Gyrkyme shook her head once, sharply. "Runners, scattered. The Red Caps are after them and securing the town. Most are east and Green Company has them. A few frostclaws, too, but dying fast. Blue is coming around from the south to cut off their retreat."

"Good. Fly back to White Company and bring them in."

"As you wish, Highness." Peri spread her wings preparatory to launching herself skyward.

"Wait." Alyx smiled and held up a hand. "Thank you for saving me, sister."

Peri winked. "Family tradition, Alyx. Be back fast with the Whites."

The Gyrkyme vanished into the night sky and Alyx turned her attention to the inn. She nodded to a warrior in her bodyguard company. He rode to the door, dismounted, and pounded his fist on the door. "In the name of the Gold Wolf, open this door!"

A few screams and panicked shouts made it out through shuttered windows. A strong male voice broke through the din. "Leave us alone. We have nothing for you."

Returning her saber to its scabbard, Alyx nudged her horse forward a few steps. "Listen to me, and do so very carefully. My troops have run the gibberers off. We own your town, but I will ransom it back to you. For every heartbeat you delay in emerging, the price goes higher."

The thunder of a horseman's approach overrode the discussion raging inside. Agitare, with a red strip of cloth flying from the spike atop his helm, reined his horse to a stop before her. He leaped from the saddle and dropped to one knee, crossing his arms, with fists jammed against opposite shoulders.

"Highness, I cannot express my mortification—"

Alyx slapped her gloved hand against her right thigh, bringing the soldier's head up. "Why are you wasting time to apologize for not having secured the town when the town is yet to be secured?"

"I didn't think—"

"You didn't, not at all." She pointed at his horse. "Get back in that saddle. I want you to report, truthfully, that you have checked every home and building for gibberers, and I want it reported before the moon slips into the Sailing Ship. Go!"

The soldier nodded, then pulled himself into the saddle and rode off. One of her bodyguard unit, a white-bearded warrior with a strip of gold cloth hanging limp from his helm, chuckled all but imperceptibly. Alyx's violet eyes narrowed and he blanched.

"Permission to aid Captain Agitare in his assignment, General?"

She considered his request for a moment. *At least Ebrius has learned that calling me Highness is not a way to deflect my anger.* "No, Ebrius, you will see to that which your position demands. The stable. An arrow from the loft killed a vylaen set to attack me. Seek the archer who kept me alive. Get going."

As Ebrius trotted his horse off, the click of a bolt being shot back sounded from the tavern and the door opened. A man emerged and the door shut after him immediately. He pressed his hands back against the door, then brought them forward, empty. He took a step toward her, then dropped to a knee, bowing his head.

"I am Quintus."

"And I am the Gold Wolf. You know of me?"

"Yes, we have heard tales."

"And you fear me?"

"No, because the stories . . ."

Alyx put an edge into her voice. "Do not lie to me, Quintus. Your fear stains your words. I prefer honest fear to lies wrapped in false courage."

"Yes, we fear you." The man's shoulders slumped a little with the admission. "How may I serve you?"

"Attend me, Quintus, walk with me. We go to your stables." She guided Valor around the tavern and Quintus quickly caught up with her. He glanced up as he paced beside her right leg. In his eyes she caught a wariness, as if she expected her to lash out at him with boot or reins.

The tableau around the stable stopped both of them

short. A half-dozen or more gibberers lay in a heap. Black-fletched arrows had stolen each of their lives. Alyx measured the distance from the loft to the targets and figured that while the range was short, shooting at night with the sort of accuracy displayed was no easy feat. *Especially the long shot.*

She dismounted and tossed Valor's reins to Quintus. Three long strides took her to a vylaen that had an arrow in one shoulder and a curious, star-shaped metal weapon buried in the other. The dark foam on the creature's lips suggested it had been poisoned.

Ebrius emerged from the stable with sword drawn. "More in here, General, many more. The gibberers lost a third of their strength here."

She nodded. "How many helped the archer?"

Ebrius squatted and studied tracks. "At least two. I have three sets of tracks overlaid on the gibberers' tracks. One is very big, one large as men go, and the third is a boy." He pointed off on a line toward the gibberer that had Peri's spear run through it. "The boy ran along that way. Looks as if Perrine saved him."

And perhaps he returned the favor. Alyx glanced from the vylaen to the spear, then looked at the tracks left by the vylaen's last steps. She could tell the beast had been looking toward the gibberer who had been speared, then turned away. In her mind's eye she could easily see the little beast following Peri's swoop, tracking her, so it could loose a spell that would kill her. The vylaen's paws showed signs of charring, from a spell gathered but not cast, which fixed the sequence of events firmly in her mind.

She thought for a moment, then nodded. "Ebrius, when the Whites get here, I want all of this recorded. Measure it, angles, everything. There's an odd weapon here and it's been poisoned. Save it, anything like it, and the arrows. I want our best archers to re-create the shot to the square, a hundred trials, on a target the size of a vylaen."

"At once, Gold Wolf."

Alyx turned to Quintus. "Who did you have in the stable?"

The man hesitated, his eyes growing wide for a moment. "Travelers. They came through before, a week ago, and back again tonight. We had no room for them in the inn, so we sent them to the stables. A man and his nephew. And a Vork, a big one, with white hair in a stripe."

"Names?"

"I don't know. I don't know them, didn't talk much to them."

Her eyes narrowed. "Pity, because one of them either tried to kill me, or saved my life. Knowledge of who they are would be ransom enough for this place."

"Stellin, my lady."

"One of them was named Stellin?"

"No, my lady, this place is called Stellin." Quintus held his hands up. "I do not know them, but they left a girl here. I can get her. She would know them."

"Go. Do it. Now."

He made to hand her the reins, then dropped them as if they were vipers when she waved him away. She crouched by the vylaen and frowned. She had been following the Aurolani raiders for over a week. They had largely managed to elude her, but her trackers read the signs of disparate bands coming together. She knew their raids would have scant military impact on the area, but razing crofts, slaughtering travelers, and, in a large enough group, sacking a town would inject a serious amount of concern into the populace.

What struck her as curious was that three warriors had killed close to a dozen and a half of the Aurolani raiders, but had not remained in town to recover the person they'd left behind, nor to speak with her. *The men who could kill this many would not fear me the way Quintus does.* Outlaws would have gladly joined her band. Their running meant they wanted to remain undiscovered, but their having fought the Aurolani suggested their reasons for remaining covert did not include their being in Chytrine's employ.

Quintus' breathless return with a girl interrupted her thoughts. "This is the one."

The raven-haired girl bowed her head. "Sephi, mistress, I am Sephi."

Alyx slowly stood and looked down at the girl. "And I am the Gold Wolf. You came into Stellin with the people in the stable. Who were they?"

The girl's body shook with a tremendous sob, then she dropped to her knees and covered her face with her hands. "It was horrible, mistress."

"Tell me, child." Alyx did not soften her voice, but lowered the volume a touch. "What do you know of them?"

"My uncle and I met them here, a week back. They left the town before we did, saying they were going into the mountains. We left in the company of hunters the next day. These three, they accosted us. They killed my uncle and the hunters, and took me." Again she sobbed, and let a silent cry of anguish finish as a pitiful wail. "They were going to keep me for their pleasure, or sell me, they said, but the gibberers drove them back here. I could tell no one. They said they would kill me, but I know you will protect me."

"Indeed, child, I shall." Alyx looked past Sephi, along the alley that ran behind the tavern. There Peri landed noiselessly. Beyond her were three riders who remained in shadows.

Alyx turned to Quintus. "My people are securing the town. Your people will return to their homes and will billet my men. We will leave tomorrow, and we will take Sephi with us. Go, make the arrangements, keep an accounting of what we owe our hosts. House Sephi here at the inn. This is where I shall stay as well."

Quintus blinked at her. "You want us to present you a bill for your stay here?"

"I don't like saying things more than once, Quintus. A

second time I may not say the same thing, understand?"
Alyx frowned at him. "The stable and this area is to be off-
limits to everyone until we are done here. And take the girl
with you. Go!"

Sephi bent forward and kissed Alyx's boots, then
Quintus dragged her roughly from the ground. "Come,
girl, you'll not be making her repeat herself."

Once they had vanished around the corner to the tavern, Alyx walked over to where Peri waited before the riders. She smiled at the Gyrkyme. "That was a clean kill with
the spear."

Peri blinked her eyes slowly. "The gibberkin was distracted." She raised her left hand, which came naturally
with three fingers and a thumb. The talons on the thumb
and forefinger had been clipped back short, but the other
two hooked nastily. "It was going to come back for the vylaen, but found other prey."

"I think the distraction got your vylaen for you." Alyx
stopped, then clasped her hands at the small of her back.
"The town is close to secure. We can show you what we did
later. By dawn we should have the battle fully reconstructed."

The smallest of the riders, a little man with a face so
wrinkled it looked like a portrait painted on wadded canvas, smiled. "I have already communicated a message of
victory to Yslin." He held up a small, rectangular slate as
long as his forearm and half as wide. "There is no reply yet
on the *arcanslata*, but the message was only just sent."

She nodded. "We did win, but we had help. A trio. A girl
who rode with them would have me believe they are cutthroats and rapists, but that does not seem consistent with
what they did defending the stable. We will conduct inter-
views, see how much we can learn of them, and have a full
report as soon as possible. It would be advisable to have
others watch for them."

The third rider, a slender man, leaned forward in the
saddle, resting his crossed forearms on his horse's neck.

"You need not be so grim, Highness. What we have seen in the week we've spent with you is beyond our expectation. You did well here; you won. The Jeranese general Adrogans will find himself a new rival when it comes to leading the fight to liberate Okrannel. You should take pride in this."

"With all due respect, my lord, I certainly would not count myself as a rival to Adrogans and I won't take pride until I know all the details. We missed a group that could have done serious harm, and I need to know how and why that happened. The trio in the stable got out of Stellin, likely slipping past Blue Company as it moved east to cut off the gibberers. Had those three not destroyed as many of the enemy as they did, well, how would we have fared? There are too many unanswered questions for me to be pleased or proud yet."

Peri laid her right hand on Alyx's left shoulder. "My sister, she is Gyrkyme in all but wings. If she chose, she could fly."

"You are no doubt correct, Perrine." The other rider, a thickset man, reached up and adjusted the patch he wore over his right eye. "Your caution does you great credit, Highness. You are indeed all that was hoped. This we will communicate to our masters."

Alyx nodded slowly. "Temper the report with reality. I have been trained to do something that will become legend. Assuming I can do exactly that *before* the act must be performed is pure folly. The saving of Stellin is a good sign, but reading the future from it is, at best, tricky. We have much more to learn and do, and your masters should know that this is exactly what I will continue to do."

CHAPTER 15

The ride south exhausted Will, and the necessity of posting a watch when they did stop to rest meant he never got enough in the way of sleep. What he found most disturbing about this was the nature of the dreams he had. Over and over again he found himself watching the winged woman kill the gibberer, then return after the Crow killed the vylaen. She enfolded him in arms and wings, hugging him to her to express her gratitude at saving her life.

To be awoken in the midst of one of those dreams produced embarrassment—and Resolute seemed preternaturally adept at knowing just when to wake him up. Will would assume his duties and return to the dreams when his watch was over; but dawn would arrive before the dreams had come to any fruition.

On the road he mentioned the dreams to Crow. The older man smiled and shot him a wink. "Not really a surprise is it, that you would dream about her? She saved your life and you likely saved hers. She was beautiful. Trysting with someone exotic like that would be an adventure."

Resolute turned in the saddle and snorted. "So would consorting with sheep, but that does not mean such things would be recommended."

Crow frowned. "Is that a traditional elven view of Gyrkyme coming from you, Resolute?"

The Vorquelf shook his head. "I'm as much of an alien creature in the eyes of my brethren as they are. My concern's for the boy's blood. Coupling with her likely won't do the prophecy any help, so I'd not recommend it."

Will arched an eyebrow. "Back up a minute. What do the elves think about the Gyrkyme?"

"Centuries ago, back before Chytrine was a threat, there was a sorcerer, Kirûn, who ensorcelled an elven prince and his band of champions. He caused them to mate with a flock of *araftii*—savage aerial creatures with the head and body of a woman, but wings, feathers, and talons of an eagle. Their union produced the first Gyrkyme, who then bred true." Crow gestured back toward the mountains where they had visited Oracle. "The urZrethi created Gyrvirgul for them, to the disgust of the elves, who see them as bestial rapeget."

A low growl issued from Resolute's throat. "It doesn't help that many of the Gyrkyme, early on, pressed claims to the properties of their fathers. Their society is a parody of elven society, or so most elves see it. But the few I've met are fierce warriors, so they've earned my respect."

The youth frowned. "You said I couldn't get a child on her, but elves got children on the *Araftii*, how is that?"

The Vorquelf shrugged. "Most say it was Kirûn's magick, which means it wasn't a natural thing at all. When it has happened, when an elf has gotten a woman with child— rare though that is—the child is accepted. For the sake of your blood though, you should abandon thought of the exotic. It's better you were dreaming of Sephi."

Will smiled. "Not so hard to do. I wonder how she's making out, given that we rode out with all her stuff, and that of her uncle."

The Vorquelf shook his head. "She won't miss ratty clothes."

"She'd probably want her uncle's book, too, and the other things."

Crow glanced over at Will. "Book? Other things?"

"Some bugboards—you know, the cedar things to keep bugs away from cloth. The book has drawings and words and things."

"Why didn't you mention this before?"

"I did, to Resolute, when we were loading up and you were tending her."

The Vorquelf nodded as he reined his horse around a bend in the game trail they were following through the hills. "He did mention it, Crow. With the girl around, there was no way to talk to you about it. The book didn't surprise me, given he's a sorcerer."

Will scratched at the back of his neck. "How did you know that?"

"The gibberer had been killed by magick and Distalus' face had been peeled. Gibberers tend to think of magickers as being possessed by the ghosts of vylaens. They peel the flesh off faces to let the ghosts out, so they can be reborn into vylaens. The more and louder the screams, the more powerful the ghost."

Will shivered, then reached back and pulled Distalus' saddlebags off the rump of his horse. He dug around in one of them and handed the book to Crow. "Maybe this will make sense to you."

Crow opened the book and turned to the place marked with the strip of wood. "The writing is coded, but we have a drawing of Stellin, marking strengths and weaknesses." He tapped the page with the bookmark. "More importantly, we have a strip here of *magilex* wood, stained to look like blackoak."

Resolute reined his horse to a stop and turned it around. "Why didn't you tell me about this before, boy?"

Will shrugged. "Probably because I didn't know about it. What is it?"

"What else did they have? Bugboards, you said?" Crow closed the book and laid the *magilex* strip against the cover. "Give them to me."

Will found the one in Distalus' bag easily and handed it to Crow. He had to dismount and run back to one of the packhorses and rummage around before he found the other one. He raced back and handed it to the man. "What do you think it is?"

Crow pressed the two pieces of bugboard long edge to long edge, with the slot connecting them across the top. He slotted the *magilex* strip in there, sliding it first left and then to the right, where it caught and held when the groove narrowed slightly. In an instant a blue flash passed over the wooden tablet and left in its wake burning blue characters.

"I can't read. What does it say?"

Crow shook his head. "I don't recognize the script. Resolute?"

The Vorquelf stared at it for a moment, then frowned. "I've not seen its like before. Probably code, like the book."

Crow snapped the *magilex* strip out of the slot and the writing vanished. "So, they each had half an *arcanslata* with them. Combining the two halves and using the mageoak to connect them, that's fairly sophisticated magick. A map of Stellin in the book with descriptions in code. I'd say they were spying for someone."

"For Oriosa." Will smiled. "Definitely Oriosa."

The Vorquelf arched an eyebrow at him. "And how did you come to that conclusion?"

"The coins in Distalus' purse. A good mix, some are fake, and none are from Oriosa."

The older man smiled. "Circumstantial proof, but interesting. Since the *arcanslata* allows them to communicate with their masters instantly, do you think they were told to look for us and that's why they followed us into the mountains?"

Resolute slowly shook his head. "If they were looking for us, they would not have spun the tale about going to Yslin. I would bet when waiting in Stellin they were told that you and I had passed through before, years ago, with Oracle. They followed, trying to track us, but failed. Because of her prophecy at the time of the expedition, she's known, so they were probably sent to find her. Her location would be of value to Scrainwood's people."

Will closed his eyes as facts collided in his head. "But, if what Distalus said about King Scrainwood is true, and he's working for Chytrine, why would the gibberers have killed Distalus?"

Crow half smiled. "While Scrainwood might provide sanctuary for Aurolani forces within Oriosa, he denies that he does the same to his peers, and will send them reports from his scouts about possible movements of Aurolani forces. He plays both ends against the middle, but because he provides value to both sides, no one kills him. Chances are Chytrine did not know Scrainwood had spies in the area."

"Or," offered Resolute as he reined his horse around and started off again, "she did and wanted them killed."

Mulling over the variety of permutations of who knew what, when, and where kept Will busy for much of the time he spent awake. They traveled east-northeast, following a river valley that skirted Yslin to the south. They kept away from towns, preferring to move through the woodlands along woodsman-tracks or game trails. Their travels took them a week—the whole of ten days—and proceeded along what Will took to thinking of as the outlaw path.

In the hills and hollows, as night fell, they would find caves or clearings where others had gathered. Mostly men, but not a few women, all of them looking lean and hungry—closer to a pack of wolves than a gathering of humans. The nature of the people surprised Will because in the Dimandowns he was used to hard men, bad men; but they seemed soft compared to those who had been chased into the wilderness. Most of the outlaws seemed almost feral. Will had no doubt that if cornered in a city, they'd tear their citified counterparts asunder.

In the city, you have enemies who want to kill you. Out here, everything wants you to die, and only the maggots will notice your passing.

Names weren't used on the outlaw path. No one asked where they were going, just where they'd come from and what they'd seen. Will figured half the replies were outright lies; and the other half were elaborated to the point of being of little use.

At one place, a green dell with some standing stones and a stream meandering past, an older man—who bore a passing resemblance to Crow—nodded as he sucked on a pipe. "I'd be being careful, were I you. Come from east, I have. Riders been asking after three traveling together: a Vork, a man, and a boy. Wouldn't be wanting you to be mistook for them. These must be desperate men, what with soldiers inquiring."

Crow laughed gently. "Not us, friend. We've done aught but kill gibberers and eat plump berries plucked from trailside. Likely King Augustus might be wanting us to show him the best bushes."

"Well, you'll find berry-picking spotty as you go on, but your other pastime, it'll keep you busy." He shook his head. "They've been a bother before, but now they're a bit more organized. Striking at farms and a few villages, which is why you'll see families on the path."

"Lots of people being driven from their homes, then?"

The man nodded. "I've seen worse. Was in Jerana when Chytrine took Okrannel. I remember them streaming over the borders. This is just a trickle, but soon enough, my friends, if she comes south, we'll have ourselves a flood."

* * *

After that night they hid themselves away from even the outlaws. The logic of the decision was as inescapable as it was simple. If soldiers were looking for them, the fewer people who saw them the better. Picking their way through the countryside off an established route did slow them down, but there were several days where only birds, beasts, and plants marked their passage.

That isolation ended the tenth day out of Stellin, at week's end. Their supplies were beginning to run low. They came across a small cultivated plot deep in the woods northeast of Yslin, almost to the Saporician border. A small wooden house sat in the middle of the plot and had obviously been constructed from the trees cleared from the field.

After a hushed conversation at the forest edge, they decided to let Will approach the house and ask if he could buy some food—meat that had been salted away, meal or flour, cheese, or anything else that might be available. The fact that no smoke drifted from the chimney suggested the building might be empty, in which case Will could employ his skills to get supplies and leave money in exchange.

The idea of leaving money, as well as the admonition to not take the best of whatever was to be found, rankled. Will fully understood that the supplies he'd be taking were valuable—*if they weren't, why would I be taking them?* Leaving money for them, though, that was just rewarding the householder for not protecting his house well enough. *Likely someone will come in, take the rest of his supplies and the money I leave behind.*

He smiled as he rode toward the house and decided he'd leave the counterfeit coins as payment. *As a lesson.*

Halfway to the house, he reined his horse around to a shallow spot in a ditch that cut across the plot. The course deviation let him see a new patch of forest past the house. There, emerging into the field from an arch of green foliage, came five gibberers leading a bearded prisoner. The naked man, whose hands had been lashed to a pole running across the small of his back, had a noose hung round his neck and stumbled forward as a gibberer jerked the rope.

Without conscious thought, Will kicked his horse in the ribs and galloped toward the gibberers. His right hand went to the bladestar pouch. His first throw spun one of the metal projectiles into a gibberer's belly. It howled sharply, then mewed and toppled over. The second throw caught the rope-wielder high in the chest. It staggered, then dropped face first to the ground, pulling the man down with it.

A black-fletched arrow whizzed past him, nipping at the upper leaves of the half-grown corn stalks. It passed through a gibberer's forearm and pierced its chest, pinning the limb. The gibberkin's outraged yip melted into a gurgle that dripped red from its nostrils. A second arrow came in with a bit more arc, passing clean through another gibberer's chest. A squirt of blood pumped out a hole in its breast, then its beady eyes rolled up and it toppled over.

The last gibberer moved from behind the captive and brandished the spear it had been carrying over its shoulder. Will reined back on his horse and the beast came around to present its flank to the gibberer. Will got a bladestar and threw it across his body, but the gibberer flicked it out of the air with the spear-point.

The gibberer charged and Will leaped from the saddle. He drew his longknife and ducked between rows of corn, letting the gibberer's first lunge slide past him. He figured he could time the lunges, move inside, and kill the gibberer, but the Aurolani soldier had other ideas. It scythed the spear to the side, smacking Will in the flank and driving him into the open. There it stalked him as an arrow whipped past its back.

Will struck a guard with the longknife, hoping Crow would kill the gibberkin, but another arrow passed ineffectually high over the gibberer's crouch. *Come on, Crow!*

The captive surged to his feet. For a half second Will

thought the hirsute man would rush the gibberer, but he
hesitated. From ground level the man appeared to be huge,
with enough muscles to make even the most brawny blacksmith envious. Those muscles bunched, and the stout pole
to which his wrists had been tied snapped cleanly across his
back. The thundercrack caused the gibberer to turn toward
him and lunge.

The man caught its spear behind the head and yanked.
The gibberer spilled forward, letting go of the spear at
the last second. It sailed from the creature's paws as the man
lunged forward and smashed his forehead down on the
beast's snout. The gibberer's cry of surprise died as the man's
left hand grabbed its throat and hoisted it off the ground.
The gibberer clawed at the man's wrist once, then Will heard
a wet crack and the beast's body shook.

The man tossed the gibberer's body casually aside. He
turned toward Will and snarled. He started forward, his
hands clawing their way down into fists.

Will stepped back, raising his hands. "Wait, I helped free
you. I wasn't going to steal anything from your house here,
honest."

The man paid his words no heed. A step further and he
dropped to his knees. Tearing at the rope encircling his
throat, the man flopped to the ground. Will heard a stran-
gled sigh, then the man lay very still.

CHAPTER 16

Alyx stood alone at the forest edge, looking down to where the plains spread out to the east. She hugged her right arm around her chest, held her chin between thumb and forefinger of her left hand. A breeze coming up from the plains teased her white-gold hair, but even the tendrils of it lashing her face did not break her concentration.

Sitting astride the Salersena River—which once, long ago, had marked the Alcidese border with Oriosa—the town of Porasena had surrounded itself with stone walls. Towers warded the gates where the river ran through the town, with chains stretched across it to prevent boats moving along. Washing fluttered from lines strung between buildings, and merchants still filled the central square with their gaily colored pavilions—though crowds were not thronging there this morning.

Green fields, clearly cultivated, surrounded the city. Along with foodstuffs moving up or down the river, these fields would have provided the necessities of life for the five

thousand inhabitants. The new crop in those fields, however, a host of Aurolani troops, did not promise life at all.
Their dark tendrils spread through the fields like fungus,
and gangly, insectoid siege machines rose amid their
camps.

Fingering her lower lip, Alyx studied the arrangement
of troops over the terrain. Across the river, several miles off,
started the foothills that marked the far side of the valley
and the current border with Oriosa. Alyx knew the raiders
had come from Oriosa. Scouts and survivors of the raids on
the border fortresses had made that quite evident despite
the Oriosan ambassador's denials. Once she attacked, the
raiders would withdraw into Oriosa, and she could not
pursue them—her guise as a bandit chieftain would be
stripped away because part of her attacking force would
consist of the Alcidese King's Horse Guards.

Replies to reports of the success at Stellin had contained
information about the force laying siege to Porasena. Raiding bands of Aurolani gibberers and vylaens had given way
to a larger, more organized force. While using *arcanslata* to
keep abreast of the situation and requesting the personnel
and matériel needed to counter the threat, Alyx had force-
marched her core unit across the nation, skirting Yslin. She
had sent a small contingent off to the capital and had them
take Sephi with them. The rest had come immediately to
the forested hills above the plains of Sena.

She heard Peri land nearby, but did not turn to look
at her.

"I never thought I would see you petulant, my sister."

"Is that what they think, Peri?"

"They are getting to that point." The Gyrkyme rested a
hand on her left shoulder. "They are restless. General Caro
is fair to bursting with ideas of what his heavy cavalry will
do down on those plains."

"And the others?"

"Caro has quite a personality, Alyx. He served with the
king in Okrannel. His fame is not undeserved. He trained

many of them, or has known of them for years. The longer you delay, the easier it is for him to win them over."

"If I have to fight hard to win them back, it's better that than forcing them to fight hard tomorrow and die down there." Alyx pointed down at the Aurolani lines. "They've arrayed themselves in a crescent on the downriver half of the plains. The river splits their lines. The troops to the west here are dead since the nearest ford is seven miles downriver—they can't be reinforced or escape. The one they used to get here is ten miles up, through rough terrain. They have no escape route. They'll be slaughtered."

Peri blinked big amber eyes. "I have scouted all over and I have seen no reinforcements lurking anywhere. It makes no sense. Must be the Aurolani commander is stupid."

"Could be, my sister, could be, but I cannot count on that. I have to wonder why he would sacrifice half his force. He had to know troops would come here to answer the invasion. The town has water, it has food enough to last for at least a month, and we can bring in supplies through the unprotected half of the city. We can just float them down the river."

"What about the river's *weirun*?"

"The river spirit, at last report, favored Porasena. It's always been very quiet and proud of the prosperity trading brings the town. This is not to say Chytrine could not have turned it, but were that to happen, I would expect to see the river level falling, causing water problems for the town."

"You think this tidbit of army is here as bait?"

"Yes, but for what?" Alyx tucked hair behind her right ear. "General Caro? That makes no sense. Breaking a premier unit of the Alcidese cavalry will really gain Chytrine little. She would do better to lay siege to Fortress Draconis, with her troops here preventing us from sending reinforcements north. No, something is going on here and I don't like that I cannot puzzle it out."

"Now, *that* is my sister."

Alyx smiled. "This leaves me only one choice, of course."

"Yes?"

"They offer us half a force as bait. I say we double their cost." She turned from the plains and started marching toward her army's encampment. "Chytrine wants us here for a reason, and we'll give her a chance to think on why that wasn't a good idea."

She walked alone into the woods, for Peri took to the air again, flying high above the brambles and little branches that tugged at Alex's tunic and trousers. Two sentries moved to intercept her, then recognition flashed on both of their faces. The man, from one of the light foot companies, smiled and saluted. The other, a woman from the Red Caps, immediately challenged her.

Alyx offered the proper countersign, then pointed at the infantryman. "At the end of your watch, report yourself for dereliction of duty to your commanding officer. I will be checking."

The man started to stammer a comment, but his companion smacked him in the chest with an open hand, then saluted sharply. The infantryman aped the salute and Alyx returned it. She kept on going, allowing the growled conversation by those in her wake to go unnoticed.

Weary soldiers dragged themselves to their feet as she passed. Those who stood proudest were her own Wolves. The others paid her the respect due to her rank, but she could read a distrust in their eyes. The other generals in the Alcidese army were well known and had a history in which one could take confidence. She was unknown, and as dangerous to the soldiers as a lordling with a gold-bought commission and a love of parading.

She walked through the wooded campsite, threading a phalanx of trees and soldiers, heading for the pavilion that had been erected in a sandy depression at the hilltop. She kept her head high, her strides long. She did not acknowledge waves or nods, but kept on going, sparing not even an encouraging glance for warriors who had bled for her in the past and would likely do so again in the future.

Two soldiers pulled aside the flaps to the pavilion. She entered and paused in the opening, allowing the flaps to close behind her. It took her eyes a heartbeat or two to adjust to the darkness. As things came into view she catalogued each emerging impression. She analyzed everything as if the meeting itself were a campaign, and she knew winning it would go a long way to winning against the forces on the plains.

A long, narrow table ran down the pavilion's center. Maps had been laid out on it—one of the valley and one of the city. Wooden blocks painted in various colors had been placed on the maps to show the location of troops, and her quick scan of their placement told her someone had been projecting movements for the next day.

Off to the left stood General Caro, with a gold goblet of wine in hand. A beefy man with white hair and dark eyes, he was as handsome as she had been told. Having been raised amid the Gyrkyme, her sense of human beauty often did not coincide with that of most others, but he was not displeasing to her eyes. He clearly had once been lean, though pendulous jowls now marred the line of his jaw, and his belly protruded too much over his belt.

Other officers, mostly younger, surrounded him. Their mild laughter tailed off as they realized she had entered the tent. They glanced silently at Caro, then her, and waited for something to happen.

Opposite that knot of people stood her supporters. Ebrius, out of his armor and looking uncomfortable for it, watched Caro and his people with the eyes of a forest bandit spying rich merchants coming down the road. Captain Agitare, wearing his company's red cap tipped back a bit on his head, had a timorous smile twisting the corners of his thin-lipped mouth. He'd been ordered to attend the meeting, but he did not know why, and clearly feared she would dress him down in front of the others for Stellin.

Lastly, Peri stood back, blinking lazily, and studying her talons when any of Caro's men allowed stares to linger too long on her lithe beauty. That was a game Alyx had watched her sister play many times, with men and Gyrkyme alike. She knew both parties enjoyed it, but found it to be pure frippery. That this flirtation seemed to sharpen the senses and bleed off anxiety was the only purpose she could see to it.

Caro set his cup of wine on the table and bowed his head to her. "Princess Alexia of Okrannel, a pleasure to see you again. Did you see anything out there this morning that will change our course of battle tomorrow?"

Alyx didn't answer, but instead crossed to the far side of the table and studied the positions. Caro had the light foot infantry coming down the slopes toward the plains, with the heavy infantry upstream. His heavy cavalry came down from the north, along the river, to crush the Aurolani forces arrayed on the west side of the river.

"A fascinating plan, General." She reached out and nudged the line of heavy infantry forward fifty meters. "The seasonal tributary forms a ditch right here. It will be an easier line to hold."

"That's true, it would." Caro smiled and retrieved his cup of wine. "However, tomorrow, I have no intention of letting the northern horde reach that line. We'll have them ridden down long before then."

Alyx's violet gaze flickered up as Caro's confederates laughed and clinked goblets together. "You aren't using the light horse battalion we have at the northern ford."

"I am, to hold that ford."

"And my Wolves."

"You are my reserve."

She chewed on her lower lip for a moment, then straightened up and folded her arms over her chest. "It is an interesting plan, General, but severely flawed. We won't be executing it tomorrow."

The man started as if she'd slapped him. "Princess, I know you have had some modest success. . . ."

Her eyes hardened. "First, General, you will address me as General. My *title* I have by dint of birth—an office in name only, since my nation has not truly existed for a generation. My *rank* I have earned."

"Earned in small-unit tactics, *General.*"

"Earned within the life span of most of the soldiers I command, General, not in the days before they were born." Alyx kept her voice low, but filled it with steel. "You and your people are here because I *requested* your presence, not because I need your guidance. I welcome your insight, but this expedition is under my command. I will make the final decisions."

"Ah, I see how it is." Caro slightly inclined his head in her direction. "You said my plan was flawed. . . ."

Captain Agitare cleared his throat. "Begging the general's pardon."

Both Alyx and Caro said, "Yes?"

"General Caro, I have served with you and with General Alexia. Just listen to her plan."

The older man smiled indulgently. "I remember you, Agitare. I once thought you had promise." He looked at Alyx. "The flaws."

"They are simple as well as glaring." She pointed to the half of the Aurolani force on the east side of the river. "These troops present a danger to your troops. We see no evidence of a dragonel in their camp, but it is possible they are hidden in their pavilions. If your King's Horse charges, they retreat, stretching your line out, and these troops across the river shoot."

The mere mention of a dragonel made some of the officers backing Caro blanch. A generation previous, at the siege of Fortress Draconis, the Aurolani horde had revealed a weapon of terrible power. Consisting of a stout metal

tube, it was filled with an explosive powder that when ignited propelled stone balls over long distances with enough
power to crush a city wall. Experiments with the one captured at Fortress Draconis also suggested that if loaded
with smaller shot, a single blast would devastate a mass of
foot soldiers or cavalry.

Alyx continued. "And we do not know if the Aurolani
host might not be equipped with draconettes, either."

Caro waved that suggestion away. "There is no proof
such things exist. They are tales made to earn the teller
a drink. Who can believe men who say they have been to
Aurolan and seen Chytrine training her troops?"

She shook her head. "Even if stories of the Aurolani soldiers being equipped with small, single-user dragonels are
fable, would you allow your troops into combat where they
could be slaughtered by such weapons? It really doesn't
matter if you would take that chance or not, General, because I will not. Until proven otherwise, I shall assume that
the eastern force is well equipped."

"And not the western force?"

Alyx laughed once. "You saw, as is evident by your plan,
that the western force is already forfeit. It's bait for a trap. It
could be that the trap does involve dragonels concealed
across the river. I don't know, but I do know that a trap
which is disarmed is a trap that won't hurt my troops. The
eastern force is the noose of this snare, and it must be eliminated.

"The other big flaw in your plan is this." She traced the
distance from the heavy cavalry's line to the Aurolani line.
"Three hundred yards at the start. That's too long a distance for you to sustain a charge and maintain unit in-
tegrity. You're better at one hundred yards. Then you are
unstoppable."

Caro held a hand up. "You skipped something. The
eastern force, how will you eliminate it?"

"Simple. I send a light foot company south, to the upstream ford. They cross to the east. The other light foot

companies will stay here in the woods to be used much as you planned to use them. Your horses will be back here, at the edge of the woods, waiting."

"That's four hundred yards from the enemy."

"I know." Alyx nodded solemnly. "The heavy infantry will be positioned here. Downriver, at the north ford, my Wolves and the two light horse battalions will cross and head south. We attack, breaking the eastern force against Porasena."

Caro frowned. "That is well and good for you, General, but it still leaves me with a thousand Aurolani troops outside the range for an effective charge. You can't think a single battalion of heavy infantry will drive them against us."

"They won't have to. The light horse and my Wolves will."

"Impossible." Caro pointed at the maps. "One ford is ten miles away, the other is seven. Your ability to attack west is limited by the same factors that make it impossible for the eastern force to support their fellows. By the time you're across the river, the western force will have fought free of the infantry and will be off raiding."

"You're wrong, General Caro, very wrong." Alyx gave him a cold smile. "Your force will be the anvil, and we will be the hammer. We have one advantage the Aurolani don't, and two days hence, that advantage will destroy their invasion."

CHAPTER 17

Resolute had come thundering up on his horse, snarled something in Elvish at Will that sent a shiver down his spine, then rode on past. He flew into the forest, along the gibberers' back trail. Will almost swung into the saddle to ride after him, but reconsidered. *Angry as he is, if he doesn't find gibberers to kill, I don't want to be around.*

The thief ran to the fallen man, but didn't get too close. He could see that he was breathing, but it clearly wasn't easy, and that blue tinge to his skin looked bad. Drawing a small boot knife, Will dropped to one knee and cut the noose free of the man's neck. His breathing came easier, but he remained unconscious, which wasn't something that bothered Will too much at the moment.

Leaving him in the dirt, Will quickly went from gibberer to gibberer, slitting throats just to make sure they were dead. He assumed Resolute would berate him for the necessity of doing that—something that showed that Will was not confident of his martial skills—but better that than his being yelled at for not making sure they were dead.

Cutting the throat of the one the man had killed took a lot of work. The man's grip had crushed the neck and pulverized the bones. Will had no doubt it was dead and felt his own throat tightening as he remembered the look in the man's eyes as he came for him.

Crow rode up quickly, leading the packhorses. He swung from the saddle, his bow still strung and an arrow nocked. He frowned at the bloody work Will had been doing. "Have you checked the man?"

"He's breathing." Will wiped his hands off on the gibberer's pelt. "He was coming for me before he collapsed."

Crow returned the arrow to the saddle quiver and slid the bow home into its scabbard. Crossing to the man he crouched, pressing two fingers to the man's neck and examining the abrasions there. "Not too bad. Blood in his hair, though, likely had a hard knock or two. Help me, we'll get him inside."

The two of them struggled to lift the huge man and had a hard time dragging him to the cabin. Will got the door open and they got the man into bed over in the back corner. The way the man overlapped it side to side and off the foot clearly indicated that the cabin wasn't his. *A rat trapped in a thimble would have more room than this man in this cabin.*

At Crow's order, Will fetched water and *metholanth*, which they used to clean the man up and pack some of his wounds. His feet were raw in places and the gash on his head looked bad after Crow cut away enough matted hair to be able to see it. Tearing apart the threadbare clothes they found in the place—which never would have fit the man anyway—they fashioned bandages. The man didn't so much as stir while they cared for him.

They'd finished up and Will had just begun to explore the single-room cabin for any hidden storage areas when Resolute returned. This caused Will to intensify his search for hiding places, but the floorboards were solid and the generally rickety furnishings held no secrets.

Resolute bowed his head as he entered the cabin. "The man?"

Crow shrugged. "Unconscious. Needs food and water, but is in very good shape otherwise. Find anything on the trail?"

"Nothing of note." The Vorquelf's silver gaze found Will easily enough. "I need to speak with you, boy."

Will forced the fearful flutter in his stomach away. "You're going to tell me what I did wrong, right? You're going to tell me I was stupid to ride up to help him when I did, right? You'll tell me this even though you'd have done the same thing."

Resolute lifted his head. The hair on his head brushed the roof, and a shoulder brushed the central beam. The expression he wore hovered between anger and a grim resignation. He slowly folded his arms over his chest and watched Will in silence for a moment.

Then he nodded. "That is exactly what I would have done, if I had seen what you saw, and *if* I were as inexperienced as you are. Do you think Crow or I would have liked seeing him being led along like a cow? You've got perhaps fifteen years in you, maybe sixteen. You were spared seeing gibberers lead your mother off that way, seeing them hack your friends to death. I wasn't, and I made the mistake you did, but I made it over a century ago."

Will frowned. "And mistakes aren't allowed now?"

"No, boy, they aren't, not for you." Resolute pointed back toward the west. "Have you forgotten the mountains? Have you forgotten that you are the person we need to defeat Chytrine? For you to launch a suicidal attack was unforgivable and irresponsible. If you had died . . ." He snarled and slammed his right fist into the side of the main beam.

Dust poured down in grey ribbons from the beam. Will wished it would cover him and insulate him from Resolute's anger. He knew it wouldn't. *I can't hide, nor should I.* Will's own grey eyes narrowed and he bared his teeth in a snarl.

"How was what I did here different from what we did in Stellin? We were all going to die there, including me, including *me*, your hope to defeat Chytrine! I came closer to dying there than I ever did here, but you didn't hide me away there. You let me be in danger. I don't understand."

Resolute smashed his fist into the palm of his left hand. "We had no choice there, boy. Here we had a choice."

"Sure, let him die."

"Stop it, both of you!" Crow rose to his feet, arms outstretched. "Resolute, the fact is that Will isn't dead. He survived the mistake. He knew it was a mistake. He slit their throats to make sure there was not going to be more of a problem. You saw that; you know it. You've made sure he knows how serious a mistake it was."

The triumphant smile blossoming on Will's face died as Crow spun, anger flashing from his brown eyes. "Don't you dare for an instant let yourself believe that just because a prophecy seems to apply to you that it truly *does* and somehow that makes you immune to misfortune. Just as things you saw in the cave were changed by your seeing them, so it could be that things change without our knowing it. And let there be no illusion on your part that—even *if* you are the person mentioned in the prophecy—this prophecy is true."

Will blinked. "It might be a lie?"

"We don't know, Will, but we've been working for the past quarter century to put things in place so it won't be. Assuming a prophecy will make things just fall into place and come true is like assuming having a road map is the same as making the journey. It's not."

Crow walked over to him and rested his hands on Will's shoulders, then crouched enough to look into Will's eyes at a level. "Risking your life to save this man, that wasn't wrong, but *how* you did it was. You didn't know if those five were the vanguard of a force, or if they had allies nearby, or if this cabin was full of them. Were they about to kill the man, yes, you would have had to intervene. You could have, however, waited, given us a signal, or done any of a number of things that would have lowered the danger."

Resolute nodded slowly. "This course we are committed to, it demands we risk our lives, but not foolishly."

Will shivered, then sagged back against the cabin's wall. "It is something *you* committed to, but you kidnapped me, made me think of this as an adventure. I was thinking of stories and legends—*my* legend, the one I'll become. You have known for always what you are doing, but me . . . ?" He frowned. "What am I doing here?"

"Life . . . saving . . ." The harsh croak came from the room's far corner. The bed and its rope mesh creaked as the large man shifted on it. He rubbed his right hand over the bandages on his throat. "Thanks."

The word came more whispered than spoken, but the nod that accompanied it underscored its sincerity.

Will levered himself off the wall and trailed in Crow's wake as the trio moved toward the bed. Crow gave the man a waterskin and helped him drink from it. The man drank greedily, with some water coursing down his cheeks and through his beard to splash on his broad chest and mat the thick, black hair there.

With his hands behind his head, catching on to the main beam, Resolute leaned forward. "What's your name?"

The man grimaced for a moment, closing his cold blue eyes, then nodded. "Dranae." He pronounced it slowly, drawing out both syllables. He placed a massive hand on his chest and repeated the word.

Will frowned. "Never heard the like of that name before."

Crow arched an eyebrow at him. "Are you certain you want to start comparing the oddities of names?"

"No."

"I have heard mention of similar before." Resolute's voice came low and soft, though still resonant. "It's an old name, an old man-name. Likely he was named for an ancestor."

Dranae just shook his head. "Don't know."

"With that knock on your head, might take some time before your thoughts are clear. I'm Crow, this is Will, and that is Resolute. Do you live near here?"

Again Dranae shook his head. "I know little."

Crow pressed the man back down into the bed. "That's fine. Rest. Rest both your head and your throat. You're safe now."

The man tried to resist, but failed and sank back down into the bed. Resolute went out to the packhorses and came back with a blanket that he spread out over the man. It barely covered his body, leaving his feet and much of his shins uncovered, but that appeared not to matter much. The man's breathing became steady.

Will slipped from the cabin and began to look after his horse. The other two joined him to likewise care for their mounts, though they conversed in Elvish and in low tones. That angered Will a bit, but his anger faded fast as the chill he'd felt before swallowed it.

What am I doing here? He knew he'd let himself be seduced by the lure of adventure—and a desire to get out of Yslin to save himself from Marcus' wrath. On the road Resolute had driven him hard, forced him to work hard, and never gave him much of a chance to think about things. While the journey had been uneventful he'd been learning, and since the cavern, they had constantly been in danger. *And now, when I do have a chance to think about things, I'm so deep in it that what I think doesn't matter.*

He realized the whole journey had been an illusion. It was a fable unfolding around him, with things like Oracle or the Gyrkyme just adding to the weirdness of it all. Even memories of the hard knocks he'd taken were fading, along with the bruises they left behind. As he thought about it there didn't seem to be anything he could identify as real, then two things rose up to contradict that.

The first was the feeling he'd had when he had been entrusted with the leaf. The most surreal part of the whole journey, his bond with that ancient leaf, felt the most real to him. That sensation had provided a foundation that made believing everything his companions told him easy. The leaf had taken him to the caverns, then the assaults by gibberers had taken over, emphasizing the opposition. One thing urged him on, the other tried to stop him, but each were different sides of the same coin that impelled him to continue.

The second was the sound of Dranae's words. Will *had* saved him and the man was grateful. His words, hoarse though they might have been, carried sincerity and opened a door into Will's understanding of Resolute and Crow. *For far longer than I have been alive they have been working to save people. I'm now a necessary part of that for them.* Will's realization explained some of Resolute's frustration, though it made it no easier to take.

Having removed the saddle from his horse, Will grabbed handfuls of grass and began to rub the beast down. In evaluating things, the thief realized he was being a fool. Chances were excellent that he'd get himself killed and no one, not once, had mentioned any sort of reward or treasure to be won. It might be all well and good that he defeated Chytrine, but if he returned to Yslin with empty pockets, the Dimandowns would echo with stinging ridicule.

And yet, even as he made that judgment, he glanced at Crow. Tired as the man was, as poor as he was, there was something in his eyes that no one in the Dimandowns ever had. Will never heard a trace of bitterness in the man's laugh. He never saw a furtive glance despite the joking around him. As much as he or Resolute might discipline Will or speak sharply to him, neither was cruel for the sake of spite.

They're not like normal folk. In the Dimandowns people focused on how to get another mug of ale for free, or a prize that would open a woman's thighs. They schemed ways to win a king's ransom, and others schemed ways to

take it from them. All they cared about was themselves—
and Marcus had been no exception. While he might have
taken orphans in and given them food and shelter, they
worked for his pleasure. *And when they come to rival him,
he gets rid of them.*

Will suddenly saw his dreams of becoming a legend
from another angle. *I want to be Will the Nimble, King of the
Dimandowns. I want to be greater than Marcus and the
Azure Spider. It will be a treasure that can't be stolen. It will
get me mugs of ale. It will open thighs. It will never die.* As
glorious as all that would be, Will suddenly realized it
lacked something.

The gratitude in Dranae's voice, the passion that would
make Oracle put her own eyes out, the fury that drove
Resolute—all of these things shook him. His vision of the
world opened up beyond the borders of the Dimandowns.
He did not suddenly decide he could be more than the King
of the Dimandowns; he just realized that for someone like
Dranae, he was more important just as Will than he ever
would have been as the lord of Yslin's slums.

Will swore and threw the handful of grass to the ground
with disgust. He shot Crow and Resolute a purely venomous glance. "I hate you both."

Resolute snorted, but Crow turned with a curious expression on his face. "And that comes from?"

"This journey. All the things you've told me. All the
things you have not told me. All of it." Will's hands convulsed down into fists. "I can never go back to being who I
was, can I?"

Crow slowly shook his head. "No."

"And it's all your fault!"

"No." The older man sighed. "It's the fault of Chytrine."

"That's easy to say, but she's never done anything to me."

"No, boy?" Resolute shouldered his way past Crow. "If
you want to think that, you can, but the fact is she's done
everything to you. If not for her, I would not be here,
Oracle would not be who she is, Predator would be some

happy gardener, the Vorquelves wouldn't be in Yslin, Crow would not be Crow. Lots of people would still be alive and your life would be entirely different."

The Vorquelf stabbed a finger against Will's breastbone. "You wonder if you could ever go back to being who you were, but you never really *were* that person at all. You were meant to be someone else. Because of Chytrine you are *destined* to be someone else. The actions of others have already determined who you *are*, Wilburforce; but we're giving you the chance to decide who you will *become* and how you will get there."

Will snarled. "You can't put it back on me. That's not fair."

"No, it's not." Resolute shook his head. "No more fair than my losing my home, my future. I'm here to stop that from happening to others. Crow is the same. You, you might have a future, but only if you're willing to fight for it. If you fail, she wins. Not only will you lose, but so will everyone else. And responsibility for that, boy, is something you can never escape."

CHAPTER 18

Sitting tall astride her horse, encased in her golden armor, Alyx studied the Aurolani encampment. She saw movement there, but heard no trumpets raising an alarm. Fires burned and sentries paced, but no one seemed to be paying any attention to the cavalry forming up to the east. She knew the gibberers and vylaens had to be able to see her as easily as she could see them, so their lack of anxiety surprised her for a moment.

Then, slowly, she nodded. The gibberers did not rely as much on sight as men did, and the breeze springing from the south meant the scent of her formation was being carried away from the enemy. Moreover, the stink of the city settled over the plain. In addition to that, she had brought her troops up at night and positioned them so they could ride in from the dawning sun. The mountains still shadowed them, while the sun's warm rays crept over the enemy camp.

The honorable thing to do would have been to have her company's trumpeter blow a challenge that would waken the enemy. Alyx knew General Caro would do that, but less to give the enemy a sporting chance than to train their eyes on his unit's banner, so they could know who they faced. *For him it would be an act of arrogance, not nobility.*

She shook her head. *War is not a place for arrogance or nobility.* She turned and gave her sister a half smile. "Are they completely gormless, Peri, or laying a trap for us?"

The Gyrkyme blinked her big eyes. "Gormlessly confident of their trap?"

Alyx laughed lightly. "That could be it. You know the two pavilions you will hit?"

Peri nodded and hefted one of the two firecocks she'd been given. The device, which wasn't much longer than her forearm, had a ceramic sphere for a nose, a cast-iron collar in the middle, and dried cornhusks at the end. It looked nothing so much like a giant shuttlecock. "The red one, and the one with the pennant. I'm ready to go."

"Go, and good luck."

"Not luck, just confidence in your plan." The Gyrkyme unfurled her wings and, with a single strong beat, launched herself into the sky.

Alyx drew her sword and raised it aloft. The Wolves, who formed the center of her line, raised their lances. The light horse units on either wing raised their lances as well, then all three battalions began to trot forward. At the signal, they would all charge. They would hit the Aurolani camp as a relentless wave of steel and horseflesh, blasting through it.

If things go as planned.

The signal came quickly enough. Peri, circling high over the Aurolani encampment, released the first firecock. The cast-iron chamber housed a bit of charcoal. When she twisted the cover on the collar, it exposed vents in the charcoal chamber. As the firecock fell, the air rushing in made the charcoal flare hot, igniting the cornhusks roughly a hundred yards above the ground. The firecock struck the red pavilion and ripped through it, then the collar shattered the ceramic sphere full of oil. The burning husks lit the splashing oil, immediately catching the pavilion on fire.

The second likewise struck its target, which then burst into flame. Gibberers began scurrying about, barking and snarling. The sounds of their voices drowned out the thunder of approaching hooves. While some ran to retrieve their arms and raise some sort of defense, others just ran toward the river.

Alyx snapped her helm's faceplate down in the last fifty yards of her charge. The Wolves had outdistanced the light horse units only because the other horsemen held themselves back a bit, as per the battle plan. The Wolves, slightly more heavily armored, made up the formation's spearhead. It pierced the thin defenses at the camp's rear and stabbed deep into the Aurolani camp.

To the right and left of her, gibberers screamed. Lances splintered explosively, whirling away transfixed bodies. Rising in the stirrups, she slashed down and past the guard of a gibberer who had failed to stab her. She was beyond him when she felt the shock of her blow connecting. Her blade's tip came back blackened with blood.

The Wolves blew through the Aurolani camp like an ill wind. On her right the Seventh Light Horse Battalion anchored itself against the river and drove into the camp. On the left the King's Own Light Horse Battalion engaged the enemy, then wheeled west, driving the gibberers toward the river. Alyx knew many of the enemy would try to swim to the other side and sanctuary, but she doubted many could fight the river's current. Fewer still would be able to fight the *weirun*, and she hoped its appetite for gibberers would be enormous.

Off to the right the pavilion that had had the pennant flying above it exploded thunderously. She felt a shock wave jolt her. *Dragonel powder to be used to sap the walls?* Flaming gibberer bodies arced through the sky. Some riders fought to control their mounts through the thunder and meaty rain, and some went down, but her steed merely picked up its pace, racing through the enemy camp. Alyx and her Wolves burst from the enemy lines and cut east as the King's Own slashed down in their wake.

Alyx smiled. *This plan will actually work.*

The Wolves hit the eastern road to Porasena at a gallop. By the time they reached the walls, the eastern gate's massive doors had swung wide and the Wolves poured into the city. Hooves striking sparks from cobblestones, they galloped through narrow streets and over a tall bridge spanning the river, then plunged down the road to the western gate. Soldiers manning the towers and above the opening gates cheered as they came on and rode down into the western plain of Sena.

The mistake that both the Aurolani troops and General Caro had made was in not realizing that the city of Porasena formed a ford over the river, and that as long as friendly troops controlled the city, passing from one side to the other was not a problem. Aurolani troops could not cross there, but she was unhindered.

The Aurolani troops on the western plain had used the extra day to prepare defenses against the Alcidese forces arrayed against them. They'd raised basic breastworks to their rear to hold off the heavy cavalry. The defenses they'd set up against a force from the city were sufficient for holding off the heavy infantry. At the commencement of the raid on the other shore, Caro's troops had appeared at the edge of the forest and started slowly forward, forcing Aurolani troops to the rear to defend, stripping the forward defenses.

The Wolves hit the Aurolani line a quarter of the way in from the end. The very end of that line had been built up to be almost a fortress itself, but up along the line, the defenses had not been so carefully prepared. Because of the line's arc, the point they hit had been removed from the threat of heavy cavalry. To defend against them the Aurolani defenders now had to rush across the Aurolani position and man their old defenses.

Peri's aerial survey of the Aurolani line had identified a gap in the lines through which the enemy had made raids. Riders raced ahead of Alyx and, under the cover of arrows from other Wolves, looped grapnel lines around the spiked logs that blocked the gap. They pulled the abatises aside, then Agitare led the Red Caps through. Alyx and her body-guards came second, then the rest of the Wolves flooded through the gap. They coursed through the Aurolani camp, cutting and slashing, riding down gibberers, shooting arrows into vylaens, and wreaking havoc.

The Aurolani forces broke. Some ran for the river, and others passed south, through their own lines, heading toward the city and the slowly advancing heavy infantry. Some started west, scrambling up the hillsides toward the waiting light foot. Most, though, fled north and away from the Wolves. They escaped in the easiest direction, grasping in their panic at the closest path out of danger.

The northern path proved illusory when it came to safety.

Alyx rode up onto one of the highest points on the Aurolani line and watched gibberers scrambling away as quickly as possible. Ahead of them, forming a dark line at the edge of the forest, the King's Own Horse waited. She picked Caro out from the center of the line easily enough. Behind him waited two riders, one bearing the unit's battle standard and the other his family's flag. The cavalry remained in place, horses stamping and snorting steam in the cool morning air. They waited, letting the enemy come to them.

She knew she had shamed him by saying that his men were at their best in a hundred-yard charge. Alyx half expected him to send them off at a greater distance, just to prove her wrong, but he did not. True to his orders, he held them back. Until the gibberers had closed within one hundred fifty yards, he did not draw his sword. He raised it slowly, then as they neared the hundred-yard limit, he slashed down and his line surged forward.

A ragged, disorganized mass of infantry is to a cavalry charge what ripe wheat stalks are to the reaper's scythe. The heavy cavalry hit the gibberers like a wall of steel. Bodies, broken-limbed and limp, flew into the air. Thrashing gibberers rose on lances as tortured pennants. Curved sabers sprayed spattered gore with each arced stroke. Hooves ground bodies into the torn earth, leaving bloodied piles of tissue to mew in their wake. Some gibberers did turn to run, but their fellows caught them up, carrying them into the heavy cavalry. It rolled over them as if they were already the phantoms they became a heartbeat later.

The charge did lose its momentum, but then Caro's troops merely resorted to their other weapons. Swords rose and fell. Maces crushed arms and skulls. Axes clove bodies and short spears stabbed. Those who had not lost their lances flicked them out, stabbing the long-bladed heads through thick gibberer bodies. The work became less fighting than pure butchery. The heavy cavalry took to it without hesitation and with all the righteous fury of warriors cleansing their homeland of invaders.

Alyx shifted her attention to the end of the Aurolani line. There the breastwork had been raised a little higher and the defenders shot arrows at riders, but most fell short. Those few that did hit only stuck in armor or bounced off. *A couple of firecocks, then raking it with arrows should weaken it.* She doubted the vylaen commanding that area would surrender, but she would inquire first, before she ordered the slaughter.

To the south and west the infantry engaged fleeing gibberers. The Wolves and the heavy cavalry met in the center of the line, then moved west, trapping gibberers at the hills. Those fleeing north strung themselves out along the river, so when the heavy cavalry turned to charge at them, the refugees had but one choice and most drowned exercising it.

Bobbing corpses slowly flowed down the river. More floated up here and there, naked, stripped of any jewelry or armor. Alyx had been told the *weirun* of the Salersena River was greedy and enjoyed offerings of gold made by the town's merchants. She wondered if the things plundered from the bodies would show up in market stalls, and the thought that they might sent a shiver through her.

Alyx dispatched Captain Agitare to offer quarter to the vylaen leading the defense of the end of the enemy line. Agitare fastened a strip of white cloth to the end of his horse-bow, approached, and tendered her offer. Power began to gather in the vylaen's palms, but before it could cast a spell, Agitare plucked an arrow from his quiver, nocked, drew, and let fly.

The scarlet-fletched arrow burst the vylaen's heart. Magickal energy trickled up its forearms like ivy growing up a tower, burning as it went. The vylaen collapsed. A sleetstorm of arrows covered Agitare's retreat. Peri screamed high above the enemy position, then a firecock exploded at its heart. The Red Caps advanced and before too long, all Aurolani resistance had breathed its last.

High in the tower that housed Porasena's mayor, Alyx attended a hastily planned noontime reception. General Caro had made certain to give her all due credit for the planning of the attack, but he did nothing to deflect the flowery praises the local merchant-princes lavished upon him. Most of them, it turned out, had taken their breakfast and tea in towers, watching the battle unfold as they ate. Their daughters and young wives entertained some of the younger officers. The women listened with wide eyes and sympathetic sighs as stories of courage unfolded and thousands more gibberers were slain than had ever been encamped on the plains of Sena.

Alyx shook her head and carried her goblet of wine out onto the tower balcony that looked north. The river unwound a ribbon of blue, flecked with flashes of silver, rolling north. It had long since carried away most of the bodies, while smoky pyres on either shore took care of the rest. The meager loot left behind in the Aurolani camps had quickly disappeared once the fighting had stopped.

"Are Aurolani artifacts selling briskly in the market?"

Peri blinked her amber eyes slowly. "Most of the real things are gone, but plenty have been manufactured. One smart man is overstriking coins with a star to mark the battle."

The pale-tressed woman set her goblet on the balcony's stone balustrade. "The people are celebrating as if this was some great victory. It means nothing. Chytrine left troops here for us to kill, for reasons known only to her. That we cost her more than she might have expected is good, but her only purpose here might have been to test us."

"Yes, my sister, what you say is true." Peri walked over to stand beside Alyx, appropriated her goblet, and drank some of her wine. "You must recognize, though, that for the people of Porasena, this *was* a great victory. This valley is their world, and we saved it for them. Could you expect them to act any other way?"

Alyx shook her head. She knew Peri was correct, but the simple and willful lack of awareness of the world displayed by the townsfolk astonished her. Alyx had seen more of the world than most of the people in Porasena; having been born in Okrannel and flown to Gyrvirgul as an infant was but the first of many journeys she'd undertaken. She'd been schooled in history and knew in intimate detail the forces and elements that had shaped the world.

And she knew the incredible threat Chytrine represented to all of it. A quarter century earlier many warriors, including her father, had died to prevent Chytrine's invasion of the south. While the effort had been unsuccessful at unseating her, it had held her hordes in check. Still, new incursions, like the siege at Porasena, indicated that Chytrine's power was growing, as was her need to project it southward.

"I understand what you are saying, Peri, but I just . . ." She shivered. "It's as if they are celebrating being dry because the first raindrop in a storm did not hit them."

"I never said it was smart, sister, just inevitable." Peri frowned. "The people are stupid from drinking too much of this wine. Vinegar is not as bitter."

"Better than the beer. It's watery and the color of your eyes." Alyx took the goblet back, went to drink, but saw something over the edge of the cup. "What is that?"

Peri's eyes narrowed as she focused on the river. "A wave of some sort, working its way down the river. It's red, bloodred."

It took a dozen heartbeats for the wave to come close enough for Alyx to see it, and she knew she wasn't getting any of the detail Peri was. The color matched her description, but Alyx noted there was no foam at the crest of the wave. It moved upstream, against the current, coming on fast.

A much larger wave surged out from the city and rose to the height of the walls. It rolled north, rising, cresting, and smashing down on the smaller scarlet wave. The red wave vanished for a second in the mist of the tall wave's crash, then a bloody waterspout stabbed up and through what would have been the wave's heart. River water sloshed up and out, over the banks, washing away dogs and setting crows to wing over the battlefield they'd been scavenging.

Fish flopped on the banks, while others floated in the channel. A few gibberer bodies bobbed up again. Huge bubbles boiled to the surface and exploded, projecting a foul stink of rotting muck.

"What was that?"

Peri shook her head. "Not certain. The big wave, that was the *weirun.* Of that I am sure."

Alyx looked again at the red stain, which had melted

from its spear-shape to an amorphous blob floating on the slowly settling surface. "Did that thing kill it?"

"The river's not dead."

The red splotch slowly floated to the western bank. A rounded and soft column of oily plasm reached up toward the bank. The very end of it resolved itself into a hand that clutched at long-leafed grasses. The rest of the red stain flowed toward this hand, as if it were wax filling a mold of a naked man. Once legs and feet had been formed, the figure pulled himself up onto the plain.

He remained naked for barely more than a second before his flesh took on the wrinkles and seams of cloth. It appeared as if his clothing were rising up through his flesh. The scarlet color drained away, leaving his clothes black, from boots and trousers to tunic. Likewise a hooded cloak flowed from him, and a black mask appeared on his face, covering him from upper lip to forehead.

His eyes remained dark holes for no more than a moment. Bright yellow-orange flames ignited there, guttering. The hem of his cloak caught a spark and also burst into flame. The fire quickly consumed the cloak, which became composed of little licking flames against which his flesh and clothes were apparently immune.

An archer on the wall below launched an arrow at the figure. The shaft sped toward its target and then, when only a man-length from its heart, slowed. It almost seemed to Alyx that it had been shot into water, or something even more viscous. The figure reached out and casually plucked the arrow from the air. He said something in an oddly sibilant tongue, causing the arrow in his hand to combust.

On the wall, the other arrows in the archer's quiver blossomed with fire. The man tore it off and others stomped the fire out while yet another colleague smothered the flames on the man's back with a cloak. Sharp, surprised shouts faded, and cold laughter from the figure stole over the city like an icy drizzle.

The figure brushed his hands one against the other to

rid them of arrow ash, then clasped them at his belt. His laughter drained away to be replaced by a voice that was both strong and melodious. Despite that, however, it brought with it no warmth at all.

"Hark unto me, Porasena, poor; town with a future no more. Celebrate victory this morn; so the morrows you'll mourn." The figure looked around, then stamped his foot to scatter a mangy pack of hounds slinking toward him. "Blood is power, and in an hour, much blood did you spill. Next will come fire, certainly most dire, and all will it kill."

The figure reached back and tugged its hood up to cover its head. Then hands shot to opposite shoulders, grasping the fiery cloak and pulled it tight around him. In an eyeblink he became a column of fire that then collapsed into a greasy black stream of smoke. The breeze wafted it toward the town and it smelled even more foul than the river gas.

Alyx drank some of the wine, holding it in her mouth until its fumes could dissolve the stink in her nostrils, then she swallowed hard. "That was a *sullanciri*."

Peri nodded. "I believe so, sister."

"So, all of this was bait to get us here, so we could see something Chytrine wanted us to see. And he was here to make sure we knew this was just a prelude."

"We would be wise, then, to leave."

Alyx upturned the goblet and shook the last drops of wine out over the city. "If we leave, there will be panic, rioting, looting. We will have saved the city for nothing. If we are going, we are evacuating it in an orderly manner."

"Not a simple task."

"No, my sister, but one that must be done." Alyx sighed. "Come with me. It won't be an easy fight, but if we turn Caro to our side, we might just be able to keep some people alive."

CHAPTER 19

Will liked having Dranae join their group. While he remained largely silent as his throat was healing up, Dranae had no problem helping out with various chores. He hauled water and firewood without being asked. He found some herbs and leaves in the Saporician rainforests that were able to spice up rabbit stew. He also didn't seem to mind taking the predawn watch, which was the one Will especially hated.

Outfitting Dranae had been difficult, since none of the clothes they had would fit him. They ended up winding a blanket around him in a skirtlike affair. At first he pulled the back of it up between his legs and tucked it in at his belly, but pretty soon just left it down at knee-height. Will thought it looked kind of ridiculous, but Resolute noted there were all sorts of sailors on the Crescent Sea who dressed similarly, raising the specter that Dranae might once have been one of them, or even a pirate shipping out of Wruona. Will questioned him about that possibility, but the man couldn't even name the pirate queen, much less remember high-seas adventures.

Crow sewed together two belts taken from gibberer corpses to make something suitable for Dranae. It circled his waist, then a leather loop went across his body from left hip to right shoulder. During the days Dranae went bare-chested, but pulled a blanket around him like a cloak as the day's heat wore off.

By salvaging more leather from the gibberers' equipment, Crow put together some makeshift sandals. Everyone agreed they'd not last long, but it was hoped that in Sanges they could find more suitable footwear for Dranae, as well as passage north to Fortress Draconis.

They made pretty good time, heading north from Alcida and into the rainforests of Saporicia. By keeping to lesser-used tracks they traveled slower than they might have otherwise, but avoided detection. Will would have been inclined to protest, if for no other reason than still being angry about how he had been pulled into the adventure, but Dranae nodded sagely when Resolute informed him of their plans. Moreover, Dranae took their security concerns seriously, earning expansive nods from Resolute and an occasional word of thanks.

The rainforests of Saporicia differed from the woodlands of Alcida in that they seemed older and far thicker. More undergrowth bordered the trails. The trees rose higher, and in the dim distances—which were not all that far, but tough to see because of the thick growth of trees—mossy giants had snapped at the base and crashed down. Stony outcroppings jutted from hillsides carpeted in rusty pine needles, dripping water down into rivulets that formed streams or sank into bogs that they bypassed or slogged through.

Will wrinkled his nose at the fetid scent of a swamp. "Why do these woods seem different than the others we went through?"

Resolute glanced back from his position in the lead. "More rain here, and less men."

"More rain, more wet. That I understand." He turned to look at Crow and Dranae. "How come there are fewer men?"

The Vorquelf answered before either of the other two could offer Will anything. "Saporicia was, for a long time, a buffer between the Estine Empire and Loquellyn. Over time, as men encroached, elves pulled the borders of Loquellyn back. Most humans settled on the coast, and around the great harbor that splits the country. During that time, though, Panqui had moved into this section of the country. They tend to keep humans out, as the dragons intend."

Will frowned. "What are you talking about?"

Resolute shook his head. "How can you be as old as you are and know nothing of the natural order of the world? First the urZrethi come into elven homelands and build mountains to chase the elves away. Then dragons come and drive the urZrethi from the mountains and make their homes in them. Dragons permit Panqui to live in those mountains or the nearby areas to discourage men from coming in. Why? Because men quarry the mountains and steal the stones to make their cities."

"Oh, and then elves come and extend their homelands to drive men away, to start the cycle again?"

"No, boy, elves do not. This is why, someday, there will be no elves left in this world."

The cold finality in Resolute's voice sent a shock through Will. He had stated, so matter-of-factly, something that meant his people would someday be driven from the world and yet, here he was, fighting to see that the cycle he described would not be broken by an invasion from the north. Will saw the logic of fighting Chytrine, since her victory would mean the destruction of the elves anyway. Still, knowing the elves would eventually have to move on meant

Will's enthusiasm for fighting would have been greatly dampened had he been Resolute.

Dranae spoke in a low voice. "Friend Resolute, that's an interesting view of the world. I have heard it suggested that elves are constantly searching for a place that is meant to be their home. If one place is not it, they move on."

Resolute reined his horse up short and turned to face them. The expression he wore seemed stuck between puzzlement and discontent. "The elves who were bound to Vorquellyn before its desecration did go *beyond*. That is your word for what they did. It does not contain the whole of it. Some say there are many worlds, like pearls on a string, and elves pass from one to another, by going beyond, or by dying and being reborn. I do not know, since this is a mystery denied me by fate."

The young thief studied Resolute's face, and tried to memorize the tone of his voice. He'd not heard its like in all his time with Resolute, save, perhaps, back at the caves. Resolute had only shown him the finely honed edge of his personality. Dranae seemed to reach him differently, and it took Will a moment to recognize the difference. *I challenge, he seeks knowledge.*

Dranae shrugged his massive shoulders. "Your telling of the natural order I have heard before. I think, though, the Panqui find dragonhaunts a good place to live because not too many men willingly come to them. This thick forest suits them."

"Have you seen one?" Will looked around, seeking to spot anything at all in the shadows. "I think I saw one as a child, in a cage, in the Dim."

Crow shook his head. "That was a man in a costume. Panqui are big, very big—at least the males are. Huge."

"You've killed one?"

Resolute laughed. "I've never gotten close enough to kill one, nor has Crow in my time with him."

"This is not something I regret, either." Crow smiled easily. "That's because they've got fangs as long as your fingers, and their hands have these nasty hooked claws they can retract. Worst of all, they have these bony plates in their skin, running from turtle-green to gold, depending on what, I don't know. Those plates will stop an arrow and probably an ax. On their faces, throat, joints, they have this black, leathery flesh. Their thick tail is very strong. They're not stupid beasts, either, and sail the Crescent Sea as pirates."

Will hunched his shoulders and kept looking around. "And we are not on the main road, why?"

The others laughed aloud. Resolute shook his head. "Boy, didn't you listen? They're not stupid. If we are being watched, they can see there is no advantage in attacking us. Besides, during the summer, they move to the coast. It's only in winter they move inland. We're probably safe."

"Really?" Will looked to the others for confirmation. Crow nodded. Dranae did as well, then smiled before snorting a quick laugh.

Will's eyes tightened. "You're all having a joke on me."

The dark-haired man shook his head in denial. "In your reaction I guess we're all remembering being your age, or younger, shivering to tales of Panqui and gibberers. The smiles and the laughs, they're not for you, but us at your age."

"I believe that of you two, but not Resolute." Will shot him a sidelong glance. "He was never my age."

"Wrong, boy. At your age I was never so innocent." Resolute gave Will the hint of a smile. "Let's hope your growing out of it doesn't hurt you as much as it did me."

Three days into their trek they could no longer move on game trails since everything converged at one point or another with the main road into Sanges. The quickest way to get to Fortress Draconis, it had been decided, would be to get a ship to sail north. If none could be had in Sanges, they knew they could sail up to Narriz and find a suitable

vessel there. Narriz, the capital of Saporicia, even offered
the option of an elven embassy that Resolute thought
might allow him to travel to Loquellyn and get a ship there.

Sanges spread out along the steep hillsides of a river valley. The river flowed down to the sea, ending in a waterfall
that split the harbor in the middle. Piers jutted like the
staves of a broken barrel into the harbor, and each one had
several ships moored to it. More ships lay at anchor in the
harbor. Even though Yslin had been a much bigger city,
Will couldn't remember having seen so many ships in the
harbor at one time.

The main road into the city cut back and forth across
the hillside south of the river, though numerous bridges
did cross it. Tiled roofs and thick walls kept the summer
heat at bay. Each building had been painted primarily the
color of old bones, but bright and gay images of animals
and flowers had been woven into paintings to decorate
windows and doorways. As they descended toward the
harbor, the buildings became older and more dingy,
though nothing reached the dark, mildewed state of the
Dimandowns.

They found an inn and were able to obtain rooms easily,
including stable space for their horses. Once they'd secured
their belongings in the room, they headed down to the
docks. Will didn't find the seaport section of Sanges all that
different from Yslin, save that the city was smaller and there
were no balloons floating high overhead to let merchants
see their ships coming in, nor were there cable-baskets
moving people above the streets. The lack of these signs of
sophistication let Will feel superior to the rustic inhabitants, putting some spring in his step.

Resolute and Crow seemed to know their way around
the town. They sought the office of a trading company and
asked directions. Cutting back through an alley, heading
away from the sea, they entered a courtyard. A building
across the way apparently was their destination, because
Crow pointed at the wooden sign creaking in the breeze

over the door. That there was a crowd of men between them and the door didn't seem to bother him at all.

Four men in red-and-gold uniforms, three of them bearing pikes, came around the crowd and converged on the travelers. The unarmed man, a plump specimen with little enough hair that it could have been easily finger-raked by a half-handed man, unscrolled a piece of parchment as the pikemen moved to hem them in. His voice came a little high, but he shouted loudly to reinforce his authority.

"By order of King Fidelius, all sailors will report to their ships forthwith. Those who are without berth will report to the Grand Pier for assignment to ships. All men of good health and five and ten years, but not more than three score, will take up arms in service of Saporicia. The defense of your nation demands this sacrifice."

He lowered the parchment. "Get in with the others."

Resolute slowly shook his head. "Your order does not apply to me. I am not a sailor, I am not of your nation, I am not a man, and I am older than three-score years. Begone."

The bureaucrat's brow furrowed above dark eyes. "You look young to me, elf, but no matter. Your companions here, they fit the bill, they're going."

The Vorquelf dropped a hand to the hilt of his sword. "They are with me, and likewise exempt."

The man glanced again at the parchment. "Doesn't say that here. I don't want trouble, but . . ."

"If you don't want trouble, go away."

The little man nodded to the pikemen, but none of them seemed eager to engage Resolute. The crowd of sailors the four men had been gathering up began to spread out and grumble. A couple of men picked up stones, and Will followed their example. Tension filled the air with curses, and the bureaucrat began to sweat.

Before violence could erupt, a slender man moved through the sailors. He looked unremarkable to Will, save that he wore a blue mask that covered him from cheekbones to hairline. The mask marked him as being from one of three nations where wearing a mask was an honor. It had all sorts of marks on it and the sailors fell silent as he strode in the bureaucrat's direction. "A minute, Warden, these are my men."

The bureaucrat turned and posted his fists on his hips. "Captain Dunhill, your ship already has a full complement of sailors. You told me as much."

"Indeed I did, Cirris, but I counted among them these men here, for I anticipated their arrival." Dunhill stepped forward and offered his hand to Crow. "Good to see you again, Captain Crow. And, Resolute, you've not changed. And these two, these are the ones you told me about, who want a life at sea?"

Crow nodded quickly. "Yes, Will is my nephew, and Dranae is a distant cousin. We apologize for being late, but travel's not been safe of late."

Warden Cirris, having rolled his parchment into a tight tube, tapped it against Dunhill's shoulder. "You should have given me their names. This is highly irregular, Captain."

Dunhill's nostrils flared. "*More* irregular than having every man in the city press-ganged, Warden?" The man tapped a small symbol painted on his mask below his right eye. "When you have earned this mark, Warden, it means you are given responsibility for your crew. *All* responsibility for it. What I choose to tell you or not to tell you is up to me. These people have reported to me, which is the same as reporting to their ship. You are done here, go away."

The ship's captain turned and waved them on after him. "Come into the office where we can speak."

Will followed in line, letting the stone tumble from his fingers so that it smacked the warden's toes. The fat man yelped, then began hopping on one foot. Hastily thrown stones by the crowd of sailors kept him dancing. Even the pikemen laughed and the tension in the courtyard evaporated.

Dunhill led them into the office of a trading company,

past tables where scribes were looking at sheets, comparing them to other sheets and scribbling things down on yet third sheets. The skritching of quill on paper set Will's skin to crawling, but that sound faded as he followed Dunhill up a back set of stairs to a larger room that clearly served as a dormitory for sailors waiting for their ships to head out. The captain waved them to a rectangular table set with benches down each side.

"You *are* Crow, aren't you? I mean, Resolute I couldn't forget, but you've changed a bit."

Crow nodded and sat. "It's been ten years. I'm surprised you remember me at all."

"How could I forget? You came to me at Yslin with a pass signed by Rounce Playfair himself, telling me to do all I could to render you aid. And then the two of you wanted me to sail north and put you ashore in the Ghost March." Dunhill shook his head. "I wondered if you'd made it back, and assumed you had. Somehow I didn't think they would get you."

"They didn't. We were fortunate." Crow looked around. "Billets here are empty, and the harbor is full. What's going on?"

"Nothing you need worry about. I can have the people below fix you up with passes that will let you go wherever you need to go. The *Seafarer* is sailing at midnight, so give me your word that you'll report in time for duty, or I'll be forced to sail without you."

Resolute rested both elbows on the table. "That's good of you, but that's not what he asked."

Dunhill smiled. "I know. It's insane, really, but reports have come in that Chytrine reached an accord with Vionna. Together they have organized the Wruona pirates into a cohesive force. Chytrine's reinforced them with her own ships. They're heading south."

Crow nodded. "Hence the king's order to ship everyone up to Narriz to defend the capital."

The captain laughed lightly. "Now *that* would make

sense, but that's not where we're going. No. We're sailing west, to Vilwan."

Resolute blinked. "Vilwan?"

"That's right." Dunhill shrugged. "For reasons known only to her, Chytrine thinks she can destroy the stronghold of the greatest mages of our age. We're going to stop her."

CHAPTER 20

At a narrow window in a high tower on Vilwan, Kerrigan Reese shielded his eyes against the rising sun. Only a quarter of its disk had risen above the horizon, but that was enough to display dozens of little black shapes bobbing on the sea, sailing toward Vilwan. The sight of such a large flotilla was unprecedented in his seventeen years of life, and he was quite certain the like of it had never been seen before that, either.

He turned from the slit window and held a finger out, visually tracking it along the spines of the books shelved floor to ceiling in his living chamber. He spied a fat volume, whispered a word, and crooked his index finger. The book slid off the shelf and floated smoothly and fluidly through the air. It came to his hand easily, but the second it touched his palm, the spell broke, and Kerrigan had to scramble to get his other hand under the book.

Even when he did that, the volume's weight threw him off balance. He stooped to catch the book, stepping forward quickly. He caught the hem of his white sleeping gown under his foot, shifted, and went down hard on his left knee. He gasped with shock and pain as the robe abraded his flesh. Hugging the book to his chest, he sagged helplessly to his left side, but kept the book from hitting the ground.

Angrily he kicked his foot free of the gown, and heard a tearing sound in the process. Rolling onto his back and lifting his feet—a task the rotund mage managed not terribly well and could not sustain for long—he saw the hem had torn out. Worse yet, a red splotch stained the gown at his left knee. The moment he saw blood, he could feel the pain in his knee intensify, and his lower lip started trembling.

He shook himself, which sent quivers running through his thick body. Kerrigan refused to cry, telling himself it was nothing, just a scrape. The fact was, though, that it *hurt*! He wanted to pull his knee closer to his face to look at it, but he couldn't with the book on his belly.

Kerrigan set the book on the floor reverently, blowing away invisible dust motes before he put it down. He pulled his knee up as far as he could and gingerly slipped the gown up over it. Breath hissed through teeth on intake, then he grabbed his thigh and pulled harder to get his knee closer to his face. His round belly hindered this attempt, but he still got a good look at the scrape across his knee, which bled a little, and mostly oozed a clear fluid.

He waved fat fingers at it, hoping the fluid would congeal in the air. Struggling up into a sitting position, he kept his knee bent and exposed. He glanced at the bloody stain on the gown, then at the torn hem, and shrugged. Kerrigan was pretty sure the gown could neither be cleaned nor repaired and, as such, would never be allowed back into his wardrobe.

That thought calmed him, so he pulled the fat book into his lap and flipped through the pages. A bold and onate scrawl—which differed here and there as other hands had inscribed things down through the centuries— covered half the pages of the book. Illustrations and diagrams also appeared, but they were few and crudely incomplete when compared with similar designs in the grimoires lining the shelves.

Kerrigan reached the point where the blank pages began, and leafed back several before he began reading. The book he held was a history of Vilwan, and was linked to the grand history housed in Vilwan's library. As with *arcanslata*, a bond had been magickally forged between this book and that one. As pages were added by the Magister Historian of Vilwan, they appeared in Kerrigan's copy of the book.

The young mage had always found comfort in the history, and studying it was one of the few tasks all of his mentors had praised. Kerrigan suspected this was because his reading gave them time free from dealing with him; and he was fairly certain they did not realize he relished the same from them. In the history he sought for clues—of what he was not quite certain, just clues in general to make things make sense.

He found a passage that addressed the flotilla off the coast and concentrated on it. The sting in his knee made that difficult, but he managed it despite the distraction. He'd used that spell many times before and, being well practiced at it, could make it work easily.

A blue glow spread from his hands to envelop the book. A little bit of it trailed off, tracing the ethereal link between his volume and the grand history. The glow sank into the golden pages, then emerged again to edge some pages earlier in the book. Starting from the front and the oldest cite, Kerrigan opened the book and read quickly. He wore a blank expression on his face as he began, but a smile slowly stole over his lips as he checked cite after cite.

He got to the most recent with a triumphant smile on

his face. A quarter century previous, when the fleet sent to save Okrannel sailed past, it had contained four dozen ships, less than half those coming to Vilwan today. He'd remembered correctly, and this pleased him. His smile bit deeply into his fleshy cheeks and gleamed from his green eyes.

And his stomach growled, reminding him he had yet to break his fast. Tucking a lock of fine black hair behind his left ear, he closed the book and tried to roll up onto his right knee. The sleeping gown rasped over his abraded knee, rekindling the sting. He hissed and almost dropped the book again. He got his fat-fingered hands around it and hugged it to him as he might a dear friend, and huddled there waiting for the echoes of pain to die.

The chamber door's well-oiled hinges did not betray its opening, but the rustle of sandal on stone did. Kerrigan looked up, surprised. He grabbed his knee with his left hand, hoping to conceal his wound. He scraped cloth against it, magnifying the sting. He cried out, then clenched his jaw, trying to keep tears back.

He bowed his head and breathed through his nose until he'd gotten himself back under control. "Good morning, Magister Orla."

The woman's robe matched the grey of her hair, and the long plait her locks had been braided into could have doubled for the cord looped about her waist. She stood in the doorway, her head up, her brown eyes bright, watching him carefully. She always watched, as his other mentors had, but looked for more than they had. Her seamed face and leathery skin suggested a hard life, but as nearly as he knew, she'd not left Vilwan more than a time or two in the last thirty years.

Strength filled her voice, and her voice filled the chamber, but she neither barked nor cooed at him. "You have injured yourself."

"Yes, it hurts."

"I imagine it does." She closed her eyes for a moment

and gestured, wrenching the history out of his grasp. It floated to her outstretched hands and she caught it easily. He hoped for a moment that she would stumble as he had, but the book's weight barely caused her to move at all.

Orla walked to the shelves and slid the book home, then turned to look at him. "I suggest something should be done about your knee."

"Yes, call a healer." Kerrigan thrust his lower lip out defiantly. "I want a healer."

"Heal yourself."

Kerrigan looked down at his knee and gently lifted the cloth away. "That is an elven spell, Magister."

"A spell you've mastered. Use it."

He brought his head up. "I am not to use it without proper supervision."

She smiled slowly, the lines at the corners of her eyes deepening. "Why persist in this game, Adept Reese? You know and I know that I will not summon an elf to be present while you heal your knee. You also know that I am not embarrassed that you have mastered a spell I could not learn were I to study another lifetime. Finally, you and I know you do not want to heal yourself because that process will hurt—hurt more than the wound does now."

"It's not a game. There are *rules*, Magister; there have always been *rules*. The rules guide me. I do everything in accord with them. The rules state that when I use elven magick, or urZrethi spells or anything sufficiently Magisterial, I shall be supervised." He spoke carefully and precisely, even a bit slowly. "If I violate the rules, I will be punished."

She closed her eyes and sighed. "Kerrigan, you know I will not sanction you for doing what I tell you to do. I am not like some of your past teachers. You know I have more latitude than others. Why won't you do what I ask you to do without this charade?"

The young Adept narrowed his eyes. "I want to see the ships. I want to go to the docks and see the ships."

"Oh, is *that* it, then?" Her dark eyes opened, and she cocked her head slightly. That motion with her head made Kerrigan cringe. "Very well, I think we can permit that, provided you follow my orders exactly."

Kerrigan nodded hesitantly. "Yes, Magister."

"Very good. First, heal your knee."

He started to get up, and held a hand out to her to have her help him get to his feet, but she shook her head. "No, do it there, on the floor."

"But the way I do the spell . . . I have to change . . ."

"And soil another robe? I think not." Her eyes hardened. "You agreed to this bargain, Adept Reese, do not make me regret it. There, where you are, you can do it."

He shook his head and kept his voice low. "It's not right."

"Do you mean to tell me you *cannot* do it kneeling there? After I have seen countless elves perform that spell on ships, on battlefields, at the site of horse-cart accidents and tramplings? Perhaps, since it is an elven spell, they are just that much better than you. Is that it?"

"No." His nostrils flared defiantly. "I can do it."

"I'm waiting. Do not make me wait long."

Kerrigan sucked in a lungful of air through his nose, and slowly exhaled it. He kept his breathing shallow after that and all but closed his eyes to minimize distractions. He flexed his fingers, then laid his left hand over the wound gently. The sweat on his palm seared into it, but he pushed that pain away.

He cleared his mind as much as he could and began the weaving of the elven healing spell. Kerrigan liked elven magick because the spells themselves seemed to be living things. Whereas a human spell would have angles and intersections, sharp breaks and sharper edges, elven spells flowed as if they had rootlets growing into the earth, or branches reaching out to embrace the sun. Human spells seemed *constructed* by comparison, and were easy to master, whereas an elven spell became a knotwork maze his mind had to travel to achieve his reward.

His left hand glowed with blue energy. Darker in hue than the indexing spell he had woven, this blue had the depth of the sea behind it, whereas the other had the fragility of a bird's egg. The energy flowed into his knee, teasing tissue to grow faster and heal, absorbing the blood and fluid, sealing the wound. As it did so the pain built. Kerrigan knew it was the sum and total of the aches and pains, itches and twinges, he would have felt while it healed. Condensed it seemed to drill straight through his knee like an arrow, then it vanished, a mind-ghost he would never summon again.

He looked up and peeled his hand away from the knee. The flesh had been reunited, with no hint of a scar. Blood still stained his palm, so he wiped it on his gown. Pushing off the stone floor with his right hand, he straightened up and felt his gown tighten around his ample middle.

He looked down at her. "Done, Magister, as you requested."

"Very good, Adept Reese." She looked him up and down, her brows creeping toward each other as she did. "Next you will remove your robe, hem it, and wash it."

"What?"

"You heard what I said, Kerrigan." Orla gestured toward the door. "I know you have servants who do that for you, under normal circumstances, but things are far from normal here. All the island's inhabitants are being pressed to other duty. Today you will clean your own robe and fetch your own breakfast."

He smiled. "From the kitchen?"

She nodded. "You can find your way there?"

"Oh, yes." Kerrigan fought to conceal a smile. While no one gainsaid him anything he wanted to eat—and servants often scurried between his chamber and the kitchen to bring more bread or soup or meat or fruit—the few times he had found his way to the kitchen, he had been enchanted by what he saw. All of his magicks were worked in the *arcanorium* above his living quarters. In the kitchen Magisters and Adepts, even Apprentices, worked magicks that kneaded dough for bread, or warmed an oven, ground spices, stirred pots. Many of those spells he knew very well, since he mixed ingredients the same way, and worked on potions and preparations with care, but in the kitchen he saw a direct link between what he studied as theory and they practiced in reality.

And the fruit of their practice filled his tummy warmly and well.

"Good, though you may be disappointed. Because of the fleet, and the need to feed the men aboard it, food is being rationed." She tapped a finger against her pointed chin. "You'll get a pint of watered ale and a small round of bread."

"I'll starve."

"Not for a long time, Adept Reese."

He frowned. The treats he could already taste turned to dust in his mouth. "Repair and wash, then eat, and *then* I may see the ships?"

"Yes."

He eyed her suspiciously. "That will give me no time, though, to see the ships because by the time I am done eating, it will be almost time to begin lessons."

Orla smiled slowly. "Ah, but you see, Adept Reese, this is what I came to tell you. Everyone is being pressed into duty—even me. I am meeting with the Magister of Combats this morning, to learn my duties. You are free until noon."

"That is what you came to tell me?" Kerrigan frowned. "You would have let me go no matter what?"

"Yes?"

"Then why . . . ?"

"Because, Adept Reese, you chose to play a game, and you lost." Orla strode simply to the door and paused halfway through it, looking back at him over her shoulder. "If you play games, you *will* lose. Consider yourself fortunate that, this time, losing did not cost you dearly. Learn from that. Given all you can do, if you lose in the future, you and those around you will likely never survive the loss."

CHAPTER 21

Fatigue burned Alyx's eyes more than the light of the dawning sun. The sleep she'd had in the previous three days could have been counted in minutes and still not threatened to fill an hour, and that had been after the long ride to ambush the Aurolani forces. With General Caro's help, she'd managed to convince the local merchant-princes that their city was doomed. Caro had carefully pointed out that if the evacuation was not carried out in an orderly manner—by which he meant that his orders would be followed to the letter—then looting would likely be the result. It would cost the merchants more than having to move on, so they reluctantly agreed to it.

Caro did not leave things to the merchants alone. The city was broken down into its neighborhoods, and the local power brokers, be they merchants, thieves, clergy, or scholars, were brought to the government tower and told how things would work. The general noted that looters would be slain immediately. At his signal a man dressed in the uniform of his own Horse Guards was brought struggling to the front of the audience hall. The canvas hood obscuring his identity also muffed his words.

Caro drew a dagger from his own belt, bent, and said to the prisoner, "Come now, do some good, die like a man." He thrust the dagger into the man's chest, allowing the bloody tip to pierce the back of his tunic, only withdrawing it when the man slacked in the arms of his fellows.

Caro had not seen it necessary to let folks know the man he'd just slain was a murderer pulled from the town's jail and dressed in a cavalry uniform.

The general looked at the assembled leaders and let blood drip from the dagger as his men dragged the body off. "As I said, *all* looters will be killed. Man, woman, child. Everyone will find enough to do carting off their own possessions, or working for those who have things they need hauled."

Tent cities were set up on the western side of the Salersena River, and merchants emptied their warehouses into them. There some carried on brisk business selling the things others would need to flee. Prices remained moderate, though, once Caro commented that usury and price-gouging were tantamount to looting.

Alyx sighed. The whole evacuation would have broken down save for the arrival of a party of riders from Yslin. They'd covered the ten leagues from the capital very quickly, and had arrived doubtlessly expecting to celebrate the great victory she'd won. Messengers sent by the advanced party sought her out in Porasena, and along with General Caro, she'd ridden back to her camp in mid-afternoon on the second day.

She and Caro had begun the liberation of Porasena at odds with each other, but the evacuation had united them. Caro had appreciated her turning power for the operation over to him. He used her stature as the architect of victory to suggest to those who did not like his orders that appeal was possible, but she sided with him at every turn. As resentment built in the city, it strengthened her alliance with

Caro. And neither of them liked being called away from the city.

The messenger brought the two of them back to her command tent, and Alyx was ready to tear into whoever had appropriated it. Caro gave her a nod as they entered, letting her know he'd be with her, but two steps in, Caro's broad form stopped, then shrank as he dropped to a knee before the man standing in the heart of the tent. Alyx caught sight of him for a second, before the tent flap closed behind her, cutting off the sunlight, but it was enough to drive her to kneel as well.

She bowed her head. "Highness, we had no warning."

"I allowed you the same warning you gave Chytrine's troops. Rise, the two of you. You serve me well."

As her head came back up she saw a smile on the man's face. Though she stood tall enough to easily see some of the white scars on his bald head, Alyx had always felt tiny in comparison with Alcida's King Augustus. In part, she knew, this came from having first met him when she was just a child. Then he'd had dark hair, and lots of it. Over the years it had thinned and gone as white as the luxurious moustaches he wore, so the king had taken to shaving his head. Regardless of what time had done to his body, adding wrinkles as it leeched hair away, it had not dimmed the vitality and power shining from his brown eyes. They revealed a man still vital in spirit and mind, which Alyx had always held in awe.

Caro stood and shook hands with the king. "Highness, this is an unexpected pleasure."

"You lie as glibly as always, Caro. The last thing you want is me here, especially if the rumors I've heard are true." Augustus turned to Alyx. "And you, Alexia, you know I am not here to usurp your victory, yes?"

She nodded and shook his hand, relishing the firm, dry leathery grip. "Our victory was for you, Highness, so usurpation is not a question."

The king smiled. "I am also not here to proclaim you to be a rival to Adrogans, but delivering your troops here and winning this victory does put him to shame. This pleases me. He might well be competent, and has even harassed Chytrine's troops in Okrannel, but I do not like having to rely on him alone. He is being pushed hard, as if he were the Norrington that would defeat Chytrine. I am uneasy with the forces gathering to support him."

"Understandably, Highness." Alyx sighed. "Despite my reservations about him, however, I would appreciate his insights on the current situation."

"This evacuation, yes. It's a bit of a thorny problem, isn't it?"

Caro nodded. "They understand the concept of clearing things out of the city, but they are without direction after that. You must have run into some people making for the capital as you rode in."

"We did. It got me thinking. Let me tell you an idea I have had." He waved them over to the map table. "It's not as clean a solution as your assault, but will work, I think."

What the king outlined was both bold and inspiring. Two leagues upriver, just shy of the other natural ford, the river's restless wandering had carved a nice valley through some low hills. The king handed out landgrants to the merchants that ceded to them vast tracts of land, provided they would remain in residence and meet other goals. The fact that half the land he gave them was in Oriosa went unnoticed in the first flush of the plan's revelation.

Smaller grants went to people of the city, giving them something they'd never had before. The king did not allow these smaller grants to be sold before ten years, but since the chance at owning land was something most of the people of Porasena could only have aspired to, incredible enthusiasm greeted the king's generosity.

Given the threat to anyone in the vicinity of Porasena, the king's retreat to Yslin would have seemed a wise course, but Augustus would have none of it. He noted correctly that if he fled to the capital, most of the refugees would follow. The king himself made several trips into the city, helping folks move their belongings out. He promised to visit them at the new city and even detailed a supply convoy that had arrived to lead the way to Newpora and oversee the settlement.

From her vantage point Alyx could already see the brown stain of a muddy track roughly paralleling the river. People heavily laden with burdens struggled along it. Little family groups moved south, jostling with enterprising people helping an overloaded mule negotiate some of the tougher spots. Alcidese warriors helped and directed.

Augustus came up beside her, letting the hood on his black, woolen cloak slip down to his shoulders. "The evacuation goes well, Alyx, and yes, I know you will tell me all praise belongs to Caro in this regard. I have thanked him appropriately."

She nodded, then pointed toward the city. "Most of the family groups are out. Now we just have the fools and daredevils. They're making runs back into the city to get things that were forgotten. Could be excuses and thinly disguised looting, but Caro has not executed anyone."

"Looting would have been an impediment to the evacuation, but now . . ." The king shrugged. "I doubt there is much of significant value left in the town."

"You are doubtlessly correct, Highness."

Augustus smiled, the corners of his mouth disappearing beneath the thick curves of his moustaches. "You heard the *sullanciri* pronounce the doom of Porasena. As I understand it, there was no hint of what or when."

Alyx shook her head. "I have been surprised we were

able to evacuate the town. I have assumed that by sundown today our job here will be done. We can slip away and leave it. The big question is whether or not we fire it."

"Yes, we should." The king looked at the town and its towers clustered at the heart. "If we leave them a place they can occupy, more will enter from Oriosa. I would just as soon deny them a stronghold here."

"Highness, I do not question your wisdom, but why do you tolerate Oriosa's harboring of the Aurolani forces?"

The king ran a hand over his jaw as he looked across the valley. "To get Oriosa to stop would require its invasion. Oriosan troops are fierce fighters, and in defending their homeland, they would be more so. As for bringing political pressure to bear, well, you know the story of how Scrainwood obtained the throne, don't you?"

"Yes, Highness. A *sullanciri* slew his mother."

"Killed her in a most horrible way. That year Oriosa was supposed to host the Harvest Festival, but it was postponed for a year because of Queen Lanivette's death. Scrainwood had once been a friend of mine, and the man I saw when my father sent me to represent Alcida at the funeral had been broken in spirit. He still had Scrainwood's feral cunning and political acumen, but what little courage had been there was gone."

The king shivered. "He does not stop them from passing through Oriosa, but he fears them so much that he keeps an eye on them. He has spies everywhere and shares his information with me, to forestall an invasion. In fact, news of your victory here prompted him to divulge some things which are useful. Chytrine is being very bold."

"So my next assignment will be?"

Augustus laughed aloud. The deep rich sound lost itself in the expanse of the valley. "You will be returning to Yslin with me. The Harvest Festival approaches, and as on the eve of Chytrine's last invasion, Alcida is hosting it. I want you there. Chytrine inspires fear in many, but you are an antidote to that fear. She may be formidable, but she is not invincible, and the peoples of our world need to be reminded of that."

"I will do as you bid me, Highness, but my place is in the field, fighting."

"I know it is, Alexia." The king's lips pressed together in a thin line for a moment, then he gave her a weak smile. "I could hear your father saying those words. He would be very proud of you, though even he would tell you that Chytrine's current move is not of your concern. *Arcanslata* reports indicate she is bringing a fleet against Vilwan."

Alyx's head came up. The value of wizards in warfare had long and hotly been debated. While it was true that even the most simple of spells could have military applications, the fact that counterspells could negate them limited their usefulness. In general, wizards were maintained behind the lines, so they could work on repairing equipment or soldiers or *meckanshii*, who were a whole lot of both.

Regardless, an assualt on the sorcerer stronghold is pure folly. She frowned. "The only way that makes sense is if she has created some grand spell, or some mechanism, that can wipe them out."

"True, though her motivation might be even more basic. The Wruona pirates are with her on this expedition, but they've harried her ships before. It could be that she wants to wipe them out, so she's pitting one enemy against another. There are plenty of leaders who should learn that to deal with her can be very dangerous."

"I wonder, then, Highness, what the troops she sent to Porasena did to offend her."

A brilliant light sparked on the plains northeast of the town. It flared argent, blindingly bright as a lightning strike, then resolved itself into the figure of the *sullanciri* she'd seen three days earlier. The Aurolani creature looked at the town, then sniffed at the air. It turned to face the hilltop where she stood with the king.

"Blood I smell, and all too well; but rare blood tickles my nose. The odor, I am quite sure, comes from our greatest of foes. All hail King Augustus, who is most chivalrous, and soon quite dolorous."

Augustus closed his eyes and hung his head, slowly shaking it. "You still try too hard, Leigh."

Though the king's words came in little more than a whisper, the *sullanciri*, despite being a half mile away, reacted as if they had scourged him. He hissed and hunched, pulling the flaming cloak around him as if it were armor. He slowly straightened up, craven no more, then pointed east.

"Behold, as foretold, Porasena no more gets old."

Alyx looked up toward the Oriosan border, then took an involuntary step back. Without conscious thought she drew her sword and interposed her body between what she saw and the king. "Move now, Highness, get away."

"No, Alexia, I've seen its like before. Running won't matter."

The dawn's sun silhouetted the creature, rendering it as black as the massive cruciform shadow that rippled down over hillside and through the fields. Once the dragon swooped below the line of hills, the ivory scales flecked with gold made it seem the work of a skilled artisan. The fluidity and grace with which it moved seemed impossible for so massive a creature, yet it seemed positively feline in its suppleness.

It dipped its left wing and soared in a tight circle around Porasena. The large blue-green eyes had whorls of color swirling through them, swiftly, as if they matched the thoughts of the brain inside the horned skull. The dragon appeared to be watching the people in the city scurry and run. It snapped idly at one person frozen on a tower balcony. Though the dragon missed the bite—the person would have been a mere morsel, lost in that maw—the person leaped back and tumbled to her death.

With a powerful beat of the wings, the dragon shot

skyward, wingtips and barbed tail tridentine, rising above the town. Several hundred yards up, the dragon tucked itself into a ball and somersaulted backward. It began to fall toward the ground, then the wings snapped out. The fall became a swift, looping dive, aiming straight at the town.

Flying barely above the top of the highest tower, the dragon vomited fire. The flash of heat hit Alyx with the force of a playful cuff, and that was but a faint ripple of the power lashing the city. The gout of red-gold fire blasted into Porasena's heart, evaporating the bridge she'd used to cross the river, then flooded through the streets. Discarded wooden furnishings and other rubbish combusted in an eyeblink. The fire knocked fleeing people forward, tumbling them as if they'd been caught in a flood, rendering them in black and then swallowing them.

The fire's roar effortlessly devoured their screams.

The fire splashed against towers, again seeming more fluid than vapor. It broke around them, not burning as much as eroding them, the way waves gnaw at sand castles. Towers, with tapestries and abandoned furnishings burning brightly within them, began to sag like overheated candles. Alyx could see where two touched and actually began to fuse, forming an arch over the inferno that was the town's heart.

The dragon circled again, letting little nasal snorts of flame roast men on the walls, or ignite the shacks of the beggars' quarter. The river carried burning debris northward. In a second circuit, and a third, the dragon sowed fire throughout the town. While no assault came as furiously as the first, Porasena blazed merrily, sending a dark grey column of smoke into the air.

The dragon circled one last time, then beat its wings and flew off to the east. Once it had again disappeared beyond the Oriosan border, the *sullanciri* walked into the town. He strode down burning lanes, his fire not quite as bright as that of the inferno. It made him easy to watch until he got into the very heart of the city.

Alyx studied the blaze intently, waiting for him to reappear, but he did not. Instead, in an instant, the fire fluttered and struggled throughout the city, as if being battered by a harsh, cold wind. The flames shrank from the edges, then fled inward. They vanished all at once, almost completely, tightening down into a burning cyclone that resolved itself into the *sullanciri* and his burning cloak.

The tiny figure sketched a bow, then threw the king a salute, again he spun, his cloak flaring to brilliance, then the fire died with an audible crack that left darkness in its wake.

Alyx blinked and looked at the town again, shaking her head. Smoke billowed from bent and twisted towers. Here and there the heat reignited fires, but they burned with pale ferocity in comparison with the dragonfire. Where the bridge had once been, now lay a basin slowly filling with steaming river water. She could almost feel the river's *weirun* writhing in scalded agony as parts of it rose in clouds of mist.

Alyx shivered though she felt not in the least bit cold. "I understand that display of power, but if the *sullanciri* knew you were here, why didn't the dragon kill you? Your loss would be a mighty blow to the forces that would oppose Chytrine."

The king slowly nodded. "Yes, but more damaging will be my reporting of what I have seen. A quarter century ago she had a dragon working for her. She enslaved it through a portion of the DragonCrown. We slew it. Men took heart in that—too much, perhaps. Now she has another."

"Won't she just send it to Yslin to slay the world's leaders when they come to the Council of Kings?"

"You would, I would, but not Chytrine." The king pulled his hood up to shadow his face. "She warned us she would return. These are more warnings. Before she defeats a foe, she wants him broken. Mark me, Alexia, the destruction of Porasena will break the will of some who oppose her. In that light, what she lost here to your victory was nothing. If we cannot unite to vanquish her, we will leave the world open to her domination."

CHAPTER 22

The repair to the hem of his sleeping gown had been faster than the recovery of his self-esteem, but Kerrigan had managed both. As he had been ordered, he sewed the hem up, sticking his fingers only a couple of times with the needle. He decided he would find a seamstress and learn some of her magicks, too, so he would prick his fingers no more. Then he washed the robe, and watching those Apprentices being punished by doing laundry, he learned to wring the garment out and hang it up on lines to dry.

None of his other tutors would have had him do that, and Kerrigan knew that Orla's reason—that there was a shortage of servants because of the fleet's arrival—was merely a blind. Every other tutor he'd had would make him work at magicks as punishment, doing mindless repetitions of spells he'd learned years ago.

He knew his tutors were manipulating him. They would show him new spells, teach him new techniques, then punish him by making him practice foundational elements.

And because this bored him, he turned more willingly and attentively to the new material they were teaching him.

Or so they thought.

Kerrigan had seen, very early on, that he had two types of tutors. The first type just cared about achievement; they had been given a goal. He never knew what it was until after he'd hit it, because that tutor would be gone and a new one would have appeared. These types of tutors were easy to manipulate. He could show some promise, suffer a series of setbacks, then rise up and do well before plateauing again. Their happiness and frustration would rise and fall with the tides. Since these tutors clearly wanted to be done with him, he could punish them by making it seem as if they would be stuck with him for an eternity.

The second type of tutor concerned himself with precision. These made up, by and large, the tutors he'd had in the last seven years. Often they were not human at all, and clearly doubtful that he could master the magicks they were showing him. Despite his being a tenth the age of some of the eldest human mages, and a tinier fraction of the age of his nonhuman teachers, he did work his way through their magicks. Most could not believe this, so they made him do things over and over again. For them he became obsessively precise—he had no choice. Orla might have ordered him to perform a healing spell while on one knee, but Magister Phyreynol would have punished him for a week for doing that.

Pleasing this latter group of Magisters was not as difficult as he would have thought. Kerrigan reveled in order and precision. He preferred peace and calm, didn't want any distractions. It allowed him to feel and experience the nature of the magick he was weaving. For him, that felt like hearing music carried on the wind. He could feel other great magicks out there, but couldn't quite catch enough hints to capture them.

Early on he found another tool for manipulating his tutors. Food. He insisted they take their meals with him. If they refused he became sulky and balky until they did. Then he would request all sorts of things, quickly discerning what they liked and what they hated. Since they ate the same food he did at their shared meals, simply by choosing what he would and would not eat he punished and rewarded them. He especially enjoyed fattening up the lean ones.

Kerrigan thought about Orla as he sat in a corner of the kitchen on a stout stool. All around him Magisters, Adepts, and Apprentices labored hard, dragging about huge sacks of flour, mixing things in mammoth bowls, feeding wood into fires to heat stoves. He wondered why they were not using magick to do things, the way they would have normally, then realized they were husbanding their magickal strength for other tasks.

Orla, he knew, would have been pleased that he'd made that observation, but she would want more. "Why?" was a question she seemed to ask incessantly. She asked him to think about things more deeply than anyone else ever had, and she demanded of him tasks that never would have occurred to his other tutors.

As he munched his black bread, Kerrigan wondered why everyone was holding back on magick. It certainly seemed true that physical strength and nonmagickal means accomplished the intended goals. It might take longer for bread to be mixed, for it to rise, and for it to bake than without magick, but it got done. The small loaf in his hand had been burned on one end, which he'd not seen before, but it still tasted good and seemed to fill his tummy.

He shrugged, fairly certain it was some command come down from the Grand Magister, for reasons known only to him. Most things he didn't understand were explained that way, and he found that explanation comforting. Whenever he asked a tutor *why* he was supposed to do one thing or another, that was always the reply.

Save with Orla. She'd always ask him to puzzle out a reason. He'd do his best and she'd accept what he said. Still, he did sense some disappointment there. She clearly expected him to have another answer. Since his answers to her were not wrong, though, Kerrigan found it beyond him to puzzle out what else she wanted him to say.

He finished his bread—excepting the burned heel that he tossed to a dog—and washed it down with watered ale. It tasted horrible, but he drank it anyway. He carried the cup to a washing-up bucket that was on his way to the door and dropped it in. The Apprentice who had her arms up to the elbows in steaming soapy water gave him a glare. He let his nostrils flare at her, then continued blithely out of the kitchen.

Kerrigan shielded his eyes against the sun for a moment, then set off down a winding pathway toward the small port. As the pathway dipped behind forested hills, he lost sight of the ocean and the ships. Despite that, the stream of people moving inland made his course easy to pick out.

Vilwan had always been his home, and while he did not often venture out of the tower complex in which he lived and was schooled, he still felt comfortable with his surroundings. The vegetation on the hillsides, while quite thick and lush, lay in a rainbow patchwork. The color was by no means uniform, since scarlet plants bore blue berries or silver flowers and so forth, but the reactions of the travelers led Kerrigan to believe such things were exotic.

Exotic is exactly what he found the travelers to be. They both amused and scared him. They dressed in an absolute riot of colors, and in many layers. They even sported trousers—he scarcely saw a robe among them—and many wore swords and daggers and carried bows and quivers full of arrows. Scars puckered flesh, yellowed and crooked teeth filled smiles, and the way some of them smelled! Kerrigan felt sure he could have found his way to the port just by following his nose.

The travelers spread throughout the island. Each type of magick had its own tower complex, with the Magisters' tower being at the center of the island. Kerrigan lived there, and tutors came to him, rather than his going to their towers to learn. Excepting those Apprentices given menial chores to perform as punishment, he seldom saw people his own age on Vilwan, and fewer still magickers of his rank.

While the procession of people onto the island had been surprising and interesting, their motion provided a general sense of order. The port itself had been given over to chaos. Ships rode uneasily at anchor, rising and falling with waves. Apprentices clustered around, laughing and shouting. Sailors called back to them, then some Adept would send the Apprentices up the gangway to help unload the ship.

Into this maelstrom of activity Kerrigan strode at his own pace. He marveled at everything, trying to memorize it all. He wanted his own record of it so he could compare it with the official history. In those pages he'd read so much, but little of it had come alive for him. Here he was seeing more than he'd ever seen before, and luxuriated in its complexity.

The sights, the sounds, the smells, the words, the accents, it all pounded into him. He rose to greet each wave of it, smiling in spite of himself. He caught glances by Adepts, saw them nod to one another. He assumed they might be talking about him, but couldn't imagine why. Here, on the docks, he felt like everyone else.

"You, how about some help?"

Kerrigan blinked his green eyes and turned to the sound of the voice. There, at the railing of a ship, stood an elf. A bulging sack hung from one hand. On the gangway below, Apprentices and young men from aboard the ship streamed like ants, hauling the sacks to a wagon.

"Did you mean m-me?" Kerrigan's voice quivered, but not out of nervousness. The elf looked unlike any of his elven tutors, for tattoos covered him, and his white hair rose from a center stripe. It took Kerrigan a moment to identify him as a Vorquelf—not because he did not know what they were, but because he'd never seen one before. The sight made him smile.

The Vorquelf nodded. "Yes, you."

"I would be happy to help." Kerrigan tugged the sleeves on his brown robe back. He flexed his fingers, extended his open hands, and began to weave a spell. As he had done with the book, he intended to float the sack from the ship to the cart. Gauging the distance and the item's weight were tricky, but the way it swayed effortlessly in the Vorquelf's grip told him it could not be very heavy.

He set himself to cast the spell, closing his eyes for a moment to compose himself, then opened his eyes again. He looked for his target, but couldn't see it. He saw others lifting their faces skyward and he aped them. He wondered what it was they were looking at because he couldn't see anything. The sky had been blotted out.

Half a heartbeat later, the fifty-pound sack of flour slammed into his chest. The impact lifted him off his feet and dumped him hard onto his back. Stars exploded before his eyes as his head smacked the ground. He bounced once, then felt a suffocating weight pressing on his chest. In a flash of anger he cast the spell he'd been readying, launching the sack of flour into the air, but he found he still couldn't breathe.

An Adept he didn't know dropped to a knee beside him. He tried to slip his arms around Kerrigan's waist, to arch his back, but his grip slipped. "He's too big, I need help."

Kerrigan kicked his legs in panic as breath burned in his lungs. He wanted to scream because his head and his back hurt, but his paralyzed lungs left him silent. Tears coursed down his face, at first from the pain, then from the laughter he heard. Through tears he saw blurred figures contorted in hilarity, telling and retelling what they'd seen.

Suddenly the Vorquelf filled his vision and straddled him. Kerrigan felt fingers dig into the fleshiness of his back. The Vorquelf lifted him, and cool air rushed into his lungs.

The mage exhaled as the Vorquelf let him down. Three more times the Vorquelf helped him breathe, then dragged his hands from beneath Kerrigan.

He stood tall above him. "Wonder you can breathe at all."

Kerrigan's face reddened immediately. He rolled on his right side to get himself up, but before he could even get a knee under him, someone else knocked into him. Kerrigan rolled away a few feet, barely had time to make sense of the shouts of "Look out" ringing through the crowd, then looked back toward where he had lain.

The flour sack landed with a heavy thump and exploded into a white cloud that slapped him hard. Kerrigan shook his head and snorted flour out of his nose. It had filled his mouth with a pasty film. He clawed it out of his eyes, then opened them as he staggered to his feet.

All around him Apprentices, Adepts, sailors, and soldiers pointed and laughed. He looked down and found himself dusted tan from the curve of his belly up, then over his arms. Those parts of himself he couldn't see he assumed were likewise coated. His face immediately burned and he wished the flour had filled his ears, so he could be deafened to the laughter.

Laughter pilloried him. Panic blossomed as his face burned beneath the flour coat. To be diminished, bullied, badgered, and threatened he'd learned to deal with, but ridicule, he had no defense against that. Alone, hurt, and mortified, he didn't know what to do. He could think of nothing, so he reacted without thinking at all.

For the first time in his life, Kerrigan Reese ran.

CHAPTER 23

Orla entered the Magister of Combats' round tower chamber, but did not descend the single step to the sunken disk in the center. All around that disk, shelves had been fitted to the walls and filled with books, scrolls, maps, weapons, bones, and other artifacts of war. Opposite the door she entered through lay a balcony, and the Magister stood there, his hands clasped at his back, watching the sea to the north.

The room would have been easy to mistake for a general's home, and not just from the items found in it. The stark and spare furnishings had nothing mystical about them, nor were they at all refined. The hardwood chairs would not encourage lingering. The cot set near the balcony had been made up, but covered only with sheets and a thin wool blanket. The drawers on one of the shelves must have held the Magister's clothes, but there were few enough of them to suggest his money did not go to filling out his wardrobe.

The Magister himself *did* wear the grey robes of a senior

sorcerer, though he was not a slave to fashion—such as it was on Vilwan. Instead, he stripped his robe down to his waist and tied the arms there as if a belt. Despite his being partially silhouetted, she could see light scars and darker tattoos on his back and shoulders.

Those shoulders had once been powerful, as had the Magister himself. In his younger days he'd had the physique of a warrior—though slender enough for it to have been an elven warrior. His head, which he shaved daily, had once been sown with long black hair that had been braided into a plait much like hers.

She cleared her voice. "You sent for me, Magister."

He waited a moment before he turned and moved back into his chamber. He seemed to age with each inch he came into the room. The imperfections that the sunlight had hidden came into easy focus. The tall, proud man she had known in her youth had shrunk, as if the weight of his responsibilities and the power he could wield had compressed him. She could still feel his power, and see it in smoldering brown eyes—reinforcing why it was foolish to judge a mage by his physical form.

"You are aware, Orla, of the forthcoming invasion. Chytrine wishes to do with Vilwan what she did with Vorquellyn over a century ago." His voice remained even, though age cracked it in a few places. "Tomorrow, or the next day, the peace of this island will be shattered."

She nodded slowly. "I question the wisdom of her assault on Vilwan."

The Magister of Combats held a hand up to forestall further comment. "Wise or not, it is a fact. We know she made a probing attack against a town in Alcida. There she lost more troops than she expected, and used a dragon to exact her revenge. She has grown more powerful in the last quarter century, perhaps more arrogant as well. She is coming and we will face her."

Orla lifted her chin. "What do you want me to do?"

The Magister of Combats smiled at her, for a heartbeat peeling back the years to a time when they had stood side by side, holding off Aurolani forces in Okrannel. "I need to inquire after the boy."

"They gave that task to you? Did the Grand Magister assume our long association would make me dull my tongue on the matter?"

He shook his bald head. "Had that been their presumption, I would have disabused them of it, and quickly. We have an invasion, and I need to know if he will be useful to me or not."

Orla snorted. "Things have not changed much since I last reported to the Council. Adept Reese is, without a doubt, the greatest human sorcerer known. His parents' talents bred true. He studies hard, but he has been raised like a horse with blinders. He knows magick, all manner of magicks. He has mastered spells of incalculable power, and is easily able to deconstruct, examine, refine, recombine, and create spells that no man has yet dreamed might exist."

The Magister nodded. "This is as intended."

"Yes, what you intended. What you all intended."

"*You?*" The Magister's eyes narrowed. "I recall rather well your being with me at his nativity. We all volunteered for that duty; we believed in that duty. Has your heart changed? Do you think we were wrong?"

"No." She shook her head resolutely. "You're correct in saying we all volunteered for that duty. All of us did, save one: Kerrigan. He was drafted against his will, before he had a will, and he has been shaped and crafted. He's been trained as a dog might, for one purpose. At least, he began his life training for one purpose, but his goal was changed as things went along."

Orla sighed and gestured south, toward the island's heart. "Have you seen him outside the times of testing?"

"No."

"You should. The entire Council should. You have no idea what his training has done to him. It was agreed—by me, too, yes—that neither Kerrigan nor any of them would be told their intended destiny. The pressure would have been overwhelming. Just their training has crushed the others, but he keeps on. Why? Because he has stopped questioning his purpose in life. He learned early on that such questions would not be answered, so he just abandoned the quest for *that* knowledge."

"Yet, by doing so, he has accomplished so much."

"True, but how useful is it?"

The Magister of Combats chuckled. "Immensely useful, if he can wield a fraction of the power you suggest. I've seen it, during testing, of that there is no doubt."

"Oh, he can, but you've seen him do it in a testing chamber." She shook her head. "In combat, arrows flying, men screaming, fire burning, and greasy smoke choking, he'd be useless. This morning, Magister, he skinned his knee. It was a wound you and I would dismiss without a second thought, but it became the center of his being. He would not cast the spell to heal it until I told him to do so, and *then* he wanted to get into a clean robe, to set himself to do it. When I made him cast it while down on one knee, when I *shamed* him into doing it, then he did. He did it well, but even then he had no distractions. In an *arcanorium* he is unequaled. In the field, I'd choose the most raw Apprentice over him."

"And yet he is the best we have." The Magister of Combats sighed heavily. "He'll be no help in the fight at all."

"He could cure some who are wounded, but I think that is it." She pursed her lips. "Put him in a ward, give him a bodyguard, and order that person to slay him if the Aurolani forces are able to overrun the island. And, no, you won't have me do it. I would refuse, and quite frankly, you need me elsewhere."

"You're right and you're wrong, Orla." A hint of a smile traced over the Magister's lips. "Were it within my power, you and I would fight side by side again, driving the pirates off."

"It *is* within your power. The defense of Vilwan is your responsibility. I may be older and slowing down, but I'm still one of the better combat mages available."

"I would never deny that fact, Orla, *never.*" He brought his hands together over the knot made of the arms of his brown robe. "The fact remains, however, that you have a more important mission than defending Vilwan. No, wait, hear me out. There actually *is* such a mission. You will accompany Adept Reese as he is evacuated from the island. It is your job to get him away safely."

Orla felt a great wave of fatigue crash through her. "You cannot be serious. I will be wasted in that job."

"Nonetheless, it is yours." The Magister of Combats bowed to her. "He is your charge, and for his fate, I have no fear. And since you think he should learn more outside the *arcanorium*, this is your chance to teach him."

Her head came up. "Oh, I see. The Council is willing to accede to my requests to do that, using the invasion as a pretext. So much better to have that than to have to admit being wrong."

"Orla, my dear friend, you know better than to question the origin of good fortune." The Magister smiled, then advanced and laid his right hand on her right shoulder. "Go strongly, teach him well. If we are not defeated, he can return. If we are, it is a good thing for the world that he will not die with us."

Will felt fair certain his ribs had cracked, he was laughing so hard. He'd dropped the flour sack he'd been carrying and clutched his sides. The look of surprise on the fat kid's face a half second before the flour sack hit him smack in the chest had been priceless. The way his expression had gone from serene confidence to sheer panic was a memory Will would run through his mind time and again.

And then, to make things better, the flour sack had flown way up, then come down hard and burst, drenching

the boy in flour. He'd run off, sobbing, leaving a misty ribbon in the air behind him.

And it was his own fault. Resolute had called to him, indicating he should get in line with the rest of them. Instead
the kid had just stood there and gestured imperiously. He'd
even closed his eyes, daring Resolute to throw the sack. *If I
had done that, Resolute wouldn't have been helping me
breathe, he'd have been skinning me alive.*

"Finished laughing, boy?"

The rime-tinged edge in Resolute's voice stopped Will's
laughter dead. "Ah, yes, I am."

"Good." Resolute caught him in a vise-grip around his
right arm. "Pick up the sack you dropped. Carry it to the
cart. Then, find a broom. Sweep up the spilled flour and
put it in that sack again."

"What?"

Resolute's eyes became silver slits. "That flour could
make up the last bread you'll ever eat. We're getting no
more supplies here. This is it. We can't waste anything."

"Got it." Will tried to pull his arm free of Resolute's
grasp, but failed.

The Vorquelf held on for a heartbeat more, then released him. "Hurry, boy."

Will stooped and picked up his flour sack, then carried
it to the cart. Dranae took it from him there and easily
tossed it into place. The cart creaked as it landed.

"Tell me something, Will." The large man plucked
another sack from an Apprentice's back and lofted it onto
the cart. "Why did you think that was funny?"

Will blinked. "You didn't?"

"Should I have? The young man was getting ready to
use magick to move that sack. He probably could have
moved the whole cart."

The young thief frowned. "How do you know that?"

Dranae hesitated for a moment, then ran a hand over
his jaw. "I just do. Seemed obvious to me. We're on Vilwan.
He's in a robe, makes a gesture."

Will nodded. "I can see that, yeah." *What I can't see is how you could have thought he was powerful.*

"Why was it funny?"

"Well, because he was knocked down. Because he was surprised, and then because he was covered in flour and ran off crying like a baby."

"Even though it was all a mistake?"

Will felt like squirming. "Well, I didn't know it was a mistake, right?"

"Even though he had obviously been hurt?"

"I didn't know. . . ."

The flesh around Dranae's blue eyes tightened. "You know how heavy the sacks are. You know that had to have hurt."

"Well . . ." Will felt his guts starting to shrivel. "Others were laughing."

"So they were." Dranae clapped Will on both shoulders, hard, sending a shock wave through him. "But they were mostly mages, too. Remember, Will, it's not a good idea to have a sorcerer thinking you've been laughing at him. You'll have a lot of trouble here on Vilwan if you forget that."

Will's expression soured. He'd not liked the boat ride to Vilwan. He'd gotten used to the motion of the ship easily enough, but had the misfortune of standing next to someone who didn't. Before Will could clean the vomit off himself, Resolute volunteered him to clean the deck. Plenty of other little jobs had kept him hopping, and then when he got a chance to sleep, it was in a musty hammock belowdecks.

His bones ached from fatigue and his belly growled. There'd not been much food on the ship, and most of it was older than he was. The hard biscuits didn't taste bad, they just didn't taste, save for the weevils in them. Will deemed it just as well that the King of Saporicia was sending so many folks to Vilwan to die, because after they'd enjoyed bad food, worse water, and a long sea journey, they'd have been ready to storm his castle and topple him from the throne.

Will talked to one of the Apprentices—easily spotted by a robe with a scarlet body—and asked where he might find a broom. The Apprentice smiled and told him they were kept at the gaming fields. She pointed toward the center of the island.

Will shrugged and set off, but an Adept in a robe of forest-green stopped him. When Will reported what he had been told, the Adept snorted and told him there were no gaming fields. "We use brooms for the same thing everyone else does, as that Apprentice will soon be reminded. Try one of the port shops here, they will have one you can borrow."

A tavern lent him a broom. The journey along the docks to it and back gave him a chance to take a look around. He found Vilwan slightly disappointing because the area around the docks, or what the locals referred to as Seatown, looked pretty much like every other seaside section of town he'd ever visited. Dirty, dingy, with a few broad, straight roads, then a tangle of muddy alleys leading back into a thicket of warehouses and ramshackle houses. While he didn't mind that, he expected something more exotic.

The Adepts and Apprentices bored him, too. Some, like the one who had been hit with flour, seemed bug-eyed, staring at the troops being shipped in to defend their home. Others sniffed like nobles, as if their blood were somehow better than his. And, from his standpoint, the most annoying thing was that none of them had money pouches. He didn't mind folks being snooty as long as he had a chance to collect a snob-tax from them.

Will sighed and returned with the broom to begin to sweep the flour up. The Adept he'd spoken to earlier came over, dragging the Apprentice who had deceived him over by the ear. "This is what you want the broom for, to collect this flour?"

Will nodded. "Yes, sir."

"Very good." The Adept glanced at the Apprentice. "You'll help him."

The Apprentice, a redheaded girl with enough soft-swelling on her chest to be only a couple years younger than Will, nodded. "Yes, Adept."

Will brandished the broom, then nodded toward the sack. "Just hold that and I can sweep the flour into it."

As she slowly bent to the task, Will dragged the broom through the flour. It seemed to him that the broom, bristle-bare as it was, did a better job raking than it was sweeping. Will made several passes, but brought more dirt than flour to the waiting sack.

The Apprentice gave him a witheringly depreciative glance. "You dulls. This will take forever." She gestured once and a blue spark flew from her right hand. It hit the broom dead in the middle of the stick and wrenched it from his grasp. Whirling and twirling, the broom danced through the flour and drove it in a wave to the waiting sack. In no time at all, every speck of the flour at the point of impact had been swept up, and the broom would have started in on the tracks left by the running boy, but the Apprentice called it back and killed the spell.

Will blinked and his jaw dropped open. "How? I thought he said you used brooms for what we all do."

"We do." She smiled sweetly. "We just don't use it the same *way* you do. Sack's full, I'll take the broom back for you."

He shivered. "It's from . . ."

"I know where it is from." She forestalled his next question. "It's in the magick."

Will took the sack and gathered the top of it closed. He hefted it onto his back but barely felt the strain. *If a kid can do that* . . . Images of self-propelled constabulary nightsticks cavorted through his head. *Dranae's right. Laughing at wizards is not a good idea, and stealing from them would be even worse.*

CHAPTER 24

Alyx refused to look in the mirror, and reluctantly met the eyes of the women who had helped dress her. Given her embarrassment, she would not have greeted their gazes at all, but they had slaved over her—bathing her, brushing, braiding, and fixing her hair, then dressing her. Without help Alyx could have shrugged on a full mail suit faster than they were able to get her into her golden gown. *And the armor would move easier and leave me feeling so much less vulnerable.*

She did not resent these two women and their help. While she had been dressing herself for decades, the garments she'd worn while with the Gyrkyme had been simple—barely more than sacks. The Gyrkyme, with their wonderful plumage, hardly had need of fashions to make themselves more attractive. A scrap of cloth here or there would suit the most modest, and modesty had not been one of Alyx's concerns until well into puberty. Even then she followed society's conventions more to save others embarrassment than herself.

But she could never have donned the gown that had been chosen for her without help. Long, flowing skirts dragged on the floor, forcing her to wear shoes with toes that reared back and up, like a snake preparing to strike. With each step the serpentine toe kicked the hem of the gown out from beneath her foot. The skirts themselves gathered at her slender waist, at the edge of a stiff bodice into which she had been tightly laced. She could hardly breathe, and bowing at the waist was a flat impossibility as the leading edge of the bodice extended down to fully protect her femininity. Above the top of the bodice, which scarcely hid her nipples and barely contained her bosom, a slender, wispy silken scarf swirled from one wrist across her shoulders to the other. Alyx, feeling trapped in the gown, likened the scarf to a golden chain linking silk manacles.

She sighed, but not very deeply, since the bodice would not allow her to draw a proper breath. For the women's help she had been grateful, but the reason they had been present rankled. Just over a decade before, on her sole previous trip to Yslin, she had been given a similar gown and left to dress herself. She studied the gown as she might a battlefield, then put it on. Since lacing it tight would have been impossible without help, Alyx had posited that it had to be worn with the lacings forward and that was how she dressed herself. She liked the stiffness against her spine, and while the lacings did bind over her breasts and belly, having nothing more to cover her presented no problem for someone raised by the Gyrkyme.

Luckily her aunt had come to check on her and was able to correct the problem before she had left the room. *They should know that I learn from my mistakes.* She would have ventured another sigh, but felt reluctant to waste her breath. Instead she smiled and bowed her head to the women. "Thank you for your help."

They curtsied deeply, the both of them, sinking into a puddle of skirts, then rising slowly. "It was an honor to serve you, Highness."

Alyx smiled beneficently at them as they left the room. She started to reach around behind her to unknot the lacings, but a quick knock on the door barely preceded the tiny squeak of it swinging open. "If you do that, you'll spill out of the gown and scandalize everyone."

Her violet eyes blazed as the man slipped into the room. Shorter than she, and on the fuller side of a medium build, he wore his black hair long and raggedly cut. His moustaches drooped well past his jaw, but his goatee remained a triangle of black surrounded by the white flesh of his chin. Gold hose clung to his legs and a gold tunic clothed him, with a tabard of black over the top of it. A winged horse rampant, in white, emblazoned his chest.

His eyes widened in shock as he met her hot stare. He pulled back, and splayed a hand against his chest. "Have you forgotten me, cousin?"

Alyx's jaw opened for a moment, then she smiled. "Misha?"

"The very same." He bowed very low, sweeping a golden cap from his head and dusting the tops of his shoes with it. As he straightened up, he smiled. "I am now styled Duke Mikhail, of course."

"Of course." She moved to him carefully and kissed him on both cheeks. "Not quite the same cousin with whom I shared a dream raid."

"I've grown up, as have you." He stepped back and his smile broadened. "Perhaps I should not have been so opposed to their arranging our marriage."

Alyx caressed his cheek. "Sweet Misha, you promised, and I know you would have sooner stabbed yourself through the heart than to violate your word."

He shrugged. "Truthfully, cousin, I'd take you for a wife in a heartbeat, save that relatives I hate would then be related to me yet one more time."

"How are they?"

"Some are truly dead, others walking dead. A few of us, we are realistic." Misha shrugged and grabbed a handful of his long hair. "The customs they impose on us are not that hideous. Remaining unshorn for the summer, to mourn your father's passing—as our grandfather did and does—is not difficult. What they do to the younger ones, and the way they are crossing our bloodlines, well, my father tells me they have always meddled."

"And they sent you to get me?"

His brown eyes grew wide again. "Duke Mikhail? By all the gods, no, little Alyx. If they knew I was here they would all be angry. I just wanted to make sure that you would recognize your cousin and know you had an ally in there."

Another knock, this one far more stout, rattled the door. Mikhail danced over past a screen in the small room, and almost slipped in a puddle of water leaking from the wooden bathing cask. He ducked down behind the cask and nodded to Alyx.

"Enter."

The door swung slowly open, letting the stone archway frame a small but strongly built man. As had Misha, he wore black over gold, but appeared more striking because of his full snowy mane and beard. He had no moustache and his flesh bore the bronze tint of a lifetime spent under the sun. In a few places, on his hands, and in one spot on his forehead, puckered scars resisted coloring; but otherwise the man was robust and the picture of health.

Though Alyx had not seen him in over a decade, she could not mistake him for anyone else. "Uncle Valery, it is good to see you."

The older man's face brightened as he entered the room and hugged her. He kissed both her cheeks and the brush of his whiskers tickled her cheek and throat. "Alexia, of you my brother would be so proud." The man's deep voice became gravelly with emotion.

He took a half step back, then straightened. "It is my duty and honor, profound and deep, to conduct you into the Crown Circle." He extended his right arm, which she took by slipping her left hand through the crook of his elbow, then he led her sideways through the door and into the corridor.

Fortress Gryps had once been the largest fortification in all of Yslin. It had been supplanted by Fortress Libertas out on the eastern point to guard the entrance to the harbor. King Augustus had been kind enough to make Fortress Gryps available to the Okrannel exile community, not as a permanent dwelling place, but a societal hub. For special gatherings, the titanic stone structure—with its vaulted ceilings and stone columns, friezes and tapestries—became transformed into a place in which the glory of Okrannel was resurrected.

Alexia knew nothing of the fall of her nation. She had been borne away to Gyrvirgul in the final days of the war against Chytrine. The nation had fallen and her father had retreated with loyal retainers to defend Fortress Draconis, far to the north. He had died there and she had been given over to the Gyrkyme to raise and train.

She had grown up being told that the Gyrkyme stewardship of her life was her father's final wish. By the time she grew old enough to question the truth of that—having heard that her father's manner of death precluded the communication of any last wishes, no matter what the songs said about it—she had wondered why her grandfather, her aunt, uncles, and cousins had not wanted to care for her themselves. Not long after that point she took her previous journey to Yslin, to be presented to the Crown Circle for the first time.

After that event, she did not wonder further why they didn't want her, but simply rejoiced in the fact that the Gyrkyme did.

On her uncle's arm, with the long skirts catching at her legs, she drifted through a fortress that had been transformed. The tapestries—some new and bright and exaggerated, others ancient, stained, and dour—all bore images from Okrans history. The newer ones seemed more imagined than real, with a number having a dreamlike quality to the pictures that revealed their inspiration.

She shook her head and hoped her uncle would not notice. The Okrans nobility, having been driven from their homeland, had come to Yslin and taken up residence. King Stefin had vowed to remain until Okrannel was liberated. The court in exile became known as the Crown Circle, and the Crown Circle determined and dictated that which was and was not part of Okrans life. While the effects of the edicts lessened with each league from Yslin—such that the refugees living in Jerana viewed them with mild amusement or deep contempt—they had the rule of law in Yslin.

One of the edicts had required each noble child at the age of fifteen to undertake a sojourn to Okrannel, to sleep on his native soil for a night. Somehow it became believed that the dreams one had during that night were prophetic, and these prophecies took on the same sanctity that the Norrington prophecy held for the Vorquelves.

At seventeen years of age she went on her journey, along with her uncle Valery, a troop of loyal retainers, and her cousin Misha. She should have gone at fifteen, as Misha did, but it took two years for the Crown Circle to get over their pique and grant her permission to go. The two of them had ventured into Okrannel and slept, then shared their dreams, refining them in the telling, so they would be suitably impressive for the Crown Circle.

Her throat tightened for a heartbeat as regret choked her. She'd have told the Crown Circle nothing of her dream, save for how they had looked at her when she was first presented to them, and later how Grand Duke Valery had silenced everyone so she could share her dream. The delight on his face as she told him what she had dreamed, the pleasure in his voice as he'd ordered someone to fetch her tea with milk and sweetened until thick, that had convinced her that what she had done was right.

Her uncle again smiled at her with such delight as two

liveried courtiers opened the door to the Grand Hall. "Come, my dear child. You are awaited."

Thick incense cascaded down in phantom ribbons from censers mounted high on massive stone pillars, filling the room to knee high with a pungent fog. Oil lamps provided illumination, but scant little of it. Men and women hid in the shadows, each wearing gold, but with black over it. Alyx alone had been permitted the right to wear gold unshrouded, and she chose to imagine that the gasps she heard from behind beards, hands, and fans were from the shock of wan light reflecting off her gown.

The Grand Duke led her forward at a stately pace. He clasped his left hand over her hand, locking it down against his arm. She felt no tremor in him indicating he thought she might bolt. Instead, as he walked deeper and deeper into the long room, drawing nearer the distant end, his steps became more certain and serene.

When last he'd led her forward she had been a gangling child who twisted and gawked at all those shrinking back. Now he brought her, a woman grown and a warrior trained, before the Crown Circle, and the sheer pride of it bunched the muscles of the forearm where her hand rested.

Finally they stopped three meters shy of the throne squatting at the hall's far end. She bowed her head to her grandfather, after the fashion of warriors greeting one another, then curtsied awkwardly. The night-shrouded women flanking the throne began breathing again when she curtsied, exhaling the breath they'd gathered when she'd given King Stefin a warrior's nod.

Her grandfather sat slumped on the throne, his crown slightly askew and sunk low, as if the man's head had shrunk. He looked almost a child wearing his father's raiment, but those dark eyes had a deadness to them that no child ever could have possessed. The man sat there, crushed down not by years alone, but by the hand of Death as it vaulted him to kill his eldest son and kill his nation.

The old man's eyes flicked up and held her stare for only

a moment. He had vowed he would not die until his home-land had been liberated. Many people who undertook such vows did so halfheartedly, but those who made them with full knowledge and intent often suffered for their temerity. In the brief moment her grandfather looked her in the eyes, she could see he was a prisoner of his own body.

And he sees me as his liberator.

King Stefin mumbled something, his parched lips barely moving. One of the women behind him moved forward, and despite the thickness of the incense in the air, Alyx caught a whiff of the moldy scent rolling off the woman. Alyx, who had not wavered when charging through Aurolani battle lines, shivered in this woman's presence and had Valery not still held her hand against his forearm, she would have taken a step back.

Scent far more than sight of the cadaverously slender, hatchet-faced woman sent Alyx reeling back through the years to when she was first presented. At that time the king had been more animated and actually smiled at seeing her. Grand Duchess Tatyana had not even made an attempt at a smile. Though only a decade older than the king, she was his aunt, so he gave her great latitude. She'd swept forward and grabbed Alyx roughly, twisting her this way and that, humming and hawing as she did so.

Then, with her sharp, bony fingers, she'd pried the girl's mouth open and thrust fingers in to count her teeth and probe her mouth. Alyx struggled, gagging as fingers hit the back of her throat, but other fingers dug deeply into her forearm. The woman hissed at her malevolently and shook her to stop her struggling.

So Alyx bit her.

She didn't draw blood, though she knew she could have easily, simply by shifting her jaw to let her molars slice through the crone's thin skin. Tatyana wrenched her fingers out of Alyx's mouth and held her left hand up as if she expected her fingers to be a couple digits shy of whole. Alyx pulled free of her right hand and stepped back, not caring that the hem of her gown tore. She set her feet and balled her fists.

Tatyana advanced only as far forward as the king's side. "His Highness says he is pleased to see his fated granddaughter again."

"As am I pleased to see *him*." Alyx knew Tatyana caught the emphasis. "And you, Great-Aunt Tatyana, you are well?"

"As well as can be expected when one's heart aches from breathing foreign air, sleeping on foreign soil, pining for one's homeland."

"It is a burden, yes." Alyx wished the gown's bodice would allow her to suck in enough air for a decent snarl. Tatyana, whose reputation as a mystic had grown over the years, served as the king's closest advisor and often interpreted his unintelligible remarks. Many of the new traditions handed down from the Crown Circle originated with her. A year or so after the fall of Okrannel, she'd had a vision that led her, covertly, to undertake the first dream raid. She also was the author of edicts concerning fashion that, Misha had once noted, seemed more designed to make sure exiles did not resemble the population of the lands where they dwelt than it did any preservation of Okrans tradition.

Again King Stefin mumbled, and Tatyana's sharp expression softened slightly as her lips twitched into a smile. "His Majesty says he is pleased you could join us this night. News of your victories has preceded you, and they make us most proud."

Alyx bowed her head toward the wizened figure of the king. "Too much has been made of these battles, Grandfather. My forces merely slapped the snout of a bear sniffing about for food. When it chooses to slap back, things could be much worse."

"I think, my darling niece, you are overly cautious." Tatyana's ice-blue eyes focused distantly for a moment. "There are those who see great victories in your future. Even you, yourself, have seen them."

"I recall." Alyx's eyes tightened. Tatyana often retreated into a chamber deep in the bowels of Fortress Gryps and remained there for days at a time. Servants kept it filled with incense smoke and hot air—Alyx had heard it said that sitting in a smokehouse with hams would be more hospitable—so her great-grandaunt could be transported to a place where she saw visions. Her visions, when not concerned with the conduct of Okrans exiles, always touted the liberation of Okrannel, with Alyx at the head of a multinational army that would sweep through the nation and into Aurolan itself, to destroy Chytrine.

The problem for Alyx was not the enormity of that crusade. Given sufficient forces, support, and some luck, she knew such a campaign could be won. Tatyana's visions always included some climactic battle in which the back of the Aurolan army would be broken. Alyx realized it would take a much longer campaign using entirely different tactics, but when she returned from her dream raid with Misha, she said her dream mirrored the visions of Tatyana.

Alyx's lie had kindled great hope among the Okrans exiles. Word of her victories in the east and west, modest though they were, must have again enflamed the exiles. With her entrance into Yslin in the company of King Augustus, clearly the Crown Circle anticipated the day of Okrannel's liberation looming.

Alyx again shivered. *And the Vorquelves have waited five times as long as we have for their homeland to be freed.*

Tatyana raised a finger—one of those Alyx had bitten—and let her smile flatten. "The time has come, child, for you to fulfill the destiny your father chose for you. He died so you could live. Your duty is to free Okrannel. You are *our* champion."

Another voice, strong and male, filled the chamber from back near the doorway. "I trust, Grand Duchess, I would be included in your statement."

Alyx turned as quickly as her gown and uncle would allow, pleased to let Tatyana's venomous glare speed past her.

Through the incense fog came King Augustus. Where Okrans exiles wore gold, he chose silver. He had donned a black tabard, with the winged horse rampant on it, but the silver gorget hanging from around his neck above it displayed a half fish, half horse that he had chosen as the ensign of his reign.

Walking beside him, in gold and black, though more of the former than the latter, came Queen Yelena. A robust woman who matched her husband in height, her brown hair displayed only a few strands of grey. Her brown eyes sparked fiercely. Tatyana did not shrink from the queen's glare, but neither did she escalate the war of expression.

Alyx found herself smiling despite the tension in the air. The stories of how King Augustus had rescued Yelena from an overrun Okrannel while destroying Chytrine's army of ravagers had been retold in endless variations. As a little girl, Alyx had delighted in them all. She took great pride in being distantly related to Yelena, and the queen had been Alyx's hero. More than one of the songs sung had told of Yelena and Augustus fighting back to back, saving each other—and in the often savage and always martial Gyrkyme society, nothing could have been more romantic.

Tatyana's voice came in a hiss. "Okrannel's debt to you, King Augustus, can never be repaid. Through Alexia we will find a way to free ourselves and burden you no more."

"Burden me?" Augustus lifted the queen's hand to his mouth and kissed it. "You are of the blood that sustains my wife and my heirs. How could you be a burden to me? And this, your granddaughter, Majesty, you know how well she has served me and my people. This debt of which you speak has already been repaid. It is the other debt that needs repaying."

King Stefin croaked something. Tatyana's eyes became icy slits. "Other debt?"

"When first we set off for Okrannel, its liberation was our goal. That was a quarter century ago. We owe you liberation, and you will have it."

The mystic let a smile slash the lower half of her face. "You have given us the means. Alexia has been trained well."

"True, quite true. At the head of an army, she could free Okrannel. For a while."

Alyx had begun to nod as Augustus spoke, but her head froze with his last three words. His voice had sunk into serious tones.

He glanced at her. "Not to belittle your skills, General, for they are formidable, but we all know that if you take Okrannel back from Chytrine, you will be granted no peace to build fortifications. You will have no chance to hold your land against another invasion."

She nodded. "I cannot gainsay your vision of the future, Highness."

Augustus looked at Tatyana. "I know I am here on sufferance, for I am but married into Okrans society. Some of you view me as a brother or a son; though most see me as a landlord who has, as yet, been lenient in asking for rent. You fear the bill coming due, and you know it will soon. You have heard of Chytrine's forays into Alcida, and you know she is sending a fleet against Vilwan. So, yes, I will make a demand of you. Do not think Alexia, no matter how brilliant, can save your homeland alone.

"The Harvest Festival is but a few weeks off, with contingents arriving constantly." Augustus raised his voice so everyone in the hall could hear him. "Together, with Okrannel as a brother nation, we will unite to drive Chytrine from our lands, to cleanse them—Okrannel, too, of course. Alexia will be key in this. I beg you, in your haste for your own freedom, do not squander the person best suited to winning freedom for all of us."

The mystic crone let his words echo into silence, then slowly nodded. "His Highness says Okrannel is ever prepared to be the razored edge of the spear thrust into Chytrine's guts. We only demand that we not be wasted, and that our desires are given proper weight. If this is permitted, then Okrannel's role in the coming war with Aurolan will be obvious, clear, and will lead to total victory."

Augustus smiled. "As it should."

Tatyana nodded. "As it has been foreseen."

The murmurs of those in the room suggested they took great heart in Tatyana's words, but Alyx did not. It was less what she said, or how she said it, that left her unsettled. What unnerved her was the glance her grandfather gave her as the mystic spoke. As his dark gaze brushed past her eyes, cold cut at her spine.

She read fear in his gaze, terrible fear. Not of death, not of dying. He knew he would pass only after his homeland had been freed. No, King Stefin was terrified that he would, in fact, live forever.

CHAPTER 25

Even having the shutters closed and the heavy drapes drawn tight across them could not keep the sunlight out of his *arcanorium*. Seated there in the utter darkness, Kerrigan knew no *visible* light could touch him, but he still felt the sun's heat. *If light is what one sees, then heat is the sun's breath.*

He couldn't wait for the sun to hide its face because, as had so many others, it had witnessed his utter and complete humiliation. The Vorquelf had seen what he was doing and deliberately threw the sack of flour at him. Fifty pounds had flown through the air easily and unerringly, with no warning shouted, no whistle, hiss, or rustle to alert him. Had he not opened his eyes at the last minute, he wouldn't have had a clue as to what was happening.

Fury flared through him, and the hair on the backs of his hands rose as energy tingled and sparked from his fingertips. The memories of ridicule crashed over him in successive waves. They crushed him down, battering him, making his spirit ache the way his back and ribs and head did. He wanted to hug his knees to his chest, but it hurt.

He could have cast the healing spell that had dealt so well with his knee, but he didn't. Kerrigan told himself it was because he could not cast it without supervision, but he knew that wasn't really it. Being granted permission to cast it would mean someone agreed it was wrong for him to feel hurt. He knew it wasn't wrong—he had been grossly wrong, so being hurt was a fit punishment for his mistake.

Ultimately, though, the healing spell didn't matter, since it would never get rid of the derisive laughter that remained locked in his skull. He wasn't stupid. He knew the Vorquelf couldn't really have known what he was doing— none of the other Apprentices and Adepts were using magick. He *was* physically large, so he might well have been able to catch the sack were he used to doing such things. He wasn't, however, nor had he been set to catch it.

What pained him the most, and sprouted thorny vines that took root in his heart, was that now he knew what the others thought of him on Vilwan. Many were Apprentices who, at his age, were decades away from becoming Adepts. To them he was a curiosity, or a thing to fear. He'd heard rumors that some of the youngest Apprentices began their schooling with warnings to be good, or they would end up like Kerrigan, trapped in a tower, with Magisters for keepers.

Adepts, with whom he shared rank, viewed him with suspicion. Some clearly did not believe he could be worthy to be ranked with them. Others who had overseen tests he had performed suspected that he should have been granted Magister rank. One Adept had even mentioned in hushed whispers that the reason he'd not been so exalted was because he did so many things so well, no single one of the schools of magick could lay a clean claim to him.

And the Magisters, when they came to teach him, they always seemed to have contempt for him. Some clearly wished nothing to do with him. A few, the ambitious ones, cultivated him until he showed, with sulks and balkiness, that he would not support them and their plans—whatever they were. Orla, who did her best to thwart his desires concerning work and schedules and indulgences, did not eye him with awe.

Kerrigan had no doubt that awe was in order because he knew how special he had become. He'd harbored the secret desire to see awe on faces, hence his willingness to display his power there at the docks. He had been ready to reap the adulation he felt he'd been denied, but he had harvested nothing but ridicule.

I should have known better. He'd been foolish in thinking outsiders would understand how much in awe of him they should have been. They knew nothing, could not work magick, and, therefore, should have been of no consequence. His experience with *dulls* had come only through his teachers and readings, but his humiliation only confirmed what he knew deep down.

The fact that *dulls* had been invited in to help defend Vilwan meant nothing. Kerrigan felt certain that in a straight duel of wizards, the Magisters of Vilwan could destroy Chytrine, but she had allied herself with Vionna and her Wruonin pirates. With their own renegade wizards and vylaens, the invading forces would have counterspells to ward off Vilwanese magicks, allowing raiders to land on the island.

Troops who would be best opposed by other dull troops. *Dogs snarling while their betters fight.*

Even as that thought formed itself in his mind, Kerrigan knew it was wrong. As angry as he was—and as much as he wanted to hate the dulls coming to Vilwan—he recognized the peril they were in. That the Magisters even thought to bring them in meant there would be a lot of dull blood anointing the island. Deep in his heart he knew that his pain was minimal compared to what they would feel as they fought to defend an island that was not even their home.

The trapdoor over the stairwell rose, allowing a thin, grey light to define the opening. Orla appeared, from waist up, more of a grey ghost than normal. "If you are finished pitying yourself, we have to go."

"Go without me."

"You mistake me. I don't want to go at all, but you are too precious to leave here." Her voice softened just a bit. "I've gathered up all you'll need to take with you."

More out of curiosity to see what she had gathered than anything else, Kerrigan rocked himself back and forth to build up momentum, then finally came to his feet. He staggered a bit, then lurched toward the stairway and descended to his rooms. There, in the middle of the floor, lay a little leather rucksack stuffed to bulging, with a blanket rolled tight and tied to the bottom of it.

"That's it?" He looked at the tiny parcel at his feet and shivered. *Everything I am can be reduced to that?* "I need books. I need my other things, my supplies."

Orla cut him off from the steps back up to the *arcanorium.* "Right now we just want to get you off the island. We are not worried about supplies. Those we can find anywhere."

"But . . . *my* things, I need them."

Her voice gained an edge. "I like this no more than you, Adept Reese. I don't want the Aurolani or Wruonin going through my chambers, taking my treasures, touching everything, smashing most things, defiling others. I don't want it, but it is not my place to complain at the moment."

She twisted, showing him the rucksack on her back, which looked to be the same size as his, but filled not nearly as full. "When we return, our things will be restored to us. But for now, anything else you want you will have to carry and, frankly, Kerrigan, I don't think you can carry much more than that."

The youth stooped and picked up the rucksack. He lifted it with no difficulty, but had trouble slipping his right arm through the strap. Orla helped him get it in place. It hung heavily on his back and the straps chafed under his armpits, but he decided not to complain. He shifted his shoulders a bit to settle the load, then nodded to her.

Orla crossed to the open door and picked up a long ebon staff nearly as tall as she was. "Let's go."

Kerrigan took one last look at his room. He wanted to take a book with him. At first he thought of his favorite, the Vilwanese history, but he knew it was too heavy for him to carry. He then looked for any book, but realized they would all be too heavy.

His head hung low in defeat, he sighed and followed Orla from the tower and Vilwan. Kerrigan thought about taking one last look at his home, but he refrained. Somehow he knew that if he ever returned, he would not see it the same way he had, so the time and energy needed to burn it into his memory seemed nothing but a waste.

Following Orla, he returned to the docks and the scene of his humiliation. Though barely six hours had passed since the incident, no one made mention of it. As the sun began to sink in the west, Orla and Kerrigan came aboard a twenty-five-foot-long fishing boat, with a single sail and a grizzled tillerman. Two people crewed the ship, looking enough like each other and the captain to suggest they were all of a family, and busied themselves casting off lines and trimming the sails. Other refugees, Apprentices mostly in their early teens, huddled beneath blankets, not realizing that the trembling of fear cannot be warmed away.

The little boat made its way easily through the harbor and then out into the Crescent Sea. There the swells grew and bounced the tiny boat around. The wind had continued to blow from the southwest, which had helped speed the fleet to Vilwan. But it made the return trip difficult, forcing the captain to tack back and forth. The boat constantly ran at an angle to the waves, either bobbing strongly while sailing along, or crashing roughly into them as it came about, changing course.

Kerrigan hung on tight to the wales, but still felt as if each dip the boat took would spill him out. And since he was larger than most of the other refugees, and more portly, he could not duck when waves spattered over the sides, so quickly water stung his eyes and left his dark hair pasted to his face. His robes began to stink. He closed his nose against that scent and clenched his jaw.

The up and down motion also wrought havoc with his sense of balance. His stomach roiled, but he'd only eaten breakfast, so nausea remained at bay for a bit. He'd humiliated himself earlier with the flour, and he was determined he'd not vomit. He shook his head to clear it of dizziness, found that did not work well at all, then forced himself to suck in lots of air through his nose and exhale it forcefully. He concentrated on breathing, ignoring everything else.

He'd actually begun to control his stomach when the red-haired Apprentice sitting on his right lunged toward the wales. She might have made it, save that Kerrigan had braced his feet against the deck. She failed to hurdle his thick thighs, so she flopped down face first into his lap, then threw up.

The sour scent caught him as he breathed in. His stomach contracted and he heaved, but nothing came up. His ribs and guts ached as his body heaved again and again, starting him crying. Then a wave crashed over the bow, splashing water into his open mouth, choking him. He expelled it in a wracking wet cough, splattering it all over the Apprentice who had puked on him before she could regain her seat.

The boat continued to rock and bob on into the night, as cold nibbled away at Kerrigan's fingers and toes. He'd not so much become accustomed to the dizziness imparted by the boat's motion as lacked the energy to deal with it. Even his stomach had given up its protests.

Sodden clothes clung to him, as did the girl. Her close-ness frightened him, but not because she stirred lustful thoughts in him. He'd thought about women before, had had dreams about them. In learning elven magicks he'd been instructed in things biological and even sensual, since so much of their magick involved life. It brought with it an intimacy that he had to understand to be able to cast the spells. He'd studied hard, which meant his knowledge vastly outstripped his experience, and feeling her lying be-side him, tucked under his right arm, was certainly the closest and most prolonged contact he'd had with any female.

The idea of sex did not scare him, but the girl's vulnera-bility did. More exactly, the fact that she found sanctuary huddled against him shocked him. Warmth rose from be-tween them, and she made little contented sounds. She felt safe there, and that terrified Kerrigan because he knew he was hardly capable of taking care of himself, much less someone so small and helpless.

The tillerman's voice rose above the snap of the sail. "Belike trouble astern, Magister."

Kerrigan turned just enough to look back without dis-turbing the girl. Orla slowly made her way back toward the stern. In the distance two lights bobbed up and down. One burned a bit above the horizon, while the other appeared nestled in with the stars. Red and blue flashes appeared near the taller light.

Orla crouched near the stern. "Not another ship return-ing to Saporicia?"

"Not one of ours. Tall mast, red and blue, that would be Wruonin." The man shook his head. "Gaining on us, too. Now, if you'd be knowing some magick . . ."

She laughed. "I know a lot of it, but nothing that will speed us up. We can't run from it?"

"Nay. She's got more canvas than us. Running lamps like that, finding us, I'm thinking she's with magickers hav-ing a lend of owl's-eyes for seeing."

Orla nodded. Kerrigan raised his right hand to swipe it across his eyes, preparing to cast the sort of spell the tiller-man was talking about. *If I follow with a hawk's-eye spell, I can see them better, too.* Pushing away the distraction of the slumbering girl, he started to control his breathing again, and summoned the power to cast the spells.

"Kerrigan, no!" Orla's command came in a harsh whisper. "If they do have magickers there, they'll know those spells."

The young man hesitated. He ignored for a moment the question of how she figured out what he was going to do, and instead concentrated on the implications of her explanation. The spells she mentioned were not difficult to cast, but were not easy to learn. Of the people on the boat, doubtless Orla and he were the only ones who could use them. *And if I cast them, then they will know we have mag-ickers on the boat. They might even mistake me for a power-ful mage.*

Orla rubbed a hand over her forehead. "We can't run. We have a boat full of sick children. Any spells we can cast can be countered. We get one shot, one surprise."

"It best be good, Magister."

"It will be, Captain." She turned and pointed. "Kerrigan, my staff."

The young man grabbed it from the deck and twisted it around to bring it up from between the seats. He slid his hands down it, wiping the beaded water off the smooth wood, then extended it to her. She nodded her thanks as she took it from him.

"Captain, what do you think they will do?"

He shrugged. "If they's hunting, they'll be killing. Run over us, rake us with arrows, could be anything. Maybe they're mounting a dragonel." The man's voice rose at that prospect. "Now there would be a way to die."

"I'm hoping we won't die at all. I think I can hurt them, if they get close enough. Be ready to bring us around and run before the wind."

"Hurry, Magister. You may not know spells to be hurrying a ship, but the like ain't true of them."

A reddish glow backlit the entire ship, rendering its three masts and billowing sails in sharp silhouette. Creatures moved on the high forecastle and along the wales. Torches suddenly flared to life, then smaller fires burned. Those little fires arced up into the air and flew toward the boat, but hissed out in the sea.

"Fire arrows, then." The tillerman spat. "They just be killing."

Orla nodded, then prodded the two Apprentices nearest her with the end of her staff. "Move forward. Give me room."

They got up and crawled toward the bench where Kerrigan sat.

The old woman's eyes narrowed. "Two hundred yards?"

The tillerman nodded. "Give or take, and they're taking by the second."

"Right, get ready to run." She grasped her staff at the top with her left hand, halfway down with her right. A bright blue spark glowed at the tip. Orla brought the staff back, then whipped it forward, flicking the spark toward the enemy ship. It drew after it a slender blue tendril, thin as a bit of webbing, yet fairly crackling with power.

The conjured whip lashed the rail. Fire burned brightly where it touched wood. The spark itself snapped against a man's chest, combusting him into a black skeleton that died in a bright burst of white light. Where the tendril cut at rigging, ropes parted, steaming.

Sailors flew to the severed rigging. Some clenched lines for splicing in their teeth. Yet others grabbed both ends of a split line. A reddish glow oozed from their hands and repaired the link, leaving the rigging intact save that some sections had the angry glow of embers burning hot.

Other creatures moved along the rails. Too small to be mistaken for human, the magickal energy arcing green between their hands identified them as vylaens. One raised his hands, then cast them outward. A dozen little darts of green fire raced from him to the smaller boat.

Orla snorted derisively. With a flick of her staff, the tendril coiled into a cone around the darts. They bumped up against its walls, but failed to pierce them. She snapped the cone down, plunging the darts into dark water, where they sank, glowing evilly until the water quenched them.

Still the pirate ship came closer. The tillerman shoved hard on the rudder, swinging the bow around. Waves hammered the little boat, killing its momentum. As it started to come around, and the sails filled again, a flaming arrow pinned the man's hand to the tiller. He screamed and recoiled, but the tiller came with him, causing the boat to turn again and founder. Worse yet, as the spar came around again, it cracked Orla in the back, driving her to the deck.

Arrows flew through the darkness, ripping canvas. The girl in Kerrigan's lap screamed as one hit her above the knee. She rolled to the deck clutching her leg, looking imploringly at him. He bent to help her, fighting furiously to calm himself so he could use the elven magick and heal her, but a wave bucked the ship up and tossed him backward. His legs caught on the bench, upending him. He landed hard and wanted to cry out, but another arrow ripped through the tillerman's throat. As that man slumped over the tiller, clutching at his neck, Kerrigan felt lost.

Panic raced through him. He couldn't do anything. The boat was rocking, people were screaming. *I don't have any of my things, no space to work.* A million reasons why he couldn't do anything assaulted him, but somehow he levered himself to his feet and got his back to the mast. Swiping at the wetness on his face, he set his teeth with determination. *It's up to me, now. I have to do* something!

An arrow quenched its flames in his flesh, skewering his chest and pinning him to the mast. Pain exploded from the wound, searing and hot, sharp-edged and brilliant. Agony twisted through him, shaking him, which started new pain from the wound. He wanted to cough. When he did, he hurt anew, and tasted blood. *My blood.*

Pain, blood, the screams, the ship pounding upward, dragging on the arrow, all of it should have crushed him. There he was, far from home, wet, miserable. The girl who had depended on him lay writhing and mewing beneath a bench that bristled with arrows. Torn pieces of canvas snapped and cracked in the wind, then more arrows thudded into the boat.

Yet, despite all that, he focused on one thing. The vylaens emitted a high, keening laughter that scourged him more than all the laughter on Vilwan. The laughter before had stung badly, but their laughter clawed him and tore him. Somewhere, deep inside, Kerrigan realized they wanted to kill him, and that this laughter was just one more cruel weapon.

Not much more than a child save in one important area, Kerrigan lashed out at the pirate ship, scared and hurt. Though he knew hundreds of spells, a devastating selection of combat spells among them, he hit the ship instead with one spell he knew so very well. He'd used it multiple times, for as long as he could remember. Had he been thinking, he might even have imagined that the vylaens wouldn't have a counter prepared to a noncombat spell like that, but he wasn't thinking.

He just reacted.

Thaumaturgical energy surged from him in an invisible wave that swept out toward its target. It swelled and gathered the ship up into its grasp. He raised his right hand and the ship emerged from the sea. Water ran from the barnacle-encrusted hull in rippling sheets. Twenty feet, forty, higher and higher. Kerrigan snarled, wanting to lift the ship to the moon, then to tighten his hand, crushing it. He wanted to see splintered planks bulge from between invisible fingers, with broken spar fragments whirling through the sky, trailing lines and canvas like flames in their descent.

He knew, however, he did not have the strength to do that. So when—to his eye—the ship eclipsed the moon, he opened his hand and simply let it go.

The ship listed slightly as it fell. Some crewmen flew off while others held tightly to rails and rigging. Some of the splices failed, leaving men thrashing about at the end of lines like the knot at the tip of a whip. Those who could not hang on were flung off, spinning wildly through the air. The sails filled with air, straining masts and spars. The canvas shredded and masts cracked.

Then the ship hit the dark water. The hull had been fashioned to take the pounding of waves even in the fiercest of gales. From the height the ship fell, however, the water might as well have been granite. Timbers buckled and masts snapped like kindling. Deck planks sprang free, spinning up into the air. The ship bobbed up once, then wallowed and bubbled loudly. The canvas sails descended like tattered shrouds over the sinking wreck.

Tagothcha, cloaked in the night-dark, greedily clawed the ship down into his realm.

Hurt, coughing out bloody mist, Kerrigan watched the ship die. He slumped forward, snapping the arrow off somewhere at his back, and landed on his knees on the deck. He smiled at the sinking ship, displaying a mouthful of bloody teeth. He savored his victory for a moment, letting it consume him.

And in the next moment he knew pure dread.

The pirates had their revenge. The huge wave created when the ship crashed into the sea reached up and capsized Kerrigan's little boat.

CHAPTER 26

The grinding pain in Will's shoulders competed with the aching in his back for the part of him that hurt the most. His butt and legs weren't even close to the lead in that contest, so they just contented themselves with burning. The occasional quiver of muscles in his thighs, or the back of his arms, added some contrast, but did nothing to improve the situation.

Yet, as dusk fell on Vilwan, and Will took bucket after bucket of seawater from one Apprentice and passed it up the hill to another, his physical discomfort could only take up residence in the back of his mind. Full-blown fury occupied him, and were he not fatigued to the point of near collapse, he'd have been cursing a streak that would have had the Apprentices around him scurrying for cover. He felt humiliated and shamed—worse yet, confused—and all of that provided tinder for his anger.

The bucket brigade shipped water up the steep face of Vilwan's northern coast. Above the line of Apprentices, a good forty feet above sea level, a crenellated fortress wall gnawed into the darkening blue of the sky. Warriors patrolled the walls, appearing for only a second between merlons. At intervals of twenty yards rose slender towers, with warriors lighting fires at their crests, and Will easily made out the forms of Resolute and Crow atop the nearest.

It had been determined that the pirates would assault the island at the northernmost point, instead of the natural harbor on the eastern shore. The harbor itself had been closed after the evacuation ships had been sent out. While no one discounted a feint at the harbor, the simple fact of the matter was that the taking of the harbor would not guarantee Vilwan's fall.

The island's geography created a valley that ran from the north down toward the southeast, between two ridgelines. While gaps in the two ranges did exist, defending them would not be difficult. The valley provided the only route to the island's heart, where the central town existed. On the way the invaders would have to lay siege to the Magister of Combats' tower, since it choked the valley like a bone in the throat. Still, it lay almost five miles distant from the shore fortress, up a rise that would make taking every inch of it costly. Troops had been stationed at key defensive points all along that route to exact the blood-toll that would break Chytrine's forces.

Not that I will be allowed to make them pay. Fury shook Will. He'd not minded off-loading ships and moving supplies around, since he knew they'd need them for the fight. He could even understand the wizards husbanding their magickal strength for the coming fight. The fact that this made manual labor the order of the day, and enlisted him as a laborer, he could accept. He even understood when many of the younger Apprentices and other folks were evacuated from the island, despite the fact that their departure increased his workload.

What he hated, though, was being relegated to the status of a noncombatant. Resolute had made that decision, and had refused to listen to any of Will's arguments as to why it was wrong. When he tried to appeal to Crow, the man had just shrugged. He explained that while it was indeed true that Will had acquitted himself admirably in the various skirmishes they'd fought over the last month, each of those battles had been against small, poorly organized forces.

It didn't take a Grand Magister to figure out that the fighting would be nasty. The very idea of mounting an invasion of Vilwan seemed insane, but Will didn't doubt there was some sort of logic behind the action. One of the more effective distractions that could be used in cutting purses was to act insane. While the victim did his best to figure out why a person was mad, or just to get away, they lay vulnerable.

That hardly mattered to Will, however, because his life on the streets had taught him more than just that lesson. When in a fight, he'd learned, there was no holding back. You went out and did as much damage as you could to the enemy. And the way he saw it, the more men on the line, the more damage could be done. He wanted to be one of those men.

An Adept down at the waterline shouted something that Will couldn't quite understand. The Apprentices nearest the water stepped out of line and began hauling sloshing buckets of water directly up the way. The Adept waved them on, so Will joined the others. He carried his last bucket up, mildly annoyed that the recall happened right before it was time for his line to trade position with the guys in the empty bucket line at his back.

The ascent, though fairly short, was not easy. The rocky shoreline rose sharply over wave-smoothed stone that was very slippery when wet. It didn't offer much in the way of cover for troops advancing up it, and the only logical paths narrowed to a couple of choke points. A lot of blood would flow in those places, and as long as there were defenders able to load ballistae and other siege machines, the attackers would be hard-pressed to gain anything approaching a foothold.

Up at the top of the hill, Will emptied his bucket into

the cistern. He tossed the bucket onto the cart where others were piling theirs, then he located the little nook where he'd put his belt with his longknife and bladestar pouch. He buckled the belt on, inched the longknife into place over his left hip, then looked toward the tower where he'd seen Resolute and Crow.

With a creak and a clank, a man eclipsed his view of the tower. "You're Will?"

The youth nodded and tried not to stare. "That's me."

"I've been sent to show you your place. Follow me."

The man turned away and started walking off away from the tower. Will wanted to protest, but the man—*no, he's a* meckanshii—held such utter fascination for him that he couldn't help but drift in his wake. The man's left leg, from mid-thigh down, had been replaced by metal posts and gears. Wires and tattered bits of ringmail hung about it like lace. His left hand and forearm had likewise been replaced with an articulated claw that had two fingers and a thumb. Over the arm and thigh, and even on up to the shoulder, mail had been grafted onto his flesh.

Will had long heard of *meckanshii* but had not seen them before. A company of them had arrived from Fortress Draconis late in the night, landing on the north shore. How Dothan Cavarre, the Draconis Baron, had known to send them no one could even begin to guess, but they had been welcomed. From what little conversation he'd heard repeated, most of the *meckanshii* viewed their defense of Vilwan as a defense of their homeland, though none of them had actually come from there.

The man glanced back over his shoulder at Will. "Come on, boy, I'm not limping too fast for you, am I?"

Will shook his head and caught up quickly. "I never . . ."

"I can tell by the gawk." The man sighed. "It's this way, Will. I was a miller's son in Gurol. About your age, maybe a bit older, I fell into the stream, lost my arm and leg to the wheel. No elves around to fix me, so my family sold me to the Draconis Baron."

"Sold you?"

"Stipend, for my services. They knew I wasn't coming back. I wasn't good but for begging, so they took the gold. I wanted to go. Up there, at the fortress, the Draconis Baron had all sorts of magickers—elves, men, urZrethi—working on us. The last time Chytrine tried to take the place, she used a spell that reversed the healing of the wounded. Well, each of us is crafted individually. One spell won't take us down. She'd have to know us each to undo the magicks."

Will blinked his grey eyes. "Can you feel with those things?"

"A sense of where they are, yes, but hot and cold, soft, no." He shrugged. "The magick helps me keep my balance, but we all train a lot. Not very quiet, so we're not good at sneaking, but in a standing fight, we do just fine. Name's Gerhard."

"Will, but you know that."

"That's a fact." Gerhard led the way down a broad stairway that switched back and forth, and across a courtyard to a thick, squat building with narrow windows. A stout bit of wall came out and around at a right angle to shield the north-facing doorway. They passed through into a round foyer about twelve feet in diameter, then up a narrow stairway that opened into a large room. To the right and left more stairways led upward.

A blond Adept waited at the top of the stairs. "Thank you, Captain."

"My pleasure." The *meckanshii* gave Will a curt nod. "You'll be here with Adept Jarmy."

"I want to be out on the line."

"I'm sure you do, son." Gerhard brought his left arm up, slowly opened his claw and then snapped it shut. "Everything in its time, everyone in their place. Your place is here. Keep him safe, Jarmy."

Will watched the soldier leave, then turned to face the Adept. He dimly recognized him. "So, have a broom for me to do some sweeping up?"

The Adept's brown eyes narrowed for a moment, then he nodded. "Oh, yes, yesterday, at the docks. No, nothing like that. Come with me."

Will followed up the stairs, past one floor to the uppermost level. They walked south along a corridor, then turned right into a room with a low ceiling. A long slit, akin to an arrow port but running parallel to the floor, had been carved in the north wall. They moved to it and through it Will could see the fortress wall, the moon-washed ocean, and a bobbing legion of lights marking the incoming fleet.

Will swallowed hard. "That's a lot of ships."

"It is, and not even all the ships Chytrine has."

"What do you mean?"

Jarmy's jaw muscles bunched. "Some ships have made it to Sanges. The pirates were out among them, destroying boats. They were making war on children, so there will be no quarter given here."

"How many were lost?"

"We don't know. Too many." Jarmy pointed to the north. "It is starting."

Will frowned. "And we wait here?"

"Until it is time, yes." The Adept looked down at Will. "They might not need us."

"And if they do?"

"We will stop them." The Adept turned his face to the north and Will leaned forward against the stone. Out there, in the darkness, he could make out little, but things soon resolved themselves in stark detail.

One ship had turned itself to parallel the fortress. Before Will could even begin to wonder why it would do that, three gouts of flame erupted from each of the fore and aft decks. A heartbeat later a volley of thunder shook him. Down below, at the wall, a projectile hit a merlon and shattered the stone like glass. The soldiers who had been standing near it simply disappeared, while others went down, writhing, torn by stone fragments.

Another projectile missed the wall, but slammed down

into the catwalk beyond it. The stone skipped off it, leaving a small crater, then bounced down through the courtyard. It clipped a running man, tearing away his right leg, then vanished from Will's sight. The remaining shots hit the fortress wall, spilling people to the ground, but not killing them.

"What was . . . ?"

"Dragonels, a half dozen of them." Jarmy patted the wall. "The Draconis Baron might be stingy with information, but the people we've had there creating *meckanshii* have been observant. The dragonels could take down a tall tower, but short and squat like this will slow them down."

From within the fleet came a dozen long, low ships, bristling with oars. Even at a distance the voices of the oarmasters rang out, exhorting the people to pull hard. The galleys surged forward in a staggered line. Waves slapped hard against their curiously flattened bows. Will didn't know much about ships, but they hardly looked seaworthy. *Good thing they don't have far to go.*

A shouted command from below resulted in a handful of trebuchets launching their cargoes high in the air. Several projectiles burned and one of those shooting-stars slammed into the aft of a galley. The wooden barrel burst, gushing *napthalm* all over the aft deck and down into the oarwells. Men screamed and flailed, some diving over the sides, others just collapsing. The helmsman likewise burned, allowing the stricken ship to drift off course as he went over the side.

It smashed into another galley, coming in at an angle that sheered off oars. Worse yet, the oars slammed hard into the bellies and backs of the rowers, shattering ribs and crushing spines. More screams arose from the two stricken ships. One ran aground on a hidden shoal while the other one, burning merrily, infected its foundering sister with fire.

Still the others came on, and a second wave behind them. As the first of the galleys hit the shoreline, their prows rode up over the stone and caught. As hard and fast as they'd hit, Will guessed it would take forever to get them free. About that time it occurred to him that they were never meant to float again.

The flattened bow on each of the galleys exploded outward on a jet of sorcerous green flame. Warriors—men and gibberers—poured out of the holds, yipping and howling as they scrambled up the stone. More *napthalm* barrels exploded, washing stone with fire, or catching the beached galleys. Sailors boiled out of the ships, seeking safety.

But safety wasn't to be had. Archers came up from the fortress' courtyard, nocked and drew. A rain of arrows sped through the night. Cloth-yard shafts crossed through targets silhouetted against the burning ships. One man, stuck through the shoulder with an arrow, defiantly snapped it off. As he raised the broken shaft triumphantly, a half-dozen more arrows studded his body and dropped him to the ground.

The dragonels roared again from the ship, crushing stone and scattering soldiers on the battlements. A small portion of the wall crumbled, opening a bit of gap toward the center. It occurred too far to the west to be of much practical use for the invaders, but it showed the power of dragonels.

More galleys drove themselves onto the beaches, and men emerged from them carrying large shields that they fastened together into mantlets. Arrows bristled from them as they advanced. A barrel of *napthalm* exploded near one, igniting it, and a hurled stone smashed another flat on the men carrying it. More appeared and more approached, getting positioned where they could ward vulnerable points on the ascent.

Will watched with fascination and horror, but shook his head. "It doesn't matter, does it? They still can't get up the wall. There are too many defenders."

Jarmy nodded. "That's my thinking. She's got nothing to counter the archers save the dragonels, and they're concentrating on bringing the wall down. So, unless she has something else up her sleeve . . ."

"Troops with draconettes?"

The Adept shook his head. "Not accurate enough."

"What then?"

"I don't . . . Oh, no, by the gods." Jarmy pointed toward the sky. "There, by the moon."

Will looked up and felt his stomach tug tightly into a knot.

A dragon drifted across the face of the moon, trapping itself there like an image struck on a coin. One wing came up, the other dipped, and it descended like a hawk stooping on prey. Two little jets of flame trailed back from its nostrils, flashing brilliantly from gold scales, and caressing reddish black eyes. It swooped low over the wall, and at the point the invaders could reach most easily, it let loose with an inferno.

CHAPTER 27

The liquid *napthalm* fire flowed, but the dragonfire *hunted*. Tongues licked stone merlons into vapor. It curled like ivy around a wall tower, then tightened, and molten rock gushed like juice from pulped fruit. Red-gold flames lapped at men, melting skin from bones, then devouring blackened skeletons. One *meckanshii* who had been metal from the waist down glowed red, then white, before his lower limbs evaporated. He breathed in fire, which silenced his screams, though many other throats gave voice to them, including Will's own horrified gasp.

The afflicted section of the wall sloughed and sagged to the level of the cliffsides. What had made Vilwan unassailable bare moments before now had a gap that could not be plugged. Heat radiated up from the fluid stone, but quickly enough a black crust hardened over it. The powerful sweep of the dragon's wing sent a gust to cool it, and buffeted back the first of the defenders to reach the gap.

The dragon soared into the air with fiery gold glinting from its scales. It twisted and rolled through the night sky.

The motion corkscrewed through its tail, snapping the last of the energy out through a flick of its pointed tip. It let playful gusts of fire jet from its nostrils.

Will looked at Jarmy. "Do something!"

The human mage shivered. "I could live to a thousand years and could do nothing against that."

Out in the night, on the wall, Will picked out Crow's silhouette on top of a tower. And moving toward the breach, there was no mistaking Resolute and Dranae beside him. Beyond the breach, the first of the gibberers showed up. They did not so much as hesitate, despite the howls of the first to step on smoking rock.

"Then all the dragon has to do is come back, sweep the walls . . ." Will's stomach doubled back in on itself. *They're gone, my friends are gone.*

"Not that fast, Will." Jarmy's eyes hardened. "That dragon's a bit young and flew here. That blast of fire tired it. More mature, better rested, what you fear would be true."

"So we do nothing?"

The combat Adept looked down at him. "One rule of warfare, Will. The side that commits its reserves last wins. That time is not yet come."

And our reinforcements are powerless against her reinforcements, young and tired or not. Will wrapped his left fist around the hilt of his longknife. "I have to go out there."

"So anxious to die?"

"Anxious to kill, to help my friends."

Jarmy rested a hand on Will's left shoulder. "Your chance will come."

The dragonels boomed again. Some shots slammed into the walls, shaking them. Others had shifted from using a single heavy iron ball to a flight of smaller balls. They ricocheted within the fortress, with one clicking sharply off the stone near Will. Blasting through bodies seemed to spend their momentum, but not quickly, leaving ranks decimated and black blood spilled on the courtyard.

Resolute and Dranae had moved to the breach, flanked

by men and *meckanshii*. The Vorquelf's twin blades flashed silver in moonlight, then became washed in ebony as his attacks punctured and slit. He'd moved far enough into the breach that his boots smoked, and the gibberers who fought him fell with their blood boiling on smooth rock.

Dranae had been given a mail surcoat that hung to his knees like a skirt. In the fight he wielded a warhammer, with its flat head on one side, and a wickedly curved claw on the other. A stout two-handed blow with the thing drove gibberers to the ground, then the claw would punch through armor or skulls. Even the steel butt-cap on the end of the haft proved deadly as he flicked it out, crushing a throat.

Despite their heroic effort, and the cadres of archers shooting from above the gap, inch by inch the defenders were driven back. More boats landed, disgorging legions of gibberers. Shots from dragonels raked the walls, cutting huge swathes through archers. Other shots caromed around in the courtyard killing ballistae crew and shattering at least one barrel of *napthalm*. It caught fire and quickly ignited the siege machine onto which it had been mounted. The rope restraining it burned through, launching the leaking barrel and painting a stripe of fire across the courtyard and wall.

Above it all, the dragon cavorted lazily, swooping back and forth. Then, as Crow hefted and hurled a barrel of *napthalm* into the breach and the torch that followed it started a blaze, the dragon ceased its play. It glided down low, causing all but Resolute and Dranae to duck. The grand beast came up at the end of the descent and over in a loop, then beat once with its wings and came back to clear the gap.

An earsplitting shriek sliced through the din of battle, drowning out even the dragonels' thunder. The golden dragon twisted upward, but a black shadow hit it hard from above. The gold dragon slammed into the ground—hard, very hard—making Will grab for the wall to stop himself from falling as the earth quaked from the impact. The shadow launched itself upward, its angry shriek becoming a triumphant bellow.

The gold dragon came to its feet beyond the gap and shook itself as a wet dog might. Mashed gibberer parts sprayed off it, while wet stains streaked its sides. It answered with a challenge of its own, then beat its wings once to soar above the walls.

As it rose past the walls, Will got his first sense of its true scale. For a split second he saw a man disappear into the black slit that was the creature's pupil as the beast flew into the sky. Gold scales the size of the shields warriors bore covered it, and its paws were as long as a dray wagon, horse-hitch and all included. On the downstroke the tip of the right wing hit an archer on the wall, breaking him as if he were some child's toy made of dry twigs.

From nose to tail the creature dwarfed the largest of the ships on the sea, yet the dragon it rose to fight was larger still. Covered in midnight scales save where curved scarlet stripes curled up from its belly, the second dragon had a greater bulk. Not fat, just muscular, as Dranae was in comparison to Crow. *Massive and powerful, very powerful.* Despite its greater size, it twisted out of the gold dragon's reach as the smaller creature rose. Then, with a quick strike, the black dragon nipped at the gold's left haunch, tearing a dark wound on its hip.

The gold dragon shrieked yet again and rolled through the air. It dove, twisting, then tried to level into a glide. A wingtip slashed through the rigging on a Wruonan ship. The dragon wrenched its body around to free the wing, but that smashed its tail through the ship's sides with a great snapping of timbers. The ship twisted awry, the aft going one way, the forecastle dipping toward the dark sea.

Beyond it, the dragon's tail dragged like an anchor through the water. The golden beast contorted itself and tried to roll onto its back to free its tail. It succeeded, but at the cost of enough speed that it could no longer fly. It splashed down heavily, crushing one ship beneath it, and sent out a wave that lifted some ships and swamped others.

The wave reached the shore, boosting grounded galleys higher up, then clawing away the dead on its return to the sea. Still other galleys raced forward, beaching themselves. At least one came down on the shoal that had snared others, snapping the keel and spilling its contents into the angry water.

From Crow's tower there arose a blue fireball that streaked high into the sky. Jarmy stripped his robe down to his waist and knotted sleeves around his waist. "Now, Will. Now is our time."

As Jarmy accepted a blackened staff worked with runes and sigils from another wizard, yet a third stepped to the wall and pressed his hand to it. A bluish light flowed through the mage's flesh and into the stone, tracing every seam and line throughout that small section of wall. A chill ran through the air, then the wall exploded outward. The various blocks in it arched out and hung in the air in pairs, with ten feet of nothing but a nearly transparent rainbow light between them. Other similar bridges—some tall arches, and others serpentine courses—connected the fortress to the walls elsewhere.

Before Will could ask what had happened, Jarmy and a half-dozen other Adepts dashed out onto the rainbow bridge. Most had arrayed themselves for battle as Jarmy had—including one dusky-skinned woman. Their staves began to glow with an internal light that shifted from blue to a white so bright it hurt Will's eyes. Only the symbols incised into the staves did not lose their nigrescent color and Will shivered as he recognized some of them from the tattoos on Resolute's flesh.

From one mage's staff sprang dark green creatures that appeared to be nothing but a sharp-toothed mouth with two spindly, claw-capped arms for moving its spherical body around. They bounced from the walls as had the dragonel's projectiles, then fell to devouring gibberers.

Other mages sped fireballs into the milling mass of invaders. The sorcerous missiles burned swathes through the invaders until some vylaen countered that spell. Still other of the mages dueled with vylaens, snuffing their spells and quickly fighting back with others.

Jarmy moved from the head of the bridge and leaped down into the gap at Resolute's left. He whirled his staff as might a stickfighter, then let it graze the stone around him. Where the staff touched, blue flames guttered, describing a circle he clearly intended to hold free of gibberers. His challenge did not go unanswered. The staff spun with supernatural speed that let the blunt wooden rod slice through limbs as if it were honed to a razor's edge, or smash skulls with the weight of a sledge.

The Adept who had created the bridge looked at Will. "Go now, or remain here. I can hold this only so long."

Will nodded, then streaked out onto the bridge. He sprinted as fast as he could along it, for with each footfall it seemed to sag a little. Nearing the wall, he leaped the last ten feet. As he soared through the air, he saw the last of the blocks fall away and his illuminated path vanish.

He landed on both feet, but skidded and went down on blood-slicked rock. He slid to the wall and huddled there with his back to the stone. The dragonels boomed, their light flashing over the fortress' seamless face. The impact of a ball against the wall pitched Will onto his face. Smaller balls clattered off the walls and a man fell thrashing in front of Will, half his skull missing and leaking brains.

The thief scrambled back away from the corpse, but before he hit the wall again, a hand closed on his tunic and dragged him to his feet. Crow pulled the youth back to the shelter of the tower. "You shouldn't be here, Will."

"But Jarmy said . . ."

The way the flesh puckered at Crow's scarred cheek hardened his expression. "Come on, up to the top."

"But I want to fight . . ."

"You can help in other ways."

Crow gave him a shove up forward, so Will ascended the tight, circular staircase on hands and feet like a dog. He rose through the trapdoor, then involuntarily ducked down as the dragonels roared once more. A tremor ran through the rock and Will found himself face to face with a woman whose leathery skin had only begun to show her age.

"I'm Will."

"You're willful, to say the least."

She rose and Will did as well. He peered out from between merlons at the long, thick line of invaders snaking its way up the cliff face. From his previous vantage point he could only see some of the landing area and realized only now that Chytrine had brought in far more in the way of troops than he had previously imagined. Greenish fire sparked here and there, marking the locations of vylaens. They traded spells with Vilwanese defenders and, more often than not, the gibberers around them would fall to arrows the archers shot at the vylaens.

Out on the dragonel ship, oars started appearing and a crew worked a winch to pull up the fore anchor. "Crow, they're going to move the ship."

The white-haired man nodded. "Bring it around to shoot at the gap."

"Can we do anything to stop them? Magick? Something?"

The sorceress snorted. "I'll give you a dagger if you want to swim out and hole the hull."

Will frowned. "Can you just magick it?"

"Watch." She gestured dismissively at the ship with her left hand, launching a blue spark that shot in toward it. When it neared the ship, it hit something that shimmered. Color bled through it, at first blue, then slowly fading into green. As nearly as Will could see, some sort of bowl covered the ship.

"You can't get a spell through?"

"That's just the outer layer of many, I suspect. I *could* get through, it would just take a lot of time." A snarl lit her features as she cast a spell with her right hand that lanced blue fire through the chest of a vylaen. "The enchantments Chytrine has worked on that ship are as tough to break as are those animating the *meckanshii*."

Will nodded thoughtfully, as if that meant something to him, then deepened his scowl. "If we don't do something, the dragonels will clear that breach."

"Which is why you're here and not down there." Crow nocked an arrow and drew. He let fly and a gibberer folded around an arrow through his belly.

"Can't you shoot a fire arrow at it?"

"It's out of my range, as well as that of our ballistae."

Another blast from the dragonels clattered shot off the walls. A few men went down, but others had taken to ducking when the dragonels' light flashed, allowing them a chance to find cover. This set of shots swept closer to the gap. The next would certainly be able to shred the defenses and while many gibberers would die at the same time, more than enough were set to pour up the beach and flood through into the fortress.

They will die. Though Resolute, Dranae, and Jarmy were holding their own, even their most heroic effort would not protect them against the dragonels' devastating power. *They will die well, and so we will sell our lives soon after.*

The black dragon eclipsed the moon and sailed past the dragonel ship with the casual ease of a seagull drifting above a fishing boat. Wings outstretched and sweeping stars up like nets, its tail out and shifting to steer, the dragon did a lazy circle around the Aurolani ship. It dipped its head toward the ship and up from the deck came a quick lance of green fire. The magickal strike splashed over the creature's right forepaw, trickling verdant lightning along scale edges and sparking off the tip of a long claw.

If the sorcerous bolt hurt the dragon, it gave no sign. The black did pull its head back up, then canted it to study the ship again with its right eye. The dragon's head jerked up and down three times, and at the end of the third, it spat out a roiling ball of golden fire.

The ball fell through the sky like a fiery comet, then hit the bowl protecting the ship. The fire spread slowly, like honey poured over a dumpling, dripping down the sides. The fierce light from dragon's fire brought a premature dawn to the north coast of Vilwan, yet Will got no warmth from it at all.

As the fire flowed down to the water and raised steam, the bowl shuddered and contracted. Black splotches appeared on the bowl and fire flowed around and drained through them. Suddenly the fire geysered back out through those holes, then the bowl evaporated as a thunderclap tightened the water and battered the island. Debris, some flaming fragments, other dark bits of things unidentifiable, stippled the water, holed other ships, and bounced from the cliffs.

All that was left of the dragonel ship was a smoking hole in the water that closed fast in a wash of froth and flotsam.

The circle of debris sprayed out far enough to carve into some of the gibberers, but left the bulk of them alone. The black dragon swooped low, but spat no fire. Will hoped it might snatch a clawful in passing, but it did not do that, either. Instead it continued out and away from Vilwan, dipping low enough only to snatch the downed gold from the water and haul Chytrine's dragon away in its claws. The gold protested, but another nip quieted it.

The departure of the black might have heartened the invaders, but not nearly as much as the loss of the dragonel ship breathed new hope into the defenders. Men who had cowered beneath the walls now rose, shooting arrows, casting stones or spells down on the horde. Combat Adepts plied spells that raked magickal fire over the Aurolani forces toward the rear. While vylaens might use magick to douse the flames, singed fur still stunk, burned flesh still blistered, and the screams of half-broiled gibberers inspired fear in their comrades.

The horde fragmented. The back ranks fled to their galleys and streamed over them like ants over rotten fruit. From the courtyard arced more barrels of *napthalm*. Stones flew, clicking and clacking their way down the cliffside. More spells split mantlets or loosed demons that lashed out with unbridled ferocity.

At the gap *meckanshii* surged forward, driving a wedge deep into the gibberer front. The close quarters meant no one had space to swing a weapon effectively, but the *meckanshii* were as much weapon as they were human. Mechanical hands closed over faces and crushed muzzles. Sharpened metal claws stroked throats and pierced chests. Gibberer blows that would have flayed flesh or lopped off limbs clanged from metal, leaving the *meckanshii* unhurt.

At the water, gibberers cast away weapons and stripped off armor. Will had no idea if they could swim or not, but plenty made the attempt. Their hope lay in the galleys that had towed the landing craft behind them, but the Wruonin captains of those vessels seemed ready to weigh anchor and pull for their distant home. Between the gibberers and these ships, dark shapes coursed through the water. Will knew what lay beneath the triangular fins splitting the waves.

The *meckanshii* and other warriors drove the gibberers back to the cliff's edge. Ranks toppled backward, some of them rolling downhill and cutting down others of the horde. The stalwarts in the front lines fought as hard as they could, but the implacable *meckanshii* would not be denied. The last of the gibberers died at the top of the hill, leaving the Vilwanese and their allies in sole possession of the heights.

From the tower top, Will watched the remainder retreat to the sea. At least one vylaen survived long enough to magick a galley off the shore. Gibberers swam to it hurriedly, undaunted by a cask of *napthalm* exploding at the shore and coating the water. Other shots missed the ship, allowing the defenders to watch a comedy of tangling oars as the boat bumped its way through burning hulks. Somehow it did get going north and started crashing its way through waves with its blunt prow.

From the gate, a blue jet of flame stabbed into the night. It resolved itself into something resembling a crossbow quarrel. It moved slowly but heavily through the dark, kissing shark-gnawed corpses with cold light as they bobbed in the water. Finally it arced down and in at the base of the ship's forecastle. Decking burned for a moment, then the ship went nose down. The helmsman spilled from the wheeldeck and gibberers clung screaming to oars as the aft came up and the black waters greedily sucked the ship down.

Will glanced at the gap and saw Jarmy standing there. His staff, still glowing white-hot, pointed toward the sinking galley. His shot had clearly blown open the landing hatch, letting the sea pour in. *But why?*

Then Will remembered. The pirates had slain some of those who had been fleeing Vilwan. *He said no quarter given, but that was just murder.*

Looking around at the bodies in the water, sliding down hills, and hearing the cacophony of the wounded pleading for succor or death, Will got his first glimpse of the future. *Her attack here was insane, and failed horribly. Launching it made no sense.*

He shook his head. Senseless or not, her attack left people broken and bleeding and dead. He clearly understood why Crow opposed her and would always oppose her. That he should want to do the same struck him as right, but the slaughter told him that was madness.

He hoped, when tested, he would have the strength to make one choice or at least the luck to avoid sinking into the other.

CHAPTER 28

The pain attendant to a cough brought Kerrigan to consciousness, but the sharp stab of a finger in his chest is what snapped his eyes open. He looked up into a broad bestial face with pebbled flesh of a mottled green-brown. The tall ears had tufts of black hair on them, and a shock of black hair covered the crest of the creature's head. Its dark eyes widened in surprise, as did Kerrigan's eyes. The magicker screamed and the creature jumped back.

The scream made Kerrigan cough again, which sent pain shooting through him. He rolled onto his right side, clawing weakly at the sand with his left hand. His robes were soaked, and the dawning sun had not yet risen high enough to have dried them. He coughed yet again and spat, but only saw a little blood on the sand.

The creature that had awakened him leaped over him, landed, and turned, spraying sand around with its thick tail. It squatted on its haunches, with clawed hands on its knees, and canted its head to the side to study him. Then another of them joined the first, and a third—with the last two looking slightly smaller and hiding behind the squatting one.

Kerrigan's mind raced. He recognized the creatures from his studies, and this made his heart sink. The Panqui were known for being savage and cruel. He would have tended to discount the stories he'd read of them, but every so often a ship bound for Vilwan fell prey to Panqui pirates.

The pain in his chest drew him back to the battle against Chytrine's pirates. A piece of the arrow still remained in him, with about an inch of it tenting his robe. He recalled having smashed the pirate ship, but after that, after the black wave of cold water had overturned the boat, he had no memory. He glanced back along the beach, and past the Panqui, but saw no other bodies and scant little flotsam and jetsam.

Orla, dead. The girl, dead, all of them, dead because of me. He hammered a fist against the sand. Any of a hundred spells could have destroyed the pirate ship without raising a ripple in the water. Properly employed, the spell he'd used to destroy the pirates could have boosted his boat out of the archers' range. He could have shielded them against arrows and magick.

But he had not. *I killed them. I killed them all.*

The Panqui approached on knuckles and short bandy legs. It sniffed, then reached out a finger and poked Kerrigan's ankle. The Adept drew his foot back. He tried to scoot backward, but had the success of a beached whale at gracefully shifting his bulk.

The other two Panqui started hooting, then moved out and around away from their protector. They darted in at Kerrigan, slapping at his thighs and head. He ducked one blow, then snarled as an openhanded slap smacked his left thigh. He rolled onto his back, then a cuff caught him across the head.

The smaller Panqui grabbed his arms as he raised them to protect his head. They hauled him to his feet and spun him around. The world swam, so Kerrigan staggered.

Another cuff over his right ear drove him higher onto the beach, into drier sand, then another spun him around and sent him back toward the sea.

The larger Panqui moved in and bellowed at Kerrigan. The magicker yelped and retreated. One of the others shoved him hard. Kerrigan stumbled and went to one knee, then a kick in his back drove him onto his face. He tasted sand, felt it grit in his eyes, then coughed yet again, spitting out bright red blood.

That made the Panqui hoot and holler louder. Their shrieks rose to a panic pitch, as a grunting built, then exploded into a furious roar. The ground shook as something landed before him, scattering the three Panqui. The two smallest screeched and scrambled into the water. The larger one backed away, barking angrily.

A growl answered him.

Kerrigan blinked his eyes, letting tears wash the sand from them, and looked up. A fourth Panqui towered over him, easily half again as heavy as the smaller ones, and a head taller than the larger. Whereas their scaled flesh had been pea-green, his had a deep evergreen hue, with faint spots of dark brown and black dappling bony plates. Silver stripes worked down the bony-armor scales on his spine and tail, and the occasional silver hair appeared on his ears and head. The creature glanced down at Kerrigan and the human read no compassion in the Panqui's dark eyes.

The first Panqui bellowed a challenge and charged. The larger one answered and rushed forward. The smaller one aborted its charge and started to turn when the larger swatted it, spinning it down into the sand. The first Panqui rolled and came up to its feet unsteadily, then flopped onto its back, with its thick tail coming up between its legs to curl over its genitalia and stomach.

The largest stood over it and screamed. It sprayed sand over the downed creature, dumping it in handfuls, kicking it, and sweeping it along with its tail. The smaller Panqui mewed helplessly and curled into a ball, hugging its head with its hands.

Kerrigan levered himself up and got his knees under him. He did his best to suppress a cough, but it squirted out of his mouth. Bloody spit dribbled down his chin and he smeared it into a sandy red paste with the back of his hand. His breath came short and laced with pain.

The youth had no idea when his savior would turn his attention back to him, but he entertained no illusions about how quickly the Panqui would dispatch him. His only chance for survival lay in being able to use magick to defeat the beast, but with a piece of wood in his chest and his lung bleeding, he couldn't concentrate enough to cast the battery of spells needed to save himself.

He raised his right hand to the piece of arrow and tried to poke the broken end back through the hole in his robe. He couldn't quite get it, and even the slightest pressure on the stick caused enough pain to make him gasp. He closed his eyes to concentrate, then something shut the sun out. He opened his eyes to find the big Panqui seated there before him.

Without ceremony, the creature reached out, grabbed the robe, and ripped it open. The Panqui's nostrils flared as it sniffed, then closed again. "Woundsour."

Kerrigan's jaw dropped open. "What?"

"Woundsour. You die." The Panqui settled back on its haunches. "No life woundsour."

"Not true." The youth winced as he tried to get a good grip on the arrow fragment. Part of him wondered what he thought he was doing, since he knew he had neither the courage nor the strength to pull it free. He could barely get his thumb and two fingers on it. If he cast a spell to pull it free—the same spell he'd used to destroy the ship would do nicely—he didn't think he'd have the strength he needed to heal himself. *But I do this or I die.*

The two smallest Panqui emerged from the water and

clung to each other, tittering. The largest snarled at them, then looked to Kerrigan again. "Stick gone, woundsour remain."

"It has to go." Kerrigan started to tug on it, then moaned and his fingers slipped off bloody.

The Panqui regarded him closely, then leaned forward. His right paw fell heavily on Kerrigan's shoulder, holding it rigidly in place. The Panqui's left hand came up and its left thumb and forefinger slid along the shaft. Pure agony ignited in Kerrigan's shoulder as the Panqui pressed the skin back, exposing more of the shaft. The creature grasped it firmly and then, with a little twist, ripped it free.

Kerrigan shrieked and hunched as far forward as he could. Sobs shook him and tears poured down his face. He gulped in air, then coughed it back out. His pain and terror redoubled as bloody bubbles accompanying a hiss burst from his shoulder. Pus and blood dribbled down over his chubby breast. He opened his mouth in a wordless cry, his lower lip quivering, then found himself shoved roughly back.

The Panqui towered over him. "Soulsour."

The abruptness of the shove shocked Kerrigan. He sniffed and wiped his nose on a sleeve. "What?"

"Woundsour, you die. Soulsour, you dead." The Panqui snorted dismissively. "Not worth Lombo's time."

The Panqui sat back down, then turned his face away, showing Kerrigan his strong profile and jutting muzzle.

"No?" The mage struggled back to his knees. "Watch, Lombo."

Kerrigan cleaned his right hand off on his thigh, then pressed it to the wound. The hole in him ached and bubbles broke against his palm. He forced himself to press hard, and bit back a gasp at the pain. Breathing in through his nose as deeply as he could, Kerrigan closed his eyes and ordered his mind. He took the jagged edges of the pain and smoothed them into the flowing twists of an elven healing spell, sucking more and more pain into it to power it.

The spell cast did as it was supposed to do and sped healing. In doing so it exacted a price, and that price was Kerrigan's feeling every bit of pain and discomfort he would have if the wound had healed normally. Months of agony condensed into ten seconds, then twenty. A half a minute passed with the pain getting stronger and more intense, but Kerrigan held steady. He dug his nails into his shoulder to keep his hand in place even though it felt as if a red-hot iron shaft was being thrust into his shoulder to burn the wound clean.

A minute and the pain still built. He ground his teeth together against it. His body shook and he wanted to vomit, but he kept that in, too. Another heartbeat and another. Sweat burned into his eyes and seeped salty into his mouth. He lifted his head and snarled, but refused to cry out.

Then the pain broke so sharply Kerrigan was certain he must have heard it snap. He opened his eyes, then peeled his hand away from his shoulder and found unblemished skin there, all pink and healthy. He breathed quickly, but painlessly, his chest heaving. He brought his right foot out first, then his left, and staggered to his feet somehow.

He looked down at Lombo. "Woundsour no more."

The Panqui looked at him, then sniffed. "Man have elf magick?"

Kerrigan nodded confidently. "I do."

Lombo exploded from the ground and hit Kerrigan with a flying tackle that folded the youth over his right shoulder. Kerrigan would have screamed if he could have, but the blow drove the wind from his lungs. Before he could say anything or do anything, the Panqui had scampered up the beach, along the trunk of a fallen tree, and into the branches thirty feet above the ground. They raced along one branch, then Kerrigan's stomach lurched as the Panqui leaped out, through the air.

Another branch and lots of foliage slowed their fall, then they swung up and around. Branches creaked and groaned as the Panqui moved through the trees. The creature's tail didn't grasp tree limbs, but Kerrigan got ample view of it swishing this way and that, counterbalancing them as they flew between trees.

Kerrigan had no idea how far they had traveled, or in what direction, when Lombo dropped from a tree into a clearing. Sturdy structures built of logs and thatched with woven branches formed a square. The long buildings had open sides, but the eaves hung low enough that most rain would be kept out. Groups of Panqui moved within the buildings, and some children chased around in the dust between them, teasing a dog that had been tied to one corner pillar. Several Panqui lounged in woven hammocks, using their tails to impart a gentle swing.

Lombo peeled Kerrigan off his shoulder, then spun the youth around and drag-marched him over to one of the buildings. In a hammock there lay an older Panqui—Kerrigan made that assessment based on the increased amount of silver striping the creature, and the pure white of its head hair and ear tufts. Several other Panqui attended it. Kerrigan adjudged them to be female because of their pendulous breasts.

Lombo squatted near the hammock and peeled a wet bit of cloth off the elder's right shin. A mass of mashed roots and herbs had been tucked into a wound, but beneath it Kerrigan could see the broken ends of a bone sticking up through the skin. The moment the cloth came off the youth caught the pungent scent of decay.

"Woundsour bad." Lombo flattened his nostrils. "Elf magick."

"I don't know." Kerrigan glanced around and began to shiver. "I have worked it on me and on others, but humans or elves. I've never done a Panqui before."

"You have to do it, Adept Reese." The voice came from deeper within the longhouse and was accompanied by the rustle of chains. "I did what I could, but it was not enough."

Kerrigan peered into the shadows. A haggard and

grey-faced Orla leaned back against a post. A metal collar had been fitted around her neck. Nestled in her lap was the red-haired girl, her knee bandaged and, given the lumpiness of the dressing, packed with herbs. "Magister Orla, why do you let them chain you?"

She shook her head. "My back is broken. I can't run. Neither can she."

Kerrigan started toward her, but Lombo barred his path. "Xleniki."

Orla sighed. "Heal the old one and they'll let you work on us. If you don't, we're all dead."

Kerrigan shivered. "And if I fail?"

"Dead is dead, Adept Reese."

Kerrigan nodded and approached the old Panqui. Xleniki's eyes remained closed, his breathing shallow and ragged. The magicker forced himself to breathe deeply. "Magick will hurt him to heal him."

Lombo nodded once, solemnly.

"Kerrigan, no."

He glanced at Orla. "What, Magister? You said I had to heal him."

"Yes, but you have to take the pain into yourself. The shock of it could kill him."

"But, his leg, it's broken. The wound is infected." Kerrigan blinked his eyes. "It will hurt. It will hurt a lot."

"These are Panqui. Do you think dying at their hands will hurt less?"

The youth swallowed hard and reached down with his right hand. The Panqui's flesh felt warmer than he expected, and even hot at the wound. Kerrigan knew that was from the infection, but he pressed his hand to it nonetheless. The old Panqui stirred a bit, but Lombo appeared at the head of the hammock and rested his massive paws on the older creature's shoulders.

Kerrigan again closed his eyes and began to invoke the elven spell. He pushed his awareness into the Panqui's flesh. It felt to him similar to a bare foot descending into thick mud that oozed up between the toes, then a rising scent suggested it was not mud but feces. A shiver ran through him and he wanted to pull back because things felt so alien and wrong.

It was that same sense of the alien, though, that kept him there and made him plunge deeper. Having just used the spell to save himself, the memory of what his wound and pain had felt like was still fresh in his mind. He catalogued the differences between that and this wound, then located the similarities and used them to push even deeper. Finally he found the flow of pain, which pulsed bright and strong, all razor-edged and saw-toothed.

Though every fiber of his body fought against it, Kerrigan severed that flow and pulled it into himself. He forced the magick back through that channel, speeding the pain's flow by constricting it, then letting it skitter through his body. It shook his limbs and ground his teeth. Needles of agony pierced him more thoroughly than the arrow had, and the one lancing into his loins voided his bladder. His shuddering muscles sent quivers through his flesh and sweat drenched him. It coursed down his back, moistened fleshy folds over his chest and stomach, and dripped from his nose and chin.

His mind tracked every twinge, every jolt, every breath, every indignity from the warmth of urine running down his leg to the whimpers escaping his throat, but he set them aside. The keenest bit of him reveled in the strangeness of the Panqui physiology. The nature of the creature he was healing fascinated him. Where he started the spell working one way and the body resisted, he shifted and shifted again. He found the Panqui were hearty beasts who normally healed very quickly, so he was able to push Xleniki's body to a greater rate of recovery. He changed and refined the spell as he worked, trimming bits here, adding bits there. He drew on the energy his body created with his shivers and shudders, pulsing more power into the spell.

The pain soared through him, but Kerrigan didn't let it

beat him. The wonderment he felt at working on the
Panqui let him track the pain and view it dispassionately,
for even it was yet another tidbit of information, a morsel
of knowledge that only he possessed. The desire for more
drove him on and with a certain reluctance and melancholy he realized the pain was slackening and that he had
accomplished his goal.

His eyes opened and he pulled his hand away from the
old Panqui's leg. The wound had closed, the flesh had
sealed, and not so much as a trace of a scar marred it.
Kerrigan smiled and wanted to say something, but his
tongue felt leaden in his mouth, and his chest tightened.

A wave of fatigue crashed over, dragging his eyelids
down. He tried to clutch onto the hammock, but his fingers
refused to tighten. He felt the burning rasp of fibers against
his flesh, and his world went black before he could ever feel
the shock of hitting the ground.

CHAPTER 29

Leaning against a merlon in early morning, Will realized he'd been wrong when he'd thought of the black dragon's flight being like that of the seagulls. The birds hung in the air, their tail feathers flicking right and left, steering them to new updrafts, then they folded their wings and dove down onto the bodies littering the coast. Some of the birds perched on floating corpses, while others squabbled over beached carrion.

Human. Gibberer. Vylaen. It didn't seem to matter to them what they feasted on. Crabs fought for the corpses nearest the shoreline, and out in the ocean, turtles and other fish plucked at bobbing bodies. Will didn't see any sharks out there anymore. Their strikes, which had still been visible at dawn, had become sluggish as the sharks gorged themselves.

Will would have shivered, but what he was watching was in no way as chilling as the battle had been. When the Aurolani forces had been driven back, word had been sent to the troops stationed farther inland. They came forward and evacuated the wounded deeper into the interior, to the tower devoted to curative magicks. That eliminated the moans and shrieks, at least from inside the fortress, leaving the folks there to straighten the limbs of their dead and begin to mourn.

That process excluded Will. None of the people he'd known had been killed. Resolute and Dranaé had both collected cuts and scrapes—with one slash rendering Resolute's left arm useless until the elf had it magicked back to health again. The spell had not been easy to cast, and Resolute had groaned while it was being used on him, then lay down on the battlements and slept for a while.

Even Captain Gerhard and Jarmy had survived the fray. Gerhard had lost a number of his *meckanshii*, then wandered through the wounded, picking out men and women to whom the option to become a *meckanshii* would be made available. Will had no idea what Gerhard would be looking for in recruits; especially when they lay wounded in a place where spells existed that could render them whole again. Still, nods from broken warriors, weak salutes with bandaged stumps, suggested he found takers for his offers.

Jarmy, likewise, had lost people from his septet. Will couldn't determine if seven was the normal number of combat Adepts who would band together, or if groupings were made up on some other basis. He saw a few glum groups with nearly a dozen members, and one set of four who appeared to be quite happy. Jarmy just scowled, then stalked down amid the bodies, making certain the vylaens were dead and removing from corpses the things that could be talismans or otherwise magickal.

The battle frustrated Will. He'd been there, he'd seen things, but he'd not fought. He'd not so much as thrown a bladestar, and he felt embarrassed by that. By the same token, having seen Resolute, Dranae, Jarmy, and the *meckanshii* in battle, he knew the only thing he would have done was shed blood. That he knew he was weak shamed him, and that he'd not had the opportunity to prove himself otherwise led to his frustration.

"Will, you should eat."

The youth turned and nodded to Crow. He accepted from the older man a small round of bread and a wedge of yellow cheese. He sniffed the cheese and welcomed its sharp scent chasing the pungent miasma of death away.

Crow sank to the base of the wall and sat back. "Not looking down there will help you eat."

Will shrugged and sat cross-legged on the battlement. "I was thinking that I'd compared the dragon to seagulls. I think that would make the dragon angry."

The older man tore a hunk out of his bread round, then nibbled some cheese. "Just for a moment, I can see that, with the black. The way it drifted there, yes. Not much else to remind you of gulls, though."

The youth shivered. "What he did to the ship . . . How? Why?"

"How?" Crow pointed a finger at a knot of sorcerers standing atop the far fortress. "I would guess they're arguing that point now, and will come down to the dragon using Draco-magick. Dragons are old, ancient. They're also very powerful, which is why we can't let Chytrine recover the parts of the DragonCrown and reconstruct it."

"She has part of it, doesn't she?"

Crow nodded wearily. "She got part of it in Svarskya. There are three fragments hidden at Fortress Draconis. There's another in Lakaslin, the capital of Jerana. Some of the stories tell of one fragment having been in Vorquellyn. The elves say it was evacuated, but they've told no one where it is."

Will gnawed on a crust of bread. "At least it will be hard for her to get that piece, then. The one piece she has lets her control dragons?"

Crow shrugged uneasily. "Seems to. She had one dragon with her at the siege of Fortress Draconis years ago, but it died. It was a gold like the one last night, but a bit bigger.

Just having part of the crown gives her limited control, like a puppeteer with a cut-string puppet. The way I understand it, the more fragments, the better the control."

"But she'd need all of it for full control, right?"

"I don't know. See, eight centuries past, when Kirûn created the DragonCrown and used it to bring war to the south, the dragons wrought havoc. Kirûn's big mistake was that he didn't have enough in the way of ground forces to garrison the towns he took. Men, elves, and urZrethi fought back and managed to trap him. They slew him and broke the crown up.

"Nearly as anyone knows, Chytrine was his apprentice, so she might know the spells used to create the DragonCrown. Even if she doesn't, if she manages to get enough pieces together she could figure out what's missing and might be able to re-create it."

He jerked a thumb at the ocean behind the wall. "Chytrine isn't stupid, and she learned well from Kirûn's mistake. If she was willing to throw away that many gibberers in a stupid assault like this, she must have thousands upon thousands waiting to go. With the dragons to smash opposition and gibberers to hold what she takes, her conquest of the world will succeed."

Will broke off a piece of bread and tossed it into the air. A gull swooped down and snared the morsel with its bill. "And we've been heading to Fortress Draconis to get them to hide the crown fragments really good?"

Resolute walked up, towering over Will. "We need to disperse them, then kill Chytrine." The Vorquelf looked over at Crow. "The Grand Magister is here, looking at the damage. He wants to talk with you."

Crow stood, steadied by Resolute's strong hand. "I sent a message to him asking that we be given passage as fast as possible to Fortress Draconis."

Will stood and, shoving his food into his pockets, drifted after Resolute and Crow. The trio approached a knot of Adepts in their robes of green. The group opened to reveal, at its heart, a small, wizened man wearing a white robe. It contrasted sharply with his long, yellowed beard. He clutched a staff taller than he was, and he was so hunched over that Will easily saw over the man's bald head.

Crow bowed solemnly. "This is an honor, Grand Magister."

The little man did not move for a heartbeat or two, then only slightly lifted his head. "You are Crow? You don't feel like a crow."

"No, Magister, today I feel like an old man."

The magician cackled, and after a moment, the Adepts around him joined his laughter politely.

Will blinked. When Resolute had announced the coming of the man who ruled Vilwan, he'd expected someone who lived up to the title "Grand Magister." He thought of someone tall and sharp-eyed, with a noble nose, not a misshapen potatolike lump, all hunched over and slow. Power should have been coursing off him, crackling the air around him.

The Grand Magister's brown eyes slowly glanced past Crow and met Will's gaze. "This is the boy you brought?"

"Yes."

"Come here, lad."

Though the command came barely as a whisper, Will found himself unable to resist it. He stepped forward, right up to the ancient man. The Grand Magister lifted his left hand and took hold of Will's chin. He tipped the boy's head down a bit, then their gazes met again.

A jolt ripped through Will. Had the magician not had hold of his chin, the boy's head would have snapped back as if he'd been kicked by a horse. An alien presence punched its way into Will's mind. The youth felt himself stretched, then something popped. Another pop and another, distant, sounded in sequence, then the Grand Magister broke eye contact and let Will go.

Will staggered back and Resolute caught him. Will

dropped a hand to his longknife's hilt, thinking to draw and slash the old man for that invasion, but the Vorquelf's grip stopped him. The youth looked daggers up at Resolute, but the Vorquelf just shook his head.

Will shivered. *He's right. I'd not get a step closer before he could kill me.*

The Grand Magister nodded slowly. "He has promise, that one."

"Thank you, Grand Magister. This is why we want to travel to Fortress Draconis as fast as possible."

The ancient thaumaturge brushed that suggestion aside with a wave of his hand. "I cannot let you go there. You are needed elsewhere."

"Elsewhere?" Will shook himself. "Fortress Draconis is where they have the DragonCrown fragments that Chytrine will use to bring an army of dragons back here. Where else could we possibly be needed?"

"His blood is fiery. Good." The Grand Magister blinked slowly, then looked at Crow. "You will accompany the Vilwanese delegation to the Harvest Festival in Yslin. You will be there for the Council of Kings."

Crow frowned. "But, Magister, Vilwan does not send a delegation to the Council of Kings."

"Not often does a witch from the north attempt to conquer Vilwan." The old man shrugged. "Times have changed. Besides which, the Draconis Baron is attending the meetings, and you have business with him, do you not?"

"The Snow Fox will be in Yslin?"

"Yes, Crow." The Grand Magister reached out and settled his left hand over Crow's heart. "You have labored long to be prepared for the times that unfold now. The weight of your work and your reputation are needed to provide balance. Your wisdom is needed to provide direction."

Crow laughed lightly. "No kings will listen to my words."

"No, but your words will fall into the ears of their subordinates, then many mouths will share your wisdom with those who need it."

Will frowned so hard his forehead hurt. "Is being vague something wizards do, or is it just that you're old?"

The Grand Magister cackled again, but the Adepts did not join him. Instead they glared at Will. The thief shrugged their anger off—in the arena of glaring, none of them could have bested Resolute, and Will could already feel the Vorquelf's eyes boring two holes in the top of his skull.

"Wilburforce, would you pour more water into a full jug?"

"Only if I wanted to make a mess."

"So it is with being vague. You and my Adepts are full up for now, especially as concerns things for Crow." A spark flashed in the Grand Magister's eyes. "If you would permit me, though, I think I would have from you an answer that would help fill me."

"Huh?"

The magicker continued as if he'd not heard Will's puzzled response. "You saw, last night, the black dragon come and drive off the gold. Why do you think he did it?"

Will blinked. "He?"

The Grand Magister nodded slowly. "Vriisuroel is not unknown. He lives on Vael. Why would he come here after the gold?"

"I don't know. He doesn't like Chytrine? He didn't like the gold?" Will shrugged. "He sees Vilwan as his domain?"

The barest hint of a smile tugged at the Grand Magister's mouth. "A game of dominion? Interesting idea. Think on this, Wilburforce. Vriisuroel is of an ancient and noble line, but he once served Kirûn. Now he defies Kirûn's heir. Why?"

Will snorted. "He doesn't want her to re-create the DragonCrown and enslave him again."

"Ah, but that's the trick of it, isn't it? I said he served Kirûn, not that he was enslaved by him. He served willingly." The little man arched an eyebrow. "Now, after what is barely a decade in the reckoning of dragons, he no longer supports that cause. His change is to be welcomed, to be sure, but unless we understand what motivates him, we could alienate him and give that power to Chytrine."

The Grand Magister nodded toward the ocean and dim, mist-shrouded Vael to the northwest. "Chytrine's dragon was limited to talon, claw, and flame, since her control is incomplete. Free, as was Vrüsuroel, or fully controlled by the crown, the dragons can bring all their magicks to play. If Chytrine is given that sort of power, there is nothing that can gainsay her anything she desires."

Crow shivered. "We will stop her."

"Yes, you have the tools, Crow, I see that." The Grand Magister nodded once. "To Yslin with you, then. You have the tools, now you need gain the chance to use them."

CHAPTER 30

If he'd ever been taught to curse—aside from the magickal kind—Kerrigan was pretty sure he'd be grumbling all hot and nasty. His boots had shrunk because of the ocean dunking, and gotten tight and hard. He had blisters, and while it would have been an easy thing to heal them, the magick did nothing about building up the calluses that would protect his feet. Every step he took put him in agony, and the pain from walking had worked up his legs to his knees and hips.

The straps on his backpack—a musty old thing the Panqui had salvaged from somewhere and presented him with great ceremony—rubbed the flesh of his shoulders raw. Because Lombo had torn his robe open and no one had seen fit to repair it, one of the straps was actually rubbing against his bare skin.

After recovering from his exhaustion from healing the old Panqui, Kerrigan had been allowed to heal Orla and the girl. Spelling them back to health had not been difficult, and both of them accepted the pain of their healing.

Kerrigan had, when dealing with Orla, repaired the break in her back. That restored function to her legs. He'd also, as long as he was in there, taken care of some lingering damage from old wounds, clearing up some old scar tissue, reconnecting some nerves, and smoothing down some bones in her hips and knees.

As a result, Orla was marching along through the Saporician jungle at a pace that young Lariika was having a hard time matching. The old woman seemed happier than Kerrigan had ever seen her. While she did admonish him about having done too much, she seemed to enjoy being able to move spryly.

Lariika, who was happy at having survived and having her knee fixed, giggled and wandered all over. She never strayed far from the group, catching up easily because Kerrigan was moving so slowly. When they would get ahead of him—usually at the top of a small hill—they'd wait, chatting gaily about one thing or another. He'd get there and they'd allow him a minute's rest or two, then set off again.

Lombo was no help at all. In the ceremony in which the backpack was bestowed upon Kerrigan, the elder Panqui exhorted the assembled group of Panqui at great length. Kerrigan estimated the community at roughly three hundred individuals, though only fifty or so came from the immediate camp. He suspected there were a number of other villages scattered throughout the area and made a mental note to learn everything he could about the Panqui when he returned to Vilwan.

During this ceremony, about the only word Kerrigan caught was "Yslin." Xleniki then waved Lombo forward and presented him to Kerrigan. Lombo translated, indicating he would be their guide for the trip to Yslin. He went on to recount his many deeds of bravery, which set many of the Panqui hooting. Most of it sounded like local adventures, but the beast did mention a stint crewing on a Wruonan pirate ship and living on that island for a while.

On the hike, which had started the day after the ceremony despite Kerrigan's entreaties to let him rest more, Lombo had primarily taken to the trees. He'd race ahead of the group, bellowing challenges that were seldom answered. Then he'd wait in the bole of a tree between branches, watching them and more often than not munching on fruit or nuts or small, arboreal creatures that hadn't moved fast enough.

The Panqui had been generous with the rainforest's bounty, especially when they made camp for the night. He brought the best of fruits, and the group knew they were good because Lombo had generally nibbled each one to make sure. The *very best* went to Kerrigan, then the silver-haired Orla, and finally Lariika. Kerrigan tried to be gracious, but he'd carry his haul off to a nearby stream to wash it all off.

Lombo would follow him and watch him, which only made Kerrigan more miserable. The Panqui would squat in the water upstream, and the young mage feared the beast was relieving himself in the water while Kerrigan washed his food. That put him off feeding until his stomach hurt more than his feet and Lombo, thinking the fruit not to his liking, brought a live snake for Kerrigan to kill and eat.

Cold and tired, achy and hungry, Kerrigan pulled himself away from the two women and barely acknowledged them. He answered their questions with grunts and scowls, which he knew wasn't fair, but he wasn't sure what else to do. His physical discomforts did make him grumpy, but he could have gotten past them. Something else was digging at him.

On the second night out, while Orla and Lariika giggled over some private joke, Kerrigan could take no more. He turned, slowly and deliberately, and snorted at them over the small fire. "How can you be laughing? They're all dead, the rest of them are dead."

Lariika blinked her blue eyes innocently. "We're alive. Isn't that something to be happy about?"

Orla reached a hand out and rested it on the girl's shoulder. "It is, child, but that's not what Adept Reese is hinting at, is it? Out with it, Kerrigan. There's a maggot wriggling around in your mind. Let it free."

Kerrigan glared at them, and then at Lombo. At the mention of the word "maggot," the Panqui had started to come closer to Kerrigan, but the youth couldn't endure Lombo's grooming him for nits. "They're dead. Lombo has said no others were pulled from the sea."

"You don't know that, Kerrigan. Others might have been picked up by boats in the area."

"They're probably dead, too."

"Some, perhaps, but you eliminated the threat to many of them."

Kerrigan's hands closed into fists and he hammered one against his left thigh, punctuating his words. "Yes, but I killed the others because of it! The wave tossed the ship over. They all went into the sea. Its *weirun* has more meat to feed his pets because of me. I killed them. I killed them."

Faster than he would have imagined, Orla rose and slapped him hard across the face. The blow stung sharply, stunning him. His left hand rose to cover his cheek. He stared at her, openmouthed, then his lower lip quivered and he began to cry.

"Why?"

Orla straightened her robe and stared down at him. "You were becoming hysterical and that's when you stop thinking, Adept Reese. You need to be thinking right now, not feeling, not fearing. That was my first reason for hitting you."

She slowly sat, holding her hands out to the fire. "The second reason is to show you that you are no killer—though I wish to all the gods you were. Someone of your power would have burned me alive for that, as a reflex. Think about it, Kerrigan, there you were, people screaming and dying. You took an arrow through the chest in the middle of a fight, and what did you do? You used a warehouse clerk's spell. You raised that ship into the air and then dashed it like a child's toy. If you had a warrior's heart, the ship would have been just as dead."

"Yes, but the others wouldn't have. There would have been no wave."

"Your lack of thinking about consequences again betrays you." Orla arched an eyebrow. "If you'd made the ship combust, the explosion would have started such a wave. If you'd crushed the prow and had it sink, the suction would have pulled our ship down. There were dozens of other things you could have done that might have swamped or sunk our little boat, and for all you know, the damage it had taken might have rendered it unseaworthy. It could have been sinking already.

"Does that excuse you from having caused the wave that sank our boat? No. Does that mean you killed the others? No. You don't know how many were already dead. You don't know if others have survived. Yes, some, perhaps all save us, perished—but we would have been no less dead had you not acted."

Kerrigan sniffed. "But there is still blood on my hands."

"Yes, there is, boy, and likely will be much more before any of this business is concluded." Orla hugged her arms around her stomach. "This is precisely what I told them would happen."

The young Adept brushed away tears. "What are you talking about?"

"How you've been trained." She took a deep breath and let it out in a great huff. "Well, this is a new round of training. Kerrigan, you have to think about the consequences of the magicks you cast. In an *arcanorium*, with everything set and perfect, you know what they will be. You're smart enough to go beyond that, to think about what will happen in the field. You have to do that."

He nodded slowly. "I will try."

Orla sighed. "That's better than 'I can't.' And, I guess, for now, that's the best I can hope for."

* * *

They broke camp early the next morning. Orla looked around for the stick she'd been using as a walking staff, but didn't see the gnarled piece of oak anywhere. She glanced suspiciously at the fire, afraid Lombo might have broken the stick apart to feed it, but the pile of wood they'd gathered the night before had not yet been exhausted, so that solution to the whereabouts of the stick seemed implausible.

"Magister, this is for you." Kerrigan rolled to his feet and stood using a five-foot-long ebon staff to assist him. He extended the stick to her and she accepted it cautiously.

Caution bled into surprise. She knew this staff. The cool smoothness of dark wood, a tiny divot missing from where she'd once parried a gibberer's longknife, even the length and the delicate balance she could easily recognize. She spun it in her hands, then ran them down the length of it.

There was no mistaking it. *This is my staff, but it's at the bottom of the Crescent Sea!* Even if Kerrigan had somehow bargained with Tagothcha, the sea's *weirun*, and the spirit had returned the staff, there was no way he could have gotten from their camp to the sea and back with it.

"Where did you . . . ?"

Kerrigan smiled shyly. "Not really where, Magister. I made it."

"What?"

He shifted his shoulders uneasily. "When I was younger I would throw tantrums and smash things. I would get punished for it. And then, even if I dropped something accidentally and it broke, more punishment. So I kind of learned to fix things. If I touched it and knew it, I could take a like material and re-create it. Your stick, the one you have been using, I used that because it already had a link to you. I've handled your staff before, worked magick through it, so I knew it."

Orla felt a chill run through her. "You've never told anyone you can do this?"

He shook his head. "If they knew, then I would be punished for breaking things, or punished for withholding information. It's not particularly hard to do, really. A bit of construction mixed with conjuration, some concealment and clairvoyance thrown in. I could show you how it's done."

She covered her mouth with her hand. *He's married four schools of magick into one spell.* She'd never heard of such a thing happening before. A spell to create a rampart for defense might combine construction and combat magicks, or a spell to make an arrow hit a distant or unseen target might take combat and clairvoyant magicks and weave them together. She'd heard of one urZrethi spell—one she didn't think she could have mastered if she'd studied for another fifty years—that transformed a nag into a mount that could make the rider tougher in combat and invisible. That wove together combat, conveyance, and concealment magicks, and was, by far, the most complex spell she'd ever believed existed.

And yet, as a child desiring to cover up mistakes, he creates this spell? She shivered. *They have no idea what we have created in him.*

"Are you okay, Magister?"

She nodded and forced herself to smile. "I am, Adept Reese, and am in your debt here. As for learning that spell, I doubt I have enough years left in me to be able to do so."

Kerrigan's eyes dulled for a second. "You feel okay?"

"Yes, Kerrigan, thank you." She hefted the staff. "Your gift makes me feel even better. By the time we get to Yslin, in a couple of days, I think I shall feel very good indeed."

CHAPTER 31

Will alternated between being so excited he wanted to shout and dance and laugh and sing, and being terribly afraid that if anyone noticed him he'd be chucked out of Fortress Gryps or tossed into gaol or worse. Being where he was at the moment was something he'd always dreamed of, and always bragged about happening. *It's just that it never happened this way in the dreams.*

There he stood, just inside the doorway of the Grand Hall of Fortress Gryps. Crow stood there, Dranae, too, and Jarmy, as well as a bunch of other folks from Vilwan. It looked to him as if every other wizard of any stripe who had been living in or around Yslin had joined the Vilwanese contingent. Since Vilwan was extra-governmental, its party was not to be introduced and took up a position of least importance.

Only Resolute held himself apart, standing with a small group of Vorquelves. Most of those Vorquelves wore bright silken finery that matched that of the human nobles in attendance. Resolute, on the other hand, wore a heavy cloak he'd made of mangy gibberer scalps and had trimmed with vylaen fur. Beneath that he wore a good set of forest-green and brown hunting leathers, though he'd taken the sleeves off so his tattoos could be easily seen.

Will envied Resolute his choice of dress, but acknowledged that things weren't as bad as they would have been had Will been forced to dress up in the rich clothing of the nobility. Their pointy-toed shoes looked like they pinched, the collars clearly choked, and the pants had enough buttons that Will was fairly certain that if you didn't pee before you drank anything, you were never going to get them off in time to do it after.

What he'd been forced to wear wasn't much better, and he was pretty certain something else was going on that he didn't know about. Because Crow, Dranae, and he were going to attend as part of the Vilwanese contingent, they were fitted out for dressy robes that would be appropriate to their station. They gave Dranae a deep red robe that marked him as an Adept, and put two colored bands encircling each wrist. Those circles indicated what magicks he was supposed to be good at, but Will had no idea what white and green meant.

Crow had been given the grey robe of a Magister. Estafa, the Adept who had them fitted out, said he was willing to risk that rank with Crow because of his white hair and powerful demeanor. Will figured the latter comment was to flatter Crow into revealing something about himself, but Crow remained politely silent. Instead of rings around the sleeves of his robe, Crow got a robe with slashed sleeves that revealed two colors—red and yellow silk panels were used. Will didn't know what they were for, but since Jarmy had a blue robe with a red band circling the sleeves, he assumed red stood for combat.

After Resolute refused to don a wizard's garb, Estafa turned to Will and studied him for a while. He shrugged, then pulled out a black Apprentice's robe and had Will pull it on. The sorcerer tugged on it here and there, then knotted a white rope around Will's waist and nodded.

"That works fine. You're done, Will."

The young thief had smiled and tucked his thumbs inside the rope. "What's this for?"

"To hold the robe tight around your middle."

"No, no, what magick? What do I do?"

Estafa gave him an overly generous, completely insincere smile full of teeth. "Ah, well, Will, you need no stripes or slashes. You're an Apprentice. No one would believe anything more of you given your youth.

"But don't worry"—the man winked—"you're very special as it is."

Will frowned. "But there was someone who came through here who got a robe like Jarmy's, and he had lots of stripes and he looks younger than me."

"Ah, Adept Reese, yes, well, he's special in his own way, too. Getting here, he . . . well, it was a long journey overland." Estafa's thin lips curtained his teeth. "Go along now, Will. Be content to hide as an Apprentice. Best you're not noticed until it's time."

Will had rolled his eyes and departed for the room they'd given him in the wizard's tower. Throughout the voyage to Yslin, which hadn't taken more than a day, he'd found all of the wizards to be fond of speaking in riddles. He wouldn't have minded it, save that he would catch them shooting speculative glances at him. A few of them, like Jarmy, turned out to be okay sorts, who listened to his tales of fighting gibberers in the mountains and at the stable.

He'd found the tower a bit annoying. When he got his room assignment he was told it would be the second left. He went down the corridor and turned left, and then left again and found himself in a little alcove. The door opened before him revealing a small room with a bed, a chest of drawers, a round table, two chairs, and a sea chest with a big lock. He started to work on the lock with his picks, just to keep in practice, but at his touch it popped open. Inside he found clothes that would fit him. Over the next couple of days he found the selection of clothes changed depending on the weather, and at least once, green shirts predominated after he'd awakened thinking the day just felt green.

He could have taken that, but his room was *always* the second left. If he took right turns—being mindful that he was in a round tower after all—he could never find his room. If he reversed course, two lefts later, there he was. Moreover, he might take three rights and go down stairs to get to the dining hall, but his room ended up being two lefts away, with no stairs most times—though once he did come downstairs to go to supper, and his return trip to his room took him down yet another level before that second left.

As a result of all that, he never did leave the tower and reacquaint himself with Yslin. It felt good to be home again, smelling the sea, hearing the accents, watching the sun set over the mountains he'd ridden to. From his tower window he could see some of the sky-baskets move from building to building above the twisting streets. He couldn't really see the Dimandowns, since Fortress Gryps stood between his room and his old home, but just knowing it was there was enough for him.

And now, here I am, in Fortress Gryps. Having grown up in Yslin, Will knew the Alcidese government used the ancient fortress as a place for important receptions and balls. Countless thieves planned capers to get them in during some grand party. They would steal nobles blind and flee, they all claimed, but generally decided the undertaking was impossible. Seven had tried—three singles and a group of four. Of five of them Will never heard another word, but one's head appeared on a spike over a postern gate visible from the Dimandowns.

The only one who had succeeded had been the Azure Spider, and he'd stolen a coronet that was going to be presented to the king's eldest daughter, Kallistae, on her fifteenth birthday. It was common knowledge in the Dim that Augustus had vowed to shave his head until the crown was returned. The Azure Spider had left Yslin in the wake of that theft—fled according to some, gone on to better things said others. Will supported the latter view, and was glad he'd not been caught and shared the other thieves' fates.

Will shivered, but not because of the memory of seeing Mad Dick's head mounted on the wall. The thieves, when describing what they'd be stealing, had so grossly underestimated things that Will figured the collective lot of them were spinning in whatever graves they'd been dumped. Their imaginations might have been well exercised in planning their thefts, but had not even begun to break a sweat when it came to describing the nature of the swag they were aiming for.

If jewels were raindrops, some folks would be drowning. Will smiled within the shadow cast by his robe's hood as kings, queens, princes, and princesses wandered past. Heralds announced them, then the various royals slowly strode along a scarlet strip of carpet that led them to a dais where King Augustus and his wife greeted the visitors.

Just seeing the king—shaved head and all—sent a thrill through Will. For as long back as he could remember, people told stories of King Augustus and his Okrannel campaign. Had it not been for him breaking the army Chytrine had sent to further ravage the countryside, the bards would have folks believing Chytrine would be wiggling her ass on the Alcidese throne. That he got a bride in the bargain just made the tale sweeter for the telling.

Plenty of men in the Dimandowns would point out the scars they'd earned in that campaign, but Will wasn't fooled. If every one of them had been there, the army Augustus led would have been much bigger than the three thousand he had with him. Since few of the braggarts had Okrans accents, he knew they'd not been in the irregular troops that had joined Augustus. But since each of the scars came with a stirring description of battle, Will hadn't minded that they were false.

King Augustus, though, was anything but false. The bald head, the bright eyes, and the bold moustaches bespoke a man who would have been more comfortable in combat, or maybe as a pirate sailing the Crescent Sea. Augustus seemed a man made for adventure and Will's heart swelled with pride as the king greeted his guests.

Will's smile broadened as he decided that if he were thieving, he'd leave Augustus his crown.

That veil of inviability did not extend to King Scrainwood of Oriosa. Bits of grey streaked his long, brown hair, and though the mask he wore made them difficult to see, his hazel eyes shifted restlessly. Will had seen his like before on the streets. The slight hunch to the shoulders, the hyper-alertness to quick movements, those were the mannerisms of a man who had something to hide. Will would have gladly stolen everything the man had on, but he half suspected the crown was studded with paste jewels.

Scrainwood had traveled to the Council of Kings with a modest entourage. Will dimly remembered hearing the man had been widowed. His wife had gone out for a sail in a little boat and had never come back. Nasty rumors said she was living life as a shepherdess in the hills, and that whenever Scrainwood traveled, her sons came to visit her. Will wasn't sure he believed much of any of that, but of the Oriosan princes there was no sign—though the younger was said to have come with Scrainwood.

Next in came the delegation from Okrannel. From behind Will the wizard Estafa hissed cattily, "Okrannel, by rights, should have come before Oriosa. Scrainwood maintains his nation should come first because he *has* a nation. Truth is, Oriosa is more Aurolani than the Okrans Marches are."

King Stefin of Okrannel shuffled slowly along the carpet, with a crone on one arm and a middle-aged man on the other. A bevy of nobles followed in their wake to make up what had been, so far, the largest contingent attending. Even so, Will noted, they collectively possessed fewer jewels than some single personages. *If jewels were raindrops, there would be a drought in Okrannel.*

One striking woman, standing tall and with blonde hair so white it came close to matching Crow's, made up for the lack of mineral wealth amid the Okrans delegation with her lively amethyst eyes. She moved with a fluid grace that put all other women to shame, and not just those in the room. *Back in the Dimandowns I've seen women like Lumina dance the way that makes men's blood molten, but she'd be nothing compared to her. . . .* In fact, it occurred to Will he'd only ever seen one other woman as beautiful as this.

It was her! He leaned to the left, tugged urgently on Crow's sleeve, and whispered to him. "The woman there, from Okrannel. She's the one from Stellin. The one on the horse. The bandit leader."

Crow leaned a bit forward, his eyes tightened. "You could be right. Who did they say she is?"

Will shrugged, but Estafa leaned in. "That's Princess Alexia, Prince Kirill's daughter."

Crow's voice grew small. "So *that* is Alexia."

Will frowned. "You say that as if you knew her."

"I . . ." Crow hesitated, then coughed into his hand. "I recall hearing she survived her father's death, but I had heard nothing of her since then."

Estafa sniffed. "She was taken to Gyrvirgul to be raised. Rumor has it that she was exiled from court here by Grand Duchess Tatyana, the king's aunt. Having been raised by the Gyrkyme, she is a savage."

Will shot the gossipy magicker a sharp glance, then shook his head. "Don't know about your sources, but she sits a horse pretty good."

"She does indeed." Crow shared a smile with Will. "And carries that gold gown well enough, too."

The Okrans party passed slowly, but only King Stefin and Princess Alexia greeted King Augustus, so the next group did not have to wait very long to move forward. Will didn't know who the small man was, all dressed in royal blue velvet with black striping, but he knew he had to be from Fortress Draconis. Behind him came ten individuals, paired male and female, but warriors all by the look of them. That wasn't shrewd judgment on Will's part—they were *meckanshii* and had been paired such that their artificial legs and arms were to the interior of the line, with metal hands holding metal hands, as appropriate.

Crow's voice grew slightly distant. "That's Dothan Cavarre, the Draconis Baron. He's the one we'll have to convince to scatter his fragments of the DragonCrown."

The young thief nodded. Cavarre was actually the first adult at the gathering who stood shorter than Will. His white-blond hair, which he wore long and unfettered, matched his well-trimmed moustaches and goatee. The grey eyes, complete with blue flecking, searched the room endlessly and restlessly. Will had seen that sort of behavior in the streets and did not assign it to paranoia or fear as much as a habit of suspecting and hunting.

The man looked more than once at Crow, and that sent a shiver through Will.

"Who is he with?"

Crow smiled. "That is his wife, Ryhope, of Oriosa. She is Scrainwood's sister. Time has treated her kindly."

Will arched an eyebrow at Crow and the old man nodded.

"I've more than heard of her. I once saw her here, at the Harvest Festival, when last it was held in Yslin. She had a few less lines on her face then, and no hints of that white forelock in her raven hair. She did, however, have that sense of self and grace you see there. The people following them, I believe, are the leaders of the fortress' battalions, some newly promoted."

Estafa cleared his throat. "My sources there are better. The last two are new. She is Jancis Ironside, from Muroso. The man's her husband, from Oriosa. He's a bit of a prig about the masks, but I think that's because he wants something covering what little face he has left."

Will frowned. The woman looked fairly normal, since her gown was long and full enough to hide whatever was making her limp. Her left hand even had a blue leather glove on it, so if it had more than just two fingers and a thumb, no one could have known there was anything she was hiding. She did wear a mask of blue velvet, trimmed in black, which matched the uniforms from Fortress Draconis perfectly.

Looking at her husband, Will had to admit the wizard did have a point. At some time in the past, her husband must have lost most of the flesh on his face, along with a bit of his nose. Around the edges of his black mask, which was decorated with ribbons and little sigils in white, the silver mail that had replaced his skin was easy to see. Will couldn't quite be certain, but seemed to recall having seen that sort of very fine mail being worn by some of the Vorks, so he wondered if some elf had used it to repair the soldier.

Crow frowned. "Does that soldier have a name?"

"Hawkins, I believe, Sallitt Hawkins."

Will's eyes grew wide. "Wasn't he the traitor?"

The sorcerer chuckled lightly. "No, he was the brother who aided King Augustus in the Okrannel campaign. He's the one who redeemed that name from the shame."

"Sure, like someone could clear up that sort of mess." Will shook his head. "Impossible."

The Vilwanese mage snorted. "No tougher than your task."

"What?"

"The vaunted prophecy, the Vorquelf prophecy." Estafa shook his head. "Kenwick Norrington and his son serve Chytrine as *sullanciri*, yet the prophecy calls for a Norrington to destroy her. You're that Norrington, Will."

"What?" He looked over at Crow and saw distraction melting into distress on the man's face. "That's what this is all about? No, NO!"

Crow extended a hand toward him, but Will slapped it away, then turned and bolted through the door. He heard Crow call for him to wait, but he ignored him. Will snarled at guards, twitching his fingers as if preparing to cast a spell. As they recoiled, he rushed past them and out of Fortress Gryps. Weaving a confused path through the throng in the streets, Will cut north and lost himself in the Dimandowns.

CHAPTER 32

As King Scrainwood continued his diatribe at the first Council of Kings session, Alexia concluded that he not only lived up to his reputation, he surpassed it. The green mask he wore—all gaudy with ribbons and feathers sewed to it, and sigils decorating it here and there—still possessed more nobility than the man himself. The whine in his words reflected stress, but his sarcasm brought with it free-flowing venom. Seated in the second rank of the Okrannel delegation, she felt tempted to vault the table, cross to where he paced, and drop him with a short punch.

Scrainwood's upper lip curled back in a sneer, half hidden beneath his mask. "And now, as a little 'side issue,' we are told by the Vilwanese that they had the Norrington who is prophesied to put an end to Chytrine and they *lost* him? How is the presence of the savior of civilization a side issue? How is his loss trivialized so?"

Scrainwood's pacing took him across the inner ring of tables. The frontline nations of Alcida, Oriosa, Muroso, Sebcia, and Jerana all occupied that first circle, with long tables covered by banners with the appropriate arms for each delegate. Two smaller tables held the Alcidese contingent at the north side of the circle. Between them Augustus sat in a throne on a dais as the presiding officer of the gathering.

Opposite him in that first circle also sat two small tables. Okrannel had been given one out of courtesy. The other table belonged to Fortress Draconis. The Draconis Baron sat there alone, though two of his *meckanshii* officers were seated behind him.

A sorcerer in a plain grey robe stood at the second ring table given to Vilwan and folded his fingers together. He let his hands rest at his waist, so his sleeves came down and hid them. "If it would please King Scrainwood and his exalted peers, my report, if uninterrupted, would explain."

King Augustus, seated at the front of the room in a throne on a dais, nodded. "Please, King Scrainwood, restrain yourself for the moment. Give them a chance to explain."

"Yes, Augustus, I shall, though I believe their priority in reporting is reversed."

The Vilwanese representative bowed his head. "I sought to provide a chronological framework for events. As I was saying, volunteers from south Saporicia came to Vilwan to defend the island. When they arrived, we were informed that a young man in the company of other travelers likely was the Norrington of prophecy. We undertook steps to ensure his safety. They were successful and he was brought here as part of our contingent to keep him hidden and safe."

Scrainwood laughed aloud. "You failed."

"Our failure, King Scrainwood, was in not fully communicating to members of our group more than we, albeit mistakenly, thought they should know. We were distracted. When the volunteers came to Vilwan, we used their ships to evacuate our Apprentices from the island. These are the sons and daughters that all of your people have sent us.

They are the best and most talented children on the face of the earth. Each was endowed with special magickal abilities that we were honing.

"It now appears that Chytrine's strike at Vilwan had two goals, neither of which was the conquest of the island. The first was the reduction of the Wruonan pirates. Since the fall of Okrannel, and the loss of its navy, the pirates have largely been unimpeded in their predation of the lower sea. They harassed her ships heading south, so she fashioned a sham alliance with them. By enlisting them to aid the invasion, she ensured that a significant portion of their ships and personnel would be killed. Since none of her best-known ships were present, it is even assumed that Vionna might have colluded with Chytrine to cull enemies in the invasion."

The man hesitated for a moment, and his shoulders sagged. "Her second goal . . . It appears she anticipated our desire to evacuate our youngest. The pirates swept over them, sinking boats, burning them, ramming them. They slaughtered hundreds. Others drowned. Many are still missing. Of the nearly nine hundred children we sent away, fewer than fifty have managed to report."

Grand Duchess Tatyana barked a harsh laugh. "You allowed our children to be cast like so much chum into the sea? You'll find it a cold day when next an Okrans child is sent to Vilwan."

The sorcerer nodded. "Not an unreasonable statement, and one doubtless finding resonance in all your hearts. I believe this was precisely the reaction Chytrine wished to inspire. Not only has she devastated a crop of wizards, but she has salted the ground so no more will grow up. If she holds off another ten years, or twenty, their lack will be sorely felt."

Scrainwood stood at his place again. "But she will be vanquished, will she not, by this Norrington? Oh, wait, you have lost him as well."

"Yes, Highness." As the man sighed, Alexia could easily

imagine the bone-weary fatigue dragging on him. "We have people searching for him."

"But not using magick to do so, if my sources are correct." Scrainwood sniffed triumphantly. "Perhaps your dead children were the experts in seeking things out?"

The wizard stiffened. "You are welcome to impugn the competency of our leadership, King Scrainwood, but do not sully the memory of our children, *your* children, with your sneers. The simple fact of the matter is this: if we use magick to seek him out, it is possible that Chytrine or her agents might be able to use our efforts to locate him first. The reverse is, of course, true, so we have people working to cover that eventuality."

Queen Carus of Jerana raised a finger. "You suggest by this comment that Chytrine already knows the Norrington exists?"

"Yes, Highness, this is what I have been told."

"How is that possible?"

The wizard's dark eyes narrowed. "The method used, by others, not by us, to ascertain the veracity of his identity exposed his presence to Chytrine's agents. In their defense, I would say that this risk was unavoidable."

Augustus sat forward on his throne. "Why did the boy run?"

"He had not been told he was the Norrington of prophecy. When he learned who he was, well, imagine the shock. He bolted and went into hiding."

The King of Oriosa's eyes blazed. "He was known to be *the* Norrington, which makes him one of *my* subjects, and he was not told who he was? *I* was not told who he was? This is impossible."

"Were it up to me, Scrainwood, you'd still not know he existed."

The snarled voice came from the second ring of tables, so Alexia had to turn toward her left to see the speaker. She recognized the white-haired Vorquelf from the previous night's reception. He'd abandoned the gibberer-scalp cloak, which meant his tattooed arms were in full display. She thought for a moment, then nodded. *He's the one called Resolute.*

Resolute swept his silver gaze over the room. "I found the Norrington, here, in Yslin. I took him to where his identity was verified. I was taking him to Fortress Draconis, and from there to confront Chytrine. The Vilwanese had no part in this, save for transporting us back here."

King Augustus stroked his beard carefully. "I have known of you for years, Resolute, and your dedication to the liberation of Vorquellyn is well known. When I ask what I ask it is not to cast doubt on you or your wisdom, it's just to gain some information."

The Vorquelf nodded slowly. "Your sense of fairness is well known, Highness. Ask."

"Why didn't you tell the Norrington who he was?"

"He is barely a man, and that is in years alone. Not in size nor mind nor disposition is he yet grown. I found him here, in your Dimandowns. He's a thief who knew nothing of the world outside Yslin's shadows. He needed to be taught things, taught to accept his destiny."

"Accept his destiny?" Scrainwood threw his arms wide. "This boy should be accepted and feted by every nation here. He is our liberation from the scourge of the north. We would raise armies and he would carry us to victory."

The Vorquelf's eyes hardened. "You mistake two things, Highness. First, we know he is a Norrington, but we do not know that he is *the* Norrington. It could be that even now some girl harbors his child in her belly. Second, even if he is *the* Norrington, to assume his patrimony means he will be unopposed, or would give him a clue about how to direct forces to destroy Chytrine, is stupid."

"Moreover," offered the Draconis Baron, "to assume we need this child to destroy Chytrine is beyond stupid. If I re-member the prophecy correctly, it says he will kill a scourge of the north, not Chytrine. He could account for just one of her *sullanciri*—his father, perhaps, or grandfather even—

and would have fulfilled the prophecy. And we must remember that this prophecy only promises the redemption of Vorquellyn. I'm certain that the good people to my left do not find the continued occupation of Okrannel acceptable."

Tatyana stood abruptly. "We do not. And we do not at all appreciate the Oriosan attempt to lay claim to this Norrington."

Scrainwood smiled slowly. "You mistake me, all of you, in thinking that I desire to possess this Norrington, or to push him into anything he is not ready to do. No, not my desire at all. My desires regarding him are simple. First, I wish for his recovery so Chytrine cannot have him. Second, since she knows of him and is presumed to be making an effort to find him, I believe we can use him. If we do raise him up, praise him, put him at the head of an army, she will be forced to pay attention to him. She has to fear him, and that will distract her from your efforts, my brother Dothan."

The Draconis Baron closed his eyes for a moment. "I will stand corrected if I am wrong, but it seems to me that Chytrine could trigger a premature fulfillment of the prophecy by allowing this Norrington to destroy a scourge of the north *and* redeem Vorquellyn. She could bleed our forces white by contesting the island, then pulling out. This would eliminate the Norrington as a threat to her, and leave her more than capable to attack south. This is why we must strike at her, quickly and hard. I have prepared plans. . . ."

Queen Carus rose. "I must object, brothers and sisters, to the presentation of any plans at this juncture. As you know, I am new-come to the throne and while I have attended these Councils before, it was my father's clear intent to marry me off to one of you or yours before I ever got to occupy the throne. My military advisor, General Markus Adrogans, is on his way here, but is a half week out yet."

Alexia frowned. She had very little reliable information

about General Adrogans, so she tried not to judge him harshly. He did have a well-known aversion to traveling by water, and had found Chytrine's gathering of a great fleet to be ample excuse to come to the meetings overland. He should have arrived well before the Council met but Chytrine had launched an assault from the Okrans March in anticipation of his absence. Adrogans had fooled her, however, by dispatching his baggage train south slowly. His army went with it, for two days, then rode fast north, using strings of horses to speed them. They caught the Aurolani forces unawares and routed them.

The queen continued. "With no disrespect to the Draconis Baron intended, his opinion about how Chytrine should be opposed is not the only one. While the baron has been very successful at keeping Chytrine bottled up to the north—save for those small units that slip past Fortress Draconis and gather in the south to lay siege to cities—his expertise is in the realm of defensive operations. General Adrogans has had a great deal of experience in attacking, so presents another viewpoint. He, too, will be bringing plans. And, fear not, Dothan Cavarre, for Fortress Draconis is vital to them, just as a smith's hammer needs an anvil, so Adrogans will need Fortress Draconis."

Cavarre smiled briefly. "My heart is warmed that your Jeranese military sees value in Fortress Draconis. I had begun to doubt that when the troops you were supposed to send to me never arrived."

The queen nodded. "When the situation was explained to me, Baron, it seemed our troops were better used defending Jerana from the direct threat of Aurolani raids. You can ask our friends from Valicia and Gurol if we have been lax in our duty."

"I have never suggested any laxity, Highness, just a lack of foresight. Chytrine stages raids here in the south, prompting you all to fear her. You keep your troops home, which means Fortress Draconis, which has kept her legions bottled up in the north, becoming weaker and weaker. If you believe her attacks here have been insanity or foolish, she has already defeated you."

Tatyana raised both of her hands. "My lord and lady, this will do us no good. The Draconis Baron's views are well known. He believes that if we can strike at evil's root, the rest of it will wither. General Adrogans feels that if we prune back evil's foliage, there will be little left to root out. Until we have the chance to compare both plans or, better yet, get these two military minds to fashion a plan together, discussion can only force people to choose sides. What should be a military decision would become a political one, and no one would find that acceptable."

Alyx narrowed her eyes. Not only did she not like the fact that the Grand Duchess had abandoned the pretext of pretending she was speaking for the king, but the woman was urging caution and being reasonable. Granted she did not know that much about her, but everything she did know spoke to Tatyana's political nature. In urging that they abandon politics in light of reason meant she must be playing a political game.

Alyx felt a compunction to warn the Draconis Baron about what was going on, but she hesitated. The simple fact of the matter was that *if* the Jeranese plan held sway, the first point of attack would be to drive the Aurolani hosts from Okrannel. This would return to her the land of her birth, and permit her grandfather to be at peace. Whether or not that would be the best course for dealing with Chytrine, the desire to see her homeland free did tug at her.

But only for a moment. Something inside of her, something born of years of training by the Gyrkyme, pushed aside sentimentality. It was not that the Gyrkyme could not be a wildly passionate and emotional people. They could, and often were. Their life, though, had stressed for them how fragile existence truly was. Whereas a man might drink and fall to the ground, a Gyrkyme similarly intoxicated would die after taking to wing. The Gyrkyme mixed calculation with stoicism and a strict demand for the best from everyone; and these lessons had helped shape her. Later tutors came and taught her everything there was to know about the world and warfare—and she found their lessons fit very well on a foundation of Gyrkyme philosophy and training.

While the push into Okrannel would be satisfying on an emotional level, it was all but indefensible on the military side. A campaign through the mountain valleys of Okrannel would be difficult. Even if they managed to force the Aurolani troops back, the terrain meant a small number of troops could hold off a larger army, which would give the Aurolani troops time to pull back into the Boreal Mountains or the Ghost March. Unless they were destroyed, they always would pose a threat to Okrannel. The freedom they fought hard to win would be fragile, and the loss of Okrannel to Chytrine would be trivial.

The Draconis Baron, however, did not seem to need her warning. "The Grand Duchess is quite kind in sharing with us the wisdom of King Stefin. Though I only knew his son for an all too brief time, Prince Kirill impressed me with the Okrans' willingness to do what had to be done to guarantee success. It is not hyperbole to say that Kirill bought for all of us the last quarter century of freedom with his life. His sacrifice at Fortress Draconis will never be forgotten. It is my hope his selflessness will be taken to heart by all present."

Augustus stood. "My friends, I believe this would be a good place to end this first round of discussions. We agree on two things: the Norrington must be found. I have people working on that already. And since he is one of my subjects, at least for the moment, I reserve the right to direct the search for him. In other words, he is not a prize you should have your people looking for. Let them enjoy the Harvest Festival *now*, because we know they will not have time to enjoy it later.

"Second, we agree that we can come to no resolution of

the question of how to proceed militarily against Chytrine until General Adrogans arrives. Until then, we can occupy ourselves with questions of supplies and troops we can raise." Augustus' face took on a grim expression. "A quarter century ago we were warned of what was coming. Now is the time we deal with this problem, or everything we know will be buried in a blizzard of steel, fire, and fang from the north."

CHAPTER 33

Kerrigan wanted to smile broadly, but he kept his expression impassive as he strolled casually out of the tower in which he'd been given chambers. No one had said he couldn't go to the Harvest Festival. No one had exactly given him permission, either, but he was pretty certain no one would stop him from wandering out. He pulled on a dark blue robe and a matching cloak to go over it and marched past the Adepts watching the tower's door. He thought one might question him, but he sailed past unchallenged.

Once out in the street, he did let himself smile, and knew he'd gotten lucky. Orla had been called away to meetings with the Draconis Baron. She had no idea what the meetings would be about, but Kerrigan was not wanted at them. Orla had suggested he find something to do with himself and seemed utterly unconcerned about what that would be.

Her lack of concern annoyed him a little, given that he was her charge. Part of him wanted to go out and get into

trouble, just to prove to her that she couldn't take his level-
headedness for granted. He knew, of course, that to do such
a thing was stupid, so he shied away from it. Heading out to
the Harvest Festival, on the other hand, would be an adventure and wouldn't be dangerous in the least.

Out in the street Kerrigan shivered, but not because of
the slight chill coming with night. *Yslin!* It was a city, big
and sprawling, with a seaside district and temples and towers and Fortress Gryps and the palace and so much more.
On Vilwan everything was shipped in—and while there
was a bit of commerce in the port, rules governed the conduct of merchants and customers alike. Fancies could be
had, but generally had any indication of their source removed because the wizards wanted the people on Vilwan to
feel they were citizens of Vilwan, not visitors who came to
learn and then return to their own nations.

In Yslin, however, Kerrigan saw knots of people wearing
what he assumed to be their native garb. By their masks he
recognized people from Oriosa, or Alosa or Muroso—he
wasn't certain exactly where they were from, except that
they were of the masked nations. Others wore colorful and
uniquely styled dress, and spoke with thick accents that
made their words all but unintelligible.

He found this both exciting and terrifying. Part of him
wanted to run back to the tower and hide, but that part surrendered to the memory of braving a long road journey
from Saporicia to the Alcidese capital. Traveling in the
company of a Panqui had reduced many threats, but still it
was an adventure. It had left him footsore and exhausted,
so he'd slept for a day when he made it to the city. Even now
his feet hurt, but the pain evaporated as he studied the
wonders in the city.

He moved along King's Way, heading ever south and
away from the sea, moving up a gradual incline to Drygate.
Beyond it, where plains stretched out toward the distant
mountains, a small city of tents had sprung up. He could

hear pennants snapping in the breezes, and saw people
pulling cloaks closed against the night's coming chill. The
smoke swirling in from the festival grounds combined the
scents of roasting meats and vegetables into something that
made his stomach growl despite his having eaten a filling
meal before setting out.

Most of all, though, the Harvest Festival provided him a
feast for his eyes and ears. Harvest Festivals were not unknown on Vilwan. While they were held a bit later there
than in Alcida, they were a grand celebration. New students
were welcomed and sorted by skill and talent, while current
students were tested to see where they would go next.
Grand ceremonies were held to celebrate students moving
from Apprentice to Adept ranks. More solemn affairs
marked elevation to the rank of Magister, but the aftermath
of all of them involved games and food, laughter, song,
dance, and other entertainments.

Kerrigan had even been allowed to participate in the
festivals, for a day at least, each year. His mentor always
conducted him through. In the beginning there had been
other students who seemed to be following his accelerated
training track, but he'd not seen any of them for years. He
didn't know if they had failed, or just attended at different
times than he had, but he didn't think about that much.

With the distraction of the Alcidese festival, he didn't
think about it at all, nor did he think about what Orla
would say if she knew he was there. *I'm seventeen, and an
Adept who destroyed a pirate ship. I've traveled through jungle and field with a Panqui. I have nothing to fear here.*

Bolstered by that thought, he plunged into the festival.
He took care not to jostle men with swords, and contented
himself with standing at the back of crowds as they
watched warriors battle with wooden swords for the right
to challenge a champion and win a purse. It seemed obvious to Kerrigan that the paired challengers took enough
out of each other that the champion would have little

trouble beating them. He gathered the rest of the crowd
knew it, too, but the champion fought with such blinding
speed and skill that just watching him was a joy.

From there he moved on to a small theater with a puppet show. Children and a few adults had gathered on the
ground and benches to watch the puppeteers do their
work. The mage marveled at how lifelike they made the
puppets appear—especially because they were using no
magick at all. While he had learned spells that allowed him
to animate such toys, his sorceries failed to give the wooden
dolls so much personality.

Just to salve his ego he double-checked, and sensed no
magick from the puppets at all.

The play seemed to be based on one of the Squab tales.
They all followed a similar formula, and had been around
for centuries and centuries, but in the last twenty-five years
the comic villain had become the coward who survived the
previous expedition to the north. In the puppet dramas
Tarrant Hawkins had become known as Squab and would
come to advise some stalwart young hero as to how he
should handle a threat directed at him by Chytrine. Squab
would try to betray the hero to the Aurolani tyrant, but
would fail and the hero would prevail, driving Squab away.

Kerrigan didn't know that much about the previous expedition to destroy the Aurolani threat. While Heslin, the
wizard who accompanied Lord Norrington, had been
trained on Vilwan and even had ranked as Magister in
combat and concealment magicks, he had not been representing Vilwan in that effort. The Vilwanese volunteers had
gone with King Augustus on the Okrans Campaign. Of
their performance much had been written in the official
history of Vilwan. Because Heslin became one of the
ten *sullanciri*, almost nothing about him appeared in the
Vilwanese chronicle.

The audience laughed and applauded as the hero drove
Squab off. The puppeteers appeared from behind the little stage, then moved into the audience, collecting coins.

Kerrigan noticed some folks giving money, and others slinking away. He hesitated for a moment, then reached inside his cloak and opened the purse on his belt. He pulled out one of the dozen gold coins he had and deposited it in the sack.

The puppeteer's eyes grew wide. "Thank you, my lord."

Kerrigan smiled and nodded, then noticed how others were looking at him. He smiled at them, then turned and lost himself in a crowd. From their expressions he gathered he'd done something wrong, but the puppeteer certainly didn't seem to think so. He puzzled over it for a moment, then let the clink of coins and clack of a stone on wood distract him.

He moved to a tent where people—men mostly—were gathered around a hexagonal wooden platform that had railings around it. A man walked around the interior of the railings, alternately taking money from people and gathering stones from the center of the platform. The platform's center had a huge hexagon painted on it, and it was filled with many smaller hexagons, most of which were painted one of eight different colors. A few had a patchwork of different colors in them.

Contestants would pay money, announce a color they were aiming for, and pitch a stone. If it landed fully inside the borders of an appropriately colored hex, they won double their bet back. If it straddled the line, their bet was returned. If they called and put the stone on a multicolored hexagon, they won four times their bet. Members of the audience wagered back and forth among themselves about various throws, making the whole of the tent a riot of conversation punctuated by cries of joy and groans of despair.

A man sidled up to Kerrigan. "Care to be betting?"

The Adept stammered. "I-I've never . . ."

"Oh, you'll find the game is simple. You see, what you'll be doing is . . ."

Kerrigan held a hand up and sniffed. "I know the game.

We play queek where I am from, but it's a bit different there."

"It is?" The man smiled in a friendly manner. "How so?"

Kerrigan returned the smile and pointed to the man on the platform. "Well, we're not allowed to use magick to skew where the stones land the way he is."

The riot of sound intensified around Kerrigan, then turned into a riot of fact as the audience surged toward the game's owner. He started yelling, tossing handfuls of coins into the crowd. Half the people dove for the ground, grabbing up money. They generally impeded the other half of the folks who wanted to get their hands on the operator. The owner vaulted the railing and scarpered off, scattering money behind him like a farmer sowing seed.

The man who had spoken with Kerrigan grabbed his sleeve and pulled him free of the crowd. "This way. You don't want to be part of that."

Kerrigan stumbled after him, then nodded his thanks. "I didn't mean to . . . I didn't know . . . I'm not from here."

The man smiled. "I can see that, but don't you be worrying. Those of us what live in Yslin don't be liking these cheaters to come to our festival and take advantage, you know? You've done a great service here, ah, your name is?"

"Kerrigan Reese."

"Well, Goodman Reese, you've exposed a cheater." The man extended a hand. "I'm Garrow, and being as how I'm from Yslin, I'd like to officially be thanking you for what you did."

The Adept's smile broadened. "You are quite welcome."

"New-come to Yslin, are you?" Garrow folded his arms over his chest and frowned mightily. "I'm betting you're thinking we're just a lot of bumpkins, being as how we were fooled by that man. It's not true, Kerrigan, not at all. I wish you could see the city the way I do. Being as how it's my home, and a place I love, showing you about would be an honor. I'm sure, though, you've got more important things to do than to have a tour of our city."

The man sounded so disappointed that Kerrigan immediately shook his head. "Actually, I don't have anything to do. I mean, if you would be so kind . . ."

"Kind? Lad, you saved me money. Come on, come on along." Garrow waved his arm high and strongly, then set off at a determined pace. Kerrigan caught up with him, having to lengthen his own stride to match that of the smaller man. They left the fairgrounds going west and reentered the city through a smaller gate than the one by which he'd left.

Garrow proved to be a wonderful guide. He explained that they'd come back into the city by Goldgate, which led straight into the richer section of town. They wandered past some wonderful buildings with ornately decorated facades. They then went through the temple district, with Garrow pointing out the various temples.

He indicated one that had columns that appeared to be tightly bound scrolls. "That's the temple to Erlinsax, of course, keeper of Wisdom. I'd be going in there because they have a shrine to Arel; but I'm lucky enough having met you, I am."

Kerrigan nodded, but the words really didn't get through very much. Vilwan had no temple area. It wasn't that the sorcerers didn't believe in the gods, they just didn't traffic with them. More precisely, they didn't want the gods interfering when magick was being cast. Getting all the different aspects of spells in order was difficult enough without some pleased or vengeful godling getting in the way.

Beyond that, Garrow led Kerrigan downhill, toward an older section of the city. "It's the heart of Yslin really, my young friend. Over there, to the east, you have Fortress Gryps, but here, in the Dim, you have things just as vital. If you're lucky, you might see a Vorquelf or two."

Kerrigan smiled and almost started telling Garrow about the Vorquelf he'd seen on Vilwan, but that brought back a dark memory that slowly killed his smile. The Adept realized that night had full fallen and that as they moved deeper into the Dim, the section of town began to live up to its name. The lamplighters clearly hadn't gotten this far on their rounds. Kerrigan started to ask Garrow if he wanted him to make a light.

He never quite got that far because another man stepped from an alley and blocked his progress. Moving out from the alleyway came other people, kids mostly, some as old as Lariika. Grime streaked their faces and caked their hands, and wiping either on their clothes would just make their flesh dirtier. The children spread out and surrounded him about the same time as Kerrigan recognized the man.

"Y-you ran that game."

"I did, I did, and you ruined it for me." The tall, slender man scratched at his pointed chin. "You'll be paying for it, too. You've a fat purse, and it will be mine."

Kerrigan dropped a hand to his purse to protect it. "It's not yours."

The circle tightened and ridicule pummeled Kerrigan. Garrow growled. "You're a long way from home, boy. Give it over."

"No." Kerrigan pressed his lips tight together so no one could see them quivering. He didn't want to cry, but fear raced through him. He knew he had to do something, and his first reaction was to lift the gameskeeper high into the air, as he had the pirate ship; but he knew that wasn't a combat spell, and hardly would deal with all of them.

His thoughts had progressed no further when the first small fist slammed into his back, right over a kidney. Kerrigan's thick flesh protected him a little, but the shock of being hit surprised him. He began to turn, then had a small stone glance off his head. He lost his balance and went down, then the kids closed and began kicking him, clutching and clawing at him. One of them tore his purse loose, raised it triumphantly, then left a gap in the circle as he took the prize to his masters.

Kerrigan knew he should have scrambled up and

ducked away through that opening. He would have, too, but through it he saw someone he recognized. He didn't know his name, but he'd been at Fortress Gryps for the opening ceremonies of the Council. *He was dressed as an Apprentice.*

The Adept looked at him. "Help me. Help!"

The young man stared at Kerrigan, and as two of the little ruffians turned to deal with that threat, he raised his hands. "Not my fight." He ran off, and the pair of kids returned to kick Kerrigan harder.

Shocked at his abandonment, Kerrigan froze for a moment. The kicks and punches came faster and more furious, but without enough weight to do more than bruise him. Then someone grabbed his right hand and started to bend his fingers back. The sheer cold and calculated attempt to break his fingers roared outrage through him.

Kerrigan rolled toward his attacker, then rolled over him. He heard the kid scream, albeit muffled, then felt him struggle to get free. The Adept came up on one knee, unintentionally putting all his weight on the child's ribs. The child shrieked as a rib cracked.

Garrow snarled, and his partner darted forward to deliver a savage kick to Kerrigan's stomach. The Adept doubled over and would have screamed, but breath wouldn't come. Panic exploded in him. He had to act, and quickly.

He raised his right hand and triggered the spell he'd been about to ask Garrow about. Pumping his fear and outrage into it, he intensified the spell. Instead of creating a soft little ball of light, a will-o'-the-wisp to gently illuminate the night, his effort gave birth to a searing argent ball. It cast a circle of long shadows, in which people clawed at their eyes. Shrieks of pain accompanied its birth and undulated in intensity as the circle of attackers melted away blindly.

Kerrigan made the mistake of glancing at the light as it rose above his head, instantly blinding himself. He fell forward, onto all fours, trying desperately to get up and run, or force his lungs to expel the fiery vapors trapped therein, but he could do neither. He knew he must because his only hope lay in escape, and his attackers would not be blinded forever.

Then, suddenly, he heard a thump behind him and felt strong hands grab him around the waist. He was hoisted from the ground, then one arm curled around his back and shifted him onto his side. For a heartbeat he felt as if his weight had increased triple-fold, then he felt almost weightless before the impact of landing shook him. He was shifted around again, this time higher and bent at the waist.

By the time his journey ended, Kerrigan had figured out that he was being carried, and the familiar sensation of having been thrown over Lombo's shoulder in the jungle had given him a good idea as to who his rescuer was. His fingers, playing along the Panqui's armored flesh, confirmed the Adept's assumption.

The journey stopped before his vision returned, and Kerrigan was thankful it had. Lombo had set him down on a stone bench that was tall enough that Kerrigan's feet didn't touch the ground. The young man leaned back and felt rough stones behind him, but just concentrated on getting his breath back. When his lungs had stopped burning, he opened his eyes and, for a moment, thought he was still blind because all he could see were pinpricks of light.

Then he realized those lights were the streetlamps from below. *Far below!* He grabbed the edge of the bench—which turned out to really be a ledge running around the upper reaches of Fortress Gryps—and pressed himself as far as he could back into the stone wall.

Kerrigan started to say something, but the calm and easy way that Lombo perched there on the ledge beside him somehow forestalled protestations of outrage. The Panqui clearly knew where they were and had chosen to bring Kerrigan to that place. The Adept took a deep breath, then let it out slowly.

The Panqui nodded. "Slowbreath good."

Kerrigan kept his eyes on Lombo, not wanting to look down. "Thank you for saving me."

"Watch Kerrigan Lombo's job."

"You were watching me?"

Lombo gave him a quizzical look.

"Why did you do that?"

"Greywitch. Xleniki."

"You were watching me all night?"

The beast nodded, then pointed from the tower to the fairgrounds and down along the winding path through the city. "Home. Fair. Trap."

Kerrigan blinked his eyes. "You knew I was walking into a trap?"

"Man stalked Kerrigan. Kerrigan followed." Lombo shrugged. "Others made trap."

"And you didn't stop them?" The young man's lower lip began to quiver. Every bruise on his body started throbbing. "Why didn't you stop them?"

Lombo lifted his chin proudly. "Hunter, not poacher."

Hunter, not poacher? Lombo's words bounced around in Kerrigan's mind. At first they seemed ridiculous, then a dim sense of them came to him. "You didn't stop them because they were hunting me. I was their prey and you didn't want to interfere with their, ah, kill."

The Panqui nodded solemnly.

"But then why?"

"Kerrigan no prey."

The Adept closed his eyes. After only a moment's reflection he realized what had happened. As long as he had not defended himself, he had been acting as prey would. He had been a deer beset by wolves. *The moment I fought back, though . . .* "I made the light . . ."

Lombo smiled, exposing a sturdy array of fangs and rending teeth. "Prey no life, no friend. Lombo's friend has help. Kerrigan kill easy."

The young man opened his eyes again. Even though he had saved Xleniki, Lombo was willing to let him be slaughtered if he acted like prey. *If I am too stupid to live, he will let me die.* It made a weird sort of sense and Kerrigan found that sentiment an odd and distant echo of the things Orla had tried to teach him. Back on Vilwan, under circumstances where everything was controlled, he could do wonders. Out in the world, however, he was a child.

Kerrigan lifted a hand and gingerly touched the lump on his head. "Ouch."

The Panqui nodded. "Elf magick."

The Adept started to shake his head no, but thought better of it almost immediately. "No, not this time. Bruises will heal, and might remind me not to act like prey."

"Kerrigan wise."

"Kerrigan is learning." He shrugged and looked over at his guardian. "I wouldn't have killed them."

"Kerrigan kind."

"No, just not a killer." Kerrigan smiled slowly. "My first impulse isn't to kill. I can live with that."

"Dead no fix."

"Not any of the magick I know, anyway." The Adept's smile broadened. "Nor does the magick I know allow me to fly. So getting down from here will not be easy."

Lombo's jaw dropped open in a lupine grin. "Lombo get you home. On Lombo's back, Kerrigan. Home we go."

CHAPTER 34

The king has returned. As darkness began to fall over the Dimandowns, and Will slipped into the night, shrouded in an old cloak and self-confidence, the young thief's world seemed to be returning to normal. He'd been in turmoil when running from Fortress Gryps. He had known from the start that Crow and Resolute were withholding some information from him, but he'd never have guessed that their secret could be so foul. Here he had been hoping he was a prince or heir to some power or something heroic like that.

Instead he found out he was son and grandson to *sullanciri*. He shivered. That *meckanshii* Hawkins only had the shame of being the coward's brother. Could have been they were only really half brothers, or that the coward had been adopted. Anything. Hawkins could distance himself from the coward easily.

But being of *sullanciri* blood, now that was something else. That thought had pounded around inside Will's skull until he thought his head would burst. He tried to think back to his earliest memories, but he'd never heard the name Norrington associated with himself. He had been told his mother had died in a brothel fire, and that he had survived the fire, but he didn't even know that for certain. He didn't have any scars to prove it. No one he currently knew had the story of the fire from any source but him. He didn't even know if he'd heard it right.

But he had no doubt whatsoever that before Estafa, no one had ever called him a Norrington. He'd have remembered, too, since there were things worse than being a nameless orphan, and being called a Norrington was one of them. They had them in the Dim, men and women who went to work for the Yslin Constabulary, preying on those who used to be their friends. They were called Dim Lancers by some, but applying that label to a fellow denizen of the Dim, even in jest, would earn someone a beating.

The thing in the cave, the way it had come through and spoken, that did make him wonder what was going on. He thought back to what the goat-thing had said, how it had spoken to him. It had known who he was, and it was Nefrai-laysh, the one they said was his father. *Had it really spoken to me the way my father would?*

Will shook his head defiantly. That was magick, and everyone knew that magick could go as wrong as easily as it could go right. And he was a *sullanciri* and everyone knew they couldn't be trusted at all. Neither could Crow and Resolute. *My life was fine before those two interfered with it, before I had anything to do with magick.*

Will, with a stubbornness born of the streets, decided that Crow and Resolute and Estafa and anyone else who thought he was a Norrington was just flat wrong. *I'm not a Norrington, and that's it.* He'd nodded once, solemnly, and put the whole problem out of his head.

It was good that he did, since he had lots of other things to think about. He stripped off the Apprentice robe pretty quickly, just in case the magickers could track him through it. He traded it to a rag picker for some clothes that weren't truly horrible, then quickly enough slipped into a house and stole more suitable attire.

By midnight, the only thing he had of his journey were memories, and that suited him just fine. He knew he couldn't go back to Marcus and Fabia right away, largely because Crow knew about them and that would be the first place searchers would look. Officials coming and questioning Marcus would cause a problem for Will when he tried to return to the flock, but he figured he could steal something good and Marcus would forgive him. If Marcus wouldn't and Fabia liked the prize, she'd defend him.

I'll get a beating, but it won't be so bad.

The first night he needed a place to stay. He hunted around for a couple of hideaways he'd known about, but squatters already occupied them. Moving through shadows, he managed to elude city watchmen. While it seemed they were doing nothing more than making their normal rounds, Will felt pretty certain they were there to lure him out. He refused to fall prey to their plans, however.

He worked his way through the Dim, getting closer and closer to the Downs. He found Lumina easily enough, and it was just as well he had. She was in an alley with a coinmate, her skirt high, her thighs outside his, but he wasn't happy. He started hitting her and swearing at her. A hand rose and a knife blade glinted dully.

The first stone cracked the man's wrist and sent the knife flying. The second stone *thwocked* off the man's forehead as he turned toward Will. His eyes rolled up in his head and he crumpled into a squat pile there in the alley. Lumina, chest heaving, right hand over her mouth, looked down at the man, then at Will.

"Glad I found you, Lumina." Will dropped to a knee and liberated the man's purse, then stood and took her by the hand. "It's me, Will. You remember me, right?"

"Yes, Will, you're my Arel's-get."

"Fortune's child, that's me." He pulled her along with him. "You still living over the dyer's shop?"

"Yes." She let her skirts fall to cover herself and came along with him. "Will? Will. Where have you been?"

"To the mountains and the moon and back. I need a place to stay." He tossed her the flaccid leather purse. "Not much there, but will it buy me a night?"

"Yes, my little hero, it will."

At that point Lumina took the lead and conducted him back to her home. It struck Will as odd that two months ago her chambers had seemed so luxurious; he'd had better accommodations, cleaner and easier on the eyes, while on the road. And she'd been the most beautiful woman he'd known before his trip, but compared to Sephi, Lumina began to seem haggard. And compared to Alexia . . . Well, it was best she wasn't compared to Alexia.

Lumina's gratitude, however, erased the world outside her chambers, wiping awareness of it from Will's mind. Never before had Will experienced anything quite so intense. While he had kissed and fondled girls before, that had been all giggles and breathlessness, curiosity and innocence. It had been fun, and some of the memories could redden his face, but those memories were part of the world outside her rooms.

Lumina showed him passion, unstinting and unfettered. She guided him in some things with words, and in others with a motion or a sharp intake of breath. Likewise she deciphered his moans, groans and gasps, navigating by them to bring him up steep inclines of pleasure. The plateaus just concentrated things, focusing him on himself and the feel of her fingers on his skin, her warm breath on his body. Then up again and up, further and further, to the point where he thought surely he would explode or go mad.

Another plateau, rise and plateau—heights undreamt of.

Dawn greeted him after what seemed like a year of burning from the inside out. He lay there, tangled in her sheets, a boneless, sweat-dappled mass of flesh. Smiling

took a supreme effort, but he managed it for her, then fell
asleep.

He awoke again before dusk and Lumina brought him
watered wine and some bread. She kissed him gently and
bade him eat. Between mouthfuls of food he asked after
Marcus and Fabia, and begged her not to let them know
he'd returned to Yslin until he figured out what to do.

Lumina, whose beauty benefited from the soft yellow
glow of tallow candles, smiled. "No fear on that, Will.
Marcus kicked Fabia out a week ago, maybe a bit more. She
was heartbroken and took to drinking. She fell asleep in the
street, didn't wake up when the tide came in. She's gone,
and it's his fault, so he'll have nothing from me, and I've
told him such."

Will finished his meal and thanked her. "I'm going to
see to some things tonight, so I don't know where I'll be."

She nodded. "You can come back here if you want."

"Really?"

The woman smiled. "You're a thief. I couldn't keep you
out if I wanted. Besides, tonight I'll be with Predator."

"Oh." Will felt his heart tighten.

She reached out and stroked his cheek. "Will, you
know . . ."

He kissed her palm and gave her a wink. He was glad
she accepted that because he knew he couldn't speak. Will
slid from the bed and pulled his shoes on. He lingered over
a shoe a moment, swallowing the lump in his throat away,
then gave her a smile.

"If you need me, I'll find you."

She lied to him with a nod and he left. Making his way
down the stairs to the alley running behind the dyer's shop,
he threw back his cloak and invited the cold in to armor his
heart. In the previous night, when the world was just him
and Lumina, he had let himself believe she loved him. In
the real world he knew that wasn't true. It stung, a lot, but
every step away from that bed lessened the pain. The cold

wreathing his heart numbed it and Will didn't see a reason
to hope for a thaw anytime soon.

I am Will the Nimble, King of the Dimandowns. He gathered his cloak around him. *The king has returned.*

He emerged from the alley to see Scabby Jack and
Garrow, along with their crew of urchins, beating up on
someone. One of the kids grabbed a fat purse and held it up
like a trophy. Looking past her, Will caught sight of their
victim. He knew him, then realized he'd been recognized
himself. The victim held a hand out toward him, begging
for help.

Will raised his hands as Scabby Jack glanced at him, and
two of the kids started for him. "Not my fight." He jogged
off down the street, then crossed it and ducked into
another alley. He worked his way along it, then up a rickety
staircase and across a roof. He leaped the gap to another
roof, then softly padded his way across it to where that
building butted up against another. He scaled the taller
building's wall at the corner, then went up a tiled roof on
all fours.

Getting to the ridgeline, he headed along about halfway.
He got down on his belly and grabbed one of the tiles. Wiggling it back and forth, he slipped it free, then peered down
through a gap in the planking.

The opening gave him a good look at the common
room where Marcus kept the kids who worked for him.
Marcus, slender, dark, and with a nasty cast to his close-set
eyes, stood at one end of the room. A rafter kept cutting off
sight of him as the man paced, but Will could hear his voice
just fine.

"Most of you know Will. Even though he's been gone
for a bit, you remember him. I'm needing to find him. You
have to find him. You have to tell him he's to come here. No
hard feelings, no, none. I'm proud of Will, and any of you
would be happy if I were as proud of you as I am of him."

The short hairs on the back of Will's neck began to rise.
Marcus' cold tone of voice belied what he was saying, but

the kids, they were all nodding in agreement with what he said. That struck Will about as odd as their all being seated on the floor, in even ranks and rows. They'd even lined themselves up such that the youngest were toward the front, where they could see easily. The oldest were at the back and no one was whispering or slapping or carrying on. Even Ludy wasn't mocking Marcus, which was just not natural.

"So, get yourselves going. Out now, out. I need you to find Will. I've a gold Gustus going to the one who brings him." Marcus brandished the bright coin in his right hand. "It's yours, you find him. Go on, out."

The kids stood, front rank first, then the next, and so on, filing out quietly, all heading downstairs to the street. Will watched them go and realized he was safe, since none of them had gone into the south room to climb the ladder and take to the rooftops. Most who got to Will's age shied from roofs when they got their growth, and the younger kids just weren't very sharp. *And the way they went out. Very odd.*

Marcus turned on his heel when the last one left, and entered the west room, which spanned that end of the upper floor. He'd shared it with Fabia, and the only time Will had seen the inside of it was when Fabia needed help doing something or Marcus intended to administer a beating. Will did know something about the room, however, and slipping the tile back into place, he turned that knowledge to his advantage.

Back on hands and feet, he catted his way over to the chimney. A little heat and a bit of smoke rose from it, but Will figured that was from down the first floor. Marcus had a fear of fire—or so he said—and that meant they were never allowed to have one, even in winter. Will thought the man was just too cheap to pay for fuel.

The thief clung to the side of the chimney and listened. The damper had long been broken in that apartment, and Will had made himself an invisible party to conversations between Marcus and Fabia before. It had saved him a beating or two, and even had allowed him to supply one or the other of them with something they'd just discovered had run out.

Marcus' voice survived the ride up the narrow flue pretty well. "They're out there. They'll find him."

The reply to his statement came sibilant and seemed to slither up the chimney instead of echoing the way his did. Will was pretty sure this wasn't just because it was a female voice. "Splendid, sweet Marcus. You please me."

"And you, me. What you did with the children . . ."

"It was nothing. I shall show you how."

"There are many things I would like you to show me."

"I know, sweetness. Perhaps, like this?"

Silence reigned for a moment or two, then was overthrown by an explosive grunt and groan from Marcus' throat. Will wondered for a second or two where he'd heard a similar sound before. His previous night's adventure drifted back on him and his face burned. *But, but, that took hours. . . . How could . . . ? It was two heartbeats, maybe three.*

A shiver ran down his spine, then a bitter taste in his mouth made him spit. The way the kids had acted, and Marcus, something was not right at all. What made it worse was that he was pretty certain sorcery was involved. *That means hiding will be tough.*

Will's eyes narrowed. *I've never liked hiding anyway. I need to find out who is looking for me. And when I do that . . .* He smiled. When he learned who was after him, they'd have to learn that to tangle with the king was an invitation to disaster.

CHAPTER 35

Alyx awoke—then amended that, since she was conscious but couldn't possibly be awake—in a misty place suffused with soft light. She felt neither warm nor cold, and the vapor had a bluish tint to it. This confused her because she would have thought she was dreaming, but she never dreamed in color.

She rose from a crouch, but didn't remember having crouched in the first place. The white gown she wore had no sleeves, and that struck her as odd. She owned no such garment. Her sleeping gowns were all utilitarian, made of warm flannel, with full sleeves. In a pinch any of them could double as a gambeson under her mail.

The gown not only had no sleeves, but it had been woven of a fabric she didn't recognize. It was white and light and sheer, with a half cloak that hung over her back from the shoulders, and seemed to have little more substance than the mist surrounding her.

The moment she thought that, however, things changed subtly. It wasn't so much that the fabric shifted, it just felt different. And then, after a moment, she couldn't recall it having felt any differently before. Now, though, flat bands of scales covered her from nipples to stomach. More scales ran down her flanks, all the way from the armpit to hem, and the cape seemed scaled as well.

This changing gown, and her surroundings, perplexed Alyx. In the past, when she'd become aware of being in a dreaming state, that had been enough to kick her out of the dream. She'd awake with the images slowly evaporating. But now the odd surroundings didn't melt away. Frowning, she took a step forward, letting the skirts and mist swirl around her legs. The ground felt smooth and slightly cool beneath her bare feet. As she moved through the mist, it began to thin, and dark images slowly resolved themselves.

Ahead of her, perhaps a mile off, lay the top of a dark mountain, the peak still sharp. Arrayed around and behind it were dark thunderheads, with lightning flashing from deep within their hearts. Lower clouds surrounded the mountaintop like a snowfield, cutting off any view of what lay below. Even glancing down she could see nothing save hints of green where the mist parted with her steps.

When next she looked up, after only a step or two, the mountain loomed over her, barely a hundred yards off. A cavern gaped in the mountainside, and in another step she was at its mouth. Words had been chiseled into the stone around the arched opening.

"The secrets within remain secret without, for the good of all the world." Alyx read it aloud and was not impressed with its profundity, nor its gravity, if it was a warning. Still, the fact that she could read it ran against the idea she was dreaming, since she could not read in dreams.

Cautiously she took a step toward the entrance and discovered her rate of progression had returned to normal. Aside from the words at the opening, the cave appeared unaltered. Long, fanglike stalactites hung down, forcing her to thread her way through a phalanx of them. She strode across a narrow arch over a vast chasm, then down through a curving pathway that opened into a large room with a huge lake in it.

At the edge of the lake waited a boat at a quay. It had no masts and had been styled after a dragon. Torches burned fore and aft. Two figures waited at the stern, on the wheeldeck, watching her as she walked along the dock and boarded amidships.

The smaller of the two figures took a step forward, but he was not a small man at all. She watched him closely, comparing him to military men she knew. Instead of a robe he wore a black surcoat made of the same material she wore, though his was more fully scaled, as if it had been cut from the flesh of a dragon.

Her choice of the dragon image was not drawn from the ship alone, but from the elaborate headgear the man wore, as well as his gauntlets and boots. Dragonish talons capped his toes, and the fingers of his gauntlets had been similarly fashioned. The helm had a jutting dragon's muzzle, and horns and ears rose from it. What disturbed her about the helm was that the ears appeared to move, and a forked tongue slithered out to flicker around.

And those great golden eyes seem to be looking straight through me.

The mouth moved as the Black Dragon spoke. "You wish to know where you are almost as much as you wish to know why you are here."

Alyx nodded slowly. "Last I knew I was in Yslin, in Fortress Gryps."

"Part of you yet is." The Black Dragon's voice came in measured tones. The long muzzle distorted them enough that she couldn't identify his voice, but she suspected the man was General Caro. "If anyone were to look in on you, they would find you sleeping soundly."

"But I am not dreaming."

"As was explained to me, dreams are your spirit at the theater, watching and hearing, experiencing. This is when your spirit has sallied forth. It is nothing to fear, especially not here." The Black Dragon's ears flicked back and forward. "This place also allows us a bit more flexibility in choosing the image we wear."

Alyx nodded. She was sorely tempted to try to revisualize her gown as a coat of scale armor, but without knowing how to do it, the effort would likely not succeed and would prove a distraction. "Despite what you have said, I still do not know where I am."

"This is the meeting place of the Great Communion of Dragons. You have been invited to become a Communicant, and are being initiated as a White Dragon." The Black's helm smiled, revealing white teeth, while his larger, steel-grey companion did nothing. "It is a great honor."

She half lidded her violet eyes. "I imagine it is. The power expended to get me here is impressive."

"Always the pragmatist. This is good." The Black nodded slowly. "The Communion of Dragons is the oldest of the Great Societies. All others are mirrors of it. This society grew up before the Estine Empire was established. It anticipated the power into which men would grow. While many view dragons today as creatures of great rage and destructive power, our founders recognized that dragons, in their wisdom, used their power only as needed. They punish poor behavior and benignly encourage good. They are parents disciplining unruly offspring, chastening them. So we seek to perform this same function within human society.

"The other societies have similar goals, but to accomplish them, they draw from all levels of society. We select only those who, through training, breeding, and accomplishment, have proven themselves capable of handling the great responsibility of guiding humanity."

"You deem me worthy of such an honor?"

"It is my hope you will be seen to be so." The Black looked back at the steel dragonman. "This is Maroth. He is a magickal construct and pilots the ship here on the crossing. When next you come here, you will say to him,

'Maroth, take me forth.' He will bring you to the appropriate destination."

"And if we do not leave the quay, I am not initiated into the Communion?"

"It is possible that such could be the case. Were it so, however, you would not get this far." The Black wrapped his left hand over his right fist. "The summons to join the Communion, to journey here and speak with your brethren, will come often but the choice to do so is yours and yours alone. On the other side we meet and discuss—advising each other, settling disputes. There are moments, on the other side, when time and distance melt to nothing. You will always be anchored to your physical form, and what might take hours here will pass in an eyeblink. Were I seated before a warm fire, the cup of wine I hold would not have had a chance to fall from my fingers before our business here was completed."

Alyx lifted her chin. "If I join, am I subject to the orders of others? I will not betray my nation or people at the order of another."

"Other societies operate with a hierarchy that demands obedience, but not the Dragons. As you gain in knowledge, your ability to interact more fully with people expands. As I noted, we discuss, inform, and advise, we do not compel. At best you will see other Dragons gathering to oppose recklessness or unbridled ambition."

The Black grasped his hands at the small of his back. "The Communion is not a path to power. It is a means to guarantee that power is used wisely and to its best effect."

She nodded. "You know who I am. When will I have the courtesy of knowing who you are?"

"In time it will come. We each choose to reveal ourselves to other members at a point where we feel it is appropriate. I'm certain you have decided I am General Caro, but this is only because I have chosen to adopt a form akin to his." The Black spun once, quickly, and the thick-limbed, dragon-helmed figure changed as skirts flared and bosom swelled. For a heartbeat she looked very much like Grand Duchess Tatyana, but flowed into the more pleasant form of Queen Yelena. "Once you have a Communicant's confidence, you will see them as they truly wish to be seen. Until then, this game of mirrors should make you wary. I have no doubt that you would have been so anyway, carefully weighing what you were told before you acted upon it."

Alyx caught herself wondering if the glimpse of her great-grandaunt had been intentional or unintentional, then realized it didn't matter. *Game of mirrors is correct.* She smiled slowly. "You brought me here, then, to get my permission to submit my name for membership in this Communion?"

"I did, daughter."

Alyx's head came up sharply. "Daughter? You presume much."

"Please, I beg your pardon. Within the Dragons this is how we address each other. You could call me father, or uncle, were it more pleasing to you. Cousin, niece, nephew, brother, grandfather, and so on, all of these are what we use to stress our ties, not ranks and divisions."

She nodded slowly. "I clearly have much to learn . . . Uncle."

"And you will have time to learn it." He returned her nod. "If you do not mind, I wanted to offer you a word of caution in what will follow in the Council of Kings."

"And that would be?"

"You are quite competent, even brilliant—better than any expected you would be. You could easily teach everyone there some vital lessons. You taught them to Caro at Porasena. Chytrine, however, is not a foe who will fall at a single blow, and certainly not the first struck at her. Listen, learn. Observe the strengths and the weaknesses of soldiers and statesmen. Study your friends as you would your enemies, for there will come a time when you will have to treat them as such to do what is best."

Alyx thought for a second, then nodded. "Sound advice and quite worthy of adoption. Thank you, uncle."

"It pleases me that you found my guidance useful." The figure plumped back into the black dragon who had greeted her. "Have you any other questions?"

"Is there anyone in these meetings I can trust?"

Echoes of the Black's laughter fled deep into the cavern and did not return. "Augustus, certainly, and your grandfather—if you hear his words yourself. Cavarre can be trusted as well, in most things, though his bias for his realm does narrow his focus. And Crow, you can trust him."

"Crow?"

"Kedyn's Crow."

"He's a ghost, a phantasm. A legend with a Vorquelf army." She smiled. "Minstrels made him up so poor people would think someone could oppose the *sullanciri*."

"He is real. I have known him for a long time. He's not a Dragon, but I trust him regardless." The Black's golden eyes half shut. "As for the minstrel songs, if the minstrels knew a fraction of what Crow has really done, they'd not dare sing of him, since none of it would be believed."

Alyx arched an eyebrow at him. "I've heard that sort of thing said of many, but this is the first I've been told the songs play down exploits, instead of making more of them."

The Black smiled. "The entertainment value of history depends less upon accuracy than drama; and where the two conflict, drama wins."

"What of the Norrington? Do I trust him when he is found?"

"I don't know. I have not met him. I would rely on whatever impressions of him Augustus and Crow have."

"Fair enough." She smiled cautiously. "How will I know if I am accepted?"

"You'll see a sign."

"And I can discuss this with no one?"

The Black slowly shook his head. "As the warning on the

arch noted, what goes on here is confidential, and remains so. While you will remember everything, to speak of it, or write it, to make pictures or to do anything associated with it will be impossible. When you meet other members in the flesh, you will know you know them, and that you can trust them, but you will not know why. It will not concern you, either."

He opened his hands and spread his arms. "So, to the Communion I bid you welcome, and for now, I bid you farewell." His body expanded until it became a black sphere that engulfed her. Her world went completely dark and she began to suffocate.

She fought against the blackness, then threw the blanket off and sat bolt upright in bed, gulping in huge lungfuls of air. Alyx swept white-blonde hair from her face, then sank back onto her pillows.

She wanted very much to believe that what she had experienced was a dream, but too much had occurred in it that was not remotely dreamlike. And while surreal elements did predominate, the fact that she saw in color, and that she had been able to read, these spoke against the idea of it being a fantasy.

Alyx shrugged. Regardless of it being dream or reality, the experience just confirmed the things that she'd already taken as true. She could trust King Augustus, her grandfather, and Dothan Cavarre. With the first two she had a long history of trust, and with Cavarre, the impression she had gained of him in the first Council had been very favorable. The fact that he stood in opposition to Tatyana, and did so without fear, likewise spoke well of him.

The comment about Crow surprised her, and again spoke against her having dreamed. Kedyn's Crow was a legend to her, and she had no reason to suspect he would be present at the Council. She actually had doubts that he was, since a man of his reputation would certainly have been very useful and part of the discussions from the start. *Then again, his known fellowship with Vorquelves and desire to see their home freed once more marginalizes him since his goal is shared by few men.*

She ran her fingers through her hair and thought for a moment before shaking her head. *It was just an odd dream.* She shivered and tried to pull the blanket up to cover her, but it had slipped full off the bed. As she leaned over to retrieve it from the floor, a jolt ran through her.

There, on the floor, the blanket had fallen twisted in a shaft of moonlight. The way it had ended up, the dark wool blanket clearly formed a head and a tail, and one corner rose like a dragon's wing. Try as she might, she couldn't find another image to fit the figure on the floor, then a cloud slid across the face of the moon.

Her blanket lay there in a tangled heap, no more sinister than a twisted piece of bed linen.

Alyx growled at herself and snatched the blanket from the floor. "Just as well I saw it now. Saves me trying to interpret everything else . . ." She meant to add "as a sign of the Dragons," but the words refused to come.

She sighed and shivered beneath the blanket. Sleep, when it did come, brought no dream or clouds, mountains or dragons. This pleased Alyx no end, because the Council of Kings was certain to give her more than enough to lose sleep over soon.

CHAPTER 36

At first blush it had seemed like a sound plan. Will's objective had been to learn who was after him. Whoever it was had enlisted Marcus and had done something to the kids to make them behave like little soldiers. Will had seen that sort of discipline before, but only after Marcus had administered a severe beating, or after one of the older kids had disappeared.

That discipline usually lasted less than an hour, and diminished in direct proportion to the distance from the hideout. Will decided to stay out of the way for a little bit, then hunt down one of the younger kids in the group and get the information out of her. He'd decided on Skurri, a scruffy little girl about nine years old, since she was smarter than average and he'd often shared little treasures with her. The way her face lit up at any kindness had been a joy.

The hour or so he spent waiting, slowly closing in on the section of the Dim where Skurri usually worked as a mule for one of the older cutpurses, gave Will time to reflect on *why* he was being hunted. He knew it wasn't to turn him in for any reward. While he'd been a competent thief, he'd never pulled off anything spectacular enough to warrant a bounty being placed on his head. As with Crow and Resolute, there was only one reason in the world anyone would be looking for him: because of his blood.

Not being able to remember his mother, and never having seen or heard mention of his father, he had no idea if he was the Norrington of prophecy. The possibility that he might have been had never occurred to him, despite countless orphan fantasies woven around his father's hidden identity. He'd always dreamed that his father might show up one day to take him away from the streets and to a life of leisure. The possibility that his father was a Norrington just didn't enter into that scheme of things.

The Norrington tragedy was well known, and sung of in a number of varieties. Among the Vorks had arisen a prophecy that said a Norrington would lead the rescue of their island. His supposed grandfather had gone on the grand crusade and had been captured by Chytrine. She'd turned him into a *sullanciri*. As Distalus had told him, the son had then gone north to redeem his family's name, but had been turned into a *sullanciri* himself. "Blood before nation" had been the refrain of the song sung about Bosleigh Norrington's last campaign.

The idea of being a Norrington never came to an orphan, for two reasons. The first was that finding yourself related to the leaders of enemy invaders has little to recommend it. Will had seen kids get beat up for being thought the offspring of half-wit stableboys. He couldn't even begin to imagine what folks would do in taking out their fears of Chytrine on anyone claiming to be a Norrington.

Second, and far more subtle, was the fact that being a Norrington carried with it a grave responsibility and the strong probability of a tragic life. If things were to continue along the lines of what he'd seen in Crow's company, Will's life wasn't going to be full of laughter and joy. He'd be used as a weapon against Chytrine. *Whether I want it or not.*

The story of Bosleigh Norrington sent a cold chill through the young thief. The man had been a hero. He had slain *sullanciri*. Distalus had described him as Oriosa's last hero, and yet blood had won out over nation. How could he, Will, a denizen of the Dim, resist the sorts of temptations that had made his father and grandfather succumb? *Will my blood bind me to them?*

That question sent a jolt through him. The ritual in the cave slammed back full force. *My blood! I* am *linked to them. That thing* was *my father?*

"Damn them. Damn their eyes, damn their lies." Will snarled at the evasions and trickery Crow and Resolute had used. They'd first said they could tell him nothing because they wanted to protect whoever they *were* looking for, just in case he wasn't it. *But ever since the cave they've known who I was. They should have told me.*

As much as he wanted to blame them, however, he couldn't build up a righteous fury. First off, when he *had* been told who he was, he ran. They'd known he would, and they had been working to change him into someone who wouldn't. As Crow had told him, he and Resolute had volunteered for their duty in this battle. Will had not been able to do that—he'd been press-ganged just as they had almost been in Sanges.

Second, they had nothing to do with his parentage. His blood was his blood. It was his to deal with. They'd tried to insulate him as much as they could. In the one encounter with the *sullanciri*, Resolute had kicked the goat-man off him. Even on Vilwan they had placed him out of danger as much as possible.

The problem of who he was fell squarely on his shoulders. He knew Chytrine wanted him, based on what Nefrailaysh had said to him. Crow and Resolute would be hunting for him, but they'd not go to Marcus—they hadn't in the first place, trusting instead on their own skills to find him. The question remained of who else might be looking for him.

He chose to focus on that question, and started his hunt for Skurri. Will sped over rooftops, sailing across alleys, to land in a crouch or tuck into a roll and keep going. In shadows he would wait and watch. Then, down in the street, he saw the brown-haired girl enter an alley. The beggars stationed at its mouth let her pass without comment or challenge, clearly recognizing her as a creature of the Dim.

Will descended to street level by means of a stairway and darted across the empty byway. He gave the beggars a nod, then leaped over a sleeping body and trotted down to where Skurri spoke with a huddled mass of rotting rags.

"Skurri, a word."

She turned slowly toward him, first bringing her head around, then her shoulders. She stared at him unblinking, and the greenish glow in her eyes unsettled him. "He's here." He barely heard her whisper and had he not seen her lips move, he could have missed her having spoken at all.

"Little sister, who's hunting for me?" He grabbed her shoulders and shook her slightly, hoping to shock the dazed look out of her eyes. "Who, Skurri, who? Is it Nefrai-laysh?"

The little girl's eyes blazed at the mention of that name, then her voice changed, sinking into a deeper register. "You have learned much, little one. You wounded my brother, both hide and pride. Now you are mine."

Skurri grabbed his wrists hard. Biting back a yelp, Will brought his hands up, then out, around and back in a big circle. The move broke her grip, then he shoved both hands against her chest and pushed her down.

As she fell, she touched the beggar to whom she had been speaking. Green eyes suddenly ignited beneath layers of rags. A hand grabbed Will's right ankle. He stomped down on the bony forearm, heard it break, then tore his right foot free. He spun and fell, but caught himself on his hands and propelled himself toward the alley mouth.

He reached the street unhindered, but found green eyes staring at him from alleys and rooftops, even from beneath carts and in the face of a cat perched on a windowsill. He spun at a sound coming from behind him and saw a shambling mass of beggars heading for him. In most of their faces two green eyes burned, in others only a single. They weren't moving fast, but they were moving as a mass.

Will stooped to grab a stone, then pegged it as hard as he could at the leading beggar. The missile flew true and caught the humpbacked woman in the forehead. She pitched back, knocking down a one-legged man, temporarily choking the alley mouth.

He spun and headed south. Will kept his eyes open for three things: broken cobbles that could trip him up, stones he could throw, and likely targets. He avoided potholes, not wanting to repeat his disaster with the Grey Misters. The stones he snatched up came easily to hand and didn't lack for supply, but neither did targets. He threw as well as he could, and if he didn't crush a rat's skull, he usually got close enough to send the little beasts running for cover. The same was true of his former brethren, though he didn't try to kill them, just hurt them enough to make them break off their pursuit.

Will realized two things almost immediately. The first was that some serious magick was at work and appeared to be contagious. At a touch Skurri had been able to infect the beggars with it and they, presumably, could infect others. Will found it all too easy to imagine some of his younger brethren in the sewers, catching up rats, then sending them to the streets to watch him. While the green glow in their eyes meant they weren't responsible for their actions, Will didn't mind killing varmints.

The second thing was that by referring to Nefrai-laysh as "brother" the huntress had revealed her identity as a *sullanciri*. That realization hadn't taken much of a leap, since Chytrine's interest in him would have outweighed everyone else's, *and* she had sufficient power to send magickal hunters after him. *And she is using my friends against me—as she used my grandfather against his son, and against all their former friends.*

More thoughts cascaded through his mind, coming as fast as his breath and his steps. His attempt at stealing Predator's prize had come because he saw it was time to move out on his own. Yes, he had prayed Marcus would welcome him back, but he had secretly harbored the hope that Marcus might make him a lieutenant. That would have been the first step in his breaking away, or supplanting Marcus. It was his first step at independence.

Chytrine would deny him that. *She would use me against everyone.* Nefrai-laysh had described him as a key for a lock, but he was much more, and he knew it. To run from that would be impossible—Chytrine would see to it that he could never live in peace. Either he would have to be in her fold, as his father chose to be, or he would have to be dead. He was enough of a threat to her that no other options would be allowed as far as she was concerned.

His only other option, of course, was to oppose her. Because of a prophecy, he had become a target. He could fight against those who hoped the prophecy would come true, or he could fight against the woman who wanted to make sure it didn't. It really wasn't even a question of which side was right. The simple fact of the matter was that she would deny him his freedom, and that just wasn't sitting well with him.

Will cut into an alley and heard a furious screech rising. Something landed on his back and right shoulder, then a fierce stinging erupted. He reached back and caught a handful of tail, then yanked the cat from his back. The claws ripped free, the pain spiking. Will snarled, then whipped the cat against the wall, dashing its brains out.

A whirring sound filled the alley, growing louder as he ran. The alley fed into a crosscut alley, and Will was pretty certain left was the way back to the street. Before he had a chance to make up his mind, the whirring grew to the right, then stopped abruptly to be replaced by a keening voice.

"Quick, quick. Run, this way, run. Quick."

Will hesitated. Crouched there on the alley wall, clinging to a brick with two legs and four arms, the humanoid creature looked slightly longer than his forearm. A quartet of glassine wings protruded from its back, and two antennae rose from above two jewel-faceted eyes in what almost passed for a human face. Chitinous armor covered the creature and looked black in the night, though a couple of spots seemed to glow green.

Those spots weren't its eyes, however, which counted for a lot with Will at the moment, and the color was more of an evergreen, not the pale corpselight that had been chasing him. "That way?"

"Yes, yes. This way. Yes." The creature launched itself into the air with a whir of wings, then looped and sped off in the direction it wanted Will to go. Ten yards further on, where the alley opened into a courtyard, the thing dipped sharply, and a rat squeaked. The rodent rolled into the courtyard, then lay there struggling within a glistening webbing. The dark windows facing the courtyard watched blindly as the webbing contracted, crushing the rat to death.

Will sprinted after the creature and followed it to the north side of the courtyard. Through an arched carriageway he could see a street free of glowing green eyes. The problem was that a stout iron gate set with a grid of bars stood between him and freedom. He grabbed the bars and shook them, then glanced at the lock. He could have had it open in a minute, with the proper tools, but he didn't have them with him.

He turned and looked at where his companion sat perched on a crossbar. "Well, now what?"

"Wait. We wait."

"Wait for what?"

The creature shrugged. "We wait."

Will spun and put his back to the gate, then thought better of that move and stepped a pike's-length forward. That still left him deep in the carriageway's shadow, but it didn't really matter. Bleeding into the courtyard, moving through the alley as well as over the walls and down, came an army of green-eyed creatures. Rats and cats formed the flanks, with a few dogs out in front of the main body. Beggars predominated in the middle, with a few robust men at their core. Will assumed they were drunken sailors who had collapsed in the wrong alley at the wrong time.

One of the beggars shuffled forward and reached a two-fingered, leprous hand toward him. "You have a choice, Will Norrington. You come to us, now, willingly, or the pieces of your body will be shat by rats before dawn."

Will lifted his chin. "Is that the sort of bargain you offered my father and grandfather?"

"What missed in the son resides firmly in grandson." The beggar's voice became almost wistful. "Serving our mistress, you will know the fulfillment of your dreams— even dreams you did not know you had."

The thief shook his head. "It won't work."

"No?"

"No." Will smiled defiantly and hefted a rock in his right hand. "My dreams are your Mistress' nightmares."

"So be . . ."

The rock caught the beggar in his throat, cutting off his words. Will, for the barest of seconds, imagined that throw being strong enough to spill the man back into the rank behind him, and cast them back and so on and so on, until the whole of the rabble fell. He knew it was impossible, but if Chytrine was going to make undreamt dreams come true, that would have been a nice start.

And yet, while his throw had by no means been strong enough to accomplish that goal, the rabble *was* falling. Arrows and stones, crossbow quarrels and even daggers, rained down on them from the empty windows. People poured from doors, brandishing clubs with which they laid about, smashing rats, mousers, and hounds. Will's saviors shouted savage war cries and took to the combat with a merciless and efficient economy Will had seen before.

In Resolute. The youth's jaw dropped open. *They're all Vorks.*

Half a dozen of the Vorquelves entered the carriageway and interposed a wall of flesh between Will and the court-yard. They had swords drawn, and struck sparks from the cobbles as they slaughtered rats. Nothing got past them save the gurgled cries for mercy that ended abruptly with the sharp sound of stick on skull.

The Vorquelves who had made themselves into his bodyguard turned and surrounded him. Predator stood at the center of their line, and Will's breath caught in his throat. Before he could say anything, however, Resolute pulled Predator out of the line. Crow slipped through the gap and grabbed Will by the shoulders.

"Are you hurt?"

Will shook his head, then let his breath out and started shivering. Above him a second of the winged creatures had joined his guardian. They whirled and looped through a complex knot of maneuvers. Their piping voices filled the carriageway, drowning out the sounds of the wounded be-ing dispatched.

"Easy, Resolute." Predator freed himself from the larger Vorquelf's grasp, then straightened out his tunic. "I was just going to see to him."

"I recall how you saw to him before, Predator." Resolute's silver eyes slitted as he looked at the Grey Misters closest to Will. The other Vorquelves backed away. "He's not hurt?"

"Of course he's not. We were here, we saw, we took care of things." Predator flicked a finger toward the flying crea-tures. "That Spritha came to us, told us we were to be here at this time, and we'd see why, do our part for the prophecy. We were, we did, and it's done. Without your help."

Resolute growled. "You know how Spritha are. They know when to be where, but not always why. Sprynt is an old friend. He got Crow and me, brought us as fast as we could go. We got here in time to see it was over."

One of the Spritha landed on Crow's shoulder and gave Will a nod. "Sprynt. Pleased to meet the Norrington, pleased."

The other Spritha landed on Will's shoulder. Sprynt snapped a harsh comment at his comrade. The green Spritha launched himself into the air, then hovered.

"Qwc begs forgiveness, begs, the Norrington."

Will shook his head to clear it. "Um, no, that's okay. You're Sprynt, he's Qwc?"

"Impetuous. A child."

"Well, I owe him my life." Will lifted his left shoulder. "Go ahead."

The Spritha landed and clutched Will's tunic. Qwc jutted his body forward and stuck his tongue out at Sprynt.

Predator came walking over. "You *are* well?"

"Yeah. Thanks."

The sapphire-eyed elf nodded. "If I had known who you were . . ."

"You'd have hated me anyway, Predator." Will shrugged, but Qwc managed to hang on. "Doesn't mean nothing. Thanks for saving me."

The Vorquelf nodded. He looked up at Resolute. "Mind if we salvage things?"

"Help yourselves." Resolute folded his arms over his chest. "You've given us a chase, boy."

"If I weren't good at it, they'd have gotten me." Will sighed. "Okay, I accept that I'm the Norrington. I don't like it, but Chytrine is convinced of it, so I'm stuck. Short of having a child on someone, I guess I'm your man."

Crow nodded. "I know that wasn't easy."

"Yeah, well, easier than outrunning the folks hunting me." Will nodded toward the dead bodies. "There was a *sullanciri* running them, and I didn't see any kids in the crowd. I know where she is. If Chytrine is afraid of me just because of my being a Norrington, well, let's go kill us one of her generals and give her something more to worry about."

CHAPTER 37

The situation was not to Alyx's liking, not at all. She'd barely had an hour of sleep since awakening after her encounter with the Communion of Dragons when a pounding on her door awakened her again. She'd just thrown back the covers and cleared her hair from her face when the door opened and King Augustus entered.

Alyx dropped to one knee. "My lord."

"Rise, Alexia. There is a matter that needs attending to and you will have to take care of it." The king moved from the doorway, letting two stewards enter, bearing a suit of iron-studded leather armor, a short mail surcoat, bracers, greaves, and a helmet. "Dress quickly, then go to the East Tower map room, second level. They will be expecting you."

She covered a yawn with her hand. "What is it?"

Augustus glanced at the two stewards, then shook his head. "You'll learn soon enough. Good luck." Tossing her a brief salute, he exited the room and pulled the door closed behind him.

Alyx dressed quickly. One of the stewards seemed to know his way around armor, so she let him help her with the greaves and bracers. The other steward she sent off to get her a skin of water. She darted out of the room before he returned, but snagged it from him as she moved to the map room.

Inside she found a gathering of individuals, only two of whom she knew. The warrior woman in the regalia of the Alcidese Throne Guards leaned on a table in the center of the room, studying an old map of the city. Next to it was a small piece of parchment onto which had been sketched the layout of a building with the surrounding streets and alleys. Tristi Exemia tapped the map with an index finger, then brought that finger up to her lips and chewed on the nail.

"The maps conflict. What's on our royal survey map does not match the sketch."

A grey-eyed youth with a green Spritha perched on his left shoulder glared at her. "My map is right. I was there, I remember."

"I'm sure that's what you think you remember, but . . ."

Weariness entered the youth's voice. "Look, I'm a thief, right? It's my job to get these details exactly. My life depends upon it."

"And now our lives will."

Alyx moved to the table, sliding in between the large Vorquelf, Resolute, and an older man wearing a set of leathers like hers, but hiding within the shadow of a leather huntsman's hood. She looked across the table to Agitare. "Give it to me quickly, Captain."

The man nodded sharply, then pointed at the self-avowed thief. "This evening the Norrington was rescued in the Dim. He has indicated that someone he suspects is a *sullanciri* is operating out of the third floor of a building on Blackline Street at Quay Road. We are estimating an enemy complement of one adult male and thirty or so children, but the *sullanciri* used magick earlier to produce more combatants. We have no reports on the presence of gibberers or any other northern troops."

She frowned at the report. Finding a *sullanciri* out in the hinterlands was one thing, but having one in the heart of Yslin, especially as all the world's leaders were meeting, created a serious problem. They had gathered to decide what would be done about Chytrine, and yet the presence of one of her generals mocked the Council. How could they rid themselves of Chytrine when her vassals ran unchecked in the city?

On top of that, the mission itself was next to impossible. She sighed. "Assaulting up stairs and into a place where a *sullanciri* and an unknown number of troops might be, in the heart of the Dim? I don't like this at all."

The Vorquelf snorted. "You have the core of the problem. The layers around it are worse. We will be seen coming from miles away. They will run like rats into the sewers."

The man at her back spoke softly. "Then we have the problem of dealing with a *sullanciri*. Killing them is not easy. It takes potent magick."

"That could be why they sent for me." A grey-haired woman closed the door behind her. "I'm Orla, a Magister of Combats from Vilwan. Do we know which of the *sullanciri* this is?"

The thief shrugged. "She's female. She referred to Nefrai-laysh as her brother."

"They're not related, that's just how they talk." Orla rested both her liver-spotted hands on the top of her ebon staff. "That makes her one of the five female *sullanciri* and we've not seen them about much at all. Hard to know what she has."

The Norrington frowned. "She could see through the eyes of others, including rats and stuff. She could also control their actions."

"The clairvoyance is pretty easy, but it's also taxing.

Seeing through multiple eyes can drive some people insane." Orla thought for a moment. "I can probably conceal a small number of people from her watchers."

Alyx smiled. "Good, that will help." She reached out and spun the city map around so she could read it. Exemia pointed out the building in question. Alyx nodded. "What time is it?"

The Vorquelf answered. "Just nigh four. Dawn's an hour and a half off."

"Good, we have enough time, then." She glanced over at Captain Agitare. "You'll get the Wolves going and move west up near the temple district, then come down here into the Dim at the far side of our target, coming back east on Blackline. Captain Exemia, you'll start most of the Throne Guards from Fortress Gryps here, marching in good order. You'll come west on Broad Street, then cut down on Mason Road to Blackline. You'll both move slowly, putting on a big show, getting ready to converge on this point just after dawn."

The dark-haired woman nodded. "You said I would have most of the Throne Guards. Who gets left out?"

"I need six of your marines, the best of them." Alyx felt a shiver run down her spine. "Orla may be able to blind her, but a *sullanciri* will be suspicious if she has nothing to watch. We'll give her more than enough to watch, which is why she won't see the rest of us coming."

"The rest of us?" The hooded man turned to face her, and she squared up to the table, then looked at him across her right shoulder. "Who would the rest be?"

"Six marines, Resolute, Orla, the Norrington—to tell us what might be a trap or not—me and you. I know you'd not be here if you were not useful."

The Norrington smiled. "Crow's a legend."

Oh, so this is Crow. Alyx studied as much of his face as the shadows revealed. The white beard and forelock provided the illusion of age, as did the wrinkles at the corners of his eyes, and the scar on the right side of his face. His brown eyes, however, still burned with an intensity that surprised her and dispelled that illusion. She could not guess at his age, but she could see there was a lot of life left in him.

"You're Crow. I've been told I can trust you."

Crow bowed his head. "You are too kind."

"No, you'll find I'm not at all." Alyx glanced over at Agitare and Exemia. "Once we're in, we'll sound a whistle and you come hard."

Captain Exemia held a hand up. "They're still going to be able to take to the sewers, so we'll miss them."

Alyx shook her head. "No they won't. You've forgotten, the street there is called Blackline because that's what's left on the surface. High tide, which is in roughly an hour, goes up that far, causing the sewers to back up. Nightsoil gets left on the street. The sewers will provide them no escape."

The leader of the Throne Guards nodded, then her eyes widened along with her smile. "You're just going to take a longboat up Quay Road and dock right on the doorstep, aren't you?"

"Chytrine had no luck with an amphibious attack on Vilwan, so I doubt she's going to be anticipating our repeating that sort of lousy tactic." Alyx pulled the sketch of the building over and studied it. "We're only going to succeed with speed and surprise and magick. We've got to get Orla in so she can deal with the *sullanciri*."

Resolute let a low chuckle rumble from his throat. "She is not the only one who can deal with a *sullanciri*."

"I know, I've read the histories, I know how the others died. If you have any magick arrows or know where Temmer can be found, bring them." The simple fact of the matter was that the easiest way to deal with the *sullanciri* would be to assemble a cadre of Vilwanese Combat Magisters and level the building. While it would be effective, it would again underscore how difficult it would be to stop Chytrine. Part of the reason the raid had to go off successfully was to prove Chytrine could be defeated.

That's why the Norrington is here. If they succeeded with his help, that would hearten opposition to Chytrine and give her something to worry about. If they failed, nations would feel vulnerable enough that they might sue for peace on their own terms with Chytrine. Piecemeal opposition would be crushed. *If the Norrington is lost in a failed attempt, it won't matter anyway, since she won't be resisted.*

Captains Agitare and Exemia saluted Alyx and headed out. She came around the table and extended a hand to the Norrington. "I am Alexia. I'm pretty certain you don't want me calling you 'the Norrington,' and that would be pretty useless in combat."

"I'm Will. The Spritha here is Qwc." The youth shook her hand firmly. "You're the Gold Wolf. We saw you at Stellin."

The stable. She slowly turned and looked at Resolute and Crow. "It begins to make sense. Which of you shot the arrow?"

Will pointed across the table. "Crow did. I thought he was shooting at you and tried to spoil his aim. I'm glad I failed."

Alyx nodded to the man. "Not only can you be trusted, but your skill at arms is impressive."

"Spend enough time with Resolute and you learn how to do a lot of things well."

The Vorquelf nodded. "Killing things, mostly. That's what I do." He stabbed a finger against the sketch of the *sullanciri's* lair. "Just get us in there, Princess. You'll see I know my business well."

Two of the marines poled the longboat up Quay Road slowly and easily. Orla had directed them to propel the boat with a fluid motion, since that made it easier for her to conceal them. "People and animals tend to track motion pretty well. My spell will just create an illusion where our motion is attributed to something else. While folks try to track it, we will have moved past."

Crow crouched in the bow, with Will behind him and Resolute next. Alyx positioned herself in the middle of the boat, leaving Orla toward the rear, surrounded by a wall of thickly muscled marines. The Throne marines normally served on the king's flagship and were known to be very tough. Each wore leather armor and carried a pair of short stabbing swords, which would be perfect for close-in work.

Resolute and Will had come armed with gibberkin longknives. Alyx had conceded the wisdom of their choices, and the choice made by the marines, and had abandoned her saber. She armed herself with a shortsword and a small steel buckler with a punch-dagger bound into it. She could stab with it, parry with it, and any blow with the flat or edge of the shield would break bones.

Only Orla and Crow were oddly armed. The mage carried her staff, which was a bit long for use in close quarters. Alyx did not feel inclined to dispute her choice, however. Crow wore a longsword at his left hip, and a quiver of arrows on his back. His black-lacquered bow sat athwart the wales, and the arrow he'd nocked pointed toward their target.

Green eyes glowed from one of the lower windows, but didn't track their passage. Having seen the shot Crow made at Stellin, Alyx knew he could kill the owner of those eyes in a heartbeat, but doing that would alert the *sullanciri* to their presence. They all hoped she wouldn't find out about them until her life's-blood was pulsing out.

The longboat gently bumped up against the building's doorstep. Will slipped from the boat and opened the door. He peeked in furtively, then took the rope Crow tossed him to make the boat fast. Resolute entered the water without a sound on the port side of the boat, then lifted Orla clear while Alyx got out on the starboard side. The marines, drawing their swords, joined the procession and entered the ramshackle building's vestibule.

The open stairwell went up and doubled back before reaching the second level, repeating that pattern to get to the third. Will started up on cat's feet, staying low and watching for things before waving others on. Resolute followed him, with Alyx next, then Orla and the marines. Crow stayed at the base of the stairs, watching, ready to shoot at anything moving that wasn't a friend.

They'd made it up to the second-floor landing—and Will had ascended halfway to the third—when a keening wail rose from above them. A large, odd-looking, pale creature clung to the ceiling above the stairwell. It had a human face on a spiderlike body and its eyes glowed the telltale green. It opened its hands and started to drop down on the party, but before it had fallen ten feet, Crow's black-fletched arrow split its breastbone.

The thing slammed into the stairs and bounced up once. Resolute kicked it through the railing, sending it further down. All eight limbs thrashed and twitched as its call tailed off, but its silence mattered not at all. Other throats throughout the building had picked up on its shrieking and echoed the alarm. Doors opened and misshapen creatures emerged. Their eyes—and most had more than a pair and often had them scattered over their bodies—blazed with hellish jade fire.

Resolute roared past Will, slashing and stabbing at the creature guarding the upper landing. It had four arms: two human and two the forepaws of a dog. The face would have been human, save for the jutting canine muzzle with bared teeth. It snapped at the Vorquelf, crushing mail and ripping into the flesh on his right arm. Without so much as a snarl, Resolute drove a longknife through the thing's chest.

His charge carried the impaled creature across the landing and buried the blade in the wall. The beast howled, gnashing its teeth. It tugged at the longknife's hilt, trying to free itself, but it only released a torrent of blood. The creature's strength flowed out, leaving it limp and hanging there on the longknife, its feet dangling inches above the floor.

The Vorquelf roared a challenge in Elvish, then kicked in the door leading to the upper floor's central room. As he raced in, something leaped on him from above the door. He went down in a somersault, catching the creature under him as he rolled. That cleared the doorway, allowing Alyx to race in after him.

She took the room in with a glance. Clinging to walls and ceiling were more of the spiderlike creatures. What the dim stairwell had failed to reveal, the lamplight in the larger room made immediately apparent. The creatures had human faces because they were human, or had been. Magick had melded the flesh of two individuals, pressing them together, back to back, giving them four legs, four arms, and faces in the front and back of their skulls. Scuttling across the floor or along the wall, they watched, then leaped.

Alyx backhanded one diving monster with her buckler, then stabbed down through another attempting to bite her knee. She caught sight of a third scurrying along toward her, but a whizzing-whir ended in a thunk. A bladestar blossomed from the thing's forehead. The creature pitched face forward, so the bladestar bit into the wood, stopping its forward slide.

Will sent another bladestar whizzing into the room, pinning a spider-thing's foot to a wall. The Spritha took wing from Will's shoulder, then dove on one of the beasts. Qwc spat out a wad of webbing that expanded to blind the thing. As it tried to claw the webbing off, Orla stepped through the doorway and incinerated it with a sizzling gout of sorcerous flame.

About the time Resolute regained his feet and tossed the broken-necked beast aside, the door to the west room opened. A naked man-thing leaped through it, then crouched as the cat's-heads grafted onto his shoulders hissed angrily. Cat's paws had replaced his fingers and patches of fur striped his body. Green light shone brightly in his eyes, but he did not attack.

The emergence of the *sullanciri* from that same room demanded the attention of everyone, even Resolute. Her flesh and the gossamer gown she wore were of the purest white, save where radiant blue tattoos decorated her skin. Many of the patterns matched Resolute's, and fairly pulsed with power. She wore her long black hair loose and both it and the gown rode the currents of power swirling around her as if teased by a light summer breeze. The molten gold of her eyes broke as hot red lightning played through those orbs, yet the touch of her gaze chilled Alyx.

The gold eyes flashed. "Better than I could have expected here in my playground."

Orla swung the staff in line with the *sullanciri*. Fire erupted from the staff, but before it could hit Chytrine's general, the man-thing intercepted the spell. The magick engulfed him utterly, save for a droplet of fire that squirted from his back and splattered the *sullanciri*'s thigh.

It ignited the gown, but the *sullanciri* slapped it out as if it were no more bothersome than a spark. She snorted as the greasy curtain of smoke that had been the man-thing rose to the high ceiling. "Your magick, Magister, is known to me, and I am proof against it." She lifted her hand and neither it, her thigh, nor the gown showed any sign of the fire.

The *sullanciri* glanced at Resolute. "You know your magicks are not enough to kill me. Only one of you is a threat."

The *sullanciri*'s voice trailed off, then she darted toward Will. Stunned at her quickness, he didn't even attempt to back off. Green energy curled around her clawed hands and he could all but feel them tearing into his guts, stringing them around the room.

Steel rang as Crow drew his sword and interposed himself between Will and Chytrine's agent. "He's not the threat, Tsamoc here is." A milky gemstone fitted into the blade's reinforced-forte, which danced with internal light.

The *sullanciri* sprang back, then let a cold smile twist

her lips. As she reached up and took hold of the gown's shoulders, the magickal energy rose in a mist and dissipated. Broadening her smile, she peeled the garment down to her waist, exposing her breasts. "It might be, but not in your hands. You could never plunge it into me."

Crow extended the blade and it did not waver. "In a heartbeat."

She laughed, but took another step back. "You would find Myrall'mara's heart is as hard as yours, silly man, harder." The *sullanciri* nodded a salute to them, then smiled. "Now is not my time, and I shall not gloat in victory. I leave you, reluctantly, but I am called away. When next we meet, you shall think on this and know how kind I have been to you."

She circled a finger over a tattoo on her right breast. The blue of her tattoos flared brilliantly, blinding Alyx for a moment. When her vision returned, Myrall'mara had vanished. She turned to look at her comrades, but saw past them and their shocked expressions.

And she called this her playground.

A shiver shook Alyx. Where the spider-things had been, now lay the bodies of the naked children who had been transformed into them. The one she'd stabbed had become two, each struck through the heart. One bore the wound on her chest, the other on her back.

Will sat on the floor, caressing the side of one little girl's face. He brushed away the blood and tucked dirty hair behind her ear. "This was Skurri. She was my friend."

Crow slid his blade back into his sheath. "She made us make war on children. You, Princess Alexia, and you, 'the Norrington.' You and your comrades have slaughtered children. We might have driven her off, but . . ." He tugged his hood forward to hide his face.

"So that's why she let us live?" Orla slowly shook her head. "There are depths of evil I never could have imagined."

"We played her game. We made war on children." Alyx's

nostrils flared. "The slaughter of the children on Vilwan, and now this, here. As rumor of these things spread, a lot of people are going to wonder if Chytrine is truly the evil one."

Will slowly stood, wiping his bloodied fingers on his thigh. "Let them wonder. She may think she won, but she was here to get me, and she didn't. Doesn't matter what her reasons were, it was a mistake. She got my friends dead, and it's one I'll make her pay for."

CHAPTER 38

Kerrigan Reese did his best to hide the stiffness in his joints as he entered the large round *arcanorium* atop the Vilwanese tower in Yslin. The domed roof had a round opening in it, letting cool air and starlight in. Flickering flames from a dozen alcoves built into the walls provided shifting light, but more than enough for him to see the other four individuals in the room.

Kerrigan paused just inside the doorway and bowed his head. "Magister Orla. Magisters. You summoned me?"

Orla had a scowl on her face, but she said nothing, glancing at the gaunt, grey-robed man nearest the doorway. Kerrigan studied him for a moment, then felt a glimmer of recognition.

"Magister Baoth, forgive me for not recognizing you."

The man who had been one of his first tutors—concentrating on constructive magick—nodded. He still had wiry hair, which he wore short, but grey predominated over black, both on his head and in the beard he had grown.

"You honor me by remembering. These are Magisters Vulrasian of Croquellyn and Carok-Corax Ryss."

Kerrigan's eyes widened slightly. The tall elf, with jet-black hair and blue eyes, had figured strongly in the chronicles of the Aurolani invasion in which Vorquellyn had been lost. Though not known as a Magister of Combat, the elf had led a group of Croquelves and had landed them in the Ghost March. For months they harried Kree'chuc's troops, ambushing supply trains, assassinating officers, and generally creating havoc. Rumor that he and his men were approaching was enough to force the Aurolani to evacuate a village.

The urZrethi mage was someone Kerrigan had never heard of before. Like all of her kind, she was short and her flesh was the color of the earth—in this case the red of iron-rich soil. She had gathered her sulphur-yellow hair into a thick braid and knotted it with a black leather thong. As with Baoth and the elf, she wore a grey robe that marked her as being very accomplished in the arts of magick.

Belatedly, Kerrigan bowed his head. "I am honored."

"As are we, Adept Reese." The urZrethi's voice came a bit deeper than he would have expected. The elf silently nodded in agreement.

Magister Baoth produced a yellowed scroll from one sleeve of his robe and extended it to Kerrigan. "I would like you to read this over and determine if you can understand it."

The Adept took the scroll and could feel the antiquity of it. He slowly unrolled it and began to study the words. The scroll had been decorated with wonderful illuminations that connected words here and there, giving the whole thing a flow. Kerrigan immediately recognized the scroll as possessing a spell. *More importantly, the spell is complex enough that it can't be worked alone. There is much here, but much more is missing.*

He glanced up from the document. "I understand it, but it is odd. It's a human spell, I can see that, but it is jarring. It is as if it is a human transcription or adaptation of another magick."

Baoth nodded. "A fascinating observation. Can you cast it?"

"Not alone. There are things missing."

The elf studied him for a moment. Unlike Vorquelves, whose eyes were one solid color, the Croquelf's eyes had whites and even a black pupil. Kerrigan felt self-conscious as the Magister raked him up and down with an intense gaze, but he managed to forestall a blush.

Vulrasian tapped a finger against his chin. "Impressive, Adept Reese, to get that from a single reading. In fact, that is only one third of the spell. Carok-Corax and I possess the other two portions of it. Our portions will catalyze the effect."

Kerrigan frowned. "I've read of such things, of course, but never studied them. How will I coordinate with you? I'm assuming, of course, that you want me to cast this spell, otherwise why have me read it. Also, while it is a human spell, I don't believe either Magisters Baoth or Orla are capable of casting it."

"You are correct. It is an older spell, and that scroll is a transcription of an earlier one, which has since crumbled to dust. Yes, we do wish you to cast it, but it is not your place to coordinate with us, but ours to coordinate with you." The elf gestured toward him. "Strip off your clothes."

That command did make Kerrigan blush. "Magister, I would rather not."

"The spell demands you be naked." Vulrasian looked around the room. "You cannot imagine that we have not seen naked humans before. Remove your clothes and move to the center of the floor."

Kerrigan reluctantly complied. He moved to the middle of the floor and stepped down into a six-inch-deep bowl depression in the floor. While only a yard across, it was more than large enough to encompass him completely. With a word or two he could have invoked the runes and sigils inscribed in the ring around the bowl, raising a magickal shield in a column around him, but he had no sense that they were out to harm him, so he did not.

He handed the scroll back to Magister Baoth, then cast a glance at Orla, leaning there on her staff. She met his stare for a moment, then shook her head and looked down. He would have asked her what was wrong, but clearly any reservations she had about what would be happening had been overruled.

Once he'd stripped off his clothes and tossed them aside, Kerrigan stood there with his hands covering his genitals, a blush burning from neck upward. Even Orla studied his naked body—though he was pretty sure her winces came not out of displeasure with his corpulence, but at the sight of his purple bruises. The assault in the Dims had left his flesh mottled a host of ugly colors.

Baoth looked at the elf. "Will you need to deal with that before you proceed?"

The urZrethi answered. "It will be of no consequence. The reconstruction aspects will deal with it."

The elf concurred with a nod. "We can proceed."

Baoth crossed to the doorway and waved someone up the stairs. Three Apprentices entered the room, each one bearing a lidded bucket. Whatever was in them sloshed a bit, but none of it leaked out, and the Apprentices were bent over enough that Kerrigan thought they might somehow be carrying molten gold. As they set the buckets down to form a triangle around him, the Adept realized the Apprentice off to his right was Lariika.

Standing there naked before her, he broke into a sweat. Kerrigan looked up at the elf and frowned, attempting wordlessly to communicate his consternation, but Vulrasian gave no sign of comprehension at all. Instead the elf nodded to Baoth, who then gestured at the bucket in front of Kerrigan. It rose into the air and slowly drifted over him, then tipped for pouring.

The fluid came thick, more like oil or molasses than water, and had the deep ruby hue of half-dried blood. Where it touched his head it began to tingle, but that became the rake of thorns over his flesh as it dripped down his body. The sensation spread into a burning, as if he'd run naked at noon and had been sun-kissed to scarlet, then it built. He almost panicked for a moment, fearing he would burst into flame.

The excess fluid pooled in the bowl, coating his toes. The Apprentices dropped to their knees and reached down to scoop the fluid up, but Kerrigan waved them off with a half-coated hand. "You want this to coat me completely?"

The elf nodded. "It will not harm them to help you."

Kerrigan shook his head. "I'll do it." He slowly squatted and dipped his hands in the viscous fluid. He smeared it over his legs and up his thighs, along his genitals, over his buttocks. He coated every inch of him that he could touch, but his huge body made getting all spots impossible.

The girl inched around on her knees until he could see her out of the corner of his left eye. "Adept, let me help you, as you helped me."

Kerrigan closed his eyes, but nodded. He heard her moving around behind him, then felt the burning spread over his back. He did not feel her touch him until she reached up and coated his ears, then traced fingertips over his eyelids and down his nose. Her fingers drifted over his lips, then she gently tipped his chin up and coated his throat.

The fluid in his ears gave Vulrasian's voice an oddly distant quality. "Rise, Adept Reese."

He slowly stood again, the sticky fluid near his joints pulling a bit. Lariika drizzled more liquid on the places where his skin was yet bare. Once she was finished, he continued to stand, waiting, feeling as if his flesh were being dissolved.

The scrape of the lid coming off the second bucket alerted him to a change. He opened his eyes enough to catch a glimpse of a turgid ivory flow starting from the second bucket. He closed his eyes and held his breath, then lifted his face to it and let it pour down over him. The sensation of being nettle-stuck returned to his skin, then intensified. What started as pinpricks became needles, then spikes, piercing him. The fire in his lungs was nothing compared to the pain tearing at his flesh.

Kerrigan had all he could do to remain standing. His body quivered with the pain. He knew that if he squatted, he could never stand again. "Lariika, please." His words came out in a bubble of the liquid, and only when more pain blossomed on his body did he learn she had heard him.

For the most part she did not touch him, save his ears and the back of his neck, where hair interfered with the anointing. Liquid poured onto his belly flowed down over his loins, and a likewise generous distribution on his back covered his buttocks. As this liquid dried, he felt as if encased in an eggshell-thin layer of plaster, and he dared not move.

Before the pain died away, a third fluid flowed over him like sap. He could not see it, but it smelled of mint and cooled the fire on his skin. It dulled the spikes piercing his flesh. It flowed over his body faster—or maybe just seemed faster in the absence of the pain. Kerrigan smiled as it dripped down his body, and he began to spread it around before it had reached his ankles.

As this liquid numbed him, he could not feel if Lariika touched him at all. He lifted his chin, letting her paint his throat with it. He rubbed it over his genitals and backside, then lowered his head so she could do his ears and neck. Finally she traced it over his eyelids and lips.

He opened his eyes as she stepped back. Baoth eclipsed his view of her, then Orla herded the Apprentices out of the room. Baoth held up the scroll and fully unfurled it. He stood where the first bucket had, while the elf and the urZrethi moved to complete the triangle.

Vulrasian's voice came low and filled with gravity. "You

will begin, Adept Reese, and we will match you. Do not stop until it is done. We shall continue past, for a bit, but you will do the hard work. Commence now."

Kerrigan started reading from the scroll, slowly yet firmly and with the rhythm of the words. While he had only read them over once before, the spell had a cadence and sense that led one from the first word to the next and so on. The seamless chain of sounds looped and whirled, stretched taut and then loosened as syllable piled on syllable, rhymes created echoes, and refrains became sanctuaries where he could rest and gain confidence.

The two Magisters' voices mostly joined with his, but sometimes rose in counterpoint. While his words were the chain, their words helped shape it and direct it. They added color here and energy there, refining and defining what he was doing. Their sounds met his, making new words and layering meaning on old words. They erased the commonplace from oft-used phrases, added understanding to the obscure, and raised some expressions beyond comprehension.

When he finished his reading, he closed his eyes and could feel his portion of the spell taking root within him. Angular and hard, it sank into his bones. The urZrethi magick came next, all smoke and evershifting shadow. It spread like a webwork over his bones, fracturing his spell into a billion fragments. The pain of the spikes faded as new, crisp agonies shook him.

The Elvish words' soothing salve calmed his body. They flooded into the breaks, sealing and healing them. It fused them together, then spread out into his nerves and muscles and skin. He felt whole and more so—and he sensed it was more than just the stiffness of his limbs and the bruises being healed.

He opened his eyes and found himself standing in a dry depression. All of the fluid had been absorbed into him and not a trace remained on his pale white flesh. He flexed his fingers, then his arms. He took a double handful of his belly and let it flop. He was different, he knew that without a doubt, but he could not tell how.

Kerrigan looked around. "What happened? What did we do?"

Vulrasian's blue eyes narrowed. "If things went well, we have saved you great pain." The elf beckoned Orla forward with the flick of a finger. "Magister, strike him with your staff."

Orla shook her head and tossed the elf her staff. "I disagreed with your plan, so I shall not play your game. You want him struck, you strike."

Vulrasian accepted the staff, whirled it around in a circle, then snapped it down at Kerrigan's left forearm. The Adept heard it strike before he felt it, but instead of the slap of stick on skin and the attendant sting, he heard the clack of wood on rock. He'd already begun to shy from the blow, bringing his arm up, and now saw an ivory bone plate sinking beneath his skin at the point of impact.

Again the staff came around, this time hitting him in the chest. A bone plate armored his sternum, letting the stick rebound harmlessly. The staff came up at his face and glanced off a ridge on his left cheek.

Baoth laughed aloud as Kerrigan's jaw dropped open. "It worked."

"It did." The elf handed the staff back to Orla. "Your reservations, it seems, Magister Orla, were unnecessary."

"You missed the point, then. I was not concerned that he could handle the spell. I was concerned over his ability to handle what the spell has done to him."

Kerrigan frowned. "What do you mean, Magister? This is fantastic! If this had been done before, I'd not have been beaten by those ruffians in the Dim. I wouldn't have been hurt. This is incredible. I can't be hurt!"

He pulled his right foot back and kicked the edge of the bowl. His toes smashed full on into it without so much a hint of armor appearing. He did hear a crack, however, and hopped back, catching his heel on the back of the bowl. He flopped over backward, landing hard, with the urZrethi darting sideways from beneath him.

Kerrigan clutched his foot. "Ow, ow, OW! Ow. What happened? I don't understand."

Icy tones filled Orla's voice. "The magick will stop others from hurting you, but not you from hurting yourself, and that's from physical damage. Spells will kill you unless you counter them. On the other hand, get pushed from a roof and you will likely survive; leap the same distance and you'll die."

He frowned. "Likely survive?"

She nodded. "Find yourself under a big enough rock and it will crush you. Let a *sullanciri* drive an enchanted lance through you, and you'll die horribly."

"But little things, they won't hurt me." Kerrigan sat up. "Why did you think this was bad?"

Orla drew a gold coin from the purse on her belt and tossed it into the middle of the floor. "Levitate the coin."

Kerrigan arched an eyebrow at her. "You know I can do it."

"So, do it."

The Adept gestured at the coin with his right hand. It rose a foot off the floor before her staff clopped him on the shoulder. The staff bounced off bone plate, but the echoes of its impact died beneath the gold coin's ringing peal as it hit the floor.

Kerrigan looked at the coin as it accelerated through a death spiral. "I don't understand."

"It is simple, Adept Reese." Orla gave Baoth a venomous glance. "That spell is part of you now. It is always on, always working. It draws energy from you as needed, diverting that which you might need to use for other things. This puts you in the curious situation where you will be unable to help others if you are put under a constant threat. An elven archer with a keen eye and a silverwood bow could prevent you from casting a single spell just by delivering an arrow from time to time."

Her nostrils flared. "You'll watch your comrades get cut down and be unable to do anything for them, and yet you will survive. Forever you'll carry the memory of their betrayal with you. I hope you can live with that. I couldn't, nor could the only man who had this spell cast on him before you."

Kerrigan shook his head. "Who was that?"

"Yrulph Kirûn, the creator of the DragonCrown." Orla slowly shook her head. "His madness has returned over the centuries to haunt the world. You've been given this spell in the hopes you will be able to end his insane legacy. I just hope, Adept Reese, it does not lead you to leave us one that is worse."

CHAPTER 39

A half week, somber and dour, passed between the confrontation with Myrall'mara and the arrival of the celebrated Jeranese general, Markus Adrogans. In the aftermath of the slaughter, Alyx had thought about many things, though none could deflect her from remembering the torn corpses cooling, and the little sighs the children made as their bodies relaxed and forced air from lungs.

She'd seen such things before, and heard them, but never quite that way. She'd seen slain children in the wake of Aurolani raids. She'd heard the death-sighs of corpses. She'd just never been close enough to the site where children had died to see their blood yet flowing and their eyes still clouding over. *And never was that death at my hands.*

Peri had done her best to lighten Alyx's mood over the past five days, but her sister knew her well enough to back away when things would not work. Misha had tried as well. When his initial suggestions that they enjoy some diversion such as theater failed to win her acquiescence, he challenged her to train with him at swordplay. The workouts had been good, but had left Misha bruised and sore; which darkened the mood that had been started because of injuries done to those who did not deserve them.

Had she been given a choice, she would not have come to Fortress Gryps for the reception in Adrogans' honor. But the Grand Duchess saw to it that she had no choice, and had even selected for her the gown with an embroidered bodice of black and gold over gold starched-satin skirts. The gown left her uncovered from the bodice to neck and wrists, which she found uncomfortable despite having spent ample time growing up amid the Gyrkyme wearing as little as possible.

At least, with them, I was always allowed to have a dagger strapped to my thigh or upper arm. She'd actually wanted to wear one on her upper left arm, and Peri had gotten her a suitable sheath covered with the same brocade as her bodice, but Tatyana had vetoed that plan. She could have worn it on her thigh, but digging beneath the skirts to draw it would have been impossible. The Grand Duchess had allowed as how she could secret a dagger between her breasts as part of the bodice, but Alyx doubted mightily that it would remain secret for long. That particular portion of her anatomy seemed to invite inspection, especially from those odious lechers she'd have loved to stab.

Alyx had arrived at the reception early in hopes she would be allowed to leave equally early. She knew, from careful study of Adrogans' battles, that he would arrive late with a large entourage and wreak havoc. As the evening wore on and the moment of his impending arrival grew closer, Alyx had taken the precaution of moving away from the tables laden with victuals, lest she be trapped between them and the Jeranese General Staff. From studying supply reports, she knew Adrogans' troops were largely overfed, his army more of a herd than a military organization.

She moved out into the gardens, where the slight chill in the air puckered her flesh. Out there the music rose above the murmurs, bringing a slight smile to her face. She let the shadows embrace her and slowly sipped a sweet wine redolent of plums.

The particular song being played was common enough in the border area between Jerana and Okrannel that Alyx recognized it. It had different names and lyrics depending upon the nation, but in Okrannel it was a simple song about a shepherd and the wonders he saw while searching for a lost sheep. Since the fall of Okrannel the song had been changed such that the previously anonymous shepherd took on her father's name, and she was identified with the missing lamb.

The garden itself had also been remade since the fall. Stones from the various cities and battle sites in Okrannel had been brought south and set up in the correct relationship to each other. A rift matching the Dnivep River valley had been carved through the garden, though a bridge spanned it here whereas, in Okrannel, the Radooya Bridge had been destroyed. Plants native to the northern climes of Okrannel had been imported and—in what had been taken to be an ill omen by some in the exile community—thrived in a home only meant to be temporary.

Alyx laughed to herself as she realized that passing from the Jeranese reception into the garden had her moving in the same direction pilgrims did when they went for their whimsy-rests and dream raids on Okrans soil. "I doubt that the dreams I would have here would please the Crown Circle."

Her breath caught in her throat as a man standing over in the corner, near the stones from Svarskya, politely coughed into his hand. "I beg your pardon, Princess."

She turned to face him and required a moment to do so lest her skirts tangle and she topple. He wore a black tunic that had been cut just below his waist over black trousers and dark riding boots. His white beard had been trimmed, as had his hair, and he wore no jewelry or weapons. "I didn't see you, Crow."

"I know, which is why I coughed when I heard you

speak." The older man shrugged. "I knew you were not speaking to me, and I heard nothing, but I didn't want you taken unawares."

"You could have spoken earlier." She frowned. "Did you not see me? Are you night blind?"

"No, not at all." A smile softened his face and even made the scar on his right cheek somehow less brutal. "You are a vision of loveliness, and quite striking in so much gold. I was, however, like you, lost in thoughts."

Alyx nodded at the white stone tower that half hid him. "You were thinking of Svarskya?"

"I was. I was lost in the heroism and sacrifice of those who died there." He stepped from behind it and toward her, glancing back for a moment as he moved forward. "The songs of what happened abound, of course. Just seeing a stone from there makes it more real."

She lifted her chin. "You have memories of Svarskya."

"Of the battles and siege? Gods, no. I wasn't there for that."

"That is not what I suggested." Her violet eyes sharpened. "After we met, I asked about you and Resolute. I was told he brought that stone from Svarskya—emptied a tower of gibberkin and vylaens so he could prize free a stone my father had touched. They must have been good friends for him to do that, and you a good friend to accompany him on that journey."

Crow gave her a half smile. "Resolute never knew your father."

"But, then, why?" She shook her head, her hair brushing against her back and neck. "It has been assumed he did that in my father's honor."

"Oh, he did. We both did. Resolute, years ago, refused to join the expedition to Svarskya because it was not going to free Vorquellyn. In the wake of all that happened, Resolute felt that had he been along, lives would have been saved." Crow brushed his fingers over the rock. "Perhaps too little, too late, but to Resolute it is an acknowledgment of a debt he owes your family and nation."

"And why did you go?"

His face closed a bit. "I met your father. I even saw you, once, when you were an infant. Your father sold his life dearly at Fortress Draconis. He saved my life and so many others. He did what no one else could do, opposing a *sullanciri*."

"Just like you."

"Pardon?" Crow's eyes widened slightly. "Oh, Myrall'mara."

"Yes, though you say it as if it were nothing. Everyone who has opposed *sullanciri* is either dead or has gone over to them." Alyx frowned. "Why is it that fate didn't befall us? Despite making us kill children, there must have been something more."

"There was. Myrall'mara couldn't have killed us all." Crow clasped his hands together and let them hang easily down by his belt. "She wasn't prepared for combat. She had come unarmed. Despite what she said to Resolute, he could have killed her."

"How is it that you chose to go after her? You know what happened to my father. From what you said, you'd seen *sullanciri* before. It takes a brave man to do what you did."

Crow slowly smiled. "Oh, my. Had I listened to Jeranese critiques of the raid I'd not have thought of you as being subtle enough for that attack on my identity. You want to know who I am, since I claim to have known your father, but there are no chronicles of Svarskya or Fortress Draconis that mention Kedyn's Crow. You are suspicious, which is good."

That's not what I wanted to know, is it? Her frown deepened. "I actually *was* wondering what sort of man would dare challenge a *sullanciri*. The question of your identity would be part of that, true, but immaterial. You could be any one of a thousand men who had been in Svarskya and Fortress Draconis. Your name is just one you took later. In fact, in the same way that the Vorquelves take on human words as names—words full of meaning—so you have made yourself a myth with your choice. In learning who you are, your name is immaterial."

"Quite an insight for someone so young."

Alyx gave him a little shrug. "Gyrkyme wisdom, not mine. They often change names to commemorate a past deed, a fallen friend, or as part of undertaking some grand quest. The Gyrkyme who carried me from Svarskya to Gyrvirgul was forever known as Ironwing for having made the long flight so quickly."

Crow thought on that for a moment, then nodded. "I would have believed it was your insight."

"You overestimate me."

"No. I saw you study the plans for the building we attacked and lay out a plan that worked. Your modesty does you credit." His brown eyes sparkled for a moment. "And, in matching your openness, I was willing to confront Myrall'mara because of my sword. Magic weapons, elemental forces, these are what we need to destroy *sullanciri*. I had a magick sword, Tsamoc, and, well, Resolute is pretty much an elemental force."

Alyx took a sip of her wine, then extended the half-filled glass to Crow.

He took it, then smiled. "What are you drinking?"

She blinked. "I didn't want you to fetch more, I was offering you a drink."

"Highness, it would be unseemly of one so lowly as myself to be drinking from your glass."

Alyx threw her head back and laughed. "You killed a vylaen who would have killed me. You chased a *sullanciri* off. I should be fetching wine for you, but that is not the point. Were we in the field, we'd share a skin of wine without thinking about it for a heartbeat."

"Ah, but we're not in the field, are we?" Crow glanced at

the doorway back into the fortress. "Different sort of battlefield, this."

She followed his gaze. "And the enemy has entered the field of battle."

General Adrogans had arrived and was being introduced by the Jeranese queen to all manner of guests, including Will Norrington. The military man shook Will's hand strongly, having swallowed the youth's limb in a huge hand. He bent down, lowering his head to Will's level. While they were clearly being introduced to one another as the only hopes for the world, Adrogans seemed intent on making certain Will knew who was the *greatest* hope.

Crow glanced at her. "*That* particular introduction is one people have been waiting for, but there are bets about the two of you meeting."

"Oh?"

"You surrender an inch and fifty pounds to him, he surrenders twenty years to you." He arched an eyebrow at her. "The gown hampers your mobility, but it will distract him."

"Are you saying you have your money on me?"

He shook his head. "Running with Resolute I push my luck way too much to gamble. Besides, it is immoral to bet on a certainty."

She turned her head and frowned at him. "Why are you here?"

"As Will's bodyguard and guest." He sipped at her wine, then returned the glass. "All of this is foreign to Will. A week ago he didn't know who he was, and now kings and queens defer to him. If he gets lost in that, we're all lost."

"I didn't get the feeling he would." She took the glass back from him. "He seems to be a smart young man."

"You're right." Crow smiled. "So really I'm here to make sure that all the stuff he nicks is put back. Not so much guarding him from society as the other way around."

Alyx sighed as she shifted her attention to the Jeranese general. "I can't avoid meeting Adrogans, can I?"

"No. And if only half the stories about him are true, he's loud, arrogant, and the way for a foe to defeat him is to carry a mirrored shield, since General Adrogans will be entranced by the vision of perfection he sees trapped in it."

His remark caught her in mid-drink. She choked a laugh, holding the glass out in her left hand so the wine that sloshed and dripped missed her gown. She wiped her chin with the back of her right hand, flicking the excess wet off, then shook her head. "Warn me next time."

"As her Highness directs." Crow's voice grew louder as he snatched the glass from her hand. "More wine."

"That will be quite enough wine for her for now." Tatyana stood in the doorway with Adrogans on her arm. "General Adrogans, this is my great-grandniece."

"Great-grandniece? Not possible. Your niece, surely, grandniece perhaps, were you but a flower child at your brother's wedding." Adrogans patted the woman's hand on his arm, devoting his full attention to her while Alyx waited. "It would not have been out of the realm to guess you were mother and daughter, the Okrans beauty runs so strongly in you both."

Tatyana gave him a smile that withered as she looked at Alyx. "You see, Princess Alexia, skill at arms does not require a lack of social grace."

"Noted, Aunt Tatyana." Alyx kept a slender smile on her lips, letting a snarl nest in its simple lines. Clearly the honey-eyed words Adrogans poured into her aunt's ears were not meant to flatter her, since only a moron would think Tatyana's vanity so easily overrode her sense. Adrogans paid her attention as a way to ignore Alexia and put her in her place. *Or the place he sees for me.*

Alexia stepped in close to the Jeranese general and looked him eye to eye. She slid her hand forward, stopping him from grabbing her hand across the knuckles. She shook his hand carefully and strongly, not trying to hurt him, but letting him feel her strength.

"I am pleased, General Adrogans, to meet a legend."

"You do me too much honor, Princess." His grey eyes had none of the warmth she'd just seen in Crow's, and the man's steel-grey hair, while marking age as well as Crow's white hair did, in no way hinted at any humanity in the man.

Adrogans gave her a carefully crafted smile. "Besides, you and I know where the legend ends, the point beyond which all is fable. We are linked that way, the two of us really. I earned my fame at the time you were being carried off to Gyrvirgul."

Crow returned as the general spoke. Returning her refilled wineglass to her, Crow nodded, then looked at Adrogans. "I would have gotten you something to drink, but I know the general prefers being dry."

"Dry?" Adrogans frowned for a moment, then nodded slowly. "Yes, dry, I see. Indeed, yes, congratulations, Princess, on your amphibious assault on the house here in the slum. Interesting tactic to use. That's the only time I've heard of a shipborne assault approaching success."

Alyx smiled quickly. "Better success against Chytrine's troops than she has against ours, certainly."

The Jeranese general snorted lightly. "You were making war on children, she was fighting against warriors."

Crow moved to Alyx's side. "If you speak with the Vilwanese, General, you will find that Chytrine was making war on children as well. Her assault never was meant to succeed."

"Her excuse now, or one made by those who apologize for her." Adrogans slowly shook his head. "You've chased her out of this city, Princess, and I will chase her from your homeland. I've assured your aunt of this very thing. I trust you will support me in this."

Tatyana nodded. "She will. We all will and do, General." The old woman's dark eyes flashed ferociously. "The princess, as with all Okrans expatriates everywhere, stands ready to do as you bid. Isn't this true, Alexia?"

"I am certain, Aunt, that the general has no doubt of it

at all." She suppressed a shudder. "Okrannel will be liberated."

"I shall be pleased to have you join me on the campaign, Princess." He bowed, then looked down at Tatyana again. "Grand Duchess, let me take you back inside before you catch a chill."

"You are so kind, General. Good evening, Princess."

Adrogans flicked a salute at her, then steered her great-grandaunt back into the ballroom. Alyx found herself staring after him for a moment, then forced her balled right fist open. She concentrated on her breathing and made herself calm down.

Crow smiled carefully. "And you don't like him, why?"

She hesitated, sorting the reasons, ordering them, then selecting the one that annoyed her the most. "He's won victories against Aurolani forces. Of this there is no doubt, but he is a cavalry officer. I have studied his battles and he wastes his infantry. Moreover, there's never been a cavalry in the history of the world that could lay siege to a fortress. If a fraction of the rumors about what he wants to do are true, we might win Okrannel back, but we won't be able to hold it. We'll run out of personnel and supplies. He's planning for a campaign as if it is just a big raid, and it won't work."

"Then you favor the Draconis Baron and his plans?"

She shook her head. "It's true that Fortress Draconis may have stuck in Chytrine's throat like a bone for years, but that doesn't mean there won't come a time when she spits it out or swallows it whole. And his strategy, while it might bleed her white and dry, won't liberate Okrannel, the Ghost March, or Vorquellyn. We need something else, a different approach, but with the sides being chosen here, the chances of that happening are slender."

Alyx glanced at Crow and the quizzical way in which he was looking at her. "What is it?"

"Nothing, really. I've just thought, for years, that doing things in the same old way would lead to nothing changing." He shrugged. "Perhaps, with you here, and Will, there is a possibility of doing things a different way."

"That's what I will have to hope, then." Alyx sipped the wine. Where she had been expecting sweet, she got tart with an acid bite. "What? This isn't what I expected."

"No, it's not." Crow's eyes became dark slits. "An object lesson, Princess. We're not in the field, so none of it will be what you expect. Remember that and maybe, just maybe, you'll be sent into the field where new ideas might make for big changes."

CHAPTER 40

In just a week, Will had gone from being the pretender to the throne of the Dimandowns to being celebrated in the Hightown. Over the last ten days—the first full week of the month of Leaffall—Will had met more people from more nations than he'd seen before in his entire life. Just the demands on him to shake hands and sit down to a nibble or sip all but overwhelmed him.

He actually looked back with favorable whimsy to the days on the road with Resolute and Crow.

Things had started easily enough after he'd been rescued and they'd gone after Myrall'mara. The next morning King Augustus' tailor arrived at the Vilwanese tower to measure him in more ways and places than Will would have thought possible. By that evening Will had a suit of clothes on him that fit properly, and that took getting used to. Being all new and of the right size, it felt confining. Worse, anything he stole aside from a glance would be clearly visible.

With subsequent outfits, the tailor did make some

minor allowances for Will to grow into things, which made the thief feel a little better. His new status brought him access to the local nobility. He got invited to estates he could only have dreamed about breaking into. While on his visits he started to catalog all the ways he could enter and escape unnoticed, but he often found himself lost in the opulent splendor. Not only did the people have fantastic works of art, and treasures from distant lands or antiquity in their houses, but they kept pet dogs and cats who ate better, dressed better, and were housed better than the richest man in the Dimandowns.

Native resentment against the rich made him look forward to stealing from them, since it served them right for being so wealthy. Will's thinking ran along the lines that if they were looking to him to be *the* Norrington who would save their lives and their fortunes from Chytrine, they owed it to him to share some of that wealth. Since they'd end up with nothing if it weren't for him, it was *just* that they survived with a little less.

While he'd had that rationalization all worked out, he never needed to employ it. Gifts started pouring in. He'd get an invitation to a ball, and a suit of clothes cut to his measurements would arrive with it. Little boxes of tea, bottles of wine, rare incense, and exotic foods all came for him. Some people gave him rings with the Norrington crest worked onto them, while others sent items they claimed they'd gotten from his father or grandfather or some other family member. The ones Will liked best just sent money as a token of their esteem.

He'd not much liked the competition from the Jeranese general. His arrival five days into Will's ascension cut into the gift trade, though the invitations to parties and meals did not slacken. While Will did like all the attention, the silver lining in the cloud of Adrogans' arrival was that the most boring and pompous of the folks at the parties spent their time talking to him, not Will. For that reason alone Will didn't slip the emerald ring off Adrogans' hand whenever they were once again introduced to each other—though Will knew he could have it off the man in the blink of an eye, with the general being none the wiser.

All of those invitations, however, paled in comparison to the one that had brought him to the estate housing King Scrainwood and the delegation from Oriosa. As estates went, it wasn't the biggest or best he'd been invited to, but it did have some odd architectural elements appropriate for people who wore masks. The servants did not use masks, being lowborn and mostly from Yslin. Between the public areas of the house and the more private chambers, curtains and screens limited how much a visitor could see. The door for each of the private chambers had been set back from the corridor to allow for the placement of screens or drapes, and even the lighting in the corridors tended to be less bright than on other estates. The resulting shadows could mask the residents even when they were unaware they were being watched.

Will had seen enough folk from the masked nations to view them as unusual instead of exotic. In the Dim they were known as Hides—both because of the leather covering their faces, and the fact that their faces were hidden. It struck the citizens of the Dim as odd that these folks wore masks in honest commerce, while the Dimkin put them on to cover themselves during illegal activity.

Of course, Will knew the tradition of wearing masks had arisen in the past, when the nobles were plotting to secede from the Estine Empire. Despite their masks having been donned for the same reason as they were worn in the Dim, no spirit of kinship existed between thieves and the Oriosans. Every so often a bright thief put on an Oriosan mask to cover his robberies. They mostly just vanished, or so the stories in the Dim went, but a few were found after having had their faces carved off and the fraudulent mask fixed to their skulls with six-inch nails.

Will shivered and looked around the long, narrow room he'd been placed into to wait. Shelves ran floor to ceiling all around it save at the narrow ends where tall double doors ate into the storage space. Everything had been made of dark wood that gave the room a cavernish feeling. Half the shelves had been slotted for scrolls, with the rest fitted out to hold books. Every nook and cranny had been jammed with volumes, even to the point where some leather-bound volumes lay over the top of others.

The thief shook his head. Unless something good had been hidden behind the phalanx of books, there was nothing of any value in the room. Clearly the house's owner thought books were worth collecting, but Will knew folks in the Dim who had amassed a fortune in pretty rocks. Neither were worth stealing, since their weight-to-value ratio ran so high. The room's furnishings, while very nice, had the sort of stout, sturdy construction that would have dwarfed Dranae and likely made them too heavy for the large man to move.

The doors in the opposite end of the room opened with a click. Will spun, then jumped back as a brassy fanfare blared. Resolute couldn't suppress a smile as he opened the doors, but it died quickly enough. The Vorquelf had put on a courtesy mask of sheer black material. Will would have described it as lacy, but he knew Resolute would at best allow that it was gauzy. It wasn't a discussion for the moment, however, so Will kept his tongue still.

Resolute had not wanted to attend the evening's ceremony. He'd not said anything, but he'd steadfastly avoided accepting any other invitations. Crow had always gone, but remained in the background. Will didn't know what had passed between the two of them, but Crow had simply informed Will that Resolute would accompany him to the Oriosan king's gathering.

The Vorquelf gave Will a quick nod, then moved out of the way. The room beyond the doors crossed the small library and possessed in depth what the library had in length. The larger room extended off to the right and left for quite a way—perhaps running the length of the house, but Will was not certain. The high ceiling's arches had been covered with colorful murals taken from Oriosan history. A small band of musicians sat in an elevated gallery at the far right end.

A carpet of emerald-green stretched from the doorway to a dais five paces away. Worked into the weave was a border of red featuring the entwined and sinuous forms of dragons. The vast majority of people crowding the dais and lining the carpet's edge likewise wore green with red trim, but only one had the royal dragon rampant in red on his breast.

King Scrainwood wore a green mask that arced down from a shock of white hair to the tip of his nose, then extended wings down to his jawline. The wingtips left his chin unhidden, though the corners of his broad smile did vanish beneath them. He clapped his hands once, then rubbed them warmly, letting light flash from the sapphire ring on his right hand. Keeping his smile inviting, he spread his hands, then nodded and beckoned Will forward.

"Wilburforce Norrington, come to me. Come to your nation."

Will, who had been sent a dark green velvet jacket and trousers, with red cuffs on the jacket and a red strip down the legs, started forward. Everyone stared at him through a mask. Most wore the guest masks akin to the one on Resolute's face—and few had eyes quite as close-set as in Scrainwood's mask—but a number were genuine Oriosans. He spotted Colonel Hawkins from Fortress Draconis, but recognized him more because of the uniform and silver mail on his face than anything else. A few other individuals looked familiar, but he assumed he'd seen them at other parties.

The irony of his being the only person in the room without a mask struck Will, but he was not certain what to make of it. Oriosans went to so much trouble to avoid being seen without a mask, and went to great lengths to keep the tradition of their wearing masks unsullied. Yet, here, *everyone* had a mask on save him.

As he drew nearer the dais, he got the sinking feeling that Scrainwood had orchestrated everything for his own benefit. *It's not so much that he wants to claim me for his country, but he wants part of my fame.* Will would have turned and run from the place just to thwart him, but doing that would have meant no more invitations. *And I'd be alone with* sullanciri *hunting for me.*

The young thief stopped in front of the dais and King Scrainwood smiled down on him for a moment. The smile had been the same warm one he'd been using since the doors opened, but, up close, the man's hazel eyes glittered icily. The king's gaze flicked up and he studied the crowd.

"We are pleased that all of you were able to attend this momentous event. Those of you who are guests here may not be familiar with the rituals through which we invest our citizens with their masks. Rarely is anyone outside the family present at such an event. And again, usually this event takes place close to Mid-Summer's Day, when the recipient is in his eighteenth year. Wilburforce, as nearly as we know, has not reached that milestone in his life, but there is no one here who can say he has not shouldered an adult's burden despite his tender years."

Scrainwood reached out with his left hand and settled it on Will's head with enough pressure that he could do nothing but stare straight ahead at the king's belly. "You all know of the Norringtons, and many of you can only think of them as monsters, but this was not always so. A quarter century ago they were here, father and son, leading the force that slew all of Chytrine's Dark Lancers. They broke the back of her army at Fortress Draconis. Had they not served the world valiantly and well, the only warmth any of us would know would be in the belly of a temeryx.

"I knew Wilburforce's father well. When a youth receives his first mask, it is white. It is called a moonmask, and for the period of the full moon he is free to explore the world and decide what he wishes to be as an adult. Bosleigh Norrington decided he would be a hero, and a hero he was, many times over, before he was granted his life mask."

Scrainwood's voice grew slightly distant. A tremor ran through his hand, sending a sympathetic shiver down Will's spine. The thief wanted to bolt at that moment, and would have, save he glanced to the side and caught the eye of a man standing behind and to the side of the king. He and Scrainwood looked enough alike—and he was wearing a simple coronet—that Will took him to be one of Scrainwood's sons.

What stopped Will from running was the dead flatness of the man's eyes. They ran more to brown than the hazel of his father's, but even the reflected hints of light could not enliven them. The slight stoop of his shoulders and creeping paunch marked the man as having been spirit-broken, and Will instantly imagined that Scrainwood would do the same to him to get what he wanted.

Let him try. Will's nostrils flared, but he didn't ball his fists or give any other outward sign of his growing anger. He even suppressed a shudder just so he wouldn't give the king the pleasure of mistaking revulsion for fear.

"With my very own hands, I gave Bosleigh Norrington his first adult mask—his harvest mask. At the same time, Lord Kenwick Norrington gave the traitor his mask, and we all know the tragic culmination of that chain of events. I like to think, perhaps, that Bosleigh ... Well, after Chytrine's *sullanciri* leader, the man who had been Bosleigh's father, slew my mother, Bosleigh came to me to ask my blessing on his mission to avenge our nation. I begged him to wait, but so full of righteous fire was he that he headed out. He had faith in the prophecy that said a Norrington would destroy Chytrine."

The young thief shivered. Songs had told the tale of his father's ill-fated quest. When hearing them, Will had always thought of Leigh Norrington as a total fool, and even now that he knew they were related, his opinion didn't shift. *He was a fool to go after Chytrine.* Will swallowed hard. *And ducklings don't stray far from their mothers.*

"We all have faith in that prophecy. And here, now, we have the Norrington who will accomplish the job. He stands here bare-faced, as he has been throughout his life in Yslin. We knew him not for what he was, but now we know him for his true nature."

Scrainwood released Will's head, then turned and beckoned quickly for the prince to approach. The prince handed his father a slender green strip of leather with two eyeholes cut into it. One had a V-shaped notch excised from it, pointing down from the corner of the eye closest to the nose. In that way it matched the prince's mask. The king's had one of those wedges chopped from each eye.

Scrainwood held the mask up high for all to see. "This is his first adult mask. We decorate them to mark our passages in life. This cut here, on the right eye, means his mother has died. The mask is green, for that is our color. And, now, I shall mark it with my seal, marking him a loyal Oriosan king's man."

The king snapped his fingers and his son fumbled at a pouch on his belt. From it he drew a signet ring that his father slipped onto his middle finger. He mouthed a word silently and the ring's flat face glowed red, though Will caught no heat from it. Scrainwood pressed the ring against the leather, right between and above the eyes. A puff of sour smoke rose from the leather. The ring came away with a sticky sound, leaving in its wake a coiled dragon in scarlet.

Scrainwood returned the ring to his son, then motioned for Will to turn around and face the audience. He did so and could feel the intensity of the stares. He blushed, so the touch of the mask to his face was cool, but not for long. The king tied the mask tightly, catching hair in it, but Will didn't cry out.

"We are pleased to present to you Lord Wilburforce Norrington of Oriosa. Let whatever he has been be forgotten, and what he will become be the subject of song and tale." The king led a round of applause, making Will blush further. Scrainwood's hands landed on Will's shoulders, holding him in place, and the flagging applause picked up for a moment or two.

"It is customary, at the time of a man receiving his adult mask, for him to be granted a gift. We would ask you, Wilburforce, what you would have of us?"

The thief glanced down at the floor for a moment, then canted his head and looked up and back. "I would, my lord, just wish to shake your hand in friendship." Will turned and offered the king his hand amid gasps and a smattering of applause.

Scrainwood hesitated for a moment, clearly caught off guard, then shook hands with the thief. Will clasped his left hand on the king's right, and the king completed the knot with his hand. Will smiled broadly and the king matched him, then gave their hands one final shake and pulled his free.

Stepping up onto the dais as the king withdrew, Will offered his hand to the prince. The young man hesitated, then extended his hand toward Will. The thief stumbled, falling against the prince, then shook his hand and backed away apologizing. "Ever so sorry. Need to learn how to see what I am doing through this mask."

"You will learn, Norrington." The prince's comment came mixed with disgust and resignation, as if he detested Will, but could not muster enough outrage to make his feelings known.

Will's head came up, but he kept his voice low. "Not easy being our fathers' sons, is it?"

The prince's eyes widened for a moment, then narrowed and died. "There are some things you will never learn, boy."

The thief turned from the prince, then stepped down to the floor and greeted well-wishers. Many of them seemed genuinely pleased, and he drew warmth from their smiles and comments, but viperish glances and weak grips told him many others did not like him at all. He assumed they were jealous, or some afraid, with the group displaying outrage all being Oriosans with well-decorated masks.

The last person to greet him offered his left hand instead of the leather-wrapped metal of his right. "I'm Sallitt Hawkins of Fortress Draconis."

Will gave him a smile. "I saw you before, with your wife, when the Draconis Baron was introduced."

"They would both have liked to be here, and send their best wishes to you, but they are away reviewing plans as the discussions about what we will be doing now begin in earnest." Sallitt's mail flesh rustled a little as he smiled. "I should return to them quickly, but I could not stay away. You know, I trust, that the prophecy says you will have a Hawkins at your side when you destroy Chytrine."

Will blinked. "I guess I didn't know that."

Resolute appeared at Will's right shoulder. "You're not incorrect, Colonel, though scholars and philosophers still debate nuances of the Elvish words used."

"I can understand that." The *meckanshii* nodded slowly. "I was too old to know your father well, but I recall how well my father served your grandfather. You've heard tales of how Hawkinses have always served the Norringtons, I'm certain. I want you to know that if you need help—need for anything—you have a Hawkins who will help you."

Will's skin tightened into gooseflesh as Hawkins spoke. Not only did he hear sincerity in the man's voice, but a conviction and desire to do his duty for Will and, by extension, the world. It didn't matter the cost—and the man's having let himself be made over into a *meckanshii* bespoke a commitment Will was unsure he could have accepted.

"Thank you, Colonel, thank you." Will nodded solemnly. "With a Hawkins and a Norrington set against her, Chytrine's nights of sleeping easy are going to be distant memories."

The man gave Resolute a nod, then turned on his metal

leg and limped away. Will looked up at the Vorquelf after Hawkins had moved from earshot. "Is what he said true?"

Resolute nodded solemnly. "There are many things in that prophecy, and what he said is but one of them."

"But this is right, him offering his service like that?"

The Vorquelf's silver eyes flashed coldly. "It is, but pairing a Norrington and a Hawkins is not enough. The efforts of good soldiers like him have to be put in a position to be effective, and we don't know if they will or not."

Will frowned. "Meaning?"

"This is a Council of Kings, boy. It is a marketplace of power." Resolute's voice became a razor-edged whisper. "For over a century Chytrine has owned my homeland, not because the world lacks the power to liberate it, but because the world leaders see no power to be harvested in liberating it. In these meetings, Cavarre will be pitted against Adrogans, and everyone else will have their own little games to play. If they forget the goal, a hundred thousand Hawkinses accompanying a hundred thousand Norringtons would accomplish nothing."

"But—but that makes no sense."

"No, it doesn't, boy." The Vorquelf sighed and patted Will on the right shoulder. "But in the eyes of a politician, they have won if their nation is the last to be devoured by Chytrine. These people will do whatever it takes to taste victory. Know that and beware."

CHAPTER 41

King Scrainwood slid a thumbnail under a fingernail and scraped at the dirt. He worked the dark ball out and rolled it between thumb and index finger, then flicked it away. He inspected his nails again, then nodded to his chamberlain, Count Cabot Marsham.

"The old witch has waited long enough; bring her."

Marsham bowed deeply, which made the varicolored ribbons hanging from his mask flutter and float. "As my lord demands."

The king suppressed his snarl until the little man had vanished behind the mask-curtain. Marsham had once done him a favor and, despite being a scheming toad, had continually made himself useful. Marsham knew how to cultivate back-alley allies, and the meeting to which Scrainwood subjected himself had been one of Marsham's manufacture.

Scrainwood would have postponed it, but Marsham had insisted it was very important. The king's head throbbed with a hangover from the previous night, for he had drunk many a toast to the honor of Oriosa and its claim on the person of the Norrington. The headache had been exacerbated by his fury with his son for having lost the state seal. What had angered Scrainwood the most about Linchmere's losing it was not that he'd actually misplaced the thing—that had happened before—but the fact that he had noticed it missing at midnight and had not commenced a search until mid-morning, after he'd awakened.

That boy has been useless ever since his mother drowned. The king shook his head. *Praise be to the gods he is not my eldest.*

The king's loss of his own ring contributed to his ill humor. The ring itself had insignificant material value, though the magick on it had proved very valuable. It also made it rather unique and possible to track down by sorcerous means. He would have preferred to have it with him, though he really felt he had little to fear from his guest, so the ring's absence would be tolerable.

Scrainwood smiled as the mask-curtain parted and Marsham led the old woman into the small library. He guided her to a large leather-upholstered chair and made to pour her some wine. She laid a thinly fleshed, liver-spotted hand on his arm to stop him, then looked up at King Scrainwood.

"Thank you very much for seeing me, Highness."

Scrainwood inclined his head. "Your request to speak with me, Grand Duchess, has honored me deeply. You come on your nephew's behalf, I shall assume."

The old woman lowered her cloak's hood, revealing white hair tightly gathered at the back of her head. Scrainwood shivered slightly as her icy gaze met his eyes, then she glanced at Marsham. "My words are for your ears alone, Highness."

Scrainwood looked up at his chamberlain. "Leave us, Marsham. Attend my son and aid his search."

Marsham again bowed deeply and departed. Had

Scrainwood not given him specific instructions, Marsham would have taken up a position just beyond the mask-curtain, where he could listen to everything without being seen. While Scrainwood was not certain what Tatyana wanted, he was sure he didn't want Marsham knowing about it until he had decided how much the chamberlain should know.

Scrainwood came over and sat across from the old woman. "He is gone. What is it you have to tell me?"

The frail old woman sat back in the massive chair. "A drop of wine first, perhaps, Highness?"

Scrainwood's nostrils flared, but he got up and poured the ruby vintage into a cut-crystal glass. Despite wanting a drink himself rather fiercely, he just served her, then returned to his chair.

"You will not join me?"

"As well you know, Grand Duchess, wine often aids speaking, though seldom helps hearing."

"So true, Highness, and seldom helps thinking—much of which you will wish to be doing." She sipped the wine, then gave him a quick smile. "Very good."

"If I like what you tell me, you'll have a cask of it by morning."

The old woman's icy blue eyes slitted. "I will accept your gift, though what I give you will grant you the continued leadership of your nation—quite cheaply at that price."

What game are you playing? "Two casks every year I am on the throne then, and you still live."

"Better." She set the glass down on the table with the decanter, then leaned forward. "In our councils I have discerned certain unanimity of thought shared by you and the Draconis Baron."

"We do not walk in lockstep, but we have many things in common. He is married to my sister. My eldest is commanding Fortress Draconis in Cavarre's absence." Scrainwood forced his eyes wide so she could see them easily within his mask. "As with every other leader, I would prefer it if he were to share with us the secret of the drag-onel, but he has so far refrained. Is he wise in assuming that if we had this secret we might war with each other? Per-haps."

She folded her hands together and rested them on her knees. "I would have thought you more discerning than that, Highness."

"Drink more, Grand Duchess, speak plainly." Scrainwood rubbed at his left temple. "I have neither the time nor the disposition for divining hidden meanings."

"I shall be blunt, then, King Scrainwood. This offer you made me, to give me two casks of wine as long as I lived or you were on the Oriosan throne—this is an offer I will live to lament the cessation of."

Scrainwood had no doubt Tatyana was too bitter to die soon, but he expected his reign to continue for a long while yet. "You think I will be unseated, and unseated by Cavarre? Perhaps you've drunk too much if you believe he covets my throne."

"No, Highness, I do not believe such foolishness. He would not take it for himself, nor for the children he's got-ten on your sister, though the throne is close to being their right. No, he would win it for your son, Erlestoke. He is teaching him a great deal and Oriosa will be better for his being on the throne. So will most of the world."

"You go too far."

"No, Highness, you have gone too far." Tatyana's voice became a rime-tinged hiss. "Do you think any of us have failed to notice that Oriosa serves as a staging area for Chytrine's forces? Cavarre sees Oriosa as an enemy at his back, so it must be dealt with. The army that assaulted Porasena, here on your border with Alcida, came from Oriosa. We all know that. While the urZrethi are tight-lipped about their affairs, stories have filtered out of Oriosa about Aurolani forces fighting with the urZrethi in Bokagul. Oriosa, under your leadership, is a putrefying wound that threatens to spill its poison throughout the world."

Scrainwood snorted. "You know I track her forces, keep count of them, and share that information with others. Her predations are kept to a minimum while our armies are honed by fighting her. Look at your own Princess Alexia. The blood on her sword has been Aurolani blood."

"A fair point, and wise." The old woman steepled her fingers. "The simple fact of the matter, however, is that if the Council decides in Cavarre's favor and does not support Adrogans' request for troops, armies will gather and march through Oriosa. You know they will prey on your people, punishing them for your dealings with Chytrine."

Scrainwood's flesh tightened as he looked down at his clawed hands. He could still see his mother's head clutched there. He could feel her warm blood dripping down between his fingers. He could see her lips moving in a final message to him, but with no lungs she could not so much as whisper. The ten seconds of life she had beyond beheading expanded into a lifetime in his memory, and each heartbeat of it tightened his stomach into a rock.

The Okrans mystic continued in a sepulchral whisper. "How easy it would be for Cavarre to send your son to Meredo to take command. He unseats you, perhaps bloodlessly, forcing you and Linchmere into exile on some little farm. He then turns its forces on Chytrine's troops in your nation, rooting them out. You know she will kill you for that, and most horribly. And you know Erlestoke would gladly let her do it, since he still lays the blame for his mother's death at your feet."

"He should lay it at Cavarre's feet, for the blame is his. He never should have allowed her to go sailing when the weather was so unpredictable."

Tatyana slowly shook her head. "Some think he was your agent in that, you know. Your wife was visiting his wife. You had no love for your spouse, as evidenced by various dalliances, and she no love for you. Did you have her thrown over the side, or did she leap?"

The king's hazel eyes narrowed. "Despite what you might think, Grand Duchess, the story of her drowning when her ship capsized was true. Had I wanted her dead, I would have arranged it later. She died before my boys had their moonmasks, and for their sake I would have wanted her to be able to look upon them pridefully as men."

"So, you will let your reign die for a crime you did not commit?"

"I will not let it die." Scrainwood brought his chin up. "You wish me to support Adrogans and his campaign in Okrannel? You know he cannot hold the nation against Chytrine if he retakes it."

"Leave the fate of Okrannel to me. Alexia is not the only person who has been trained to war. We have many who will fight and make Okrannel too problematic for Chytrine to want to retake it."

The king tapped a finger against his lips for a moment. "You will subordinate Princess Alexia's role in what is to come to a Jeranese general's role? How do you know Adrogans will not just take Okrannel and add it to Jerana?"

The old woman laughed harshly. "Alexia will study him and destroy him if he does that."

"And know of enough of him to take Jerana when the time comes?"

"That will long be after my death, King Scrainwood, and yours." The old woman reached for her wineglass again. "You will let an army march through your lands at your peril."

"I buy the freedom of my nation with freedom for yours?" The king nodded slowly. "And the reason my thinking has shifted in this direction?"

"The most basic of premises, Highness. If we fight Chytrine in Okrannel, we fight on her territory. My nation has already been ravaged by her troops. There is no reason we should offer her the chance to despoil virgin lands. Not only does supporting Adrogans liberate my nation, but it saves so many others.

"If, by supporting the Draconis Baron's plan, we invite her to attack Fortress Draconis, we invite her to expand her territory. We already know there is leakage past Fortress Draconis. It could easily be that she can bring down a sieging force that will bottle up the forces in Fortress Draconis while a yet larger army marches past, slashing down into the heartlands of the south. Only by attacking in Okrannel can we divert those troops from her invasion corridor."

Scrainwood slowly nodded. "Logical and defensible. The Jeranese have not thought about the predations of foreign armies marching through their nation?"

"Adrogans wishes only to win enough glory that he can claim the queen and throne for himself. She shares this desire."

"It will be done, then." Scrainwood nodded.

"One more thing, Highness." Tatyana's thin lips curled into a catty smile. "We could tie our countries more closely. Think on the idea of Alexia needing a husband."

Me? No, she would not give Alexia to me. "Erlestoke. He would move to the throne of Okrannel, leaving Linchmere for Oriosa?"

"You would live long enough for one of Linchmere's children to come up and be strong."

"Indeed, much to think about, Grand Duchess." King Scrainwood smiled and, rising, crossed to pour himself some wine. "I do believe I will join you now. We will share wine as we share planning the future. To your health."

"And yours and ours, Highness."

CHAPTER 42

King Augustus held his palms up toward Dothan Cavarre. "You're taking this wrong, my friend. I'm not abandoning you. I agree fully with your strategy."

The smaller man narrowed his blue-flecked grey eyes. "Forgive me, or did I mishear you advocating my sharing dragonel science with the nations in the Council?"

Augustus glanced behind him at the double doors that led from the garden into the council chamber in Fortress Gryps. Lowering his voice, he steered the Draconis Baron deeper into the garden. "What I suggested is something we have bruited about in our own councils. I was advocating that you provide companies of *meckanshii* to operate dragonels for the various nations. They would have what they want to hold others off, yet they would not be able to use it to attack their neighbors."

Cavarre sighed audibly. "Despite their being constructs of metal, flesh, and magick, the *meckanshii* are quite human. They have passions and desires, and are capable of being corrupted. Their loyalty to me and Fortress Draconis comes from our giving them a purpose in their lives. They would have been reduced to nothing, but we have made them special. They guard their old homes from the threat to the north, making their sacrifice more noble than we can imagine.

"But human they are, and were they sent here to Yslin, or to Meredo or Lakaslin, they could be seduced by life there. Promises would be made. They would be changed and turned. The secrets of the dragonel would spread unchecked. People would turn them on each other instead of reserving these hellish weapons for use on Chytrine."

The King of Alcida nodded slowly. "I know that is a risk, but if you cannot or will not even consider this sort of concession, the Council will vote to back Adrogans. The troops you need will go to him. Okrannel will become a killing ground, and I know so very well how much blood will soak the earth there. It will be an open wound that will suck warriors in, year after year."

"Exactly!" Cavarre's eyes blazed and Augustus thought, not for the first time, that madness might have tinged them. "Chytrine will keep the war there going forever. Just as Jerana has done, other nations will deny me the troops I need. Queen Carus will make trade deals and alliances that will cause other troops to be sent to Jerana and into Okrannel. Worse yet, the outcry for dragonels will rise, as if they could win that war."

Augustus shook his head. Okrannel's mountainous terrain severely limited the effectiveness of dragonels, which were slow to move and needed very specific supplies to make them function. Laying siege to some little fort only required a supply of wood and rock if conventional siege machines were to be used against it. A dragonel was useless—save perhaps as a battering ram—without its firedirt and shot.

"We will not let that happen, Cavarre." Augustus

groaned as an ache started throbbing from temple to temple. "There are enough of *us*, my brother, to counsel against that sort of thing."

Cavarre's hesitation told Augustus that his emphasis had not been misread. The two of them belonged to the Ancient and Most Secret Society of the Knights of the Phoenix. The Knights had hotly debated how things would go if the Adrogans' plan was put into effect. While some thought Adrogans had a chance at inflicting some serious damage to Chytrine's forces there, all agreed that the defenders would have a great advantage in Okrannel. That nation would serve Chytrine in the same way Fortress Draconis served the south, costing time, matériel, and lives to liberate. Given how ravaged the nation had been, keeping troops in good supply against any Aurolani counterattack would be nearly impossible, creating a second drain on the south's resources.

Though all of the Knights understood Cavarre's reasoning for keeping a tight grip on the secrets of the dragonel and even agreed with him on that issue, they had so far proven unable to exert influence enough to change the minds of their leaders. The simple fact of leakage of small groups of Aurolani troops past Fortress Draconis meant people no longer saw the place as the grand shield it had once been. Since it seemed to be failing a little bit, and they feared a gross failure, a plan that provided an offensive that would take the war to Chytrine proved very attractive to world leaders. Moving dragonels south would help allay some of the fear, but sow more trouble for the future of the Fortress Draconis strategy.

The small man snorted. "Even if I were to agree with your plan, and even if the leaders of those *meckanshii* companies were to join *us*, the secret could still get out. Moreover, demands to supply dragonels would require time or the stripping of defenses from Fortress Draconis. Think of it, Highness. They will tell me that as soon as they have dragonels to make up for the troops they are sending to me, those troops will be released to me. Until that time, however, they will support Jerana. They will do this to make me act in haste, which weakens Fortress Draconis and leaves the world open to Chytrine's predation."

"Is Fortress Draconis strong enough to hold Chytrine off right now?"

Cavarre frowned. "If it were not, she would have laid waste to it already. If I am denied the things I need, however, it could be fatally weak."

"Then you need to offer some sort of compromise." Augustus pointed back toward the council chamber. "You heard Scrainwood. He's come around to the idea that if war is joined in Okrannel, Chytrine will be forced to pull troops back from the lower nations and reinforce the Ghost Marches and Okrannel."

"He's an idiot. Chytrine has very capable leaders in Okrannel and the Ghost Marches. Adrogans has won some victories, but they have not been clean and have been the result of his having overwhelming force on his side. In Okrannel his force will be broken up and subject to ambush. Everyone seems to forget that Edamis Vilkaso—Malarkex, as she is styled now—knows how to use cavalry very well. If rumors of flocks of grand temeryces with vylaen riders running around the Ghost Marches are even remotely true, anyone who thinks Adrogans will win anything in Okrannel are as stupid as Scrainwood."

"There is a room full of them behind us."

"I know." The Snow Fox looked up at Augustus and sighed. "Chytrine has played this game very well indeed. By striking here in Alcida she has shown that no nation can escape her touch. Scrainwood and others offer the hope that she can be distracted, but they have been blinded as to her true goal: stealing back the pieces of the DragonCrown and destroying the southlands. Distraction or treasonous appeasement just delays the inevitable."

Augustus couldn't disagree. The most expedient plan to end the threat to his own nation would be to strike into

Oriosa, overthrowing Scrainwood and purging Oriosa of Aurolani troops. The difficulty of doing that would be that it would shatter any unity among the southland nations and create the impression that if people did not do what Augustus wanted, he would take their nation as well. The south would descend into chaos and no one would be able to oppose Chytrine.

The king scrubbed hands over his face. "What will you do when they vote to back Adrogans?"

"I will do what I have always done, Highness. I will defend three fragments of the DragonCrown as best I am able."

"And you won't even suggest there is room for compromise. You won't say you will consider sharing the dragonels?"

The small man shook his head. "I cannot, for they would know it for a lie. Augustus, I am neither blind to nor ignorant of the politics and all the ramifications of what we are facing here. I truly am not. However, the second I lie to your peers, they are given grounds for distrusting everything I say after that, and many will doubt things I've said long before. They will assume that I have, for my own purposes, exaggerated things to such a degree that they can refuse my funding, they can refrain from sending me troops and supplies."

"Damn and damn." Augustus raised a fist to his mouth, then forced his hand open to smooth his moustaches. "If I pull out of any agreement, I fracture the alliance we have opposing Chytrine. Nations will support you or Adrogans or, worse yet, will sue for a separate peace with Chytrine. I will have to support Adrogans if they do, and I will, to the letter of whatever agreement we reach. I'll also support you. I have that luxury, and I am certain I can influence a few others to join me. Naliserro doesn't like having a *sullanciri* claiming their nation as its home. Sebcia, Muroso, and Viarca will likewise lend you support since you are their first line of defense. I think we can prevail upon the Vilwanese as well."

"No, spare me the sorcerers. They are angry over the slaughter of the young, and people now mistrust them. They will better serve to work with the small units in Okrannel than they will with me. I have enough to forge more *meckanshii*. If I need more than that, all is lost." Cavarre narrowed his eyes. "There is one more thing we can do, though it will be difficult."

"And that is?"

"We need the Norrington in Okrannel."

Augustus frowned. "I don't follow your reasoning."

"The Norrington is the one real threat we have for Chytrine. While it has been argued whether or not he will kill her, it has been prophesied that he will liberate Vorquellyn. Chytrine has put her Croquelf *sullanciri* Winfellis, in charge of the island—her perversion of an elf watching over her perversion of an elven homeland. As long as the Norrington is out there, he poses a credible threat to the island."

"That won't happen if he is at Fortress Draconis?"

"Chytrine would rightly assume that I would not strip away troops for an assault on the island. Adrogans would be likely, on the other hand, to order such a reckless thing, especially if his troops get bogged down in Okrannel and he is making little headway. We've not got that long until winter settles in, which will be a boon to Chytrine since her troops are hardened to the cold and function so well in it."

The king nodded. "Besides which, with the Norrington at Fortress Draconis, his destruction would be added to the presence of the DragonCrown fragments to make the fortress even more irresistible."

The Snow Fox sighed. "The only thing working against Chytrine is her impatience. Slaying the young sorcerers will weaken us a generation from now. If she waited, slackening off strikes here and there, suggesting she was weak, the leadership of the world would fall to those who don't remember the horror of the last war. Internal pressures would tear the fragile alliance apart, with old rivalries springing up anew. The Okrans refugees would go the way of the Vorquelves, becoming bitter, and no one would risk their lives to help liberate their nation."

Augustus snorted a quick laugh. "She trapped herself when she sent her warning with Hawkins so many years ago. She promised that the children of today would never live to see maturity. She's fulfilled the promise with the children from Vilwan, and the urchins of the Dim. If she let things go at that, in another generation she would take it all in a walk."

"We can't give her that chance." Cavarre shifted his shoulders, then nodded toward the Council. "I will demand everything I can think of, including the Norrington. You will talk me down, and we will fight hardest over the Norrington. Perhaps, in that way, we will get what we need. If not . . ."

Augustus shook his head. "We'll get what we need. In Kedyn's name, I hope it is enough."

CHAPTER 43

Two left turns out of his door in the Vilwanese tower and Will found the room to which he'd been summoned. Because of the morning sun shining through the long, narrow room's windows, he knew it faced to the east. Will also knew that was impossible since two left turns should have put the room beside his and sharing an external wall, but his room faced west.

He would have worried about that problem, but more immediate trouble presented itself. In addition to Crow, Qwc, Resolute, and Dranae, three other individuals were in the room. The only female stood in close conversation with Crow, sharing with him the grey coloration of age. Will recognized her as the combat mage sent out with the raid on Marcus' place, Orla. The nonhuman was a Panqui—at least that's what he assumed the hulking creature to be. The sun glowed golden and brightly off the beast's bony-plated flesh. The Spritha hovered around the Panqui while the beast and Dranae both sized the other one up.

The third individual spelled trouble for Will. He

expected to see recognition flickering through the tall youth's green eyes. *He was the one Scabby Jack and Garrow had their kids giving a beating to.* Then Will smiled. *He doesn't know me because of the mask.* Will gave him a curt nod, then lifted his chin and walked over to Crow.

"I'm here."

Crow smiled benignly. "So you are. You remember Magister Orla from the other night. She has been assigned to help safeguard you from the *sullanciri.* Her aide is Adept Kerrigan Reese. Lombo is a Panqui and is accompanying them."

Orla nodded. "Pleased to meet you again, Lord Norrington."

Her words sent a jolt running up his spine. Her voice rang with respect and it chilled him.

Kerrigan moved forward for an introduction.

Will frowned. He was, after all, *the* Norrington. He would be the salvation of the world, so Orla's respect was rightly due him. Despite that, he felt uneasy and, perhaps for the first time in his life, ashamed. Everyone wanted him to be a hero, and he'd done some heroic things, but he'd not helped Kerrigan. It wasn't even that he was afraid that he'd have gotten a beating from the Garrow gang— most of them couldn't hit worth spit anyway. He'd just walked away because it wasn't his fight. *If I did that in so simple a situation, why might I not do it when I need to be* the *Norrington?*

The Adept extended a hand toward Will. "I'm Kerrigan Reese."

Will nodded. "We've met, sort of."

Kerrigan frowned. "I don't remember. . . ."

The Panqui came over, striding on knuckles and feet and crossing the distance that separated them much too quickly for Will's comfort. The Panqui took a healthy sniff of him, then nodded. "Prey-night."

"I don't . . ." Kerrigan blushed deeply.

Will slowly inched his mask up. He couldn't believe he

was hearing himself speak. "I didn't help you when Garrow's gang had you down."

The Adept's green eyes narrowed and his jowls quivered. "I called to you for help . . ."

Lombo snorted and smacked Will in the center of his chest with a casual backhand blow. "Hunter you became, Kerrigan. Lombo saw."

Will coughed abruptly and staggered back. Will was certain Kerrigan never caught the glint in the Panqui's black eyes, but Will saw it sure as dark comes with night. *If I ever do anything that gets Kerrigan hurt, Lombo will punch my heart out through my back.* Will rubbed at his breastbone, but nodded to the beast. He got a quick nod in return.

Resolute's iron grip closed on the back of Will's neck. "What did you do?"

"It's what I didn't do." Will shook his head. *If I'd kept my mouth shut, only Lombo and I would know, and we'd have our understanding.* "When I was in the Dim, there was a gang manhandling Kerrigan. He asked me to help him and I didn't."

The Vorquelf spun Will around and, grabbing his shoulders, shook him. "How could you not . . . ?"

Will slapped Resolute's hands off his shoulders. "I had other things going on at the time. I was running away from everything that had happened since I met you, and he was part of it."

Razor-sharp silver crescents regarded him coldly. "Your role is to . . ."

The thief snarled. "I know what my role is, thanks, but right then I wasn't being *the* Norrington. I was being *me.* I know that *I*—or whoever I was or am—wasn't *the* Norrington right then. But, look, I told him what I did. Kerrigan, I'm sorry I didn't help you out."

The Adept shrugged. "It's okay."

"No, it's not." Resolute crossed his arms over his chest. "I don't think you understand, boy, just how critical things have become. The Council of Kings has made their decisions. They are backing General Adrogans and the Okrannel offensive."

Will frowned. "What does that mean, exactly?"

Crow came over and waved everyone toward the table and chairs. As they moved to take places, with the Spritha lighting on the back of Will's chair and the Panqui squatting at the far end, he began to explain. "It means, quite simply, Will, that we are bound for Okrannel."

The youth frowned. "But, I mean, I thought we were going to Fortress Draconis. From there we just go north and kill Chytrine and be done with it all."

Crow, Orla, and even Resolute shared a smile before the older man continued. "Were that it would be as easy as you suggest. That was the thinking a quarter century ago, and it did not work."

"How did this happen?" Will snorted with disgust. "There's a Hawkins there at Fortress Draconis and even Resolute said I need one with me when we go kill Chytrine."

Crow nodded. "I've been told this was a point raised by the Draconis Baron. He argued long and loudly that you should be brought to Fortress Draconis, but General Adrogans claimed you for himself."

"Next time I shake his hand, that ring is mine."

Resolute scowled. "The discussion was balanced until Scrainwood threw in with the Jeranese. You want to avenge yourself on someone, he should be it."

Will chuckled softly. "Already done."

Crow's left eyebrow rose sharply. "What?"

Will's smile broadened and he dipped his hand into the pouch on his belt. "Well, the king was being an idiot and I didn't like him, so when we shook hands, I took his ring." He produced the sapphire and held it up proudly.

Orla covered her face with a hand and Crow shook his head. "You didn't."

"But Resolute just said . . . I just anticipated him."

Crow plucked the ring from his left hand and set it on the table. "Resolute, my friend, I apologize to you. Throughout our search and journeying with Will, I thought you were just being too thorough, too hard on him. I hoped he had more of his father in him, or less."

"Not your fault, Crow." The Vorquelf, who had seated himself at Will's right, turned toward the youth. "Give over your other loot."

"What are you talking about?" Will refused to flinch, refused to drop a hand to his pouch. "The king had it coming."

Resolute's voice came low and cold enough to suck all the heat out of the room. "Your choice, boy. I saw you stumble against the prince. Do you want me to believe you were clumsy? Or should I believe you were so practiced and smooth that you fooled me, even up to now?"

Will hesitated. If he claimed clumsiness, Resolute would just search him and all his gear. If he coughed up the other ring, the signet ring the king had used to mark his mask, at least Resolute would have admitted he missed the theft. The punishment would end up being the same no matter which course he picked, so the only bright spot in the whole picture was the admission from Resolute.

The thief fished the ring from his pouch and set it there with the first one. "It has magick on it."

Kerrigan, seated at Will's left, reached for the rings. Will gave him a quick, backhanded slap with his left hand. His knuckles cracked off the Adept's upper arm.

"Ow!" Will shook his hand, then sucked at his knuckles. He glared at Crow. "The prince was stupid, too."

"Will, while it might be true that were Linchmere a cow, he'd starve because he doesn't have the brains to sneak up on a blade of grass, that gives you no cause to steal from him—and certainly not a ring that serves as the king's official seal. You don't know King Scrainwood. He can be insanely paranoid and could see the disappearance of either ring as the glimmerings of a plot against him. He could use it to justify letting Chytrine station more troops in Oriosa. He could strike at allies, thinking they are out to topple him."

"I understand. I get it." Will sighed loudly. "I can get into the house where he is and put both rings back and they'll never notice. Resolute didn't see anything that night, no one did."

Orla rested a hand on Crow's shoulder. "Perhaps, given the omen of the last visit by a Norrington to the leader of Oriosa, having Will return the rings is not a good idea. In fact, if you wish, I can have them returned to the king, noting that once we heard they were missing, we undertook a search and are returning them. The remarks will be cryptic, he'll not know how and where. . . ."

Crow nodded. "That should work."

A blue aura sprang to life, surrounding Kerrigan's hands. In his left he held the king's ring and in his right, the seal glowed red. "Magick on both of the rings. The signet has a basic sealing spell."

The Adept set the ring down, then reached a fat hand toward Will's mask. Blue flashed before Will's eyes, then the hand came away and Kerrigan was nodding. "The ring made the mark on the mask. Easy way of verifying orders as coming from the king."

The Spritha's wings filled the room with a humming as the creature darted from ring to mask and back again. "Yes, yes. Same."

Kerrigan held the sapphire ring up in his left hand. "This one is fascinating because it has a rather unique spell on it. It has to be invoked and will detect hostile intent in a sphere roughly twelve feet in diameter around the wearer."

Resolute laughed. "He must never use it lest he be overwhelmed."

The Adept frowned. "It has some narrowing factors on it. One thing is that it seeks to warn him especially of enemies from the Norrington bloodline."

"He must have had it made after his mother's death

because he certainly would have fled from the *sullanciri* if he'd had any warning." Crow's dark eyes narrowed. "Why wasn't he warned about Will's stealing his ring?"

Orla accepted the ring from Kerrigan and surrounded it with her hands. A blue glow leaked out from between her fingers. She thought for a moment, then nodded. "There are a number of different answers to that question. The first is that Will might not, in fact, be a Norrington."

Resolute waved that idea away. "He is. Of this there is no question."

Lombo extended a single claw and scratched at the corner of his eye. "Thief steals. No hate."

Orla nodded in agreement. "Will's penchant for theft seems to be independent of any emotional content. When the spell was created, the mage who cast it would have provided his own sense of *hostile* and Will's thievery might not rise to that threshold. After all, he did not mean to do harm to the king, just to enrich himself. It would take some time to determine, but I suspect that was it."

Will frowned. "Maybe he just didn't have it working."

Orla nodded. "Another good idea."

"At such a gathering, heralding the debut of the Norrington?" The Vorquelf laughed harshly. "He had it working. If Chytrine wished to strike terror into the hearts of the world's leaders, she could have done it there by attacking and destroying their only hope."

Dranae, seated across the table between Orla and the Panqui, raised a hand. "So, then, we have a curious situation. *If* King Scrainwood has determined that Will stole his ring, and if the king would consider that a hostile act, then he must think Will is actually *not* the Norrington. This could explain why he is willing to have Will bundled off to Okrannel."

Will's brows beetled. *If he doesn't know I stole it, then he thinks I am the Norrington, but if he does know, then he knows I'm not? Unless, of course, he knows my theft wasn't hostile, in which case he thinks I am the Norrington. Or, if the magick wasn't working, then* . . . He raised his hands to his temples and began to massage them.

Crow tapped a finger against his lips for a moment. "Interesting idea, but I think the most simple answers are likely the best. First, he doesn't know Will stole the ring. Scrainwood is petty and vengeful, but also resourceful. He'd have called Will in, told him he was going to Fortress Draconis, and offered him a lot of money to steal a sample of the dragonel powder from there. More importantly, though, there is a more basic reason he's not sending Will to Fortress Draconis. We'd move by land through Oriosa. Chytrine has troops there, so Will would be most vulnerable. If she killed him in Oriosa, the other nations would pull the nation apart in rage, fear, and retribution."

He turned to Orla. "Please do see to it that the rings return to King Scrainwood. You might even have your envoy suggest a modification of the sapphire ring to more broadly define 'hostile.' "

Dranae smiled. "That could guarantee that Scrainwood would survive an attack by Chytrine's forces. Wouldn't Oriosa be better off with someone else on the throne? Wouldn't the rest of us be better off with someone else on the throne?"

"Scrainwood is unreliable and a schemer, but as long as he is alive, he is a problem for Chytrine just the way he is a problem for us. If he dies, her forces could back Linchmere, other forces back Erlestoke or even Ryhope. The nation would collapse, other nations would pick sides. It would not be good."

"But what if he sides with Chytrine and turns against us? That ring could prevent him from being slain when we need him dead."

Before Crow could answer Dranae's question, Resolute rapped a knuckle on the table. He glanced up at Orla. "The spell on the ring—to target the Norrington bloodline; there is something of a Norrington in the ring to allow that."

She nodded. "A hair. Probably from the son."

The Vorquelf nodded. "That which includes could exclude?"

Orla nodded hesitantly. "Your knowledge of magick does you credit, Resolute."

"I'm honored, Magister." He reached up and plucked a single white hair from the stripe running down the center of his scalp. "When you fix the ring, make sure it will not recognize me."

Will's eyes grew wide as Resolute extended the hair past him to Kerrigan.

Crow reached out and grabbed the Vorquelf's wrist. "Hunter and warrior, yes, but assassin, Resolute?"

Resolute nodded slowly. "You, a man, have pledged to see my homeland liberated from Chytrine's forces. I just want to be certain that when the time comes for me to return the favor, there will be one less obstacle in my way."

CHAPTER 44

Alyx and Peri wandered through the gardens of Fortress Gryps. In daylight, with her feathered sister beside her, it seemed quite different. The Okrans landscape seemed alive and Alyx found herself easily imagining that it would be so again once it had been liberated.

Still, in the back of her mouth she could taste the sharp bitterness of the wine Crow had fetched for her. His lesson had been perfectly on point, since the subsequent discussions about how Chytrine's forces would be dealt with had completely marginalized her. With her grandfather's agreement—as voiced by Tatyana—Alexia had been consigned to a group of advisors who would accompany Adrogans. The Alcidese General Caro would also be along on the expedition to direct his nation's contingent. He and his Horse Guards would ship to Okrannel and take command of the force while awaiting Adrogans' arrival. Alyx's Wolves would nominally be under his command.

The Okrans troops joining the expedition included both cavalry and infantry. The Kingsmen heavy cavalry unit had a large contingent of nobles, while the foot soldiers were largely peasants. Considered "irregulars," the infantry was regarded as untested and unreliable, though no one doubted their zeal to liberate their homeland. Their role would be as scouts and outriders and reserves, which almost certainly eliminated any serious participation in the sorts of battles for which Adrogans was famous.

Peri hopped up and perched on one of the stones matching a Svarskya tower. "But, in your grandfather's eyes, this is the best outcome. You will be there for Okrannel's liberation. You will take command of the nation and hold it against Chytrine."

Alyx frowned. "You are telling me, then, that a gift of meat tastes better than something you have killed yourself?"

"Normally, no, but can you bring down the sort of game Adrogans can?" Peri cocked her head to the right. "I know you, my sister, and know that you could, easily. Others don't want to trust you with the troops that would let you do it. He's won that battle, which lets him fight the others."

Alyx snarled and leaned heavily on the plinth Resolute and Crow had brought from Svarskya. "That's the problem, Peri. I could liberate Okrannel with less troops than he will. He always demands too much, he is too cautious. He's using a huge club to bash a tiny bunny."

"It might seem that way, Princess, but what if that bunny is not so small?"

She turned as Peri slid off the stone. King Augustus had slipped into the gardens and gave her a gentle smile. "I do understand your frustration, Alyx. You doubtlessly could do more with less, but my peers have listened for two decades to stories of Adrogans' skill. I've told such tales. While I tell better ones of you, the fact remains that you've led smaller groups. I would rank your successes as high, but I am seen as being biased since you have been working within my realm."

Alyx nodded solemnly. "Highness, do not think for a moment that I fault you for my situation. Everything you say is true, and I accept that. What I do not accept is how Adrogans can be wasteful of men and materials. The supplies he has demanded for our forces would feed half again as many men. While having strong and well-fed soldiers is important, having so huge a supply train creates a tempting target for Chytrine's forces. Given the rigors of traveling through the Okrans landscape, as well you proved in your campaign there, the only way to safeguard supplies would be to stretch his troops so thin that they could accomplish nothing when it comes to a battle."

He opened his hands. "You have no argument from me on that front. I would much rather see you in command of the expedition, but this was not possible. In your position you are going to be able to study him."

"I've already studied him." She sighed audibly and crossed her arms over her chest. "I've read all his reports of his battles. They are rife with sloppiness and wastefulness. If not for the sheer bulk of his troops and his good fortune at catching and wiping out smaller units, no one would even know his name. Stupid enemies do not brilliant generals betoken. There were better ways for him to have run and won every battle he's fought. Most frustrating is the fact that he was so close to seeing the best choices, and yet he turned away from them—arrogantly dismissing most, or failing to mention the others. It's all in his reports."

The king's eyes hardened. "I will not dispute that reading of him, either. The fact that you have seen these tendencies in him means you can curb them."

Alyx snorted. "I doubt he will listen to me."

"He will listen to General Caro, and Caro will listen to you. I have directed him to do exactly that, and to work with you to make sense prevail." Augustus slowly shook his head. "In the Council we hammered together a workable plan, but it was hardly the best plan. No nation gave all it could to this effort, but held back in case of failures. Everyone hedged their bets and refused to believe there was a threat of Chytrine stealing the various pieces of the DragonCrown. It's like snarling at the darkness to hope you scare off the wolf unseen. If the wolf is truly there, you know you are lost, and if it isn't, you would have been safe anyway. Since they know they will be lost if she does put it back together, they refuse to contemplate that possibility.

"The best we could have done here was simple: provide Adrogans troops to free Okrannel. Provide Cavarre troops to reinforce Fortress Draconis. Provide you an army to drive into Aurolan."

Peri blinked her big amber eyes. "Not liberate Vorquellyn?"

Augustus smiled. "I'd have suggested that as your first target, Alexia, and the elves would have demurred and raised their own force to do it."

Alexia saw the logic in how Augustus would have played things. "You would have then offered our help to the elves, yes, and they would have offered us other troops to bolster our effort, thereby keeping us away from Vorquellyn?"

The king shrugged. "That might have worked, too. I was thinking that I'd reverse it, and hint that we didn't need elves in your force, since we had the Gyrkyme."

Peri's crest came up. "And you would have let the elves dictate that we could not participate in exchange for elven help?"

Augustus held his hands up and palm-out open. "Soothe yourself, Perrine, I would not have shown such disrespect to your people. We would have crafted things so both could participate. With the urZrethi involved as well, all three of your peoples would have been pushed to excel."

The Gyrkyme let loose with a raptor's shriek that dissolved into laughter. "It would have worked."

Alyx grinned in spite of her nascent anger. "Keep that in mind, the both of you, for we may yet need to use it. The other element of the Okrans campaign that concerns me, Highness, is the opposition's leader. She is now called Malarkex?"

The king nodded solemnly. "She was once Edamis Vilkaso, of Naliserro. She could have been you, or you her, both in coloration and history. She led some of the Nalisk cavalry and was accomplished in small-unit tactics. As you have suggested, in the Okrans landscape, this gives her an advantage. She was also very smart and recognized the importance of the dragonel. She captured the one Chytrine had at Fortress Draconis. Some stories—which Adrogans dismisses—suggest she has even put together a mounted unit of people equipped with draconettes. Our archers are thought to be better at range, but a volley of shots from these draconetteers can rip men apart."

"What concerns me most is the apparent dismissal of Malarkex because she was only known for small-unit tactics." Alyx frowned heavily. "And it is not because I am similarly dismissed. I can think of a hundred ways to bedevil the invasion force. Even if I only ascribe to her a tenth of those ideas, the fight for Okrannel will be brutal."

Augustus nodded solemnly. "Alyx, I remember my battles in Okrannel. The campaign has been heralded as a grand victory, but you have read enough to know what it was. Yes, we stormed through the Ghost March and were able to unite refugee groups to escape Okrannel. The fact is, of course, that were I as successful there as many claim, you'd not be having to go off on this expedition."

"At least you understand that." She shook her head. "Too much of his plan is vague. Everyone has agreed that we will liberate Okrannel, but exactly how he plans to do that has not been discussed. It seems as if the campaign is being done more as a game than anything else. Game pieces do not bleed."

"Caution, Princess, you know better than that." Augustus shook his head. "He may not take to planning as you do, or he may not deign to share with you his planning process or both. You have to go, have to learn from him."

Alyx narrowed her eyes. "Highness, forgive me. Frustration is not something I handle well. I see so much, but I don't see an opportunity to share what I know. What I need to learn from Adrogans has been culled from his reports and his plans. He's working with the traditional divisions of Okrannel into six duchies, which would be fine, but several are political divisions that only have value to exiled nobles. The Svoin Lakes Duchy straddles a huge lake and is split in half by it and rivers. From a military standpoint it is two distinct areas and to let the lake or rivers split an army will be suicidal. And the Bhayall lowlands that surround the Svoin Duchy, they actually break down into four tactical regions. Even the Crozt Duchy has two distinct parts and I've seen no intelligence to suggest Chytrine's forces have rebuilt the Radooya Bridge, so the northernmost part of the peninsula might as well be an island."

The smile growing on Augustus' face earned a scowl from her. "What? What is it?"

"It's been a while since I've been lectured on Okrannel geography; and never by someone who has not really set foot in the country. That's an observation, not a rebuke. What you are saying is accurate, and Caro knows this. This is why it will be important for you to be there."

Peri keened a sharp laugh.

Alyx turned toward her. "What am I missing, sister?"

The Gyrkyme smoothed down over her breasts. "Just the reason we are being sent to Okrannel."

"I don't . . ." Alyx hesitated. "Oh . . ."

Augustus nodded as he rested hands on her shoulders. "That's right. You see all these things. If Adrogans does not, he'll be relieved of command. And I will not be alone in being happy that you are there to replace him."

CHAPTER 45

Topping the rise of the first hill west of Yslin, Alyx reined her horse around and looked back over the column slowly snaking from the Alcidese capital in the rain. General Adrogans had been kind enough to allow her Wolves to lead the way out of the city toward Okrannel. Alyx had ridden proudly, waving back at her grandfather's sagging form as he watched from a Fortress Gryps balcony.

The city itself defied the rain, with strong walls and tall towers refusing to be softened despite the downpour and grey sky. The riders fared not so well, with gaily colored pennants dripping limply. Dark oilskins covered each soldier. Water oozed from hems and boots, or sprayed explosively when horses shook their heads. Muddy water surged up with each hooffall, dappling legs and boots.

Her heart had swelled as they rode out of the city. There was no way it could not have, for her countrymen—a generation removed from their homeland—cheered her and the Wolves and the Okrans Kingsmen heavy cavalry battalion. Small children ran along the streets, splashing through puddles, laughing and waving little black-and-gold flags. Within the Okrans community there seemed no doubt that the expedition would sweep the Aurolani forces from the country, and they would be free to return to estates that remained pristine in their memories or in the stories of elders.

Alyx had stopped to watch the column go past, thankful that distance had muted the cheers and the cold rain had chilled prideful fires. The simple fact of the matter was that there was nothing simple about the campaign that had been proposed. Nations from the western half of the continent would be sending troops directly up through Jerana to the Zhusk highlands, in the southeast corner of Okrannel. That little triangular portion of the nation had never been conquered—before the Aurolani invasion the Zhusks had always been fiercely independent and claimed to be an autonomous state. Frequently the King of Okrannel had to send punitive expeditions into the highlands to quell rebellions. Roughly a quarter of the expedition forces would make their way there by themselves.

Over half the troops that were going to be used were infantry, with a full regiment—the King's Heavy Guards—coming from Alcida. Those troops, as well as some from Naliserro, Helurca, and the Okrans exiles, would have taken all but two months to travel the five hundred miles from Yslin to Okrannel on foot. That would have brought the invasion force into the Zhusk highlands at the start of the month of Snow. There they would have remained until spring.

A fleet had been organized to carry Caro's cavalry, the infantry, and supplies to Okrannel. With the prevailing seasonal winds, the trip would take three days. No one expected trouble from the Wruonan pirates after their drubbing on Vilwan, but delays were worked into the planning anyway. The entire force would be delivered in eighteen days, and then every six days more supplies would be brought in.

Adrogans had seized on the ship shortage to order the cavalry elements to take the land route back to Okrannel. The cavalry would arrive at roughly the same time as the last of the infantry, saving the ships one round-trip. Alyx had argued that if a significant portion of the cavalry had shipped ahead, they could begin planning their actions, but the Jeranese general demurred. He said nothing of his distaste for traveling on the sea, but Alyx knew he was letting his fear get the better of him.

He wasn't alone in that sort of thing. Tagothcha, the *weirun* of the Crescent Sea, had been an enemy when the last expedition against Chytrine had been launched a generation before. At first the warriors had tricked the spirit, then, at Svarskya, they had bribed him. She recalled dimly that King Scrainwood was said to have tossed his wedding band as an offering to the sea spirit, and that had been cited by some as the reason Tagothcha took his wife.

It seemed as if everyone who was meant to ship north was learning from Scrainwood's lesson. Soldiers offered the *weirun* gold and wine, live animals—which soon ceased being live—and any manner of valuable they hoped would make them stand out. In the case of a disaster at sea, they wanted its sovereign to think kindly of them. Alyx had heard countless tales of *weiruns* of forest, fields, mountains, and streams helping the lost and innocent, or rewarding the honest and noble. Tagothcha was well known for being capricious and greedy, but as his lust for gold was sated, so was his mischievous nature.

Because Adrogans felt bribes were beneath him, or he just had an abiding fear of the sea, over a thousand men and women set out on horseback, with three horses for each of them. A long wagon train would have also been part of their expedition, but arrangements for fodder and food had been made and supplies had been cached along their route. Every third day they would resupply themselves and have some of their mounts replaced.

Even Alyx had to admit that Adrogans had done a good

job planning out that logistical angle of the campaign, though his demands seemed inflated to her. She was willing to allow that he was just planning against delays and the sort of thievery that accompanies the establishment of supply depots. Even so, the matériel he requisitioned would have amply supplied an army half again as large as their force.

This was all part and parcel of the paradox of Adrogans. The man knew enough to make sure his troops had everything they needed to fight, but he used his people poorly. In maneuvering he surrendered speed for strength, which was a dubious proposition at even the most favorable of times. He'd clearly been successful at defending Jerana from Aurolani aggression, but his battle reports suggested luck played a bigger part in his victories than planning.

If his luck runs out before his supplies do, he's done for.

She shivered and watched the cavalry units head on down the road. Another bit of the paradox struck her as she watched them go by. Her Wolves and the mercenary legion, Matrave's Horse, were the only light cavalry in the force. They'd been given scouting duties, which made perfect sense. The three heavy cavalry units were well spaced on the road so they would have time to form up and charge if the scouts detected the enemy over the next hill or around a corner. Vilwanese warmages and various officials traveling with them were kept toward the middle of the column where they would be safest, or would do the least harm, depending upon how one chose to look at it.

His deployment of the forces matched what she would have suggested, had her opinion been solicited. That he did not ask for her advice did not surprise her. What did was that, again, he showed an intuitive grasp of tactics in how the column moved, yet that never showed up in any of his battles.

Alyx frowned and reined Valor around. She slipped back into the column behind her Red Caps. She found herself riding beside Crow. He gave her a nod. Droplets of water flicked free of his oilskin cloak's hood and one hung from the tip of his nose. He blew upward to launch it into the air, then smiled at her.

"Your Wolves have a few more companies here."

"Black and Silver were added. Gold was made a full company and I have a new squad of bodyguards." The Wolves had been a reinforced legion with a hundred fifty soldiers in it, but two more companies had been added prior to the expedition's setting out. Along with extra staff officers this brought her command up to two hundred twenty individuals. Hardly enough of a force to warrant a general in command, but both the unit and the rank had come from King Augustus, so no one complained.

She glanced back along the column. "You ought to be back there with the Norrington."

"You should call him Will." Crow shrugged easily. "I prefer riding with scouts. I'm not heavy cavalry, and I'm not well suited to letting others protect me. If you object to my presence, however . . ."

She started to shake her head no, but hesitated for a moment. Under normal circumstances she'd not have wanted him riding with her, but with Peri having flown ahead to Gyrvirgul, she had no one to talk with. While her cousin Misha was in the Kingsmen, her rank and position made it difficult to speak to him without earning him the ire of his commanding officer.

"No, not at all." She glanced beyond him as Resolute trotted his horse up and around toward the head of the column. "I suspect it wouldn't matter to the members of your band where Adrogans or I want them."

Crow laughed quickly. "Well, not to some, no; but others would obey. I would be among them."

She raised an eyebrow at him. "You seem hardly one to take orders, Crow."

"Only from those whose judgment I respect."

"I see." She easily could have taken his words as idle and flirtatious flattery, but she heard sincerity in them. Alyx turned her head and regarded him closely. "Have you formed an opinion of our leader?"

"More than one, Highness."

"Call me Alyx."

"Not if it were your dying command, Highness." The man stared at her from within the shadowed depths of his hood. "I know very well my place in the world. No, wait, I'm not saying what you think I am. Your willingness to permit me familiarity is something I cherish. As per our conversation before, I would be more than willing to share a cup with you here in the field, and count myself fortunate in doing so. My point is not that I am of common stock and therefore unworthy of such familiarity. While it's true, the simple fact of the matter is that while our missions are united right now, there could come a point in this war with Chytrine where our purposes will differ. What I have to do may well anger General Adrogans, or King Augustus, or any number of people you need to succeed in liberating Okrannel. So you will not be tainted by your association with me, we should maintain at least the appearance of formality."

Alyx frowned for a moment. "I was raised among the Gyrkyme. Save for wings and down, and a veneer of manners from tutors, I am Gyrkyme. They do without all these games, so I have a hard time seeing them."

Crow nodded. "As did I, until events forced me to open my eyes to them. And, even at that, I barely avoided blinding."

"I understand what you said, Crow, but I will take issue with a point."

"Please, Highness."

"You suggested my purpose was to liberate Okrannel. This is true, but only halfway true. My goal is to keep it free. The only way to do that is for Chytrine to be destroyed. Our purposes, then, are more tightly interwoven than you seem to think."

The older man pursed his lips for a moment, then nodded. "You're right, Highness, thank you for correcting me."

"Something that will be rare, I have no doubt." She smiled at him. "So, you were saying you had developed many opinions of General Adrogans?"

Crow glanced back down the column to where the Jeranese Horse Guards rode. Their oilskins had been dyed a rich brown, with a white crouching panther on their left breasts. Their lances stabbed defiantly toward the sky, as if threatening to rip the clouds open in retribution for the rain. They surrounded Adrogans, warding him within the forest of lances.

"At the reception I decided he was arrogant, but that was not a difficult opinion to reach. After that I had a chance to observe some of his people—not his officers, but his troopers. He has them well trained. They care diligently for their horses. They do drink but not to excess, and I saw no witless bragging or brawling. Mild provocation earned harsh stares before fast fists."

"You see, then, the paradox I do."

"The difficulty is in judging which image is correct. If he is truly the sort of leader who can inspire men and instill such discipline in them, well, this explains his victories. If, on the other hand, he is incompetent and arrogant, well, pride in their unit could inspire his soldiers to make more of themselves than their leader demands."

"That second case does not bode well for our campaign."

"Hardly the worst thing we have to worry about." Crow leaned forward on his saddlehorn, then twisted his shoulders to the left and right to loosen his back. "The Gyrkyme who will join us will be very useful, but the elven infantry being shipped over from Loquellyn will refuse to work with them. The Nalisk infantry will have something to prove because the *sullanciri* leading the Aurolani comes from Naliserro. The Okrans Kingsmen and Volunteers likewise will feel a need for heroics, which will make yet more difficult leading a force with so many elements of differing sizes and skills."

She nodded in agreement. "Then there is the whole matter of the size of the force we will be opposing. The reports we have are vague and old, so Chytrine could be reinforcing the country, or could just let us fragment ourselves and then send more troops in to sweep us up piecemeal."

"Possible, but unlikely."

"Why?"

Crow shrugged. "The last thing she wants is to have the world truly united against her. Driving her forces back in Okrannel would give people the taste of blood. It would tell them she was vulnerable. That she counterattacked and smashed them could be dismissed as desperation on her part, and bad luck on ours. She would have shown herself to be vulnerable, which would mean we'd keep coming. What she needs is to snap our spine in Okrannel, then crush Fortress Draconis. If she does those things, the resolve to oppose her will evaporate, and she will be able to negotiate truces with nations so she can eat up their neighbors."

Alyx flicked a drop from her nose with her finger. "You've thought a lot about her motives."

"I've had a long time to think about them. A generation ago she warned us she would be coming. Why?" He sighed. "So we would panic and be on alert, then tire and become complacent and then forget how to fight and why we wanted to fight. She comes again and we panic, which is never a good way to enter a fight."

She nodded. "Is entering battle behind Adrogans going to be a good way?"

"I don't know. At least he's been fighting for a long time." Crow smiled slowly. "He may have his own reasons for *why* he's fighting her, but at least he knows *how*. As omens go, that has a lot to recommend itself."

CHAPTER 46

Will certainly found himself enjoying his second trip west much more than the first. Resolute's apparent uneasiness with large groups of people meant he stayed away from Will, especially when Will elected to ride with the Horse Guards or the Kingsmen. Even the Savarese Knights—men who resembled Dranae in coloration and build, though slightly smaller—let their stern demeanor slip a bit when he rode among them. They seemed to like having *the Norrington* in their midst, and the chores that Resolute would have made him do were often taken up as part of some soldier's duties.

Aside from Resolute, only two other members of the expedition gave Will any cause for concern. One was Lombo. The Panqui, while apparently having seen Will's abandonment of Kerrigan to a street gang as the right thing to do, still watched him and studied him. It wasn't anything as unnerving as having his footsteps dogged per se, but every so often he'd find the Panqui squatting beside a line of his footprints, probing them with a finger, or lowering his muzzle to sniff at them.

Will didn't feel he was so much being stalked as it was that Lombo was measuring him as a threat. The thief did notice Lombo doing that to some other folks, or at least seeming to, but not with the frequency Will saw in regards to himself. It also annoyed him a little that Lombo seemed to function like a body servant for Kerrigan. After all, Kerrigan was nothing compared to *the Norrington*, but did Will have one person seeing to his needs?

The thief shrugged. It was probably just as well that Kerrigan did have the beast caring for him, since he seemed incompetent otherwise. There were hundreds of things that Will knew how to do that Kerrigan couldn't. It did not slip Will's mind that most of these things were skills Resolute had forced on him in the first western trip, but he conveniently let that fact drift into the back of his mind. The little bits of friction between Orla and Lombo over how Kerrigan should be handled also pleased Will.

Qwc and Dranae seemed to be weathering the trip well. Because of his size, and the requisite size of the mounts needed to carry him, Dranae spent a lot of time with the men of the heavy cavalry units. The mercenary Matrave had one heavy cavalry company in his legion and even offered Dranae a job. When the column camped and contests of strength became the night's entertainment, Dranae became a prohibitive favorite, especially in wrestling matches.

Qwc became a favorite as well, but for entirely different reasons. The green Spritha flitted about almost constantly, marveling at things that were quite ordinary. Troopers caught on very swiftly that his innocence could be used. When riding through an orchard, one might bet Qwc a feather that the Spritha couldn't possibly fetch an apple from the top of the tree. Qwc would dart to the goal, harvest the prize, and win his feather, or button, or whatever other bit of trash the soldiers proffered.

On top of that, everything Qwc did seemed to have added consequences. More than once he returned from some sojourn through a field with a buttercup-blossom helm planted firmly on his head. Half the time he didn't seem to notice or know how the flowers had gotten there, but when it was called to his attention, he set it at a jaunty angle and soared through tight spirals that made him dizzy.

Whenever Will saw him, he couldn't help but smile, and often laugh. Even Resolute's normally vile mood lightened in the Spritha's presence, which Will marked as a victory right up there with defeating Chytrine. When Qwc would win his bets, he'd bring his loot to Will for evaluation and storage, announcing, "Trusts you, Will, Qwc trusts you. Safe treasure now."

Even that statement, delivered sincerely, earned laughter since everyone knew Will was a thief by trade. Still, it was the soldiers who were swindling Qwc who were having it pointed out to them that the Spritha trusted Will. That had a gradual and good effect on the soldiers. After the first few days on the road, fewer and fewer of them eyed Will suspiciously as he wandered through the camp at night.

Not that their precautions could have stopped me from taking whatever I wanted. Will smiled. They knew their trade, and he knew his. Will wasn't certain how what he knew what to do would defeat Chytrine, but he was content to figure it out as things went along.

Late on the second day the column approached the town of Stellin. Arrangements had been made to camp north of the town in a farmer's vacant field. Will found Crow and was preparing to take care of his mount when one of the Jeranese troopers rode up to him. The man dismounted and handed Will the reins to his horse.

"General Adrogans will be riding into the town. He wishes you to accompany him, Will Norrington."

Will glanced at Crow and Crow nodded, then began to rise.

The trooper waved Crow back down. "The general wishes the Norrington to accompany him alone. He will be well warded."

Crow's eyes narrowed. "Very well."

The trooper helped Will into the saddle, then pointed out where the general and a squad of lancers were waiting. Will gave the horse, a big bay gelding, a touch of his heels and the beast responded quickly enough that it almost bounced Will out of the saddle. The lancers parted as Will rode up, and spread out so any conversation Adrogans and Will might have would go unheard.

The expedition leader nodded a greeting to him. "You are tolerating the trip well."

Will shrugged. "Horses are doing the work."

"True enough." The general kept a smile on his face, but Will knew it for nothing more than a polite mask. "You have been to this town before?"

"Yes, a month ago. Crow, Resolute, and the princess were there. Not much to see."

"But it must be seen." The man's grey eyes became slits. "Tell me, Will, what do they say about me?"

The question, delivered quietly, sent a jolt through Will. "No, sir."

Adrogans' eyes widened and his nostrils flared. "What?"

Will raised his chin. "You want to know what they say, ask them. I'm no wagtongue who betrays friends."

They rode on in silence for a moment, then the trace of a smile tugged at Adrogans' mouth. "Then I have no fear of you betraying my words to them?"

"You're not a friend."

Adrogans' smile broadened. He turned and regarded Will more closely. "You're right in that, of course, but I *am* an ally. We share a common enemy and, together, we will cause Chytrine much discomfort."

Will nodded. "I want to kill her."

"An admirable goal, yes. Doing that will require us to work together. A working alliance such as we need can only be formed on the basis of mutual trust." His eyes narrowed again. "So, tell me, why should an accident of birth make me trust a feral little thief?"

"Why should the fact that you're luckier than you are arrogant or egotistical make me trust a general?"

Adrogans chuckled. "So, that's what they think about me?"

Will's cheeks immediately burned. "You tricked me. That doesn't build trust."

"No. You're right. It doesn't." The general's face settled back into impassiveness, though passion threaded through his words. "It does give me your measure, however. You are loyal, but a bit immature, and possibly impetuous. You do have spirit, however, and the instinct to strike. Properly trained and employed, these are invaluable skills.

"The simple fact is, Will, that success requires that I trust you. I do believe I *can* trust you, but I needed to discover how far."

The thief growled. "How far is that?"

"Far enough to know that you can serve in a role that is more valuable than bait. You're sharp enough to see that this is the role in which you have been cast. We're on a campaign. There is nothing to steal. You are a rallying point for those who need to believe Chytrine can be defeated, and you are a target to distract her."

Will nodded. "You don't have to be the Grand Magister of Vilwan to figure that much out."

"Another good point." Adrogans ran a hand over his jaw. "You will have to understand, Will, that I approach this campaign as being very important. I know how much it means to everyone involved. I will conduct it in the manner I best see fit and I am fairly certain that you and your acquaintances will come to feel that I am ignoring you or your advice. If I see a role for you or them, I will use you. If not, you will remain in reserve—and no amount of mumbling or cajoling will change that."

"So our job is to do nothing unless you have something for us to do?"

"Yes."

"What if we don't agree with what you are doing?"

Adrogans raised his chin and stroked his throat with a gloved hand. "I was given command of this expedition for a reason. I know I have detractors, and am roundly criticized for a variety of reasons. Curiously enough, despite all the criticism, I do win my battles. This fact is always underplayed."

Will frowned as they topped a rise and looked down on the village of Stellin. "What if what they say about you is true, though? What if they're pointing out things that will mean you lose? The next battle could be that, you know."

"I know that far better than you, Will, and take countless precautions against it." The man watched him for a moment, then nodded toward the town. "Come on, it's time the people of Stellin see the salvation of the world."

Adrogans applied spurs to his horse, and Will's mount followed eagerly. A small crowd of people began to spill out of the Hare and Hutch. As they reined up, Will recognized Quintus moving to the fore.

The general brought his horse right up to Quintus, forcing the man back a step. "I am General Markus Adrogans of Jerana. You have, of course, heard of me and are in awe. Scant little time for that now. Bow, mouth your obeisances, and we can dispense with further ceremony."

Quintus staggered back, then dropped his eyes and lowered his head. "We are honored, my lord."

"Yes, yes, of course you are." Adrogans sniffed, then wrinkled his nose. "You are further honored that I have brought with me the Norrington, your countryman and the salvation of the world."

The people gasped and bowed in Will's direction. He

was surprised that none of them recognized him, but with his mask on, and further masked by the introduction, the chances they would connect him with his past visits were nil. *Unless* . . .

He glanced about for Sephi, but didn't see her. He wanted to ask, but that would definitely make them recognize him, and he didn't want that. He wasn't sure why, but part of it came from the hope sparking in the townsfolk's eyes. *If they knew who I really was, it would die.*

Adrogans clapped his hands, once, loudly. "Yes, well, you are thrilled, without a doubt. Easy to see, which makes this easier on all of us. Some things you must do. First, everyone is to stay away from Northmont. As arranged, my army has taken it over. The provisions are adequate though uninspiring. Have you, in this fine establishment, a cask or three of brandy that I can requisition? Two thousand men do develop a thirst."

The tavern's owner wiped his hands on a stained apron. "Not that much, my lord. I could fit a wagon with ale casks, and brandy for you, if you want."

"Splendid." Adrogans nodded at one of his soldiers. The man tossed the innkeeper a fat leather sack that rang of gold coins when the man caught it. "Now, I do require fifty head of cattle to be driven to Northmont by morning. We will pay in good gold, of course. Headman, divide this herd among your people, so no one will be unduly enriched nor impoverished by my request. Make the choices by lot, if you must. Any provisions we leave behind at Northmont should be taken into the town stores, to be held against our return, or for the depths of your winter need."

Will caught sight of a half-dozen young men with satchels. Each carried a bow and a quiver full of arrows. Slightly older than he was, each one had a sloppy, eager grin on his face. Their intention to join the army was quite evident in their expressions.

Adrogans clearly saw them as well. "Good, I see Stellin has a militia. You'll need it. Guard your town well, men.

Your presence means I don't have to detach a squad of my finest. One less worry for me, one more worry for Chytrine."

A shiver ran through Will as he listened to Adrogans. While some of the arrogance and pomposity he'd seen in the man in Yslin remained, another aspect blossomed beside it. In those few words he went from dashing the hopes of farmers' sons to incorporating them in his force and leaving them with the clear impression that their presence in Stellin left him indebted to them. Not only did that forestall a ragtag horde of untrained, unequipped, and inexperienced youths following in his force's wake, but it guaranteed they'd fight even harder to defend their village if the time came to do so.

While that new side certainly was born of the shrewd and analytical person he'd talked to on the ride into the town, the two Adrogans seemed as different as air and earth. Adrogans was manipulating the townsfolk of Stellin with the skill of a swindler bilking a victim. When Adrogans rode away, the folks in Stellin would be left thinking of a distant and arrogant man, dedicated to leading a force to kill Chytrine. *And they would think that force was twice the size it really is.*

Adrogans glanced at him. "Come, Lord Norrington, our work here is done. I bid you, fine people of Stellin, my hearty thanks and wishes for a safe future."

With that, Adrogans reined his horse about and the whole of his party began riding back to Northmont. Will held his horse back a little, not wanting to pull up next to Adrogans or continue their conversation. *If he wants to speak to me, he can slow down.*

Will shivered again. He admired Adrogans' skill at manipulating the people, but this opened up a bigger question for him. *Is he manipulating the rest of us?* The thief took a quick census and could name four different versions of Adrogans: manipulator, arrogant-socializer, incompetent-warrior, and shrewd. He wasn't sure which one he believed in, then shook his head, since they all inhabited the same body.

Perhaps it's just like me. No one could see the Norrington in me until the time came. He glanced at Adrogans' broad back as the man rode on. *Let's hope the true Adrogans will make himself apparent when his time comes, too.*

CHAPTER 47

While intellectually Kerrigan knew there would be some point in his life when he would again be dry and warm and his stomach would be full, emotionally the day seemed as far away as Vilwan and his tower chamber. Though not even a half week into the trek, he felt as if he'd already reached Aurolan. Working their way up through the mountains of Gyrvirgul, the riders got drenched by rain and, worse, some freezing rain. Everyone said it was unseasonable, which most of the troopers translated into meaning *magick* and clearly wondered why none of the Vilwanese legion could do anything about it.

The warmages ignored the glances and whispers from the troopers. Kerrigan had done his best to explain that the warmages were no more suited to controlling the weather than soldiers were to brewing beer or sailing a ship. Whenever he offered that analogy, at least one of the soldiers would comment that he knew all there was to know about brewing or sailing, and that specific example tore down his generalization.

Kerrigan did acknowledge that he was managing to annoy the soldiers, but they didn't help at all. His snoring, he came to understand, was not appreciated, as it might alert the enemy to their presence. The sheer absurdity of that proposition—given the excessive smoke from their fires, for example—led him to be disappointed in the soldiers. Their little prejudice against snoring would make sense in another setting, but the column was so obvious that snoring would make no difference. His logic won him no friends, however, as the small-minded soldiers found it easier to cling to their notions instead of actually thinking.

In some ways he envied them their dullness, since it allowed them to rejoice in the simple and banal. They were overjoyed, for example, in the fact that they could eat pretty much as they pleased, since the rations they were issued were generous. Kerrigan hated it, since salty, dried beef and biscuits hard enough to crack rocks were hardly the sort of fare he liked. More appealing fare, like local fruits and vegetables, had to be shared out on an equal basis, and nothing he offered the Spritha to fetch him things brought a positive response from the creature.

Qwc's rejection of his offers underscored the isolation he felt. The warmages accepted Orla. All of them were younger than she was, and her attempts to keep up with them tired her out. This meant she had little patience for dealing with him. When they did speak, she demanded he take care of little camp jobs that Lombo was happy to perform. It made no sense to Kerrigan to be given those jobs, so he did them slowly and sullenly.

Orla did order him to drill with the warmages, but those efforts quickly ended in frustration for everyone involved. With proper preparation, he was able to counter any spells they cast in his direction. He carefully chose the spells he would use to attack them, and diligently worked them. The warmages would anticipate him and raise defenses, but his attacks came with such strength that they blew through the defenses. They learned nothing from him, nor did he learn from them, so he withdrew from their company.

Lombo provided him with some companionship, but the Panqui was as much out of place with the expedition as Kerrigan was. The beast would range far and wide, disappearing for hours at a time, then return bearing some flower or knot of wood or another oddity that provided Kerrigan a moment's diversion. Far too infrequently did Lombo bring Kerrigan something he could eat.

Most frustrating of all was Orla's order that he should not use magick to make things better for himself. It would have been child's play for him to enchant a leather bucket so he could fill it from a stream a quarter mile downhill, but Orla would not hear of it. Kerrigan countered by offering to work the spell such that he would provide water for more people—even the entire expedition. She refused, forcing him to walk to the stream and fill his bucket. It made no sense to him for him to have to do that, though he did notice comradely nods from the soldiers traveling likewise to the stream and back.

As his horse plodded along the narrow mountain track, the young mage just closed his eyes. Grey sky, mists, rain, wet rock, and wetter soldiers were all there was to see. The walls of the canyon through which they rode rose to the clouds and even the twisting tendrils of mist that descended to tease pennants bored him. Worse yet, they frustrated him because he would have loved to put together a spell to duplicate the effect, but Orla would never let him test it.

Kerrigan rubbed a hand across his belly as it rumbled. The oilskins he wore over his robe didn't do much to keep out the cold. He shivered and sniffed, then snaked a hand out from beneath his cloak to wipe his nose on his sleeve. The wet wool stunk, but snorting the scent back out would just make his nose run more.

Then his horse stopped. He heard a gasp from the rider

in front of him. Frowning sourly, Kerrigan opened his eyes. He blinked once while they focused, then he, too, gasped.

The trail had curled up and around a small rise, then continued snaking on down and toward the west. Another branch curved off to the right and opened a dozen yards on into a huge arch. Two towering figures, both male, had been carved from the stone and formed the arch's sides. They faced forward, staring forbiddingly out and down toward the riders. Their wings, spread behind them, formed the arch itself on the interior, and pointed east and west externally.

The horse before his moved again, and Kerrigan followed. His mind reeled. He knew the legend of the Gyrkyme. Kirûn had captured an elven prince and his retinue, then used magick to make them mate with *Araftii*—mythical, bestial bird-women. The resulting offspring had been the first of the Gyrkyme. The Gyrkyme had bred true, but were viewed by the elves as rapeget and beasts. The elves would have nothing to do with them, and for their own reasons, the urZrethi created Gyrvirgul as a homeland for the Gyrkyme.

Until seeing the artistry of the arch, those facts had been sterile and lifeless. The urZrethi created mountain strongholds—Kerrigan knew that as certainly as he knew there were ten days in a week, three weeks to a month. But seeing the arch, it hammered home the effort necessary to raise such a place from nothing. He recalled that many men felt the urZrethi had created Gyrvirgul out of some animosity for the elves, but that arch alone suggested to him that there was something greater that had motivated the urZrethi.

The arch rose to a great height above him, and for a half second he thought it terribly inefficient. Looking up, tracking the lines of little torrents dripping down, he spotted shadowed archways high in the passage's ceiling vaults. A smile blossomed on his face when he realized that among men such height would have been an extravagance, but this arch served a *winged* people. That there was a level path suited to the passage of horses should have been more the surprise than the height.

The pathway continued on into the mountain, switching back several times. Flames danced in sconces just above eye level and did little to reveal any color on the walls. Their swaying shadows and golden light did teasingly conceal and display the friezes that had been worked into the walls nearest ground level. They appeared quite idyllic, with Gyrkyme figures soaring together, or gathering fruit and hunting. Clearly more scenes had been worked above, and the lack of light in those upper reaches suggested to him that the Gyrkyme had superior night vision.

He almost passed a hand over his own eyes to invoke a spell and let him see what they saw, but he hesitated. Oddly enough he found himself completely indifferent to what Orla might say about his using magick to let him see in the dark. Instead, he refrained because until he'd seen the entrance to Gyrvirgul, it had been nothing but a name, a fact. It had lacked life and majesty and mystery. By using magick he could easily reveal its secrets, but in doing so he would once again relegate it to the realm of facts. *In knowing too much I can kill it and I don't want to do that.*

That realization surprised him. His entire life had been centered around *understanding.* To opt out of wanting to understand something ran counter to everything he had learned or done. Even so, it felt right on a level he'd not experienced before.

The passageway leveled out and ended in a massive conical chamber alive with light. The room could have easily housed the entire Grand Magister's tower. Dark archways swirled around in a helix on the walls, while a massive fire guttered in the chamber's heart. *If each of those archways leads to a home . . .*

Gyrvirgul, using that measure, did not house as many people as a metropolis like Yslin, but certainly was home to several thousands. *Which is far more Gyrkyme than I had any idea existed.*

Flames leaped skyward from the balefire. Kerrigan watched a fiery tentacle twist and curl upward, then smiled despite having his vision momentarily stolen by the darkness it left after its collapse. When he could see again he caught sight of Orla waving him over to where she waited with Will Norrington and the others. He reined his horse in their direction, then found Lombo loping beside him.

Kerrigan dismounted as best he could, and knew enough to still cling to the saddle so his legs wouldn't collapse. "Magister, this is incredible."

The grey-haired combat mage nodded. "It is indeed. I had no idea."

Kerrigan caught a quizzical note in her voice. "Did you know we were coming here?"

Orla shook her head as Crow came walking over. "None of us did. We were passing through Gyrvirgul because to go around the mountains would have added days to the journey. I was riding with Princess Alexia, scouting out our route, when Perrine found us. Originally she had come here to gather the company of Warhawks who will join our force. When she related all that had happened in Yslin, including the presence of General Adrogans and the Norrington in our party, Ausai Tirigo dictated that the expedition should be brought here, housed, welcomed, and feasted."

Kerrigan's stomach rumbled at the last bit of news.

Orla glanced reprovingly at her charge for a moment, then away again. "You've been here before, in your travels, Crow?"

The old man shook his head. "Me, no. The urZrethi hid this place very well. Had the Tirigo not wished us to find it, we would have continued on by none the wiser. As nearly as I know, our host will be fifty times the number of men who have seen this place before. Princess Alexia was raised here, but prior to her arrival, it had been at least a century before a man walked in the heart of Gyrvirgul. Since then, the few other men brought here were her tutors."

The man hastily added, "And I only know this because I was present when Peri extended the invitation to the princess. She filled me in on the details as we rode."

Will smiled and puffed himself up a bit. "Well, we are a pretty special company. Not really a wonder they wanted to meet us."

Crow laughed. "Ah, I didn't make myself clear. The Tirigo wanted us here not to honor us. They're planning to honor the princess, and we are here to bear witness to that honor. They are very proud of her and they want no question left of that fact in anyone's mind."

CHAPTER 48

Once within the massive domed chamber of Gyrvirgul's heart, Alyx tossed Valor's reins to Captain Agitare and vaulted from the saddle. She stripped off her oilskins and tossed them to one of the chirping fledglings that huddled in the shadows. The youngsters caught the cloak and began to tussle over it. From the corner of her eye she saw one of the Talons emerge victorious, and that surprised her not at all.

She laughed aloud, once and sharply, molding it as well as she could to match the Talon's victory shriek. She was less concerned that her Wolves might have heard her make such a sound than she was by embarrassing the Gyrkyme by not making it. Had she been alone, she would have abandoned human decorum entirely, stripped herself down to a sword-harness, and have begun the ascent to her family home. Not having that option, she flicked off her gloves, tugged off her boots, then climbed up the stonework decorating a column supporting the hollow's vaulted roof.

Her climb did bring a burn to muscles too long removed from such exertion, but that only made her smile. Alyx had been two years away from Gyrvirgul. She'd been aware of missing it, but until she rode into the grand chamber again, she didn't realize how fierce the ache in her heart had been. *So many other things filled my time and attention, but none of it could fill the want of my home.*

She swung off the column on the highest of the Talon levels and ran down the narrow ledge to a big round hole. She ducked into it, shrieking a greeting. She dropped to a squat there, just inside the entrance, then smiled happily down at the quintet of Gyrkyme waiting for her.

Perrine stood there, flanked by her mother, Lanlitgri, and her father, Preyknosery. Her parents, Talons both, had bred true in her and in her brother, Octras. Both siblings shared their parents' dark brown down over their backs, the dappled brown-and-white down on their breasts, and the striking dark design around their eyes and down their cheeks. Octras, being male, was larger than Peri, but gave nothing away to her in martial skill or fierce splendor.

Alyx was pretty certain she'd never seen the fifth Gyrkyme before. Female, obviously, and jet-black save for bright red fletching on her shoulders and the forward joint on her wings. That coloration, and her slender, slighter build, marked her as being from the Swift caste. Seeing Octras hold her closely, Alyx had no doubt certain Talon mavens were regretting his loss to the next generation of warriors.

Alyx leaped to the chamber floor and found herself smothered in hugs and kisses. She wished she'd torn her clothes off before, and had to content herself with the warm caress of down over her face and hands.

"I have been away too long." She wanted to say more, but emotion choked her. She pulled back to wipe away tears. Preyknosery helped her, leaving talons sheathed as he brushed his thumb over her left cheek. She took his hand in hers and pressed it to her cheek, then turned and kissed his palm.

The elder Gyrkyme smiled. "This nest will always have room for you, Alexia."

"Thank you."

Octras stroked Alyx's shoulder, then squired the Swift forward with his other hand. "Sister, this is Sergrai, she who will be my wife."

The Swift smiled shyly and extended a hand to Alyx. The princess clutched the hand delicately, then drew Sergrai into a hug. She felt an initial stiffness, but it melted quickly. Sergrai gave her a quick peck on the neck, then they parted.

Alyx nodded. "Pleased to meet you, Sergrai. Octras, I see, is still very lucky."

Sergrai nodded, then tucked herself under Octras' arm.

Strong hands grasped Alyx's shoulders and spun her around. Taking a step back, Lanlitgri studied her for a moment with a sharp amber eye. "You look well, as near as I can see."

"Yes, Mother, I am very well." Alyx smiled. "Better now, and honored at the invitation to return."

Peri keened quickly. "I was going to kidnap you if they didn't agree to your return."

Preyknosery shook his head. "Her intention, which echoed through Gyrvirgul, sparked quite a debate among the Plumes and the Wise. Perrine told many a tale of your adventures."

"She told of the Norrington, and fighting a *sullanciri* and the dragon!" Sergrai's dark eyes widened. "And she told the stories very well."

Alyx nodded. "Lauded by a Swift for your taletelling, sister? High praise indeed."

Peri smiled proudly. "I even was called to tell the stories to the Tirigo himself. He ended the debate and said he would make you a Wing."

The princess blinked. "But . . ."

Preyknosery settled a hand on her left shoulder. "Yes, it is awkward to be given that title when you have no wings."

Alyx held her hands up. "No, no, it's not that. It's that I've done nothing to deserve such an honor. You, you earned the title Ironwing a hundred times over. What I've done is nothing."

"No, daughter, what you have done is to make all of us proud." Preyknosery pressed a three-fingered hand to his breast. "I am a Talon, not a Swift nor a Plume, but even I understand what you and your success mean to us. Because Kirûn was responsible for our creation, we have always been tainted. When your father entrusted you to us, for your raising, and when Augustus convinced others that you should be left here, they began to see us differently. Not the elves, surely, but men. Augustus and others sent their best to teach you what we could not. What they saw changed how men see us."

"That's not anything I did, but what was here and seen when outsiders came in."

"A point debated among the Wise, to be sure." Ironwing smiled. "You might say you have done nothing. You have missed all you did to grow up here. We are not men. We do not treat our young as do men. You survived here. You thrived here. There were those who saw you as being a sneakbird—placed in a nest to be raised over our own. You proved them wrong, all without having wings. You've earned your title. Your life proclaims it."

Alyx started to renew her protest, but Peri grabbed her by the shoulders. "Sister, you'll sputter and wonder and protest, but it's done and done. Now we have to get you ready for the ceremony."

"Um, sister, I only have road clothes with me. Between us we have the fashion sense of a grub-worm."

Peri winked. "That's why Sergrai here has offered to help us get ready."

"It would be my honor, Princess."

Alyx hesitated only for a heartbeat, then nodded. "You'll make it so I give the Gyrkyme all due honor?"

"Wings alive, dead, and yet in shell shall be proud."

"Good." She glanced at Peri. "What will the Wolves think?"

"Who cares? They are only walkers." Peri slid an arm around Alyx's shoulders and guided her to the wallhole leading to her old sleeping chamber. "You are one of us, and that is all that matters."

Will smiled, largely because he could straighten to his full height in the little room he'd been given, and Crow could not. It wasn't Crow's discomfiture that gave him cause to smile, but that he didn't have to worry about bashing his brains out on the ceiling. The Gyrkyme had led his little company into a corridor that circled the main area, but at a distance. Off it branched other smaller corridors, and dark holes dotted their walls. Beyond the holes, which were small enough to force Will to duck his head, lay small, cylindrical rooms with bedsteads carved from the rock, and a series of small niches where gear and lit lamps could be stowed.

Will remained silent until the black-and-red-winged Gyrkyme left them. She'd been no taller than Will, and her wings had been half formed. In fact, he just assumed she was female because her build was so slight, though she exhibited no breasts, nor the curves of even someone like Alexia's aide. Will assumed she'd just not hit puberty, when her body and wings would develop.

Crow groaned as he stretched out on the woven straw mat that covered the stone sleeping ledge. "Warm, not wet, slightly softer than the ground last night. It will do."

"You're going to sleep?"

"As opposed to?"

"Go exploring." Will pointed back out in the general

direction he thought the fire was. "Did you see all that stuff? This place is huge, the whole mountain is hollowed out. And the Gyrkyme, did you see them? There's the ones that are like hawks, then the raven that guided us here. There have to be more and . . ."

"Will, this might not have occurred to you, but we can't just go exploring."

"Sure we can. It's easy. I didn't see any guards posted about or anything." He interlaced his fingers and bridged them. "The decorative columns will be easy enough to climb. . . ."

Crow rolled up on an elbow and narrowed his eyes. "I have two points to make. First, given your early career, it might have escaped you that if people want you to look around in their domain, they will offer an invitation and take you on a tour."

Will wrinkled up his nose. "I know that, but they might have forgotten."

"You know better. The second, and far more important, is this: you are *the* Norrington. The Gyrkyme are our allies. They want to help us. Their inviting us here is extraordinary, and as their guests, we will be on our best behavior."

"Okay, is this just because you're old?"

Crow rolled onto his back and laughed aloud. "Oh, ouch, Will." The man continued to laugh, then wiped tears from his eyes. "That was funny."

"It wasn't meant to be."

"I know, which made it even more so." Crow looked over at him. "There are times I think you grasp the gravity of our situation, and others, like now, when I know you've forgotten it."

"I haven't forgotten it." Will sat down on his bunk, facing Crow. "It's just that there are times it's boring."

"Like the battle on Vilwan?"

"No, that was very exciting." The thief smiled quickly, then let the smile die as a shiver shook him. "And it was pretty horrible, too."

"That's the way of these things, Will. You can listen to countless campaigns reduced to song, but they only touch on the parts that excite or horrify. If songs are sung of our mission, they *might* mention our visit here, but they'll certainly forget rain-soaked camps, cold meals, roads churned to mud by thousands of hooves."

Crow smiled. "So, I choose to sleep right now. When we're needed, they'll come for us and we'll be rested."

"Well, I can't sleep."

"Then if you must go running off, at least pull on some dry socks. Your squishing around in those boots will give you away."

Will grumbled, but pulled his boots off, then peeled off his socks. He rung them out and draped them in one of the niches. He rummaged around in his saddlebags for dry socks, pulled them on, then decided to lie down for a moment. He refused to groan aloud as Crow had, but his back ached as the muscles eased themselves.

He shifted his shoulders a bit, then closed his eyes. *Just until my back stops hurting.* He thought about what the dark, shadowed reaches of Gyrvirgul's upper levels might hide. Before avarice could blossom full into a fantasy, the darkness he contemplated smothered him with sleep.

Will had nothing but the complaints of his belly to suggest how long he'd slept. A small, brown-colored Gyrkyme had come for Crow and him. In rather subdued monotones the envoy told them the time of the feast had come. Each of them was handed a diaphanous silken strip of cloth that would have served as a scarf or loincloth, and their guide said he would return once they were ready.

The young thief looked at Crow. "I've almost gotten used to dressing for feasts, but I don't have any of those good clothes."

Crow smiled. "I'm not sure this is my size either." He tugged off his doeskin tunic, revealing a trio of parallel

scars running from collarbone to hip through a thick
thatch of white hair. Various other scars decorated his body
here and there, but nothing could come close to matching
the long ones for size or age.

"The Gyrkyme don't use much in the way of clothes, so
they don't really care if we dress or not."

"So you'll make that into one of their loincloths?"

The old man shook his head and looped the silver cloth
into a sash running from right shoulder to left hip. He
knotted it at his hip and tucked the tails beneath his belt.
"Not that I'm expecting it to be cold around that fire, and
the food should be hot, too, but why take the risk?"

Will raised an eyebrow at him as he rolled the cloth and
tied it around his head in a headband that passed just above
his mask. He tied it off neatly and left it with long flowing
tails hanging down his back. "So you're not trying to hide
your scars? Three long ones like that could have come from
a Gyrkyme hand."

Crow frowned for a moment, then shook his head. "I
thought you'd seen these before. I guess not. They're not
Gyrkyme."

"What, then?" Will frowned and thought. "Frostclaw
tracks?"

His companion nodded. "It was a long time ago. A
frostclaw decided to play with its food before it ate."

"I don't remember a song about that being sung of
Kedyn's Crow."

"There isn't any. Dull tale anyway. Headband looks
good." Crow threw Will a wink, then stood and ducked his
head to follow their guide. "I'm sure you'll find the feast far
more entertaining."

Will wanted to maintain a respectable amount of dis-
dain, but the Gyrkyme made that difficult. It seemed as if
the entire expeditionary force and population of Gyrvirgul
had been gathered around the balefire for the night's feast.
The outer ring of attendees weren't actually down on the
floor, but sat and stood on the ledges all around the central

chamber. They seemed, to Will's eyes, to be young, without fully developed wings, and roughly grouped by type as the rings ascended from brownfolk to very colorful and larger Gyrkyme.

On the floor, however, things became very interesting. The visitors had been arranged by company in seven ranks, starting with one man, then two, then three, and so on until the seventh rank of seven. The remaining two members of the company—usually the senior officer and most decorated soldier—were pulled off into a separate mixed group of special guests. The visiting triangles pointed in at the fire, then inserted on either side of them were triangles of Gyrkyme, seven ranks deep, that pointed away from the fire. It took two rings to take up all the human guests, then a third ring made entirely of Gyrkyme handled the rest.

Only the expedition's special guests had been given the sashes and individual taste dictated how they would be worn. Resolute wore his as a breechclout and was nothing short of magnificent. Muscles rippled beneath flesh adorned by twisting tattoos. While the Gyrkyme with their brilliant plumage were breathtaking, Resolute matched them for splendor in his own way.

Kerrigan had likewise decided to observe Gyrkyme custom, which was pretty much the last thing Will needed to see. He figured that Kerrigan and Dranae massed about the same, but Dranae had it all arranged better and chose, as had Crow, to employ his cloth as a sash. A few others made it into a headband or armbands. Orla went the armband route, but instead of letting the ends hang free, she braided them down her left arm and knotted them off at her wrist. Qwc tied his around his waist, letting it trail after him like silver smoke as he flew, and Lombo had used his as a neckerchief, tying it with a big floppy bow that looked ridiculous, but Will felt no inclination to point that out.

Ultimately, though, it fell to Alexia to put all others to shame. She actually wore three sashes, the other two being black and gold in addition to the silver. The black one, silken and not sheer, she wore as a loincloth with the ends hanging down to her knees. The gold cloth, likewise opaque, circled around her neck and then crossed down to cover her breasts before being knotted at the back. The silver cloth circled her waist, holding the loincloth in place, with the loose ends hanging at her left hip.

When she appeared a gasp melted into murmurs amid the assembly. Will found her to be beautiful well beyond imagining. She'd always been pretty, and had haunted a dream or two of his, but her selection of gowns and her war kit had never displayed her charms so clearly. More impressive than just her physical beauty, however, was the regal bearing with which she moved beside the Tirigo. She'd always been graceful when Will had seen her at receptions, but never so free and fluid. Here, home, among those who raised her, she felt completely at ease and able to relax, which made her yet more alluring and attractive.

Her noble presence also somehow elevated her above and beyond the position where Will had seen her before. As always he had thought of people in relation to his legend as Will the Nimble. Watching her move to the place of honor next to the leader of the Gyrkyme, he realized that she was a heroine of her own cycle of songs. Just as Kedyn's Crow and the Azure Spider were sung of in the Dimandowns, she would entertain the world's nobility. If Will the Nimble were ever to be sung of in one of her songs, he would play the fool, of this he had no doubt.

He laughed to himself. *And if she were sung of in any of my songs, I'd play the fool.* An accident of birth had thrust him into a position where he could be a hero, but she'd clearly been meant for this through generations. He knew, no matter the prophecies and portents, that she would be more important to the world than he ever would be. Though he could feel a little piece of his dream dying, he made a silent and solemn pledge that he'd make any effort needed to help her succeed.

Alexia had been given the place of honor at the Tirigo's

right hand. The Tirogia, the leader's primary queen, sat at his left and to her left came General Adrogans. The Jeranese military leader opted to wear his strip of cloth as a loin-cloth. Though softer than Resolute, with fewer scars and no tattoos that Will could see, his flesh didn't sag and pool as Kerrigan's did. Adrogans maintained a sense of dignity de-spite being nearly naked.

The Tirigo managed to put everyone to shame regard-less of dress. He'd donned a silver breechcloth, with black and gold ribbons edging it. He bade his guests seat them-selves while he yet stood, then spread his wings in a most incredible display of plumage. His crest rose, flashing iri-descent green feathers that spiked two feet above his head. Scintillating blue feathers covered him all over, save for shiny black on his face and breast, but the design worked into his wings made him yet more impressive. There, with hints of red and green surrounded by blue, two eyes looked out at the assembly. The gasps that had greeted Alexia rose again, then sank into a hushed and reverent silence.

"Honored guests, a prouder day has never dawned in Gyrvirgul. Before this, our pride had been marked by Alexia's arrival as an infant. Now, her return as a powerful and storied general makes our breasts swell with admi-ration. Likewise, our awe at your campaign to destroy Chytrine is limitless, and this feast is but a small represen-tation of our gratitude for your efforts on behalf of the world."

With that he furled his wings and sat, then nodded to a blackwinged Gyrkyme. That figure clapped once and mo-tion returned to the room.

Gyrkyme youths began to serve, passing through the ranks to hand out large bowls the size of washbasins Will had seen in the private chambers of rich households. Oth-ers moved around after that, with small wheeled carts dish-ing up rice and all manner of foods, both hot and cold. If there was a pattern to the delivery, Will could not figure it out. He just rotated his bowl to get each new offering in an empty spot.

The vast majority of food Will had consumed in his lifetime had consisted of crusts and scraps, moldy cheese, weak broths, and fruits or vegetables easily stolen or scavenged from garbage heaps. While the fine foods offered at the various receptions had greatly expanded the universe of his culinary experience, it in no way prepared him for the sweet, savory, and spicy fare served to him that night.

To eat, they'd been given small wooden paddles, shaped much like a spoon, but flatter and very flexible. A small dollop of rice would be teased from the center of the bowl, mixed with meat in a sauce, pressed together into a little disk, then scraped up and popped into the mouth. Sometimes the food just gushed sweetness over his tongue. Yet others exploded with a head-clearing aroma that set the area behind his face afire. To start he'd gobbled quickly, but the first big gulp of spicy food had set his nose to running and made him slow down. Henceforth he attacked things more modestly.

Sweat gathered on his forehead and ran down the back of his head. He glanced at Crow, who likewise sweated, and Resolute, who shaped his little food patties with great deliberation and precision. Both of them seemed to be enjoying the meal and a quick inventory of what had disappeared from their bowls indicated Will's tastes ran closer to Resolute's than Crow's.

The Tirigo waved away service after a point, and the servants withdrew from the area. When the last of them had left, the soft tones of flutes and horns began to drift down from the vaults of the great chamber. Will looked up, as did everyone else, and caught a quick glimpse of something plummeting freely from the room's highest point.

The item resolved itself into a huge long banner of black fabric, unrolling as it fell. Gold letters in all manner of scripts decorated its entire length. Will had no idea what they said, but the way they flashed in the firelight gave them a majesty and power. The banner's tail snapped audibly as it finished, then a tongue of flame from the balefire licked at it.

In an instant the entire banner exploded into a white-fire ribbon. Its brilliance stole Will's night sight, but as his vision cleared more swirling descended from the darkness above. Gyrkyme, black save for the red on shoulders and wings, wove their way in an intricate aerial dance. Some dove toward the ground, then swooped low, while others tightly circled, wingtips all but touching. Gyrkyme chased one another, reaching for the trailing ends of gold loincloths, banking and arcing, diving and then climbing with powerful wingstrokes.

The clash of cymbals underscored the music that accompanied the winged ballet. It changed pace from slow to frenetic, shifting from coldly cultured to barbaric. Will couldn't take his eyes off the dancers and envied them their freedom. Their cries, which came in unison at breaks in the music, rang with pure pleasure that summoned a wide grin to the little thief's face.

After far too short a time, the company circled overhead so fast and so low that the breeze of their passing tousled Will's hair and tugged at the ends of his headband. Their circle tightened, then they descended, grounding themselves. They knelt and their wings overlapped in a black-and-scarlet disk surrounding the fire. Their bodies heaved with breathing, but they kept their heads down and hidden.

Applause, unbridled and enthusiastic, arose from the humans, while keening calls from the Gyrkyme echoed through the room. The joyous cacophony filled the air as the entertainers had once done, and showed no sign of slackening. Will clapped his hands as hard as possible, and whistled as loudly as he could. He'd never seen anything like that performance before, and couldn't imagine seeing its like again.

The Tirigo rose, his dark eyes reflecting the golden firelight, and slowly the chamber drifted back to silence. He smiled, his crest rising, then bowed his head to the dancers. "The beauty of your offering does more honor to our daughter than words and awards could ever imagine." He clapped his hands once, allowing the dancers to rise and filter out of the room to a renewal of applause.

Once they had departed, the Tirigo bade Alexia stand. "We have, among us, a tradition of honoring the best among us with the title 'Wing.' The triangles in which you are seated mimic the pattern in which we fly, and that individual at the point acts as a guide. That position is the most difficult in a flock, not only because of leadership responsibilities, but because it demands the most physical strength. Those of us who follow have our wings lifted by the winds our leader's labor produces.

"Our Wings are known among us by their honorific. He who became Alexia's father, after bringing her here from far Okrannel, is known to us as Ironwing. Taken beneath his wing, Alexia became the leader you know her to be. Now, with you, she shall return to Okrannel, to fulfill the mission for which she has been trained. From us, in acknowledgment of all she is and her value to us and the world, we proclaim her to be Goldwing."

A small brown Gyrkyme approached bearing a cloth-covered tray. The Tirigo took a gold chain with a gold feather amulet on it and settled it over Alexia's bowed head. The feather rested just below her throat, against her breastbone. He slipped her hair out from beneath the chain, then bowed to her.

Alexia swallowed hard, then smiled carefully. A hand rose to touch the amulet, then she closed her eyes for a moment. When they opened again, it was to the accompaniment of applause and vocalizations by the Gyrkyme. Her smile broadened. She pressed a hand to her lips for a moment, then looked out over the assembly.

"Thank you, Ausai Tirigo, and you, the Gyrkyme. Here I

was always the fledgling, the one whose wings never sprouted. You could have pitied me and reviled me, but you did not. All of you accepted the mission my father had given Ironwing." She opened her arms wide. "While you see no feathers on me, the fact is that I am fletched with all you taught me about courage, honor, determination, and nobility. There might be some who would say my blood made me a diamond, but without your efforts I would have been dull and gone unnoticed.

"To be named Goldwing, this . . ." She faltered for a moment and glanced down before continuing. "It is a dream we have all shared here, and yet I do not think myself worthy. Your confidence in me shall be an investment, and I shall make it pay handsomely for you. Whatever successes I have, all shall know they would never have been save for you."

Alexia's eyes hardened as her gaze swept over the men present. "And you, my comrades, you now know the proud and beautiful womb from which I emerged. Together we will be born again of Gyrvirgul. West and north we'll go to the land of my birth, and together we can once again make it a home."

CHAPTER 49

Though it was likely just her imagination, Alexia felt a tingle run through her as she rode across the border from Jerana into Okrannel. A granite obelisk, which had once stood tall but had been hacked and cracked to where she could see the jagged top from on horseback, marked the line between the two nations. She smiled, taking no offense at the broken obelisk, since the weathering proved it had been vandalized long before the Aurolani forces had ever invaded Okrannel.

It did feel good to be in Okrannel. As with her previous journey, when she engaged in her dream raid, she concentrated to see if her blood would sing with joy at her return. So many of the other exiles reported such things that part of her wondered at how normal she was when it didn't happen to her. Though disappointed years ago, and a bit yet even now, she didn't worry about the silent fluid in her veins. *The romance of a return has nothing in common with the reality.*

Alyx couldn't allow herself to be fully at ease, however,

and again not because of the presence of Aurolani forces. The coast road brought the army past the Jeranese port city of Ooriz and up onto the Zhusk plateau. The plateau was home to a native people who, while primitive, had proved defiant and elusive. Adrogans, in explaining that he'd set up his headquarters on the plateau, said that the Zhusk hated the Aurolani more than they did Okrans or Jeranese warriors, hence their willingness to help in the war.

The Zhusk had long been a problem for both kingdoms. As mountain tribesmen they normally presented very little of a threat to either nation. Occasionally, however, a leader would form up a company of bandits who would raid down into the Svoin basin, into Ooriz, or even up into parts of the Crozt peninsula. Expeditions sent to punish them might catch a few, or burn some villages, but the heavily forested plateau prevented the sort of pitched battles that might break Zhusk power forever. Fortunately the Zhusk's complicated clan system usually had them fighting each other, which reduced their outside threat, though it did hone their martial skills.

The obelisk, in fact, had been destroyed by the Zhusk who never accepted that a portion of their plateau had long ago been ceded to Jerana. While Alyx took Adrogans at his word that the Zhusk were allies for the moment, the potential for trouble could not be ignored. She feared less for her personal safety than she did for Zhusk support vanishing when needed. *Still, if Adrogans is inclined to trust them, I won't undermine his position unless necessary.*

The journey to Okrannel from Gyrvirgul had taken a full week and then some—twelve days—though the travel had not been particularly hard and they had made good time. Having a full company of Warhawks available for long-range scouting virtually eliminated the threat of an ambush. Midway through Jerana several of the Gyrkyme were sent to Lakaslin to report to Queen Carus. Adrogans did impress Alyx by using multiple couriers for the same message, requiring them to get a receipt with their delivery that allowed him, on their return, to know exactly who had been given the message and when.

The fact that he used winged messengers instead of *arcanslata* did surprise her. She asked him about his choice and expected some frippery in reply, but he grew serious for a moment. "Physical messages I can seal and send myself, limiting those who can read them. With an *arcanslata*, at the very least, the mage who sends the message knows what I've written. *Arcanslata* are useful when speed of communication is vital, but secrecy is another matter entirely."

The messages to the queen did include some sensitive information. On the road north the expedition did meet the Gurolans Stoneheart Battalion. The heavy infantry marched along at a solid pace, and were quite willing to march further during a day than the expedition required. While rather taciturn and keeping to themselves in camp, at night they gathered together and filled the evening with rousing ballads of valiant deeds from their history.

The expedition arrived at Adrogans' base in midafternoon on the last day of their journey and Caro immediately ceded command back to Adrogans. The army spread out through a valley, the center of which had been cleared for years. At the camp's heart lay a collection of daub-and-wattle huts with thatched roofs that were clearly of Zhusk manufacture. Spreading out around them, grouped by nationality, were the troops that had shipped up from Yslin. Helurca, Alcida, Jerana, Naliserro, Valicia, and Loquellyn were all well represented and the cavalry companies soon joined their countrymen in setting up their own camps. The Vilwanese, Gyrkyme, Savarese Knights, and the mercenaries all staked out their own territory a bit further away from the village center. The Gyrkyme picked a small hill toward the northeast that provided them height from which to fly, and had the added advantage of being as far away from the elves as possible.

Alyx turned her horse over to one of her Wolves, then marched along with General Caro to the longhouse where

Adrogans dwelt. The building was easily twice as deep as it was wide, and the third of it nearest the door was devoted to sleeping mats and baggage. Neither the accommodations nor their arrangement supported the image of Adrogans as fop. That illusion would have been impossible to maintain given the way the rest of the longhouse had been laid out, but the lack of pretense surprised Alyx.

The vast majority of the building had been given over to maps hung from walls, and a huge table on which Okrannel had been modeled. Little wooden blocks had been painted up with the appropriate regimental colors and placed on the landscape, representing the coalition forces gathered to oppose Chytrine. Oddly enough, Alyx noted, given the map's scale, the placement of the headquarters showed them to be twenty miles north of their true position. *Does he suspect a spy here who might give us away to Chytrine?*

Aside from Caro, Adrogans, and herself, and a half-dozen Jeranese troopers applying calipers to maps and carrying measurements to the model or vice versa, the longhouse held only two other individuals. The male, scrawny and small, with skin darkened by dirt and sun, smiled gap-toothed at them. What little hair he did have was worn long enough to cover his shoulders. Beads and bones—strung round his neck, piercing his ears, or affixed to his leathery flesh with small metal rings—appeared to be Zhusk talismans of power. A woven loincloth secured by a braided leather belt served as his only clothing.

The woman could not have been more a contrast, for she shared Alyx's light coloration, though her eyes were a deep cerulean. Her clothing, which consisted of pale leather trousers, moccasins, and tunic, had curious adornment. The seams had been overstitched with running strips of leather knotwork. Alyx knew enough of her homeland to know this woman was from the Guranin highlands to the west, and had she been able to read the knots correctly, she could have deciphered which clan and town claimed her.

Adrogans smiled. "General Turpus Caro you already

know. Phfas of the Zhusk and Beal mot Tsuvo, I present to you Princess Alexia of Okrannel."

The Zhusk broadened his grin and cackled a bit, but said nothing intelligible.

The Guranin warrior dropped to one knee and bowed her head, letting her blonde hair ripple down to veil her face. "It is an honor of unknowable proportion to be presented to you, Highness."

Alyx nodded slowly. "The honor is mine, and the glory is to Clan Tsuvo. The ability of the highland clans to hold off the Aurolani is legend among the exiles, but for you to have arrived here, crossing through their lands, requires courage that only runs in highland veins."

Phfas snorted. "Ask who guided them here, Svarskya."

The princess cocked her head as the Zhusk made the capital's name into a curse. "Forgive me, Phfas, but the identity of their guides I had long since puzzled out. Not only would they not have found their way here, but they could not have remained without the forbearance of the Zhusk. Just as they would not be here, neither would I, since it was in these forests as a babe I slept in the arms of Preyknosery Ironwing. Without your blessing, neither he nor I would ever have left Okrannel."

The little man cackled. "You were here, so you had already left Okrannel."

"A point lost on the enemy we both face."

Phfas tugged on a bone carving of a raven set into the extended lobe of his right ear. "Hearing wisdom from Svarskya is an omen of hope."

Adrogans stepped to the large model of the countryside. "In the hopes we have more such omens, please, if you would join me."

Beal rose and slipped past Adrogans. Alyx slid around the other side of the table to stand beside her, leaving Adrogans and Caro at the southern border. Phfas hovered near the corner with his beloved plateau, crouching so that little of his face below his eyes was visible.

The Jeranese general narrowed his eyes. "This represents the current strategic situation as nearly as we can make out. Our forces here number approximately seventeen hundred cavalry and three thousand infantry. Our object is to descend from the plateau here and lay siege to Svoin. The city, back when the Aurolani forces conquered it, was home to nearly twenty thousand men, women, and children, with a small Vorquelf population. We believe, at the most, that the city now houses a quarter that number. It serves as the headquarters for one of Chytrine's regiments and is supplemented by a Vorquelf legion."

Caro shook his head. "Vorquelves working for Chytrine? I can't believe that."

Phfas' head bobbed as if floating in a choppy ocean. "The witch has them hunt us, but they fail."

Adrogans nodded. "It would appear there are some Vorquelf hostages being held by the Aurolani. I don't know that we can liberate them prior to the siege, but any plan to do so would be one I would be willing to entertain."

Alyx frowned. "Slipping a force into an enemy-held city, to find people who might or might not exist, and get them out while an army is laying siege to the city would be suicide."

"Does that mean you won't take the assignment, Princess?"

Alyx's head came up. "What?"

The Jeranese general's eyes half lidded. "Just a question, inspired by your raid on the building in Yslin. It strikes me as a puzzle you and your compatriots might be able to solve."

"Perhaps we could, but there are larger issues I'd prefer to address." Alyx pointed to a set of twelve wooden blocks set halfway between Svarskya and Svoin, in the heart of the Bhayall lowlands. "This Aurolani regiment would appear, if I read the markings right, to be mixed heavy and light infantry, heavy and light cavalry. What is its makeup?"

"Light Aurolani infantry is gibberers led by vylaens. Heavy is gibberers with a fair number of hoargoun backing them. No sighting of draconetteers among them, but the heavy infantry do include some men." Adrogans frowned. "The giants are ponderous and slow, but tough to kill."

"So legend has it, General." Alyx smothered a growl. "My father died at one's hands."

Beal rested a hand on Alyx's shoulder. "It was a *sullanciri*, Highness. Nothing less could have slain your father."

"I appreciate that thought, mot Tsuvo, but to somehow let ourselves believe hoargoun are not deadly in and of themselves is foolish." Alyx looked over across the table at Adrogans. "The cavalry is temeryces?"

"Light is frostclaws, yes. Heavy is made up of grand temeryces carrying armored men and gibberers. Again, no draconettes."

"And the *sullanciri*?"

Adrogans pointed to Svarskya on the north coast nearest Alyx. "Malarkex remains there with two regiments, one of foot, the other of cavalry. The red flag there in the city indicates our information about her placement is too old to be reliable. The yellow flag on the road regiment means it's three days old, whereas the green in Svoin tells us it's current."

"Communicated to you by Vorquelves who venture out and 'die' in expeditions against the Zhusk?"

Adrogans smiled as Phfas cackled. "You are very perceptive, Princess."

"You're too kind." Alyx sighed. "The problems with liberating Svoin are overwhelming. The road regiment is in a position to lift the siege on the city. The land around Svoin, if your map is at all accurate, is marshy, and this summer was far from hot enough to dry it out. As a result cavalry will have a hard time operating there. Bringing in siege equipment and moving it will also be tough."

The Jeranese general shook his head. "It was not a wet

winter, nor has the summer brought a lot of rain. While the watertable there is high, the lake is down. The earth will be solid enough for our purposes."

"That is good then, but for all sides." Alyx chewed her lower lip for a moment. "If the city holds out for any time at all, bringing a relief force down from Svarskya means we'll be caught in the basin. Fighting our way free will be bloody."

"I agree, but when we have the city, repulsing the relief forces will be easy."

"It's rather optimistic to suppose you can take Svoin with what we have and repair it fast enough to hold Malarkex off; and that's provided that she takes her time coming down from Svarskya."

Adrogans waved away her protest. "The city won't hold out long enough to matter. Our scouts report no hope of that. Guranin raiding from the highlands down into the Svarskya region will pull some Aurolani forces west, putting at least two rivers between them and our position. There are many details, of course, to be dealt with, but I have no doubt we will accomplish our objectives."

Alyx glanced up at General Caro. "What do you think?"

Caro stroked a hand over his chin. "Risky, but feasible. Realistically, Svoin is the only objective we could hope to take and hold before winter sets in, and I don't want to be on this plateau when snow begins to fly. Plans will have to be modified depending upon locations of enemy troops, their strength and the like, but if the intelligence proves good, I can see proceeding."

She nodded her head slowly. "I see. Well, I look forward to working out the details of the campaign."

Adrogans shook his head. "You needn't concern yourself with them."

"What?"

"That's for General Caro, his counterparts among the other forces, and me to do. I need you to work on saving the hostages. In the next building over we have a layout of the city. We have their locations determined as best we can."

Her violet eyes blazed. "You're not serious."

"Oh, but I am." His chin came up as he gave her a frank stare. "Saving them will be critical as far as the campaign is concerned. Saving them will provide people with hope and a reason to resist if their positions are overrun. It will also earn us the gratitude of Vorquelves, and I would not mind having their volunteers join us. Lastly, Phfas says it must be done."

The Zhusk shaman nodded once.

Alyx blinked. "I think your last reason is the paramount one, and I need more explanation than that."

"In fact, Princess, you do not." Adrogans gave her an infuriating little smile. "You have your task. If you fail, so will we. There is no one else to whom I could entrust the planning and execution of this mission."

Alyx frowned. "Why would you hate me so?"

The Jeranese general frowned. "Hate you? It's your ability I admire, Princess. I'm giving this task to you because it is the one problem here I cannot solve. If you can, the liberation of Okrannel may actually be possible."

CHAPTER 50

Will slung his blanket around him like a cloak in an effort to cut the chill creeping through the camp with dusk. Qwc, who had launched himself into the air as Will began the move, flutter-buzzed back to resume his perch on the thief's left shoulder. Will smiled despite the light sting of a wing hitting an ear.

"Easy, Qwc, I have use for that ear."

"Hearing praises, hearing." The Spritha reached out and tugged on his ear. "Hit they get, hit, because big they grow with praises."

"That's not true."

"Lie, foul lie."

Though the Spritha's voice remained light, and Will caught not even a hint of a whiff of malice in the words, they did sting. Most of the soldiers in the camp had seen him in passing in Yslin, and clearly stories about who he was and what he would do had raced through the camp faster than the red pox. The cavalry troops supplemented stories with what they had seen and heard on the road—

which shouldn't have been much since he didn't do anything but ride, sleep, and talk. Despite that, soldiers gave him smiles and nods when, three months earlier, they'd have cuffed and kicked him back to the Dim.

Part of him could understand what they saw in him. The fact that a prophecy said he'd finish Chytrine made them happier and more confident. Having him on their side meant they had an edge in battle. Chytrine's defeat was preordained and now the only tough work would be convincing her of that fact.

Will did notice one subtlety in the good wishes and brags folks made within his earshot. Jeranese forces regularly linked him and Adrogans as an unbeatable pair. The Okrans forces included Alexia when praising him, and most vocal were the Guranin highlanders.

The Zhusk tribesmen tended to stay away from Will, which surprised him. Phfas, the headman, had looked him over very thoroughly, running hands through his hair, checking his teeth, tugging on his arms, examining his hands and feet. The old man spent a long time staring him in the eyes, and whenever Will would glance away, Phfas hemmed and hawed, or hawked and spat, muttering something Will couldn't understand at all.

Will found the Zhusk tribesman as intriguing as he did intimidating. Whereas Resolute had decorated himself with tattoos of magickal import, Phfas had all sorts of bone carvings, stone figures, and metal bits clipped into his skin. Will couldn't be certain, but he thought some of the talismans were replaced from time to time, or moved, but no scheme or reason for doing so presented itself to him.

What intimidated Will, and made Phfas something more than an old man he'd have dismissed as insane in Yslin, was the strength in the man's hands. Steely fingers poked and prodded Will. When the old man pulled on his arms, or gave him a shove, Will lost his balance. And the one time he tried to shove back he felt as if he could have more easily moved Gyrvirgul.

Something just isn't right about Phfas. Whatever it was, Will couldn't figure it out, but he was happy that the Zhusk and his people kept away from him. Will would have asked Resolute what was going on, but the Vorquelf had been in a singularly poor humor since the first night, when Alexia had called them together to talk about the coming campaign and the battle for Svoin.

Will returned his attention to Qwc. "You really think I listen too much to what everyone is saying about me?"

"More, listen more to Alexia, that is what I think." Qwc pointed with two arms toward the longhouse where Alexia had been planning her part in the campaign. "Help, Will, help them."

He sighed and tipped his head back, closing his eyes. "Resolute keeps chewing on me because Vorks are working for Chytrine. I know why that makes him angry, but what did I do?"

"More, you can do more."

Will growled, then rolled his shoulders, opened his eyes, and marched into the village. "You have an annoying way of being right, Qwc."

The Spritha laughed, flew up in a loop, then turned, flying backward, waving Will on. "Will, brave Will, smart, Will, smart."

Qwc flew on and made a grand show of struggling to push the curtain in the doorway aside for him.

The thief ducked his head and, entering, quickly scanned the room. Alexia, Perrine, Crow, Beal mot Tsuvo, and Orla crowded around the table. Orla hid a yawn behind a hand, and the others had fatigue shadows beneath their eyes. Back in the far corner Kerrigan had collapsed and snored lightly. Opposite him Resolute rasped a whetstone along the edge of a longknife. Of Lombo and Dranae he saw no sign, and he even glanced up into the rafters to see if the Panqui had hidden himself in the shadows up there.

Crow acknowledged his entrance with a quick nod. "Welcome back."

"Thanks." Will approached the long table in the middle of the building quietly, less worried about breaking Alexia's concentration than giving Resolute something to complain about. The situation on the table hadn't changed that he could see since early that morning. A half-dozen buildings bore flags that indicated that hostages had been held there, but the situation flags were all yellow, indicating the information was fast slipping into uselessness.

Alexia shook her head. "I agree, sister, that if the hostages could paint some sign on lintels, or hang rags out of windows, that you and the Warhawks could fly over and scout their positions. The difficulty comes in two areas: a quick move of the hostages would invalidate your information, and more hideous, if someone betrays the signals, we'd be drawn into traps."

Orla frowned. "Spells could locate the hostages, provided things close to them could be smuggled out of the city and used to make a link to them. The difficulty there is that the use of magick might alert the Aurolani forces to our mission, or could be altered to lead us into a trap."

Alyx slowly shook her head. "The whole thing could be a trap. I can't fault Adrogans' assessment of the benefits from rescuing the hostages, but the cost will be excessive. Phfas is pushing to have us do this, and I don't like that at all."

Beal nodded. "Princess, I understand your reservations about Phfas. You know that we highlanders have no love of the Zhusk, but since I have been here, there are things I have learned. Nothing quantifiable, but Phfas has an insight. I think he sees the land differently than we do and that, perhaps, the rescue of the Vorquelves will influence the *weirun*. The simple fact is, however, that as long as we are positioned to rescue the Vorquelves, we will have Zhusk support. Without it, the campaign will not succeed."

The princess sighed. "I know, which is why we're doing this. We need to consolidate the hostages. If we can't use magick without detection, then infiltration is our only other option. Is that feasible?"

The Guranin woman reached out and pointed at each suspected haven as she counted them.

Will scratched at the back of his neck. "That detecting magick thing, how does it work?"

Before Orla could answer, Resolute growled, "Stop wasting their time, boy. You don't know anything about a military mission like this. When we get in and need locks opened, then you will be useful."

Crow looked over at him. "What are you thinking, Will?"

Will shrugged abruptly, unseating the Spritha.

Qwc grabbed at Will's tunic with all four hands, dangling down over his left breast. "Sorry, very sorry." Climbing up hand over hand over hand, the Spritha righted himself.

The thief shrugged again, more subdued this time. "Well, I was thinking that Resolute is right. I don't know about military stuff. I'm just a thief, so I'm looking at it the way a thief would. Now, if I was out to steal a hundred things that had been split up for safekeeping, that would be tough. So I was thinking that maybe you could convince the Aurolani to bring them all together. Or at least they could move them to places where you knew they would be."

The Vilwanese warmage arched an eyebrow. "Detecting magick works into this how?"

"Okay, you've been thinking about trying to go in through the sewers, right? Come up as close to these buildings as possible, inside them if you can, right?"

Alexia slowly nodded. "We have to get in unseen and that's the easiest way."

Will smiled. "Okay, couple parts to this plan. The first is to make them think their places for holding the hostages aren't any good. If I were going to steal stuff, I might break in and leave indications I was there, as if I almost got caught. If we got folks into the sewers and used some sort of magick so the Aurolani *did* detect it, we could make them think we were scouting out where the hostages were."

Resolute rose from his chair and crossed to the three-dimensional map of Svoin. "They would know where we were going to strike, so they would move the hostages."

"Right, and Peri or one of the Warhawks could be flying high and see them move. We find out where they are that way. Since there are only a few buildings that are solid enough to use to hold the prisoners, it narrows down their choices."

The Vorquelf's silver eyes tightened. "That's relying too much on the stupidity of the enemy, boy."

Beal nodded in agreement. "Besides which, if we show the Aurolani that we can come in by the sewers, they will have troops ready to ambush us when we do come through."

Will smiled. "And how will they know we're coming?"

Resolute snorted. "What's the answer you're looking for, boy?"

The thief sighed. "What I'm thinking is that they will have their vylaens looking to detect magick in the sewers. They will send squads of gibberers down there looking to get us."

Crow frowned. "I thought we wanted to avoid that, Will."

"Yes, so I was thinking if there was a way to make something like sewer rats magickal, they would end up detecting the rats as they moved around."

The Vorquelf shook his head. "No such spells."

"Couldn't we tattoo them like you?"

"No, boy." Resolute shook his head. "The tattoos are difficult to get and require an intelligence to make work. Magister, am I wrong?"

Orla shook her head. "There's no spell that will make the rats give off traces of magick."

"Forgive me, Magister, but that's not exactly right. There isn't one *now*, but I could make one up." Kerrigan yawned, then rubbed sleep from his eyes as he struggled into a sitting position. "It could be done, and fairly easily."

Alexia whirled. "Really? How?"

The fat Adept rolled to his feet. "Well, it would be a variation of the *arcanslata* spell, triggered through the Law of Contagion. We would take a large rock and shatter it. Each piece would be linked to every other piece. We enchant them to strengthen that bond, then tie a small piece to each of the rats. A larger piece remains behind and a mage will pulse a spell into that larger piece, which would then be passed to the smaller pieces. If he made the big rock glow in the dark, the smaller rocks would also glow. Any vylaens looking to detect magick would pick up on that spell. And the beauty of this system is that different mages could use different spells—as could the same mage, creating different but similar traces, confusing the vylaens into thinking it is a huge invasion force."

Will nodded and pointed to Kerrigan. "Exactly."

Resolute raised an eyebrow. "You mean to say you understood what he said?"

"Um, well, not exactly, but it sounded like it would work."

"It will work." Kerrigan nodded once, setting his jowls to quivering.

"It actually could work." Orla leaned heavily on her staff. "The trick will be getting ourselves into the city. If we don't use the sewers to get in, we will be highly visible."

Alexia turned back to the map and tapped a finger against her chin. "Perhaps not. People are still catching fish and otherwise making use of the lake. Perhaps we should have our people join the city residents as they return to Svoin."

"That would mean that our people would be unarmed."

Crow rubbed a hand over his face. "I may be so sleepy that I don't see what you do, but unarmed people aren't going to be able to rescue the hostages."

"You're right, Crow, but our people will only go *in* unarmed. I would like to employ the Warhawks in nocturnal raids on the city. They'd shoot arrows, use spears, and otherwise make life miserable for the garrison forces on the walls. In the aftermath of those raids they should be able to drop bundles of weapons and light armor which our Vorquelf confederates can hide. If that is not feasible, we use Will's plan to overwhelm the vylaens by picking a route in that will have no rats. Unless the vylaens plot magick against an existing map of the sewers and notice an area where there is no activity *and* send forces there, we ought to be in quickly."

Orla nodded. "We can pick a route determined by where they place the hostages. We head back out through the sewers, or perhaps fight our way to the docks and take a ship out."

Peri flicked a taloned finger against one of the larger ship models in the port. "Firecocks would slow pursuit."

"Good thinking, sister." Alexia looked at the people assembled around the table. "Flaws?"

"There are some, certainly, Highness." Crow placed his left hand on Alexia's right shoulder. "I suspect none of us is sufficiently rested to spot anything more than the obvious ones at the moment."

The Vorquelf leaned forward, resting his elbows on the edge of the table. "The entry into the city is very risky, but getting the hostages out will be more so. Securing a building and holding off the Aurolani forces isn't going to work because they will overwhelm us at some point. A fighting retreat through the sewers or streets will kill the hostages. We need to be able to evacuate them quickly. If we had a thousand Warhawks we could just fly them all to safety, but we're stuck in that regard."

"Yours is an excellent point, Resolute, as was Crow's."

Alexia hooked blonde hair behind her right ear. "I suggest we all get something to eat, then get some sleep and come back at this tomorrow morning. I'm sure there is a solution to Resolute's problem, as well as any others we may spot."

She smiled and nodded her head toward Will. "And, thank you, Will, for your insight. You're right, this wasn't a military problem so much as it was a theft. We'll steal the hostages away from Svoin, somehow we will, but this is a wonderful start."

Will beamed at her praise, and didn't stop all evening, despite Resolute's scowls and Qwc's teasing. He even smiled as he drifted off to sleep, and that smile broadened as he dreamed. Not because he dreamed of Alexia, but because he dreamed up a solution to Resolute's problem. He awoke with enough of the dream still in his head to reconstruct the whole of it. And Will the Nimble, King of the Dimandowns, knew it would work.

CHAPTER 51

Alexia had found Will's plan for dealing with the hostage evacuation intriguing. She took pleasure in Adrogans' look of surprise when the thief explained it, but he agreed to it a bit too quickly for Alyx to feel truly comfortable. The plan, while imaginative, required logistical and matériel support that she didn't think the expedition had. Dealing with those details, however, passed from her hands to Beal mot Tsuvo. Adrogans had another job for her.

The Jeranese general announced his immediate intention to march to Svoin. "Your Wolves will accompany the Zhusk in a reconnaissance-in-force. I want to know what is out there before us. You're to watch and not engage large forces. But take on smaller bands, learn what you can of Svoin and Aurolani forces; this will be important."

Adrogans allowed her to supplement her Wolves with Resolute, Crow, Dranae, Peri, and two other Warhawks. He said he wanted the Norrington kept close to work with Beal on the hostage rescue, but both of them knew risking Will on a scouting mission was stupid. His presence with the main body would raise morale, while his loss in her company would irreparably damage it.

The reconnaissance force consisted of just shy of three hundred soldiers. The Zhusk tribesmen rode stout little mountain ponies that navigated tracks clinging to the sides of hills and mountains with an amazing amount of heart. The trails they rode wound down deep into valleys where thick vegetation hid the sun, and past long waterfalls that spawned rainbows from their mist. The Zhusk, while not seeming to pay that much attention to their surroundings, appeared to be preternaturally aware of how far Aurolani forces had come into their territory, and often pointed out campsites or other signs of invasion.

The distance between the camp and Svoin, as a Gyrkyme might fly, should have only taken four days to traverse on horseback. The army's main body would move far more slowly, taking close to a week to make the journey on foot. Alyx shuddered to think how the supply wagons would make the arduous trip, and didn't mind having Adrogans saddled with that problem. *Given that he's requested half again as much support as he requires, he can lose a lot of it and still have a viable force when we reach Svoin.*

The reconnaissance force kept its rate of advance slow and cautious. It meant they'd not outdistance the main army, precluding an Aurolani force slipping undetected between them and setting up an ambush. For the most part Alyx's force traveled to particular objectives as quickly as was prudent, then sent scouts out laterally and a bit forward on the wings to get some inkling of what the next day would bring. Reports were prepared with care and sent by Gyrkyme back to Adrogans who, in turn, acknowledged them and requested information about certain targets.

Three days out, entering the foothills that separated the plateau edge from the downslope into the Svoin basin, scouts reported activity at an iron mine. Human slaves overseen by gibberers, vylaens, and at least one Vorquelf were pulling ore from the mine and loading it into carts drawn by mules for the long trek back to Svoin. The city's smiths would transform the raw ore into iron and steel.

In consultation with Agitare, Crow, and Resolute, Alyx decided to take the mine and free the prisoners. Given that scouts only reported a dozen Aurolani troops present at the site, the Wolves would easily take the prize. Alyx elected to wait until darkness provided cover for both Zhusk and Alcidese soldiery. That also gave them a chance to stop the wagon train leaving the mine.

The wagon train consisted of a half-dozen creaky old wagons with six mules pulling each, and two human slaves per wagon. A Vorquelf with long flowing black hair, eyes of a deep blue, and decorated with a few tattoos rode at the head of the column, while two gibberers with pikes walked at the back, and one walked along at each side of the middle of the procession.

Peri kept watch over the wagon train while a dozen Zhusks accompanied Resolute, Crow, Alyx, and Phfas on a fast advance along game trails that paralleled the road. The Zhusks and Crow carried bows, Resolute his longknives, and Alyx her sword. Phfas carried no weapons. Alyx had been afraid he would slow the ambushing squad, but he showed great agility and stamina moving through the forests. They all managed to work up a sweat as they hurried on foot to a small hill where the wagon train would have to slow its already torpid pace to get the heavy wagons up to the crest.

They reached the ambush site well ahead of the wagons. Alyx split the Zhusks in half, sending six with Crow to the far side of the trail. Both sets of archers were positioned so their shots would not strike each other, meaning they were ordered to shoot at an angle down the trail instead of straight across. Alyx, Resolute, and Phfas remained toward the uphill side of things, since Resolute had his own idea for dealing with the renegade Vorquelf.

With everyone in position, they waited. To her left, Resolute remained all but motionless. Since his silver eyes had no pupils, Alyx couldn't even guess what he was looking at. In some ways she imagined he was not really studying the scene before him, but pulling some other vision from his memory. He seemed too calm to be preparing for combat. She shivered. He had to be one of the most frightening individuals alive.

Phfas sat cross-legged on the ground and brushed his fingers over plant leaves and flower blossoms with a childlike abandon. He lifted up mats of wet, brown leaves, then watched the chaotic scurry of ants carrying away egg-cases. His motions, and the light humming he engaged in, would not betray the ambush, and gave him a youthful innocence she had not suspected he could possess. There were moments, though, when the humming faded, the smile froze, and the eyes grew distant, that made her wonder if he were not sharing Resolute's vision, or seeing something entirely different. Something dark and nasty, not for a child at all.

Alyx herself studied the trail, noticing how sunlight dappled leaves and the ground, shifting and swaying as light breezes teased the trees. The pragmatic part of her mind took comfort in the fact that the wind was coming up from the plains, so her troops would not be betrayed by scent. The more romantic part of her relished the wind's soft kiss on her cheek, and the way it cooled her neck and face. Then pragmatism would kick in again, causing her to loosen her sword in its scabbard and inventory her belt and boot daggers with a touch.

She wondered, for a moment, how Crow was occupying his time. He certainly had an arrow nocked. She found it easy to imagine him picking at the black lacquer coating on his bow, chipping off pieces of it to reveal the silverwood beneath. Only elves made silverwood bows, and she'd never seen one styled like the horse-bow Crow carried. Such a weapon in a man's possession meant the elves felt him worthy of such an honor—and the fact that he'd hidden his bow's nature while in Yslin was cause for curiosity.

Phfas brought his head up sharply, which broke her out

of her reverie. Resolute just stretched and rose to a knee. Down toward the base of the hill the wagons stopped and the slaves on the second one started to unhitch their mules so a double team could be used to haul the first wagon to the top of the hill. The gibberers milled around in a knot toward the back of the procession, while the Vorquelf rode his black stallion halfway up the hill, then turned in the saddle to watch those behind him. In addition to a sword on his hip, the Vorquelf had a silverwood longbow resting athwart the horse's shoulders, and a sheaf of arrows in a saddle quiver before his right knee.

Resolute slid silently from cover and barked harsh words in Elvish.

The mounted Vorquelf's horse came around as the silverwood bow came up. The Vorquelf nocked, drew, and released in an eyeblink. Since the plan had been for them to take him alive if at all possible, none of the archers had been instructed to shoot him. *And even if one had, no one could have shot before he did.*

Alyx looked toward Resolute, certain she'd see an arrow quivering in his chest, but he stood there, startled and wide-eyed, still unharmed. Nothing obstructed her view of him, or the arrow slowly revolving in the air, barely a yard from his breastbone. The leaves surrounding the hole in the foliage through which she looked did quiver, matching the palsied tremor of Phfas' extended left hand.

Elsewhere bowstrings sang and gibberers howled. Crow whistled loudly, letting everyone know the gibberers were down and dead. All that passed into the background, however, as Resolute raised his right hand and plucked the arrow from the air. He studied it for a moment, then cast it back over his shoulder.

The other Vorquelf snapped a comment in Elvish, then returned the bow to the saddle quiver. Bringing his right foot up over the horse's neck, the Vorquelf slid fluidly from the saddle and drew a straight longsword. Clad in sleeveless leathers as was Resolute, the Vorquelf waved him forward.

Resolute drew both longknives and advanced. The window in the foliage collapsed, forcing Alyx to shift around to watch the road. Phfas joined her, a bit winded, his skin glowing with sweat. His mouth opened in a silent cackle that sent a shiver through her.

Resolute stood taller than his foe, and it wasn't just the spiky height of his white hair that gave him that advantage. In every way he was bigger than his enemy, but the smaller Vorquelf didn't seem concerned. He dropped into a fighting stance, still waving Resolute toward him, then dashed forward in a quick attack.

Resolute sidestepped the lunge, twisting to let it pass from left to right along his body. He flipped the longknife in his right hand around so the blade lay flat against his forearm, then raised that forearm to parry the backhand slash his enemy launched. Continuing his forward momentum inside his foe's guard, Resolute brought his left elbow up. He smashed it into the Vorquelf's face.

The Vorquelf staggered for a half step. Resolute's right hand came around, the longknife coming back off his forearm. With one quick swipe, Resolute could have laid the Vorquelf's throat open, but instead he just punched the black-haired elf in the face, snapping his head around to the left.

The Vorquelf stumbled back two steps and Resolute ate up that distance with one strong stride. The silver-eyed Vorquelf kicked his enemy full in the stomach, dropping him to his knees. The other Vorquelf abandoned his sword and clutched his stomach, then retched his last meal into a thick puddle. Behind him his horse shied away.

Resolute grabbed a handful of black hair and yanked the Vorquelf's head back. Blood from his nostrils melted into the vomitus running down his chin. Resolute snarled barbed words at him, then released him. The defeated Vorquelf vomited again and hunched so far forward that the ends of his hair sank into the puddle on the road.

Alyx emerged from hiding, glancing at the arrow on the

ground, then up at Resolute. Pure fury contorted his face, matching the tone of his words. She didn't want to know what Resolute had said, nor did she need to know. The other elf held himself, his body wracked with sobs.

Resolute snorted. "He says his name is Banausic. I'm sure he picked it when he started working for Chytrine. At least a quarter of a century ago he had a sense of shame."

"Resolute!" Crow, coming up from where the Zhusk worked on freeing the wagon crews, stopped short of Banausic. The Vorquelf had dragged himself over to his sword and was bringing it to hand. For a heartbeat Alyx feared the elf would plunge it deep into his flesh, but he remained hunched over and brought the point nowhere near his heart or belly.

Instead he let the blade lay flat in his palms and raised it in Resolute's direction.

Snorting again, Resolute walked over and kicked the sword out of the other Vorquelf's hands. "Why would I want a sword that couldn't beat a longknife? Even the name Banausic is too good for you. You should be known as Wretched or Pathetic or Nothing."

The utter contempt in Resolute's voice brought his foe's head up. "Perhaps Irredeemable would suit."

"You better hope not, or you'll leave a lot more blood on the road here." Resolute slowly shook his head. "You want to be of use to me? How many Aurolani troops at the mine?"

"Sixteen. Four vylaens, eight gibberers, two men overseers, and two spies within the slave crew." The Vorquelf glanced back down the road. "The redheaded driver is also a spy."

"And my reason for believing you is?"

Banausic's head snapped up and his blue eyes blazed. "You defeated me. I offered you my sword."

"Chytrine defeated you. You offered her your sword."

The kneeling elf's nostrils flared. "I offer you my word of honor. My family . . ."

"Your family is dead. All our families are dead. If you had any honor I'd not have found you here."

"I did what I had to do, to stay alive." Banausic sighed and seemed to shrink. "I knew this day would come. There are things I've seen, things I know that you need to know."

Resolute's eyes narrowed. "So tell me."

"No, I can tell you much, but not all these things. I'll tell you what you need to know to take Svoin. The other things . . . If I tell them, she'll know, and will kill me."

"This is pathetic." Resolute shook his head solemnly. "I should kill you for that transparent plea for sympathy alone."

"Not if you want to redeem Vorquellyn." The Vorquelf swiped a hand across his mouth, smearing blood over his cheek. "I'll be Pathetic, if you want. Anything, it doesn't matter. Take Svoin. Kill Malarkex. Once she is dead, I will tell you all I know and you will be glad I did."

"And why is that, Pathetic?"

The Vorquelf spat blood onto the ground. "After the fall of Okrannel, they took me home, to Vorquellyn. I saw Chytrine create one of her *sullanciri* there. I know what else she wanted to do and why she failed. I don't know how to stop her, but I know how to undo much of what she's done."

He tapped a slender finger against his head. "It's all up here. Kill me now or let me die, and Vorquellyn will be lost forever."

CHAPTER 52

Keeping a journal, Kerrigan decided, would keep him sane—if it didn't drive him crazy first. The idea of chronicling his adventures had come to him after he caught a chance remark by Resolute in the wake of one of Will's rhymes. The Vorquelf had said, "If that's the best you can come up with for a bit of song, minstrels will let your history die."

The Adept refused to admit to himself that a strong part of his motivation was a shocked indignation at the idea that Will might be remembered in song while he would be forgotten. Almost instantly his mind flashed back to the grand history of Vilwan and how a chronicle of his adventures might be a vital chapter in the history of magicians. After all, he'd survived the culling of the innocent, he'd fashioned a new magick to save a Panqui, had lived through a brush with deviltry in Yslin, and had visited Gyrvirgul. That alone would have been enough to make a nice little travelogue, but the coming siege of Svoin and his role in saving the hostages, that would be a truly heroic tale.

Will worked on his little rhymes and songs, but Kerrigan eschewed that route for his chronicle. He didn't reject it because he had no facility with rhymes and couldn't have carried a tune in a bucket; minstrel's immortality was just too common and clearly meant for the illiterate. Civilized people were capable of writing, and a written record was far less mutable than one that had to be learned by rote and crafted to pander to the needs of the audience.

Will's song will be entertainment; *I will create* history.

The difficulty with creating history was that it required a bit more in the way of matériel than did a song. For all that General Adrogans had requisitioned ample food and supplies, writing materials seemed scarce and tightly controlled. The general, it seemed to Kerrigan, had a near-pathological fear that someone might use the sort of spells that created *arcanslata* to enchant his stock of paper. As he wrote out orders and exchanged information with the queen in Lakaslin, those messages could then be read over by the enemy. Because of Adrogans' paranoia, his paper stocks were kept under lock and key.

This lack of paper frustrated Kerrigan no end, which made it difficult for him to sleep. One night, as he wandered the camp, he happened upon a trio of Jeranese Crown Guards. The one in the middle had a piece of paper and clearly was trying to read what was written on it, but from the way he twisted the paper left and right, it was pretty clear he was not having an easy time of it.

The tallest of the warriors slapped the reader furiously on the shoulder. "You sure it says my Flora is having the baker's boy?"

The reader shrugged. "Them's the words, Fossius."

Kerrigan smiled sheepishly. "If you wish, I could read it for you."

The trio eyed him suspiciously, then Fossius gave the reader a shove in the back toward him. "Let him have the letter."

The Adept took it and began to read, though the script

was certainly not Vilwanese cursive, which made it a bit difficult to decipher. "Ah, here it is, Fossius, your Flora is wet-nursing the baker's son. The baker's wife had twins and it says here that she's a small woman."

Fossius smiled proudly. "That's right, little slip of a thing; and my Flora, she'd help out since our girl's about ready to be weaned. And you had me all worried there, Pirius."

Kerrigan finished reading the letter, which appeared to have been written by a neighbor and included local gossip as well as news for each of the three men. They desperately wanted to reply to it, and Kerrigan agreed to write their return letter, provided they get him blank paper. Word spread through the camp fairly quickly about what he was doing, and men began bringing him every scrap of paper or leather or even strips of cloth they could find to write on.

Even as the camp was packing up to head out for Svoin, Kerrigan's scribe business thrived. Will's mutterings about how silver could be had as payment instead of paper told Kerrigan how well he was doing. He felt pretty certain that Will wished Kerrigan was taking in coin so the thief could steal it. The Adept put all his paper scraps into a leather-bound, wood-slat folio a Helurcan officer offered in return for Kerrigan's writing down some of his Steel Legion's history, then gave the folio to Lombo for safekeeping.

Kerrigan didn't realize how well he'd truly been doing, however, until two of the Jeranese Horse Guards came for him. Each man grabbed an upper arm and quick-marched him to Adrogans' longhouse. They deposited him just inside the doorway, then retreated, leaving the young mage alone with Adrogans and Orla, both of whom stood in close conversation on the other side of the large map of Okrannel.

Orla nodded, then Adrogans turned and narrowed his eyes. His voice, full of import and gravity, filled the longhouse easily. "I don't believe, Adept Reese, you wish to be a problem for me, do you?"

"No, sir, no."

"But you have become one." Adrogans slowly shook his head. "You've produced a volume of correspondence that will severely weigh down any Gyrkyme courier."

"I didn't, I mean—"

The general held a hand up. "When I want you to talk, I will give you leave to do so, do you understand?"

Kerrigan opened his mouth, then snapped it shut and just nodded.

"You're right, Magister, he can learn." Adrogans narrowed his brown eyes. "The weight of correspondence is not the problem, Adept Reese; it is the volume of it. Orla has assured me you really have no understanding of how things work, so I will explain it to you simply. The missives you are producing have to be read by my staff before transmission to see if they reveal any information that would be useful to the enemy. The reports I send to Lakaslin, the orders I send out, are coded, so the enemy would find them useless if they were to stop a courier. The letters, though, might have little details, like someone reporting that he'd named a mountain 'Eagle's Nest' because of its profile. That would tell the enemy that our camp is within sight of such a place. Do you understand?"

"Yes, sir. I could edit out all those references in future letters."

"You could, yes, but you won't." The Jeranese general smiled slowly. "I will provide you a list of things to substitute for such observations. The truth of things won't matter to the people back home—just getting a note is what will matter. To the enemy—and if you do not believe there are spies in Lakaslin you are even more naive than I would choose to accept—the information will misdirect them and put them where I want them."

"But, that would be lying. To the people, I mean."

"It would, yes, but would they rather have a lie that keeps someone alive, or a truth that would kill him?" Adrogans slowly smiled. "I understand you have amassed a collection of paper scraps, often half of a letter where you used the back of a sheet for a reply. Is it as motley as the notes you've produced?"

"Yes. I was going to write a history on them."

"A history. Interesting." The man stroked a hand over his chin. "I will give you a bound journal for your history, Adept Reese—ink, quills, whatever you need—but I need something in return. You will take your stock of scraps and you will write letters on them, mythical letters, from soldiers."

Adrogans approached the map and pointed to an area near the mountains that split the central lowlands from the Crozt peninsula. "This force will number three thousand, complain about short rations, long marches, and my insane plan to draw the Svarskya garrison south to relieve Svoin, while they strike north to liberate Svarskya. You've already heard the concerns of soldiers in the letters you've written. Can you compose this mythical correspondence?"

Kerrigan frowned. "I can, but I don't understand why."

The general cast a glance at Orla. "He might be brilliant when it comes to magicks, but you've really taught him nothing else, have you?"

She shook her head. "It is my duty to expand his awareness of practical knowledge, but there is so much he must learn."

Adrogans waved Kerrigan closer, and pointed to Svoin on the map. "We're taking that city. We have roughly enough troops to do it, but we will need time to build siege towers and some of the other things we'll need to do the job. The forests will provide the raw matériel, so all we need is time. The problem is that Malarkex can easily bring a relieving force down from Svarskya that will force us to withdraw.

"This army we have here is large, and casualties are expected. The other day we lost a man to a snakebite and we used magick to preserve his body. I can place him in a courier's uniform and place him here, where Malarkex's scouts can find him. They will read the notes and assume there is indeed a force in the mountains, working their way toward Svarskya. I have Zhusk out there creating the signs of encampments. It won't fool them for long, but as long as they hesitate, I get some of the time I need."

Kerrigan smiled. "You're creating an illusion."

"I am, with your help. You can double the size of my army with a little ink and paper."

The Adept nodded. "I will do it."

"What you are doing will have to be our secret."

"Yes, sir, I understand that."

"Good, very good. Orla assured me you could be very powerful, but I suspect even she did not know your power might lie in other talents." Adrogans clapped him on the shoulders. "And, Adept Reese, this history you will write . . ."

"Yes, General?"

"Don't leave anything out. I suspect your observations here will be the closest of any to the truth."

Somehow Kerrigan managed to juggle all the things he had to do, and no one was more surprised about it than he was. He'd gone from being an Adept to being a historian, a scribe, and a *counter*-spy, which he thought was much better than being a plain old spy. He worked hard at getting the fake correspondence completed before the army started on the move, but also wrote a couple of notes while riding in a wagon since he assumed the jiggled handwriting would add verisimilitude to the note.

He didn't work on his history while moving. Kerrigan did feel it would be a bad thing if he wrote about the deceptive letters in his journal, so he only made veiled references to writing notes for soldiers. If he were ever allowed to tell the full story, he could expand those notes and make sure all the details were there for future generations.

His desire to chronicle everything as openly and

honestly as possible did force him to take more notice of the world than he might have otherwise. Though they were hideous to look at, for example, Kerrigan did study the crucified forms of the two human spies at the iron mine, taking down their names and other details. He tracked down the wagon drivers and heard from one of them a story of how a Vorquelf's arrow had stopped in mid-air before it killed Resolute. He assumed the story was probably wrong since the difficulty of casting such a spell was enormous—just the preparation time would be too great, much less figuring out how, magickally, to identify the arrow sufficiently to stop it.

He did decide that he should ask Resolute about it, but that decision retreated in urgency as he imagined the snarl and snapped answer the Vorquelf would likely give him.

Kerrigan found his observational skills sorely tested as the army wound its way down out of the forested hills toward Lake Vriyn and the city of Svoin. Three rivers fed down into the lake from the south, originating in the mountains on the Jeranese border. One broad and sluggish river, the Svoin, flowed north from the lake to eventually join the Svar River on its journey to the Crescent Sea.

The city itself had a crescent of high walls with higher towers to protect the landward approaches. The land actually rose toward the city, which had been built on a rocky plateau, with a meandering roadway rising to the main gate. From the distance Kerrigan could see some of the city's interior, but not too clearly. For curiosity's sake, and that of his history, he wished he was back in Yslin, with its balloons and cable-baskets that would give him a Gyrkyme's view of the city.

The area around the city was clearly land that had once been under extensive cultivation, as plots were level and stones had been used to set up boundary markers and some walls. Only a few fields had grain in them and as the army approached, human slaves from the city came out to harvest what they could. Orla explained this was to deny the invaders much of anything, and to emphasize that point the fields that couldn't be cleared were burned.

If that bothered Adrogans at all, he gave no sign. He detached a portion of his force to remain in the forests to chop down trees for the siege towers, catapults, mantlets, and rams. In the fields he deployed his infantry in a great arc to cut the city off from the land. The inability to blockade the port meant there would be no starving the city, but beginning a siege this late in the season meant that starving the city into submission was not an option anyway.

"Either we take it by force before the snow begins to fly, or we retreat," Orla explained. "As dry as the ground is now, it will be a complete morass come spring, and blanketed with snow throughout the winter."

Aside from the cavalry units out scouting or protecting the woodcutters, the rest of the horsemen were placed well back of the infantry lines. They could easily be brought into action against any force coming out from the city, and were in position to deal with any relief force coming down from Svarskya. The most obvious point for such a force to enter the basin was along the Svoin River, but Adrogans scattered scouts throughout the hills in case the *sullanciri* decided not to be obvious.

Kerrigan diligently and carefully recorded all the details about Adrogans' deployment. To his mind, the general had everything under control. As soon as the siege machinery moved up, Svoin would fall, and the history of the Okrans campaign's first victory would be his.

CHAPTER 53

Alexia held an arrow by its fletching in her right hand and tapped it against her left palm. The paradox that was Adrogans continued to haunt her. King Augustus had told her that she was present to take over for Adrogans if he proved to be a fool, and half the time she felt he clearly was. Then he would go and do something that would make her reconsider, at least for a minute or two.

The layout of the troops for the siege made her take heart, at least a little bit. The Jeranese general had arrayed his troops to screen Svoin from any landward force, but it did stretch them out. He placed a force astride the coast road to forestall any troops coming down along the Svoin River from the north. Alexia would have placed it further north, in the hills through which the road ran, but she did concede that its current placement would stop any advance and allow the cavalry a chance to flank the Aurolani attackers.

Adrogans had even mixed his troops intelligently. Heavy foot occupied the center of the siege line, with light making up the bulk of both wings. The Gurolans Stoneheart Battalion had been placed as the road force, and Alexia knew they'd hold long enough for cavalry to be deployed. The cavalry had been broken into four parts, with her Wolves and the Okrans Kingsmen given the northernmost position. They'd be the first to attack any relieving force. The other forces, with the Savarese Knights and Alcidese Horse Guards in the center, were arrayed to the south, with two groups positioned to guard the baggage and supply area to the south. The Jeranese Horse Guards acted as Adrogans' own bodyguard troops and were stationed to the south, near his headquarters.

Also to the south was the woodworks where the siege machines were being assembled. As they were completed, with trebuchets and ballistae the first things produced, they were deployed with the infantry units. Once they got their siege weaponry, they inched their lines forward. Three hundred yards seemed the effective range of the wall-mounted weapons in Svoin, and the infantry advance invited shots.

Adrogans even used the Warhawks as Alexia would have. As the Aurolani forces shot at the ground forces, Warhawks used firecocks to set their siege machines ablaze. An indiscriminate use of firecocks would have set Svoin on fire, which none of the invaders wanted, so the Aurolani stopped shooting fairly quickly. They were clearly intent on saving their shots for the final assault, when they could do the most damage.

He implemented the hostage-rescue plan, and the first infiltration of the city had been successful. Mages reported increased magickal activity in Svoin in response to magick being used in the sewers. Kerrigan and other mages worked on enchanting stones and fragments. Even the orders to gather rats from the city and surrounding area didn't seem too odd when it was accompanied with the rumor that the Zhusk claimed rats would make a fine stew that thickened the skin.

The Zhusk, however, provided her with one of several questions that Adrogans evidenced no intent of answering. The Zhusk *combatants*—she wasn't sure the word "warrior" fit well—wandered everywhere, had no single place they seemed to gather, and answered or ignored questions at their own whim. An overwhelming number of them appeared to be older, and aside from a knife and a knotted club, none of them carried weapons.

Alexia was well aware of the stories of Zhusk tribesmen and how damnably galling their defiance of Svarskya had been during her grandfather's day. Zhusk fighters had been the stuff to frighten Okrans children, even in exile. She recalled Misha hoping, on their dream raid, that they'd not encounter a Zhusk. "Better a thousand gibberers than one Zhusk," he'd breathed in a hushed whisper.

She'd have dismissed them as useless, save that their arrows had found their marks during the liberation of the mines. More troubling, however, was Phfas' ability to freeze an arrow in flight. That spoke to power she did not understand, and this troubled her because she had a hunch that Adrogans was relying on it.

Alyx had asked Orla to explain what she had seen, but the Vilwanese warmage had no answer for her. "A spell could toughen armor to stop the arrow from penetrating, but what you describe . . . I can't see how it would work." Resolute had been even more taciturn than usual on the subject, and Crow shrugged when asked about it.

Phfas merely cackled and scampered away when she approached him for clarification.

Another of Adrogans' behaviors that perplexed her was ordering the troops to dig into the earth and set up breastworks. This wasn't out of the ordinary, save that the water table in the area ran so high that a foot or so down, water began to weep into the holes. Adrogans' orders required the soldiers to dig here and there, in some crazy-quilt pattern that, according to Peri after a flyover, made no sense at all. Rays extended out from Svoin in all directions, taking a field that had been solid enough for cavalry action and turning it into a quagmire.

Even that would not have been much of a problem, since much of the damage was done well behind the lines, but the arrival of scouts from the northern hills changed all that. They reported seeing two Aurolani forces. One, which they estimated to be two battalions of infantry, was coming down the coast road. The other, likewise having two infantry battalions and one of mixed cavalry, was coming straight south, through the mountains, so it would be coming in northeast to the siege line.

Leading that force was Malarkex.

The Aurolani camped in the forested hills a mile to the north, placing scouts on the ridgeline. A company of heralds came south, to the edge of the fields, and planted legion standards. The nine-skull banner represented a legion that had been at the siege of Svarskya. Alexia recognized no others by description, and when the Okrans Kingsmen heard of the nine-skull banner they wanted to ride out and take it.

She ordered them to stay put, then went off to find General Adrogans. On her way to his tent she felt a hand land on her right shoulder. She shrugged it off and turned to snap an order. She assumed the person who had touched her was her cousin Misha, hoping she'd rescind the order concerning the taking of the standard—no one else would presume to touch her. To her surprise she found Crow catching up to her, matching her long-legged strides.

He clearly caught the glare in her eyes and pulled his hand away. "Forgive me, Highness, but you'd not acknowledged my calling your name. I should have known better. Another time."

A hint of disappointment flashed through his brown eyes, sparking a twinge of regret in her. "No, Crow, please. I am preoccupied, and going to see the general. Perhaps it is best I don't go in there angry."

"Angry?"

She sighed. "Things here are neither ordered nor chaotic. You clearly have had military experience, and the camp is well run, yet Adrogans has had people doing things that make no sense." She waved an arm toward the north. "All the digging has made a battleground into a patchwork of ponds. We have a large force camped to the north, and yet we're not shifting troops to preclude an attack. I need to understand things, but I'm certain he won't explain them, which is why I am angry."

"That certainly makes sense. Adrogans does make it difficult to trust him."

"And yet we must." She shook her head. "You didn't find me to listen to that, however. What can I do for you?"

Crow gave her a devilish smile. "I'd heard you issued an order forbidding anyone from heading out to steal a standard."

Alyx's jaw dropped. "Don't ask, Crow. You, of all people, should have known better than to even think of such foolishness."

He shrugged. "I've spent a quarter century with Resolute. Compared to some of the things we've done, stealing one of those standards would seem the height of deliberate brilliance."

"That may be, but you know those standards are a trap."

"Of course." Crow smiled, his right cheek tightening around his scar. "Resolute talked to some of the warmages, and the standards are fair pulsing with Aurolani sorcery. To touch one would be death."

"So, what do you want of me?"

"I just wanted to make sure your order forbids the *stealing* of a standard, nothing more. Though we're not part of your command, we will abide by your orders and your wishes."

"You're not going to get yourself killed, are you?"

"No, Highness." Crow's voice softened. "That would leave you saddled with Will, Adrogans, and an angry Resolute. I'd not do that to you."

"Good." She hesitated for a moment, tempted to forbid Crow from doing whatever he had in mind. She knew she could, in fact, take him at his word and that he would obey her. By the same token, she trusted him to avoid being stupid. Unlike her cousin or so many others, Crow wouldn't follow through with a plan just because he said he was going to do something. If it proved impossible, if no one else's life was at stake, he would withdraw.

Alexia gave him a sincere smile. "I don't want to know what you are going to do. Before you do it, though, find Peri and she'll give you the challenge and response for our lines, just in case they would be of use."

Crow winked at her. "I thank you for your trust. We won't betray it."

"I know. Arel be with you."

"Save Arel's help for dealing with Adrogans."

"You'd scorn the gods?"

He smiled. "I have Resolute. He does that for me; besides, I've long since run through any luck I ever had the right to claim."

Crow turned and gave her one last wave, then wove his way into invisibility within the smoke and chaos of the camp. Alyx watched him go. She smiled because she realized she did not fear his failing to return. *He'll be back, with a tale to tell. And somehow, I imagine, that will be the only good I hear today.*

General Markus Adrogans turned from his study of the battlefield maps and nodded to Princess Alexia. "Good afternoon, Highness. I've heard of your order and I approve. Thank you. Will there be anything else?"

The fire that sparked in her violet eyes didn't surprise him. "There are many things, General Adrogans." She glanced at Phfas, the tent's other occupant. "I would speak to you alone."

"Say what you have to say, Highness."

"I would not embarrass you."

"I doubt you could." He folded his arms over his chest. "Please don't waste my time."

She lifted her chin slowly and deliberated, choking back anger. *That is good, Highness, that you manage to control yourself so well.* Adrogans raised an eyebrow, but got no further reaction from her.

"General Adrogans, you clearly are aware that we have five Aurolani battalions prepared to strike at our rear. You've shifted no forces, issued no orders to address this problem. My Wolves and the Kingsmen are positioned to bear the brunt of any attack. We do not protest this, but we are cavalry and without infantry support, we are not going to deter Malarkex."

Adrogans nodded. "That is a problem, yes, but one I will remedy."

"How?"

"A fair question. You have to trust me that I will deal with it. You are well advised to prepare your troops, for you will be fighting tomorrow. You will be the key to crushing that relieving force."

"How can I trust you, General?" The Okrans warrior stalked over to the battlefield map and stabbed a finger at it. "The two battalions coming down the lakeshore route will hit and hold against the Stonehearts here. If they send more forces out from Svoin they catch the Stonehearts from behind, and will push the Okrans Volunteers back into them, breaking the end of our line. Malarkex brings her forces forward to prevent us from flanking her forces and presses us hard on that same flank. If we successfully counterattack, she pulls back into the hills and has us at a severe disadvantage. At worst she gets more troops into Svoin."

Adrogans nodded slowly. "I congratulate you on your analysis, Highness. I suspect this is exactly as Malarkex has seen it. You forgot to mention that your line of attack on her is muddied, but her path to the Stonehearts is fairly clear."

Alexia's nostrils flared as she glanced sidelong at him. "Don't mock me, General. You ask me to trust you, to believe you have everything under control, but you hide things. That does not promote trust. You know I am a competent leader, a good leader."

"You betray yourself, Highness, for it is clear you do not think I am the same."

"I have evidence that speaks for and against it, General."

"I see." He narrowed his eyes. "Understand something, General. I know very well who you are and how you have been trained. I do marvel at your analysis. Your planning skills are splendid. You have done more with fewer troops in your engagements than I would have thought possible, and I have learned from reports of your battles. Yes, do not be surprised, I have read of you."

Again she lifted her chin. "And I've read of you."

"And you find flaw with my tactics."

"I do."

"It could be that I am at fault, or . . ."

"Or, General?"

"Perhaps the reportage of my battles has been faulty?" Adrogans let his voice harden. "Do not take this as criticism, Princess, but while you have been being trained, and trained so very well, I have been here, fighting the Aurolani. What I have learned in all that time has imparted to me a knowledge of Aurolani tactics that I will make good use of here. Malarkex has not yet deigned to engage me, so tomorrow will be a momentous day. One for which I have been preparing for decades."

Alexia nodded. "I grant you have that knowledge."

"Good. The other thing I have learned is that loyalties waver and fail. I know, for example, that there are forces in Lakaslin who do not like me and see me as a threat. They would be perfectly happy to see me die here. That there are conduits which guarantee my plans make it to Chytrine, I do not doubt. I do not ask you to trust me, I demand it.

That I do not seem to trust you is because I cannot, lest I chance betrayal."

"Trust is not a river that flows in only one direction, General Adrogans."

"In my army it is, Princess. It has to be." The Jeranese soldier snorted. "Quickly, then, you know it benefits me not at all to betray you. I gain nothing by putting you into a position to be killed. I want Okrannel in your hands. It buffers my home against the Aurolani, if nothing else, and the merchant princes of Jerana drool with the prospect of profits to be gained in helping Okrannel rebuild. Half the Okrans nobility in exile have married daughters of the Jeranese merchant class, and these same people will reward me very well to bring your nation back to life.

"Moreover, Princess, I have great respect for you and your skills. The positioning of your troops was not an accident, since I had to assume Malarkex would come to relieve Svoin, and come from the north. I wanted you there, not to waste your forces, but to provide you the chance to strike and draw first blood from those who have deprived you of your nation. Your troops are wonderful. I can count on them, so they are the tip of a lance I want to drive into the Aurolani forces."

Alexia nodded. "Thank you."

"So, Highness, while I cannot and will not trust you with information you have no need to know, I do trust you will do everything you must to defeat Malarkex. How, you will see, as needed, but the way to victory will be clear for you."

She frowned. "I do not like this."

"No, I don't suppose you do, but that is a flaw in your training. You were trained to be a great warrior, and you are, but you were not trained to accept orders. I am not one of your tutors, but I do not shy from presenting you this lesson."

Alexia snorted lightly. "If it is not a profitable lesson, I will hold you accountable."

"If things go wrong, we'll have an eternity in the grave to ponder our errors." He sighed. "I do have an order. We will have a cold camp tonight. No fires."

Irritation creased Alexia's brow. "Malarkex is not going to be counting campfires to see how many of us there are. That information has likely been signaled to her from the city, and they have had ample time to tally our number."

"Trust, Highness, trust."

Her eyes narrowed, then she nodded once. "We will be ready to go at dawn?"

"Not unless she forces it. Get a meal into the troops, then fight by mid-morning, I think."

"We'll be ready."

"Good, Highness, I am counting on you."

She gave him a salute and he returned it. He watched her until she departed his tent, then glanced over at the cackling Zhusk. "What is it?"

"If you fail tomorrow, she will be a deadly enemy."

"If I fail tomorrow, I will be ready to die." He shook his head at the little man. "Is everything ready?"

"Yes, all ready. We will keep our half of the bargain."

"And I will mine." Adrogans drew in a deep breath and let it out in a heavy sigh. "This is the one time Chytrine will underestimate us, so we have to make the most of it. Gods and all else willing, we will do just that."

CHAPTER 54

Dawn could not come quickly enough after a night spent in a cold camp. The night had not actually been that cold, though the moisture in the air made it seem much more so. The lack of hot water for tea or to cook up what would be some men's last meal did not sit well, but rumors passed quickly enough through the camp that fire was a tool Chytrine could use to spy on them. It actually got creative, equating tongues of flame with wagging tongues—an old soldier's legend that gained new life one more time and served to quiet some grumbles.

The night had remained peaceful save for two things, neither of which became truly clear until the sun's first light crept down to shrink the plateau's shadow. In the dark, the people in Alexia's position had been able to hear sounds coming from the direction of the Aurolani standards. She could see nothing, but anyone who had a moment to spare kept watch in that general direction. She almost asked a Vilwanese warmage for the lend of a spell to see what was happening, but she quickly assumed that because such spells would be available to the Aurolani vy-laens, Crow, Resolute, and their allies had worked counter-spells to cover themselves.

Even knowing she'd not see anything, she did watch from time to time, and two hours before dawn her efforts were rewarded. A bright flash of fire as silver as Resolute's eyes split the night. The circle of standards was burned into her sight as black silhouettes. Within it, another stan-dard—half again as tall as the Aurolani ones—had been raised. It proved as gruesome as those surrounding it, com-prised of a crucified vylaen on a stick. His body writhed as silver lightning played over it—likewise twitched and danced the bodies of gibberers trying to haul him down.

Subsequent green and red sparks flared as gibberers were blasted against the Aurolani standards, triggering the horrible magicks that had been worked into them. The screams and howls ran from outrage to pain, then darkness closed in again, disturbed only by yellow flames guttering on bodies and broken shafts of standards.

That single act seemed to warm many men beyond what a hot meal would have done. Crow and Resolute slipped back through the lines all but unnoticed, with Dranae in tow. Each of them had sooted their faces and ex-posed flesh black, and had dark cloaks covering them. When Alexia saw them, they were doing their best to con-tain their giddiness. Aside from some minor cuts, and a few weals earned from slashing underbrush, none looked worse for the wear.

Alyx smiled at Crow. "There was some excitement out there."

Crow nodded. "Was there? We were out for a constitu-tional—loosening up old bones before the coming battle." He winked at her.

She returned the wink. "Clumsy of the Aurolani to trig-ger their own trap."

Resolute swiped a rag over his face, reducing his com-plexion to grey. "The Aurolani are not always as smart as

they should be. You might warn General Adrogans that he
wants to keep people away from the standards, a hundred
yards at least, east and west. Someone left caltrops all
around there, poisoned ones. Boots might stop them, but
thick gibberer foot pads won't."

"Noted, thanks." She glanced at Dranae. "And you'll
continue this charade?"

"What was done is more important than who did it,
Highness." Dranae smiled broadly. "There will be heroes
enough to laud tomorrow. This was a lark. That will take
courage."

Alyx nodded slowly. "But first blood is to us. Thank
you."

Crow returned the smile. "Don't thank us. Thank whoever did it. Dranae is right, and the last thing needed now is
distraction, with all that is going on."

She smiled tightly and walked away from them to oversee preparations for the coming battle, which was the second thing that disturbed the night's peace. In setting up the
forces for the siege, Adrogans had broken the infantry
down into six groups. He kept the Stonehearts in position,
but pulled his second group back to cover their eastern
flank. The next unit in line, which consisted of the Okrans
Volunteers and a full regiment of the Alcidese King's Heavy
Guards, was split into four parts. The Volunteers, who were
a battalion of light infantry, covered the gap between the
Heavy Guards and the unit to the west. The Guards broke
into three wings, with two battalions in the center, one each
left and right, drawing a line to screen Alexia's cavalry from
the Aurolani forces.

The deployment took place in the dark, with Zhusk
scouts leading the troops into position. The discipline of
the Alcidese troops made the maneuver possible. As the
morning's light filtered onto the battlefield, the Heavy
Guards with their blue surcoats over ringmail, round
shields, and long spears stood in a strong line to oppose
Chytrine's troops.

While they waited for their enemies to take the field of battle, the troops ate from dry stores and drank, knowing they'd likely not get a chance for another meal until much later in the day, if at all. Most appeared to be in good spirits as she rode among them, but she noticed some who were dour or nervous. Many used daggers to dig hasty little holes in the ground, tucking a scrap of food or a coin into the earth in an effort to appease the *weirun* of the city. She suspected few who observed that superstition hoped to be saved from death, but instead wished that their spirits would not be bound to haunt this place.

As the sun rose and mid-morning approached, the Aurolani legions spilled from the forest to the north in dribs and drabs. Bereft of their standards, which still smoked in a blackened circle to the west of their line, they gathered nonetheless. Occasionally a gibberer would venture in that direction, then he would yip and howl, grabbing one foot. Sometimes he would hop about, but most times he would just drop and die twitching.

The legions did not mass as heavily as the Alcidese did, though rising from their midst were hoargoun. Pale of hair, eye, and flesh, and given to growing long beards and longer hair—both of which were sometimes braided with black ribbons—the glacier giants stood easily three times as tall as a man. Their legs had the stockiness to carry them, with big flat feet that let them walk over snow without sinking. Alexia wondered if Adrogans' creation of the chain of ponds had been designed to make the battlefield swampier. Though it put her cavalry at a disadvantage, it also would slow the giants terribly. Most of the oncoming titans favored clubs, but at least two had massive, double-bitted axes and one appeared to be wielding an iron mace that looked as if it had once served as the clapper for some huge bell.

As ragged and hideous as the Aurolani infantry appeared, the cavalry was both colorful and impressive. They drew themselves up in smart ranks, long lances held so that sunlight glinted from the sharpened foot of steel at the end of each one. To the right and left, three hundred strong, were lighter cavalry legions consisting of frostclaws with vylaens or gibberers mounted upon them.

Alyx had seen temeryces before, but seldom alive and certainly never mounted. From their noses to the tip of their stiff tails they'd been shrouded in iron-studded leather armor, tight-fitted yet supple enough to let her see the rippling of their muscles. The powerful legs, which were birdlike in design, sprouted three toes, the interiormost of which had a huge sickle-shaped claw designed for slashing. Their narrow heads had two amber eyes that looked forward and a mouth bristling with sharp teeth. Without riders the frostclaws would be formidable enemies, so slaying their masters did nothing to eliminate their threat.

The centermost legion of heavy cavalry was yet more magnificent, for they rode grand temeryces. Whereas their smaller counterparts had snowy feathers covering them, the grand temeryces wore a brilliant rainbow plumage that was mirrored in the layers of multihued leather that made up their armor. Some had colorful crests rising from within the leather hoods they wore, and the ribbons dangling from the face armor made Alyx wonder if Chytrine wished her beasts to mock Oriosans for some reason.

Gibberers mostly, but a few men, rode the grand temeryces. Steel encased the riders and their lances ended in horrid, tridentine claws designed to punch clean through armor, rending and tearing what they found beneath it. The riders bobbed up and down as their mounts advanced, each powerful leg more than capable of bearing the weight of beast, man, and steel.

Leading them came Malarkex, and the first sight of her made Alyx's mouth grow dry. The temeryx the *sullanciri* rode had the size of a grand temeryx, but was covered in a jet-black plumage that the rising sun burnished gold. Whereas the other beasts had amber eyes, or gold, even brown, her mount's eyes burned the yellow-orange of a coal, and even had fleckings of ash to darken it. Wisps of smoke rising from the beast's eye sockets made Alyx wonder what she was truly seeing, but the temeryx was nothing compared to its mistress.

That Malarkex was female Alyx discerned by knowledge of who she had been, and nothing more. In Edamis Vilkaso's shifting form there were no clues as to her gender. A black cloak shrouded her and appeared to burn, much as had the cloak of the *sullanciri* at Porasena, but Malarkex's garment remained black for the most part. A jagged webbing of red appeared around the hem, outlining little bits of shadow that leaped away to evaporate. Her eyes, which glowed from within a closed steel helm, had the same steel-silver hue as her curved saber. The blade appeared to be no more natural than its owner, for it reflected no sunlight. Instead, it coruscated with a pale green fire that slithered snakelike up and down its length.

A courier from the Jeranese Horse Guards rode up to her. "Compliments of General Adrogans, General. He thanks you for the information about avoiding the standards. His orders for you are as follows: the Heavy Guards will advance three hundred yards on the signal, and set themselves. At the next signal, a gap will open right and left, with the Kingsmen going left and your Wolves right. You are to flow with the current as a mighty river to drown your enemies. Do you understand these orders?"

She nodded. "Simple, a bit lyrical. They are understood." She made a mark on the receipt the courier presented her, then summoned the commanders of the Kingsmen and the wings of the Heavy Guards, relaying their orders to them. They headed off to communicate to their subordinates, then sent messengers back to her to let her know the orders had been understood.

Crow came riding up to her side. "The general is letting you deal with Malarkex?"

Alexia nodded, then glanced back toward the tent that

served as Adrogans' home. Smoke rose through the hole at the center and Zhusk scouts were carrying buckets of water up to it. "It would appear he wants a warm bath while we fight. My only real concern is that the Kingsmen's charge will likely drive the Aurolani troops east, which will carry them more to our rear."

"Yes, but it will prevent them from linking up with the legions coming down the lakeshore." He turned in the saddle and pointed back toward the second cavalry formation. "General Caro and the Savarese Knights seem to be up and about as well. They can range west as well as east, so could easily be our reserve."

"No debating that." She sighed. "I know there are things I am not being told. I have to hope, have to *trust* that General Adrogans knows what he is doing."

"Do you?"

Alyx frowned, considering her previous encounter with the task force's leader. "For now, yes, I must. Do you?"

Crow nodded, then rested his left hand on the pommel of his sword. "I have to. Scant few of us here today have the means to kill a *sullanciri*. I trust Adrogans will get me close enough to do it. Edamis was always bold and resourceful, so doubtless knows how she wants the battle to go. I hope Adrogans will find a way to disappoint her."

"I share your hope, Crow. I want to stop her and break their backs." Alexia drew her saber as heralds blasted out an advance. "Ride with me and we'll both get what we want."

Will fumed at having to wait back with the baggage train as the trumpets blared to send troops forward. Crow had explained very clearly why he couldn't join the battle. While they had no doubts about Will's combat skills serving him well, the simple fact was that he had no military experience. The key to winning the battle would be discipline and training; Will's lack of each was precisely the sort of thing that could get him killed.

Much as he hated it, Will had accepted that. At Vilwan he'd been too tired and too confused to make any sense of the emotions he was feeling. He watched Crow and Resolute get ready to ride off and it occurred to him that, very realistically, they might die. The very thought of that thickened his throat and tightened his eyes.

Such emotion felt very alien to him. He'd formed attachments to other kids in Marcus' gang, but they'd never been in the position where they had a good chance of dying. Kids did die, and others disappeared, but there was never really any time to anticipate their going away—one just dealt with it after the fact. Marcus would always make those situations into a learning experience, which meant beatings until everyone understood how bad it was to be stupid.

As much as he didn't want his friends to die, and as much as he didn't want to watch them die, the heralds' blaring advance drew him from the relative safety of the baggage area up to the hill where Adrogans had his tent. The Horse Guards stationed there to ward folks off just smiled and nodded at him, which allowed him to steal up to the hilltop and hide in the tent's shadow.

In the distance the Alcidese Heavy Guards marched forward across what was fairly level ground. The landscape actually did rise a bit toward the north, but not so much that it would give the Aurolani an advantage. The ranks moving forward rippled as some men stepped into little valleys, then walked out the other side. Their heads might dip for only a step or two, but it gave the whole formation the illusion of being decorative cloth caressed by a lazy breeze.

The bristling of long spears did partially dispel that illusion. Pennants waved and snapped from some spears, and those in the forward ranks were carried low, pointing at the enemy. Tightly packed as the infantry were, with a second and third rank angling their spears forward, they would present an impenetrable wall to the enemy cavalry.

Behind the infantry, likewise sporting spears and lances, came the cavalry. The dolorous black tabards on the Okrannel Kingsmen somehow made that unit seem more substantial. Though it had been unproven in combat, the desire to liberate their homeland fired the hearts of every man and woman encased in steel there. Their horses wore heavy armor as well, fitted with spikes and hooks, and some even had banners streaming back from little posts planted behind the saddle.

To the right rode the Alcidese Wolves. Their blue tabards had a slash of gold from right shoulder to left hip, and a stripe on the left shoulder had been made of the color of the company with which each rider fought. They appeared to be every bit as colorful as the grand temeryces toward which they rode.

Three hundred yards forward of where they had started, the infantry came to a stop. Spears rotated forward on a command, presenting man-made thorns eager to pierce Aurolani flesh. With one throat, the Alcidese troops voiced an ancient war cry that sent a shiver up Will's spine.

Blood and bone, for our home;
King, kin, and nation.

Will's heart swelled even as his growing smile rubbed his mask over his cheeks. *Oriosa may claim me, but I am Alcidese.*

Drummers within the Aurolani formations pounded out an advance that started their lines surging forward. They kept roughly even across their line, despite their center moving through the cavalry formation. Will was left with the impression of a wolf hiding its teeth, but the threat was still there.

Closer and closer the Aurolani troops marched. The hoargoun moved to the fore of their legions. They hefted weapons capable of blasting huge holes in the Alcidese formation. A swipe of a club would clear spears, spinning the men who wielded them into their companions, wreaking havoc.

And the center, it's never closed. They are planning something.

Will frowned, concentrating, trying to puzzle out what the Aurolani were trying to do. His efforts came to naught—half because he had no experience, and the other half because of the sounds coming from the tent. Amid the cant of the Zhusk, which he recognized but did not understand, Will caught gasps and groans, as well as an inhuman creaking and set of popping noises. He didn't know what it was, but he knew it wasn't right and that, regardless, Adrogans should be out there figuring out what Will couldn't about the Aurolani.

Without thinking the young thief darted around the curve of the tent and slipped inside. It took his eyes a second to adjust to the darkness, but what he saw in that moment took his breath away.

Adrogans, naked, bloody, bound to a cruciform rack above a watery hole in the ground, had pierced his breast, stomach, thighs, and arms with iron nails. Smoke choked the tent, the smoke of sizzling flesh. One Zhusk held a glowing nail in a pair of pincers, while another grabbed a fold of Adrogan's flesh at his left shoulders. Muttering some sibilant curse, the Zhusk shoved the nail home, while a third hung an oddly shaped weight from it on a slender cord.

Before Will could sound an alarm, the old Zhusk headman turned and gestured at him. The man's hand quivered, then tightened into a fist. Will felt all the air crushed from him, then his sight darkened.

He never felt himself hitting the ground.

CHAPTER 55

Markus Adrogans barely caught the flash of light betokening Will's entry to the tent, and scarcely heard his smothered gasp or the sound of his collapse to the ground. The agonies pulsing through his body demanded most all his attention, as red-hot iron pierced his flesh, as his joints twisted and ground with his struggles. His chest felt fair to bursting with the scream he kept locked in, and in a momentary surcease, he harshed out a whisper.

"More, still more."

He clenched his jaw tight, closing his throat, as nimble Zhusks pinched skin into tabs through which they thrust burning metal. To the skewers they fastened wires, on the end of which hung talismans. They tugged and pulled, reigniting nerves that sent waves of pain surging through his body. The sweat covering his body seared into wounds, blood streaked him, boiling when rivulets hit some new piercing. His flesh and blood rose from him in a dozen little streams of sacrificial smoke, the stink of it further torturing him.

He opened his mouth to request more, he needed more and wanted more, but instead his body protested with a wracking cough. Phfas snapped a word—Adrogans made no sense of the sound, but knew there was a sense to it. The ropes at his waist and wrists parted, the pain in his shoulders eased for a moment, then he slid forward, feet first, as the rack tipped down. His sweat- and blood-slicked body picked up splinters from the rack as he glided off.

For a moment he flew free, wrapped by nothing but air and agony, then plunged into the quenching water. It engulfed him and consumed him, subsuming him as well. It flowed over him, cooling the metal, shocking away the heat in his body, penetrating him with a frigidity that numbed him. He slowly descended, his weight and speed accepted by the water, bled off by it. It supported his tired arms and let him dangle there, effortlessly, as if his body, for heartbeat after heartbeat, had ceased to exist.

Adrogans opened his eyes and found himself in union with the water. Through it, through the moisture in the ground, he was able to spread out, seeing and hearing, feeling and smelling. At once he was part of the battlefield. He could see it all, see the Aurolani infantry splashing forward. He could feel himself running down their bodies, soaking their fur as they came on. The temeryx claws tore at his flesh, horse's hooves pounded it.

Blood flowed into it.

At once he could sense it all, everything. The whirl and swirl of battle, the skirling song of the wounded shrieking, the husky chuff of a chest pierced by a spear, it all came to him. The warm spray of blood, the heavy thump of a body hitting the ground, and the shudder of a spear-butt, planted firmly in the earth, accepting the weight of an impaled temeryx before bowing and shattering, peppering warriors with splinters, the fearful clawing at the ground by a wounded frostclaw, the scrabbling of the broken-legged rider beneath it, and the fearsome war cry of a warrior, sword in hand, advancing to finish both; all of these things made up the tapestry of battle for him.

Tapestry. Dimly, in whatever part of him remained human, the inappropriateness of that word struck him. It suggested beauty and artistry, yet what writhed over the landscape was a carpet of pain and death, of blood and torn flesh, shattered limbs, ended dreams and unending nightmares. As sword cleaved flesh, so it rent the mind and soul, compounding the damage and creating wounds that would never heal.

Adrogans focused, narrowing his perceptions to those of more human proportions. He rose over the battlefield with the morning mist, watching as the Aurolani lines hit and engaged the Alcidese infantry on the left wing. Hoargoun swung clubs that shattered some spears, but others rose and thrust, sticking the giants here and there, fending them off for a moment. Pendulum-like, the clubs came back, breaking hafts, but leaving the hoargoun stickled as if the infantry were some iron porcupine and their spears quills.

Through the open center came the Aurolani cavalry. The light cavalry hit the engaged line, tearing into it. Likewise, at the center, the heavy struck hard. The grand temeryces leaped well past the spears, soaring over the front lines, to land heavily, crushing men into the mud. Claws rent armor, opening flesh, tearing spines, then teeth flashed and men spun away with half a face or less one arm. Though some spearmen did catch temeryces in mid-flight, even the weight of a heartstuck frostclaw was enough to smash down the soldiers between it and the ground.

And Malarkex, the *sullanciri*, came hard and sliced into the Alcidese formation with the ease of a schoolmaster scattering children with a whip. Of her he could feel little save hatred and fury, and her black mount tasted of blasphemy. Sleek though the beast was, it had been long dead before being magicked to serve her. No heart beat in its breast, no lungs pumped, but a feral and malign spirit did strengthen its limbs and speed its reactions.

About her and the circle of death her sword harvested around her he could do nothing, but he had known that forever. She was not his to destroy, but she was only part of the battle. The whole battle was the key, and all he had gone through was designed to let him win.

Adrogans reached out, splaying his fingers, letting sensation return to them long enough for him to feel the water flowing within his grasp. He willed his fingers to flow into the water, extending his reach, integrating him with the realm in which they fought. Part of him, fearful of being lost forever, resisted, but he overrode it.

What I do must be done.

His head slowly nodded, bobbing lightly. Then he set his face in a fierce grimace and tightened his hands into fists.

Twin geysers erupted on the battlefield, jetting thick columns of brown water high into the sky. One carried lead elements of the Aurolani infantry's center into the sky; the other knocked a hoargoun reeling. The columns vaporized, leaving a rainbow behind them, and a quagmire oozed up to ensnare the Aurolani center.

Behind Alyx and her Wolves, heralds sounded a signal. The Alcidese left and center were fully engaged and could not maneuver, so the Okrans Kingsmen had no path opened for them. Then the Alcidese right pulled away, providing an avenue for the Wolves to charge, and to Alyx's amazement, the ground hardened and dried, cracking as if baked by years of drought. Raising her sword, she dug her heels into Valor's flanks, leading the Wolves into a charge that would catch the Aurolani heavy cavalry in the flank.

She had no idea how or why the battlefield was shifting. The flow of water smacked of magick, that much was clear, and she quickly assumed Chytrine's forces would find a way to reverse the spells. The little lake growing up to keep the Aurolani right at bay would eventually shrivel, but that would be a problem to handle later. The hard ground beneath her horse's hooves meant the charge could generate speed and power.

Some of the grand temeryces on the flank turned to face the charge, but it scarcely mattered. The sheer mass and weight of the charge blasted frostclaws back, sometimes spilling riders to be sliced and crushed amid prancing claws and stomping hooves. Mostly they were driven back into the flanks of their fellows, trapping the other heavy cavalry, leaving them unable to maneuver or defend themselves. Lancers on either side of her skewered beasts or riders.

The Wolves drove a spearhead into the heavy cavalry with one legion, then the other swung out wide to the right, passing in front of the mired Aurolani center to hit the infantry left in the flank. Agitare led them in that daring move, rising in his stirrups, waving his sword, and lustily shouting orders.

His Red Caps ate into the Aurolani left like a cancer.

The heavy cavalry's cohesion evaporated as the far flank broke under pressure. The Alcidese King's Heavy Guards pushed one company forward to bedevil the milling riders and protect Agitare's legion's rear. While that saved their countrymen, it still choked the lane the Okrans Kingsmen needed to engage the enemy, trading the nip of a dagger for what would have been the bite of a sword.

Shrieking in a voice that mixed the howl of a biting boreal wind with the scream of a gutted cat, Malarkex reined her mount around and leaped it into the Wolves' formation. The temeryx's claws laid open a horse's flank, shredding ringmail as if it were cobweb, and carried away much of the rider's leg. The *sullanciri*'s saber swept around in a blow that would have chopped the rider in half, but Crow's straight-bladed sword intercepted the blow and parried it high.

Malarkex's temeryx turned quickly and scythed its tail

through Crow's horse's legs. They snapped like wet twigs, rolling the horse in the air with the quick violence of the blow. Crow kicked free of the saddle, launching him away from the horse, but awkwardly so. He landed hard on his right shoulder and though he rolled to his feet, a riderless horse hit him from behind, stunning him and pitching him face first into the mud.

The *sullanciri* spun her mount and leaned down for a stroke that would have opened Crow's spine from ass to at-las. The sudden jolting of her mount to the right carried the cut wide as Lombo hit the temeryx's left flank with a shoulder. Looking much like a bundle of burning rags, Malarkex flew from the saddle. The temeryx craned its neck around to snap at the Panqui, but quicker than its flashing teeth, Lombo grabbed its head jaw-and-crown and wrenched.

Alyx reined Valor around and drove at the rising *sullanciri*. The Aurolani leader ducked the cut, then slashed at Valor, laying the horse's belly open. Alyx leaped from the dying beast and managed to keep her feet. The shadowy warrior drifted toward her, blood-vapor rising from her blade, then slashed, but Alyx parried the blow low, then cranked her armored elbow around to smash Malarkex in the face.

Her elbow passed straight through the *sullanciri*'s head, sending a shock through Alyx as if she'd just plunged full on into an icy river. Alyx stumbled a step past, then whirled just as Malarkex reversed her direction. The *sullanciri* did not so much spin as turn inside-out, her faint and hate-filled face suddenly appearing where the back of her hooded head had been.

Again Alyx parried a cut, then slashed back, but got nothing but black mist and a wave of cold traveling up her sword in return. She backed away from her foe, realizing the enthusiastic slash had left her open, but the *sullanciri* did not press her advantage quite yet. Drifting forward, like a wind-driven cloud, Malarkex moved toward Crow's still form, forcing Alyx to intercept her.

Over and over they traded blows, with Alyx's strikes rending vapor and reaping cold. Frost formed on her blade and already her fingers felt numb, but she kept fighting, kept moving. She knew she was a better swordsman than the *sullanciri,* but it mattered little when her blade couldn't draw blood. Any of a number of her cuts would have put a normal foe down, and fleetingly she wondered if she would join her father in having died at the hands of a *sullanciri.*

Malarkex feinted with a low slash, then came up high and from the right. Alyx raised her sword to block, but this blow came in harder and heavier than any before. The *sullanciri's* sword notched hers and, worse yet, blasted it from her grasp. Alyx tried to dance back, knowing the next cut would open her armor and flesh, but her heels caught on something and she toppled back.

The *sullanciri's* blow whistled harmlessly past.

Alyx rolled to the right, away from any return cut, and found the hilt of a sword with her left hand. She came up and around, wrapped both hands around the hilt. The straight blade had an opalescent gem set in it at the forte. Shaped like a keystone, the gem pulsed once, fiercely, and warmth filled her right hand anew.

She stepped forward, straddling Crow's body, for it had been his shoulders that caught her heels, and brought his sword up in a guard. She caught Malarkex's low slash easily, turning it aside, then lunged forward and arced Tsamoc skyward. On a normal foe the tip would have been located between the knees, and the upward cut clove shadow where it would have sliced groin.

Malarkex screamed and the shadow gushed down into an inky puddle beneath her. Another cut, frightfully weak, threatened to slash Alyx at the left hip, but Tsamoc parried it high and around, then chopped down into the *sullanciri's* back at the right flank. The shadow figure wavered for a heartbeat, then its dark essence poured out onto the ground, with only the stain and the bouncing saber to mark where it had stood and fought.

Alyx stared at the sword with the pulsing gem in it. *Magickal sword, indeed!*

The battle rolled around Alyx, with temeryces snapping, men screaming, howling gibberers charging at her. She refused to give ground, standing there over Crow, spattered with mud and blood. Some gibberers made it to her, but only after threading a gauntlet of lances and swords, or the blurred backhand flick of a Panqui paw. More than one gibberer had its bones pulverized by those swats, and yet more would have save that Lombo seemed to take a singular delight in pouncing upon riderless frostclaws and crushing their skulls between his fists.

Trumpets sounded behind her lines, and she could hear the Alcidese infantry rallying to advance. More trumpets answered, but from the north, which surprised her, but she had little attention to spare in puzzling out why. The lead elements of the Aurolani center had just struggled from the swamp when the water drained from that basin. She braced herself for their onslaught, hoping to sell herself dearly, when trumpets blared again, and the thunder of hooves overrode the frenzied pounding of Aurolani war drums.

From the north, three legions of Jeranese light cavalry crashed into the Aurolani rear. On the right the little lake separating the Alcidese King's Heavy Guards from the Aurolani flank vanished as Jeranese heavy infantry marched in from the northeast. Already flanked, the Aurolani left pulled back, crowding the center, making both crumble.

Then, to her own left, more horses came charging hard. The Okrans Kingsmen, unable to come through the Heavy Guards, had ridden around and come from the west, rolling up that flank and grinding the Aurolani right wing between themselves and Agitare's legion. Hoargoun, stuck with spears and bleeding black, wavered and toppled as lances pierced their thighs and sabers whittled away at their shins.

Mad, milling gibberers ran every which way, with a few flowing toward Alyx just by pure chance. Tsamoc made short work of some, and Resolute's arrival made shorter work of others. The one grand temeryx that leaped toward her would have been a horror to deal with, but a geyser of steam caught it in mid-flight, parboiling it. Though not quite dead when it landed, it could do little but mew and hiss, so Alyx beheaded it with a stroke.

Resolute caught the reins of a riderless horse and motioned to Alyx. "General, ride."

"No."

"Yes, you must." Resolute nodded quickly at her. "I'll see to Crow. And you'll see to him when you return Tsamoc. Now, General. It will finish things."

Alyx nodded and mounted. As she raised her sword, the Alcidese host gave a great shout, which the Kingsmen echoed. From further back the rest of the siege force cried out and cheered. The Heavy Guards tightened their formations and surged forward, sweeping past Crow's body, constricting and crushing the Aurolani force.

From horseback Alyx gained perspective and realized what had happened. Somehow, from somewhere, Adrogans had conjured up a full battalion of light cavalry and a whole regiment of heavy infantry. Both were from Jerana and clearly had been lurking in the hills. The mist rising with the water on the field had screened the Aurolani from the threat to their rear and flank until too late.

Things began to fall into place for her. The excessive requisitions for food had not been extravagance on Adrogans' part; he was feeding another whole army on the leavings of the expedition. He'd kept their existence hidden from her, from everyone, meaning he feared a spy in the midst of the rulers. She began to wonder if all his battle reports had been manipulated to read poorly, to make it seem as if he won by luck instead of skill or cunning. And she wondered if they had been so written to deceive Chytrine.

I'm not sure I owe Adrogans an apology yet, but he has earned a lot more trust.

The heavy infantry, both Jeranese and Alcidese, linked up and drove west. The Kingsmen and the Jeranese light horse preceded them, nipping at the flanks of the Aurolani formation that had come down the road and had been stopped by the Stonehearts. The Aurolani legions began to withdraw, but the Stonehearts advanced. The Aurolani legions broke and the cavalry slaughtered them as they ran for the hills.

CHAPTER 56

It surprised Alyx to see Crow bare-chested and sitting in a chair in the shadow of the Vilwanese warmage pavilion. He raised his left hand in greeting and she noted with some satisfaction that the glow from the little brazier near his booted feet didn't show any new wounds on his body. His right shoulder was discolored, and she was thankful the evening's wan light didn't let her see the true colors there. That he held his arm close and tight to his ribs, half hiding a trio of scars on that side of his chest, did not surprise her at all.

She frowned at him. "Should you be . . . ?"

Crow smiled easily and pointed at an empty chair beside him. "Please, Highness, sit. I cannot thank you enough for risking your life to protect me. Resolute told me what you did. Lombo, too—you impressed him mightily."

Alyx laughed. "It's mutual. The way he kept the gibberers back, and the temeryces . . . you wouldn't believe."

The man nodded. "He regrets it, you know, of robbing you of those kills. He thinks he was selfish."

"So I live to forgive him." She smiled. "How do you fare?"

Crow shrugged, at least with his left shoulder. "While you were off leading the reconnaissance of the Aurolani camp, Lombo carried me back here. Kerrigan was going to magick me back to health, but I told him just to see how much damage had been done first. Bumps and bruises, knot on my head. I told him to see to others. I'll be fine."

"Why are you still here, then?"

He pointed a finger at the tent. "Will's in there. He was with Adrogans, watching the battle, when he fainted. Will's resting. He came around but doesn't remember anything since last night, which puts us in the same position. I don't remember much past talking to you."

"You had a long night out there with Resolute and Dranae. How are they?"

"Doing very well. Resolute has some scratches. Dranae has the bite pattern of a frostclaw on his right thigh, but it never got much through his mail or skin before he killed it." Crow nodded toward the battlefield. "They're out there, helping the wounded, finishing the gibberers. Resolute will have enough longknives to make a galaxy of bladestars. I guess the Vilwanese are looking for some folks to become *meckanshii*. I'd be lucky to be among them if not for you."

Alyx reached out and patted him on the knee. "You saved my life, too, you know. After she'd disarmed me, I'd have been split in two except that you tripped me and sent me below that slash."

"Quite by design, I assure you, Highness."

"Ah, then it was also by design that you left this for me." Alyx unsheathed Tsamoc. "Your sword is what finished her, you know."

"A carpenter builds the house, not his hammer."

"You know, Crow, I think we're both wasting a lot of time being so polite. Fact is that you saved one of my men from death, but that was happenstance since you'd gone straight for Malarkex. Don't deny it. You knew she had to be finished, and I agreed. You stopped her, then I stopped her. We both stopped her. We've killed a *sullanciri.*"

A grimace flashed over Crow's face. "'Ware saying that too loudly, Highness, for only ill has come to such folk. Bosleigh Norrington now *is* a *sullanciri.* Tarrant Hawkins is dead by his own hand. I like neither prospect for you."

"And for yourself?"

"Neither as well." Crow accepted Tsamoc from her, then used the sword to lever himself stiffly out of his chair. "No, Highness, stay seated. I'll just put Tsamoc with my other things and fetch us some wine. You once said you'd willingly share a skin with me in the field, and I know they have some inside. Give me but a moment."

She nodded and watched him go. With his white hair and beard, walking as stiffly as his injuries demanded, she could easily imagine him being of an age to court her great-grandaunt—though the thought of that pairing sent a shudder through her. Tatyana was cold enough that Malarkex would have felt a burning coal by comparison.

Alyx leaned back in the camp chair, listening to the creak of the wood and canvas from which it had been constructed. The brazier's warmth slowly bled into her, melting away little aches and leaving only fatigue in return. She closed her eyes for a moment, relishing the kiss of heat on her cheeks, then felt a jolt run through her.

Though she knew her eyes were closed, she could see the camp and the glowing fire and Crow's empty chair. In addition to that, the Black Dragon stood before her, across the fire from her. Red highlights slithered over his scales and along his arm as he raised a hand in greeting.

"Forgive me, daughter, for so abrupt an appearance. I cannot be long, the strain is great. You must go to Adrogans. Wruonan pirates went overland to Lakaslin. The Azure Spider managed to steal the DragonCrown fragment *and* destroy the *arcanslata* with which the capital communicates to Mallin on the coast. The theft wasn't noticed for we don't know how long, so it could be on the island already."

Alyx nodded. "I'll tell him. We'll send a force."

The Black Dragon shook his head. "You can't tell him, daughter, for nothing I've said to you will pass your lips. You'll find a way to make him learn. You will. Go to him, now."

She jerked upright in her chair, her hands tight on the arms. She blinked, half expecting to see the Black Dragon where Crow now stood with alarm on his face.

"I didn't mean to startle you, Highness."

"Never mind that. We have to go talk to Adrogans."

Crow slung the wineskin over his left shoulder and started immediately through the darkness toward the hilltop where Adrogans' pavilion glowed softly like a phantom mushroom. "I haven't seen him today, but I've not been looking. There's still a Horse Guards cordon around his tent, however."

"It doesn't matter."

He frowned. "What is it?"

Alyx opened her mouth to tell him, since the Black Dragon had long ago told her she could trust Crow, but the words disintegrated between her mind and her mouth. "I can't say, but it's urgent. You have to trust me."

"With my life, Highness."

They reached the edge of the cordon, which surrounded the base of the hill upon which the tent was perched. A horse soldier tried to stop Alyx by getting in front of her and telling her she couldn't go up, but she just kept veering, forcing him to twist and turn. When he finally grabbed at her left arm, she pulled free of his grasp and backhanded him with a blow that spun him to the ground.

Two steps further on, halfway up the hill, a Horse Guards sergeant stopped her. "Highness, with all due respect . . ."

Alexia's head came up and urgent fury dripped from her words. "Respect, *Sergeant*, would mean you'd be leading me, not stopping me. Stand aside, or General Adrogans will know of your conduct."

"His orders I'm following, Highne . . . General."

Crow cut to the left, so the sergeant grabbed him by the right arm. The man roared with pain and the soldier recoiled, letting Alyx shoot past. She reached the crest of the hill while the sergeant huffed and puffed up after her, only to find the entryway barred by Phfas.

The Zhusk headman shook his head slowly. "He is to be left alone."

Alyx lowered her voice, but kept her anger constant. "Were I reporting on the battle, or any number of other matters which are as trivia to what I need to say, I would leave it until morning. Stand aside."

Phfas' little brown face squeezed in on itself, all but hiding his eyes in a webwork of wrinkled flesh. "Go away, Svarskya."

"Phfas," Adrogans called quietly from within the tent, "let her pass."

The headman moved aside, then quickly intercepted Crow. Alyx glanced at him, but Crow shook his head. "Go on. I can wait."

Alyx slipped past the curtained entryway and saw Adrogans struggling to rise from his bed. He wore a loincloth, very much after Zhusk fashion. More important, talismans had been fastened to his swollen, mottled skin, and decorated him as they did Phfas. *But so many more, and bigger.*

Adrogans regarded her with half-lidded eyes. "My mother, you know, came from Okrannel. She was a merchant's daughter bound to be wed to a merchant family in Mallin to seal an alliance. They traveled the coast road and Zhusk raiders kidnapped her. Jeranese soldiery rescued her—the younger brother of her intended groom, in fact, led them. When she reached Mallin it was apparent, by her own admission, that she had been despoiled. The warrior, my father, had developed a great affection for her, so the alliance was sealed through their union, and I was born three seasons later."

The man walked slowly to a side table and poured out two goblets of wine, nodding toward her to take one. "It was not until I led troops into the Zhusk domain that I was recognized for what I was—a half-Zhusk bastard. Phfas saw that in me, and more. Through his offices I was accepted, which is why the Zhusk have let me operate here for years. Despite my acknowledgment of my link to them—a link I have kept quiet for fear your grandfather would disapprove of me—I had not undergone full initiation into their societies."

Alyx accepted the wine, though barely tasted it. Her message burned urgently in her, but the quiet power of Adrogans' confession forestalled her speaking of it. Instead she nodded at him. "The talismans."

"The Zhusk are a primitive people. They acknowledge the gods and the *weirun* but tend toward dealing with things more primal. They call them the *yrûn*. Water, air, fire, earth, a host of other elemental things, all of them share an essence. While a river might have one *weirun* and a lake another, they both share the same *yrûn* essence. They can be manipulated and controlled."

He gestured toward the doorway. "You wondered how Phfas stopped the arrow that would have split Resolute's heart? The *yrûn* of air is his companion. After he was prepared and pierced, they threw him from a cliff. Had they not bonded, he would have been dashed on the rocks and killed. Because of their bond he hardened the air, saving himself much as he made it intercept the arrow."

"And you are bound to water? You produced the geysers, swamp, and lake? The mist, that was you?"

Adrogans smiled slowly. "When you come to the initiation late, and you have a certain amount of power yourself, wisdom, philosophy, the *yrûn* seek you as much as you seek them." He touched the talisman on his left breast. "Water wanted me and I it. And fire, which is why the skewers were heated, and earth, which is why they were metal. Wood for the splinters in my back, and water, which quenched the burning. But, largely, it was another, the *yrûn* of pain, who is mine. I could see through the water out there, I could feel through the earth, but I also saw and heard and felt and tasted and smelled through the pain."

He snorted. "She will be a harsh mistress, pain will, but ours will be a long and passionate affair. I'd delayed long enough my initiation, and the first time, the time when the bonds are formed, this is when you have the most power. I am not saddened I used it here and now."

"Nor am I." Alyx nodded solemnly to him. "General, this will sound insane, but do not think it so. You need, with your *arcanslata*, to send a message to Queen Carus."

Adrogans' eyes hooded. "What makes you think . . . ?"

"Trust, General, trust. You earned mine today by bringing your hidden forces into play. I think I earned yours doing what I did, killing a *sullanciri*. You need to trust me in this, you need to communicate with her, now. It is vital."

The Jeranese general hesitated for a second more, then moved the wine decanter and tray with two more goblets to the ground. The tabletop it had been on slid to the side to reveal a hollow, and from it he withdrew one of the magickal communications devices. He slid a bead of wood from the top to the bottom of a narrow side and glowing words in a tiny delicate script filled the surface.

Alyx could not read the words at that distance, but she did not need to. Adrogans stiffened, then his shoulders began to sag. He turned and looked at the princess as the words faded.

"You know about this how?"

Alyx shook her head. "I've earned your trust in reporting to you so you could learn it. How is immaterial. Say it came to me in a dream and be done with it."

Adrogans tossed the *arcanslata* onto his cot amid a tangle of blankets. "A fragment of the DragonCrown is on Wruona. Vionna wishing to play in a game that is worlds above her, and the Azure Spider is abetting her desire. If she gives it to Chytrine . . ." His voice faded.

"We have to stop her." Alyx hesitated. "We cannot pack the army up and send it off, since we do not have enough ships to assault Wruona."

"Agreed; we have just enough to do as bad a job there as the pirates did on Vilwan. If we were to shift the army, Chytrine would know and know why soon enough—if her agents in Lakaslin don't already know. I'll tell the queen to spread the tale that the theft was a blind for us to move the fragment to a place no one knows about, to make it impossible to steal. It will cast doubt on the tales of spies and the pirates."

"That will forestall immediate action, General, but Chytrine will have to move to get the fragment. Vionna will tell her of it as soon as she is able. We have to move fast."

Adrogans nodded. "You'll have to do it, Princess, you and your band of friends."

"My band of friends?"

"Crow, Resolute, the others."

"But we've been preparing to rescue the hostages in Svoin."

"I know, but their lives will mean nothing if Chytrine gets that DragonCrown fragment. This operation will be the same as the rescue. Infiltrate, locate, appropriate, and evacuate."

"No, no, no." She stared at him. "It is not the same at all. We don't know Wruona, we've not been in Port Gold. The place will be full of pirates. . . ."

"Not as full as it was a month ago."

"No, it's impossible. We don't know the place—" But before she could continue, shouts arose from outside. She turned toward the doorway as Lombo barged in, dragging two Horse Guards who were unsuccessfully trying to detain him. Behind him, Phfas and Crow entered the tent.

One of the Guards, the sergeant she'd encountered

before, slid to the ground and saluted. "Begging your pardon, sir, but . . ."

"I understand. Dismissed."

As the two soldiers departed, a Spritha sailed through the doorway and perched itself on Lombo's shoulder. The Panqui nodded, then looked at Alexia. "Port Gold, Lombo know. Stealing there easy."

"You see, General, optimism."

The Panqui growled. "Escaping, very hard."

Alexia exhaled slowly. "I know some Panqui have been pirates, but you were . . . ?"

Lombo pounded a fist against his chest, spilling Qwc from his perch. "Lombo best pirate. Get into Port Gold easy."

Adrogans raised an eyebrow. "Easy?"

The Panqui nodded. "Pirates never suspect Lombo."

"Why not?"

Lombo flashed a mouthful of teeth in a terrible grin. "They think Lombo dead."

CHAPTER 57

Kerrigan shifted uneasily in his chair. The journey from the Zhusk plateau had taken an easy week on the descent, but the trip back there and beyond to the Jeranese port of Ooriz had been accomplished in three days. Three very *long* days, riding horses to the point of exhaustion and pushing the riders even further. All of their road camps were cold, not out of fear of discovery or lack of wood, but lack of time. In a couple of Zhusk villages they did pick up new horses and got some warm food, but otherwise they pushed hard enough that even Lombo was all but dead with fatigue.

Finally, in the wee hours of the morning, they arrived at the port. Lombo led them straight to the docks and quickly they divested themselves of their road clothes and found items a bit more colorful and fragrant with which to disguise themselves. Both Alexia and Resolute had to dye their hair—she opting for black while Resolute picked an icy blue.

Kerrigan had spent his life wearing robes, so shifting to

boots, pantaloons, and voluminous shirts layered with the sleeves slashed to show a rainbow of colors felt completely alien to him. He hated wearing a kerchief to hide his hair until he saw how good it looked on Dranae. In fact, the two of them had similar enough of a look that the others cast them as brothers who had gone to sea together.

Kerrigan waited with Dranae and Orla in a small quay-side tavern with low beams, lower lights, and clientele that seemed happily at home amid either. Orla had adopted fishwife garb, but gave every evidence of being ready to tuck her hem up into her belt as needed to work a ship. Dranae, while he wore layered shirts like Kerrigan, had opted to retain his kilt—in keeping with other sailors they saw.

Alexia and Lombo had gone off to finish the negotiations for a boat to take them to Wruona. Crow, Resolute, and Will were watching over them, with Qwc and Perrine poised to help or run messages as needed. The two winged members of their company were not among the races given to being pirates—by virtue of their being so rare outside their homelands—so they were to keep out of sight and would travel in the crow's-nest or belowdecks.

All the others made suitable pirates—even Will, as small as he was. He'd almost been left behind at Svoin because of his size, then it was pointed out that he might be able to talk the Azure Spider into turning the DragonCrown fragment over to them. No one, including Will, thought that was very likely, but it was a chance they could not pass up. And, if he couldn't talk the Azure Spider into giving it up willingly, Will could always steal it.

It felt good to Kerrigan to be out of a saddle and sitting still for a bit. He wasn't looking forward to getting back out on the sea, especially since just thinking about his previous journey had him breaking out in a sweat. More annoying, however, was the flat prohibition against his writing things down in his journal. During the trip he'd had no chance to record any observations, and in port Orla had warned that his writing would be viewed with suspicion. While he didn't want to believe her, he did note that she didn't carry around her staff, to look even less like a wizard.

The difficulty of wanting to appear to be a sailor exacerbated a problem stemming from the battle before Svoin. He had seen a lot and found it overwhelming. He wanted to discuss it with others, but on the road no one had enough energy for such a discussion. And while hiding in the guise of sailors, such discussions would be grossly out of character.

And that's if anyone would want to indulge me.

Because of the loss of the boat he'd been on, Svoin was not really the first combat he'd ever seen, but it certainly was the first between armies. The histories he'd read had all been dispassionate and judgmental, assessing the mistakes made by this commander or that, including lists of casualties and the like. He'd read them more as stories than anything else, and thought himself prepared for Svoin.

He found it had been difficult to remain dispassionate when screaming men begged like children for help or death. The one elven unit, a battalion of archers, had two magickers with them. He and the two of them were the only magickers capable of actually healing people, but there were some wounds no magick could repair. They could assure that a man who'd had an arm or leg struck off, or his genitals or half his face bitten away, would live, but those they saved didn't always see that as a blessing by any means.

Several of the men he worked on begged him to write letters for them, and he assured them he would, as he had in the past. What he remembered, however, were not the ones who asked, but the ones who were beyond asking. *Dead before their letters reached their homes.*

The sheer carnage, the way the muddy earth had been churned with the violence of charge and countercharge, the way some weapons had bitten so deeply into bone that they could not be dislodged; these things all exploded past the safe boundaries in which he had confined his concept of warfare. The majority of bodies he saw had grievous leg wounds and defense wounds on arms as well as the death blows that had rained down on head and chest. In short, the deaths were not clean, one-stroke affairs, but acts of butchery in which a man was crippled with a leg blow, in which he cowered and fended off blows with his hands until his efforts ebbed and he was dispatched. Multiple killing wounds to head and chest bespoke the fury of the attackers.

He didn't take such evidence as an indictment of warfare. A philosophical debate over the evils of war always ended up with two conclusions. The first was that war was evil. The second was that there were times when war was inescapable because some individuals desired the subordination of others to their will. Defending freedom was not evil, and blood spilled in defense did not stain as deeply as that spilled in aggression.

What the signs of violence did was to redefine the world. On Vilwan his existence had been simple and peaceful, idyllic even, despite the difficulties he'd had. The slaughter on the sea, or the beating he'd taken in Yslin, these could all be explained as aberrations, the acts of evil people. That preserved his basically safe sense of the world. Svoin, however, showed him that even good people were capable of savagery.

Am I? He couldn't deny that he'd killed the pirates in the ship he'd smashed, but he'd really visited the violence on their ship. *If I had stopped to consider that I was doing it to people . . .* He shook his head and glanced at Orla. She'd attacked pirates more directly and hurt them, but it did not make her evil.

Could I do that? Could I kill if I thought about it? Kerrigan shivered. *Do I really want to know the answer?*

Will wasn't certain if he was happy or not, and this annoyed him. He skulked his way through the darkened streets of

Ooriz, heading for the Broken Keel tavern to collect the others. Lombo and Alexia had struck a deal for passage on a small ketch, supposedly used for fishing but not outfitted for the same and undoubtedly a smuggling vessel. Trade with Wruona could be highly profitable, especially in the area of basic goods like grain and beer—the kinds of things that were vital for life but seldom part of prizes taken at sea.

Will did know he liked being away from the army and back in a town. Camp life had not suited him particularly well—especially because everyone knew who he was. Having been raised to cultivate anonymity, even the most benign of attention grated on him.

He also had chafed beneath the story of his having fainted because of the slaughter in the Svoin battle. He couldn't remember much beyond heading up toward Adrogans' tent, which meant he had to contend with a sense that something important was missing from his memory. When he'd awakened they told him the battle had been won and that he was fine, but his ribs had ached and felt as if he'd been wrestling with Lombo.

And Will was pretty sure that fainting shouldn't have made his ribs ache.

There was one thing he regretted about leaving the camp, and that was his inability to participate in the rescue of the hostages. Adrogans had been able to locate a handful of men who had criminal backgrounds in his army—armies in general had more such folks, but the Okrans campaign had included fairly elite units, which cut down on the underclass population. These men, including Will, had been assigned to the various squads who would go in and rescue hostages, because they could open locks or shackles or anything else needed to free the people.

It surprised Will that he didn't want to be there to garner praise for his hand in planning the rescues. Nor was he craving the action of the rescues, because he knew—just as with a well-planned theft—there would be little or no action if things occurred as hoped. Instead, and this really astounded Will, he wanted to be there to help because he felt some responsibility for getting the hostages to safety.

Will eyed responsibility as he might a strange and growling cur. Through his life he'd been responsible for himself. The prophecy made him responsible for a lot more, but that all seemed vague. He'd been able to define his enemy as Chytrine, which helped him focus, but that also narrowed the conflict to him versus her. The hostages had become involved without his really being aware of it.

But as long as he was going along on the rescue mission, his own sense of invulnerability had held they would succeed. Now, in the back of his mind, he could see hostages being hurt or killed in the attempt, and every drop of blood that leaked from them was accounted to him. *Because if I were there, they would all be saved.*

Part of him knew that was nonsense, but he couldn't get past it. And not getting past it surprised him. In the past he would have just walked away from such responsibility—*as I did with Kerrigan there in Yslin.* Not being able to do that—and not wanting to do that—burrowed into his mind and festered.

It would have driven him utterly and completely mad save for the nature of the mission that called them away. Despite the prophecy and all the training he'd been given, he really knew very little about the DragonCrown and its pieces. He accepted that for a fragment to be out of the hands of responsible folks was bad, and much worse for Chytrine to get her hands on it. Seeing what a dragon under its influence could do at Yslin was more than enough to convince him of that latter point.

He agreed that they had to get it back, which pretty much meant he had to *steal* it back. That meant he'd be going up against the Azure Spider. The very idea of that sent a thrill through him, and a lot of fear came in its wake. The Azure Spider was sung of from shore to shore and lauded as a swordsman, lover, and thief. Will had always hoped, as the King of the Dimandowns, to surpass him; but stealing something from his own stronghold had never been part of the plan.

Will had wracked his brain to try to remember all the details about the Azure Spider that he'd heard Marcus mention. He wished there had been some simple flaw to the Spider, like his having pledged always to honor an orphan's request, or vulnerability to some complex fencing move. About the only thing he did recall was Marcus contemptuously suggesting that the Spider never hung on to a prize for long because once the thrill of stealing it was over, the man lost interest. Will wanted to count on that as being a help, but he'd learned enough in planning the hostage rescue to avoid relying on the stupidity of the enemy.

The thief entered the Broken Keel and threaded his way to the table where his companions sat. Kerrigan looked more of a clown than sailor, but it easily disguised who he was. Dranae and Orla looked their parts. They finished their ales before rising, which Kerrigan did not do. Will took the young mage's mug and quaffed the last of it.

Will gave them all a nod. "Tide runs in an hour. We're going on the *Pumilio*."

Dranae rested his hands on Kerrigan's shoulders and steered him through the crowd. "No trouble?"

"None yet."

"That's good."

"For now anyway." Will dropped in behind the large man and sighed. "I just hope we're not saving it all up for later."

Alexia waited on the dock while Lombo stood on the wheeldeck with the helmsman. She shifted her shoulders uneasily. She did not like feeling hostility and menace just over the horizon without the familiar weight of ringmail on her body. She did acknowledge that the lighter weight of the clothing she wore would give her added speed in fighting, and that this would balance out.

Another source of anxiety came from the blade she wore on her belt. After the battle she had recovered her own saber, but the fight with Malarkex had left the metal brittle and the blade well notched. Adrogans had insisted that because she'd killed Malarkex, she'd earned the right to the *sullanciri*'s sword. Aside from being a suitable reward for her valor, it had the added benefit of being magickal in nature. This gave her a weapon to use against other *sullanciri*.

The idea that she would face more of them did trickle some dread into her belly. Crow had warned her not to expect too much of the blade when it came to dealing with Chytrine, since any weapon she had a hand in creating certainly would not do her harm. He did agree with Resolute, however, that the blade would be most effective against Chytrine's creatures.

Alexia had taken some time to try it out, dueling with Crow. Because Malarkex's sword was a saber, it wasn't entirely suited to fencing, but the weapon's balance and weight did let her put considerable power into speedy slashes. She found Crow a skillful foe and was able to really test some of the weapon's limitations, but always held herself back despite Crow's ability to defend himself.

The aspect of the blade she hated was how it made her feel about fighting. With the heat and flow of the duel came a dispassionate and cold distancing of herself from it. There came a point where all affection for Crow bled away, quickly followed by any sense of humanity he possessed. She began to see him as lines of force, as muscles to be severed, organs to be skewered, bones to be shattered, and joints to be dissected. The blade took the science of anatomy and dueling and overlaid it on the fight. In killing him or anything else she would be doing nothing of any more consequence than solving sums or calculating positions by the stars.

What dismayed her is that part of her hungered for that detachment. Warfare, she knew, could largely be reduced to numbers and position, angles, vectors, and timing; quantitative factors that dealt with qualitative elements like morale and tradition as fractional variables one did one's best to eliminate entirely. Warfare as science completely discounted pain and suffering. The motives behind why any engagement had been fought became immaterial, and the casualty lists just more statistics to factor into computations for the next battle.

Alexia allowed her mind to wander that far before she reined it back in. Having a leader of such a disposition was valuable to Chytrine because it promoted the infliction of hideous casualties on the enemy without a second thought. Were Alexia losing a battle, she would withdraw to preserve her forces for a later conflict, but Malarkex would have been willing to commit everything to hurt the enemy as much as possible. Overwhelming casualties would sap the will of the southlands to fight, and that was the victory Chytrine desired.

But Chytrine had not reckoned with the sorts of sacrifices men like Adrogans would be willing to make to stop her. Chytrine viewed the efforts of individual warriors as immaterial, for even the most successful campaign depended upon the supplies flowing from the south. A vote in some distant Council would stop Adrogans cold. Adrogans' effort had won such a victory that likely Svoin was lost, but political maneuvering could result in the city's abandonment and a cessation of the campaign.

Alexia wished Adrogans luck, since she had no desire to see him or her cousin or anyone else in that campaign dead. She had the most dread for the fate of Beal mot Tsuvo's people, but a great deal of hope for them, too. The hostages would be rescued—most of them, anyway.

While she had wished Adrogans luck, she'd not wished him *all* luck. She had little doubt they'd be able to get into Port Gold. She felt pretty certain they would be able to locate the fragment of the DragonCrown, and she even had a glimmer of hope that they could steal it back. Getting it off the island and in safe hands, however, she gave a small chance, and of their getting away without casualties she held no hope. Still, leaving a DragonCrown fragment available for Chytrine was not an option: and getting it back was worth any risk—including the Norrington's possible death. His skills as a thief made him invaluable to the raid.

She looked up as Will came leading the trio from the tavern. Behind them Resolute and Crow slipped from shadows. Above, unseen, Peri and Qwc flew past to perch in the small ship's rigging. *Ten of us to steal one of the world's most valuable items from an island teeming with bloodthirsty pirates. Who will bleed? Who will die?*

Alyx forced a smile onto her face. "This way, my friends. Welcome to the *Pumilio*. Watch your head when you go below, it's built for midgets."

Crow laughed. "As long as it's more dry than wet, can we complain?"

"No," she agreed, letting her hand linger on his left shoulder. "When we look back, in the grand scheme of things, any discomfort on this voyage will likely be minor indeed."

CHAPTER 58

Markus Adrogans gingerly shifted his shoulders, reseating the weight of the mail surcoat he wore. The metal garment had a leather gambeson between it and his flesh, but still tugged on the raw piercings. The pain had faded to a dull but persistent series of aches in the four days since the battle that saw Malarkex's death.

He looked to Beal, who stood there in lighter leather armor worked with her clan's knotting. "Your preparations for rescuing the hostages are complete?"

She nodded solemnly. "Save for one detail, General."

This brought Adrogans' gaze around to meet that of a raven-haired Loquelf. "I recall. Mistress Gilthalarwin, I was under the impression we had reached an understanding concerning your Blackfeathers and their part in the rescue."

The elf bowed her head in his direction. "We had, General, before the plans were modified yesterday. Before there had been a respectable interval between the employment of the animals and our participation. Now we will be called upon to coordinate with them. This cannot be done. It will not."

Adrogans struggled to hide his fury, and Phfas' cackle from the corner did not help at all. Will Norrington, having grown up in Yslin, had suggested that balloons be used to evacuate the hostages. Magickers could heat rocks that would produce hot air and make the balloons rise with hostages in baskets. Guide ropes on the ground would draw the hostages from the city while the Blackfeathers shot archers and vylaens trying to bring down the balloons. The balloons were to have been delivered by the Gyrkyme Warhawks, who would then have no further role in the rescue.

A final review of planning had located several flaws in the enterprise. They'd not been able to produce enough balloons to complete the evacuation quickly. More important, a vylaen who could simply cast a spell to chill the balloons could bring them down, killing the hostages. The plan had subsequently been modified, but had a more immediate role for the Gyrkyme, and the Loquelves refused to work with them.

The human general slowly folded his arms over his chest, his mail rustling as he did so. "Mistress Gilthalarwin, you have lived centuries to my decades and view things with a perspective which I have scant chance of understanding. I know better than to threaten you and your Blackfeathers with death. I am not in the habit of killing allies. I know the censure and scorn of men amount to nothing to you, for every one of us here will be dead soon enough by your reckoning.

"You put me in an awkward position, however, and I don't want to be there. I don't think you want it known that you put me there. That position is this: you force me, as a man, to once again rescue Vorquelves. Once again I have to do what elves could not. *And* you force me to use the Gyrkyme to do it. The children for whom you have abrogated your responsibility for over a century, you place their fate in the hands of men and those you see as beasts."

The elf shook her head. "You have no idea. . . ."

"I have a very good idea, a wonderful one, mistress." Adrogans' eyes became slits. "You see the Gyrkyme as rapeget, the mating of elves with animals. You see the *Araftii* in much the same way as many Jeranese and Okrans see the Zhusk. I was gotten upon my mother by one of the Zhusk, but I was accepted by all sides."

Gilthalarwin snorted and waved his comment away dismissively. "Zhusks are demonstrably men, so your example does not pertain."

"But the Gyrkyme are demonstrably not *Araftii*. They might not be elves, either, but they certainly are not beasts."

The elf's dark eyes blazed at that suggestion. "The discussion is closed." She lifted her chin. "You will, I have little doubt, give us an assignment where we shall be killed because of our temerity."

Adrogans shook his head. "No. Go home."

"What?"

Even Beal looked a bit surprised at that command.

The general opened his hands. "Mistress, you have missed the point of this entire exercise. Chytrine wishes to shatter our unity so she can pick us apart piecemeal. Your subordination of good sense to race hatred aids her in this quest. I won't have it. You are free to go. I would only ask you give your parole that you will not fight against us and in her favor."

The elf's jaw dropped open. Adrogans was not certain if her shock was born of his impugning her honor and loyalty, or merely because she'd never expected a man to speak to her in such a way. He actually didn't care if it was either or both, or something else entirely.

He glanced at Beal. "Phfas will put his best archers with you. That should be fifty or so. The Nalisk Mountain

Rangers should also suffice. Please tell your people that their sacrifice shall inspire us all. Their courage will live forever with the Vorquelves they save."

Beal nodded, tossed Adrogans a salute, and turned to leave, but the elf caught hold of her shoulder. "Wait."

Adrogans raised an eyebrow. "Parting words, mistress?"

The elf's features sharpened. "What you ask of us is unthinkable."

"Ah, and asking my people to bleed and die isn't?"

Gilthalarwin shook her head. "You do not have nearly as much freedom as you pretend, General. You know that all of us will be torn apart by those who would judge us in the dawn's light."

"Then better to be damned for a winner." Adrogans pointed a finger at her. "Which would please you more? Never hearing your action criticized, or suffering all that criticism so just one voice of one survivor can be raised in protest at how unfairly you've been treated?"

The elf fairly trembled as she sorted thoughts from emotions. The elves' deep-seated hatred of the Gyrkyme was clearly irrational, for the Gyrkyme could do nothing to change their nature. At the same time, that hatred was as much a part of their lives as believing dawn would follow dark. The difference was that the hatred could be voided without changing the world's mechanisms.

And for the sake of justice and the hostages, it would have to be.

Gilthalarwin snorted, then set her shoulders. "You'll tell the Gyrkyme to fly clear of our areas of responsibility."

"Your archers are too good to mistake them for gibberers."

"General, you will tell the Gyrkyme to stay free of our areas."

Adrogans nodded slowly. "I will do that."

The elf bowed her head. "We'll be ready. You are still set to go at dusk?"

"You and the Gyrkyme see so well in the dark, the

operation is possible. We will prepare today, look as if we will go at dawn, but it will be tonight we go."

The elven archer nodded slowly. "You risk much in a night action."

"Lake tide will be running high, back-flooding the sewers. We'll get gibberers down in there and trap them. It won't be much, but it will help." Adrogans looked to Beal. "Pass the word to the warmages. Their ratting operations will commence mid-afternoon. By dawn we'll have Svoin."

From her post on the southern edge of Svoin, Beal mot Tsuvo watched the sun's disk touch the western mountains. In the highlands they'd have had an hour more of sunlight, but already the mountain shadows crept across the valley, caressing the far lakeshore, chasing ships to harbor. She watched the sunset, and the colors it streaked into the clouds; not worrying that she might not see another sunset, and taking great comfort from the lack of bloodred suffusing the clouds.

To the east trumpets sounded and the sieging force began its tightening of the circle around Svoin. Ponderous siege machines inched forward, approaching the piles of stones that had been placed to feed them. Trebuchets with their massive arms that would hurl huge stones to smash the walls rolled in. Beside them came ballistae, resembling giant crossbows, speeding spears, and long arrows that would rake the walls of defenders. And behind them, along cleared alleyways, crawled the siege towers, crowded with brave soldiers who would rush onto the battlements and sweep them of defenders, provided their towers were not smashed or burned before they could reach Svoin's defenses.

Smaller ballistae and catapults on the walls and in towers shot at the attackers. The marshy ground before Svoin did not serve the defenders well, since a stone would stick instead of bouncing madly through ranks, shattering limbs, pulping bodies. Even so, one stone struck a mantlet straight on, reducing it to a cloud of splinters and blood, then skipped further to crush another soldier.

On the far side of Svoin's east gate fire blossomed. A flailing gibberer fell flaming from the top. Others fought furiously, beating at the fire consuming their ballista, while overhead a Warhawk looped to celebrate his firecock's direct hit. Arrows reached up toward him, but slowed as they flew, and he contemptuously snatched one out of the air and hurled it back at the gibberers.

More firecocks exploded, and flaming missiles arced out at the siege towers. One tower caught and men leaped from it while warmages scurried around to extinguish the blaze. Defiant shouts from the walls and brave cheers from the attackers dueled before combatants were close enough to be fully engaged.

Lots of shouting arose on her front. A trebuchet and two ballistae had moved forward, supported by the Blackfeathers and the Nalisk Rangers, but her own people snarled and cursed as a siege tower refused to advance. It had moved not an inch since the start of the action. Men dug at the wheels and cursed, others scurried about with torches, and chaos reigned.

The gibberers on the walls hooted and hollered. Flights of elven arrows discouraged some, while the explosions of firecocks cleared whole portions of battlements. Drums pounded and gibberers moved along the walls toward the east gate as a ram rumbled down the road. Mantlets and shields covered the men dragging it forward and arrows soon studded them as the defenders fought to slow its advance.

The trebuchet on her front finally reached its position. Crews pounded in anchors while others hauled mightily on the cables and blocks that pulled down its long arm. At the base, beyond the pivot point, a wooden box filled with stones to act as a counterweight slowly rose. Still other men rolled a three-hundred-pound stone into position, then fixed a sling about it. The ends of the sling were attached to the trebuchet's arm, then a lanyard was pulled. The counterweight fell and the arm rose, then the stone arced through the night sky, all but invisible.

The stone struck with great impact, pulverizing itself and the wall block it struck. A merlon teetered a bit above the crater. Several gibberers had been knocked from their feet, but appeared otherwise unharmed. The city's walls, being as massive as they were and so well built, would require lots of pounding. Because the trebuchet would use missiles of different weights, because it would settle with each shot, because wood could crack and ropes fray, the chances of hitting the same spot over and over again were minimal.

The southern front in the siege could not credibly be thought a threat.

Which was exactly as intended since that front was never meant to get people *in*to Svoin, but get them out.

Three firecocks exploded in succession on the walls, which was the signal Beal had been waiting for. In the backlight she could see more gibberers shifted toward the east and this brought the hint of a smile to her face. She glanced at the Vilwanese warmage near her. "Adept Jarmy, get your people working now. That was the signal. We have no time to lose."

The triple explosion to the south caught Adrogans' eye and he focused on it. His flesh tingled, the *yrûn* of pain trickling into him the things being felt within the city. The thrashing and suffocating of gibberers in the sewers formed a basis onto which the overwhelming fear of the wretched humans trapped in Svoin had been layered. That fear had been brewing for days, since the men feared a slaughter by the gibberers, and the gibberers feared much the same by the attackers.

He pushed past the sensations and studied the battle.

The signal from the south meant the hostages had been gathered into the appointed place. He could only wonder at the battles waged by Guarnin clan Bravonyn in gathering them together. A chill ran through him as he imagined the keen wails of highland widows.

High on the walls near the gates, green fire blossomed into balls that streaked down at the ram. The sorcerous fire exploded against the shields, knocking men down, warping metal. Those who lived scrambled to their feet and back into position or withdrew, and others advancing in the ram's shadow surged forward, moving from pushing to pulling. The engine crept ever closer to the gate.

Ballistae swung around to pepper the area from which the magick had been launched. Sheaves of arrows shot up, some bouncing from merlons, others transfixing defenders. Other flights of arrows arced up high over the walls, to fall like rain amid the gibberers and vylaens.

Trebuchets hurled their stones, some hitting the gate and others slamming into towers. Firecocks exploded. One bolt of green fire lanced upward, instantly igniting a Warhawk who spiraled through death throes to slam into the ground and burn before the walls.

Adrogans started down the hill from which he had watched the siege begin and mounted his horse. He accepted his helmet from Phfas' hands, settled it over his head, and cinched the chinstrap up tight. By the time he reached his Horse Guards, the ram had reached the gate.

By the time they break it, we will be ready to plunge in. He drew a deep breath, then trotted his horse forward with the Horse Guards behind him. Beyond that gate would be death and pain, which minstrels would turn into valor and glory. For a fleeting second he wondered whether the ability to make that transformation marked them as fools or supreme magicians, then he dismissed such speculation and set his mind for war.

CHAPTER 59

Will worked in the rigging, helping to get the mainsail furled as they sailed into Port Gold. The passage itself had been relatively quick and even safe, despite making considerable sail during the night. The ketch's crew knew how to handle the boat very well, and accepted the added help. Will's role in going aloft was to keep the sailors away from the crow's nest, where Peri and Qwc had remained until just before dawn; then they saw the island and winged their way to it.

Resolute looked different in his disguise as a pirate, and even acted differently. He clearly knew his way around a ship, wore layered shirts with ease, and anticipated orders about the handling of the sheets. His blue hair appeared black in the night, and there were times when Will forgot who Resolute was. This was especially true when Resolute reeled off a string of nautical terms that could have been Aurolani for all Will could make heads or tails of them.

Make dry or wet of it would be the way sailors would say it, I think. Will shook his head and came down the lines to the deck, then worked forward to the bow. Port Gold, which was located on the northern coast of Wruona, had a natural harbor warded by a spit of land that came out from the east, leaving a narrow but deep channel to the west. The sailors had said that Tagothcha held sway until the bay, then its own *weirun* took over.

From the ocean, and in the haze of mist that had not yet burned off by mid-morning, Port Gold looked as if it were a colony of mushrooms growing up the trunk of a tree. The highest hill was to the northeast, with a stronghold built upon it. Curving down and around to the low point at the northwest of the semicircular harbor, the hills slowly shrank and softened. Landward there was no wall to mark the edge of the city, but the hillcrests limited Will's view beyond that. Further distant, to the interior, a volcano overgrown with jungle commanded the island's heart, and the smugglers had said a few tiny settlements had sprung up near smaller harbors.

Aside from the castle, which had been built of grey granite blocks, the habitation looked pretty crude. Some buildings had a log construction, but they sagged next to daub-and-wattle hovels that once had been whitewashed. The closest thing to a finished building appeared to be those built out of scraps from hulls.

As could be expected, the best, most solidly constructed thing in the town were the docks. A half-dozen large ships lay at anchor or tied up to the docks. Will didn't recognize any of them from the siege of Vilwan. But one—the grandest and most beautifully painted, with black from the waterline up to a red stripe and then white on up at the forecastle and afterdeck—that one he knew had to be Vionna's *Ocean Witch*.

Lombo ambled forward with Kerrigan in his wake. The Panqui pointed past the *Witch* to a slightly smaller ship painted in brown, green, and white, with a white shark on a red field emblazoned on the stern. "That ship, Lombo's ship."

The mage arched an eyebrow. "The *White Shark*? But the song I heard last night in Ooriz said Tremayne Reach is its captain."

Lombo snorted. "Put Lombo out for oceanswallow."

Will wasn't certain what the Panqui meant by ocean-swallow, but it didn't sound too nice. The Panqui didn't bother to explain and instead just sat perched at the bow like a gargoyle. The thief figured that if Reach was as super-stitious as any sailor he'd seen in Yslin, Lombo's return would be taken as a fell omen indeed.

The ketch lowered a small boat that came around, took up a bowline, and pulled the ship to the docks. Before the crew could tie her up, Lombo had bounded from the ship and scampered along the docks to the collection of ware-houses and taverns beneath the castle. The Panqui ducked into a darkened alley between two buildings and Will marked it well.

As fast as possible the company boiled from the ship and followed Will as he led them on into the streets. Even at mid-morning nothing much stirred, including rats and other vermin. The absence of the same near middens and in other alleys—combined with a few fleeting tracks in mud—marked Lombo's passage. As they neared his desti-nation, however, sound surpassed sight as the surest way of determining where he was.

It didn't hurt that he blazed the trail by tossing a sailor out through a doorway and into the alley before them. The tavern had no sign per se, just the bleached jaws of some huge shark. The plaster on the building had that same sort of weathered ivory color, save where urine stained it in lit-tle wedges, or the green of corroding copper from the roof sheathing dripped down the walls.

They fought an outrush of fleeing sailors to get into the tavern. The interior made it easy to tell what had happened. A straight line of overturned tables and scattered chairs—with sailors trapped beneath, draped over, or hiding be-hind them—ran from the doorway to the large round table in the back corner. At the back wall, Lombo had a slender, red-haired man by the throat, and the man had both hands wrapped around Lombo's left wrist. The man's feet dangled well above the ground and his face had taken on an unhealthy purple color.

Crow stretched a hand out. "Lombo, you'll choke him."

The Panqui nodded as the man's eyes flashed. "No choke."

The Panqui's hand convulsed once and the man's head jerked up about three inches. Will shivered as Lombo tossed the man aside. The way the man's head lolled about made Will mindful of the gibberer whose throat Dranae had crushed.

Crow winced. "The late, lamented Captain Reach?"

A couple of sailors nodded, but Lombo barked sharply. "No lament."

Sailors, unable to determine if that was just a statement or order, did their best to compose themselves and slowly set the tables to rights. The bartender, one-handed though he was, gathered up as many pewter tankards as he could in one go. Some sailors helped him, while others staunched wounds, and at least two of them tried to pop a third's shoulder back into its socket.

Lombo did his part by setting the big table up again, returning a massive chair to its upright position, then hauling Reach up and sitting him in a chair at the Panqui's left hand. Lombo even put a feathered cap back on the man's head, pressing it down so it would stay on. Continued pressure appeared to compact the man's neck enough that it kept his skull seated solidly.

Will remained in the shadows, with his back to the wall, in the corner nearest the door. He noted with some satisfaction that Orla took up a similar position on the door's other side. Resolute, Crow, and Alexia appropriated a table toward the middle of the tavern, while Dranae and Kerrigan seated themselves at the bar.

Lombo seated himself imperiously and adjusted his

throne, then summoned a sailor with the crook of a taloned finger. "Go, make *Shark* seanow."

The sailor, an ugly man whose face had clearly been kissed more by steel than lips, hesitated for a moment, then nodded and headed out. A couple others looked after him, and Lombo dismissed them with a wave of his hand. One or two of the remaining sailors pulled up chairs around peripheral tables, while others just drifted toward the door and out.

The bartender bowed deeply as he approached Lombo's table. "What would Cap'n Lombo be having?"

"Wait."

Will wondered what Lombo wanted to wait for, and his answer wasn't too long in coming. A man strode through the doorway within a half hour of Reach's death. Hard and lean, the man wore leather bracers on his forearms and a wide, iron-studded belt around his middle. Between knee-high boots and that belt he wore loose pantaloons of blue silk, which would have looked silly save for the deadly earnest in the man's stride. His head had been partly shaved, and tresses of long black hair had been gathered back into a queue that reminded Will of the warmages on Vilwan. Because he had no shirt, it was easy to see the rainbow-scaled snake tattoo curling around his body. Will couldn't see where it started, but the head rested on the man's left shoulder.

The man's hard-eyed gaze swept over Will and Orla, but they did not register as a threat. Will figured the man was very confident or stupid, since the two steps he took into the tavern left his back open. Will slid his right hand down to finger his bladestar pouch, but a slight glance from the man made him doubt he'd be able to draw and throw without being detected.

The man balled his fists. "Lombo, you shouldn't have come back. You should have stayed dead. Did you tire of Tagothcha's company, or did he of yours?"

"Talk, talk, Wheele." Lombo slowly rose from his chair and planted his fists on the table. "Alone now."

"And soon dead." The man's right hand swept up and began to weave through a complex series of motions. Off to the left, Kerrigan gasped, which brought Wheele's head around. He started to say something, probably connected to the puzzled look on his face, when a flash of gold hit Wheele on the right. It flowed over him like bowspray, at first contorting his back, then snapping him forward into a little heap.

Will got up to check him, but Orla was there first, waving Will back with her hand. "Stay off him, lad."

The thief stopped dead in his tracks, and half because of her warning. The other half came as the tattoo writhed and shifted a little. It didn't move much, but that was much more than Will wanted to see.

Lombo designated two sailors to drag Wheele off to Vionna, then settled back down to wait. The tavernkeeper brought him a huge bowl of ale, then set about making food for the rest of them. Will took his meal with Orla, much preferring her company to Resolute's.

"That tattoo, Orla, I've never seen anything like it."

The old woman nodded as she sopped up the yolk of an egg with a dark crust of bread. "They've been rumored for years, but that's the first I've seen."

"What was it?"

She frowned, then lowered her voice. "When the heroes went to fight Chytrine, a Vilwan-trained mage was with them. He had been sent to work for your grandfather because the elven prophecy was not precisely the first indication that the Norrington bloodline would be important. I don't think your grandfather had any inkling of how powerful Heslin truly was. Perhaps, in Svarskya, he caught a glimmer of it when Heslin, all alone, undid defensive magicks woven to protect the Vilwanese consulate.

"In that action, Heslin was badly wounded, perhaps even killed."

Will nodded. "He became one of the *sullanciri*."

"He did, indeed. He is known as Neskartu." Her brown

eyes focused distantly. "Chytrine, if portents are to be believed, set him to creating a school of magick akin to Vilwan deep in Aurolan. Men like Wheele, men who have some talent but no patience, they go there to learn the easy path to magick power."

The thief raised an eyebrow. "Easy path?"

"Oh, the avarice in your voice, Will." She shook her head. "The spells we teach on Vilwan are not the only way to get that effect. As a thief you know a lock can be picked or it can be smashed. Smashing it takes less skill, and might be more effective, but it comes with danger. So it is with magick. The Vilwanese spells are safe and require skill; the magery Wheele knows does not."

An explosive laugh and a blur of color bouncing into the tavern interrupted any further explanation of magick. A human dwarf, with foreshortened limbs and clad in a motley riot of bright colors, rolled, leaped, and danced through the tavern, then vaulted onto the seat of a chair. The dwarf tipped it over, letting the back rest against Lombo's table, then boldly strode onto it as if Adrogans himself.

"Captain Lombo!"

The Panqui smashed his palms down on the table, jouncing the dwarf into the air an inch or two. "Pet Nacker."

The dwarf bowed, then capered around in a circle before resting his fists on his hips. "I am bid by the most terrible Vionna, Queen of Wruona, to welcome you. Word of Reach's wreck has flowed into her ear and fits well and warmly. She bids you and your companions to sup with her as day bleeds into night."

"Lombo agrees. Deliver message."

The dwarf laughed aloud, then dropped into a cross-legged seat on the table. "I told her you would. I am to guide you. I'll wait here and save myself the long walk, so you and I can talk, and I can learn of your life after Vionna ordered it taken away."

* * *

Will shook himself out of a near stupor. As storytellers went, Lombo might have a lot of material to work with, but pulling it out of him two or three words at a time didn't make for a rousing performance. Nacker kept at it with a tenacity that surprised Will, making him quickly suspect that what the dwarf lacked in height he made up for in intellect.

The dwarf called an end to the day's chatter as midafternoon ebbed toward dusk. Lombo scooped Nacker up in an arm and led the procession that wound up the hill, through alleys and unpaved streets with eroded gullies on either side. The absence of cats and chickens and other animals, save skinny, whiny, quick dogs, made Will of a mind to wonder what sort of meal they'd be heading to in the stronghold.

He saw no sign of Peri or Qwc, but he had no doubt they soared through the night, unseen, above them.

From the bay they'd seen walltowers, but the stronghold itself occupied the entire hilltop, with thick walls supplementing sheer cliffs on the south and east sides. While coming up through the last switchback and the long tunnel piercing the walls, Will could see both how old the stronghold was, and why it would have been tough to take. The hilltop sunk away, so the main courtyard and tower didn't appear to be very tall when seen from below, but grew as you came up onto the hilltop. It struck Will that some of its levels might have been built into the hill itself.

His guess turned out to be correct, for they entered at the base of the tower and proceeded down tall steps to a vast room with vaulted ceilings and pillars to support them. A spiral staircase worked up into the entryway wall, leading to the tower's higher levels, but Will had nary a care for them. The large room served as Vionna's treasury, with gold bars stacked hither and yon, casks of coins filled to bursting, bolts of cloth draped over ornate furnishings, weapons racked, stacked, and piled, and a few works of art hung crookedly from walls or pillars.

In the center of it all a long table had been set with gold plates and cutlery. Multi-armed candelabras grew up like trees in three spots and candles burned at the ends of each branch. Crystal goblets in trios were stationed at each place, baskets laden with bread, platters with steaming heaps of meat filled the spaces between settings and the candles. Pirates in clean clothes stood by the walls as servants or guards, and Will wasn't certain he liked them in either role.

At the far end, standing before a tall, thronelike chair, a handsome woman beckoned them forward. Somewhere between Alexia and Orla in age, she had rich brown hair, long and unbraided, half hidden beneath a red kerchief. She was clad in a black silk blouse and silk pantaloons, and wore them much better than Wheele ever had. She smiled and waved gloved hands toward the chairs.

"Lombo, you'll be here beside me. Your friends, around us." Her smile smoothed out slightly. "I am, as you have surmised, Vionna."

Each of them moved to a place, leaving two open. The seat at her right hand remained empty until a tall, slender man wearing a turquoise tunic with a webwork of black over one side came down the stairs. He paused toward the bottom of them, looking up innocently as if surprised at their presence, then gave each of them a nod.

As the man looked at him, Will's mouth gaped, then he blushed and looked away. The mental image he'd carried for years of the Azure Spider merged with reality. Little details didn't quite match, like the man's dark hair being more fine than curly, but that didn't matter. The ease of his movements, the supple grace of his lean limbs, the hint of a smile he gave Alexia and Orla, all of it provided Will with a clear understanding of why Marcus hated the man.

Will started to speak, to introduce himself as one of

Marcus' protégés, but the words caught in his throat. Partly it was because of the sheer awe he felt being in the Azure Spider's presence—even his having rubbed elbows with royalty had not prepared him for this meeting. Beyond that, however, he realized the Azure Spider had paused precisely for effect. As innocent as it had appeared at first, his holding his position just a heartbeat too long revealed the truth to Will.

He may have been a hero of mine, but would a true hero do that? Resolute never would, nor Crow nor Alyx or any of his companions. That revelation shook Will and slowly closed his mouth.

Oblivious to what had run through Will's mind, the Azure Spider swept to Vionna's side and kissed her cheek.

"Forgive me for being late."

Vionna nodded. "This is the Azure Spider, and the reason you're here."

"Lombo came for ship. Lombo's ship."

The pirate queen shook her head. "You'll forgive me, Lombo, but I do not believe in coincidences."

She reached out and pulled a small silver cover off a dish at her place. Resting there on a bed of green velvet was a sapphire the size of a goose egg. Will knew his gems and knew that even discounting the gold setting, the deep blue stone was worth a king's ransom and then some.

Vionna lifted it in her left hand and held it up so Will could see the candlelight spark a cross in it. "Yes, this is the Lakaslin portion of the DragonCrown. This is why you have come to Wruona. You might even be able to leave with it."

Resolute's eyes tightened. "Name a price."

"The price is not for me to name. That's up to you, my guests." She nodded once, then her smile broadened. "Ah, we are complete. Now we can begin."

Will saw something coalesce from the shadows at the top of the stairs. Slender, but not so tall, wearing a cloak that appeared to be fledged with little licking tongues of flame.

"It's rather simple, you see. For the DragonCrown to go with thee, just outbid me." The *sullanciri* Nefrai-laysh sketched a bow, then descended. "This auction, of course, I will win, so, pray thee, let the bidding begin."

CHAPTER 60

A century earlier men had fashioned the gates of Svoin from thick slabs of oak, overlaid and cross-braced. Long iron bolts, set every six inches, held the wood together, while pitch had sealed it and time had stained it. Behind the gate three separate stout bars set in massive iron brackets held the gate closed. The doors had taken no damage during the Aurolani siege, since, at that time, men had opened them, believing promises of gentle treatment in exchange for cooperation.

When the ram reached the gate, the men who had been pulling it came round behind to push. The ram itself was a simple affair, little more than wheels and a framework that suspended a long log on cables. The log had been capped with iron to give it weight, and the iron had jagged teeth twisting this way and that to let it nibble into the wood. Over it all had been built a roof that already bristled with arrows and even burned in a couple of places.

The soldiers working the ram tugged back on ropes to swing the ponderous piece of wood away from the gate.

Ropes slid through rough hands as the log reached the apex of its rearward arc, then swooped forward to pound the gate hard. The blow resounded loudly, as if an ax had bit deeply into a stump. The log shivered and rebounded, with the men hauling back to aid that rearward momentum, then released it again.

The iron head slammed heavily into the gate, and the teeth did their job, exposing white wood and half-uncovered iron bolts. Again and again it bit, not terribly deeply, but as it came away splinters and wood chips littered the ground. Left alone it would gnaw its way through, though the sheer force of the blows could easily rip the gates free of the walls before its hunger had been sated.

Defenders did all they could to stop the ram, but ballistae shots made the ramparts above the gate a very dangerous place to fight from. Firecocks washed it in flames, and arrows swept away defenders. Firepots lobbed from further away seldom made it to the ram itself and arrows shot at long range did strike some soldiers, but rarely penetrated armor.

The siege towers inexorably crept closer as trebuchets and catapults flung stones high into the sky. They crashed down, splitting merlons, crushing rock, wearing away the stone walls. Adrogans knew that with so little time they could never bring the walls down fully, but he didn't want that. Collapsed walls would be too difficult to repair in time to defend the city from any sort of counterattack. What he needed, and what by Arel it appeared he might get, was enough of a breach at the top of a wall for the defenders to have trouble opposing the men in the siege towers.

A sharp crack and the scream of metal focused Adrogans on the gate. The right side gate had begun to sag and the upper hinge had torn free. Another pounding blow, and another, widened the gap at the top. Men shouted and shifted the ram a foot or two right, concentrating on that door. Each hammering blow shivered it.

Gaps appeared between the timbers, then the weight of the doors became too much for the final hinge.

Shrieking like an eviscerated frostclaw, the hinge tore away and the gate sagged back. The other hinges held for a heartbeat, then pulled free of the stone, allowing the entire gate to flop backward. The leftmost section ground against the entryway's side, so it never lay flat but the right side did, crushing gibberers that had been waiting behind it.

The men at the ram shoved the engine forward one more time, filling the opening. While the wheels couldn't get up and onto the downed door, the ram itself acted as a partial plug. Some defenders squirted out around the edges, only to be cut down as soldiers brought swords to hand.

The trickle of defenders soon stopped, and Adrogans knew why. He signaled and a trumpet blared. The men at the ram pulled the siege engine aside and there, waiting at the far end of the tunnel, stood a phalanx of gibberers with shields and longknives. They clogged the furthest end of the tunnel, and slowly piled debris before them. They meant to hold up any attacking force, trapping it in the tunnel, so the warriors in the chamber above the tunnel could use the murderholes to pour arrows and boiling lead down on the attackers.

Two small ballistae had come up as the ram was pulled aside. Both shot into the tunnel, launching thick spears and sheaves of arrows. Transfixed defenders went down in droves. More appeared to fill their ranks, and the explosion of a firecock behind them did kill some, but it did not disperse them.

Adrogans drew his sword and raised it aloft. *Only one thing will clear that hole.* "On me, Horse Guards, form up. The liberation of Svoin is at hand."

Beal watched as the warmages worked feverishly and their efforts paid handsomely. The sorcerers heated larger stones, and Zhusks created a small breeze that sent air over the stones to fill sealed silken sacks. These sacks rose, carrying with them ropes, which were attached to a length of stout cable. At the far end of the cables a Gyrkyme pulled, tugging the floating line toward Svoin.

Both cables streamed out from the top of the siege tower. That tower had never been meant to move an inch, but instead had been built in place with logs driven deep into the ground for stability. Each line was over six hundred feet in length and weighed a considerable amount in and of itself. The balloons lightened the load for the Gyrkyme, who would anchor the heavy rope in the town, then her people would take up the slack in the line.

The Blackfeathers advanced toward the wall, shortening their ranges and feathering any defender who so much as flicked an ear in the open. The trebuchet continued to loft stones, battering a section of wall in hopes of cutting off defenders. Ballistae shot and shot again, finding fewer and more elusive targets, but treating quite harshly those they did hit.

A Gyrkyme came swooping low from the city and sliced a dagger through the rope holding the first balloon to the line. As he continued cutting them loose, Beal snapped an order and her clansmen rushed to the siege tower. They took up the thick end of the line and began to pull. Their booted feet churned the ground into mud, but inch by inch the slack left the rope.

The top of the tower braces were set and the rope was tightened off. A trumpet blared then and was answered from the Svoin building into which the hostages had been gathered. Only the twitching of the line told Beal what was happening until she saw the first person sweep past a fire burning on the walls. Clinging to both ends of a rope, hanging below the strung line, a Vorquelf came sliding along to freedom with her skirts snapping and flapping out behind her.

The wooden gate just below the uppermost level of the

siege tower flopped down. Two men grabbed her as she reached it, and a third freed her hands of the rope. The metal slide, which had been fashioned from a bracer, was snapped back off the line and tossed up to the top of the tower where a Gyrkyme waited to fly it back into Svoin.

Beal joined the others in laughing and shouting. The only thing the plan had going for it had been audacity, and the audacity had paid off. Clan Bravonyn had gathered the hostages in one building and the ropes had been anchored there on its roof. Because the building was taller than the walls and the tower, the slide worked. One by one, Vorquelves slid through the night to freedom.

As the Jeranese Horse Guards moved into position to strike, two catapult crews levered their machines around and loaded logs thickly swathed in oil-soaked rags. Torches ignited the missiles, then the catapults hurled them flaming into the night. Thick black smoke trailed in their wakes, obscuring stars, but the explosion of sparks marked their landings. Both hit true, bouncing off the downed gates, lodging themselves firmly in the middle of the tunnel.

Phfas came up and extended a hand toward the tunnel. A slight breeze picked up, fanning the flames and drawing from the burning rags a thick cloud of black smoke. Much of it rose to pour up through the murderholes, while the rest billowed along to fill the tunnel.

The Savarese Knights, three hundred strong, trotted forward under cover of the pall and formed up in ranks ten abreast. The first company moved to the fore and, a hundred yards from the gate, kicked their horses into a charge. Only the first rank had their lances deployed, as the ranks following could not be sure in the smoke what they would be stabbing. With visors on their helmets closed, the heavily armored Knights vanished into the smoke in a curiously echoed clatter of hooves.

Behind them came the next company, and the next, the first of three legions thrown into battle.

A Gyrkyme Warhawk swooped low from the sky and screamed that the Knights were through, but Adrogans already knew that. He felt the shock and pain of the gibberers being stabbed and thrust aside, the choking of their lungs, the stinging slashes of swords, and the ripping jolts of lances piercing flesh.

Adrogans gave his horse some heel and led his legion forward, moving into a gallop at the gate. Hoofbeats thundered as his horse raced over the gate, then a break and a sharper, harder sound as shoes met cobblestones and sparks flew. In the smoke he could see nothing to guide him, so he went by feel, directing the horse toward the center of the channel. The clatter and crash, ringing peal of steel on steel grew louder, then suddenly he was through, his eyes tearing, into the streets of Svoin.

Adrogans reined his horse left and charged down South Crescent Road, which ran inside the wall. His saber rose and fell, slashing at the few fleeing gibberers. They died obligingly and quickly, screams dwindling fast, and on he raced.

A thousand yards along the road, heading due east, he found his target. Gibberers choked the road, intent on assaulting the building from which the two ropes extended over the walls. As he approached, one gibberer managed to loop a rope over a line, which stopped a Vorquelf's slide to freedom. The Vorquelf hung there as stones and sticks flew up, and an arrow pierced her thigh. She screamed. Men shouted at her from the building to hold on, but she could not. She fell into the teeming mass of Aurolani troops and they tore her apart.

Her death agony exploded in Adrogans, leaving him numb and cold as his horse plunged into the gibberkin mob. The sheer impact of a galloping horse slamming into creatures snapped spines and broke ribs. Adrogans slashed to his right, kicked to his left, even raked one gibberer's throat with a spur. He cut at the looped rope, then yanked it free, not caring about the clawed hands scrabbling at his legs.

Then the rest of the Horse Guards hit the crowd in a wave of flesh and metal. Bodies spilled into bodies. Horses reared, lethal hooves flashing. One kick lifted a gibberer and tossed him a dozen feet backward, while his dented helmet and much of his skull went twice as far.

The Bravonyns in the building cheered as the Horse Guards lifted the siege on their position. Up on the city wall a vylaen stood, preparing a spell. He jerked as two arrows crossed in his back, punching through his chest and pitching him off the rampart.

The gibberers broke and dashed into alleys or sprinted down streets. Adrogans dispatched riders to kill those they could, then scout out the city. His intelligence from the Vorquelves had been good but old, and while he was fairly certain the walls had demanded three-quarters of the defenders in the city, that still left a battalion gathered somewhere. He needed to find it and destroy it before the leader could disperse it with orders to fire the city and slaughter the inhabitants.

Adrogans quickly dismounted and entered the building being used to evacuate the hostages. He passed through the packed crowd of Vorquelves, doing his best to ignore haunted faces, and worked his way to the roof. He took quick comfort in the fact that he saw no golden glow betokening buildings burning, but he had no confidence that that situation would last.

A Guarnin captain tossed him a hasty salute. "They're going fast, General. We've lost a few—to arrows, to just being weak and dropping off lines—but most are escaping two a minute, each line."

Adrogans nodded, then called out to a Gyrkyme who landed to drop off more of the bracers. "I need you to over-fly the city. I need to know where the enemy is gathering."

The Warhawk nodded and set off, quickly vanishing in

the night. As he waited for her return, Adrogans watched Vorquelves come to the roof, get secured on the lines, and launched. Some screamed in terror, and a few in delight, which caused smiles to blossom all around.

The Warhawk returned and pointed toward the center of the town. "They gather there, General. If we had more firecocks . . ."

Adrogans waved her remark away. "Go east. Find General Caro and give him my compliments. Tell him they are in the market square and will be oriented south. Tell him to use the Kingsmen as well."

She launched herself into the night again and Adrogans made his way back down to the street. He dispatched two riders to bear the same message to Caro, then gathered his legion and headed north toward the market square. His troops filled the road five abreast, expanding to ten as the streets widened near the market.

It surprised Adrogans that the windows above remained shuttered and darkened. The lack of curiosity of the inhabitants puzzled him. He shivered when considering that most places might be empty. Or, worse, that the population's spirits had been so shattered that nothing could bring them hope.

At the edge of the market he halted his troops. Three hundred Aurolani infantry filled the market square. Most were gibberers, with a vylaen for every ten. Scattered throughout were a handful of hoargoun. Adrogans suspected the giants had been in residence in the huge temple to Erlinsax at the west end of the square. The open arched doorway would have admitted them without having to lower their heads.

Adrogans rode forward of his line. "Throw down your weapons, strike your banners."

The gibberers hooted and hollered at his command. Their legion banners were boosted higher in the air and waved, part defiance, part taunt. Vylaens snapped orders and ranks closed. Shields and spears deployed on the front facing him. One hoargoun bent down and then straightened up with a long granite curbstone in his hands, ready to hurl. In their movements Adrogans almost read a nobility, but that vanished with his recollection of the Vorquelf falling to her death.

Then Caro's Horse Guards burst into the square from the east, catching the Aurolani formation in the flank. The charge drove a huge wedge into the formation. The hurled curbstone did take down several horses and riders, but couldn't blunt the attack. Vylaens shouted more orders, trying in vain to reorient their troops.

Then the Okrans Kingsmen hit from the north. The Kingsmen literally sheered off a third of the Aurolani battalion, driving it back toward the temple, then encircling it and shrinking it until finally even the last embattled hoargoun went down.

Adrogans did deploy his Horse Guards, but only let them police the square's perimeter, picking off fleeing Aurolani troops. His people could have added nothing to the main fight and would have only robbed Caro of a full sense of victory.

The Jeranese general slowly let a breath out. *It would appear we did win here this evening, and the butcher's bill won't be too high.* The next move would be Chytrine's, and Adrogans shivered. *The price exacted for winning the city was light, but the charge for keeping it, I have the feeling, will be very dear indeed.*

CHAPTER 61

Will stared at the creature standing opposite Vionna at the far end of the table. *That thing is my father?* He shivered, feeling cold ooze into his marrow. As much as he had come to accept being a Norrington, and even *the* Norrington, having the orphan's dream of some wonderful father coming to claim him replaced by having to acknowledge this thing as his father came hard.

He shook his head. *That's the thing that consumed my father. I refuse to be his son.*

Alexia, who stood on Will's right, between him and Lombo, turned to face Vionna. Will took that as a sign of her trust in him, for she wore a dagger at the small of her back. It would have been simple to draw it and plunge it into her. *If I were my father's son . . .*

The princess lifted her chin. "You want us to name a price for that portion of the DragonCrown? How do you know we will pay? How can you trust *her* agent to pay?"

Vionna seated herself in the tall chair and leaned back, bringing her booted feet up onto the table. She held the sapphire before her as if it were a crystal goblet of wine, turning it to admire the light moving in it. "Well, Alexia, I would trust you if you gave me your word—and if you remained behind as my guest until the price was delivered. As for Chytrine, I have ample evidence that she rewards those who serve her rather well."

Crow forced a laugh. "You need only look down the table to see your reward."

The *sullanciri* bowed his head graciously. For a heartbeat light played in those blue eyes as it did in the sapphire, then they went dead. "To rule all that is small, or a small part of the all. One option to choose, one option to lose."

Resolute stood opposite Alexia, between the Azure Spider and Crow. He glanced at the *sullanciri*. "Is that your bid, then, a portion of all Chytrine will conquer?"

"Still full of unrest, fury clogging your breast, Resolute seeks to contest where acquiescence is best." Nefrai-laysh slowly grinned, then lifted a turtle to see what awaited him at his place. "If the bid pleases her heart, it's good for my start."

"It pleases my heart greatly, thank you." Vionna lifted an eyebrow and looked to Alexia. "Your turn."

"He bids the future, a future he does not own. Chytrine's conquests will be contested; she will lose."

"But not if she has this, will she?" Vionna laughed lightly. "Here is the trick. Even if I were to give this to you, Alexia, and your fine band of heroes here, you would never use it. You would never command dragons, and without them, you could not prevail against Chytrine and her allies. So, yes, he promises that which he does not have, which his Mistress does not have, but is more likely to get if she is given this portion of the crown."

Will shivered again as the cold calculation of Vionna's words sank into him. Across the table the Azure Spider listened and nodded, his expression betraying no surprise at her words. He had clearly heard them before, had reckoned on their value, and, it seemed clear to Will, had agreed with her reasoning even before the robbery. In fact, in the absence of such a discussion, Will could not imagine the Azure Spider having undertaken such an adventure.

That portion of the DragonCrown in Chytrine's hands would mean suffering and death for thousands. Stories of the misery of Svoin's residents, of the melting of the town of Porasena, even visions of the dragons at Vilwan, all these made clear to Will the evil that Chytrine could wreak with that piece of the DragonCrown. To think about that and further undertake to get it into her hands marked a level of depravity Will had not heard of outside terror tales for children—and those were all clearly fiction.

Crow usurped Alexia's answer by pointing past Orla and Kerrigan toward the *sullanciri*. "So you would become like him, willingly supping on the suffering of the world? He was once a man, you know, an honorable man."

The *sullanciri* looked up from a picked-over bird carcass and snarled. "By a friend laid low, as well you know. It was quite the blow, Crow, and you can't say it's not so. A man I once was, and ne'er again will be, but better to be this, than to skulk about as thee."

Nefrai-laysh sucked on his fingers from where he'd been tearing meat from the fowl, then nodded. "Have they no bid, no treasure hid, to sate avarice thine? Then end the game, a winner name; the gem goes to Mistress mine."

It occurred to Will, in a heartbeat, that Vionna had never intended to auction off the gem. Nefrai-laysh had arrived to take possession of it. Vionna would next offer them to Chytrine's lieutenant. And for this band to fall to Chytrine would be even more of a blow to their allies than the loss of the crown fragment.

He couldn't allow that to happen.

Even as he reached his conclusion, a whirring buzz sounded in the chamber. In the corner of his left eye Will caught a flash of green as Qwc flew between the ankles of a pirate at the stairs, then vanished beneath the table. Will raised his right hand as the Spritha popped up before

Vionna, beating his wings furiously as he stopped, then spat a mouthful of webbing in her face.

The pirate screeched and clawed at her face as her chair tipped and began to fall. Qwc neatly plucked the gem from her hand and started to fly back, but the weight of the gold turned his flight into a fall, which landed him with a thump on the platter that had held the gem. The Azure Spider clapped the turtle back down, trapping the Spritha.

That would have ended the brief drama save for Will sliding the dagger from the sheath on Alexia's back. In one fluid motion he whipped the blade forward. The knife was a thick, cumbersome thing with no balance at all, but it flew as Will wanted it, smacking the *sullanciri* full in the face. Nefrai-laysh staggered back, more from surprise than hurt since the hilt had hit flat across his face, then laid his right hand to a swordhilt and drew a longsword that moaned piteously.

Resolute swung a fist, catching the Azure Spider full in the chest and knocking him back away from the table. The Spider went down, but slewed his legs around and came back up. He drew a swept-hilted longsword with an extraordinarily narrow blade, then lunged at Resolute. The Vorquelf parried with one of his longknives, and lunged with the one in his left hand. The Azure Spider danced back adroitly and parried, carving a little curl of steel from Resolute's blade.

Crow swept past Kerrigan and Orla, bringing Tsamoc to hand. He intercepted the cut Nefrai-laysh had meant to kill the warmage, then parried it high and chopped back down at Nefrai-laysh's right leg. The *sullanciri* retreated quickly, but not quite quickly enough. Crow's straight blade nicked him, spraying black blood that smoked when it hit the ground.

"I bleed, I plead, but you will die, say I." Chytrine's creature attacked, whipping his blade about quickly, as if it were a willow wand. Crow parried one cut and let another slip past his left flank. He tried to spin away from the reverse slash, but bumped into Kerrigan, knocking the corpulent youth against the table. Nefrai-laysh's slash sliced through Crow's multiple shirts, tracing a thin and reddening line over his right hip.

"Ah, just for thee, a scar to cross the three!" the *sullanciri* brayed.

Kerrigan's bashing into the table proved providential. Lombo had already turned away and had armed himself with two bags of gold coins, which he used as flails against several pirates. Alexia had drawn her sword and engaged Vionna, likewise moving away from the table. Dranae, to Will's left, had picked up an iron candlestand and was using it to duel with two pirates while Orla thrust her right hand at another, triggering a gout of brilliant flame that engulfed him for a heartbeat.

The only member of the pirate crew left unaccounted for was Nacker, who had bounded up on the table. He grabbed the turtle covering Qwc in his right hand, and had a serving fork in the left, ready to spit the Spritha. Kerrigan's bounce against the table shifted it enough to topple candelabra and the dwarf. The turtle came off, Qwc spat a mask of webbing into Nacker's face, then looked at Will. "Help Qwc, quick."

Will grabbed the edge of the table in both hands and vaulted himself up to kick the dwarf squarely in the chest with both feet. The dwarf grunted and flew past Resolute as the Vorquelf trapped the Azure Spider's blade between his longknives, then shoved the slighter man back. Reaching out, Will grabbed the platter on which Qwc lay and slung it down the table to Kerrigan.

The spinning Spritha's scream all but eclipsed Will's shout of "Help Qwc." The thief scrambled to his feet on the table and grabbed the turtle in both hands before leaping off. He brought the turtle down with all his might, clanging it over the Azure Spider's head. The man groaned, then collapsed as Will's body slammed into him. Will rolled off the legendary thief and came up into a crouch with his back against a thick stone column.

At the head of the table Vionna and Alexia dueled. Their blades matched in length, giving Alyx an advantage in reach. Vionna turned her lunges, but only at the last moment, and more than once retreated, trading ground for whole skin. Ground quickly surrendered however, as her retreat backed her against an open chest of gold coins. She sat down abruptly and Alexia approached with her blade leveled at the woman's throat.

"Yield or die."

Nefrai-laysh drove at Crow, coming in at an angle that kept the man trapped against the edge of the table. Crow parried one slash, but kissed the table with his blade as he moved to block the next blow. The *sullanciri*'s next cut would have laid him open hip to hip, but Resolute lunged forward, sliding on his knees, and deflected the blow. The Aurolani's blade sliced through the longknife as if it were smoke, then came up and around in an overhand blow that pared three-quarters of Resolute's other longknife away.

Resolute threw the hilts at Nefrai-laysh. The *sullanciri* batted one wide, but the other thumped against his chest. Resolute twisted to his feet and backed away, but Chytrine's plaything advanced, slashing. Resolute leaped away again and again, but each cut came closer to separating him up from down.

Will hooked a toe beneath the guard on the Spider's sword and kicked it up into the air. Rising, he grabbed the blade's curiously leather-wrapped forte in his left hand. He felt a sting where his last two fingers touched bare metal, then tossed the sword to Resolute. "Catch."

The sword was not the only thing flying through the air. Vionna flicked her left hand forward, launching a trove of gold coins into Alexia's face. The princess batted some away with her free hand, but others hit her. She recoiled from them and her advancing foe, then caught a heel on

Vionna's toppled chair. Alexia went down, hitting her head hard on the stone floor, and the pirate queen loomed up over her, with her sword poised to impale the princess.

It likely would have spitted Alexia, save that Crow grabbed one of the candelabra and lunged, catching Vionna's swordhand in the device's tangled arms. Hot wax splashed over the pirate's face. She spun, tearing the candelabra out of Crow's grasp. He kept coming, slamming his body into hers and pitching her into and over the treasure chest. It slid down, half burying her in a shower of gold.

Resolute snatched the sword from the air in his left hand and turned Nefrai-laysh's next cut easily. The Vorquelf's right fist came up, clipping the *sullanciri*'s chin and driving him backward. The dark creature stumbled back, bumping into the table. A feral grin twisting across his face, he parried Resolute's next lunge with his left hand, grabbing the blade. Nefrai-laysh hissed as Resolute slid the blade free of his grip, then smeared black blood over the dining table. For a half second the black puddle smoked, then it burst into flame, and fire ran the length of the table.

Nefrai-laysh gave the elf a quick nod. "Another piece of prophecy has been given to thee. Be wise, be well, for in agony you will dwell. This is true: death in pyre, born in fire."

The *sullanciri* snapped his head backward and brought his heels up. His cloak merged with the flames on the table, then he vanished, leaving the table burning and thick smoke gathering.

"Resolute, some help here." Crow had Alexia on her feet, with one hand thrown over his shoulder, but she was all loose-limbed. The elf edged past the table to get her, while Lombo and Dranae rushed forward and scattered the pirates standing between them and the stairs. Orla followed them, and Kerrigan trailed behind her. He still carried the platter with Qwc on it, and the Spritha hugged himself tightly to the sapphire.

Will headed out as swiftly as he could, which meant he

paused only to loop a couple of gold chains around his neck and pluck up a leather pouch that felt and weighed as if full of gemstones. Deciding to act the rear guard, he drew a sword from among those stored in the treasury and prided himself on the fact that his choice had not been the most ornate, but a bit more functional than that.

Will followed the others up the stairs and out into the courtyard. The guards at the gate gave them no trouble and Will wondered why until he saw Peri crouched over their bodies. The Gyrkyme crossed to where the princess hung between Resolute and Crow and peered up into Alexia's eyes.

"More will die for this!" Peri slashed taloned fingers through the air. "More, many more."

"She had a knock on the head, Perrine; she'll be fine. We need you to get the DragonCrown fragment out of here." Crow pointed with his free hand toward Kerrigan and his treasure.

The Gyrkyme shook her head. "I won't leave her."

"You must, Peri." Crow let his voice soften slightly. "You know she would tell you to take it. She'd entrust it to you as she was entrusted to your father."

"Yes, but remember what happened to the other Gyrkyme that tried to escape with a piece of the DragonCrown. They died in Svarskya."

Resolute nodded. "But they were not Preyknosery Ironwing's daughter."

Peri's head came up at that. "Where do I take it?"

"Where, Qwc knows where." The Spritha stood on the platter and hefted the sapphire onto his shoulder, then staggered back against Kerrigan's chest. "We fly, Perrine, Qwc knows where."

The Gyrkyme took the gem from him, then narrowed her amber eyes. "If something happens to her . . ."

"Never." Crow shook his head adamantly. "I promise."

Orla patted Perrine on the back. "Get going. You've not a moment to lose."

The Gyrkyme and the Spritha launched themselves sky-ward, then circled the tower once and dipped down to the south. They vanished beneath the far wall. Will nodded, happy to see them away, then looked to his companions. "How do we get out of here?"

Lombo let loose with a thunderous hooting so loud that Will clapped his hands over his ears. In the distance a half-dozen similar howls answered him. "Lombo's ship."

"*Your* ship? I think not." Wheele, backed by a crowd of pirates, strode through the tunnel and stopped at the courtyard's edge. "Orla, your master detected the traces of your magick on me. He sends his compliments."

Orla moved forward, interposing herself between Wheele and the others. "Stay behind me. He's mine."

"He said you were brave, more brave than intelligent. I'll enjoy telling him how you died." The man laughed and drew a slender wand from the top of his right boot. "I had this wand from his hand for me to use against Vilwan spawn."

He spun the wand between his fingers, then snapped it into his palm and thrust it at her. A green jet of flame lanced out at her, but Orla gestured casually and deflected it to the ground. It ignited the granite there, pooling for a moment, leaving dancing flames to splash their shadows over the courtyard's walls.

Orla slowly began to circle, only a quarter of the way around, then pivoted on her right foot. Her left foot came forward, toward Wheele, and her left hand came up. A gold spark flew at him as if it were a bee intent on a blossom. Her right hand also came up and flicked a scattering of other sparks toward the tunnel.

They hit the walls, rebounding, splitting and spitting, then swooped down into the pirates. The first spark touched a man and he burst into flame. Another who parried the spark with his ax found its blade molten and dripping. The pirates shrieked and ran, including the burn-ing man.

The spark hit Wheele square in the chest, and the serpent's head darted its tongue out to lick the magick up. The man shivered for a second, then burst into flames. But he laughed aloud. "You make it too easy, Orla, as he said you would. You've sacrificed yourself for your friends, and I shall have them, too."

Wheele flicked the wand at her and a jagged green bolt of lightning stabbed her through her bowels. It tossed her back against Kerrigan. She grabbed the silver platter and tore it from his grasp as she fell at his feet.

Kerrigan screamed in fury and flashed both his palms at Wheele. A starfall of gold sparks swirled and curled out at the man. They tightened down into a coruscating lash of light that flayed some flame away, but mostly was sucked into the fire. Wheele's magick blazed more furiously.

"Your apprentice is a fool, Orla. He watches you and does not learn. Your magick cannot harm me."

"My magick, no," she gasped as she pointed a quavering hand at him. "But yours . . ."

With the jerked and pained gesture, Orla sent the silver platter riding a wave of magick through the air. It spun slowly, easily, but always with a purpose, soaring, not drifting toward him. It picked up speed as it flew, turning faster, with the firelight flashing from it, over Wheele, the keep, and the walls. The platter tipped upright at the last moment, passing broadside through Wheele's fiery armor.

It was in that last second when Wheele realized the threat.

The metal glowed red, then white. It hit him heavily, smothering him like a wet sheet. It poured thickly over his head and shoulders like molten wax. The man's scream was not enough to bubble the fluid metal, but his tortured expression did contort it. Viscous silver flooded his mouth and splashed down his body, then flames flared. Black smoke billowed around him for a moment, then vanished along with most of the flames. Wheele's smoking corpse knelt in the center of the courtyard with its head thrown back and its silent silver scream pitched at the cold stars.

His wand clattered to the stone.

Lombo scooped Orla up into his arms. "The wand, the wand," she murmured before she went limp.

Will beat her apprentice to it, then chased him from the citadel. He resisted the temptation to outdistance the blubbering mage, and likewise didn't thwack him across his ample buttocks with the wand. Instead, he tucked the wand into his belt, turned to watch their backtrail, and brandished his sword at any shadow that looked the least bit menacing. Because of his efforts or in spite of them, the company made it to the docks unmolested and set off quickly on their escape.

CHAPTER 62

Kerrigan sat on the *White Shark*'s afterdeck, his legs crossed, his hands clutching a slender ebon staff across his knees. He stared intently at the luminous wake trailing the ship, seeking any sign of pursuit. His line of sight had no impediment as the taffrail and several posts had been torn away, leaving a gaping hole between him and the sea. There had been no ships sighted since they left Port Gold's harbor, but he dared not let his vigilance slacken.

Behind him crewmen grunted and strained, lines creaked, and the sails and pennants snapped as the *Shark* headed east. Flying through the city, they had encountered no trouble and had reached Lombo's old ship quickly enough. Perrine and Qwc had gotten there before them and released the four Panqui who had been held in chains as galley slaves. They slew the men loyal to Wheele and Reach, and the rest of the crew gladly decided to sail under Captain Lombo again.

The Panqui had carried Orla below to the largest cabin and had laid her in a berth. Kerrigan had followed, hoping to heal her, but Orla roused herself enough to send him back up on the deck. "Stop the ships, Adept, or we are lost."

On deck it had been close to panic. Sailors dropped into the galley benches and took up the oars to get the ship moving, while others cut the anchor lines or lowered sails. Lombo barked orders loud and fast. The crew responded admirably, and the ship got under way, leaving the harbor by the light of the flaming stronghold.

Kerrigan had felt his face burn shamefully. He had clearly seen that Orla's spell had not worked to destroy Wheele. Why did he assume that more and more powerful of the same would do it? As he had watched the man's sorcerous armor incorporate his magick and grow stronger, he had searched for spells that could counter it, snuffing the fire and Wheele, but there were so many choices and Orla lay dying and . . .

The Adept had shaken himself, determined to make amends. As the *Shark* pulled away, he moved to the after-deck and studied the ships. He forced himself to be calm, to ignore all the chaos around him, then reached out with the spell he'd used to destroy the other pirate ship. He chose Vionna's *Ocean Witch* as his first victim. He did not pluck it out of the water, as he needed to preserve his strength to deal with each ship in turn. Instead he took hold of the mast and started it shaking as if it were beset by an incredible gale. He worried it, working it back and forth, then, with a big push, drove it down through the keel.

Water geysered up through the holes in the hull and deck. Sailors scattered, diving for the bay as the first ship began to wallow. Kerrigan shifted his attention to the next largest and the next, tearing away rudders, snapping masts, crushing the galley deck, and breaking oars apart. After that he tightened his right hand into a fist and pounded it down on his leg. With each blow a piece of pier exploded, chasing sailors to dry land.

His last blow, delivered through tear-filled eyes, had

crushed the taffrail. Lombo had grabbed his hand before he could further smash the ship and held on until Kerrigan's rage had fled, taking with it his strength. Sobs had wracked him, so Lombo scooped him up and carried him below, placing him in a chair beside Orla.

Part of Kerrigan wanted to fall asleep, but he didn't let himself. Instead he levered himself to his feet and cast a diagnostic spell over his mentor. The impressions he drew from her were of a severe burn, akin to the sort of wound one would create by casting a lightning spell at a target. Kerrigan had cast the same diagnostic spell on a rabbit that had been hit by such a spell and felt similar damage.

That kind of damage he could have healed, but before he could start working on her, Orla's eyes flickered open. "No, Kerrigan."

He'd blinked. "I want to fix you."

"No. Check again. Traces of magick."

Kerrigan had cast another spell on her, one used for detecting magick, and he did find some residual magick in her. That surprised him, because a combat spell like the lightning spell couldn't have left an impression behind. *Traces are only left when something is enchanted.*

He switched to a forensic spell, one that probed in faint degrees. It tested the edges of enchantment and was employed by scholars on Vilwan as a way to puzzle out the nature of enchantments on all manner of items. In casting the spell he immediately got a sense of two spells lingering there. One was active, slowly poisoning her, and the other had quiet tendrils wrapped around the first. What surprised him about the second spell was that he got so small an impression of it that he almost missed it. A mage of lesser talent certainly would have.

Kerrigan had straightened up and thought for a moment, and then a moment longer. *Just as Wheele's shield ate up my spell and increased his, could this second spell do that to the first, hastening her death?* He wanted to do something, but didn't know what.

He gathered up her hand in his. "Orla, you have to help me. If you don't, you'll die."

She winced, her face grey and pinched. Her brown eyes opened only slightly. "I'll die anyway." The words came in a rush, with her chest rising before, and descending fast as she spoke. "When you healed me . . . you fixed more, yes?"

Kerrigan nodded slowly. "Simple things. Wear and tear."

Orla smiled slightly. "That's why I'm not dead yet."

"What?"

"Heslin knew who would hunt him and his." She paused for a moment, her eyelids dipping. Her body shook with a new jolt of pain, but she gave his hand a squeeze. "The wand . . . read my magick, modified the spell cast. Heslin liked finesse. Tailored it to kill me. But I'm not me, because of you."

"I'll make you more not you. There are two spells in there. One is poisoning you. The other is shielding it." Kerrigan smiled, forcing confidence into his words. "All I have to do is to split the two spells, then eliminate the first."

Orla closed her brown eyes, but nodded. "Yes, but you cannot."

"I must. I can figure it out."

She shook her head without opening her eyes again. "Kerrigan, you were not fashioned for that work. They made you a bludgeon. This needs a stiletto."

"I know, I'll get the wand."

"No!" Her adamant outburst left her weak, then coughs shook her. "No."

"But it cast the spell, so it should help me reverse it."

"No." She freed her hand from his. "Go to the deck. Stop pirates. Do what you can. Send Resolute to me."

Bewildered, and not a little hurt, Kerrigan left Lombo's cabin and stepped down to the next one. Peri, Resolute, and Crow had crowded themselves around the berth in which Alexia lay. He waited in the doorway and nodded to Resolute. "Magister Orla asked for you, Resolute."

The Vorquelf left the room, but there still was not

enough space for Kerrigan to enter, even if he'd been inclined to do so. He just stared down at Alexia, where she lay
with a bloody rag wrapped around her head. Unlike Orla,
she looked peaceful and had a healthy color to her skin.
She's not dying.

Resolute poked his head out of Lombo's cabin and
called for Crow. The white-haired man got up, clearly reluctantly, his clothes still red with his own blood, his shoulder dappled with Alexia's. He squeezed past Kerrigan,
hissing slightly as his cut side brushed against the Adept's
belly.

Kerrigan reached out and caught Crow's right arm. "I
can fix that for you."

"I'm sure you can, son, but heal Alexia." Crow gave him
a grim smile. "Another scar on me won't matter."

Under Perrine's watchful eye, Kerrigan cast the same diagnostic spell on Alexia as he had on Orla. She'd had a hard
knock on the head, but her skull hadn't been broken. He
gladly took on the pain of her healing, of the reknitting of
her scalp, scourging himself for having failed Orla at least
twice.

In the dark he returned to his post on the afterdeck. He
took a chunk of the smashed taffrail and smoothed it in his
hands. Watching the sea, and working idly, he reshaped the
wood with magick. Once again he re-created Orla's staff,
then sat there, caressing it.

As the sun came up, splashing orange light over the
deck and pitching his long shadow deep into the sea, Kerrigan's eyes burned. He would have welcomed sleep, but still
held it at bay. He'd not been able to save Orla, so he could at
least honor her last directive to him.

Footsteps sounded on the deck behind him.
"Kerrigan . . ."

"I've not the time to heal your side, Crow."

"Don't need it, thanks. Resolute sewed it up while we
spoke with Orla. She wants to talk with you."

Kerrigan rolled onto his knees and found Crow

crouched there, with his right hand held up to stop him. "What?"

"She wanted me to talk to you first. About the wand."

The Adept snorted. "What would you know about that wand?"

Crow rested his elbows on his knees. "About the wand, nothing, but about Heslin and Chytrine, far too much. Nefrai-laysh was once Bosleigh Norrington. The last time Chytrine came south, he acquired a sword known as Temmer. It made him invincible in battle, and as you saw back there, he needed that sort of help. He could not stand against Resolute or me without some sort of ensorcelled weapon.

"As great as Temmer was, it exacted a fearful price from the man who wielded it. It took him over, slowly, and controlled him, ultimately destroying him. With that example, Heslin could easily have built such safeguards into the wand. If you think about it, it is the perfect brake on any apprentice who might wish to rise above his station."

Kerrigan slowly nodded. "And a trap for me?"

"That's what she fears."

The Adept snarled and punched a fist against the deck. "If I had acted faster, if I had been smarter, he never would have hurt her." Kerrigan pounded his fist against the deck again, then just flopped down on the oak and began to cry.

Shock ran through him as Crow grabbed him by the shoulders and hauled him up against a solid portion of the taffrail. "Listen to me, Kerrigan, and listen very well. If you blame yourself for Orla's injuries, for her death, you will diminish the sacrifice she made. You saw her step forward to deal with Wheele. You heard Wheele say her sacrifice was what doomed her. She knew what she was doing from the beginning, and to blame yourself dishonors her nobility."

Kerrigan hung his head. "I would never do that."

"Good. Now look at me, son, right in the eyes, look at me." Crow's brown eyes blazed and the scar on his face had become livid. "We all make mistakes, some of us more than others, but we all do. I gather you've been shielded from the results of mistakes."

"I don't make them." Kerrigan remembered the weight of the flour sack smashing him in the chest, and the kicks and punches of the urchins in Yslin. "Not many of them, anyway."

"You're a long way from Vilwan, Kerrigan. Out here mistakes hurt, missions have costs. Orla is badly hurt and might die, we might all have died, but Chytrine has been denied a portion of the DragonCrown. At Svoin she lost a *sullanciri*, and her pirate ally lost a huge portion of her fleet. I'm not suggesting that Orla's life is in any way worth so little as all that, but even she is happy at the damage we've done.

"My point, though, son, is this: We learn from our mistakes. We have to. You can figure out what you think you could have done better, then resolve to do it. I need you to do that. *We* need you to do that." Crow poked him in the chest with a finger. "*You* need to do that, for us, for Orla, yes, but for yourself most of all."

Kerrigan closed his eyes and furrowed his brows, feeling the finger hard against his chest. Some of what Crow said made sense—in fact, most of it did, though Kerrigan's fear of losing Orla, losing his last link to Vilwan, shook him.

The Adept slowly nodded, then looked up. "You said she wanted to see me?"

Crow nodded, then stepped back, crouched, and handed Kerrigan the staff. He accepted it, then climbed down to the main deck and into the companionway to Lombo's cabin. He found Orla half awake, speaking in a whisper to the Spritha, who sat on her pillow. Qwc nodded and flew out of the cabin.

Orla smiled weakly as Kerrigan drew up a chair. "You've come."

"Yes, I brought you this." He laid the staff on the bed beside her and wrapped her left hand around it. "Good as new."

"Thank you." Her lips formed the words, but they came with but the ghost of a whisper.

Kerrigan moistened a cloth and brought it to her lips so she could suck in some water. He held it there until she nodded, then tossed it back into the bowl at his feet. "Crow told me about the wand. I understand."

"Good. You must promise . . ."

"I promise I'll not use the wand."

"Yes, that. And other things."

"What?"

Orla lay there breathing hard for a half minute or so, then nodded. "You can't return to Vilwan."

He shook his head. "I don't understand."

"Promise me."

"I promise, but why?"

She continued as if he'd not asked his question. "Follow Crow. Follow Resolute. Promise."

"I promise." He covered her left hand with his. "Tell me why."

Orla turned her face toward his. Pain washed over her face, but he knew it was not physical. "There are destinies, Kerrigan. Will's was writ in prophecy. Alexia's inscribed in blood. Yours was forged. . . ."

"Forged?" He hesitated. "Forged as in by a blacksmith, hammered of steel, or forged, faked, untrue, a charade?"

"Those who forged it will think the latter." She shook her head slightly. "I know it's the former. Vilwan will destroy you now, in fear. That cannot happen."

"Why would they do that?"

"They wanted you to be many things. You could be any of them, but not all." Her smile slackened. "The world needs you to be you. You know how to do much. You must decide what it is you must do."

Orla's eyes closed and her breathing evened out, though remained shallow and labored. Kerrigan remained with her and slowly succumbed to sleep, though it was not very deep nor restful. Every time he awakened, he glanced at her, hoping to see she was better, but clearly she was slipping away.

The *Shark* had sailed due east since leaving Wruona. Qwc had sped forward of the ship, reaching Loquellyn four hours before they did. He bore a message to the Loquelves and they sent a ship out to meet the *Shark*. On it had come two of the best healers available at Rellaence. They roused Kerrigan from his sleep and shooed him from the cabin before setting to work.

Kerrigan yawned and stumbled down the companionway to check on Alexia. Perrine had continued her vigil and now lay swathed in a blanket on the bed, with Alexia sitting on the chair in the corner.

She smiled up at him. "I owe you thanks, Adept Reese. I've been hit hard in the head before, and never recovered so quickly."

He shrugged. "I was glad to help someone."

A shriek rang from Lombo's cabin. A wave of sorcery pulsed out from it and cut at him. A fiery ethereal blade seemed to slash a line straight through his middle, numbing his legs and dropping him helplessly to the companionway deck. He shivered and shook, then grabbed one hand with the other to stop the shaking.

Alexia leaped over and past him, meeting Crow and Resolute following two crewmen from on deck. In the corner of his eye, between their legs, Kerrigan saw one of the Loquelves being dragged from the cabin by the sailors. He appeared to be completely stiff-limbed, as if he'd been dead for a while. The other elf staggered out. Resolute caught him and dragged him up on deck.

Alexia returned to Kerrigan's side as the prickling of feeling returned to his legs. "How are you doing?"

"Get me up. I want to see her." He pushed off the deck and bulkhead, trying to lever himself up, but Alexia's gentle pressure on his shoulder kept him down. "Please, I have to."

"No, you don't, Kerrigan. You don't need to see her like that. She'd not want you to. Peri, help me." Alexia took one of his arms, the Gyrkyme the other, and dragged him over to the still-warm cot. They forced him down into it, ignoring how the ropes and frame creaked in protest. "You're staying there and sleeping, Kerrigan. You dream about Orla and all she wanted for you, all she expected of you."

Alexia looked up at Peri. "He doesn't get up. Sit on him if you have to."

Peri nodded and easily shoved Kerrigan back down into the bed as he made a feeble attempt to rise. "Stay there, Kerrigan. If I must choose between disappointing my sister or drawing your blood, you know what I will do."

Kerrigan nodded and slumped back on the bed, finding its warmth seductively inviting. The blanket Perrine spread over him had an exotic scent that he distracted himself by trying to identify. His concentration soon eroded and sleep again claimed him.

CHAPTER 63

If there had been a virtue to a nighttime attack, Markus Adrogans decided, it was that it hid the deplorable conditions in Svoin. The reasons no one had been looking out from behind shuttered windows were simple and terrifying. First and foremost, there were very few people remaining in the city. Second, those who did remain were grossly malnourished. Third, for a generation they had learned it was worth their lives to avoid being seen.

The men they had freed from the mines had been long enough away from Svoin that they had no idea of the true conditions therein.

The Vorquelves had not dwelled on the plight of men in the city, and had apparently willfully allowed Adrogans and his people to assume they were no better off than the men. The simple fact of the matter, as it turned out, was that even the most wretched of the Vorquelves was far and away better off than almost any man in Svoin. Adrogans imagined that Chytrine ordered such kind treatment of the Vorquelves to build resentment among men against them.

The Svoin Vorquelves had subverted that policy by helping men when they could—they keenly felt the debt owed to men from the time of the evacuation of their homeland. Still, the Vorquelf errors of omission were understandable because even Adrogans would have thought otherwise of risking so much to save so little.

Svoin had once been a city of twenty-five thousand, which made it the largest city in the south. It benefited from trade with Jerana, and the nearby hills had once produced wonderful wines and iron ore. The lake had provided a great deal of food, and nearby farming settlements had supplemented the food supply in exchange for trade and manufactured goods. Trade up and down the rivers had been brisk and brought Svoin a fair bit of prosperity.

After a quarter century under Aurolani rule, the population had shrunk below five thousand, with the best off being the fisherfolk. The lake still provided a fair supply of fish, which became the staple food, along with lakeweed and some grains from fields cultivated by slave labor.

Adrogans had toured the town and everywhere had seen emaciated, hollow-eyed people covered more in open sores than rags. One man had been picking at scabs, making them bleed, and refused help when Adrogans had ordered one of the Zhusks to treat his sores. The man said, "No, my lord, the gibberers, they don't like eating us crusty ones."

That statement had sent a shudder through him, and for a moment he was able to see what the city was to the Aurolani. It wasn't a gathering of people, a center for trade and industry—which is how he would have evaluated it were he looking to take it. No, for them it was one big stockyard. They could cull men as they wished, torturing them, eating them, letting their disappearances inspire fear.

The fearful glances he got as he rode through the city told him much more than the people wanted. They clearly had done things, unspeakable things, to survive. What would he do if gibberers had come down his street looking for a meal? Would he hide his own family? Certainly. Would he point them to someone else? Not actively; he hoped Kedyn would grant him the courage to avoid that. But passively? And forced to choose between his mother and a brother or brother-in-law, what choice would he make?

Fortunately, the Jeranese general hadn't been called upon to make those choices. But he knew making them would have been mortally wounding, and verified this by the suffering that had been etched deeply into the faces of the people, even some children. But he was certain there were stories of heroism, too, with parents offering themselves to save children; little resistance movements that fought back, even momentarily.

The principle of death before dishonor was overrated, he felt, but dying to escape the misery of Svoin, that was a sane option in a place where he was certain no hope had dwelt since King Augustus rode into Jerana.

General Caro emerged from the building the Alcidese Horse Guards had commandeered as a headquarters. "A moment of your time, General?"

"I was just coming to see you, Turpus. Have you completed the survey?"

The large man sighed heavily. "There are no food stores worthy of the name. The Aurolani seemed to think that anything above a starvation diet would cause people to riot or attempt escape. The boats only have a limited number of nets. We have them out there catching as much as they can, and we'll smoke lots, but we need more than fish."

Adrogans nodded. "What of the plan to send foraging teams into the hills? The vines have been untended for ages, but still grapes grow. We saw that coming in."

"That's all fine, sir, but it will be our people. Lifting a grape is beyond most folks here, and those who could work are terrified that the gibberers will be back. If not for the Vorquelves, we'd have no one to even look at heading out. They're a game bunch."

Caro shook his head. "I'd say we evacuate them to Jerana, but they won't make it. Not sure wintering here will be possible, either. I don't mind telling you I don't like this place."

Adrogans felt a shiver run up his spine. "I confess I always feel a bit cold here myself. But, you are right, we can't move them out. I do think relocating them all to one section of the city, to consolidate food delivery, storage, and such is a good idea. Beal has her people working it out. That's the plan I want to use."

A brown-and-white Gyrkyme Warhawk landed in the street before General Adrogans, folded his wings, and bowed. "General, I have news."

"What is it, Lansca?"

The Gyrkyme looked up with large amber eyes. "Northeast of here comes a rider. He bears a flag of truce. He is Aurolani."

"How do you know? Is he a gibberer or vylaen?"

"He appears to be a man, General; but he rides a fiery horse that flies with dragon's-wings."

Caro and Adrogans exchanged glances. The Alcidese cavalry commander smiled. "Do you want company when you meet with him?"

"What makes you think I'm so foolish to meet with a *sullanciri* bearing a flag of truce?"

"I'd do the same in your position."

"And would you want a companion?"

Caro barked a laugh. "I would, a big one, with a magick sword. Since we have nonesuch here, I offer myself as a poor substitute."

Adrogans nodded, momentarily regretting giving Malarkex's sword to Alexia. *I hope she has used it well.* "I will wait for you by the east gate."

Caro tossed him a salute and ran off to where the Alcidese had stabled their horses. Adrogans turned and nodded to Lansca. "Thank you, Warhawk, for bringing me the news. Please find Beal mot Tsuvo and inform her of where General Caro and I are going. There is no need to attend us. She should send word to Gilthalarwin and the other commanders, then prepare to defend the city."

The Gyrkyme nodded. "And Phfas?"

Adrogans smiled. "I suspect he is already waiting at the gate."

The Warhawk soared skyward, clearing the road for Adrogans. He gave his horse a touch of spur and negotiated his way through Svoin. He'd seen the city once, long ago, as a child, when it was big and foreign, with the market teeming with sights, sounds, and smells, especially the smells. *My mother bought me sweet ginger.*

He smiled at himself, wishing for some ginger to settle his stomach. As he expected, Phfas waited for him at the gate, riding in some decrepit donkey-cart. They said nothing as they waited for Caro, then the trio of them rode out of the city and onto the battlefield. The siege machines had long since been torn apart to provide fuel for fires, but the scars they'd left in the earth remained.

Phfas pointed to the northeast where a rider and flaming horse rode in a little circle around the area where the Aurolani banners had stood. Aside from the flames, it would not have been that remarkable, save that the horse's hooves came no closer than four feet to touching the ground. Adrogans saw no indication of the dragon's-wings, but he assumed a creature made of fire could likely fashion body parts as needed.

He did see a flag of truce. Phfas raised a rag on the end of a stick, and the rag was largely white. While the rider did not appear to be looking in their direction, once their flag rose, he reined his mount around and galloped toward them.

It was a bit disconcerting that while his mount's hooves did not touch the ground, earth flew behind him as if torn up by the horse, and little grassfires marked his passage.

Caro glanced over at him. "You've heard the tales?"

Adrogans nodded. "This would be Nefrai-kesh, he who

was once Kenwick Norrington. Svoin must have rated more highly in Chytrine's thinking if she sends the king of her *sullanciri* to contest it."

"Perhaps killing Malarkex attracted some attention."

"Perhaps."

The Dark Lancer hauled back on his reins, bringing his firehorse to a halt. The beast snorted and a wave of warmth washed over Adrogans, but did nothing to chase away the chill he felt. The rider, whose fiery cloak and cowl had been fashioned from the flesh of a grand temeryx, nodded once to them, then thrust his flagstaff into the ground. The truce flag fluttered as heat came off him.

"I am Nefrai-kesh, and am come from the court of Chytrine. My Mistress bids me congratulate you on your conquest of Svoin." The *sullanciri*'s eyes, like those of a Vorquelf, had no discernible pupil and instead were a mélange of white and blue, as if thin, wispy clouds were blowing through a winter sky. "I would add for myself that your tactics of deception were most impressive, General Adrogans. Malarkex did send part of her force to hunt your mythical army, and she came here to die."

Adrogans nodded. "Thank you. And so you are here to negotiate the terms of Svarskya's surrender?"

Nefrai-kesh fell silent for a moment. Adrogans saw something flicker through his eyes, as if he were trying to remember what humor was, trying to recall irony. Then the *sullanciri* simply shook his head. "Were you able to deliver your force there inside a week, I might indeed, but reinforcements are already on their way. The reason I am here is to tell you that I will not harass your evacuation of the city."

The Jeranese general could not hide his surprise. "That's most kind of you. Unbelievably kind, in fact."

"I would give you my word."

"You would understand my not taking it."

"Yes. A deceiver hates to be deceived." Nefrai-kesh nodded slowly. "As you will, then. I grant you this. No Aurolani troops will you see here until spring. The Svoin basin is yours for now. In the spring you will be divested of the city."

Caro frowned. "You'll forgive me, but this makes no sense. We can and will reinforce this city. Chytrine might think we are restocking a larder for her, but she will find it a difficult one to open."

The *sullanciri* snorted. "None of you are stupid. What purpose do you think Svoin served for us? What purpose do you think it serves? You cost us three thousand troops and a *sullanciri*. The latter hurts, but the former? A fraction of the host we have assembled. And what did you win but five thousand mouths that cannot feed themselves? Bring in your food. Bring in your troops, your carpenters and masons, your merchants and exiles. What they will see will turn their stomachs.

"Every one of them will consider how his family will fare when we come to take his home city. You might never capitulate—you are military men, warriors. But merchants who pay taxes? Minor nobles? Other people of influence, when they are given a choice between facing this living death or negotiating a peace, what will they do? You won a victory, but your prize is a viper's nest. If we had defeated you, that would have served our purpose. Losing to you did as well."

All Adrogans' thoughts about what he would have done came flooding back. He closed his eyes for a second, then shuddered. Finally he opened them and put an edge in his voice. "But we did win, Nefrai-kesh. We killed a *sullanciri*. That will give people heart. And we have Svoin."

"No, Markus Adrogans, you do not have Svoin." Nefrai-kesh slowly swept his gloved right hand out to encompass the city. "The purpose the city will serve for us now, this we have discussed. And, General Caro, your estimation of Svoin having been a larder is not incorrect. It is also incomplete."

Phfas hissed. "Poison."

"Yes, little Zhusk, poison was our aim. We poison the soul of the people, and we poison the soul of the city." The *sullanciri* raised his right hand and splayed his fingers out. They closed ever so slightly, as if he were feeling for something ephemeral. He found it and his hand contracted into a fist. Yanking back hard with his right hand, he pulled something ethereal from Svoin.

Adrogans saw the entire city shimmer for a moment, as if he were viewing it across a desert plain. Something thin and white drifted from the city. It resolved itself first into a beautiful young woman of dazzling white, but she quickly aged and took on the dark color of a thunderhead. Her dowager's hump forced her to keep her eyes low, and she moved more unsteadily than a cart with a broken wheel.

"Yes." The *sullanciri's* word came with a hiss. "This is the *weirun* Svoin. What was once proud has been brought down, as shall all who oppose Chytrine. You have your victory, General Adrogans, but you have won nothing. You cannot heal Svoin before spring. This spirit is broken, all but dead. So is Svoin, and all attempts to change that will fail."

Nefrai-kesh opened his fist and the *weirun* dissipated into a grey fog that stole back into the city. Adrogans could not suppress the shudder caused by the fog's cold caress. Phfas' skin had become tinged with green, and Caro had paled.

The *sullanciri* reined his mount around and trotted off several yards before the flames flared and dragon's wings sprouted. He rose into the air, then turned and tossed them a salute. "Come spring we will duel, our armies our weapons, Okrannel the prize. I welcome the contest."

Adrogans said nothing, but returned the salute. In silence he watched the Dark Lancer rise into the sky and head north to Svarskya. He spat in that direction, then spurred his horse forward and kicked over the truce flag.

Caro growled. "He's not the only one who welcomes the contest."

"I don't."

Caro looked at Adrogans wide-eyed. "You don't?"

"No. We saw here that our friend will be anything but a gracious loser."

Caro ran fingers back through his white hair. "That's true. He's right about Svoin. There's nothing we can do to save it."

Adrogans nodded. "I concur. That leaves us one course."

"I'm not following you."

"That speaks well of you, then, General Caro." Adrogans turned to look at Svoin. "Our course is simple, yet difficult. The only thing for Svoin now is for us to put it to the torch."

CHAPTER 64

Will had been in the ratlines studying the Loquelven ship when the scream sounded from the captain's cabin. He'd slid down to the deck by the time the sailors and Resolute had dragged the Loquelves out into sunlight. The first had gone grey, and his skin had gotten all scaly. The Loquelf shook a lot, and pieces of his flesh flaked off, littering the deck. His lips had been pulled back to expose his teeth, but it looked about as unlike a grin as possible.

The other Loquelf was able to move, but his hands had been contorted and locked like claws. They'd also been blackened, maybe even burned; to Will, they looked a lot like charred branches.

The thief was pretty sure the first Loquelf was a deader, which surprised him, since he didn't think elves could die. The second appeared to be in a lot of pain. Resolute sat him down and the Loquelf just rested his forearms on bended knees, tears streaming silently down his face.

Will looked at Crow. "What about Orla?"

Crow just shook his head. He signaled to the ship

alongside the *White Shark.* "You need to take these two back, get them to Rellaence. Hurry, we can't help them here."

A half-dozen elven sailors poured up over the side, leaping from their lower deck to the wales of the pirate vessel. The first two hesitated on seeing the state of the magickers, then an officer moved to the fore and issued orders in Elvish. He asked a question and Resolute answered. The officer seemed surprised when Crow nodded in agreement with the Vorquelf's reply.

The elven officer and his crew helped the two magickers into the Loquelven galley. Will got a chance to study the ship, which rode lower in the water, resembling a shark more than it did a human ship. It had been made of silverwood, which Will learned was rare based on the prices he knew a small box made of the stuff could command. He'd never actually had his hands on any, but there was always brisk trade in elven artifacts among men, so Marcus had always urged his charges to be alert for such things.

The elven ship had a stout ram at the bow, which rode below the water level. The decks sloped up and then flattened out, save where they rose to the forecastle. The main deck had places for rowers, though the ship had no oars, nor any place to put them. The single mast split the distance between forecastle and afterdeck, and the ship's stern tapered back and down. Will saw no rudder, though the wheel was clearly visible on the afterdeck. How the ship moved he wasn't certain, but the rowers pulled hard to move the ship off and the ship did leave a well-churned wake to mark its passing.

The Loquelves had left a harbor pilot on board to guide the ship into Rellaence. Will wondered if the elven homeland was akin to Gyrvirgul in that one could not find it unless invited. The idea seemed to make sense until he remembered that Vorquellyn had been conquered by the Aurolani, and he was pretty sure no Vorquelves would have guided Chytrine's troops to the island's shores.

Then again, if someone did . . . He shivered and walked over to Crow and Resolute. "What happened?"

The Vorquelf frowned. "They assumed that Orla and Kerrigan knew too little of magick. She and the Adept had worked out some of what the spells affecting her were. I told them what she had told me, but I was dismissed as well. They proceeded to unravel magicks they did not fully understand, and they paid a fearful price."

"Is it going to kill them?"

"Arrogance should, but it will depend." Resolute looked out to the east. "If they were truly the best healers in Rellaence, yes, it probably will."

It took the *White Shark* four more hours to reach Rellaence. The elven pilot brought the ship in from the northwest, through a narrow channel, then hard to port. The high cliffsides had been covered in green, with sea breezes teasing broad, flat leaves that glistened with spray and sunlight. Birds that nested in rocky niches swooped out to greet them, calling defiantly as they soared effortlessly around the ship.

As the *White Shark* came around the headland, the harbor opened up to display Rellaence and the winding silvery ribbon of river that plunged east and deeper into Loquellyn. The splendor spread over the landscape all but dragged Will to the bow so he could study it. So many elements presented themselves he could concentrate on one for only a heartbeat before the next distracted him, and the next, overwhelming him with intoxicating intensity.

More than the visual stimulus worked through him, though. Grand groves of silverwood trees with their argent foliage dancing and flashing would have been more than enough to occupy him, but he could feel the trees as easily as he could see them, or hear their leaves rustle. Something in the very nature of Loquellyn seemed tangible, but not like the heavy air of a humid day. Instead it felt friendly and accommodating. Not a lover's caress—not quite that intimate—but still inviting.

He couldn't identify it exactly until its opposite floated up from memories. There had been countless times in his youth when he'd felt hunted and alone, oppressed and fearful, as if he could have vanished and his passing would have gone unnoticed. Here, sailing into Loquellyn, he knew he would be missed and mourned even after so brief an introduction.

The city itself barely looked like a city because trees and plants predominated. Buildings did rise up through the foliage canopy, with a tower here, an exposed wing there, and glimpses of warehouses near the docks. Even such utilitarian buildings, however, had ivy growing up over them, and flowers blossoming in niches.

The buildings themselves had a different nature from anything Will had seen in Yslin or beyond. Not only were they not built of stone, but their wooden construction had a curious flow to it. As nearly as he could tell from a distance, it appeared as if the buildings had been assembled from pieces of trees that had been barely altered. One tower with crenellations and all appeared to have been a huge piece of driftwood that had been worn smooth and grey by the sea's waves. In other places branches and trunks had been fitted together like a puzzle. As the ship drew closer, he sought any sign of joints, but he couldn't see them, and windows and doors appeared to be natural hollows and knots in the wood.

That didn't mean there was no shaping or woodworking, because doors and shutters had clearly been fashioned instead of grown. Light and dark woods, silver, red, and brown even, had been inlaid together to create pictures and heraldry, or to trace out words in an ornate and twisted script. Will couldn't read a word of it, but the soft forms and the flow of the letters enchanted him.

Two small elven boats came out from the pier and took bowlines from the *White Shark*. The human and Panqui sailors shipped their oars, and the sail was furled then lowered, as the elven boats dragged the pirate ship to the dock between two of the shark galleys. Elves made the ship fast, but before anyone could alight, an elven delegation made its way down the pier.

Qwc rode on the shoulder of a white-haired elf with a long face and square jaw. He bowed his head as he came aboard. "Greetings to you, Captain Lombo. I bid you and your people welcome. I am Dunerlan and will be honored to be your host."

Lombo seated himself on the deck and sniffed the air. "Richlife, this place. Lombo is pleased."

Dunerlan opened his arms and his smile broadened. "To all of you, welcome." His head came up and the smile tightened as Kerrigan emerged from the cabins and Perrine came after him. Several of the other elves backed up a bit when they saw the Gyrkyme, but Dunerlan's right hand came up to forestall any comments.

"Qwc, when you told us of Peri and how she helped you fly the DragonCrown fragment to safety, you did not mention she was . . ."

"Female? Qwc said female."

"Indeed, but you left us with the impression she was a *Spritha* female." A look of concern flashed over the elf's face. "This could be difficult."

Will frowned. "Why?"

Dunerlan gave him an indulgent smile. "You are the Norrington. I am honored."

"And you're not answering my question." Will sighed heavily. "I mean, I know the stories about how the Gyrkyme were born and everything. I know you think she's an animal, but I know she's not. First time I ever laid eyes on her, she'd spitted a gibberer that was about to have my guts for garters. She's fought, she's scouted, and she carried off the DragonCrown fragment."

Another of the elves, a slender female with blue eyes and auburn hair, moved to Dunerlan's side. "A trained animal would do as much for its master. She was just following orders."

"Yeah, but she didn't want to take the fragment. She didn't want to leave. Alyx, I mean Princess Alexia, had been hurt and she was concerned for her, but she put aside her personal worries for the good of the world." Will's expression hardened. "Ain't an animal I know of, and damned few men, would do that."

The elder elf raised an eyebrow. "An interesting point for debate, Will Norrington."

The thief folded his arms across his chest. "Well, add this in. If you're not welcoming her, you're not welcoming me. I don't go where she's not welcome."

The elves behind Dunerlan looked surprised and huddled together in quiet conference. The female made to speak to Dunerlan, and Qwc flew off so she'd not be speaking through him, but Dunerlan waved her back after a few whispers. "Would you take full responsibilities for her actions?"

"Of course."

Dunerlan nodded, his expression easing. "Then your pet will be allowed into Loquellyn."

Will's eyes blazed. "She's not my pet."

"No?"

"No!"

"Yes, Will."

Perrine's quiet comment brought Will around wide-eyed. "No, Peri, I won't let them treat you like that."

The Gyrkyme smiled. "Yes, Will, it will be permitted."

"But . . ."

She smiled. "It is part of elven tradition, one we respect." Peri's voice rose and remained clear. "When someone new is invited into an elven home, they are sponsored by a member of that family. The sponsor takes responsibility for the actions of the guest. These Loquelves are here to act as our sponsors, which is a great honor for us. You, Will, are being asked to be my sponsor. I thank you for accepting that responsibility. I will neither embarrass nor disappoint you."

Will wanted to continue his protest, but the effect of her eloquence on the elves stopped him. Most of the crowd behind Dunerlan had shrunk and gone white. Dunerlan had a curious smile on his face, and the female seemed both intrigued and afraid.

The thief glanced at Peri. "Are you sure?"

"Quite."

"Well, if that is the way of things, okay."

Dunerlan clapped his hands once. "Very good." The leader of the elves turned and began to introduce the various hosts to their guests, which gave Will a chance to pull Perrine aside.

"Why are you letting them do this? And don't give me that tradition stuff."

Peri winked at him. "It's simple, Will. We're bound for Fortress Draconis. In one of the elven galleys, the journey will take five days, perhaps less. On horse it will take close to a month to get there, and I'd have to be flying around the long way, through Saporicia."

Will nodded. "I hadn't thought about that."

"Goldwing and I worked it out as we came in." Peri shrugged. "I can put up with a little discomfort if it helps us, and if we get to dispel some myths about the Gyrkyme for them, all the better."

"Oh, we'll do that, all right."

Dunerlan finally approached Will, and the female came in his wake. "Will Norrington, this is Trawyn. You will be staying with her."

Will glanced up into the female's blue eyes. "Think there will be enough room for me and my 'pet'?"

"I should hope so." She gestured toward a silverwood grove on the north side of the harbor. "The palace is, after all, large and quite accommodating."

CHAPTER 65

Will woke with a start, then sank back against the soft mattress and luxuriated in the warmth of the thick quilt covering him. Since he'd left Yslin he'd not had such comforts, and since leaving Svoin, sleep had been snatched here and there. He stretched and couldn't even find traces of aches he'd known from the days past.

He opened his eyes and lifted his head a little, glancing over at the corner of the room. Perrine had taken several of the pillows from his big bed, and a couple of spare blankets, to form a little nest for herself. She'd positioned two chairs and stretched a blanket between them for some privacy, and it took Will a second or two to register that the cloth she used as a halter and loincloth had been draped over one of the chairs.

Will immediately blushed, then turned away from her. A stray ray of sunshine lanced through the window and poked him in the eyes. He yipped, then rolled onto his back again, all but blinded. Peri rose from her nest in an instant, unconscious of her nudity, leaving Will both happy and sad that he'd been sun-dazzled.

"It's okay, Peri. Just had the sun in my eyes."

The Gyrkyme nodded, stretching her arms and wings out. The room, which had an ovoid shape, was large enough that she could spread her wings wide. The wood's dark hue all but matched the color of her feathers as they played along over the smooth surface. Unlike a man-home, the walls were not flat, but instead flowed more naturally, with large niches fitted with cabinets, and smaller ones supporting flowers and other foliage.

The door to his chamber opened and two servants of indeterminate age—*heck, all elves look ageless*—swept in before Princess Trawyn. One of the servants bore towels and clothes, the other had a tray set with fruit, cheese, and warm, fresh bread from which steam still rose.

Trawyn smiled at him. "Good morning, Will. I have fond hopes you slept well."

"I did, very well."

Her smile grew. "Splendid. We hoped the repast we prepared for you would be restful."

"Huh?"

Trawyn began to tick things off on her fingers. "The wine, not too strong nor bold, the bread from fine-ground flour, the soup with a variety of vegetables, yet not too spicy. Fish, not meat, so as not to introduce inflammatory humours into your blood. We hoped it would work for a man."

"Oh, right." Will forced a smile on his face because he'd not really understood what she'd said. After a month of army food and what passed for the same on a ship, fresh food served hot had filled his belly and he found it very easy to curl up around it and drift off to sleep in a warm bed. "And thank you for having food sent up for Perrine."

Trawyn did not look in Peri's direction, but nodded. "More is coming for her presently. After you break your fast, bathe, and are dressed, I thought you might like to take exercise in the garden. Your . . . friend may stretch her wings. After that we will join the royal councils as they discuss your plans for the DragonCrown fragment."

Will heard disapproval in her voice, more for the fragment plans than for Peri taking wing. Before he could ask what she was thinking, one of the servants set the tray with his breakfast on his bed and withdrew along with Trawyn. The other servant walked to a spot in the oval to the right of Will's bed. He traced a finger over and around the grain in the wood. Noiselessly a panel in the wall swung out, bringing with it a bathing tub of seamless wood. The tub itself began to weep and a fragrant steam twisted up from the water being collected therein.

Will ate quickly and tossed Peri what he would have taken to be an apple save for the bluish tinge to the skin and a melon scent. The elven servant either missed the toss, which did take place when he was not looking, or had decided to ignore anything having to do with this strange human and his abominable pet.

After finishing his meal, Will bounded from the bed, doffed the borrowed nightshirt, and slipped into the tub. He scrubbed himself well using a soap that smelled of flowers—less because he was worried about how clean he had to be than because the servant looked ready to apply a brush to him if needed. Will sent the elf off to take away the empty dishes, which seemed to offend the servant somewhat.

Once the door had closed behind him, Peri laughed. "They'll be talking about you for years, Will. Imagine asking a body servant to perform a scullion's duty."

"I don't think anyone will notice. I brought a pet Gyrkyme to Loquellyn. They'll be talking about that forever." Will shivered as a thought occurred to him. "If elves live a long time, does that mean those servants will be servants forever?"

Peri shook her head. "Chances are very good that he

wasn't a body servant yesterday, and might not be one tomorrow."

Will shook his head, spraying water from his hair. "What?"

"Elves are not strictly bound by caste the way we are." Peri sat and hugged her knees up to her chest. "This is one of the things elves hate about the Gyrkyme. Because of my coloration, I am a Talon, fit for war. Plumes are our nobility and leaders; Wise is the caste of our philosophers. Among us, as your mother was, so shall you be, and those things do not change."

He grabbed a towel and wrapped it around himself as he emerged from the tub. The basin slowly absorbed the water, just as the wooden floor drank in the puddle around his feet. Will used a second towel to dry his hair, thinking as he did so. "But, Peri, do you ever want to do anything else?"

She shook her head. "War is what I do best. It is the duty my people have for me. I could no more perform well the duties of a Swift than one of them could make war. Our society is stable because of our system."

"But, if you wanted to write a poem, you could, right?"

"Having a duty to perform in one area does not preclude having abilities to perform well in other areas." The Gyrkyme shrugged. "We're not mindless, just focused on our duty. All else, of which there is much, is secondary."

Will tossed his towels on the floor and began dressing. The body servant returned in time to collect the towels and nightshirt, which he carried away. The scullion reappeared and slid a small bucket with fruit and some meat in it across the floor to Perrine. The servant left before she could start eating, but did not close the door after herself. Will walked over to do that, but Trawyn appeared in the doorway before he could.

The elf reached out and tugged on the shoulders of Will's tunic, then smoothed the sleeves. "Very good. The seamsters will be pleased their work fits so well."

"It does." Will returned to the bed and sat there to pull

on his boots. They were the only piece of clothing that the elves had not taken away and replaced. Will did notice that they'd been cleaned and polished, which impressed him. He smiled, figuring he looked good enough that he'd have targeted himself as a rich man from whom a fortune could be stolen in a crowd.

Trawyn nodded as if she'd read his mind as he stood. "Quite suitable. Now, if you will, we shall repair to the gardens."

Peri emerged from her nest, with her clothing in place and a couple of apples speared on talons for the walk. "Please."

Trawyn affected not to have heard her, so Will nodded. "I think we're ready."

The elven princess took Will's arm and guided him through the palace wing, along corridors that had not been laid out in an exact line but instead meandered, akin to a termite's track through wood. Various niches housed statuettes or pretty rocks, and the veins in some of the wood swirled around and into ghostly murals. While all of it was quite fetching, Will did have the feeling he was being taken along a minor corridor because they had Peri in tow.

They emerged through a tunnel that resembled a long, rootlike projection and into the garden. Soft moist mosses covered the earth beneath the spreading boughs of thousands of trees. In their branches were nestled hundreds of different flowering plants. Some grew right there on the branches, with their roots and stems projecting into the air. Others were clearly cultivated so their vines rose up and around the host trees, while others had been raised in pots that had been inserted into niches. The combined effect of color and fragrance overwhelmed Will at first, and his stopping only a couple of steps into the riot of color clearly pleased Trawyn.

Peri breathed in deeply, then unfurled her wings and struck skyward. Trawyn watched her go, the smile on her face not slackening a bit—at least not until she noticed Will glancing up at her. Her blue eyes narrowed ever so slightly, but the smile broadened and carried up into them.

"The palace gardens here in Rellaence are renowned among the homelands for their variety of plants. We have samples here from every homeland, even Lost Vorquellyn."

"Raising them so the Vorks will have something to bring home when the island is reconquered?"

Trawyn nodded. "When you redeem it, Will Norrington."

Will smiled and let her lead him on a whimsy course through the garden. Many of the plants were or resembled some of those Resolute had taught him to recognize. Where things got rather unfamiliar were in the silverwood and mageoak groves. In the boughs of silverwood trees grew plants whose fruits and flowers looked a lot like body parts or animals. Trawyn explained how the elixir made from a heart-shaped leaf would promote good heart health, or a foot-shaped fruit might be good to get rid of a toe fungus when made into a poultice and applied liberally.

Mageoak had a lot of plants that had similar shapes, but these had magickal powers. "Here a heart-shaped leaf could brew a tea to make love grow."

Will pointed at a feathery flower. "And this one?"

Trawyn stiffened. "It is a legacy plant, grown only to preserve it. We do not use it now."

"What did it do?"

"It is known as dreamwing. It let fancies fly during sleep and, being a powerful drug, deluded some into thinking unorthodox thoughts. It's not been used in centuries." She tugged him away from the purple flower with gold edging. "There is a pond where we may relax, over here."

It seemed pretty clear to Will that she didn't want to talk about dreamwing, so he shifted the subject. "I heard that servants aren't always servants here, which would be tough, given that you live a long, long time."

Trawyn spread her skirts and sat, then patted the greensward beside her. "That's quite true. Your body servant of today might head to sea tomorrow to fish, then tend the garden the day after."

Will sat. "Isn't that confusing? Who would know what needs to be done?"

She laughed lightly, then tapped a finger near her right eye. "Your Resolute, his eyes are a solid color. He was not bound to his homeland as we have been to Loquellyn. Because of our being tied to our land, we know what the tasks are that we are called upon to perform."

He shook his head. "I don't understand."

The princess smiled carefully. "You know that the Spritha learn from the world that they must be at a specific place, at a specific time."

"Yes."

"It is similar with us, though not quite as urgent. At times we know we are to go learn from a particular person, or to teach them, and the skills that are acquired then are used as needed. Were Loquellyn under invasion, our calling would be to fight, so to war we would go. The Blackfeathers headed to Okrannel because that was what would serve Loquellyn best. When they return, they might farm, they might sweep; they could do anything."

"Even be a princess?"

"No, not that." She frowned slightly. "Intermarriage with those from other homelands is not discouraged, and each elf is linked to the land of his birth, regardless of where his parents came from. Within a homeland, however, the nobility is born of generation after generation of individuals linked to that homeland. Our link to it is stronger, therefore our responsibility is deeper and greater. Our path is a bit more rigid."

Will thought he heard a longing for the freedom others had. "More responsibility, and you have to lead. Is that why your hatred for Gyrkyme is so strong?"

Her eyes widened in shock. "I have no hatred for your . . . friend."

"Ha! You can't even say her name. And you don't look at

her, not if anyone can see you doing it." He scowled. "If that's not hatred, I don't know what is."

"It's not hatred, dear Will." Trawyn's voice softened. "Others may hate the Gyrkyme, but I do not hate your Perrine. There, I said her name. But you are correct, I have difficulty looking at her."

"I'm not convinced."

"It's not hatred, Will, truly it is not." The elven princess shook her head solemnly. "She is akin to the Vorquelves—because of Aurolani evil the Gyrkyme and the Vorquelves are forever barred from fulfilling their elven nature. They cannot become part of their homelands. Knowing how much my connection to Loquellyn completes me, I mourn their lack of that bond. I cannot look at her because in her I see what she could have been without evil's taint, and the reality of her is too painful for me to bear."

Kerrigan Reese stood a man-length away from the wooden bier upon which Orla's shrouded body had been laid. A single sunbeam poured through a small, high window, illuminating her body. She looked far smaller lying there than she ever had in life.

The pirates had used some sailcloth to sew up a shroud for her. They'd used a bright crimson canvas, which was coincidentally appropriate since that was the color worn to indicate skill at combat magick. He was pretty certain neither Lombo nor the crew realized that, but he felt sure Orla would have appreciated it.

Even though she didn't wear red around me. He thought back over his brief association with her. She'd not taught him combat spells—he'd learned all she knew and more before she ever became his tutor. Instead she had tried to train him to function as a warrior. He could see that at this remove, and saw how he had failed her. He'd been taught so much that he could do almost anything, and she had been trying to teach him how to decide, how to take responsibility and act.

He glanced back to his right, to the elf standing behind him in the solemn, dim chamber. "Thank you for letting me have this moment with her. We can proceed."

Arristan glided forward, silently, and took up a position opposite Kerrigan across Orla's body. The elf spread his hands out, letting his palms play a handspan above the shroud-covered body. "It is still there. Lomardel and Osthelwin were foolish to dismiss you and ignore Magister Orla's concerns."

Kerrigan stepped closer to her body and held up the block of mageoak he'd asked his host to provide the previous night. A foot long, and three inches on the smaller sides, it felt lighter than he would have thought. He caressed it with his right hand. "If you would open the shroud, please."

The brown-haired elf gestured languidly with one hand and the stitching snaked free, letting the shroud sag open. He spread the cloth over Orla's stomach and the putrid stench that rose choked Kerrigan. He swallowed his gorge back down, then set the block in place against her grey flesh, covering the wound. The top of the block touched her wrists where they crossed over her heart. He made sure it settled in, concentrating on her stomach so he would not look up at her empty face.

Arristan's brown eyes flicked up at him. "You are certain you can do this?"

Kerrigan nodded slowly. A discussion with Osthelwin had revealed that both the elven healers had detected the dual spells that Orla had warned them about. They used magick to sever the spells, then discovered the shielding spell was something of an illusion. The reason Kerrigan had found it difficult to define was because it pulled in magickal energy and once it had enough, it exploded, casting off one of a variety of spells at the mages who were plying it with magick. Kerrigan's investigatory spells had been insufficiently powerful to trigger the shield spell, but the elves had provided it more than enough energy.

When Orla's body had been removed from the *White Shark*, Kerrigan had detected the spells as still active and warned others of the danger. As the elves discussed things, Kerrigan mulled the problem over and came up with a solution. Impressed by his thoughts on the matter, the elves decided to let him try to get rid of the spells.

It never occurred to him that in letting him try his solution they put no more of their own people in jeopardy. Arristan agreed to help him because he was Kerrigan's host and his skill at magick ran to conjuration and construction spells, not curative, so he was not needed to deal with his stricken brethren. Loquellyn's healers had their hands full trying to help Osthelwin and Lomardel, with hopes sinking for the latter with each hour.

Kerrigan took a deep breath, then let it out slowly. Again he stroked the wooden block and trickled magick into it. He used the spell he'd employed to make Orla's new staff, slowly reshaping the wood. *Magilex* took well to being thaumaturgically manipulated, with the wood taking on the viscosity of thick sap, allowing itself to be pushed, pulled, and pinched into a new form. Kerrigan worked with a broad outline for the physical shape, and concentrated on altering the block's essence so it matched Orla in every way possible.

Kerrigan wasn't certain how long it took for him to have the *magilex* block changed into a simulacrum of Orla, but the sunbeam had long since moved off her body by the time he was done. He'd come up with his plan without using Wheele's wand or even touching it—though he did use what the renegade mage had said about it. He reasoned that if the wand allowed him to identify her spells, then crafted a response to her, he should be able to locate those elements of her essence that the wand had used. Once he had them, and instilled them into the mageoak model, the spells lurking in her decaying flesh could be lured out, mistaking the block for her.

Arristan glanced down at the Adept's handiwork. Settled against Orla's womb lay a small wooden statuette of a woman. It could easily have been taken as a grave offering that would be entombed with her. "You are certain of this next part?"

Kerrigan rubbed at his eyes. "Not wholly, but I think it should work." Again, following how the spell seemed to track along the lines of energy back to the mage casting a spell, Kerrigan touched the simulacrum and used it as a conduit to cast a simple diagnostic spell. At the same time Arristan used a spell to make the simulacrum more receptive to enchantment. Kerrigan's spell teased the Aurolani magick with the impression that its target, Orla, was again available. To enhance that impression, he altered how he cast his spell to more closely match the elements that identified Orla.

The Aurolani spell slowly stirred. Kerrigan made his magick trickle in along Orla's arms, then withdrew the tendrils of it. Heslin's magick moved from her guts upward, through inert flesh, following the ethereal residue. Kerrigan pulsed a bit more power in and the Aurolani spell quickened.

"Careful, Adept, very careful." The elf swiped at the sweat on his brow with his left hand.

"I will be." Sweat burned into Kerrigan's eyes. His finger stroked the simulacrum and magickal tendrils flicked at the malignant spell. Little by slowly, inch by inch, he lured it up to her left shoulder and then let it flow down her arm and out the wrist, into the wooden doll.

The doll shook, then opened its mouth in a soundless scream before trying to bite Kerrigan's finger. All it got was a mouthful of dragonbone armor, then Arristan killed his spell and the doll froze with fury etched into its features. The human mage picked the doll up and with a simple gesture the elf magically sewed the shroud closed again.

Arristan wiped his face with a sleeve. "The magick has left her. She can rest well. That thing you should have destroyed."

Kerrigan shook his head. "No, it won't hurt anyone now."

"How can you say that? From here I can sense that the magick is still active."

"Yes, but it has a severe limitation. It didn't kill Orla outright because she had been altered in her nature when I healed an injury. The spell that killed her produced a toxin that poisoned her. When it jumped to your healers, it produced the same toxin, which could be fatal to them, but much less so than to a man. Even with her dead, it continued to work, consuming her body, and would have continued until nothing was left of her. Now, the spell is trapped in wood, so it will start dissolving this block. If I were foolish enough to let it jump into me, it would be far from lethal, since I'm not made of *magilex*."

The elf frowned. "From what you are saying, however, it will eat up the wood, destroying it anyway. What's to be gained by letting the spell do it instead of a fire?"

"Time." Kerrigan looked down at the block and past it to Orla's body. "Time to study the spells, see how they work, and see what can be done to make sure they no longer spread Chytrine's evil."

CHAPTER 66

Princess Alexia felt a bit conspicuous wearing the uniform of a Loquelven Goldfeather. Her clothes matched those worn by Dunerlan, who, as her host, led her into the Rellaence council chamber. Dunerlan, despite being of royal blood and the queen's consort, had served with the Goldfeathers and wore the rank of Master at cuff, collar, and shoulder. The waist-cut jacket with gold body and black sleeves trimmed with gold gave way to black pants and knee-high boots.

The chamber had been meant to house the city's deliberative body, but the vast majority of seats remained empty despite the coming discussion. In many ways the chamber reminded her of a wooden bowl that had been turned on a lathe, then set with high benches along one semicircle opposite the delegate seats. The benches had a gap between them with a throne occupying a recessed and raised dais.

All of Alexia's companions were present, but not all of their hosts. Trawyn occupied the throne as her mother's representative. Though Dunerlan was the queen's consort, he was not Trawyn's father—Alexia had been led to believe her father had been the consort a century before Dunerlan rose to assume that post. Arristan and Dunerlan each took up positions behind the high benches, while a handful of other Loquelves filled the four remaining seats.

Alexia sat next to Crow in a row of four chairs in the center of the room. Resolute and Will filled out that row, with Kerrigan, Dranae, and Qwc behind them. Lombo would have nominally been part of that row, but he sat on the floor. His chair had been pulled back into a third row and there Perrine perched.

Trawyn smiled and Alyx could not avoid thinking the slender woman wasn't much more than a child, despite her having lived for centuries. The clear skin and large blue eyes suggested youth, and her high voice did little to dispel that illusion. The Loquelf even wore a simple gown that, were it not made of so fine a red silk, might have been the sort of thing with which a young human girl would clothe herself.

"In my mother's name, I thank you for coming here. We will discuss the petition Princess Alexia has made for us to convey you to Fortress Draconis with all dispatch. Before that, however, I have news of Svoin, sent to us by the Blackfeathers. I apologize for the lack of details, but it is all that General Adrogans would permit to be communicated."

Alyx smiled, knowing that if Adrogans was still censoring communications, he was alive and concerned with Chytrine's people learning about his position and disposition of forces. This suggested victory in the siege, and that boded well for the campaign's continuation in the spring.

Trawyn creased her brow. "He reports that Svoin was taken. It has subsequently been burned."

Will's cheer at the news of the victory died aborning as Trawyn completed her statement. "What happened?"

The Loquelven princess shook her head. "We do not know. The Vorquelves were saved almost in their entirety.

The Blackfeathers will continue to serve beneath Adrogans. There is no indication of casualties, but requests for Blackfeather supplies would suggest they were light for our people."

Alyx frowned. Clearly something had gone horribly wrong at Svoin. *If Chytrine had used a dragon to set the place alight, why wouldn't she have used it to destroy our sieging force? And if Adrogans had to burn the city, what could have induced him to do that?* Where he would go, what he would do without Svoin as a base remained an open question, since the Zhusk plateau had not been a place where they wanted to winter.

She shook her head. *I will trust Adrogans knows what he's doing. I have no choice.*

Trawyn pressed her hands together. "Princess, the queen's consort did communicate your request to my mother. Your plan, of going to Fortress Draconis in one of our galleys while sending the *White Shark* south as a decoy, is wise. We would further disguise your movement by adding to the force heading north. Our Steelfeathers and Iron Horse legions will accompany you."

Alyx smiled. "Thank you, Highness."

The Loquelf nodded. "We will pay the *White Shark*'s crew to make the journey south under the command of one of Lombo's Panqui lieutenants. Their journey should suffice to make Chytrine think the DragonCrown fragment from Lakaslin will be in King Augustus' hands."

"Good. That will let us get the real one to Fortress Draconis." Alyx nodded. "Your assistance is greatly appreciated."

Resolute glanced at her, his argent eyes flashing. "Not so quickly, General. There is more."

Trawyn smiled indulgently in Resolute's direction. "You are so quick, Resolute. It might be an endearing trait."

Alyx cocked her head to the left. "Is there a problem?"

Dunerlan splayed the fingers of his right hand on the benchtop, then arched his palm and spider-walked his fingers back a bit. "The concern we have is that you plan to take the Lakaslin fragment to Fortress Draconis. Given the rumors of Chytrine's troops massing to assault the fortress, you would be providing her more incentive. She will learn quickly enough that you are there and she will assume you have the fragment with you."

Crow stroked his beard. "You mean to say, my lord, that there will be increased incentive if we are recognized as being at Fortress Draconis, and you want to avoid the possibility of further rewarding Chytrine if she succeeds in her siege."

The elder elf nodded. "A good point, Crow."

"Then why let us go at all?" Crow opened his hands. "The handful of us, even supplemented with your troops, are not likely to tip the balance against Chytrine, and you seem to think her intended siege is a credible threat."

A blonde elf in a military uniform tapped her bench with a forefinger. If the steel-grey of the uniform bodice and the rank insignia were any clue, Alyx assumed she was the mistress who commanded the Steelfeathers. "To assume the threat is not real, that victory is not possible, is imprudent. The very presence of the Norrington could make a considerable difference in the fight."

Resolute waved that comment away. "Speak clearly, mistress, for my companions do not know the shadings of the Elvish terms in which you think. Because the prophecy says Chytrine's defeat will come at his hands, you need to have him brought into direct confrontation with her. Any conflict where they oppose each other is one she could lose. Without the boy being there, you think she cannot be defeated."

Alyx narrowed her eyes. "If Resolute's right, then incentive is not germane, but reward is. Chytrine has one fragment now, which gives her control over at least two dragons. There are three more fragments at Fortress Draconis. We would bring a fourth."

Trawyn nodded. "And there is no good reason for you to do so."

"Not true." Alyx sighed. "Vionna pointed out that we would do nothing with the DragonCrown fragment, so she might as well give it to Chytrine. By doing that she could increase the chances of Chytrine paying her for the fragment. This got me thinking that perhaps what we truly want to do is to assemble the pieces of the DragonCrown we do have, and use them to oppose Chytrine. . . ."

The majority of the elves reacted frigidly to her explanation, so Alyx let her voice trail off for a moment. "You clearly do not think this a wise idea."

Dunerlan folded his hands together on the bench. "Its wisdom could be debated for centuries, but the horrors of the war caused by the DragonCrown's first employment do still haunt those of us who lived through it. I fought against Yrulph and his legions, losing many friends and even my brother. The simple fact of the matter, though, is that your plan will not work. Aside from Chytrine, a handful of elves, and perhaps some of the urZrethi, there's not a mage in the world capable of wielding that sort of power."

Arristan shook his head. "That's not true, my lord."

Dunerlan's brown eyes widened. "What? Who?"

The elven mage nodded toward Kerrigan. "I believe the young Adept there could do it. Yesterday I witnessed his great facility for magick."

The queen's consort recoiled. "Put the power of the DragonCrown in the hands of a child? Yrulph Kirûn was twice that boy's age when he conceived of the thing. What it did to him, what it did to the world . . . No, it cannot be permitted."

Resolute shot to his feet. "What if it is the only way to destroy Chytrine? What if doing that is the only way to free Vorquellyn?"

Dunerlan's nostrils flared. "A child arguing in favor of a child does not a swaying argument produce."

Crow rested his right hand on Resolute's left forearm and dragged his friend back into his chair. "His point still stands, my lord. Will conveyed the fragment to Kerrigan. Perhaps Kerrigan is the means by which Will defeats Chytrine."

Before Dunerlan could reply, Trawyn cleared her throat. "Adept Reese, you have had time to study the fragment?"

Kerrigan nodded. "A bit. On the ship and then again a little, yesterday, with Magister Arristan."

"Could you use it?"

The fat magicker shifted his shoulders uneasily. "We talked about that after studying the magick. It would be akin to playing music on a fiddle with only one string. I could get sound, yes, but music would only come with more strings."

Dunerlan pointed a hand at Kerrigan. "An apt analogy, into which should be factored this: Chytrine has the songs written for that instrument, but you do not. You would have to learn to use it, in a short time, and under pressure. I am given to believe you do not function well in such situations, Adept, do you?"

Kerrigan's jowls quivered and his lower lip trembled. He shook his head, then glanced down at the ground.

Trawyn frowned. "My lord consort, your opinion on this matter is well understood and you need not embarrass our guests."

Dunerlan blanched. "Yes, Highness. Please, Adept Reese, accept my apology. The strategy suggested is a dangerous one, but one worth investigating, including your role in it."

Resolute laughed. "If that is true, my lord, and we leave you the Lakaslin fragment, will you produce the Vorquellyn fragment so Kerrigan could have two strings to study?"

Trawyn shook her head. "We have no knowledge of that fragment's location, Resolute."

"Loquellyn always says that, but we know the fragment came here."

The princess wagged a finger at him. "You may have seen it evacuated from Vorquellyn, Resolute, but you do not know it came here. I remember the night the refugees began arriving, and I saw no fragment. But this is an old discussion, and bears not on our current topic. While it might be agreed that reassembling four segments in Fortress Draconis *could* help defeat Chytrine, the possibilities of that are slender, and the consequences of letting her get those four segments would be catastrophic."

Will raised a hand. "Why don't we just make a new DragonCrown?"

Stunned silence greeted his suggestion, so he filled the silence with an explanation. "She's trying to put together the old one, but with Kerrigan and Arristan and other magickers you ought to be able to assemble something that was better. After all, there's more than one fiddle in the world, isn't there?"

Dunerlan's voice grew distant. "Alas, it is the strings that are so rare, Norrington."

Trawyn's brows arrowed in with concern. "The question would remain, Will, about whether or not such a concentration of power is a good thing. Yrulph Kirûn was, by all accounts, a good man before he created the DragonCrown. Could we chance creating another monster just to defeat Chytrine? Setting your own house on fire to deny your goods to a thief is effective, but would be cold comfort once the thief and your house are gone."

Will sighed. "Well, it was a suggestion."

Alyx smiled over at him. "And one we might still have to use." She shifted her gaze to Trawyn. "Given your comments, I would assume that we can have your assistance if we choose to leave the Lakaslin fragment here. We would only do so in *trust*, since it belongs to Jerana, not us."

Dunerlan dismissed that idea with a quick shake of his head. "Lakaslin lost it, you took it from pirates. Legally you have a claim to it under the maritime laws by which most nations abide, including Jerana."

"I wasn't speaking of legality but morality. Jerana still has a right to it and we acted as their agents in retrieving it. It would be held in trust."

"Until such time as Jerana could prepare a proper home for it, yes, it would be held in trust." Trawyn nodded. "We would then be pleased to convey you to Fortress Draconis."

Resolute and Crow gave her quiet nods and Alyx opened her mouth to agree with it, then closed it quickly. She hesitated for a moment, then nodded herself. "When do we leave?"

Dunerlan smiled. "Tide runs just past midnight, if that will suit you."

"It will, thank you, very well."

Alyx sat back and nodded as Dunerlan told her he would be waiting for her outside. She let the elves file out, then turned her chair around and faced her companions. "That was the proper decision, right?"

Resolute and Crow reiterated their agreement. Will shrugged, Kerrigan less vehemently, and Qwc with all four shoulders. Dranae smiled and said yes, while Peri gave her one of those easy I-trust-you expressions.

"Good, I wanted to make certain."

Crow frowned. "You almost said no."

"Not no, per se. Look, they want Will there because, as Resolute said, he's the key to defeating Chytrine. There was room to ask them for more things to get us there. More troops, anything we wanted." Alyx rested her hands on the back of the chair, and her chin on top of them. "I almost asked them to stop treating the Gyrkyme like animals."

Peri laughed. "Just as well you did not, sister, for that would have forced some Gyrkyme to stop hating elves."

Dranae scratched at his beard. "Do you think they would have done that?"

Crow shook his head. "The princess wouldn't have had that authority, and the debate about it would have lasted longer than I have. Your hesitation, Highness, speaks well of you. You knew it was a political impossibility, even though it is the just and right thing, so you held off."

"Yes, it was something like that." Alyx scowled. "Or, could have been my courage failed me."

"Better it fails you in this than in battle, Highness." Resolute stood and stretched. "I pledge this, however. When Vorquellyn is liberated, we will not forget the role of the Gyrkyme in its restoration. There will be one homeland in which the Gyrkyme are not only welcome, but revered."

CHAPTER 67

The ships left Rellaence just after midnight, with a blazing rope of stars twisting through the clear sky, pointing the way toward their eventual goal. Four ships made up the flotilla, with one war-galley bearing each of the elven legions, one for the companions, and the last—a bulky transport that looked more like a whale than a shark—for the Iron Horse's horses. All four ships moved at the transport's pace, but it made enough speed for their trip to take them no more than a half a week.

While their hosts were quite pleasant and even helpful, Alexia found them to be reserved as well. She assumed part of that was because of Peri's presence, even though she could detect no slights, deliberate or otherwise, in how the crew treated her. All meals were communally served in the cabin where they hung their hammocks to sleep, and the sailors serving them were cordial.

Alyx felt an unease growing in her as the ships rounded the Loquellyn headland and started the long run up toward Fortress Draconis. She tried to dismiss it as the chill bite of the winds, but the dread bubbling in her throat told her otherwise.

She stood at the bow of the boat, with misty spray dappling her skin, staring off far to the northeast. The sun was dying behind her, casting the mast's long shadow out like a lance. *A dark lance.* She shivered and hugged her arms around herself.

"If you will permit me, Highness." Crow draped an oilskin cloak over her shoulders. "With night coming on, it will get cold."

She reached up and pulled the cloak tightly around her body. "Thank you, but it will be for naught. It's not the cold that's making me shiver."

Crow nodded, leaning forward on the rail, letting the air brush his white hair back. "Fortress Draconis is a fell place. It's changed over the years, grown darker, nastier."

"My father died there."

"I know. I was there. I saw. I mourned." Crow fell silent and stared toward the far horizon. Tears gathered in his eyes, and Alexia knew they were not from windwear. "A quarter century ago Fortress Draconis determined the fate of the world. It broke Chytrine's army. If it does so again we will have to finish the job this time."

Alyx glanced back at the few folks gathered on deck, knowing the others slumbered below. "Lord Norrington had a group of heroes to help him, and he failed. We have you and Resolute, and half-grown children, myself included. A fresh crop of *sullanciri* just waiting to be harvested."

Crow swiped at his face, then glanced over at her. "You don't believe that, do you? You don't believe you would become one of Chytrine's creatures, do you?"

"No." She frowned. "At least, I hope not, but then I think of Vionna and her pragmatic assessment of our situation. We place limits on what we do, what we are willing to do to win, and our foe does not. When I think of Lord Norrington or his son, heading forth full of righteous indignation and burning with the desire for justice, then see how they were turned, I have to wonder. Am I—are we—foolish in thinking that our sense of justice can armor our minds, that our desire to make people safe can ward our hearts? Chytrine has murdered children—happily, perhaps gleefully—and yet when we look at the bodies, we're the ones who feel the pain. We're the ones it drains."

Alyx pointed off to the northeast. "I'm certain my father shared Lord Norrington's convictions. They traveled together, they planned together. Would my father have been with him on that last expedition? Undoubtedly. My father could be one of the *sullanciri*."

Crow raised an eyebrow. "So you think you could have been one as well? You think you might become one?"

Alyx nodded, feeling a small worm crawl through her guts. "It's not having Malarkex's sword or anything like that. All my life I've been disciplined and fighting hard. Fighting to succeed in an alien culture, then fighting to live up to a reputation. I've fought to be worthy of my father's heritage."

She smiled. "It's here, with you, with Resolute and everyone else that I feel a freedom I've not known before. Your expectations for me are the same as the ones you have for yourself: that we will work together, do everything we can to stop Chytrine. We're the arbiters of our own destiny, but bound to the goal of stopping her.

"Being given complete freedom, though . . . It seems so seductive."

"Of course it does, but you won't succumb to it." Crow's voice came low and rich. "You know that no matter what she promised you, she would demand a price. So in offering to strike the chains from your spirit, she'd just fit you for new chains. Freedom, which is what you desire, is illusory as long as she lives. The only way you *can* succeed is through her destruction."

Alyx slowly nodded, then reached out and rested a hand on Crow's shoulder. "I believe you're right, Crow, but in

case you're not, in case I suffer a moment of weakness . . .
You're capable of killing a *sullanciri*. Don't let me . . ."

A jolt ran through Crow. "You're asking more than you
know. I can't agree, and not because I want you to suffer
that fate. If I agree, then you lose that last bit of impetus to
resist. You have me in reserve, as your final check."

"You wouldn't let me, though. . . ."

Crow straightened up and took her hands in his, brushing his thumbs over her knuckles. "You'll never be a *sullanciri*, Highness. Of this, I have no fear. Chytrine will think
that you, like all the others, can be broken, but I know you
can't. That gives you the advantage of her, and in the end,
her underestimation of your resolve will be her undoing."

Once again dressed in the multiple layers of a pirate,
Kerrigan came on deck an hour after the cry had been
given that Fortress Draconis had been spotted. Their speed
still gave them a couple of hours before they would reach
it, and to the north, paralleling their course, a couple of
Aurolani war-galleys paced them. Though Kerrigan knew
little of sailing—most of his knowledge had been picked up
on this voyage—with the prevailing wind coming from the
west, it should have been easy for the Aurolani galleys to
come down and engage them.

Why they didn't, he didn't know, but he'd stationed
himself near the port bow in case they decided to make a
run. In his mind he went over the spells he would cast:
shearing off oars, snapping the mast, or, better yet, destroying the rudder. While he could easily hole the hull, he also
knew that if the ship had any magickers aboard, they would
be defending against just that sort of attack.

He knew he likely could overwhelm any sort of defense
they might offer, but the vision of how Wheele had turned
his spell into an advantage haunted him. Battering past defenses would be useful, but only if he knew the nature of
those defenses. Much easier was attacking in ways the

enemy was not prepared to handle. Even a minimal effort would work in that situation, and easily, whereas bashing away against a foe who has anticipated your attack would be disaster.

The reluctance of the Aurolani galleys to close allowed him to shift his attention to Fortress Draconis and he discovered, to his surprise, that they were closer to it than he imagined. The morning fog had hidden the horizon, and since the fortress was known for the Crown Tower, he had assumed the distant structure was far taller than it appeared to be. In fact, as the rising sun burned the fog off and details became sharper, Kerrigan discovered that the tall, elegant fortress of a generation ago had been replaced with a squat, brutish, brooding structure that looked akin to a thorn-ridden granite horn that had erupted from the earth, then had been snapped off all ragged and raw.

The Aurolani galleys still made no attempt to stop the elven ships as they sailed into the harbor on the fortress' northwest quarter. Instead, they took up stations meant to keep the ships from fleeing, which would have seemed utterly useless save for the ill omen their action represented. *If they want to stop us from running, it means they think there is something we will want to run from.*

The fortress showed no signs of distress. The elven ships hoisted a series of flags in a pattern that had been sent to them by *arcanslata* before they left Rellaence, then sailed unmolested into the harbor, past the hulking slab-sided little fort that capped the causeway and shielded the harbor. Sharpened spikes stabbed out from the walls, and from the various slits and ports jutted the brass muzzles of dragonels. Though Kerrigan had never witnessed their power, what he knew of them left no question in his mind as to why the Aurolani galleys had remained beyond their range.

The little harbor fort, hexagonal in shape, had thick, stout walls that sloped toward the sky at a gentle angle. The thickness at the bottom would make them very tough to undermine, which would prevent them from coming down easily. Kerrigan saw none of the crenellations of other fortress walls—lookouts just paced on a recessed walkway, exposing only their heads and shoulders to the enemy. While passing close to the fortress meant the guards could not see the ship, there was no way any ship would have gotten that close to the fortress were the dragonels operating.

The ship came to a pier and tied up smartly enough. The elves rigged a gangplank and Kerrigan followed Lombo off, then joined Alexia and the others in the company of a tall man with brown hair and hazel eyes that could barely be seen beneath his green mask. His steel-grey uniform had a rampant dragon embroidered in dark green on the left breast and a crown on the right. Given the green of the mask, Kerrigan assumed he was from Oriosa.

The man's voice came a bit stiffly, as if he were straining to be proper. He addressed himself to Princess Alexia. "Highness, the Draconis Baron sincerely apologizes for not being able to greet you himself, but he has pressing business. He will brief you, later, but asked that I conduct you on a tour and answer your questions. Your baggage will be taken to your rooms. You will be housed here, in the Crown Tower."

Will cocked his head. "Not much of a tower."

Their guide's head came up, with a touch of shock quickly melting into bemusement. "I shall explain as we go, if that is to your liking. I'm Erlestoke. Like you, of Oriosa. You must be the Norrington."

The thief nodded. "And you look much more like a prince than your brother."

That remark tightened Erlestoke's smile. "So I have been told. This way, please." He led them up around to a long ramp that was broken at several points by a sharp downslope to a narrow trench. "You will find these trenches in various places around the fortress. Men waiting herein can easily defend the stretch of ramp below, and in the unlikely event a ship were to get into the harbor and unload a ram or some other siege weapon, this would catch it up."

Continuing on up, he slapped a hand against the sloped face of the fortress wall. "You've not seen this sloping type of wall elsewhere, I will warrant. The Draconis Baron, in conducting experiments with dragonels, discovered they are very effective at bringing walls down because they can concentrate their missiles on a specific point. They become a long-range ram in that way. Low, thick, sloping walls deflect the projectiles, minimizing damage."

"Unless you happen to be under them when they hit." Will tried to scramble up the wall, got a few yards up, then slowly slid back. "Pretty effective against attackers, too."

"More so, even, when boiling oil washes down them." The prince pointed at the spikes. "Grabbing those won't help. Most are sharp, many are poisoned, some break away, and others hide surprises."

Reaching the top of the ramp, the company cut back and forth between two small walls that acted as a baffle to slow attackers. "These walls likely won't last long against a determined enemy, but long enough for us to get a battery targeted to deal with them."

Kerrigan felt a shiver run down his spine. Erlestoke spoke simply and easily about things, but the mage's racing mind filled in all the details. Back down the ramp he could imagine seeing a ram caught in one of the trenches. He saw sheets of boiling oil coursing down the walls, splashing over attackers swarming up the ramp. He saw gallant defenders holding the narrow baffles, could hear a trumpet calling them back.

And then the enemy pours through.

As Kerrigan emerged from the baffle he found himself staring down the black maw of one of the dragonels. Cast of brass, this one had a muzzle that looked like a wolf snarling. He quickly cut to the side, slamming into Dranae. Kerrigan bounced off and fell to his knees, fully at the metal wolf's mercy.

Erlestoke smiled as he ascended the last bit of ramp and patted the dragonel on the head. "Please, forgive me that trick. It is a tradition here, to show our visitors what an enemy will see. Some of our dragonels have names—this is Thunderfang and was one of the first dragonels the Draconis Baron cast. Chytrine's dragonel had a dragon design to it, but Dothan Cavarre found that wolves, bears, cats, serpents, frostclaws, and eagles worked just as well. Now, to save metal, our dragonels are not all so fanciful, though we do have at least one monster per battery."

The magicker struggled to his feet, then brushed his knees off. He struggled up that last bit of slope, then followed along the top of the fortress' western wall. The joint of two sloping walls created a point upon which a dozen of the dragonels had been positioned about six feet beneath the top of the wall. Their muzzles pointed out through tall, slender ports that allowed for them to shift the aim left and right through a ninety-degree arc. This overlapped their shots with those of the harbor fortress and allowed coverage of the ramp on the northwest face.

Erlestoke invited them to get close to the big brass cylinder on a wheeled truck. The dragonel crew—*meckanshii* all—used ropes and blocks to pull the weapons into place, then levers to shift the point of aim. Likewise levers raised the cylinder so shims could depress the aim and shoot at ships close below.

"These are what everyone wants to see. These are dragonels. They're fed a diet of firedirt, which is packed in tight, then a projectile. We've been using iron balls to great effect—one big one for ships and many small ones for crews. It really doesn't matter what you load on top of the firedirt, it gets vomited out very fast. Provided it survives the blast, it will go through almost anything it hits at a fair range."

Erlestoke accepted a small horn and poured a fine black dust from the narrow end into a hole atop the dragonel, near the butt end. "Firedirt comes in three grades: gravel, sand, and dust. Dust gets used here. Small grains to small holes, bigger to bigger."

Will peered closely at the powder in the dragonel's hole. "What is it? Where do you get it?"

The Oriosan prince laughed heartily and the *meckanshii* joined him. "That, Norrington, is the question my father and every other head bearing a crown would love to have answered. The Draconis Baron worked long and hard on the formulation. Only the *meckanshii* know how to make it, in what proportions the parts are mixed, how it is cured. I don't know; I just know what it does."

Erlestoke reached out a hand to take a slowly burning bit of match-cord from one of the *meckanshii*, but he stopped and looked at Kerrigan. "You're the mage, yes?"

He nodded.

The prince waved everyone away from the dragonel, then pointed a hand at the powdered hole. "If you can make fire, please."

Kerrigan concentrated, then flicked a finger at the dragonel. A spark, gold and scintillating, shot toward the hole and the powder there immediately began to smoke. A heartbeat later, as Prince Erlestoke leaped back, a gout of flame thundered from the dragonel. The weapon recoiled along well-worn ruts in the stone and even before the smoke had begun to clear, the *meckanshii* crew had leaped to the process of reloading and readying the dragonel again.

The smoke made Kerrigan's eyes water, and the blast had set his ears to ringing. Lombo grasped him by the back of his shirt and directed him back away from the battery. They joined the rest of the company on the wall and Kerrigan found Erlestoke looking proudly at him.

Kerrigan smiled. "Was that acceptable?"

The prince nodded solemnly. "If I need a master detonationist in the siege, I will draft you.

"You are too kind, Highness," Kerrigan tried to hide his smile.

"Not at all." Erlestoke waved his hand back toward the fortress. "Let us continue."

Kerrigan ducked his head and followed in silence as Erlestoke conducted them through a tour of the rest of the fortress. They made a quarter circuit around the irregularly shaped structure's outer walls. Beyond them, to the northeast, east, and southeast sat three smaller fortresses, akin to that which warded the harbor. A swelling hummock connected them to the main fortress and Erlestoke indicated that supply tunnels ran beneath the ground to connect the buildings. Each of the smaller fortresses bristled with two dozen dragonels, guaranteeing a murderous cross fire for any troops storming the fortress. Moreover, the main fortress and the smaller ones could cover each other, so taking them would be a bloody affair as well.

Erlestoke then led them off the wall and in through the city, heading toward the Crown Tower. The city, he explained, was known to the locals as the Maze. "It takes a bit of getting used to, but once you do, you can get through it quickly. An invading army, on the other hand, will be broken up and cut to pieces."

As he led them into the Crown Tower, through a tall arched doorway, he pointed a hand toward the sky. "Twenty-five years ago the Crown Tower was three times taller than it is now. As you know, the DragonCrown fragments were housed in the very top, and a trap set there slew a dragon which Chytrine had commanded to take them. Right up there, molded into the wall, is that particular dragon's skull."

The beast's bleached bone stood out starkly from the grey stone. The hollow eye sockets peered down and Kerrigan imagined he saw someone hidden there, looking down at them. The skull itself was nearly thirty feet long and twenty wide toward the back, and had teeth so large a man would have barely rated as a morsel.

Erlestoke continued his commentary. "Because the dragonels are so effective at bringing towers down, the Draconis Baron lowered the tower and reinforced it. It is, however, still the home to the DragonCrown fragments."

Erlestoke led them through the tower, up stairways that ended in corridors requiring them to move across the tower to pick them up again, or to traverse baffles. Getting to the top of the tower would not be easy were it defended, and the tower itself boasted many *meckanshii* guards. Most of them seemed to have armor grafted onto their skin in a metal carapace that had been decorated with hooks and blades and spikes at elbow, knee, and heel.

In the archway before the fragment chamber, Erlestoke turned to Kerrigan. "Please, no magick in here. There are defenses worked into this place that I don't know about, much less understand, and I don't want to find out about them right at the moment."

Kerrigan nodded, then entered the chamber behind the prince. The stone-walled circular room had no windows and no decoration, save for three stone plinths occupying the corners of a triangle centered in the room's heart. On each of them rested a massive gem set in gold, virtually identical to the fragment they'd rescued on Wruona. The nearest one, a huge ruby, cast bloody reflections over the floor and walls. The center stone was a yellow gem with the qualities of a sapphire, though its light seemed muted. The last, a green stone with blue flecking, did glow with its own light, though not nearly as ostentatiously as the ruby.

Erlestoke allowed all of them to study the stones for a moment, then folded his arms over his chest. "In the south, when people think of Fortress Draconis, they think of the power of the dragonels. They forget that these three stones would allow Chytrine to unleash forces that make dragonels toys."

They followed Erlestoke back down to the bottom of the tower, where a knot of soldiers pressed into duty as servants greeted them. Each warrior conducted one of the company away, save for Kerrigan. Erlestoke smiled. "I'll be your guide, if you don't mind."

Kerrigan couldn't think of anything to say, so he just wandered along with the prince, remaining silent. They moved quickly into the tower's depths, ascending several floors, then coming to a dark door. The prince knocked once, then opened it into a large room with shelves full of books. For a moment Kerrigan could imagine himself back in his rooms on Vilwan, but the sight of the Draconis Baron rising from a chair quickly dispelled that notion.

The small man smiled. "Ah, very good, Kerrigan Reese, I'm glad you came. I am pleased you are here, and regret that I did not speak with you in Yslin. I was uncertain of your identity at that time."

Kerrigan blinked. "My lord?"

Dothan Cavarre smoothed his moustache with his left hand. "It has been reported to me what you are able to do magickally. In some ways I find this curious, and in others merely a confirmation, but this leads me to ask you something."

The Draconis Baron's fast speech left Kerrigan waiting to catch up, then he nodded. "Please, my lord, if I can be of service."

"Oh, I think you can." Cavarre waved him deeper into the room. "We shall talk. If I hear what I expect to hear, you can perform a service for me. A great service, for which I shall forever be in your debt."

CHAPTER 68

After a moment's reflection Alyx realized she wasn't surprised seeing Crow at Kirill Square. After the tour she'd retired to her room and dropped into bed for a brief nap. She'd not intended to sleep until first light, but her body had a different idea. She didn't have nightmares and, in fact, had no dreams at all. As she woke very rested, she wondered if the Draconis Baron had somehow had the fortress magicked against dreams, preventing Chytrine another possible point of access.

She'd dressed quickly, choosing from the clothes that had appeared in her room's wardrobe while she slept. Unseen servants had filled it with the pirate garments the elves had cleaned and repaired, as well as the Loquelven Goldfeather uniform and more suitable local garb. She chose the standard grey Fortress Draconis uniform, which, in her case, had a winged horse rampant on the left breast, and a crown on the right. Both of them had been embroidered in white, but traced in black, the significance of which she did not quite grasp.

Down in the mess hall she grabbed some bread and a mug of hot soup. She drank the soup as she threaded her way out of the hall, past tables full of people from every nation and species. She noted that instead of a national insignia, the *meckanshii* wore a sword crossed with a wrench, surrounded by a toothed gear-wheel, embroidered in the color appropriate for their nationality. Alyx also noted that they tended to congregate together and not share much with the other troops—but she could not be certain if that was because they no longer thought themselves part of their nations, or if their countrymen shunned them so they'd not have to look at what they might become.

Munching on her roll, she left the Crown Tower, exited the grounds through one of the five gardens surrounding it, and headed east toward the place where her father had died. She'd heard that a memorial had been raised to him, or at least that was how she'd had it from her family, but none of them had ever visited. What they had described, however, in no way matched the reality.

The entire square behind what had once been the inner gate had been preserved intact despite the reconstruction, while all else around it had been changed. The stones around the gate had been half wilted by dragon's breath, with tendrils of stone frozen in place as if they were sand being blasted back by a spray of water. The gateway itself sagged a little, the cobbled courtyard was unevenly paved. Missing stones had been replaced by newer ones, and she had no doubt that the stolen ones had been broken down into talismans soldiers carried into battle for luck.

Over on the north side of the gate, just inside the wall, a mountain of candles burned before a crater that had been smashed into the wall. Little strips of paper, cloth, and parchment fluttered from where they had been jammed between rocks and into cracks. Ivy had grown up around the crater, but no branches intruded upon it. Amid the candles stood a number of statuettes of various sizes, made of anything from terra-cotta to bronze, all representing her father.

The sight of it choked her, bringing tears to her eyes. She'd been ready for some grand monument, with a huge statue: her father in a heroic pose, dominating the square. That was what her grandfather and her great-grandaunt thought was here. *They would hate so humble a display.*

She did not. She understood it. These were the offerings, the signs of respect everyday warriors were showing him. To them he was another warrior, a man who gave his life to defeat Chytrine. They didn't need to see him resurrected in some heroic statue—the crater itself told them everything they needed to know about his courage. This courage they venerated and hoped they would know, too, when the right time came.

Crow slowly rose from setting a candle into place. "Good morning, Highness. Forgive my intrusion."

Alyx shook her head. "I'm the one who intrudes, Crow." She walked over to him and got close enough to feel the heat wafting off the candles. "I had always imagined something ostentatious and gaudy."

"Something your father would have hated."

She nodded. "Yes, exactly, but something Aunt Tatyana would think barely adequate. The candles I understand, and the statuettes, but the paper? They look like prayers."

"They are."

"But my father isn't a god."

Crow smiled softly. "First, to those who were here that day, his intervention was nothing short of divine." He pointed at a two-foot statue that was covered with a rainbow of melted wax. "King Augustus had that first statue fashioned after the Alcidese custom of ancestor worship. Others who didn't quite understand took it to have another meaning and, well, you know how soldiers are with their superstitions. There are many who claim your father didn't die here, but moved into another plane of existence."

She shook her head. "That makes no sense."

He shrugged. "Fact of the matter is, Highness, that your father was most roughly treated by the *sullanciri* who killed him. As for your father's body, well, recognizing him wasn't possible. Stories sprang up about how he'd not died. People accosted by roving bands of bandits or Aurolani would tell of a warrior answering your father's description who would save them."

"But those stories are nonsense."

"They might be, but some people needed them to be true, Highness. Every other hero from that time, save the Draconis Baron and King Augustus, is dead or has joined Chytrine. People needed a hero to oppose her, and some chose your father for that role."

She narrowed her eyes and regarded him closely, recalling the nighttime raid staged before the battle on the Svoin plain. "Some of those rescues, they were you and Resolute, weren't they? You didn't mind the stories being spread, so Chytrine would waste time and resources looking for a hero who didn't exist."

"Nothing that was done was anything your father wouldn't have done, were he alive. I'm sure he took great comfort in people being saved. But, please, don't be angry. We were not mocking him or his memory."

"I didn't suppose you were." Alyx frowned. "You stopped, though, why?"

Crow scratched at the back of his neck. "We realized that Chytrine could easily use one of her *sullanciri* to make it look as if your father had been taken, had gone over. When Bosleigh Norrington did just that, we were glad we'd stopped. Besides which, once Leigh became a *sullanciri* we had to start our search for the Norrington of the prophecy. We knew it wasn't Leigh, so the hunt became paramount."

Alexia shivered despite the heat swirled up from the candles by a breeze. "As I grew up, the world was painted for me in very simple and stark terms—Chytrine had killed my father, had taken my nation, and I was to undo all of that. As a child I saw it as a grand adventure. As I grew up and was trained, I learned that it wouldn't be easy, but there were glimmers of hope. I never imagined that others would oppose her as you have, but now I see that all these efforts are going to be required to stop her. Ultimately, all of us who are arrayed against her will have to make the same choice my father did, make the same sacrifice, or at least be willing to do so."

"But you've always known that anyway."

"Yes, but I didn't really grasp that others were willing to do it, too. I saw it as my duty as his daughter." Alyx pointed at the candles and other offerings. "This shows me a host of different paths that are leading to the same goal. Only by pulling everyone together will we succeed."

The blast of a trumpet from the north cut off any reply Crow might have offered. Other trumpets repeated it urgently. Crow took Alexia's hand and started sprinting with her through the Maze. The course forced them to run west a bit to go east again, but soon they reached the fortress' outer wall and ran up the ramp to the eastern Lion battery.

Coming up over the hummock between Fortress Draconis and the smaller fort to the east, two riders raced along toward the main gate there to the southeast. Both men rode hard and one had an arrow sticking from his right shoulder. He wavered in his saddle a bit, but managed to hang on. The other rider waved her hand in a salute, then apparently gave some sort of hand signal that caused the *meckanshii* captain at the battery to call down to the gate and order it opened.

The narrow sally port in the gate swung open, admitting both riders. The wounded man swung from the saddle in the courtyard while his companion spurred her lathered horse on into the Maze. Alyx watched her go, then looked up and saw an Alcidese balloon rising on a tether above the Crown Tower. A basket hung beneath it with two observers, their attention focused to the north.

Alyx knew the two riders were scouts—that much was obvious. Equally obvious they'd been in a fight and rather ominous was the fact that a squad consisted of ten individuals. She couldn't imagine part of the squad abandoning their fellows, unless the information they had was vital and the fight already lost.

Soon, a number of flags hung from the balloon. The breeze plucked at them, snapping them crisply. On top of the Crown Tower other flags rose and fell on a flagstaff there, apparently in answer to the signals from on high. Neither she nor Crow could figure out the exact information they conveyed, but both of them knew what was coming.

Within an hour their worst fears were confirmed. Chytrine's host had come from the north, down through the Boreal Pass. Cavalry came first, with renegade men riding horses, and gibberers and vylaens on frostclaws black or white. Armored figures rode the grand temeryces, but their metal shells hid their identities. Still, a number were tall and slender enough to be taken for elves.

The cavalry came down into the plain just north of Draconis Pond, which warded a portion of the north wall. They formed up just beyond the range of the dragonels in the northeastern stronghold. Behind them came Chytrine's artillery. Teams of a dozen frostclaws drew small dragonels, while drearbeasts in pairs or fours moved the larger weapons. The drearbeasts were of a size to make a full-grown bear seem to be little more than a yearling pup, and their white fur would have rendered them all but invisible in the frozen Aurolani wastes.

Wagons loaded with firedirt and shot for the dragonels came next, then infantry. Alexia had been used to ragged lines and unruly sounds coming from her enemies, but these troops moved smartly, with discipline and in silence. Their standard, a cloven ox skull painted red, was one she recognized from a variety of reports. While they had not always been victorious in their various raids, they had always fought hard.

Beyond them came a legion of large men and gibberers

who shouldered weapons the like of which she had not seen before. "Crow, are those draconetteers?"

The older man raised a hand to shade his eyes, then slowly nodded. "You can see they're carrying their draconettes and that other stick with the horns on the top. They rest the barrel of the draconette on it and shoot, then reload and shoot again. Accuracy isn't much over fifty yards and the rate of shots is must slower than that of an archer."

"Then why use them?"

Crow sighed. "Archery takes a lot of training, but shooting a draconette does not require so much."

"You've fought against them before?"

He smiled. "I've eluded them before. I've never been hit, but I helped Resolute dig a ball out of another Vorquelf. The ball broke the arm and it hasn't been quite right since. Got him some magick help, but too late."

Alyx frowned. "But, Resolute, with all his magick, I would have thought . . ."

"Him, magick that *heals*? No." Crow stared hard at the smallest of the wheeled weapons that started to filter onto the plains. "I wonder what those are. I've not seen them before."

She looked out, following his line of sight, and saw a series of two-wheeled metal things being pulled by a single frostclaw each. They looked nothing so much like a frog squatting with its mouth open, though most of the creatures decorating them were more reptilian and toothy than any frog. Clearly the weapons belonged in the dragonel family, but their exact purpose she could not puzzle out.

Legion after legion came into the field, with cavalry and heavy infantry screening the assembling artillery and supplies from the castle itself. The infantry set about digging trenches and using the dirt to create revetments, behind which dragonels and their volatile firedirt could be stored.

The Aurolani troops started to cheer, and Crow pointed north. "There she is, riding in the open this time."

Alyx looked north and found herself staring at a woman driving a chariot drawn by two grand temeryces, flanked by two more, and followed by yet one more pair. She wore a rainbow cloak of semitransparent silk, while her gown was a wispy sky-blue and far better suited to a boudoir than a battlefield. Long golden tresses floated on the wind, as did her cloak and skirts. She seemed tall and strong and ageless, though Alyx admitted the considerable distance made all of those assessments suspect.

She saw Crow shift his shoulders. "What is it, Crow?"

"Someone walking on my grave. Perhaps riding over it." He glanced over at her, the reddened scar very apparent on his ashen face. "Just seeing her with hair like yours, strong and tall like you, I wonder if she shaped herself to be like you, or that is mere happenstance."

"Shaped herself?"

He nodded. "Like the urZrethi, she can mold her shape to whatever she desires. In Boragul she'd taken on the appearance of a demi-fledged urZrethi queen. The way she is out there now, that's how she appeared twenty-five years ago."

"Is she urZrethi?"

Crow shrugged. "I don't know. They deny it, but that is no surprise. Kerrigan might know of magicks that would allow her to change shape—I've always assumed she had mastered such things in her lifetime."

Alyx slowly nodded as more and more troops poured into the area. Against any army raised in the south, Fortress Draconis would have been impregnable, but the Aurolani host had dragonels and much more. The fortress itself had a garrison of nearly seven thousand, but her army boasted easily three times that number and there seemed no end in sight for her troop train.

A black, cruciform shadow raced over the landscape coming from the west. Alyx saw it drift toward the Aurolani lines, then turned and, shading her eyes, looked up. Drifting lazily above the battlefield, like a hawk hunting vermin, a dragon hung in the sky. Gold glinted from its scales, then it slowly spiraled down and came to a landing beside the pavilion being raised for Chytrine.

Crow pointed. "See the wound on its hip? That's the dragon she had at Vilwan. I wonder why the old black didn't kill it?"

"I don't know, Crow, but I have a feeling that this dragon isn't going to die as easily as the last one she employed here." Alyx crossed her arms over her chest. "And if we can't kill it, stopping Chytrine will be all but impossible."

CHAPTER 69

Rather a curious thing to be called a garden, isn't it?"

Will looked up from his contemplation and saw Princess Ryhope of Oriosa, the Draconis Baroness, standing just inside the garden gate. Will tried to straighten up, but since he was sitting on the railing of a little bridge, his motion threatened to topple him backward. He grabbed the railing and heard it creak, but it held and he was able to avoid the short drop to the dry streambed beneath him.

Her comment had been completely correct, and he acknowledged it with a nod as she picked her way from one stepping-stone to the next on the winding path to the bridge. Despite the growing gloom of night, the blanket of white stones on the ground made it easy to see every bit of the garden, and to see that aside from the hedges bordering it and a couple of trees tucked next to the walls, nothing grew there. Instead larger stones rose from the white like islands from a storm-whipped ocean, and the darker trail of stones in the streambed split that white sea cleanly in half.

Ryhope smiled. Will found her to be a handsome woman, with the strong chin, full lips, and straight nose that her mask allowed him to see. The twilight helped as it hid wrinkles and the light threading of grey in her hair. She wore a grey gown with a dragon rampant in green on it, similar to the design embroidered on his shirt's left breast. Over her right she had a crown, whereas Will had a sword. Ryhope moved fluidly and lightly, as if the stones really were water and she wished to stay dry, lifting her skirts girlishly until she reached the bridge.

She watched him closely for a moment, then shook her head. "There are little traces of your father in you. I can see it, just a bit, in the eyes, the chin. Your eyes are lighter than his, of course, your hair darker, and he was a bit bigger than you. Not much, but a bit. Quite dashing when he wanted to be."

"Did you know my father well?"

She clasped her hands before her and said nothing. The rhythmic pounding of Aurolani war drums filled the dark silence before her returning voice banished them. "I knew him. Not terribly well, since I only met him briefly, during the Harvest Festival, but he made quite an impression on me, on my brother, and even on my mother."

She laughed lightly. "Had things been just a bit different, I could have been your mother."

That sent a jolt through Will. "I thought you said you didn't know him well."

Ryhope nodded, her eyes pale. "He and I would have been paired, for he was a hero, the slayer of three *sullanciri*. He surpassed his father, but his injuries here prevented his joining his father on the fateful expedition. He returned to Oriosa, to Valsina, to recover. News that his father had been seduced into Chytrine's service hit him very hard. He had not recovered from what had gone on here and that was another blow. My mother could not have allowed us to marry, had either of us tried to pursue it."

Will frowned. "I don't understand."

She smiled indulgently. "I am of the Oriosan royal house. My desires are nothing when placed against the needs of my nation. It was deemed desirable for the Draconis Baron to have a connection to the nations of the south, so I became his bride. Like you, I had a destiny visited upon me, and I hope your destiny is as fruitful as mine has been. I have grown to love my husband, and I love our children. What I once feared I now praise every waking moment."

The thief pointed east. "Even with Chytrine out there pounding away, ready to destroy this place?"

Ryhope mounted the bridge, then leaned back against the railing beside him. "You know Adrogans was successful in taking Svoin. You saw a *sullanciri* die there, if I am not mistaken."

"Something like that, yes." Will squirmed a little, refusing to admit he'd fainted. "But losing that battle hasn't stopped Chytrine."

"No, it hasn't, my point exactly." She raised a hand and pointed at the Crown Tower. "You see that dragon skull there? That is the skull from the dragon that died right here, died in the pond. Chytrine lost the last time she tried to take Fortress Draconis. It cost her dearly, and we had already lost Okrannel. That defeat didn't stop us, nor did hers stop her."

He frowned. "I'm missing your point, then."

"My point is simply this: whether or not Fortress Draconis falls to Chytrine, the only way we lose is if we stop fighting. The only way we win is to stop her from fighting. Ripping the heart out of her army here will do that quite effectively."

Will looked at her curiously. "You don't think she can take this place, do you?"

"I know better than to assume she can't." Ryhope shrugged. "I've spent over two decades here learning how difficult this place will be to take. It will be a big bone in her throat and could easily choke her to death. We might not beat her, but Adrogans or Augustus, they could finish what we start."

Will scratched his head. "Your voice is nicer, but you're as depressing as Resolute."

The Draconis Baroness threw her head back and laughed aloud. "Well, pragmatism and realism are an antidote to minstrel songs, yes; but I don't mean to make you melancholy. I will admit, however, this garden can have that effect."

"Really?" Will shook his head. "I don't know why anyone would think that. Sure, it doesn't have flowers or fruit or anything, but I'm not much for all that anyway. I mean, this bridge is lovely, and the way the stones lay on the ground and the big ones come up, I can almost hear gravel waves breaking against them. Looking out I can see what a Gyrkyme flying over the sea might see with islands and everything."

"You don't find it a bit stark and forbidding, cold even?"

"Well, maybe the white is a little bright, but you have to look at how everything is covered and the little swells and curves and stuff. I mean, maybe if you see it as white rocks over dirt it's dead, but I guess that's not what I see. I mean, it is, of course, since that's what it is, but there's something more here, there is life in the rocks. It makes me think."

Ryhope nodded thoughtfully. "I've been told your father spent a lot of time in here, thinking, composing poems. It was a peaceful time for him, before the last battle."

Will slapped his hands against the bridge railing. "You mean he might have been sitting right here, in this very spot?"

"I don't know, but . . . perhaps he was. It could be that the railing has been replaced in that time, but yes, in this garden."

Will began to smile and look anew at the garden when something thumped him solidly on the chest and shoulder, somersaulting him backward off the bridge. He came all the way over and landed on his feet, but pitched forward onto his hands and knees quickly enough. Above him, on the bridge, he heard Ryhope struggling and the tearing of cloth. "Run, Will, run!"

The thief came up in the dry riverbed and saw two dark forms, wings unfurled, clutching at Ryhope with clawed feet. The things had human-sized torsos and heads, but no arms, short bird-legs and claws, and wings about equal in size to those of a Gyrkyme. Will wasn't sure what they were, but when one turned its hag-face toward him and hissed, he knew they weren't friendly in the least.

Will cocked his right hand back, then let fly with the stone he'd grabbed when he pushed off the ground to stand. The rock sped true and smashed the creature clutching at Ryhope's hair in the face. Its hissing shrank into a sigh that ended with a thump and grunt when it hit the bridge railing, then flopped off to the streambed.

Will's second stone missed the other creature's head, but he'd shifted his aim at the last moment to avoid hitting Ryhope. He caught the beast in the left wing, near the shoulder, and clearly snapped the limb. A thin sliver of metal gleamed in Ryhope's right hand. She'd drawn the dagger from a sheath at the small of her back and plunged the curved blade into the beast's breast, angling up under the ribs. She twisted the blade back and forth quickly, then wrenched it free.

Blood splashed over the bridge a second before the creature landed and twitched. Will darted under the bridge, grabbing up a heavier stone in both hands. As he emerged he raised the big rock, then swung it, dashing out the brains of the creature he'd felled.

He started to straighten up, but Ryhope joined him in the streambed and pulled him back down in a crouch. "There may be more."

"What are they?"

"*Araftii,* the non-elf half of Gyrkyme." She smiled. "If we live through this, we can add feathers to our masks— and *Araftii* feathers are rare indeed. Chytrine did not use them in the last war, but she probably decided she wanted something to counter our Gyrkyme and their firecocks."

"So what were they doing here?"

"Scouting. Chytrine probably told them to kill any targets of opportunity, and we looked pretty defenseless. If they'd managed to kill us, imagine how disheartening it would be for people to know they were not safe even here."

Will smiled. "And now she'll have to think about the two we killed. Maybe we just pluck a few feathers and send the rest back, with our compliments."

"Not a bad idea." Ryhope reached down and pulled the rear hem of her skirt up between her legs and tucked it into her waistband. "I'm going to run to the tower door there."

Will hefted two rocks. "Anything wings its way at you, I'll get it."

She reached down and yanked a handful of feathers from the dead *Araftii*. "So they'll know what we're up against."

He nodded and weighed the rocks in his hands. "Go."

Ryhope set off and moved nimbly from stone to stone, staying low. She ran fast and reached the doorway unmolested. She waved Will to her. "Quickly."

The thief leaped from the streambed and sprinted as fast as he could toward the doorway. The white stones proved poor footing, slowing him. He pushed off with his left foot to cut right, onto the stepping-stones, but slipped and went down instead. A whoosh of something swooping through the night, the light brush of feathers against his face, and a quickly receding hiss told him how closely he'd been missed.

Coming up to his knees he looked left, hoping to see the *Araftii*. He was able to pick out its dark form, wings spread, wheeling around on its left wingtip to come back at him. He readied one of his stones, but it ducked back down beneath the level of the wall and he lost sight of it for a moment.

What he did see clearly, however, was a flash of white, followed by a hideous squawk and then a triumphant shriek. White stones showered everywhere as Peri slammed the *Araftii* into the ground. She perched there on its back, her wings furling, her toes curled into the creature's plumage. The Gyrkyme reached down, grabbed the *Araftii*'s head at jaw and crown, then twisted mightily, snapping its neck.

She lifted her face to the sky and shrieked again.

Will shivered and stood slowly. "Peri, thank the gods you got it."

Peri sprang from the body and spread her wings enough to tuck Will beneath one as she herded him to the tower door. Ryhope already had it open and shut it after the two of them had entered. "You're not hurt, Will?"

He rubbed at his left shoulder. It felt sore, and he was surprised to find his tunic was torn and his hand slick with blood. "I didn't even feel it."

Ryhope tore a strip out of her skirt, wadded it up, and wiped the blood away. "A couple of cuts, not very deep. A stitch or two will close them."

Will nodded. "Peri, how did you know they were about?"

"Qwc wanted to go bug-hunting—something about northern moths being tasty—and invited me along. We were on top of the tower when we spotted them." She looked at the bloodied talons on her right thumb and forefinger, then licked them. She wrinkled her face. "Sour, but better than moths. Anyway, a clean kill is never bad."

Ryhope raised Will's left hand and used it to press the cloth to his wound. "We need to get you taken care of, Will. Thank you, Perrine, for saving us."

The Gyrkyme snorted. "Well, what good is a pet if she lets her master get killed by *Araftii*?"

Ryhope raised an eyebrow and Will blushed. "Please don't ask."

"As you desire, Lord Norrington." Princess Ryhope laughed warmly. "Knowing that first blood has gone to us, and at the hand of the Norrington no less, is more than enough for me this night. It's not a great victory, but one that will hearten our people, and that could make all the difference in the coming battle."

CHAPTER 70

The next morning, at first light, the gates of Fortress Draconis opened and a cortege rolled forth beneath a white flag of truce. Three carts carried five shrouded *Araftii* corpses among them, with Alexia, Crow, and Resolute riding out to lead them. Alyx felt a bit apprehensive in that role, since she held no command position at Fortress Draconis. In fact, she had discovered, the black thread outlining the embroidery on her tunic marked her as a noncombatant in the fortress' scheme of things.

She actually harbored no illusions about safety when it came to accompanying the bodies. The Draconis Baron had asked the three of them to ride out because she had killed a *sullanciri*, and both Crow and Resolute were capable of the same. That they were also expendable counted for a great deal. *If she refuses to honor our flag, we will perish in a thunderborn hail of metal.*

As she rode from the gate she marveled at how the path sloped down, raising the spiked walls around her, higher and higher. The menace of the dragonel batteries became even more real to her. In the blink of an eye the greensward over which they rode would become twisted and torn, muddy with blood and sown with broken, screaming bodies.

They rode into the shadow of the easternmost stronghold and stopped. Crow planted the truce standard in the ground. Alexia resisted glancing at the stronghold and at the small sally port at its southwest corner. The Draconis Baron had told them they could retreat there if Chytrine attempted to murder them, but she doubted they could cross the hundred yards to safety if the massed Aurolani batteries spoke as one.

A guttural cry went up from the Aurolani lines. Two individuals, the one on the grand temeryx bearing a flag of truce, emerged from the Aurolani formations. The rider had been encased in metal armor that appeared black at a distance, but showed signs of rust and pitted corrosion as he came closer. His mail coif allowed her to see his face, all withered and dried, his nose shrunk to the point where his nostrils had just become slits in the middle of his face. His leathery lips were pulled back to expose black teeth. His eyes had a milky film over them and viscous, puslike fluid ran from his nose to drip from lips and chin.

His companion, another *sullanciri*, required no mount. Her legs had been stretched and reshaped to resemble those of a temeryx. Black feathers covered her body, save for a brilliant sulfur crest, a splash of same on her throat, and a slender V running from shoulder to loins and back up over each breast. Her dark gaze flicked from face to face amid the trio.

The urZrethi *sullanciri* pressed clawed hands together. "My Mistress welcomes this chance to offer you mercy. I am Ferxigo. This is Ganagrei—he who was once Brencis Galacos. I speak for Chytrine in this matter. These two I know, but you, you would be Alexia of Okrannel."

Alyx shivered, feeling as though the *sullanciri*'s soft, supple words had somehow stripped her naked. "I am

Alexia. We are not here to discuss mercy, but to return the bodies of your dead *Araftii*. You may tell their brood they died well. The Norrington slew the first, elven archers two more. The Draconis Baroness and the daughter of Preyknosery Ironwing dispatched the others. We would understand, given this ill omen and the presence of the Norrington, if your Mistress chooses to withdraw from the field. As the morrow is the Draconis Baroness' birthday, we would offer you a day of peace to return north in her honor."

Ferxigo closed her large eyes and slowly shook her head. "Your kindness will be unnecessary, as the unfolding of events will make apparent. We would wish, however, the Draconis Baroness all peace on her day, and will attempt to conclude things such that she may be granted same."

The princess nodded. "Haste will cost your Mistress dearly."

"And you shall be forgiven a statement made in ignorance." Opening her eyes again, Ferxigo looked at Crow. "You know surrender will save lives, will make things painless."

Crow snorted. "If you still had a soul, you would recognize the agonies surrender brings. Never. Please, tell her that. Never."

The urZrethi laughed and Ganagrei started a hideous chuffing that sank into a gurgle as dark fluid dripped through his lower teeth. The shape-shifting *sullanciri* smiled, revealing sharpened peg-teeth. "You have a price. It will be wrung from you at one time or another."

Resolute growled. "You won't be there to collect it."

She laughed again, harshly. "No, I shall perhaps be in your homeland, razing Voragul, or in Okrannel or Oriosa, amusing myself. You will all likely be dead, and as Ganagrei demonstrates, death is no bar to entering my Mistress' service."

Rising on her hind legs, Ferxigo looked beyond them at the wagons. "As for those bodies, they are of no use. Were

my Mistress in the habit of rewarding failure, there would
be many more in line for use than these. I shall not bid you
farewell, for this day will not be kind to you. I think I shall
bid you reason, so you can find the true path through what
shall follow."

Ferxigo turned and raced back toward her lines.
Ganagrei followed, after a moment's delay, leaving his flag
of truce stuck in the ground. As the two *sullanciri* rode
clear, activity increased on the Aurolani side of the field.

Crow reined his horse around. "Dump the bodies, turn
the carts; hurry. Come on, behind me." He urged his horse
forward and plucked the first carter off and onto the back
of his saddle. Alyx got the second driver and Resolute the
third, then they galloped as fast as they could back into the
fortress.

From behind them Alyx heard a series of *crumps* that
cracked at the edges, then a series of explosions that shook
her. The din echoed off the fortress' walls, pounding her,
and something whizzed past her head, but she couldn't tell
what it was. She ducked her head as she followed Crow
through the sally port in the main gate, then she dismounted and ran up the ramp to the Lion battery to see
what was happening.

The crumping sounds continued, slightly lagging behind the flash of fire and puff of smoke from the squat
dragonels she'd seen the day before. Crow pointed to the
sky and she could see dark dots arcing high into the sky.
She followed one in its flight and saw it hit the ground, then
it exploded and metal fragments flew, some striking sparks
from the fortress walls. Another actually exploded in the
air, barely twenty-five feet off the ground, tearing the turf
and making it dance like the surface of a puddle being assaulted by raindrops.

All that remained of the wagons, horses, and *Araftii*
were smoking splinters, twitching horseflesh, and black
feathers incongruously drifting gently to the shredded
greensward.

The little dragonels—Will dubbed them skycasters—shifted their aim and began to rain their projectiles down on the eastern stronghold. Air bursts blasted soldiers from the walls, tearing some apart and just knocking others about with the concussion. Some of the thunderballs—another Willism—bounced down into the stronghold's central courtyard and exploded with a bright flash. Yet other balls skipped off the walls to land in the field to explode, and one or two failed to detonate at all.

Will, who leaned on the battlements between Crow and Dranae, wondered aloud, "Why aren't they shooting back?"

Alyx pointed toward the revetments shielding the skycasters. "They're beyond the range of our dragonels. It scarcely matters, though, because those thunderballs can't take the fortress. That requires troops, and they will get into range."

Drums began to pound behind the Aurolani lines. Ranks sharpened up. Crude ladders were passed from the back to the fore to be borne by squads of gibberers. Alyx estimated the distance they would have to cross to be eight hundred yards. At a dead run it would take them two minutes or so to reach the stronghold.

The Aurolani troops did not run, but instead moved forward in an organized manner, marching in time with the drumbeats from behind the lines. Slowly they came on, pace by pace, fearless, chanting, legion after legion, advancing across an eight-hundred-yard front with the wings paced a bit quicker so all sections of the formation would reach the stronghold at the same time.

Seven hundred yards, six, then five. At five hundred yards the first rippling explosion from the stronghold cut loose, spewing fire and iron through thick grey clouds. The iron balls smashed down into their formations, splashing bodies, bouncing, crushing others and on until spent. One shot blew through a hoargoun's chest. The giant peered down at the dripping hole torn through it, then flopped forward, squashing gibberers.

Vylaens snapped orders and the formations' ranks contracted. They continued their orderly march, leaving the field behind them strewn with bodies. Onward and onward, unwavering, filling the gaps, getting closer and closer.

The other strongholds began to shoot as well, crisscrossing the field with sizzling metal. Gibberers fell, with whole swaths scythed through their midst, but still they kept coming.

Smoke began to clog the battlefield, affording Alyx only little glimpses of what was going on. When the Lion battery began to fire it made the condition worse, since the acrid, bitter smoke seared her eyes and made them water. Even so, the smoke and tears couldn't hide the fact that the sheer number of Aurolani troops, and the rate at which the dragonels could be recharged and set off, meant the stronghold could never kill enough to prevent the troops from reaching it.

Worse yet, the long dragonels on the Aurolani side of the field were being shifted. Dragoneers hitched them to frostclaws and pulled them to new positions, closer positions, laying them anew. Crews worked to aim the guns, then fire them, hurling iron balls against the stronghold. Dozens of dragonels got shifted closer for the attack, but they all selected the same target, blasting away at a vylaen's command.

The Aurolani fire slammed into the stronghold. Many balls—most of them, in fact—skipped high off the sloped walls, but each pulverized a little crater into the previously smooth surface. Some snapped off spikes, others clipped the top to rattle around inside the small fortress. A few, a precious few, however, shattered the casements around a dragonel and one even struck metal. The ball knocked the dragonel askew, crushing one crewman and scattering shot.

The lost dragonel meant less metal flew at the advancing troops. Again and again, the Aurolani dragonels hammered Draconis dragonels. The stronghold's dragoneers shifted their aim to fire back, knocking out one or two, but by that point the gibberers were already laying ladders to walls and beginning to swarm up.

Defenders mounted the walls and skycasters sent thunderballs among them. The Aurolani didn't seem to mind that the occasional misdirected shot blasted a hole in their own formation, since the majority fell true. Grey-clad defenders reeled away as thunderballs burst in the air. Others thrust with spears at gibberers, or tried to pry their ladders off the stronghold's walls, but the mottled fungus of gibberers clung stubbornly and climbed ever higher.

At least one dragonel fired into the gibberers climbing in through the fireport, blasting bits and pieces of them out over their fellows. Others continued in over the goreslicked stones. The other strongholds and Fortress Draconis itself shifted battery aim to pound the walls, scraping gibberers off, but never enough, never quickly enough.

Alyx looked over at Crow. "The stronghold is lost."

He nodded, suddenly looking far older and more weary. "With its loss, the other strongholds are weaker. We've not enough dragonels to hold off those masses of troops. When she said her invasion had been premature twenty-five years ago, she was right, because if she had come with these numbers then, she would have won, dragonels or no."

Will brushed the *Araftii* feather on his mask back away from his nose. "And Chytrine hasn't even used her dragon."

"No, she hasn't." Crow raked fingers through his beard. "Either she suspects Cavarre might yet have a way to deal with a dragon, or she wants to suggest the fortress is beneath its efforts. Either way, I'm glad it's not being used."

"Hardly matters, does it?" Alyx looked out over the battlefield. The firing from the eastern stronghold had ceased, and gibberers danced jubilantly on top of the wall. The occasional shot from the fortress skipped through them, but had no material effect. As the smoke began to clear, the true shape of things became apparent because Chytrine's host had barely been decimated in taking the stronghold. Already dragonels and legions shifted north and west to drive at the stronghold there.

She sighed. "We just can't kill them fast enough."

Will shrugged. "Taking a stronghold isn't going to be as tough as taking the fortress. I'm betting we can stop them."

"I know that we *must* stop them, but I'd not bet on it." Alyx gave him a bit of a smile. "It's a bet that will be paid with your life."

"Ever since Crow and Resolute found me, my life's been the ante." Will thrust a finger toward Chytrine's pavilion. "She's been trying to win it for a long time, and we'll just have to make sure it takes even longer. Whatever it takes, we'll do."

CHAPTER 71

The northeastern stronghold had fallen shortly after dark. The backflashes of dragonels on both sides had split the night with hellish red light, providing glimpses of shattered bodies, troops splashing through blood-puddles, and a writhing mass of gibberers crawling up over the stronghold's walls. Alexia watched until her eyes burned, happy that smoke and fatigue blinded her at the end.

Not even the ringing blasts of the dragonels and thunderballs could deafen her to the screams of the dying. As darkness fell and fires arose in the enemy camp, she retreated to the Crown Tower. She could not bring herself to count the fires over there. Even the most conservative of estimates represented a force Fortress Draconis could not resist.

Sleep came quickly and ended cleanly, though the way the sheets had tangled around her legs showed it had not been an easy night. Part of her had hoped to visit the Dragon Society that evening, so she could seek counsel. She wasn't certain if the way was blocked to her by magick, or if she hadn't sufficient need to be able to travel there. She hoped for the former, and dreaded the latter.

When she awoke, she found more to dread. She avoided breakfast and went immediately to the walls. All signs of the previous day's conflict could be seen despite the low fog swirling over the battlefield. Shambling forms moved through the mist in the distance, halting and jerking oddly, but all drifting toward the Aurolani position. Up at the nearest stronghold, bodies were being slid down the walls. Spikes caught them and spun them all loose-limbed like rag dolls. They finally sloughed off the stone surface and lay in heaps.

She couldn't figure out why the gibberers were casting their own dead out until a shining figure, a slender slip of a woman, emerged from the stronghold's far side. Alexia immediately recognized her as Myrall'mara, the *sullanciri* who had been a Vorquelf. As the luminous female bent down and caressed a gibberer body, it jerked to life and stood, though it had one arm missing. She touched another body and it clawed its way up despite having lost both its right arm and leg. Magick blazed crimson from the *sullanciri's* right hand. The empty arm socket of the undead gibberer melded with that of the other, forming a three-legged, two-headed monster that awkwardly stumped its way back across the battlefield to the Aurolani camp.

As if in answer to Alyx's unvoiced question, one of the Draconis dragonels roared. It had been aimed well and filled with scatter-shot—a good twenty-four pounds of iron balls the size of an egg yolk. The metal hail ripped through the reanimated gibber-thing, vaporizing its skulls, splintering limbs, and shredding its pelt. Gobbets of its hide and flesh splashed over the stronghold walls and slowly slid down.

The blast had caught Myrall'mara as well, spinning her around and smashing her flat against the stronghold's pitted surface. One ball had opened her skull, leaving a chunk of it hanging down over her left ear, fastened only by a strip of scalp. Her left eye rested on her cheek. Several balls had pierced her torso and her left thigh had been opened and her femur cracked.

The *sullanciri* scooped a handful of brain tissue from her shoulder and packed it back into her head, then snapped the skull back together. The designs on her pale flesh blazed silver, hiding her for a moment in an iridescent cloud of fog. As the light faded, she stood, unblemished. She clutched at her stomach and doubled over, then vomited blood and the shot her body had absorbed.

The princess shivered. Not only could they not kill Chytrine's living troops fast enough, those that were not chopped down into tiny bits could be recovered. Alexia didn't imagine that the reanimated troops would be good for much in the way of tactical maneuvering, but that had never been an Aurolani strength. The undead would be a slow, mobile shield for the living troops, requiring their destruction all over again.

A messenger arrived and conducted her back to the Crown Tower. He led her to a large room full of book-lined shelves. The Draconis Baron and his wife were there, along with Prince Erlestoke and the rest of her companions. Kerrigan, whom she had not seen since their arrival, looked as haggard and unrested as the others.

Dothan Cavarre waved her to a chair in the front of her seated companions. "Last night, Chytrine conveyed a message here by *Araftii*." He nodded toward an unfolded document on the desk behind him. "It mocks our offer to let them retreat in honor of my wife's birthday. She is willing, in honor of the nation of Ryhope's birth, to allow all non-combatants and people of Oriosa free passage to the south, and safe conduct to their homeland."

Alyx shook her head. "That makes no sense at all."

Cavarre arched a pale eyebrow. "Actually it is quite

shrewd. It instantly confers on Oriosa some sort of favored-nation status, which others will resent, thereby making the alliance to oppose her weaker. Moreover, it suggests that she is capable of leniency and even charity, which will prompt some to negotiate their own peace with her. And this is if she chooses to keep her word and let you go."

Will laughed aloud. "If you think she'd let us get away free, you're insane."

The Draconis Baron inclined his head slightly to the right. "I doubtlessly am, but I should like to avail myself of her generosity."

His wife clutched his shoulder. "I'm not leaving you. I'm not taking our children away from here."

He raised a hand and patted hers. "You must, beloved, for if you do not, no one else will leave. I would not have you go away, for I have no desire at all to see you slain; but I desire even less having my troops see their families slain. I need you to be an example of brave sacrifice, my dear, so others can do what is right.

"You will recall that Chytrine prophesied that when she came again, the children of that day would not see their own offspring mature. The children of that day are my warriors today, and I would thwart her prediction."

Ryhope looked down and said nothing, but a tear traced its way along her cheek and hung at her chin for a moment before she turned away.

Alexia narrowed her eyes. "You have called us here for what reason?"

"I want you to lead the expedition south."

Will shook his head adamantly. "No, no way. You know the prophecy. I'm the one that beats her. I go away and you can't win."

Cavarre raised a hand to stop Will. "Your understanding of things is far too shallow, Will Norrington. The prophecy refers to the war, not one battle or another. Perhaps by leaving here you will be preserved for a greater victory."

The thief snarled. "I keep hearing this 'perhaps' over and over again. 'Perhaps' I have helped stop her by giving the lump there the Lakaslin fragment. 'Perhaps' I've helped by taking this mask or by being at Vilwan. I'm done with perhapses. I want her done, and done here and done now. I'm sick of this perhapsing."

"Noted, Will Norrington." The Draconis Baron looked up, tapped his right index finger near his right eye twice, then gathered that hand into a fist. "It must be clearly seen by others that your retreat is the only course open, the vital course."

Alyx opened her hands. "It's laudable to evacuate the noncombatants, the children, but you don't need us to do it. You've got competent troops, and Prince Erlestoke can lead them."

The Oriosan prince, who stood deeper in the room than Cavarre, turned from the window. He had his arms tightly crossed over his chest. "I'm not going. I'm staying here. I must."

Cavarre never even looked back over his shoulder at him. "And if I ask you to safeguard your aunt and your cousins?"

"I would entrust them to Alexia and the troops we will send back. Colonel Hawkins will see to her safety. And while I might be able to replace him there, he can't replace me here. You've trained me too well to let me go."

"And if I order all Oriosans to go?"

Erlestoke laughed. "I'll throw away my mask and become an anonymous soldier. I'm not going, and that is final."

Alyx nodded. "I agree, fully. Let me be an anonymous soldier, too. This idea of sending people south is folly. You know she will have to assume we are smuggling DragonCrown fragments away, so she has to attack us."

Cavarre smiled. "She will want to assume that, but she also knows it is impossible to do. The dragon is here, in part, because he has a sense for these things. Were even one to move south with you, she would know more than some and even her vylaens would know."

Kerrigan raised a hand nervously. "But moving the innocent out, um, we know she has killed children before. It's fine that you say you want your soldiers to know their children are away, but what if she just captures everyone, makes them into hostages? How will your men fight then?"

"No less hard than they would fight were their kin here."

"But you would leave them feeling helpless if they knew their loved ones had been slain because they were away from their protection." Alyx shook her head. "No, this doesn't make any sense at all."

"Actually, it does." Crow stood and stepped forward. "I think Cavarre is right, we have to lead them south. We've all seen what Chytrine did yesterday. We know what sort of havoc her weapons can wreak, and Fortress Draconis is well suited to opposing her. Can you imagine how quickly the castles and keeps to the south will fall to her weapons? Conventional tactics won't work against her, and unless we can warn the south about what is coming, the sacrifices here will be for naught.

"And, Princess, I think *you* have to be the one to lead the expedition. Not only will you be believed, but you have the best chance of being able to formulate strategies to deal with the nature of her thrust."

Will shot from his chair. "I can't believe this. Crow, you're running from a fight? Resolute, you're not going to go. You'll stay and fight, right? I'll be there right beside you."

Resolute shook his head. "I go south with the expedition."

"What?" The thief looked aghast at him. "How can you . . . ? Why?"

The Vorquelf snarled and stabbed a finger at Will. "It's your fault. My preference would be to stay here, but now I can't. Crow, find me when we're to leave."

Resolute stood abruptly, disentangled his sword from the legs of his chair, then stalked out. Will, his face red with anger, darted after him. The others watched them go. Alyx looked from them to Crow and tried to read his face.

"You really think we have to lead them out of here?"

He nodded solemnly.

Alyx looked at Cavarre. "We won't have enough horses for everyone, so we'll be moving very slowly."

"I am assuming a pace of ten miles a day. It's four hundred miles to Oriosa, so that's four weeks. It will take you a week to reach Sebcia, and I will send messages by *arcanslata* letting the appropriate authorities know you're coming. You'll carry supplies for two weeks with you, get more along the way."

She nodded slowly. "It will take a week to clear the Black Marches. Chytrine won't come after us until she has reduced this place. Her cavalry can make three days to our one. Hold out for four days and we will be deep enough in Sebcia to be safe."

"I'd put the margin at five, but I concur." Cavarre sighed. "I've taken some steps already to see to your safety. You'll only have small units with you, but you are quite skilled in fighting with the same, aren't you, Highness?"

"It seems I will be put to the ultimate test, my lord."

The Draconis Baron nodded, then looked past her at Crow. "You know she will send a *sullanciri* after you."

"Its head or mine." The white-haired man smiled grimly. "I'm honored that you trust me with your wife and children."

"I've studied your exploits for a long time, Crow. I've never seen anything that gave me any reason to question your courage or dedication. We're birds of a feather, and I entrust them to you without reservation."

Cavarre opened his hands and gave them all a solemn nod. "I wish you good fortune and all speed."

Crow offered the man his hand. "Confusion to Chytrine, and death to her troops."

Alexia rose and placed her right hand on the top of their hands. "Death to her troops and more. Much more."

Will finally found Resolute in the stone garden. He couldn't believe the Vorquelf had eluded him so easily, but after a quick hunt he'd found him. He expected Resolute to bolt, but the elf simply regarded him with cold eyes and a colder sneer.

"Do you think I'm a coward, Will?"

"I didn't think so before, but it looks like you are one now." Will's nostrils flared, brushing the edges of his mask. "So now you run and you blame it on me? Talk yourself into believing that you'll be saving my life? Well, I want to be here. I want to fight her here. Didn't you hear me when I said that?"

"Most clearly."

"Then what is this running about? You're not using me as an excuse for your heart going weak."

The Vorquelf's eyes narrowed as his chin came up. "Whenever you're done, let me know."

Something in the chilly tone of his voice warned Will off continuing. "Go ahead. What do you have to say for yourself?"

"The reason I will be leaving *is* your fault, but not because I have fears for your survival or mine. We could die here, we could die on the road. The chances of all of us making it to Sebcia are slender, and Oriosa is not really any better. I fear nothing, least of all death."

"Then why are you going?"

"Early on in our journeys, you asked me why I fought with longknives. I told you I preferred them but there was more. Being an elven warrior is a great honor. When one is bound to a homeland, he knows his calling, knows what he must do, and being allowed to take up a sword is close to the greatest responsibility an elf can be given. Because I am not bound to my homeland, I knew I would never have the sense of being called upon to take up a sword, so I've not. I've studied them, trained with them, but never taken one as my own."

Will frowned. "But you're wearing one now."

"I am." Resolute slowly drew the long, slender blade. Without the basket-hilt and the leather wrapping it, Will almost didn't recognize the sword as the one the Azure Spider had owned. "Long before you were born, before your father was born or his father before him, Oracle told me I would be given a sword by Vorquellyn's redeemer. This is it. The sword's name is Syverce. It's old, very old."

The thief pointed to the forte, right below the crosshilt. "It has a hole in the blade."

"That's the eye of the needle." Resolute's voice lost some of its volume and power. "A long time ago, when there were more elven homelands than there are now, each of the homelands had a Syverce. They were all made by the same swordsmith, from the same ore. They're fashioned and named after the needle we use to sew shrouds for the dead."

"But elves live forever."

"Many do, or choose to move beyond this world, as did all the adults bound to Vorquellyn. Accidents do happen, and in those cases a normal Syverce will do to sew the shroud. The swords, however, call elves to do a terrible duty. An elf who takes one up does so to slay someone."

"That's an assassin's sword?"

"Yes and no; mostly no. If an elf chose to go against the calling of his homeland, to rebel, well, only madness could be the cause or the result of such a thing. That elf becomes a danger and someone has to eliminate him."

"Couldn't one of the mad ones just pick up a Syverce and start killing himself?"

Resolute extended the sword to Will hilt first. "Take it."

Will reached for the sword, but the second he touched it, he whipped his hand away and shook it hard to rid it of the terrible sting. He started to yell at Resolute for tricking him, but he dimly remembered having felt a similar but muted sting when he'd touched it before. "I don't understand."

"It's part of the magick worked into the blade. If you're not meant to have it, it hurts you. The Azure Spider had wrapped it up in leather and wore gloves to take most of the sting away."

"Will it kill *sullanciri*?"

The Vorquelf nodded. "I'm certain of it. Winfellis and Seethe will die beneath it."

"Seethe is Myrall'mara, right? She's here; you can kill her here."

"I can't, Will." Resolute sighed. "Up until you gave me this sword, my focus was redeeming my homeland. The straight line to that was through Chytrine. It was a grand goal, a great goal, a worthy one; but it was also very selfish. Down through the decades I have done good in its pursuit, but that's all been by happenstance. If people benefited from my killing Aurolani, fine. If people being in trouble attracted Aurolani for me to kill, better yet."

"How did Syverce change that?"

"The blade doesn't sting me. I'm supposed to have it, even though I'm not bound to a homeland. It's odd, since the homeland it came from has long since vanished, so it has no home, same as me. What it tells me is this, Will: I have a greater responsibility than seeing to my selfish goal. Thwarting Chytrine by making others safe is more valuable, more powerful, than just killing her troops."

Will shifted his mask up to the top of his head so he could give Resolute a proper frown. "You mean to tell me that after all this work to make me realize that I had this greater responsibility to the world, that you never saw that for yourself? You weren't bound by the rules you had me playing by?"

Resolute laughed aloud. "It doesn't seem fair, does it,

Will? Perhaps I was bound by them all along, but I just re-fused to acknowledge it." He played his fingertips over the flat of the blade, tracing them over Elvish sigils. "I suspect the Azure Spider stole this blade from some collector and never knew what he had. He had to steal it, though, was *fated* to steal it, so it would fall into my hands, courtesy of you."

"You're welcome."

"Am I?" The Vorquelf gave him a sly look. "If you thought I was relentless about drilling home your greater responsibilities before, it will be as nothing now."

The thief rolled his eyes. "I wonder if Chytrine is hiring? You can just stab me now and she can bring me back to life."

"Won't work that way, Will, not if I stab you with this."

"Why not?"

"It's the magick on the sword. You've seen me reanimate the recently dead."

Will shivered. "Yeah, I have."

"Well, when someone dies, their thread in the tapestry of life is cut. The magick I use, the magick Chytrine uses, splices that line back together. It's not as good as the origi-nal connection, hence the poor quality of life. Syverce, however, not only severs that connection, it knots it off—hence the needle's eye. There's no thread to splice. Die from Syverce and you are dead forever."

"There's something to look forward to." Will sighed. "We have to go, then, huh?"

"Their children will live to sing of their glory."

"Or avenge them?"

The Vorquelf nodded once. "Or avenge them, but only if you and I fail to accomplish the tasks fate has assigned us."

Erlestoke knocked on the open door to Alexia's chamber. "Forgive me, Highness. I wanted to return your sword."

The pale blonde woman glanced over at him as she tightened the last strap on a saddlebag. "I sent it to you because I wanted you to have it." She nodded toward Crow, who sat on the foot of her bed. "The Draconis Baron noted a *sullanciri* will come after us and Crow can deal with it. That leaves at least two here, and Malarkex's sword will let you kill any you face."

The man smiled and stepped into the room. "I appreciate the gift, but you killed Malarkex. The blade is yours by right. It is too precious to be given away."

Alexia straightened up and looked down her slender nose at him. "To tell you the truth, my lord, I don't like the sword. It's not to my taste, doesn't feel good in the hand. Your armory here yielded me a suitable replacement. I insist you keep it."

Erlestoke started to speak, but Crow eclipsed him. "Save your wind, Highness, for once she has made up her mind, she cannot be swayed. We know how savage things will be here. That sword will be an advantage and you will need all you can get."

The Oriosan prince nodded to Crow. "It would be a pity, then, to lose it to the enemy."

Alexia shouldered her saddlebags. "Chytrine created it; she can make more. I suspect creating *sullanciri* is a bit more difficult. Killing them is bound to distract her."

"I'd like to hope for something more than that, but I won't complain if that is all I get." Confidence surged in Erlestoke's breast as Crow stood, then waved Alexia toward the door. "I'll do your gift justice."

"Of that I have no doubt." She rested her hands on his shoulders. "Your people will be safe. We'll see to it."

"And of that I have no doubt." He smiled at her. "Safe journey."

"All courage." Alexia turned to go, then stopped in the doorway. "Do you have a message you want me to tell your father?"

Erlestoke started to shake his head, but hesitated. "Yes, I

suppose there is. Tell him for me, for the sake of his nation, not to live his whole life a coward."

The Okrans princess blinked her violet eyes. "Those words, exactly?"

"Anything less, he'd not notice." Erlestoke sighed. "Anything less and he'd know they didn't come from me."

CHAPTER 72

Alexia rode out in front of the refugee column and then pulled to the east a bit, keeping herself between the people and the Aurolani host. The sun blazed in the sky, making it unseasonably hot. The mail she wore over a padded gambeson weighed her down and kept her uncomfortably warm, but she wasn't going to doff it for all Chytrine's promises that she would let the refugees leave unmolested.

The noncombatants exited Fortress Draconis through the small southern gate. Chytrine's southern wing had pulled back to give them ample passage to the south. The women and children who could walk did, many struggling with packs stuffed to overflowing with clothes, blankets, rice, dried meat, dried fish, and what few mementos they couldn't bear to leave behind. Because so many of them were Oriosans, it was not uncommon to see them bearing the mask of the folks left behind, and to see those soldiers wearing makeshift masks.

Alexia understood that sacrifice on one level. Oriosans

were often defined by their masks, and families kept those of relatives to marvel at and venerate, if not worship. By giving their life masks to the refugees, the Oriosan soldiers were escaping along with their families. *An Oriosan without a mask is all but dead anyway.* These warriors were ready to sell their lives dearly and already counted themselves among the dead.

The Oriosan soldiery had all been given leave to head south. Dothan Cavarre had, in fact, ordered the Oriosan Scouts to accompany the refugees, and had assigned a *meckanshii* legion made up of Oriosans to the column as well. Other Oriosan soldiers, either the very young with families, or the very old, joined the refugees, while the rest remained to fight. Often those who wanted to leave changed places with Scouts who wanted to remain, allowing everyone to suit themselves.

It struck Alexia as odd that the Okrannel campaign had begun on a cold, rainy day, yet everyone riding from Yslin had been of high spirits. Now, riding from Fortress Draconis, under a blistering sun, she felt hollow inside and knew from the expressions on various faces that she was not alone.

Crow rode out to where she waited. "We have roughly two thousand people: five hundred are soldiers, another hundred are adults who've seen battle before. The rest are women and children, just shy two bairns to each adult. Twenty wagons with supplies, a hundred horses, mostly draft."

She looked at him. "Are you certain this is the right thing?"

He sighed. "I can't say I'm certain about anything, but I know this has to be done. Cavarre wouldn't have suggested it unless it was for the best. We have to make it work."

Alexia rested a hand on his shoulder. "We will, Crow."

The line of refugees snaked its way south, led by the *meckanshii*. They took up a position just inside the range of the southeast stronghold's dragonels and the refugees were

directed to move behind them and to the south. It seemed
ridiculous that a hundred men and women, half flesh and
metal, could stop the Aurolani forces if they chose to sweep
down and crush the refugees, but their formation went unchallenged.

The only movement on the Aurolani side came from
the golden dragon. It slithered toward the south, not deign-
ing to take to wing. It kept its body back behind the line described by the most forward of the Aurolani troops, but
jutted its muzzle out toward them. Nostrils widened, but
no flame burst forth. The creature sniffed and pulled itself
up in a very feline pose, even wrapping its tail around its
feet. It watched closely but did nothing.

Back in the line Kerrigan, Lombo, and Qwc came
through, shepherding a group of children. The little
Spritha's aerial antics delighted the kids, and Lombo provided transport for a couple of toddlers. Kerrigan had a
walking staff and a cadre of a half-dozen tiny boys trailing
in his wake, as if he was a goose and they his goslings. The
portly magicker shouldered his own pack, and had those
belonging to the two smallest kids hanging from it, but he
kept his eyes warily fixed to the east. Were the Aurolani to
come, Alyx felt certain Kerrigan would defend his charges
unto death.

As the wagons finally rolled from Fortress Draconis and
the southern gate closed, warriors lined the walls and
raised their weapons in a salute. Various voices shouted,
then the defenders gave throat to a grand *hurrah*! Again
and again, three times three, they voiced it. The refugees,
who had shuffled from the fortress fearful and tearful,
could not help but be heartened by the cheer. Adults
straightened up, children marched along more smartly, and
passing troops returned salutes.

Alyx reined her horse around as the last of the wagons
passed her position, then rode with Crow to join Resolute
and Will at the rear of the procession. They rode in silence
to where the *meckanshii* waited, then let them move out as

a force screening the column's left flank. The column snaked south for a mile to a line of low hills and began to slip through them. The riders mounted one of the taller hills, then turned to look back at Fortress Draconis.

The princess slowly shook her head. Already the Aurolani troops had begun to move forward and the dragon soared lazily over the battlefield. "I know we have to do this. I accept that. It doesn't stop me from feeling like a coward."

Resolute's eyes became argent slits. "Just remember, Princess, they have the easier job. All they have to do is kill. We have to survive. We're not just guarding their families, we are burdened with their hopes and dreams for the future. And we must succeed, or all that will be as dead as they soon will be."

From the Crown Tower roof, Erlestoke watched the last of the refugees head south and waited to see if Alexia turned to look back at the fortress. He hoped she would, and perhaps even look for him. He entertained no romantic notions about her—at least no more than any man would when looking at such a striking woman. Erlestoke's emotions had been fully engaged, and his mistress and their son were amid the refugees. Colonel Hawkins said he would look out for them, but Laerisa had agreed that she would be given no preference, and no attention would be drawn to her or the boy in case Chytrine did snap them all up.

He hoped Alexia would look back and get a glimpse of the maelstrom that was about to engulf Fortress Draconis. There was no denying that the speed and power of the Aurolani assault had surprised the defenders. Skycasters and thunderballs were weapons they had neither imagined nor anticipated. The damage they had done had kept the Draconis Baron awake long hours, thinking, dreaming, about how he could counter them. Without an example of a thunderball to study and dissect, however, designing countermeasures proved very difficult.

Erlestoke smiled. *But Chytrine is not the only one who has developed new weapons.* He fervently hoped Alexia and the others would realize that those who remained behind did so not to die, but to kill lots of Aurolani. *And we are very well prepared to do that.*

Drums began pounding behind the Aurolani lines. Undead legions started forward and dragonels massed near the northern wall. A smaller contingent toward the southeast could be moved quickly into position to strike at the main gate. *And the dragon could strike anywhere.*

He glanced over at the Draconis Baron. "Where do you want me? North at Hydra battery, or at the main gate with you at Lion?"

Cavarre considered for the moment, then pointed north. "Your people are there. That's where I will need you. When she makes her drive at the main gate, I will be ready and have you ready to command my reserve."

Erlestoke snapped a salute. "As ordered, my lord. In case I don't get a chance later, I want to thank you for all you've taught me."

"You were an apt pupil, so it was my pleasure." Cavarre returned the salute, then half smiled. "A question if you don't mind."

"Please."

Cavarre tapped a finger against his own nose. "You're still wearing your life mask. You didn't give it to Hawkins to take south?"

"He would have refused, wouldn't he? Would have told me to bring it myself." The prince shook his head. "Besides, do you think I want my father to have it?"

"No, I don't suppose you do."

Erlestoke smiled. "If you find me, promise me you'll toss my mask into the sea. My body, too, if there is anything left. I'll rest better with my mother."

"Consider it done."

"Any wishes for yourself?"

Cavarre laughed and patted a hand against the Crown Tower's thick walls. "I grew up in one Fortress Draconis, and I built another. I'll haunt this place, thank you very much. Now, you best get going. Tell Colonel Tatt to signal all soldiers to their posts."

Erlestoke nodded, then retreated through the tower. He found the *meckanshii* in charge of Signals and passed on the baron's command. Outside he worked his way north to the northernmost battery. He ducked his head and slipped into the first of the two dragonel lairs. A dozen of the weapons pointed in each direction, out toward the stronghold the Aurolani had taken the previous night. The dragonels each had a serpent's-maw at the muzzle and scales worked on the body, hence the designation of Hydra battery.

Captain Gerhard snapped a salute that the prince returned. "Dragonels sighted and treble-shotted. They won't be happy."

"Good. The tunnel is still intact?"

"Main tunnel fitted with nets and flooded as planned." The *meckanshii* officer smiled with a squeak. "We waited until some were coming up before we flooded it. Probably got a half-dozen squads."

"Don't let them relax down there. Their dead troops aren't going to be stopped by a little water in the lungs."

"Yes, sir." Gerhard went over to a speaking tube built into the wall and shouted an order down to the troops waiting in the dark. An acknowledgment echoed back up. "We're ready."

"Good." The drums outside began pounding to a crescendo. "They're coming."

Beyond the fortress walls the Aurolani troops began their march forward. Behind them the skycasters launched their thunderballs. More skycasters spoke from the captured stronghold, arcing the explosive spheres deep into the Maze. The bombs detonated in the air, or on the bounce, spraying metal fragments everywhere. One stray piece zinged into the battery, narrowly missing Erlestoke, and clanged impotently off Gerhard's left arm.

The *meckanshii* looked at the bright scar on his arm. "I'll need more paint after this is done."

The stronghold's dragonels—which had been captured when it was taken—could not easily be brought to bear on the fortress' battery, while the reverse was not true. The Aurolani had widened the fireports to give their dragonels more play, but that just gave Gerhard and his gunners bigger targets to shoot at.

The stronghold's dragonels spat fire and steel, skipping balls off the fortress. A few stone fragments from a shattered casement ricocheted through the battery, but the crew paid no attention. Their weapons had been long since aimed, with the ranges measured to the inch, the powder load and shot weighed carefully, the dragonels properly angled and primed. Erlestoke nodded and Gerhard snapped the order for his men to fire.

The dragonels boomed and rolled back in recoil, their missiles vomited out on a gout of flame. Smoke choked the battery and a heartbeat later the floor shook as the lower level fired. Erlestoke's ears rang and his eyes watered, but the breeze swirled smoke out of the battery, revealing men sponging the weapons and hurriedly reloading them. Past them the stronghold came into view, with its shattered fireports. At least one dragonel had been blasted free and slid down the exterior wall, while the others had been scattered about. At least one gibberer dragoneer hung from a ragged fireport, while parts of others oozed out elsewhere.

Beyond the stronghold, things looked more ominous yet. Some Aurolani troops had advanced using the stronghold as cover, but now they crept around it and kept coming. The undead, misshapen creatures came first, shuffling and shambling. Overhead sailed more thunderballs, but their distant explosions failed to hide the husky grunts and groans of the undead as they approached.

Gerhard, his face sooty from the first barrage, gave Erlestoke a quick nod. "Loading with scatter-shot, that was the plan."

The prince nodded. "Good. Looks as if they are moving their dragonels up."

"Two batteries, twenty dragonels or so." Gerhard stepped over to the speaking tube. "Ready on the flamers, ready in the hole."

The Aurolani dragoneers got their weapons moved and positioned, a bit back of the stronghold, giving them a clear line of fire at Gerhard's battery without exposing them to Eagle battery to the west. They rammed home powder and shot, then aimed their field pieces. The *meckanshii* waited until slow-burning match-coils had been distributed to fire the weapons, then shouted down the tube. "Fire the hole!"

Knowing what was coming, Erlestoke backed to a wall and hunkered down a bit. In the first siege of Fortress Draconis, back when he was still a child, Chytrine had only one dragonel and a limited supply of firedirt. The wagon carrying it had ventured into the fortress through the shattered gate and got trapped in a cul-de-sac where it caught fire. The resulting explosion leveled a portion of Draconis town.

To minimize the chances of that happening in the future, the Draconis Baron had ordered all magazines in which the firedirt was stored to be built underground, and charges for the dragonels were to be conveyed up to the batteries. The tunnels between the fortress and the strongholds ran underground at a level slightly above the magazines, and once the Aurolani had taken the strongholds, those tunnels had been fitted with nets and flooded.

Little side tunnels, which ran parallel to the main tunnels, and slanted down to the magazine level, had not been flooded. UrZrethi sappers had clambered down through them, broken into the darker reaches of the magazines, and opened a fair number of firedirt kegs. They then laid a trail of powder back through the side tunnels and, at the order, set light to the powder.

The Aurolani dragonels spoke loudly, crashing iron balls into the battery. One glanced off a dragonel's barrel, skewing it around and knocking the fireman flying, then the ball smashed the loader against the wall, crushing his right arm. The loader yelped, and his arm hung from his shoulder a useless mass of twisted metal and broken wire. Stone fragments from the wall tore at his face, where mail had not replaced flesh, while the misshapen ball pirouetted around the middle of the battery, then sagged over on a flattened side.

About a minute later, the first of three explosions shook the stronghold. It sounded like a muffled thump, but the second explosion's rumbling boom swallowed it. Jets of fire spurted here and there, smoke rose, but that formed a mere prelude to the final titanic blast. A volcano erupted from the stronghold's heart, pitching dark flecks of stone, decking, and creatures into the air, then the fire brightened from red to searing silver-white. The walls burst outward, dark stone divided by spiderwebs of white, with pieces growing smaller and smaller, then smoke condensed and rose while the explosion spit debris in every direction.

Stones and pieces of wood from flooring blasted through the fireports. The shock wave hit, jolting dragonels, cracking mortar, and loosening paving stones set in the battery floor. Erlestoke found himself flying for a second, then ended up in a heap on the ground, sputtering from the dust and smoke. He swiped at his eyes, smearing dust with tears, then shook his head to clear it of the ringing. He snorted to rid his nostrils of that dry scent of dirt, then felt blood dripping from his nose.

Smoke swirled and thinned, and the prince saw Gerhard laughing and pointing. Nothing was left of the stronghold save a smoking rubble pit occasionally stirred by fiery flares and small explosions. The Aurolani vanguard had been shredded with shrapnel, covering the field in blood and twitching bodies. The undead that had survived the blast did claw at the ground, dragging what was left of their bodies forward, closer and closer to the fortress. Erlestoke couldn't see the Aurolani dragonels, though a powder wagon burned merrily and exploded, knocking down other troops.

The prince crossed to the speaking tube and shouted down into it. "Flamers deploy!"

Hidden amid the wall spikes were some hollow tubes. At his order a valve was thrown open and a hidden oil reservoir drained out through the nozzle. In the bowels of the wall a combat mage triggered a simple spell, igniting the stream of oil. A stream of liquid fire arced out, trailing a curtain of black smoke, incinerating the undead and living alike.

Gerhard and Hydra battery started up a steady fire, with barrages coming every couple of minutes. Solid iron balls reached out to carve furrows through formations, while closer in scatter-shot blasted whole squads to pieces. Yet even with them firing as fast as they could, and the deadly streams of burning oil, the Aurolani troops got closer and closer, and the stronghold's rubble served as a breastwork behind which other dragonels could be hidden.

Erlestoke retreated from the battery and felt a chill as a black shadow coursed over him. He looked to the east and saw the main gate burning, the stone melted away. The gold dragon circled and swooped, then perched itself on the Crown Tower. With a swat of its tail it dashed the flagstaff to flinders, casting down the grey flag with black dragonskull on it. The dragon crouched on the tower's thick edge, its talons crushing stone. It did not stretch itself out over the top of the tower, as its predecessor had done.

The dragon had learned from the previous assault. A quarter century ago a dragon had torn open the Crown Tower's roof and had been impaled by a trap the Draconis Baron had previously arranged. Though this Crown Tower was far too small and squat to allow for the same defenses as before, the dragon took no chances, and began to claw away at the masonry and expose the fragment chamber.

The dragon had learned, but so had the Draconis Baron. Throughout the Maze lay other strongholds, blockhouses in which food and supplies were stored preparatory for a siege. Into each of them had been built a large dragonel, one far too big to be moved or reloaded with any ease or speed. Each had been laid so that it pointed at the top of the tower, one at each cardinal point of the compass. Using an intricate pulley, gear, and lever system, the aim could be adjusted ever so slightly, but with as large a target as a dragon, such minor adjustments were unnecessary. Sorcerers assigned to the fireteams used *arcanslata* to confer, and when the dragon began to tear through the wall, casting great blocks of granite to tumble through the town below, the fireteams were given the order to fire.

The grand dragonels did not quite go off as one, but it hardly mattered. The huge weapons had a bore the diameter of a common warrior's shield, perhaps two and a half feet across. An iron ball that size would have been impossibly heavy and the charge needed to lift it would have exploded the weapon. Scatter-shot, even made up of fist-size balls would have worked, but against a dragon's armor would not have done much more than shatter a few scales and anger the beast.

The Draconis Baron, having once used a single long needle to skewer and kill a dragon, decided to repeat his use of that weapon, but multiply it. Each grand dragonel had been loaded with a wooden canister, a cylindrical barrel a yard long and filled with wax. Into the wax had been sunk eighteen yard-long steel flechettes with razored tips thickened for penetrating armor. As the weapons detonated and the fire expanded to fill the metal tube, the canister accelerated. The fire melted the wax and blasted the canister apart, then sped the flechettes with an incendiary push.

From the south needles lanced through the partially healed wound on the dragon's thigh, ripping it open anew and causing the limb to falter. The western arc's dragonels' shots did not all hit, but several pierced its cheek and one exploded its left eye. The northern arc proved most accurate, peppering the dragon over its right side, skewering its paw, flank, foot, wing, and tail. None of the wounds were fatal, but the needles plunged in deeply, tearing muscle and spilling fiery black blood.

The shots from the east, the stronghold from which Cavarre had issued the order to fire, struck hardest and best. They caught the dragon full on in the back, stickling shoulders and neck. They screwed themselves in tightly, splintering bone and further rending tissue. One, in particular, struck for great effect.

As the dragon leaped up from the tower and opened its wings to strike for safety, the left wing failed to respond. That one needle had severed a nerve, numbing the wing. The gold dragon's hale wing pumped mightily, and its tail lashed savagely, tearing through the fragment chamber. The wing's thrust began a somersault that the tail could not stop, and the half-blind dragon crashed down hard into the Maze, smashing its head against a stronghold before it disappeared amid the dust of collapsing buildings.

Erlestoke yelped with joy, then shot down a ramp and ran toward the building where his company of troops awaited him. He pointed to the east, back toward the ruined main gate, but before he could tell them to move out in that direction, something clanked heavily behind him. His men's eyes widened and some of them ducked back. The prince looked to his left and saw one of the thunderballs lazily rolling through the air as it bounced past him.

For the briefest of moments he tried to memorize the details on the device so he could describe it for the Draconis Baron.

About the time he realized he was never going to share that information with his mentor, the thunderball exploded.

CHAPTER 73

Alexia did her best to peel away as much anxiety as she could about the evacuation. She freely admitted to herself that, all things considered, it was going better than expected. They got further along than planned that first day and by halfway through the second they'd reached a supply cache that Dothan Cavarre had set up in the event he needed to detach troops and have them operating to the south. Kerrigan managed to get through the spells warding it, and the cache provided a plethora of supplies, including enough weapons that every adult could arm themselves.

The rest of that second day had been devoted to the *meckanshii*'s acquainting the noncombatants with their weapons. Alyx harbored no illusions that being armed would make the adults into anything even vaguely useful as a fighting force. Even so, being given something to do to defend their children buoyed confidence and banished some fear, so that was to the good.

By that second night, however, she faced a grave decision. Peri had reported, and a quick scouting foray with

Crow and Resolute had confirmed, that the refugee train was being stalked. Aurolani cavalry had moved south on a course that paralleled theirs. They stayed to the east, cutting the refugees off from the Tynik River, which they could have forded above Yavatsen Bend, then rafted down to Sebcia. Because of their position, the Aurolani could curve around and herd them back north to Fortress Draconis anytime they wanted to.

The question she faced was whether or not to let the refugees know the Aurolani had already come after them. Not only did the Aurolani pose an immediate threat to them, the import of the cavalry being detached and sent south would be clear to everyone. Since the cavalry would be largely useless inside the fortress, their being given this mission suggested Chytrine was having no problem with the troops left behind.

The fact that the dragon had not winged its way south to stop them belied that, but Alyx expected to see it at any point. She wasn't certain whether or not Chytrine had ever intended to honor her pledge to let the refugees go, but that speculation was immaterial. The simple fact was that Chytrine had no reason to honor that pledge, so Alyx saw no harm in assuming she would renege on it. Letting them go had been a game, and clearly Chytrine had tired of it, therefore ending it.

She waited one more day before making her decision. In that time she was able to determine, to the best of her abilities, that two cavalry legions had been sent after the refugees. One consisted almost entirely of frostclaws, with vylaens to direct them. That unit had been broken down into companies that ranged forward of the line of march and served as the main body's eyes. The other unit was heavy cavalry and the *sullanciri* Ganagrei was in command.

Against them she had six hundred troops, but only the *meckanshii* could be considered heavy infantry. The Oriosan Scouts would have been ideally suited to the fight, but two-thirds of them had remained behind in Fortress

Draconis. While the soldiers who filled out the Scouts' ranks were game and had their families to defend, they weren't well versed in fighting through light woodlands.

In fact, the only thing Alyx had going for her was terrain. The road south wound through forested hills that provided some wonderful defensive positions. Peri scouted ahead and picked out a perfect spot for them to make a stand. Two streams carved a flat-topped, lozenge-shaped hill that was large enough to hold the refugees. They stopped prematurely and immediately set about digging in and throwing up breastworks. The troops moved out to the west and south, taking up positions on the hillsides beyond the streams. The single genuine Scout company pushed further on and a bit north, finding a spot they could defend easily. The *meckanshii* formed the heart of her line, with the other Scouts to the south, and the assorted troops and irregulars to the northern flank.

Waiting there with the *meckanshii* as dusk fell, Alyx knew that if an attack were to come, it would be in the night because the Aurolani forces had the advantage in the dark. She needed to take that advantage away. She had her troops gather wood for bonfires behind their own positions, but she had to be careful because the forest was rather dry, and the prevailing wind was moving toward the east. Roasting her own people in a forest fire wasn't something she wanted to do.

Visiting that same fate on the Aurolani, on the other hand, was something she would not mind at all. As the uppermost horn of the moon's crescent arose in the east, Resolute, Crow, and a couple of *meckanshii* started a fireline roughly five hundred yards to the east. Quickly enough the fire spread, roaring up over ancient pines with an orange hunger. Smoke poured east, borne on the breeze, and she imagined that if that didn't get the attention of the Aurolani host, nothing would.

* * *

Back in the refugee camp Will checked his pouch of bladestars for the dozenth time. He'd not wanted to be left behind with the women and children, but Alyx had taken him aside and pointed out that because everyone knew the prophecy, his presence would stiffen the spines of those left behind. The fact that Kerrigan would remain as well made him feel a little better, and the way the fear in the eyes of some refugees lessened when he walked through helped even more.

An old infantry captain had been left in charge, though the two most able warriors present were Lombo and Dranae. Lombo squatted in the middle of everything, playing with children, while some parents lined the dirt piles rimming their hilltop. Dranae walked the line, speaking to everyone, smiling, laughing, and nodding reassuringly. His air of quiet confidence set everyone at ease. Back between the line and the children waited the rest of the parents, fingering spears, swords, daggers, and, in a few cases, big rocks.

Will wandered over to where Kerrigan nervously stood, alternately frowning into the darkness and looking down at his hands. The Adept hadn't bothered to switch back to robes at Fortress Draconis and instead wore a mélange of old pirate clothes and, next to his skin, a uniform tunic from Fortress Draconis.

The thief looked at him. "You have to get this right, you know, no mistakes."

Kerrigan snarled. "I know!" His hands curled down into fists. "Can't you leave me alone? Just go away."

The Adept tried to turn away, but Will caught his arm and turned him back. "Hey, Keri, there's no going away here."

"Don't call me Keri."

Will snorted. "Look, you're nervous, I'm nervous. We have a lot of people here counting on us. Counting on you, mostly, because you're the one who has the big part to play."

"I know how important it is."

"Good. I want to make sure you're here with us."

"What does that mean?" Kerrigan's face screwed up tight and he crossed his arms over his chest.

Will stepped in close and kept his voice low. "We get away from the pirates, the elves put you to work. On the ship to the fortress you're quiet, not talking much except with the elves, then at the fortress you pretty much vanish until it's time for us to go, then you spend all your time with the kids. You've been avoiding us—those of us who were with you at Wruona. I think that's because you think we blame you for her dying."

Kerrigan blinked. "You think what?"

The thief kept his voice low. "I don't think it was your fault, nobody does. It wasn't your fault at all. So you don't need to be hiding or nothing anymore."

The Adept raised his chin. "You think that's what I've been doing?"

Will smiled. "Seems pretty obvious."

"Does it?" The magicker's eyes narrowed. "I hope you're a good thief, because, as a mind reader, you're really, really bad. That's not what I'm thinking at all. I'm not hiding and I haven't been hiding."

"No? Why didn't I see you around the fortress, then?"

Kerrigan hesitated. "I was sleeping. I was tired and sleeping."

Will snorted. "Okay, sure, if you say so." The thief backed away, opening his hands as firelight flared to the east. "Just as long as you're with us now . . . and *awake* . . . that's all that counts."

The fire did provoke a reaction from the Aurolani host. Green magick shot from the darkness, suppressing flames, then vylaens rode through, with frostclaws following them. The temeryces galloped forward, bobbing almost comically on their powerful legs, then leaped toward the *meckanshii* positions, hissing and screaming furiously.

It seemed to Alyx to be somewhat less of a battle than a riot. Crow struck from behind a tree, shooting arrows as fast as he could. He shot at vylaens and those he missed often found one of Resolute's bladestars buried in them. With their leaders falling, the frostclaws still attacked, but lacked cohesion. While more than capable of rending and tearing with their teeth and claws, they chose their targets by whatever criteria existed in their little minds, not with a goal toward rolling up a flank or breaking a formation.

The defensive preparations the *meckanshii* had made confounded the frostclaws. Some that leaped over the front line found themselves trapped in ropes and nets strung through tree branches. Others that soared past the warriors' spear-points discovered the ground sown with sharpened wooden stakes that pierced haunches and bellies. The close-set trees did make it difficult for the stiff-tailed beasts to turn quickly, and, like as not, a nip at a soldier would get them a mouthful of metal, not flesh.

The *meckanshii* fought demoniacally, slashing back at the temeryces with claws of their own. The fighting broke down into small knots of warriors thrusting and jabbing, or grappling and clawing. Alyx almost wished for Malarkex's sword again, for it would have allowed her to revel in the violent chaos and throw herself completely into the fight. As it was, her blade sang, slashing throats, cutting off limbs, while frostclaws shredded her mail and eventually scored the flesh beneath it.

The light cavalry company did its job, for it engaged the *meckanshii* in time for a heavy cavalry company to come blasting through. The larger frostclaws and their riders leaped through the resurgent flames, undaunted and uncaring. Weaving through trees, they came swiftly, aiming their charge at where the *meckanshii* center had been driven back. Some riders did lean too far one side or the other and were blasted out of the saddle by a tree, and a few others did have their mounts falter and fall when they impaled themselves on the spikes. The majority of them, however, blew through the heart of the *meckanshii* line and disappeared into the darkness.

Ganagrei did not. He reined his grand temeryx back, then snapped guttural orders at those riders who were engaged with the *meckanshii*. Out of the darkness whizzed a bladestar. It burst the big frostclaw's left eye and sank a point into its brain. The creature convulsed hard, then leaped into the air and landed harder, before collapsing and sagging to the side.

The *sullanciri* rolled to its feet, none too quickly nor with much agility, but it uncoiled its armored form, then reached down and tugged a double-bitted broadax from its saddle sheath. The weapon came up and around quickly, then flashed down, striking sparks from a *meckanshii's* metal arm as it mangled the limb beyond recognition.

Sallitt Hawkins whirled away, his twisted arm and the force of the blow spinning him to the ground. The *sullanciri* raised the ax to kill him, but before the blow could fall, an arrow stabbed through Ganagrei's right eye. The undead thing staggered back a step or two, allowing Hawkins to scramble to his feet. The damaged warrior cast about for anything he could use as a weapon.

Crow advanced and tossed him the silverwood bow. "Keep that for me." The white-haired warrior then drew Tsamoc and the gem set in its forte glowed brilliantly, washing color into his beard and hair.

Ganagrei snarled and slashed at him, but Crow blocked the slow blow simply enough. The man cut to his left, then slashed Tsamoc at the *sullanciri's* stomach with a disemboweling blow. The Aurolani creature grunted and the armor glowed at the point of contact, but failed to part. Ganagrei backhanded Crow with a mailed fist, catching him between the shoulder blades and sending him sprawling.

The *sullanciri's* good eye glowed a gangrenous green as

it stalked toward the downed man. Crow got back up quickly enough and parried another blow. He lunged, then tried to cut up into Ganagrei's armpit, but the sword skittered harmlessly off the glowing armor.

Crow danced back as another slash tried to bisect him, then chopped his sword down, double-handed, on the creature's forearm. Sparks flew argent from where Tsamoc caught the *sullanciri*'s armor. The blade traced a little silver scar on it and left a dent, but didn't even come close to penetrating it. The dent glowed green, then the armor screeched as the metal resumed its original shape.

Alyx's mouth went dry. The *sullanciri* were vulnerable to magickal weapons. By fashioning magickal weapons for her generals, Chytrine made them formidable, but by enchanting armor for Ganagrei, she made him invincible. *Tsamoc might be able to kill him, but first it has to cut him, and Crow can't punch through that armor.*

Again and again Crow struck at Ganagrei. A slash nearly severed a triangle of mail from the *sullanciri*'s mail coif, but the scrap swung back into place as the creature advanced and the rings interlocked in a green light. The *sullanciri*'s blows, though ponderous and heavy, came closer and closer to striking home as Crow began to tire. The man parried many blows and sidestepped others, but one slash scored the flesh over his ribs, and a second laid open a stripe on his left thigh.

Crow began to retreat, glancing behind him as he did so. Drawing the *sullanciri* further from the battle, the man picked up speed in his withdrawal. The Aurolani creature came after him, moving faster. Ganagrei mumbled something unintelligible, then reached up and snapped the shaft of the arrow in half, casting it aside.

Alyx cut down a gibberer with a slash that parted upper jaw from lower and angrily thrust its body aside. She could only watch as Crow ran to a thick tree, put his back to it, and extended his sword in a thrust that would impale the *sullanciri*. Ganagrei laughed hoarsely as he figured out

Crow's desperate ploy. Magickally armored as he was, he might be spitted on the sword, but he would certainly crush Crow.

The *sullanciri* sped up. He pulled the ax back with his right hand and swept it in front of him in a parry meant to batter the sword out of line. Likely the precaution would have worked, but Crow had already pulled his blade back at the last second. The man cut to the right, clearly intent on letting the *sullanciri* batter itself against the tree, then finding a way to kill it.

The plan almost worked. Ganagrei crashed into the tree's trunk with a hideous clang. Bark flew. The *sullanciri's* head hit so hard that the impact drove the remnant of the arrow through the back of its skull. The broadhead tented the mail coif, popping a few rings, which glowed furiously green as they attempted to reconnect around the arrowhead.

It would have worked, had Crow been quicker. The cut to his left leg meant he didn't push off as strongly as intended, so when the *sullanciri* slammed into the tree, Crow's leg remained trapped between it and the trunk. The man's thigh and shin snapped more easily than the arrow had. Crow screamed and fell at the base of the tree, clawing at exposed roots to drag himself away as the *sullanciri* rebounded and tottered backward.

The creature's breastplate showed full signs of the impact, with a cylindrical dent running from throat to waist. The metal groaned as a green magick washed over it in waves. Ganagrei arched his back as if that might help return the concave armor to its original convex form. With a final ping the armor righted itself, then the *sullanciri* looked about. The monster slowed, then deliberately oriented on Crow and his crooked leg.

"Crow, no!" Alyx shouted and threw her sword at the *sullanciri*. It clanged off his back, no damage done. The *sullanciri* took no notice of the blow as it stooped and hefted its ax again. Alyx darted at the thing's back, but knew she would never reach it in time, and had no idea what she would do if she did.

Luckily for her, it didn't matter.

"Ganagrei!" Resolute's voice cut through the battle din. "You've forgotten something!"

The *sullanciri* turned toward the Vorquelf, his good eye searching for the threat the words implied. All Ganagrei saw was an elf with a stick in his right hand and a sword in his left. Had the *sullanciri* been capable of registering fear, that sight would have inspired none.

A blue glow illuminated one of the tattoos on Resolute's right forearm. A heartbeat later the stick in his hand burst into flame. The fire made it readily apparent that what he held was more than just a stick, it was the back half of an arrow.

The other half of which lay buried in the *sullanciri's* brain.

Flames jetted from Ganagrei's nostrils as the undead creature clawed at its own face. The arrow's shaft burned hot, bubbling steaming brains out the *sullanciri's* ears. The fearsome creature danced awkwardly, like a man having taken a mouthful of very hot food, then tripped and fell, thrashing on the ground. Resolute stalked over to it and drove Syverce straight down through its forehead, twisted and yanked it free, leaving a little volcano erupting through the creature's skull.

The night air carried the war cries of men and the piercing shrieks of the temeryces back to the camp without distortion or diminution. Will waited beside Dranae, feeling nervous and edgy. He couldn't tell if the sound was getting closer or not, and peering out into a darkness virtually untouched by the distant fires did little for Will. Lombo barely flicked an ear in the direction of the fighting, but that didn't help Will much, since the Panqui delighted in killing frostclaws with his bare hands.

When the Panqui finally stirred, Dranae shook the infantry captain's shoulder. The man looked up, then called to Kerrigan. "Now, please, Adept."

Over toward the south end of the line, Kerrigan raised a hand and waved it. A shower of sparks shot from his fingertips, each growing into a glowing blue-white ball about the size of a man's head. They floated across the ravine toward the east, then lodged in the branches of the trees. They cast a harsh light that made for sharp shadows beneath the underbrush.

The light also made it easy to see the frostclaws moving through the forest. Will was glad of the light because he couldn't hear them, especially above the gasps and wails of the people on the line. While other adults herded children to the other side of the camp, and many others formed a wall between the oncoming enemy and their offspring, the hundred or so people on the line prepared themselves and waited for the order they had been told would come.

Some of the frostclaws leaped from the far end, trying to reach the camp through the air, but the distance proved too great. Those creatures landed deep in the ravine, scrabbling to gain purchase on the steep wall. They slid down toward the stream on a river of old leaves and fresh earth, but eventually checked their retreat and started to pick their way back up again. Their fellows, which had run down the far side, filled the gaps in their line and scaled the hillside.

Behind them came the heavy cavalry, starting a hurried descent.

Dranae nodded to the captain. "Now."

"If you please," came the man's voice, loud though quivering a bit, "fire!"

As Crow had explained, a draconette might be inferior to a bow and arrow in terms of range and accuracy and the rate at which missiles could be shot, but it required little, if any, training. When they'd opened the weapons' cache they'd discovered an ample store of the Draconis Baron's early attempts at creating draconettes, along with firedirt and shot. None of the warriors on the trip had been members of fire companies—those men and women would never have left Fortress Draconis—but the *meckanshii* knew enough about the weapons to instruct people in their use.

The draconette irregulars rose and pointed their weapons downslope. Fingers tightened on triggers, slow-burning matches ignited dust, and the weapons fired in a ragged, smoky volley. Several did fail to discharge and two blew up, killing the shooters, but the rest performed admirably.

Shot ripped through frostclaws, filling the air with feathers and littering the ground with thrashing bodies. Wounded creatures screamed and clawed blindly in agony, rending hale and wounded fellows alike. Some frostclaws, though wounded, continued their scramble up the hill, while others that had gone untouched climbed ever closer to the top.

The heavy cavalry splashed through the stream. Dranae pointed to Kerrigan. "Now, Adept, now!"

The infantry captain gave Dranae a sour look because of the usurpation of his authority. Will noticed that, then shifted his gaze to where Kerrigan moved up to the top of their breastwork. He became a thick, black silhouette against one of the will-o'-the-wisps, and swept his hand out with a near theatrical calm.

More sparks shot from his fingers, but these did not drift lazily and glow softly, they sizzled and plunged down into the smoke choking the little rift. In no time they reached their targets, and as instructed, everyone in the camp ducked for cover.

It had been readily apparent to Alexia that the draconetteers would get one volley. The chances of their being able to reload and shoot again in the midst of a battle were slender. Moreover, having shot flying around in the camp was just as likely to strike friend as foe, and was more likely to do so since there would be far fewer of the enemy.

Because the chances of a prolonged firefight were nil, the *meckanshii* filled three small casks with firedirt and shot, then buried them at the base of the eastern slope. Kerrigan's sparks plunged burning into the earth, passed through the wood, and ignited the powder. The resulting explosion destroyed the casks, casting wood and earth about.

And spraying lots of shot up over the western side of the valley.

Crouched down with the others, all Will saw was a series of bright flashes, accompanied by sharp thunderclaps. Dirt rained down along with some smoldering leaves. As the explosions' echoes faded, he caught more screams, more wails, but just enough war cries punctuated them that he knew the job hadn't been finished.

People surged to the breastwork, and Will along with them. One Aurolani rider crested the breastwork and a half-dozen spears impaled its temeryx thigh and breast. The gibberer slashed with a longknife, notching one of the spear-hafts, then its mount went down and started to roll back into the ravine. The gibberer leaped free, but went down as someone twisted the spear between its legs. Swords and knives flashed, hands clutched at it and dragged it back where others tore it to pieces.

Will whirled bladestars at shadows moving through the smoke. Dranae stepped up beside him and shouldered a draconette. A mounted gibberer emerged from the smoke. Dranae fired and the ball dented the creature's helmet. The rider pitched back off into the smoke while the grand temeryx cut across the slope and came up.

Its angled run brushed aside thrusting spears and it bore straight at Kerrigan. The magicker stared at the creature wide-eyed, but didn't move. Will whipped a bladestar at it. The weapon grazed a leg, cutting it, but not delivering enough poison to drop it.

Lombo pounced on the rainbow frostclaw with the ease and delight of a cat attacking a wounded bird. The Panqui's weight crushed the creature down. It shrieked furiously and turned its head back to bite him, but Lombo's hand just circled its throat and squeezed. The shriek became a shrilled hiss that ended in a loud pop.

Others of the Aurolani heavy cavalry appeared on the far side of the ravine. They waited there, peering down into the smoke-filled valley, trying to decide if they should ride down or not. Lombo picked up the big frostclaw and hurled it at them, but the beast didn't quite make it. A couple of spears arced over, but did no damage, then Kerrigan pointed his finger and cast a spell that exploded an oak tree, peppering them with burning splinters.

The riders quickly took off to the south and soon sounded distant trumpet calls. Will wasn't certain what they signified until he saw one gibberer crawling his way out of the ravine to the south.

Dranae, who had reloaded his draconette by then, ended the gibberer's flight with a single shot. The smoke below had begun to thin and as Will looked down, he kind of wished it hadn't. The twitching, and the way it made the ground look as if it were alive, or at least dying slowly, bothered him more than the painful cries.

He glanced over at Kerrigan. "Can you stop the light?"

"Our survivors need a way to find us."

"Then leave one, or string the others further away." He pointed down into the pit. "If any of the children look, it might give them nightmares."

The magicker moved to the top of the breastwork and looked down, then recoiled and would have fallen save that Will stepped up and steadied him. "Yes, you're right, Will." He gestured and the lights sailed out toward the east. "No one needs the memory of seeing that."

CHAPTER 74

General Markus Adrogans handed the *arcanslata* to the signal mage who had brought it to him. "Please acknowledge the message without comment."

The mage bowed and left the Jeranese military leader standing there with Phfas and Beal mot Tsuvo in the dawn light. He looked at both of them, then slowly shook his head. "Four days ago Chytrine allowed about two thousand Oriosans and noncombatants to head south from Fortress Draconis. There is no word on their fate. According to the last messages from Fortress Draconis, the Aurolani have entered the fortress."

Beal paled. "Fortress Draconis has fallen?"

"It appears so."

"And word of Princess Alexia?"

"The refugees went out under her command. They are bound for Oriosa, so we might eventually hear if they make it." Adrogans scratched at his unshaven throat. "They're looking at a trek of over four hundred miles, over a hundred to Sebcia."

Phfas shrugged his bony shoulders beneath a thread-bare cloak. "They will not be wanting for supplies. Their journey is as nothing."

His disgusted tone prompted a surprised chuckle from Adrogans. "Uncle, our journey is difficult, but do not minimize theirs."

All around them, the refugees from Svoin began to stir as the sky brightened. Men and women—*with far too few children*—looking all stick-and-sinew thin crawled from beneath blankets thicker than their skin. Some people stumbled down to the river to drink or bathe—and far too few of them bathed, having long since become used to the colonies of body lice that infested them. Others just sat in one place, dazed, disoriented, hovering between life and death.

Adrogans had been given no real choice. Svoin was a dying place, a fetid pit of misery. It would never and could never allow the people there to heal. As quickly as they could, his troops had gathered up all the supplies available and started herding refugees toward the north, where they harvested what they could from the hills. Beginning in the southeast quarter of the city they set fire to it, burning everything. They saved the docks for last, allowing the arson teams to escape onto the lake and sail up the river to join the refugee caravan at the Svoin River ford.

The two possible places to take the refugees were the Zhusk plateau or the Guranin highlands. While the land of the Zhusk was closer, the housing and supplies available there could never have supported five thousand sick and malnourished people. The highlands, by way of contrast, had actual cities. The various clans had their own towns and villages and had already begun to compete with their rivals in shows of generosity concerning the refugees.

Guraskya lay a hundred miles from Svoin by conventional routes. Adrogans' troops could have made the journey in a week, or even half that, if he'd wanted to push them hard. The refugees, on the other hand, were hard put to go five miles in a day. Sometimes the last of them had not even started to move before the head of the column stopped and began to make camp.

And the bodies of the dead marked the roads all along the route.

The Aurolani forces made no serious attempt to harass the refugees. Caro led the Alcidese cavalry and deployed them as a screening force. They'd caught and killed small knots of Aurolani scouts, as well as rounded up and moved into the refugee train crofters scattered through the Svoin basin. The soldiery carted off all the grain and livestock they could find, then burned the farms to deny them to the Aurolani.

Beal mot Tsuvo regained some of her composure. "We have made it to the most critical point in our journey. Once we put the Gurakovo between us and the Aurolani, their ability to strike at us is gone. Already the people of the highlands are preparing to help these people."

"I think you're right, Beal, and I hope you are right even more." Markus Adrogans sighed heavily. "It will be a long winter. Assuming we survive it, we'll have to make the best of every free moment. We'll be planning what we'll sow when comes the spring."

"What we'll sow"—Beal smiled—"and what we'll harvest."

"Indeed." Adrogans nodded solemnly. "And perhaps even figure out how we'll be able to bring it all to market in Svarskya."

The *sullanciri* Ferxigo shifted her form so she had knees to bend in obeisance to her Mistress. She lowered her gaze as Chytrine moved along the narrow corridor. Gibberers shrank back against the walls as if the touch of a stray strand of Chytrine's hair would be a whiplash. Their eyes darted to the glowing, silver-white form of Myrall'mara drifting in Chytrine's wake, knowing well she would kill them at her Mistress' whim, then find any number of ways to employ their remains.

Chytrine swept into the small room carved into the bedrock upon which Fortress Draconis had been built. The featureless room would have been pitch-dark save for Myrall'mara's glow, and the scintillating light of the gold-bound yellow gem resting in the top of the stone throne at the room's heart. The DragonCrown fragment had been set in a small recess there, well above the head of the chair's occupant.

The Aurolani Empress walked to the throne and reached a hand out to grasp the man's chin. She turned his face to the right, then the left. She released it, letting his head loll onto a shoulder, then turned toward Ferxigo. "This was Dothan Cavarre?"

"This is what is believed, Mistress."

"He is dead, but not a mark on him. How did he die?" Chytrine held her right index finger up and it quickly lengthened into a slender hornlike needle. "Did you pierce his vitals and I've missed the sign?"

"No, Mistress." Ferxigo pressed her hand to the ground, wishing she could melt her feathered form into it. "Your desire was for him to be taken alive. He is as he was found."

Chytrine slowly nodded. The dragon's thrashing tail had scattered the Crown Tower's DragonCrown fragments. Her soldiers and Dark Lancers had labored hard to recover them. Upon examination she determined they were counterfeits. The magick on them, which had caused the dragon to believe they were in the Crown Tower, had been a sophisticated spell of great strength, but could only function over a relatively short distance. The fakes were linked to the originals by this magick, drawing their magickal identity from the originals, so her hunters were able to employ the counterfeits and use that link to locate the originals. After days of searching, this was the first they had recovered.

That they still remained in Fortress Draconis did not surprise Chytrine. Just as the Draconis Baron would not entrust dragonel technology to anyone in the south, she had known he would not disperse the crown fragments. Cavarre had seen his duty to protect them as being sacred and his very presence here, protecting one with his life, clearly indicated his depth of commitment to his duty.

Extending her arm, reshaping it to add several feet to its length, she plucked the DragonCrown fragment from its perch. The stone's warmth was as expected, for the fragment she wore between her breasts felt similar. She looked at the setting, at the tabs and notches, the Aurolani script incised into it, and knew the two pieces she had would not fit together. One of the two others hidden in Fortress Draconis would bridge the gap between these two stones, and she could forge links to bring the fourth into concert with them.

That would be for the future, however. For the moment she stroked the yellow stone's surface and focused on it. She projected her mind into it and there, deep in its depths, she sensed a distant presence. It was ancient and unknowable, and a bit surprised at the intrusion. Anger began to gather, so she pulled back and her awareness returned to the room.

Chytrine pointed at Cavarre's body. "You will take it to what is left of the tower and have it bound to the forehead of the dragon skull there. It will remain until the birds have picked it apart and the bleached bones fall to ruin along with the rest of this place."

Ferxigo glanced up as her Mistress spoke, then bowed her head once. "It shall be as you desire."

"Very good." Chytrine glanced at the Vorquelf *sullanciri*. "And you, my pet, will arrange for guards to haunt the tower. Cavarre's people will emerge from their warrens to rescue him. You will make them pay dearly for their defiance. They do not realize that they stand naked before the might of a fierce north wind. You will teach them why this is folly. They will learn this lesson well, and then so shall their brethren to the south."

Erlestoke cupped his hand around the end of the slow-match and blew on it until the ember glowed golden red. Across the street, barely visible against a pile of rubble, a *meckanshii* pointed south twice. The Oriosan repeated the gesture twice, counted to two, then stood, shouldered his draconette, and fired.

A puff of smoke obscured his first target, but a gib-berer's guttural scream told him he'd hit. Bringing his right hand off the trigger, he cranked the lever from alongside the foregrip up and back to the stock, then returned it forward. The lever pushed other levers and turned gears that rotated and locked into position the next of the dra-conette's four barrels, as well as cocked back the match hammer. He brought a powder horn up from his right hip, primed the weapon again, sighted, and fired.

A second gibberer went down, this one clutching a ru-ined belly. Across the street the *meckanshii* also shot, drop-ping her second target. The Aurolani squad had begun running at them with the first two shots, and kept coming despite the second shot coming so quickly.

Erlestoke worked the lever again, primed, and shot, get-ting off his third shot inside a minute. This one spun a gib-berer around and set his longknife clattering off a wall before he hit the street. The *meckanshii* missed with her third shot, but only by dint of a gibberer tripping in his haste and going down.

Other warriors—*meckanshii* and full-fleshed men, elves, and one urZrethi—emerged from the shadowed ruins behind and beside the remaining gibberers. The Aurolani troops realized, belatedly, that they'd been lured into a trap. Their process of enlightenment ended prematurely and painfully. The ambushers dragged the dead bodies from the street—dispatching those who were not yet dead before making their bodies disappear.

Erlestoke and the *meckanshii* watched the street, then retreated down into the warrens below Fortress Draconis. Hidden stone doors slid into walls, permitting them passage, then sealed the way behind them. They'd found ample evidence that Aurolani searchers had trailed after them in the past, but their secret paths remained undiscovered.

The prince patted Colonel Jancis Ironside on the shoulder. "You shot well."

"As did you, Highness." The Murosan smiled beneath her mask. "Keep shooting that well and we will be even, soon."

He laughed and followed her down a set of spiral stairs that opened into a long, narrow room. In it their squad had gathered—twelve veterans from throughout the world, united in contesting Chytrine's ownership of Fortress Draconis.

In this mission they had fared well, and they knew there were other groups, some larger, some smaller, who were doing likewise. The Aurolani troops had succeeded in breaching the main gate and occupying the eastern quarter of the city. They'd also taken the Crown Tower. The southwest quarter had been fighting hard and the entire northern arc had resisted Aurolani penetration. The Aurolani had brought dragonels into the Maze and used them to blast buildings apart to root out opposition, but the troopers made them pay dearly for every block they cleared.

Erlestoke remembered nothing of the two days following the point when the thunderball exploded in front of him, but Castleton, the only survivor of his fireteam, had filled in the gaps. The prince had been severely wounded, but Jilandessa, a Harquelf healer who had been at Fortress Draconis for decades, had repaired the damage. By the time he was ready to resume fighting, however, organized resistance had broken down. Soldiers fled to the sewers and into a network of warrens few admitted having known existed.

The prince handed his draconette to an old *meckanshii* who functioned as the group's armorer. "Perfect match of load to shot. The aim remained true at all ranges."

The old man smiled, revealing a mouth only half full of teeth. "And you saved one shot?"

Erlestoke nodded. They had a limited number of the quadnels. The shooters entrusted with them only used three shots, saving one for emergencies as they pulled back. "It's the one ready to fire now, so draw it carefully."

"Sure, Highness, and next you'll be telling your grand-mother how to suck eggs." The man pinched the slow-match out with a mechanical hand. "Glad to have you back."

"Good to be back." The Oriosan turned away from him and crossed to the table in the center of the room. Two of the people who had done the close work had taken a pouch from one of the dead gibberers and were unfolding a map they'd found in it. Crudely drawn, it showed the fortress, with a heavy charcoal line around what, apparently, the en-emy felt were fairly secure areas.

The Loquelf, one of the Steelfeathers, looked up as he tapped the map with a finger. "They may think they own this area right here, but they don't move through it during daylight hours. It's ours if we want it."

"I know, but you know we don't want it." Erlestoke smiled. "They can have it for as long as they want to pay the rent in blood."

"I know, Highness, I just want us to raise the rent."

"In good time, Ryswin, in good time." The prince shook his head, marveling at the absurdity of his having to sug-gest patience to an elf. "Remember, as long as we are trapped here, so some of her troops will be trapped here. Fortress Draconis might not have caught in her throat and choked her the way we wanted, but now it's a hungry maw nibbling away at her troops. She wanted it, she's taken part of it, and we'll keep gnawing away until it drives her insane."

"Or," piped a youthful soldier from Savarre, "until the armies of the south come up and smash her."

Erlestoke gave the youth a quick nod. "Or until then, yes. That won't be until the spring, however. We'll see, by then, just how much sanity Chytrine has left."

CHAPTER 75

All the aches and pains, all the fatigue Kerrigan had been feeling, vanished as the road south straightened and the border posts marking the line between Muroso and Oriosa came into view. Their journey was finally at an end, and they'd actually survived.

After the grand battle they'd faced some harassment by the remnants of the force Chytrine had sent after them. Alexia had managed to organize their troops so that they punished the ambushers rather severely. Sebcian troops also came north and caught the Aurolani in a trap of their own, scattering them and shepherding the refugees into Sebcia.

Once in Sebcia, Alexia, Ryhope, and their companions had been given fresh horses and passes that allowed them to speed south. Sallitt Hawkins led the way despite his mangled arm, and Ryhope had insisted some woman and her infant child be brought along as well, for reasons Kerrigan didn't understand. He likely could have discovered who she was, but he'd kept himself apart from the others during the journey. He'd had lots of practice driving his mentors off by being pricklish and sulky.

He felt a little bad for Will because the thief had accused him of freezing when the grand temeryx had come for him. Kerrigan had aptly pointed out that because the temeryx was a predator, and predators tended to go after things that acted like prey; by not moving, he was not presenting himself as prey to that creature. Will had refused to believe that explanation and had laughed, so Kerrigan feigned being hurt. Resolute berated Will for his behavior, so Will did his best to stay away from Kerrigan, and the others left him alone as well.

The Adept touched his heels to his horse and urged it forward to where Alexia and Crow rode. He smiled at them as his horse pulled even. "We're almost in Oriosa, yes?"

Alexia smiled. "We are. It's good to finally see you in high spirits, Adept Reese. We're safe, and now we can rest."

"Oh, I know." Kerrigan glanced beyond her and at Crow. "And your leg, it is still okay?"

The older man nodded. "I appreciate the work you've done on me."

The Adept's smile broadened. Crow had been in a bad way by the time they got him back to the camp. Kerrigan had worked on the broken leg, healing it up some, but lacked the strength to complete the job. He set the bones and started their repair, but couldn't finish it without drawing on Crow's own strength. As with the Panqui Xleniki, Kerrigan feared that to do that would kill Crow.

The next morning he'd come to complete the repairs, and to even fix up some other stuff as he'd done with Orla, but Crow stopped him. "As long as I can sit a horse, that's all I need. Work on others who have been hurt."

Kerrigan could tell, even looking at Crow's leg now, that it was swollen and hurt him, but he respected the man's wishes. "If you want or need any more help with your leg, when I'm rested, I'd be glad to be of service."

"Thank you. And thank you for riding up here to share that."

Kerrigan said nothing until they rode past the stone pylon marking the border. "That wasn't the reason I caught up with you. Princess, I have a message from Dothan Cavarre. He made me promise I wouldn't say anything unless it was an emergency or until we reached Oriosa."

Her violet eyes glittered. "Go on."

The Adept reached into the wrinkled folds of his many shirts and produced a leather bag. "In here I have a fragment of the DragonCrown."

"What?" Alyx gasped at the news. "How did you? I don't understand how . . ."

Kerrigan nodded at Crow. "The Draconis Baron must have told you about it, Crow, since you agreed to help smuggle me out with it."

The princess turned to look at her riding companion. "You knew?"

The man shook his head solemnly. "I knew the Draconis Baron thought it was vital that we head south. I did not know why, beyond his hoping to have his wife and the other Oriosans evacuated. This I will swear. Had I been told what we were really doing, I would have refused. I thought there was no way we could smuggle a portion of the DragonCrown out of Fortress Draconis without the dragon detecting it."

The Adept let the gemstone slip back next to his skin. "The Draconis Baron had long ago created three duplicates of the real fragments. He hid the true fragments away, but the magick on them linked them to the decoys, so the dragon thought all the parts were still in Fortress Draconis. The Draconis Baron had a long talk with me—I guess Arristan had sent him a message about me courtesy of a Steelfeather. He had me make up a new duplicate, a better one, for one of the fragments—the ruby one. I strengthened the spells. If we had had more time I could have done more; but he said the Red was the most important of these. . . . If Chytrine gets her hands on my duplicate, she'll know it's not real."

Alyx and Crow exchanged glances. They said nothing as Sallitt Hawkins spurred his horse forward to meet the cavalry company riding toward them. Ryhope and her children followed in the *meckanshii*'s wake, while the others let their horses drop to a walk.

The princess blinked, then slowly smiled. "Well, this is a victory of sorts, I guess. We've cheated her of two crown fragments."

"That's not the only thing." Kerrigan's voice came a bit low and he shifted his shoulders uneasily. "I did something else while I was there. I hope it will work."

Crow watched him closely. "What was that?"

"The magick they used on Orla, it was bad, really bad. It pulled away magick strength and stored it up to trigger another spell. I put one of those in another fragment. If she notices it I'm sure she can take it out and fix it. If she doesn't, though . . ."

Crow ran a hand over his beard. "What will the magick do?"

"I didn't have time to do much, so it's a variation of an illusion, really subtle, almost nothing at all." The Adept's face hardened. "It will make her certain that no matter how much she knows about what we're doing, there's something else, something hidden, something she can't trust. She'll always be looking to be betrayed. She'll be haunted."

Alexia reached out and rested her left hand on his right shoulder. "You may not think that is much, but it could be everything. You've done well, Adept Reese, very well."

"I'll do more, Highness."

"I'm sure you will." She gave him a broad smile that made him flush.

The princess' attention turned away from him as the cavalry company came closer and spread from column into line. The line curved around them. She reined her horse to a halt and Kerrigan did likewise. Behind them a squad rode off with Ryhope and her children, leaving Sallitt Hawkins in the middle of the road, cradling his twisted arm against his stomach. With him remained a civilian, a young woman.

Will rode up and pointed at her. "I think that's Sephi."

A civilian rider urged his horse forward. He wore a thick medallion on a chain around his neck. "I am Call Mably, magistrate for the town of Tolsin. We welcome you to Oriosa. We have made provisions for your stay with us. We hope you will be comfortable."

Princess Alexia nodded. "I am Alexia of Okrannel and these people are . . ."

Mably held a hand up. "We know who they are, Highness. Your identities were sent by *arcanslata* from Fortress Draconis. We have been anticipating your arrival."

The magistrate reined his horse over to block Crow. "You're known as Crow, Kedyn's Crow?"

"I am."

Mably nodded. The Oriosan cavalrymen drew horse-bows from their saddle scabbards and nocked arrows. "By order of Most High King Scrainwood, you are placed under arrest. You will be confined in Tolsin until proper authorities come to conduct you to Meredo."

Alexia dropped her hand to the hilt of her saber. "I believe you're making a terrible mistake, Magistrate."

Mably's voice became ice-cold. "The mistake will be yours if you interfere, Highness. These men will kill you, will kill any of you who interfere."

Crow reached out with his left hand and grasped Alexia's right. "Don't do anything, none of you. This isn't worth your lives."

Crow looked Kerrigan straight in the eye and added, "When secrets come to light, they can become deadly. This one should have remained hidden and didn't, but the price is not yours to pay. It's mine."

Crow lifted his chin. "I give you my word that I'll do nothing to escape. Leave my friends alone."

"You think I would take your word for that?" Mably beckoned two soldiers over who bracketed Crow, stripped him of his weapons, and tossed them on the ground. They bound his hands behind his back, then one took his reins and led him off.

Kerrigan wanted to do something, but Alexia shook her head. The riders led Crow back through their line and on toward the town. Sallitt Hawkins turned his horse south and galloped off, leaving a trail of dust that swirled like fog over Crow.

Sephi waited, smiled, then trotted off in Sallitt Hawkins' wake.

Alexia kicked her horse forward. "I demand to know what is going on here. Nothing Crow has done could have warranted this sort of treatment."

Mably looked at her, surprised, then laughed. "You really don't know who he is, do you? Your Crow was tried in absentia for treason a quarter century ago. Your Crow is the Traitor. He's Tarrant Hawkins and when he gets to Meredo they'll give him the death he so justly deserves."

ABOUT THE AUTHOR

MICHAEL A. STACKPOLE is an award-winning game and computer game designer, as well as a novelist. He is best known for his eight *Star Wars* novels.

In his spare time—of which there is not much when undertaking massive tomes like *Fortress Draconis*—he plays indoor soccer, rides a bike, reads a lot, travels, and serves as a Frisbee-flinger for Saint, a Cardigan Welsh corgi. He lives with Liz Danforth and Ruthless, Saint's great-grandmother, in Arizona.

His website is www.stormwolf.com.

The saga of Will, Alyx, Kerrigan, and the others will continue in *When Dragons Rage* (I know, I know, write faster).

Be sure not to miss
the next thrilling installment in
The DragonCrown War Cycle

from

Michael A. Stackpole

WHEN DRAGONS RAGE

Coming in trade paperback in
December 2002

Here's a special excerpt:

With his arms flailing unsuccessfully to control his flight, the Tolsin guardsman landed hard on the round wooden table, shattering it completely. The short drop to the ground forced a grunt from him and caused his tin-pot helmet to bounce off. It clunked and danced across the floor, striking Call Mably full in the knee, which was, for Alexia, a consequence unintended but hardly unwelcomed.

Mably—a scrawny man with brown eyes and thin lines of hair covering his pate—hissed and clutched at his knee. He glanced up at her with a hot glare. He wore a leather mask of Oriosan green that had been festooned with a variety of marks and little badges to stress his authority as Tolsin's magistrate, and its gaudy display only served to undermine the glare's heat. He straightened up at his table in the Thistle-down Tavern, and did his best to keep his voice even.

"To what do I owe this honor, Princess Alexia?"

Alexia took one step forward, pinning the guardsman's right hand to the floorboards. "I came to visit Crow, but this man was under the mistaken impression that no such visit would be allowed."

Mably's nostrils flared for a moment, then he picked up a small steaming bowl of mulled wine. "He was not mistaken. The traitor is to be allowed no visitors."

Alexia frowned and turned her head partway to the left. She let her own gaze fall over a few of the tavern's patrons near the fireplace. As they abruptly looked down, pretending to mind their own business, she spoke softly. "If I heard you correctly, Magistrate, you said Crow would be allowed no visitors."

"I did, Princess."

"And you are under the mistaken impression that rule would apply to me?"

"I am."

Alyx walked over to him, the golden mail surcoat she wore rustling as she went. She leaned down, her gloved hands pressed firmly to the table, her nose a gnat's length from his. "I noted your impression was 'mistaken.'"

Mably's eyes hardened as much as they could, which meant they avoided looking as runny as soft-boiled eggs—but not by much. His voice tightened, rising in register. "I recall that. It was not."

"Ah, very good. Then consider this. I am a Princess of Okrannel. I am of the same rank as your King Scrainwood. King Augustus is married to a cousin of mine. If I were to choose to deem your prohibition an insult, then demand satisfaction of you, what do you think would happen? Do you think any of your people would stand against me? And do you think that if I slew the lot of them, you included, I would be censured or punished in any way at all? Don't nod, Mably. You might not be the smartest man alive, but you are not that stupid. I want to see Crow. I *will* see Crow. *Now!*"

She straightened up and hooked her thumbs behind the round buckle of her belt.

Mably reached for his wine coolly, but the ripples in the liquid as he grasped the bowl revealed his fear. He raised his left hand, flicking it casually toward the back of the tavern. "The princess wishes to see the prisoner. Let her pass."

"You are most kind."

Mably's voice grew cold. "Even you would not imagine you would be allowed to wear a weapon."

Her eyes tightened. "You have my word of honor..."

"Yours, yes, but not his. You see my predicament, Princess. Your sword belt, please."

Alexia unbuckled it and slid it off. Then she rebuckled it and hung it from a peg on one of the tavern's wooden columns. Unrestrained by the belt, the mail hung on her like a girl's summer shift, rustling loudly as she crossed to the back corner. There, a corpulent guard struggled to his feet, pried a wooden chair off his ample buttocks, then moved it aside from the trap door leading down into the cellar.

As the man opened the door, she took a lantern from a wall peg and turned the wick up. The opened trap door revealed a steep set of ladderlike steps, and cold and moist air washed over her as she descended. The guard closed the door over her head and the scraping sounds from above indicated he'd resumed his post. She listened closely to see if Mably was ordering him to keep her imprisoned, but she heard nothing. A pity. While she hoped the magistrate would do something stupid, he was too much of a coward to strike openly.

Since it was a small town, Tolsin didn't have much need of a gaol to house prisoners. When Crow had arrived someone had decided they needed a place to keep him—and the best option turned out to be the root cellar below the Thistledown. Alexia was fairly certain that Mably owned the tavern or had an interest in it, and that the Oriosan government would be charged for keeping Crow safe.

As nearly as she could tell, the preparations for housing Crow had been kept to a minimum. A corner of the cellar had been cleaned out and a patch of straw had been spread down. An eyebolt had been hitched to a rafter and from it hung chains that ended in manacles. The chains were long enough that Crow could lie down, and that surprised Alexia.

The light from her lantern finally touched Crow himself, bleeding some color into what had been the white ghost of a figure huddled in the corner. He'd been stripped of his clothing, and while his long white hair and beard suggested antiquity, his body was still that of a younger man. His left leg remained slightly swollen from broken bones that had only been partially healed by magic. A single scar started at his hairline to the right side of his face, came down over his cheek, then picked up two companions at his collarbone, which in turn traced down past his hip and thigh to his knee. A plethora of other scars, all white with age, crisscrossed his body.

Alexia gasped—not because of his nakedness or the scars, but because of the new livid bruises on his chest, his arms, legs, and face. His lower lip had been split and his left eye was all but swollen shut. A crust of blood matted the hair at his right temple and one bruise on his chest clearly bore the imprint of a bootheel.

Her gasp snapped his good eye open. Anger rather than fear flashed through it, then the right corner of his mouth tugged back in a smile. "Princess. I am honored. Forgive me for not getting up."

Alexia shook her head and crouched down, setting the lantern at the edge of the straw. "They beat you?"

"They were provoked."

She frowned. "You went with them peacefully. You wouldn't do anything stupid."

He snorted, and his smile stretched the split lip. "Your confidence in me is gratifying. I am afraid I did provoke them."

"How?"

He raised his hands. "They'd looped the chain high enough that I couldn't lie down." His right eye sparkled as he separated his hands, then, quickly, slammed his wrists together. The manacles hit hard with a muffled clang, then the right one sprang open. "A manacle is only as good as the spring that keeps the catch shut. I unwound a bunch of the chain from around the rafter. After that I helped myself to some of the provisions down here. They have some passable wine in that cask over there, and there is some good cheese in that wooden box."

Alexia smiled in spite of herself. "So, I shouldn't have been worried about you at all?"

He winced as he shifted more fully onto his left hip. "Not concerning my hunger. As it was, they decided I had some sort of key in my clothes, so they took them. Then they decided I needed a lesson."

"I'll make sure they get you some clothes. I'm freezing myself down here, and I've got a quilted gambeson on under this mail." She rubbed her gloved hands over her arms. "You won't have to endure the cold tonight."

He shrugged. "I've been in far colder climes and survived, but your kindness is appreciated, Highness."

"Crow, you should call me Alyx."

"Highness, we have been through this before."

"Times are different, Crow. Before you didn't want any familiarity because you said our causes would someday force us apart. You didn't want to be a liability. I didn't know what you were talking about then, but now that I do, it doesn't matter."

Crow snapped the manacle back around his right wrist. "Highness, I wasn't thinking about who I had been when I said that. And I must apologize for misleading you. I would have gladly shared with you all I knew of your father. I didn't know him long or well, but I respected him. That I could not act to save his life is the single greatest regret of my life."

"Crow, I said none of that mattered." Alexia sank forward onto her knees and pressed her palms to her thighs. "Yes, I do want to hear from you about my father, but we have a more pressing problem. Mably's intention is to take you to Meredo where you will be executed."

Crow nodded slowly, then rested his head against the corner. "He's taken pains to let me know my fate. In great detail, in fact. I gather he's hoping to ride one of the horses they use to tear me apart."

"Crow, I'm not going to let that happen."

"Princess, there is nothing you can do to stop it. We are in Oriosa. Scrainwood has hated me for a very long time, and he has cause to do so. I knew, coming back here, that I risked my life. The simple fact of it was, though, I had to. I had to get Will to safety, return Ryhope, and get whatever it was the Draconis Baron wanted gone from the fortress away."

The scrabbling of a rat in the straw caught her attention for a moment, then she looked back at him. "You're wrong that I can't do anything to save you."

"Highness, I have no doubt you could save me." He laughed lightly. "You could toss me over your shoulder as if I were some lace-laden damsel in a bard's song and cut your way out of here, but then what? It's not that you can't save me, it is that you *should not*. Remember, you're here to convince the crowned heads to commit to fighting Chytrine. Allying yourself with me will not help you.

"Scrainwood hates me because I know he's a coward. Twenty-five years ago I told the crowned heads that they were cowards. I told them Chytrine had vowed to return. For them to follow the plans of anyone associated with me will make people question their leadership and judgment."

"If they were that foolish or cowardly, it should be called into question."

He shook his head. "I won't debate that point. You have to remember that if you are going to lead forces to oppose Chytrine, you *need* forces to lead. If you make rulers choose between you and the appearance of competence, what choice do you think they will make?"

"That doesn't hold for all of them, Crow. Queen Carus of Jerana is fairly new to her throne. She's not bound by her father's judgment. What's been done to you is an injustice."

"Yes, but an injustice that has endured for over two decades. The men who beat me weren't even born when I was stripped of my mask, but they believe every single thing they've been taught about me since they were children. Even if you and King Augustus and Queen Carus stand up and say it was a mistake, they won't believe you.

"But, Highness, you are right. Queen Carus can claim she was deceived about me. You have to take a lesson from her and claim that, too. You have to walk away from me. You have to claim that I fooled you, and you have to be angry about it. Don't let my efforts here be wasted. You'll gain by renouncing me, and your gain will be Chytrine's discomfort."

Alexia shook her head so adamantly that her thick blonde braid lashed past her shoulder and almost whipped his cheek. "No, I'm not going to do that. I've thought about this. A lot. You're a friend. You saved my life. I care about you, and I don't abandon people who matter."

"Princess, I won't drag you down with me."

"You won't drag me down. As you said before, I am strong enough to carry you, Crow." She stood and looked down at him. "I have a plan. It will save your life, and it is frightfully simple. I'm going to marry you."

Crow knelt there, his mouth open, then slowly began to chuckle. His shoulders shifted, then he sagged back into the corner. "Oh, very good, Princess. Cruel to joke with me like that, but very good."

"It's not a joke, Crow."

His head came up, his right eye a crescent slit full of fear. "It had better be a joke."

"No. It works perfectly. I marry you and you become my Prince Consort. This raises you to such a level of nobility that Scrainwood cannot carry out a summary execution. You will get another trial, since a trial *in absentia* is not recognized as binding in any treaty between Okrannel and Oriosa. Moreover, you were tried on charges of treason, and since you will become a citizen of Okrannel when we marry, the charges will no longer apply. The best they could do would be espionage and that would fail because you would have to be tried before your peers, and no royal would want that sort of precedent set. Scrainwood *could* demand personal satisfaction for any insult you gave him, but we both know he won't do that."

"Forgive me, Highness, but are you insane? Your plan might be clever, but it is wasted. You will burn a lot of political capital and for no good reason."

"I hardly think you are 'no good reason.'"

"Highness, listen to me, please." Crow's hands curled into

pale fists. "Your loyalty to me...I can't tell you what that means, but it is misplaced. You have to make sure Will can oppose Chytrine. You have to see that Kerrigan fulfills his potential. You have to raise an army to destroy Chytrine. You can't let yourself be distracted by my fate."

Alexia stepped toward him and crouched again, her shadow spilling across his scarred flesh. "What I see clearly is that *your* fate is tied up with mine, Will's, Kerrigan's, Vorquellyn, and Chytrine. If I let you die, I'm letting the world die." She reached out and stroked her right hand over the left side of his face, keeping her thumb from touching his black eye. "I'm not letting either die. We'll get a priest in here and have him marry us this afternoon."

"No." Crow shook his head. "Even if we did marry, no one would believe it. It would be assumed to be a trick, which it would be."

"They would have to believe it. We would have witnesses."

"They would say they lied."

She snorted. "They would not dare say *I* lied."

"They would, just not to your face. Before you they would say that I tricked you into it. No, Highness, abandon this plan."

"Crow, it will save your life."

"And ruin yours." He reached up and took her hand in his. "Princess." His voice dropped to a whisper. "Alexia, promise me you won't do this. I won't agree, so the effort will be wasted. Don't. Please."

She squeezed his fingers. "You will resist, won't you?"

He nodded.

"Then I will have to find another plan." She stood slowly, then leaned over and picked up the lantern again. "I am not letting you die."

Crow's right eye sparkled. Was that a tear forming in the corner? "Just worry about the world, Highness. The world you can save. Nothing else matters."

* * *

Kerrigan Reese huddled as best he could in the shadows and shivered. The cool night air had little to do with his discomfort, as he was bundled up against it and swathed in black woolen clothes that rendered him invisible. He even sank to one knee, as did the expedition's leaders, though he knew he'd be at a sore disadvantage when called upon to move quickly.

Kerrigan shivered because the last time he had engaged in this sort of secret operation, Orla had died. Granted, the streets of Tolsin were not the streets of the Wruonin pirate haven, and the local constabulary was not a band of bloodthirsty cutthroats who just happened to have a *sullanciri* visiting them. Still, he'd made a mistake then, and his mentor had paid dearly for it.

Well, at least the princess thinks this is a good idea. He let his shoulders slump a little. *Then again, she's not here.*

In front of him, shrouded in black, Resolute and Will knelt to study the Thistledown Tavern. The squat, two-story building didn't look like much, with its thick thatched roof and tiny windows. The dim light leaking out from behind the warped glass suggested the miserly distribution of candles, but that suited their purpose perfectly.

Two men stood beside the door on guard duty, stamping their feet against the cold. The two of them might have been enough to daunt Tolsin's criminal element, but not the crew that had assembled that night. Resolute could have slain either of them in an instant, and Will was no slouch in combat. Dranae—a massive human warrior, with dark hair, a full beard, and blue eyes—crouched beside Kerrigan. The man towered over him and weighed more than he did, despite not having an ounce of fat on him. Kerrigan would have loved to be that strong, but his life on Vilwan had not exactly been physically demanding. Dranae carried a short wooden staff that hardly looked like much of a weapon, but in a strong man's hands it could break bones.

The last two members of the company carried no weapons. Qwc, a Spritha, clung to the eaves of the building against which Kerrigan huddled. The lack of light made his green carapace look black, but his four wings still managed to flicker as if trapping starlight. His upper pair of hands smoothed his antennae while the lower pair and his feet kept him anchored to the wall. Though only a foot tall, Qwc's speed and ability to fly made him useful.

His voice buzzed low. "Just two, just two there."

Resolute nodded. "Lombo?"

Kerrigan glanced back over his shoulder at the creature hulking there. The Panqui was an intelligent beast who had once been a Wruonin pirate until he had been betrayed and almost slain. Huge, with bony plates armoring his flesh, long retractable claws, and a jutting muzzle full of teeth, he looked more than sufficient to tear the town apart, much less two guards before some tavern. In battle against Chytrine's forces the Panqui had gleefully attacked and killed Grand Temeryces, coming away without a scratch.

Lombo raised his muzzle and sniffed, his ears flattening back along his skull. "Two outside. More inside. And Crow."

The Vorquelf nodded, then turned back to look at Kerrigan. "Your turn, Adept. Can you do it?"

Kerrigan frowned for a moment, then flicked fingers at the building. The spell he cast sped unseen at the tavern, then raced back to him, allowing him to view it with *mageyes*. For him, the night's gloom vanished and the building lit up, with each living creature glowing more brightly than the candles. Aside from the two men by the door, three more people occupied the upper floor. One was sleeping and the other two were . . .

Kerrigan blushed and refocused on the ground floor and the basement. Four men remained in the tavern itself, and he picked up two more individuals in the cellar. They were very close, but one lay on the ground while the other fairly blazed with activity. "Someone is down there with him and is kicking him."

Will turned, eyes narrowing. "Stop him."

The young mage opened his mouth to explain that while casting the spell in question was simple, focusing it to hit the people in the basement would be trickier. But the look in

Will's eyes indicated that an explanation would be wasted. While Kerrigan knew his Vilwanese tutors would have berated him soundly for using his skills in an illegal activity, he drew in a deep breath, set his shoulders, then opened his palms and let the spell ripple out.

The magick flowed out effortlessly, moving through the night like fog. The two guards collapsed in boneless heaps by the door. Within the tavern itself, the sleeper upstairs burrowed deeper into the covers and the other two relaxed into sleep; even falling out of bed didn't waken one of them. The guards on the ground floor toppled to the floor or sagged in their chairs. And in the basement, the man who had been kicking Crow dropped to the ground as if he had been poleaxed.

Kerrigan smiled and Will began to head toward the building. The magicker grabbed his wrist. "Wait."

"Why?"

A series of staccato thumps sounded from around the building. Plump little creatures fell from the eaves and a couple more plopped down from the roof. Will craned his head forward, then shivered. "Rats?"

"There will be more inside, so be careful."

The Vorquelf raised a hand and pointed to the building. Qwc flew straight away to it, then keened a high tone. The others followed in his wake, with Lombo hefting the two fallen guardsmen. Dranae and Kerrigan appropriated their spears and helmets, then took up the guard positions while Will unlocked the tavern door with a click. Lombo, the Vorquelf, and Will disappeared inside. The Spritha then launched himself into the air and began a circling patrol.

Kerrigan really didn't expect much trouble. Princess Alexia and her Gyrkyme companion, Perrine, had hosted a dinner for Call Mably and the other local nobility. They'd all been seated well above the salt, while the present company had lurked below it, pretending to drink far too much and stumbling off to bed while the others engaged in discussions of world affairs and other important events. None of the guests would be allowed to leave until Alexia declared the festivities at an end, and she'd not do that until Qwc returned and let her know the night's adventure had succeeded.

Dranae fitted the dented helmet on his head. "Your control of magick is impressive, Adept Reese."

Kerrigan blinked. "Oh, no, I was very sloppy." He toed one of the sleeping rats. "If I had concentrated, I could have gotten just the men. Oh, and the dog in the corner, too. I just let the spell go and got everything in there. I should have been more precise."

"But, Adept Reese, I was under the impression that outside the realm of combat magicks, humans did not have the discipline necessary to work magick on living creatures. In fact, isn't the spell you used part of an elven healing regime to make the injured sleep while other healing spells take effect?"

"Well, yes, but . . ." Kerrigan frowned. "On Vilwan I had elven instructors. I just did what they taught me to."

"You learned your lessons very well."

"How is it that you know about magick?" Kerrigan tried to keep his voice even. "No disrespect intended, but . . ."

"But I hardly seem like a scholar?" The big man shrugged and tapped the helmet over the left side of his head. "You know that Crow, Resolute, and Will rescued me from a squad of gibberkin. They had made me a prisoner and hit me in the head. I don't remember anything from before I joined with Crow, so I can't answer. Could be it was something I overheard while on Vilwan, fighting the pirates. There were elven healers there, so that's probably the answer."

Kerrigan nodded easily. "Elven magick is very difficult to learn because it is different than human magick. Human magick you construct, whereas elven magick flows and grows."

Any further discussion of magick ended with the tavern door opening. Resolute emerged first and Lombo followed, dragging a guardsman in each hand. He sat them beside the door, with their backs against the building. Will exited last and relocked the door while Dranae and Kerrigan returned the helmets to their respective owners.

Resolute frowned as he took the helmet Kerrigan had put on the man's head and turned it around properly. "It's done."

Kerrigan smiled. "It worked?"

Will laughed. "Perfect, Kerrigan. When all this is over, you and me are going to be unstoppable. You drop the guards, and I'll get the goods."

The Vorquelf glanced down at the thief. "You didn't steal anything, did you, boy?"

Will's nostrils flared. "That wasn't part of the plan. No."

"Good. Then move."

The five figures hustled away from the tavern. Kerrigan hesitated in the shadows from which he had cast the spell. "Do you want me to wake them up?"

"No."

"Yes."

Kerrigan looked first from Resolute to Will. "Which?"

The Vorquelf shook his head. "Let them wake at dawn as they normally would."

Will groaned. "But that means the guy in the basement will stay sleeping."

"Let him. It just postpones things."

Dranae raised an eyebrow. "The one who was kicking Crow? What did you do to him?"

Resolute shrugged. "The ladder down into the cellar is steep. He fell. Broke his leg."

Will nodded. "A really nasty break, too, with the bone poking out and everything."

Kerrigan blanched. "You broke his leg deliberately?"

"I wanted to break both of them, and then stuff his thumbs up..."

"Enough, Will." Resolute urged them on through the town, pressing a hand over Kerrigan's spine. "There are times, Adept Reese, when petty evils need to be met with painful retribution. The man will recover, but anytime he goes to kick someone else, he will remember. It's not much of a victory, but for this night's work, it will do."

The rustle of feathers that announced Perrine's arrival came more quietly than the dawn's scrabbling of waking pigeons in the eaves. Alyx smiled and leaned out the window as the Gyrkyme folded her wings. Perrine had the coloration of a falcon, which was common for the Gyrkyme warrior caste, with dark brown feathers over shoulders and back, which shaded to cream dappled with brown over her breasts and belly. Large amber eyes flickered with intelligence, though the brown fletching around them did make her look as if tears had stained her face. The fierce grin belied any sadness, however.

"You were right, sister, they gathered at the far end of the town, thinking to go around as they headed to the capital. Lombo has squatted in the gate, and seems oblivious to the two guards beating him with sticks."

Alyx shook her head. "I'd best get down there in case he decides to notice. Will you . . . ?"

Perrine screeched happily and launched herself into the morning air with a powerful beat of her wings. "Not too much blood, I promise."

"Thank you, my sister."

Alexia turned and stalked through her room, leaving her baggage and sword behind. As was her custom, she had braided her hair into a thick queue and tied it off with a black leather thong. She'd attired herself in a simple doeskin tunic and trousers to match, though they had been dyed black. She'd tucked them into her boots and belted the tunic with a wide belt into which she had tucked her gloves. Accustomed as she was to wearing her coat of mail, she felt light and almost naked without it as she flew down the stairs and out into the street.

It didn't take her long to cross the distance from the inn to where Call Mably and his squad of guards had gathered. Lombo still squatted in the gateway, with the splintered bits of sticks littering the ground around him. Perrine perched on top of the gate, gazing balefully down at Mably, and Qwc had lighted on Crow's shoulder. Around them, various townsfolk had begun to assemble.

Alexia smiled as she broke into the circle and grabbed hold of Mably's horse's bridle. "Magistrate Mably, had you told me you intended to leave at this hour, I would have adjourned our celebration earlier."

Were it not for the green mask he wore, Mably's face would have had no color. Alexia revised her initial assessment quickly, for his eyes were rather red and his skin actually hinted at the color of his mask. She resisted the temptation to spook his horse, which easily would have spilled him from the saddle and quite probably induced vomiting.

"Princess, I thought not to trouble you with such a mundane thing as moving the prisoner."

"You might not think I have an interest in that, Magistrate, but where my husband goes, so go I."

Mably's red eyes all but bugged from his mask. "What?"

Even Crow's head came up. "Princess, don't." He clearly wanted to offer more of a protest, but lacked the energy. He'd been set in the saddle and tied there; his wrists were also heavily bound. A threadbare grey blanket had been thrown over him, but fell only to mid-thigh, letting everyone see his bare, bruised legs.

Mably raised his head. "You claim this man is your husband?"

Alexia nodded. "He is."

"She's lying."

Mably smiled. "He denies it, Princess."

"He's delirious, and no wonder, after the treatment he's had at your hands." Alexia smiled warmly. "As well you know, Oriosan custom does allow a wife to travel with her husband while he is being taken for judgment."

"Judgment has been rendered, he is bound for punishment. The custom does not apply." Mably snorted. "Besides, he denies you are married."

"And you have maintained he is Hawkins, the Traitor, who is a notorious liar, so how can you believe him?" She ld up her left hand and thumbed a gold ring around her 'h finger. "We are wedded. We were wedded in a ceremony in Kedyn's Temple at Fortress Draconis. Prince Erlestoke was a witness."

Crow growled. "Mably, you are not so much a fool as to believe this, are you?"

"Hush, beloved." The princess looked from Crow back up to Mably. "Look at his hand, Magistrate; you'll see his ring. Even the most simple of magickers could tell you our rings are linked as they should be after such a ceremony."

The bureaucrat snarled. "He had no ring when we took him into custody."

"Your search of his person failed to find it."

"You had no ring on last night."

"You simply failed to see it." Alyx snorted. "A consequence of being blind drunk, it would seem."

Mably shook his head once, hard, then hissed in pain. "Princess, you know the only magicker worth the name here in Tolsin is Adept Reese, and I would trust what he says about those rings. You are lying."

"She's not lying."

Alexia turned and saw a slender, dark-haired woman emerge from the crowd. Anger flashed through her, and above the gate Perrine's wings unfurled. *That is Sephi, the woman who betrayed Crow to Scrainwood. What is her game?*

Mably's head came up. "What are you prattling on about, girl?"

Sephi's eyes blazed. "I said she is not lying. They *are* wed."

"More nonsense."

"Is it?" Sephi's voice took on an edge. "You know well who I am, Call Mably. I am the king's eyes and ears. I was sent here to confirm the Traitor's identity. I know all about him, and I know they are wed."

The magistrate shifted his shoulders. "Why didn't you tell me this before?"

"Magistrate, you are only meant to know that which the king wishes you to know. Are you smarter than he is? The king's answer to that question would differ from yours, I am certain." Sephi shook her head. "I reveal this knowledge to prevent you from doing something stupid, like parading a

Prince of Okrannel through Oriosa naked. I will not have you embarrassing our nation."

The magistrate slumped in his saddle. "This is not right. There was no ring on his finger."

"That's because the princess is lying."

"Shut up!" Mably's shout silenced Crow, but clearly cost him mightily. He breathed hard for several seconds, then glared down at Alexia. "This *is* trickery, I know it. I will not be made a fool."

The princess stepped back and opened her hands. "If you choose to call me a liar, I will demand satisfaction of you. You may choose between that, or believing the king's spy here and letting me accompany my husband to Meredo."

"Just you, Princess."

"Of course, just me. And my bodyguards."

Mably groaned.

Alyx smiled. "You know they will be there regardless, Magistrate. Do not fight a battle you cannot win."

"This is a skirmish, Princess, and one you have won." Mably drew himself up in the saddle again. "In Meredo the battle shall be decided, and it shall not be in your favor."